I0646633

A Novel of Nazi Art Theft

in WWII

THE ART PROCURER

By
Jeff Ridenour

This book is a work of fiction. Names, characters, places, and incidents are the product of the author's imagination or are used fictitiously. Any resemblance to actual events, locales, or persons, living or dead, is coincidental.

Publisher: Karlsbad Middleford Press **KMP**
Charleston, South Carolina

Copyright © 2013 Jeff Ridenour
ISBN: 0989629635
ISBN 13: 9780989629638

for

Ronda, of course,
who introduced me to
the paintings of Franz Marc

Acknowledgements

I would like to thank my father, Julian Ridenour (1919-2007), for sharing with me over the years numerous incidents -- some comical, others harrowing -- that happened to him in WWII, several of which I include in modified forms in the novel.

My dad might have been the only soldier in WWII who went through basic training [Camp Croft, Spartanburg, South Carolina] three consecutive times, first as an Army infantry recruit, second as a paratrooper recruit, and finally as an Army Air Corps recruit.

Later in the war he became one of the Tampa Bay Volunteers, a group of seven pilots whose adventures took them from landing U-boat-hunting B-25's on Greenland's glaciers to flying photo reconnaissance P-38's in New Guinea and the Philippines, notably filming the entire east coast of the island of Luzon from fifty feet above the beaches, in order for Douglas MacArthur to find the perfect beach on which to fulfill his "I shall return" promise.

When the Japanese attacked Pearl Harbor, my father, age 22, was a student at what is now known as the Cleveland Institute of Art. Yellowing photos indicate he was both a very good painter and a superb sculptor. When he returned from the war he had a wife and son to support. Never again did he take up sculpture, and only in his late seventies did he once again put paint to canvas.

I also wish to acknowledge the contributions of my father-in-law, Rinehart Rutschman (1912-2006). Over the years, he passed along many of his large family's tales and descriptions of Wasterkingen, Switzerland, where he was born. The village is where I describe it -- on the German border north of Zurich, on the north side of the Rhine River near the Rhine Falls. His family immigrated to St. Joseph, Missouri in 1914. During WWII Rinehart was first a merchant seaman on Atlantic crossings, then a gunner in the US Navy in the Pacific.

And very special thanks to my wife and editor, Ronda, for her (nearly) infinite patience as we raced to make connections, dragging heavy baggage through countless Hauptbahnhofs, and when, more than once, I got lost driving a rented Škoda through the twisting backroads of Bavaria. *Habst du meinen ewigen Dank, Liebchen!*

Nothing is more delusional than to suppose for a moment that any art has ever existed solely 'for art's sake'.

Durch Die Hintertür Der Kunstwelt
[Through the Backdoor of the Art World]
-- Hugo von der Heydt, 1905

Prologue

Monday
July 20, 1992
Hohenfelde, Germany

"The locals call this kind of swirling fog *Der Grauergeist*, The Gray Ghost," a pudgy fellow with a ratty beard and wire-framed glasses said when he caught up with Selby Parker and Ingrid Sundstrum just as they reached their rental car. "Legend has it children have disappeared right off their front porches in this sort of mist, never to be seen or heard of again. Snatched by *Der Grauergeist*, folks claim."

The man introduced himself to Selby and Ingrid as Roger Broadwell, born and raised in Yorkshire but now a resident of Kiel for the past twelve years. He said he ran a one-man travel agency specializing in providing British tourists "sun, sand, and sea", which corresponded to the company logo stenciled on the ten-passenger min-van parked outside the Seeblick Inn, where they stood now. *Seeblick*, sea view, was a stretch, Selby decided before he and Ingrid had gone inside for a late lunch.

"I couldn't help overhearing your asking the proprietor about farms in the vicinity of Todendorf, just down the road. I'm pretty familiar with that little village myself, there being a lighthouse near the beach that makes a nice photo opportunity for my customers – excepting on a day like today, of course. Are you interested in buying some farm property? Because if you are, I might be of help to you in that regard. I could take you there. Not today, of course. I've got my paying customers. But tomorrow perhaps?"

I'd sooner go to Treasure Island with Long John Silver, Selby thought. Couldn't help overhearing, could he? Selby calculated the man's table of tourists was twenty feet from his and Ingrid's. Nor had he and the proprietor exactly shouted at one another. Still, Selby had begun to discover that information on Karl Vollmer was proving difficult to come by. So, despite his annoyance with the man, he decided he had better be willing to accept an offer of help, even from such a smarmy chap. So what if the grubby fellow was consummately skilled at overhearing conversations not intended for his ears. Selby had to concede that was no doubt a useful trait in a tour operator eager to satisfy his clients' travel-related curiosities, as in "Oh look, Dear, I wonder what that hideous-looking building might be," as the van sped by this or that *Bau* or *Gebäude*.

"No. We're not after property. We're trying to trace a man who might live, or have once lived, in a farmhouse somewhere near Todendorf," Selby said.

"The man's name?" Broadwell asked, toying with his beard.

"Surname's Vollmer. Karl Vollmer."

"Can't say as I've heard of him. How long ago did he live hereabouts?"

Selby smiled. "He disappeared sometime between the middle and end of 1945."

Roger Broadwell cocked his head and gave a low whistle. "Just after the war that never happened."

Selby nodded. "Yes. That war." Germans were still loathe to talk about, even acknowledge, World War II, an attitude Broadwell was obviously familiar with, Selby thought.

"Makes him what? Seventy? Eighty years old?"

"Eighty-six," Selby said.

"Probably dead, " Broadwell said. "Even wars that don't happen take a lot out of a man."

"Still, there's a chance."

"Just disappeared, did he?" Broadwell snapped his fingers. "Poof?"

"He was a member of the SS."

"Ah! That explains it. Probably skittered off to Argentina, Paraguay, or some other sympathetic place," Broadwell said.

Ingrid finally spoke. "We'd like to check out possibilities a little closer to home first."

"How do you figure him for SS?"

"Archives in Berlin," Selby simplified.

"Suppose you'd mind telling me what you want with this SS bloke."

"You suppose correctly."

"Not exactly my business anyway, is it?"

"Not exactly."

"Official business, eh?"

Selby pointed a finger at Broadwell as a mild admonishment.

"Sorry. Not my business. Right?"

"Not your business."

"Where'd you come from?" the tour operator asked Ingrid.

She announced, "I've been working in Berlin."

Broadwell peered over his glasses at Ingrid. "But you're Swedish, I bet."

"Yes."

Broadwell eyed her from head to foot. "Lovely." When Ingrid's eyes narrowed, he hastily added, "Lovely that you're Swedish is all I meant. Splendid people, yours. Keep their noses out of other people's business."

Which is more than can be said for you, Selby thought.

"And you'd be a Yank," he said to Selby.

"Yes."

"New York, I'm guessing, from your accent. I'm pretty good at accents, if I say so myself."

"Which you just did."

"Still, you're a bit too laid back for a New Yorker."

"Would you prefer I fulfill your stereotype?"

"No, no. Mellow suits me just fine."

Nationalities, personalities, and pulchritude finally established, Selby asked, "Any suggestions who else we might ask in this vicinity? We've been through Todendorf once already. Not much of a place and no one is talking."

And now the Seeblick's owner had professed complete ignorance about any goings on in "distant Todendorf", the distance between his establishment and Todendorf consisting of a vastness spanning all of seven kilometers. But then the proprietor struck Selby as another one of those northern Germans whose memory conveniently failed regarding any World War II issue except who started the war and who lost it, assuming it ever happened. Having spent part of his career in Hamburg and Berlin, Selby was well aware that citizens in northern Germany, both young and old, believed The War That Never Happened, as Broadwell called it, was both started by and lost by Austrians and Bavarians, Catholics and Occultists.

"Go to the pub in Todendorf. There's only one," Broadwell explained. "Zum Alten Fritz is it's name. A bit out of the way, even for that pissant burg. Turn off the main road and head toward the lighthouse. It's about a quarter mile. Plenty of old timers there, most of them spending their sunset years making sure the pub's tap lines don't freeze over from inactivity. I have to admit that more than once I have lent my own expertise to their efforts in that regard."

"Zum Alten Fritz," Selby repeated.

Broadwell nodded, adding, "And no need to mention my name."

"Okay."

"In fact –." A sheepish look.

"I might fare better if I didn't?" Selby said, grinning.

"We all make enemies," Broadwell gave as his defense.

Selby thanked the man and unlocked the doors to the rental car. As he opened the passenger door for Ingrid, Broadwell, ogling Ingrid unabashedly, said, "And another item I wouldn't mention."

"What's that?" Selby said.

"Your missing man's affiliation with Himmler's bunch. Might as well walk in and invite all the regulars to stand up and join you in singing the *Horst Wessel Lied*. Best you'd leave it be that he was a simple farmer."

"Actually, he was a fisherman," Selby replied. "But thank you for your help and advice."

"Glad to be of service," Broadwell shouted as he retreated backwards toward the inn door, his eyes still fixed on Ingrid.

The sign on the gated fence leading to the Vollmer farmhouse read, Schlimmerfeld & Horne, A.G..

"That's odd," Ingrid said. "No one at the tavern mentioned the Vollmers not owning the property any longer. Who do you suppose Schlimmerfeld and Horne are?"

Selby said, "We'll obviously have to try to find out. But let me tell you from experience, trying to nail down even elementary details about German corporations is as hard or harder than your attempting to establish the provenance of an obscure fifteenth-century painting."

The sign's paint was peeling; the wires binding it to the chain-link mesh were rusting. Only the padlock looked new.

"What now?" Ingrid asked Selby as they stood in the fog, denser here even than closer to the coast.

"The sign doesn't say 'Keep Out'."

"Yes, but that does," she said, pointing toward the padlock.

"It must be saying it in *Plattdeutsch*, which I don't *versteh*." Selby fiddled with the lock for a minute before deciding climbing over the gate was quicker and easier.

Ingrid shrugged. "I'm game and you're the spook." Then she scrambled over.

Selby winked and said, "I just hope I'm a match for *Der Grauergeist.*"

The patrons sharing *Gemutlichkeit* in the stale-beer-and-cigarette-smoke atmosphere of Zum Alten Fritz had proved willing to chit-chat about both the Vollmer farm and about the Vollmers themselves, but only after Selby broadcast the lie that Karl Vollmer stood to inherit a substantial sum of money from an anonymous friend in Munich, provided Vollmer could be found. That lie loosened tongues more quickly than Selby's offer to buy a round of drinks.

The tavern crowd's narrative of the Gray Ghost tale differed in one critical aspect from the brief account told by Roger Broadwell. According to the tavern tale, Karl Vollmer's grandfather, Wilhelm Vollmer, had not only farmed that particular piece of land since before the turn of the century, but made the farm prosper by fertilizing its soil with the flesh and bones of dozens of young children. Wilhelm Vollmer was in fact, according to the legend as it was accepted in Todendorf, *Der Grauergeist* incarnate. And, when Wilhelm himself disappeared -- as in vanished, not died -- his grandson Karl inherited not only one third of the farm but *all* of the ghostly traits attributable to his grandfather.

Once on the porch, Selby handed Ingrid a pair of thin rubber gloves, then donned a pair for himself.

"You came prepared, I see."

"In case we weren't welcomed by a brass band."

Moments later Ingrid whispered, "You picked that door lock like a professional burglar," and tiptoed past Selby into the farmhouse foyer.

Selby gave her a what-can-I-say gesture, then followed her in and shone his flashlight around. "A tidy ghost, I'd say."

"Makes me think the outside of the building is left deliberately shabby," Ingrid said, wiping a finger across an end table and shining her own flashlight beam on her hand. "Dusted recently, I'm sure."

"Well ventilated, too. No musty smell," Selby added, then walked through the dining room toward where he supposed a kitchen would be. Ingrid followed him.

Opening the refrigerator, Selby found only an open box of deodorizing baking soda. The freezer compartment was empty except for full trays of ice cubes. When he and Ingrid had finished checking cupboards they had found nothing.

"Not even mouse shit," Selby remarked as he peered beneath sink and found nothing but plumbing.

"Just obsessive orderliness," Ingrid said and sat down on a kitchen chair. "Somebody's been here recently, but I doubt it was Karl Vollmer. Men aren't this fastidious."

"You might be surprised," Selby said, sitting down across from her.

"Are you this neat?"

"I'm afraid not."

Ingrid said, "I'm slowly starting to think maybe Vollmer went south, followed the underground Church railroad. Maybe Broadwell is right. And maybe good old Roger knows something he's not telling us."

"I disagree," Selby said. "If Vollmer'd headed south, he would have stuck with his colonel, Zeitz. Or have caught up with him.

No. I think he stayed here in the north. At least until –." Selby took a deep breath, then let it out slowly.

Ingrid, impatient, finally said, "—until what?"

"Until it was safe to move the two paintings. Or dozens of paintings. Why just two?"

A shrug. "The colonel was clearly obsessive about Marc's *Tower* and the Raphael was serendipity," Ingrid said.

"We also know that the colonel included Klee's *Moonlight Over the City* when he tried to cut a deal with Lieutenant Wynerson."

"The Klee and Raphael are not all that big, but *The Tower of the Blue Horses* is huge. How many other paintings could Vollmer or his colonel deal with?"

"Exactly. Huge. If either one of them could deal with *The Tower*, we must suppose they could deal with a whole museum's worth. Well, of course, I'm exaggerating, but in for a *pfennig* --"

"While they sat right under the Allies' noses?" Ingrid said, incredulous.

"Remember. Early in the war they moved nearly thirty crates of Amber Room panels around as if the crates were no more than a deck of pinochle cards to them."

"Every inch of their way secured by a German army that, at the time, was invincible," Ingrid pointed out. "Nor was it entirely a piece of cake. Remember that Vollmer lost a forearm while shunting the boxcars to a side rail in Königsberg."

"There's that," Selby conceded. "But what about the rumor that, at practically the same time, Zeitz picked Herman Göring's pocket and moved that booty to Switzerland?"

Ingrid Sundstrum smiled, and in a mocking voice, said, "There's that."

Selby stood and pushed his chair carefully back under the table. "We won't solve anything sitting here speculating. Let's check out the rest of the house."

Ingrid pointed to the chair Selby had sat in. "Neatness rubbing off on you?"

Selby chuckled. "No. But my mother had very strict table rules. Putting my chair back before I left the table was one of them."

"Sounds like my kind of woman."

"She was a pretty special lady."

Nothing interesting turned up in any of the bedrooms. Dressers were empty, the beds stripped to their mattresses, closets bare. The only thing Selby and Ingrid found remarkable in the parlor was the absence of even the slightest vestige of an ash in what was clearly an oft-used fireplace. So they ventured into the cellar.

"Not quite so orderly down here," Ingrid said, shining her flashlight on a pair of broken chairs, a piece of a leg missing from one, the upholstery on the other's seat slashed, its stuffing shredded and hanging out.

"And the maid forgot to dust," Selby said after blowing on a shelf and watching a small cloud swirl like the fog outside. He directed his light beam to a distant corner. "What are those?"

Ingrid walked to where his beam was pointing. "They're stone crocks. Twenty-gallon size, give or take."

"What are they used for?" Selby asked.

"Making sauerkraut usually, although any vegetable will do. Meat, too, for that matter. Brining."

Three crocks sat in a row, each with a thick lid atop it. With difficulty Ingrid lifted the lid from the one nearest her, knelt down, and stuck her head inside the crock.

"What are you doing?" Selby asked as he walked to her side.

Ingrid came up, took a deep breath, then put her head in the crock again.

When she lifted her head she said, "Sniff for yourself."

Selby got down on his knees and smelled the interior. Straightening himself, he looked at Ingrid. "I don't smell anything. What am I missing?"

"Sauerkraut. It's very, very faint, but I can smell it."

Selby tried again. Still nothing. "So? You said that's what they're for."

"Maybe women are better smellers, too, yes?"

"I'm in no position to argue that, although maybe age plays a role as well."

"That aside, there's something wrong here."

"Besides upstairs neat, downstairs messy?" Selby said.

"Yes. Let me explain. My Grandma Katerina made sauerkraut in her basement. So did lots of my other relatives. None of them would consider for a moment letting fermenting crocks sit out in the main part of their cellars. No matter how smooth and heavy a crock's lid, the smell always manages to creep out. So everyone I know who ferments cabbage has a separate crypt-like room as part of the cellar. Air-tight on the inside; vented only to the outside of the house. One of my jobs, as a little kid, was to help my mother seal the inside door once the crocks full of cabbage were placed inside the crypt for six weeks. We used a mixture of sand and mud. And before we closed and sealed the crypt we had to check the reinforced grating over the vent to the outside to make sure air could get out but rats and other little critters couldn't get in."

"So where's the crypt here?" Selby asked.

"That's my point. I don't see one."

Selby let his flashlight beam pan each cellar wall slowly. Nothing.

"It's got to be here. Grandma's crypt extended beyond the house, went out under the back porch."

Selby rescanned the rear wall.

"Over there, I think," Ingrid said excitedly. "Behind those wood panels."

With his pen knife Selby poked at and pried the seams of several sections of wall until one joint separated, allowing him to remove the panel. With the first panel gone, a second one popped free.

"That's it!" Ingrid said, shining her light where the sheets of wood had been. "One more and we've got it."

"Not even locked." Selby said when he had laid the third panel on the cellar floor.

"But it looks like a tight seal," Ingrid said, running her hand around the edges of the half door, the bottom of which began three feet above off the floor. "Shall we open it?"

"It might be bobby-trapped," Selby said.

Ingrid sighed. "You can take the agent out of the field but you can't take the field out of the agent? Is that you?"

"I haven't been retired all that long," Selby said defensively.

"Stand back," she said. Then she gave the door a tug.

"Allow me," Selby said, easing Ingrid out of the way when the door failed to open. On the second hard pull the door opened and he shone his light into the crypt.

"No *Grauergeist*, I hope," Ingrid said, peering over Selby's shoulder as he bent forward to look inside.

Selby stood aside in order for Ingrid to get a better look.

"My God! Frames. Empty frames. Look at them all. You were right. Half a museum's worth at least," she said, bumping her head on the door latch in her excitement.

Selby climbed into the crypt and quickly discovered he was unable to stand up straight. When he moved deeper into the small room and began shoving painting frames aside he saw something new. "Don't come in, Ingrid."

Behind him her voice echoed, closer than he expected. "Too late. I'm right behind you."

Selby aimed his light at the floor near the rear of the room. "A skeleton. With a human skull," he said, centering his beam of light toward the lower right rear corner of the crypt.

"Children? Victims of *Der Grauergeist*?" Ingrid gasped.

Selby dropped to his knees and crawled forward, maintaining his flashlight's focus until he reached the skull. Though no forensic anthropologist, Selby, in his long career, had witnessed enough grisly exhumations of victims of Cold War intelligence killings to turn toward Ingrid and say, with confidence, "This is an adult who was shot at close range through the back of the head."

BOOK ONE

Parallel Lives, Converging

1937 - 1945

1

Wednesday
June 9, 1937
University of Chicago
Harper Quadrangle
Spring Commencement

At the conclusion of the convocation ceremonies Martin Wynerson elbowed his way through hundreds of other milling graduates and their families until he found his sister, Madeleine, waiting for him on the steps of Rockefeller Memorial Chapel.

Six inches shorter than Martin, as well as four years younger, Maddy, as she was known by her friends and family, kept her brother standing two steps lower than where she stood in order look him in eyes. "We're all so very proud of you, Martin."

Madeleine was almost always Maddy; Martin was *never* Marty.

"Thanks, Maddy. At least *most of us* are proud of me."

"Daddy is, too. He really is," Madeleine insisted.

Martin shrugged. "I don't think so, but I'm willing to pretend he is."

"You should have heard him tell the hotel clerk 'My son is going to become a doctor today,'" Maddy said.

"But not a physician," Martin reminded her. In as deep a bass voice as he could muster, Martin imitated his father. "Son, you could have been a lawyer or a medical man. Instead, you want to waste your life staring at moldy old paintings."

"That was last year," Maddy claimed.

"I promise I'll behave myself around him," Martin said, then plopped his mortarboard cockeyed on Maddy's head of long blonde hair. Again in a faux-bass voice he said, "Madeleine Sue Wynerson, I hereby confer upon you the title of *Doctorus Historicus Artisticus,* with all the rights, privileges, and duties attendant thereon."

"You made that up. I know some Latin."

"Yes, I made it up. So what?"

"Stop with the mocking, Martin. People might think you're not sufficiently proud of yourself."

Mostly I'm just plain relieved, Martin thought to himself. Relieved to be finished with being a graduate student, finished with Chicago winters, finished with listening to my father bleat on and on about his life's disappointments – I being foremost among them.

"What about your plans for graduate school?" he asked his sister. "You still interested?"

"You'll be proud to know I'm putting together my application now for library school."

Martin gave her a puzzled look. "You're already a librarian."

"Yes, but with an advanced degree I can work at a college like Macalester or Carleton or even the University of Minnesota."

"Where do you intend to apply?"

"Next year the Wisconsin Library School is being integrated into the University of Wisconsin. So I want to go there. It's the closest to home. I wish we had one in Minnesota, but we don't. Maybe some day."

Martin decided to spare her his scornful opinions on life in graduate school. "I think it's a great idea, Maddy. Have you told our parents yet?"

"Sort of."

"And?"

"They seem supportive."

"Lucky you."

"Come on, Martin. Mother and Daddy are waiting for us across the street by the ice rink," Madeleine said, tugging playfully at Martin's black gown.

"Yes. Let's go face the music – again."

"Martin! Promise you'll not say something rash to Daddy."

Just as Martin was mulling whether to make such a commitment, he heard a familiar voice behind him. Turning, he saw his thesis advisor, Clement Moore, waving and calling his name as he hastened toward him, his bald head glistening with sweat on the warm – for Chicago – day.

After making introductions between Professor Moore and Madeleine, Martin said, "Professor Moore is spending his summer in London and Cambridge, Maddy. Doesn't that sound exciting?"

"Very! Are you British?" Maddy asked.

"I lived in London for several years, but actually I'm from Dayton, Ohio."

"You sound a bit British."

"An affectation, I confess, young lady. At bottom I'm just a vain old man."

"Martin thinks you're wonderful."

"And I think the world of your brother. In fact, if you don't mind, I would like to steal Martin for a few minutes to discuss a travel proposition with him."

"Are you taking him to London with you?" Maddy asked.

"Something even better," Professor Moore said.

"Do you know about this, Martin? Are you keeping secrets?" his sister said.

Martin shook his head. "Run along, Maddy, if you don't mind. I'll join you and the folks as quickly as I can."

Walking west along 59th Street with Martin at his side, Professor Moore began, "Elliott Parker is going to Germany next month for three weeks. He would be honored to have you join him."

Martin was stunned. "He doesn't even know me," Martin stammered when he recovered his power of speech.

"Actually, he's read your dissertation. I sent it to him."

Elliott Parker had already made a name for himself in art history. Not yet forty, he was a full professor at Harvard, having previously taught at Brown and Cornell. His journal articles and books on modern art were standard reading in nearly every art history graduate department. His theory that all of Modern Art is, in large part, a rebellion against the noun, was legendary. Parker was an expert on both the paintings and writings of Paul

Klee, and a cornerstone supporting his theory was Klee's remark in 1920, one that Martin had committed to memory, that *"Formerly we used to represent things visible on earth, things we either liked to look at or would have liked to see. Today we reveal the reality that is behind visible things, thus expressing the belief that the visible world is merely an isolated case in relation to the universe and that there are many more other, latent realities."*

Klee's view, Parker had written, was a nod to Plato and Kant, though Plato would scarcely nod back, given the Greek philosopher's uncompromising opinion that art and poetry ought be held in contempt, in that their representations were twice removed from reality. One of Professor Parker's most famous journal articles, Martin's favorite, consisted entirely of an imaginary dialogue between Plato and Klee on the meaning and value of Modern Art.

Martin was in such awe he almost felt he was having an out-of-body experience when he heard himself say, "I've heard you say you know the man, but I failed to realize you knew him well enough to send --."

"Elliott and I were classmates at Yale. But my reason for interrupting your family graduation celebration is that Elliott needs an immediate answer in order to make travel arrangements for you."

"But you know I have to go off to Washington. My new job... find an apartment... start preparing for fall semester," Martin blurted. "I'd love to go, but --."

"Hear me out," Moore said.

"I'm listening."

"Elliott was in Berlin in 1936 for the Olympics. Had a cousin from Dartmouth on the American track team. He was appalled by what he saw. The Nazis, that is. But now it's getting worse. Seems Hitler's propaganda toadies have cobbled together an exhibition that will open in Munich next month. They've gathered more than six hundred works from over thirty German museums, all the pieces falling into the Modern genre. The bloody bastards are calling their show *Entartete Kunst*."

Martin translated, "Degenerate art."

"The Nazis clearly take Elliott's theory seriously. After all, the Germans like to suppose they invented the noun. Twist them into a mile-long string, like barbed wire, till they get caught in your throat."

"Professor Parker intends to pay a visit to this exhibition?" Martin asked.

"Indeed he does. Thinks it a grand idea to take you along. His wife, Kate, doesn't care to go. They have a two-year-old son, Selby. Kate's much younger than Elliott, by the way. In any case , Elliott's parents will stay with her and her son. Thanks to her parents, Kate owns a fancy estate overlooking the Upper Hudson."

"I'd love to go, but even if I had the time, which I don't, I can't afford such a trip."

"That's not a problem. Elliott has wangled some money from the government to pay for it all. Don't ask me how. He has a knack for that sort of thing. Wish I did. And as for your getting set up in your new teaching position, I've spoken to your department chairman about Elliott's wanting to take you along."

Martin interrupted. "You also know Frank Therrigold?"

"Elliott knows him. Introduced him to me indirectly. The telephone's a splendid invention – sometimes. Anyway, Doctor

Therrigold thinks your going is a fine notion, the better to prepare you for your teaching assignments. And as for your living arrangements, Hayden Arsdale is taking a two-semester sabbatical, as you probably know. Off to Greece to stare at urns, I believe Therrigold said. In any case, Professor Arsdale has decided he would like a house-sitter in his absence. So his place is now yours for nine months, rent-free. Somewhere across the Potomac, in Alexandria, I think Frank said. So it's all arranged, assuming you're willing."

"My God, yes!" Martin said, thrilled beyond imagination.

"You're to meet Elliott in New York on the last day of this month and sail for Bremerhaven the next day. Until then I've arranged to put you up in university housing here and feed you until it's time to leave for New York, at which time you'll go by overnight coach on the New York Central. You can discuss the details when Elliott calls me at my home tomorrow night to see if you've accepted his offer."

Martin felt as though his head was spinning. "I'm simply overwhelmed, sir. I don't know what to say."

"Just say you'll do it and then you can run along and share your good news, or rather your *added* good news, with your nearest and dearest."

Martin wanted to turn a somersault, but decided that would be a bit much, not to mention he might get tangled in his gown, break a leg – or worse, his neck – and end up spending July in the hospital instead of participating in an incredible adventure. He settled for saying, "I definitely accept."

———————

Monday
July 19, 1937
Munich
Opening Day of the *Entartete Kunst* **Exhibition**

Having walked the kilometer and a half from his father's art gallery, Rainer Zeitz paused at the intersection of Königinstrasse and Prinzregentstrasse to relight his meerschaum pipe and stare at the long queue forming at the Hofgarten Gallery, on the far side of the intersection. Directly in front of him, across Königinstrasse stood the Haus der Deutsche Kunst, where only yesterday he had listened to Adolf Hitler himself give the inaugural address at the newly opened exhibition halls, heard *Der Führer* proclaim that "Art which… relies on small, in part interested and in part blasé cliques, cannot be countenanced."

His cousin, Anna Stahlinger, had promised to meet him at the Hofgarten in time to be among the first to see the collection of works by artists no longer 'countenanced' by the Reich. He had hoped to bring along his father, Werner, but that possibility proved too much to hope for. The father-and-son talk in the storage cellar of his father's gallery had failed to persuade Werner to attend the exhibition the old man had already condemned as the most outrageous insult to German culture ever conceived.

Rainer had hoped his father would find some grounds for compromise, with him and, more importantly, with the Reich, just as Anna's father, a museum director in Stuttgart, had done. Otherwise, no telling what might happen to the outspoken old man. Most likely, and at the very least, the Party will close his gallery, Rainer thought. At worst --. Well, he didn't want to contemplate that. The thought of his father in jail was unbearable. But that is what will happen if he doesn't curb his tongue, Rainer was certain.

Just then he sighted Anna waving to him from across the street, in the queue. Rainer signaled back by holding his meerschaum aloft. When he joined her in line an old woman behind them snorted and muttered under her breath something about how rude the younger generation had become.

"Perhaps you would care to step ahead of us, Frau --. What is your name, please?" Rainer said quietly, but with just a trace of menace.

Not knowing who Rainer might be, or who he might represent – a ranking member of the Party perhaps – the old woman replied, a small quaver in her voice, "No, no. It's all right. One person, more or less, in front of me is no big matter."

Rainer turned to Anna and winked. Then said, loud enough for the old woman to hear him, "The older generation are such a sniveling lot."

Anna gave him a stern look. "Do you include your father in that remark?"

Rainer laughed. "His form of complaining hardly qualifies as sniveling."

"How serious a quarrel did the two of you have?" Anna asked.

"Not very. Rather than give his real reasons for not joining us, he made the excuse that he had to finish making provision for the two American art professors who arrive from Dresden by train this evening. I know he's already settled their Munich arrangements."

"Has he made any further mention of what he plans to do about the gallery?"

"Sell it, he says. Maybe even give it away, he said in a particularly nasty fit of pique. I hope he's joking. He even says he's looked into leaving Munich."

"Where would he go?"

"London, he claims."

"He can't be serious," Anna said.

"Can't he? He said to me, 'Many of the artists whose works are being put on this humiliating display are people I know -- and respect. How can I continue to call myself an art dealer? How dare I even show my face if I carry on as if what is happening doesn't matter? That business as usual is acceptable?'"

"I know he's upset, but I was hoping --."

"I'll give you an example of how upset he is. With me, especially. He says I disappoint him far more than Hitler, Goebbels, Göring, and the rest. He asked me what I suppose will happen to all these paintings after the exhibit is over. I tell him I don't know. 'Well,' he says, 'I know. They'll all be destroyed in a big bonfire, with hundreds of Party members dancing about the flames. And,' he adds, 'You, my son, will not only be there, you will be among the first to strike a match.'"

Anna shook her head. "He can't believe that."

"He can indeed."

Anna took a deep breath before looking at Rainer gravely. "Is he right? Would you?"

Rainer toyed with his pipe for several moments, looked up at the sky, then back down at Anna before saying, "I'm not sure."

2

Four years later --

Monday
September 15, 1941
Gatchina Palace
45 kilometers south of Leningrad

Dust stirred by a mechanized army on the move filled the sky and gave the sun a swollen, pallid look as it descended behind the palace's center parapet. Rainer Zeitz climbed from the BMW sidecar, removed his goggles, and stared up at the dull limestone façade of the palace, then upward at the sun. Turning to his aide and driver, he said, "How much daylight remains?"

Karl Vollmer, holding the rank of *SS Hauptscharführer* -- the Army's equivalent of an *Oberfeldwebel,* a Master Sergeant -- extended a pack of cigarettes with one hand, slapped dust from his uniform with the other. "Sunset yesterday came just before 7:30." Karl looked at his watch. "Four hours."

Rainer paused before accepting a cigarette. Having misplaced his cherished pipe somewhere between Riga and Tallin, he now forced himself to smoke unpleasant army-issue cigarettes rather than forego nicotine altogether. "We'll only be here an hour or so. I want to be at the front before sundown."

"No treasure here, *Sturmbannführer*?"

"A few bits of Meissen, some Faberge china and silver, and several tapestries that might interest *Reichsmarshall* Göring."

"No paintings?" Karl asked, looking incredulous.

Rainer pointed to Karl's canteen, which his aide then handed to him. After washing the dust from his mouth he said, "Only a few minor water-colors. But in any case, we'll leave everything for the others to examine, supposing, of course, the Russians left them behind." He then lit the cigarette and inhaled deeply.

Karl shrugged. By *others* he understood his *SS Sturmbannführer* to mean those members of the 2nd Special Battalion, one of the four *Einsatzgruppen*, Special Task Force units under Baron von Kunsberg assigned to the Eastern Front. They had been left in Estonia to finish packing artwork from the Tallin City Archives, but were expected to join them before the week was over -- *after* the czars' summer palaces in Pushkin were safely in German control. Von Kunsberg's previous work in France for Foreign Minister Ribbentrop made him untrustworthy in the eyes of Himmler, although the *Reichsleiter* in the end decided the baron's men could be highly useful, according to Rainer's account. But, as a precaution, Rainer had been assigned to precede the baron's extra-military *Sonderkommado* groups and to keep watch that their deeds reflected Göring's, and SS interests, not anyone else's.

Karl disliked the baron intensely and supposed his *Sturm-bannführer* did also, although Rainer was too politic to let his attitude show. Better that they worked independently of the baron. Karl was not so naïve, however, as to suppose Rainer did not have Himmler and Göring pulling some of his strings. Rainer's most important cachet, however, and the one that had proven most useful in dealing with anyone who dared cross him, was the *Führervorbehalt*, a Hitler prerogative, which included a letter of instructions signed by the *Führer*, which Rainer carried with him and protected as though it were life itself. How his commanding officer came by such a document, Karl neither knew nor cared. He did know Rainer had never met the *Führer* in person, though he had met Himmler several times. He wasn't sure about Göring.

Standing in the vast courtyard, Rainer closed his eyes and bowed his head, oblivious to the roar of the dozens of courier motorcycles and supply trucks coming and going. The palace was now temporary headquarters for General Eric Hoepner's Fourth Panzer Group, spearhead of Army Group North's drive toward Leningrad. Sleepless since leaving the ammunition train that carried Karl and him from Tallin to Narva, Rainer wanted nothing more than to lie down in the shade of a palace wall and dream of less frantic days before the war. But time was critical. He could sleep when his immediate mission was complete. That this palace still stood, mostly intact, boded well for his assignment. When Rainer looked up again he scanned the ramparts of the palace, pleased the Russians had chosen not to put up a serious defense of it.

Behind him Karl said, "What a drab-looking building. It looks more like the SS *Junkerschule* we attended than a czar's palace."

Rainer nodded wearily. Of the monochrome limestone, he said, "The drab color, I'm told, changes color with the movement of the sun. Too bad we won't be here long enough to tell."

"It still looks dull as a prison," Karl said.

"Did you know that the czars used to review their troops right here where we are standing?"

"Horse parades, no doubt."

"Picture Cossacks in bright red tunics." Rainer pointed to a turret rising above the third floor of the palace. "The view from there must have been spectacular."

"Cossacks," Karl snorted. "Barbarians. All Russians are barbarians for that matter."

"Some, however, possess an artistic flair," Rainer said. "That is why you and I are here."

"I thought we came to recover German art the Russians stole from us."

"That, too."

Karl nodded indifferently. "Shall I find us quarters to rest for a while before we push on, *Sturmbannführer?*"

"No time. I said I want to be here no more than one hour. Find the soldiers' mess and feed yourself. Then look for the motor pool and bring us back something more dignified than --." Rainer waved toward the motorcycle. "Meet me back here in precisely one hour." Suddenly realizing his uniform was as dusty as the BMW, he slapped his cap at his tunic and trousers. A brown cloud formed around him and he stepped away, patting at his tunic pocket. As Karl walked away Rainer called out, "Pick us up more cigarettes. A better grade if you can manage." He tossed his half-smoked Eckstein on the ground.

"This is not Berlin," Karl said boldly. He pulled a full pack of the same brand from his tunic and offered them to Rainer. With reluctance Rainer accepted them. Karl was right. He was not only no longer in Berlin, but within a few kilometers of the front lines. I should have sought out a tobacconist in Tallin, he told himself. Bought a new pipe, bought a decent pouch of cut to put in it, supposing I could find any. Rainer judged the army-issue Raulino pipe tobacco indistinguishable from cow dung.

"Shall I bring you something to eat?" Karl asked.

"No. I'll see what the Wehrmacht feeds their frontline officers." His culinary expectations were low, but he could always hope. He reminded himself that, arriving in Tallin the same day the Wehrmacht had forced encircled Russian army units to exit by sea, Rainer had seen for the first time what battlefront enlisted soldiers eat and decided he'd rather starve. No such cavalier attitude possessed him now. No telling when the next opportunity to eat something other than Russian road dust might present itself, he thought sullenly.

Inside the palace a clerk directed him to the second floor, where he found General Hoepner's aide, a man named Franz Emmert, standing at the back of an ornate parlor stripped of furniture as he listened while a Panzer major gave a briefing to a roomful of officers on the disposition of the Russian Fifth Army defending Leningrad. Rainer recognized the colonel from the clerk's description.

"Colonel Emmert?"

The man turned and slowly took in Rainer's still-more-brown-than-black SS uniform. "You must be Zeitz," he said. Whether his omission of Rainer's rank was deliberate Rainer couldn't judge. "How did you manage to get here?"

Rainer explained his two-day itinerary.

"Too bad you're not the ammunition train. We could make better use of you."

Rainer was well aware of his unpopularity, or rather, the unpopularity of his role as *Kunstverschaffner*, art procurer, in the eyes of Wehrmacht officers and soldiers. This particular assignment especially, he knew, would grate on those who wore *feldgrau*.

"I understand your dismay, Colonel. But let us not dwell on it. I am counting on you and *Generaloberst* Hoepner to see that I reach the proper frontline commanders in time to explain Berlin's instructions."

"We already know Berlin's 'instructions', as you call them," Colonel Emmert said forcefully.

"Then you know that I am required in this instance to reinforce these instructions personally."

The colonel did not try to mask his disgust. After a deep sigh, he said, "Come. Rather than interrupt proceedings here, I'll show you on a small map where you need to go."

Operation Barbarossa, Germany's blueprint for the invasion of the Soviet Union, called for Army Group North to strike from Poland across the Baltic states of Latvia, Estonia, and Lithuania toward Leningrad, then to capture the city named for the most revered of all Russia's czars, Peter the Great, and now renamed for the father of Soviet Communism, Nikolai Lenin.

Russian resistance had stiffened near Novgorod, 200 kilometers southeast of Leningrad, as Army Group North crossed out of Latvia and Estonia in a sweeping counter-clockwise arc. The marshes and small lakes that made up the tedious landscape south of Leningrad proved inhospitable to the broad-front advances that had brought the Germans this far. Instead, the terrain proved ideal for small units of Russian infantry and sappers to stall German blitz tactics. Yet, despite mounting losses of men and materiel, the German army ground slowly forward toward its primary objective, Leningrad. Just south of that huge city lay the village of Pushkin and the summer palaces of the czars – Rainer Zeitz's primary objective.

The hour since he had left Karl was up. Having examined routes on the colonel's map, Rainer now stood on the palace ground waiting for his aide to return. Short of time after allowing Colonel Emmert to brag at length of what he knew of the terrain between Gatchina and Pushkin, Rainer only had time to grab a slice of bread and a piece of stale cheese from the officers' mess before returning to the parade ground to wait.

No Karl. So he sat on the ground and nibbled at his bread and cheese, checking and rechecking his watch. His food eaten and still hungry, he lit a cigarette. Five minutes later a camouflage-colored VW Kubelwagen with its top down came into view. The front-hood-mounted spare tire was missing, but Rainer was thankful simply not to have to travel another kilometer in the damned motorcycle sidecar. No point in his worrying about a flat tire until it happened.

"What kept you?" he snapped at Karl as his *Hauptscharführer* held the side door for him.

As he slammed the door and returned to the driver's seat Karl said, "The *Leuntnant* in charge of the motor pool insisted I was to drive you to the front with the motorcycle and sidecar. I gave him your rank and told him a sidecar was unfitting for a major to meet a general. Then he tried to tell me motorcycles were all he had available."

Seated, Rainer pulled out the pack of Echts and lit one as he watched Karl brush away imaginary flecks of dirt from his crusher hat before repositioning it on his head. "So then where did this vehicle come from?" He patted the back of Karl's seat.

The aide turned and grinned. "I gave him your name."

"The motor pool lieutenant knows me?"

Karl shook his head. "Not personally. But the lieutenant said, 'I was told by a Colonel Emmert to accommodate your... officer.' He started to say *asshole officer*, but caught himself and said *assertive officer* instead. Apparently this Colonel Emmert has made you famous here already."

"Yes, I know. The colonel made himself quite clear: He doesn't like me or my instructions." Rainer said, reflecting again on the Army's disapproval of his current task. "My requests do not always coincide with what is easiest for the Army," he muttered to himself. To Karl, "Drive. I want to reach General Kruger's field headquarters before sundown."

With Leningrad now within a single day's push, two at most, and with the summer palaces of the czars only kilometers ahead of the lead units of Army Group North, Rainer understood that he and he alone wielded the power – via Berlin – to prevent the czars' great summer estates from being destroyed by the German military juggernaut. The sooner he detailed his requirements to the commander at the front the better. Rainer now knew from Colonel Emmert that the orders just issued by General Loeb, commander of Army Group North, directed General Walter Kruger's First Panzer Division to spearhead the attack designed to overrun those Russian Fifth Army defensive positions concentrated in the immediate area of the palaces at Pushkin.

Karl shifted the Kubelwagen into gear and slowly pulled away from Gatchina Palace, stopping only at the moat to allow three messengers on motorcycles to cross the bridge leading into the vast parade ground. Over his shoulder he called back, "I told the lieutenant that, unless he gave me a car suitable to your rank, I could promise him that he himself would end up driving you to the front on the motorcycle and that you would make him walk back alone in the dark."

Rainer shook his head, only slightly amused, and leaned forward to say, "Thank you for making me appear to be an even bigger asshole than I really am."

Over the noise of the car's engine, Karl shouted, "You're very welcome, *Sturmbannführer*."

Though nine years older than Rainer, Karl Vollmer had been a friend since Rainer's childhood, since the first time they had met, when Rainer's father had taken the family to vacation on the Baltic Sea at a rental home in the resort town of Hohenfelde, east of Karl's hometown of Brodersdorf, on the east side of Kiel Inlet, north of the city of Kiel. Karl's parents, Otto and Myra Vollmer, ran a small seaside café and gallery called Kunststall, where Rainer's family often ate and discussed art with the locals. Rainer and Karl met because Karl had worked as a deckhand on his older brother's fishing boat and had invited Rainer to join him and his brother, Klaus, for a day at sea. From that day forward they had been fast friends, differences in their ranks notwithstanding.

At the outbreak of the war Rainer had sought Karl to be his aide and had clashed with the SS bureaucracy in Berlin to get him. Only *Echt Deutsch*, true Germans, were permitted to serve in the SS. Because Karl's mother grew up in the small town of Parnu, Estonia, and because Karl's parents had died in 1935, and because official records showed his parents lived in Parnu in the year Karl claimed he was born, 1903, and because of the Russian takeover of Estonia in 1914 resulted in the loss of many birth records, and because he had no birth record to prove otherwise, Karl could not demonstrate his native-born German status to the satisfaction of the SS purists and was officially proclaimed *Folk Deutsch*. Because, because, because. Yet, with much help from Rainer's cousin, Anna Stahlinger, Rainer tracked down Karl's birth and baptismal records in the village of Todendorf, on the sea east of Kiel, where Karl's parents had come to visit Karl's grandfather at the old man's nearby farm, when Karl arrived two weeks prematurely.

Records in hand, Rainer had finally been able to satisfy Berlin's SS bureaucracy.

At the junction of the main road and a narrow lane Karl and Rainer stared mutely as a Wehrmacht burial detail loaded the bodies of German soldiers onto an open-bed truck. Scattered in a nearby field appeared to be dozens of dead Russians, left where they had fallen, all together in a small area.

Seeing the Russian corpses, Rainer shouted to Karl, "How long has it been since you had a chance to speak Russian?" Without waiting for an answer, he said, "Perhaps we will see some Russian prisoners up ahead. You can talk to them."

Over his shoulder, Karl replied, "I don't think so. I overheard men talking in the mess tent. We aren't taking prisoners."

Rainer turned, looked back at the cluster of dead Russians, and fell silent.

As the small Kubelwagen approached a line of panzers pulled off to the side of the road waiting to be refueled, Karl said, "Despite two days' of dust on our uniforms, we are much too clean, *Sturmbahnführer*. Perhaps we should baptize ourselves with a bit more of the soil of Mother Russia before we proceed any farther. Otherwise, those ahead –" he gestured vaguely in the direction of Leningrad " -- will judge us tin soldiers," *Zinnsoldaten*. "Worse. They will think us dandies."

Karl's vanity amused Rainer. Karl had not needed military life to teach him to fuss about his appearance. He was always fastidious, Rainer remembered. "Perhaps we should not have dusted ourselves off so diligently back at Gatchina. Yet I rather suspect the frontline soldiers will pay us no mind," the *Sturmbahnfrührer* said. "We mean nothing to them."

Suddenly Karl honked the car's horn when, as if to make his commander's point, a panzer crewman began to walk slowly across the narrow, gravel road, oblivious to the oncoming car. A second honk failed to draw the soldier's attention. The man stopped to finish rolling a cigarette instead.

"Go around him. He has other things on his mind," Rainer said.

"He'd better pay attention or he'll get himself killed," Karl said, as he swung the right-side tires of the car into slippery grass.

"Don't worry. He'll be alert enough when his panzer rejoins the advance."

Past the indifferent tank soldier, Karl eased the Kubelwagen back onto the gravel road, then looked in the rearview mirror to see the soldier make a half-hearted obscene gesture toward the car. Ahead, in the middle of the road stood another grimy panzer crewman, staring at the oncoming vehicle, but making no effort to move aside. Rather than honk, Karl again took to the grass, this time far enough to make all four tires spin as they grasped for traction.

When the second road soldier was behind them, Rainer again leaned forward, this time asking teasingly, "Don't you wish to be thought of as a *Stutzer*, Karl?" Rainer used the word for a dandy more common in his native Bavaria. Earlier Karl had used the word from his mother's Estonian *Volkdeutscher* vocabulary, where a dandy was a *Geck*.

"I guess I don't care all that much what these men think. We are not like them," Karl said.

Rainer patted Karl on a shoulder once more. "No, we're not. In fact we're not even soldiers of any kind, are we? Let alone tin soldiers. We just happen to wear the same uniforms."

"Soldier or not, you still must deal with General Kruger," Karl said.

"So I must."

"He will not be easy."

"Do you think not?"

Karl said, "By reputation he is a soldier's soldier. He served in France in 1914."

"Then he has no one to impress. Least of all me."

White smoke, grey smoke, black smoke began to mingle with thick dust and hung like an eerie fog ahead of them. Rainer had never ventured so near the battlefront before, had never witnessed, outside a Munich funeral parlor, so much as one dead man, let alone so many. Again they encountered Wehrmacht burial details scuttling about, hastily retrieving German dead, assiduously ignoring any body not dressed in *feldgrau*. Late summer wild grasses and thistle should have scented the air but other odors dominated, choking odors worse than the dust and smoke. Rainer took off his goggles and wiped away sweat and grim. Overcome momentarily by swirling dust, he coughed a heavy, choking cough. His throat cleared, he inhaled deeply. His nostrils filled with a mélange of smells: gunpowder, diesel fuel, cigarette smoke from soldiers idling in the grass. And, most overpowering of all, burnt hair and rotting flesh.

"Keep it on the road!" he shouted from his place in the rear seat, as Karl let the car's right-side tires slide off the compact gravel and into twisted, matted grass.

"I am trying my very best, *Sturmbannführer.* As you can see, the soldiers will not respect us. They will not move."

Though the panzers lined the left edge of road in disciplined fashion, their crewmen idled randomly. Some lolled beneath temporary canvas canopies tied to the tanks' treads. But others chose to sprawl in the grass on the right side of the road. Others squatted by makeshift fires built in the middle of the road, while still others wandered aimlessly back and forth across the road, oblivious to their surroundings, cigarettes limply dangling from the corners of their mouths.

Finally, Rainer caved into Karl's continuing exasperation. "Run over them, if you must. Then the others will get the idea," Rainer said, trying to sound serious.

"But *Sturmbannführer* – "

"Honk your horn!" Rainer stood up from his place in the rear seat and, as the driver swerved again, braced himself against pitching out onto the grass himself. Blasts from the horn evoked not so much as a curious glance from the indolent troops. Rainer slumped back into his seat. "Do your best," he said to Karl.

At last they reached the small town of Krasnogvardeisk, where the 41st Mechanized Infantry had halted, waiting to be re-supplied. Beyond, the road to Pushkin stood jammed with transport trucks waiting to move soldiers of the 269th Infantry Division, already rearmed and fed, forward in support of First Panzer.

The final five kilometers took three quarters of an hour to complete. The sun was sinking quickly when they reached First Panzer's temporary field headquarters, consisting of a pair of folding tables and a single chair. The air was thick with the smell of cordite and Rainer could hear sporadic small-arms fire coming from well beyond the most forward tanks. Before he could exit the car someone stepped away from a circle of men bent over one of the tables and strode quickly toward the Kubelwagen. Offering neither a salute nor a greeting, he announced, "I am Major Hartmann." Then demanded, "Who are you and what is your business here?"

Rainer stepped from the car. "*Sturmbannführer* Zeitz. I am here to speak to General Kruger."

The major scowled. "For what purpose?"

Rainer turned to Karl. "Wait here." Enough of these pompous intercessors, he thought. Sidestepping the major, he marched toward the tables. He had rehearsed his upcoming conversation with the column's tank commander and hoped his rehearsal would not prove ineffective. Or worse – pointless, for being too late. He understood that battlefield generals do not debate military tactics with lower-ranking, non-combat emissaries, however cogent the underling's petition. That Rainer was present at all – and from Berlin – was likely to enrage any commander worth his commission.

Amid the diesel roar of tanks eager to advance, amid the smell of cordite all around, amid the sound of distant artillery, Rainer braced, saluted, then introduced himself to General Walter Kruger, commander of First Panzer Division. Only when Rainer finished did the general look up from his maps – without returning the salute.

"I am here, Herr General, on behalf of the *Führer* to convey personally his desire that German forces capture entirely intact any and all works of art rightfully belonging to the German people, having been stolen from them by the Bolsheviks. My presence is his gesture to demonstrate the utmost importance of this, his own, directive."

General Kruger gave Rainer a cold stare. "My orders, Major, are quite simple at this point. I am to press forward toward Leningrad, seizing all ground between here and there, killing any and all Russians who stand in my way, kill them by any means at my disposal."

"But that does not including destroying all buildings that stand in your way. Nor all buildings' contents, Herr General."

"So you say."

"So Berlin says," Rainer emphasized.

"Oh, now it's *Berlin* says, not the *Führer* says. Well, my orders come from the OKW, from no one else. And their directives are always approved by the *Führer* himself. The *Führer*, I repeat. Not Himmler, and certainly not *Reichsmarshall* Göring, who I know perfectly well is behind all of this. If Göring wants to make himself useful, he should be sending more airplanes, not some arrogant *Kunstverschaffner*. This is a military campaign, you fool." He pounded the map table. "These are tanks, not camels. And this Russia, not Egypt. We are here to destroy an enemy, not to gather baubles from the graves of Pharaohs."

"Wrong, Herr General. We are here to reclaim German treasures from the halls of the czars. That, too, is our mission. Your mission."

The general looked out into the smoky distance ahead of him. "Treasures," he said softly. Looking at Rainer, he said, "You are welcome to whatever treasures remain when my tanks finish blasting the Russians ahead of us from their excellent defense works. Reclaim them from the rubble."

"You would pulverize the most cherished work of Fredrick the Great?"

The general stared at him.

"The Amber Room lies just ahead of you in one of the summer palaces in Pushkin. The *Führer* himself insists that it be saved at all costs."

"At all costs," the general sighed.

"Yes."

"Damn you. Damn all of you. This is no way to fight a war. This is madness."

"Whatever your cost, the Amber Room must be spared destruction. My orders are to dismantle it and return it to Germany," Rainer said.

The general gestured for one of his aides. "Colonel, escort this man to the rear of the column. Stay with him until we have fought our way beyond the village of Pushkin. Then, after we have taken the czars' summer palaces, see that his orders are followed. Give him whatever assistance he requires. But, under all circumstances, keep him from me. I wish never to see him again. Understood?"

The colonel saluted smartly. "Yes, Herr General." To Rainer, "Come."

Rainer, too, saluted. "I'm sorry to be so difficult, Herr General. Our duty to the Fatherland is not always simple or easy.

I regret that so many more of your soldiers may die that art may live. But those are our orders. Keep in mind I speak of German art. Great German art. Reclaiming such works is part of restoring German honor."

General Kruger glared at Rainer, then gave him a dismissive wave before returning to stare at his map table.

3

Monday
September 15, 1941
Washington, D.C.

Martin Wynerson left his office in the art department at George
Washington University and walked two blocks north on 23rd
Street to Washington Circle. Although Elliott Parker had kept
in touch regularly with him, *regularly*, as Martin had calculated,
amounted to approximately a dozen times in the four years since
they had journeyed together nearly the full length of Germany,
from Berlin to Munich and several cities in between, listening
to whispered horror stories about the state of the arts inside the
Third Reich, culminating finally in seeing the grotesque display
of what the Nazis were pleased to label Degenerate Art. Keeping
in touch, for Elliott Parker, had amounted to half a dozen one-
page letters and as many five-minute phone calls from Boston.
The purpose of each letter and call was to inform Martin of the

latest shocking bit of news leaking out of Germany regarding the desecration of art by this or that political arm of the Reich.

Now, as Martin stood waiting for Elliott Parker to pick him up, he remembered vividly the phone call from Elliott on Armistice Day, 1938. Because the holiday fell on Friday, Martin had planned to spend his three-day weekend in New York City, catching an early morning train and planning to visit the Nierendorf Gallery. Karl Nierendorf had fled Germany in 1936, though his brother Joseph chose to remain in Berlin and continue to operate their gallery there.

By incredible coincidence, it seemed to Martin, Elliott's call was to announce an invitation from Karl Nierendorf himself, whom he had first met in New York City the day before Martin sailed for Europe with Elliott Parker. The purpose of Herr Nierendorf's invitation was to solicit Martin's help in deciding which of the one hundred fifty paintings by Paul Klee now in the gallery's possession would display in the space the gallery owner intended to allot the Klee exhibition. Martin's joy at having been asked to help was inexpressible. Or so he told himself.

The New York Nierendorf gallery instantly had become a haven for refugee German artists, the latest being Franz Xaver Fuhr. What pleased Martin most about Karl Nierendorf was that during the earlier part of the decade, before leaving Germany, the man held private exhibitions in his own home for selected guests and once the featured artist had been Martin's own favorite, Franz Marc, a member, along with Klee, Vassily Kandinski and others, of the Munich-based Blue Ride Group.

As Martin thought about it later, Professor Parker's phone call that morning became Martin's first foray into the realm of art-related intelligence gathering. Well, his first stateside. The trip to Germany a year and half earlier served the same purpose.

After extending the Nierendorf invitation to Martin, Elliott's call had ended by asking Martin if he had read or heard the news of the events that had occurred all across Germany on the previous Wednesday night, November 9th, the concatenation of which was now being referred to as *Kristallnacht*.

Martin had not. So Elliott explained to him that nationwide attacks were instigated against Jewish synagogues and businesses by the *Sicherheitsdienst*, the intelligence branch of the SS, whose chief was a brutal man named Reinhard Heydrich. The pretext, according to Elliott, was the assassination of a German embassy official in Paris two days earlier by a Polish Jew. Pillaging and looting followed, hence the name given to the events, which referred to streets strewn with broken glass following the rampage by Heydrich's thugs.

The second purpose of his call, Elliott had explained, was to ask a favor of Martin, the favor being that Martin ask a colleague in the art department at GWU, that colleague being Morris Gottlieb, to try to find out the status – post-*Kristallnacht* -- of one of Gottlieb's close friends and a fellow Jew, Hugo Helbing, the owner of the leading art auction house in Munich. Elliott had been assured recently by German refugee art historians at Harvard that Gottlieb might still maintain contact with Helbing, though perhaps indirectly.

Martin had promised to seek Morris out and ask him about Herr Helbing, inquiring, even as he promised, if he had permission to use Elliott's name. Parker had assured him it was okay, told Martin that Gottlieb already knew of Elliott and his work, making Martin wonder why Elliott had not contacted Professor Gottlieb directly. But Martin thought better of asking, assuming Elliott Parker had his reasons. Much later Martin decided the reason was that this was Elliott's way of starting a slow immersion process whereby Martin found himself pulled inextricably into the American apparatus for keeping track of, and eventually tracking down, the objects of German art plunder.

As it turned out, Martin now remembered, Professor Gottlieb eventually found out through his sources that Hugo Helbing's art auction house had undergone *Entjudung*, a word Professor Gottlieb could barely force from his mouth. It meant de-Jewification, the counterpart of which was Aryanisation. Of Helbing himself, Gottlieb learned nothing, which did not bode well for Herr Helbing – and Morris Gottlieb knew it.

In any case, two weeks later he received a second call from Elliott, thanking him for passing along his request to Professor Gottlieb, adding that Gottlieb had been in touch with him directly, something Morris himself had not mentioned to Martin when explaining what little he had been able to unearth.

In the meantime his three-day trip to New York had turned out splendidly, Martin now recalled. Karl Nierendorf actually listened to my ideas, implemented several of them in fact, he thought, still highly pleased.

At the time of the phone call asking the favor Martin knew Elliott was part of an organization at Harvard that called itself the American Defense/Harvard Group, a group of art historians – many of them recent German immigrants – whose task was to track and identify art works confiscated by the Nazis inside the sphere of German occupation.

And now Martin stood waiting. Elliott had invited him to a meeting at Georgetown University – a little *Treff*, Elliott had called it – with a pair of professors there who, by whatever means, maintained contact with anti-Nazi elements inside German-occupied territories, people willing to risk their lives, and perhaps their families' and friends' lives, to keep the outside world informed on whatever local details they could ascertain about Nazi art plundering.

Martin walked as far as the south side of Washington Circle when a taxicab stopped beside him. Elliott Parker rolled down a rear window and gestured for Martin to climb in. "Good to see you again, Martin. Hope I haven't kept you waiting long."

"I just arrived myself, sir," Martin said. "I could have walked, you know. Or taken a bus. It's not that far."

"Of course, but I wanted to go over a couple items again; make certain you understand the transitory nature of whatever news may be passed along to us. Much of it will be third or fourth hand and many weeks old in some cases. For the nonce it's the best we can do, I'm afraid."

For the nonce. Martin snickered to himself, even though he recalled hearing Elliott Parker occasionally served as a set-design consultant to an amateur Shakespeare troupe in Cambridge. In keeping with an out-of-time sense of identity, Elliott wore a homburg and carried an umbrella, even thought the day was perfectly sunny and the weather forecast predicted no rain.

Elliott said, "I'm eager for you to meet the two priests. Actually, I believe you've already met Father Troquier."

Martin nodded. "I was panel member at a colloquium at the Museum of Modern Art last spring and Jean-Marcel Troquier also was on the panel. We had coffee together afterwards. He struck me as a very accomplished scholar and definitely a cheerleader for French art. Father Rokosz I have not met, but he is held in high esteem by people I respect."

Elliott said, "Both are good men. And knowledgeable. Each has contacts unavailable to me, unavailable to our government. But again, how reliable their contacts are, I cannot confirm."

Martin nodded. "Do you have contacts of your own?"

Elliott Park paused before saying, "I do. Unfortunately many – most, in fact – are or were in Germany. I hear nothing from any of those still in the Fatherland – except for one who manages to skip back and forth between Bavaria and Switzerland." With a sigh he added, "I'm not even sure if most of them are still alive."

The cab turned right on 35th Street, then left on O Street, dropping them off in front of the entrance to Healy Building at Georgetown University. While some students sat on the grass enjoying the afternoon sunshine, many more queued in lines to board city busses lined up in front of the grassy commons. Elliott tipped the driver generously, then turned to Martin. "The fathers' offices are back in the Walsh building, but we're meeting them in front of Dahlgren Chapel on the Quad. More privacy. Both men are suspicious types. I'm afraid they tend to imagine German spies behind every pipe-smoking sophomore wearing a fraternity sweater. But then the horror stories each has heard coming from their homelands, as Hitler spreads his venom in an ever-widening circle across Europe, would put a saint on guard."

"I think I understand, sir," Martin said.

"You are sworn to secrecy, Martin, even though I'm in no position to ask you to raise your right hand and take an oath."

"Yes, sir."

"Feel free to speak, to ask questions," Parker said. "But --."

"But what?"

"I understand you have taken exception to the Vatican's role – or lack of same – in invoking its moral persuasion to try to stop Nazi art confiscation in occupied countries."

Martin nodded. "I believe I've made a remark or two to that effect." *What big ears you have, Grandma*, Martin thought, more amused than offended that Elliott would keep such close tabs on him. The remark or two had been made to colleagues at a sherry party reception given for new graduate students by his department chairman, Frank Therrigold, at the chairman's house in Arlington at the beginning of the semester.

"More than one point of view exists on the subject of where His Holiness stands on the entire Nazi issue. I understand the Curia itself is deeply divided between those who cheer Hitler, thinking him an angel of the Lord, Christendom's best -- perhaps only -- hope to crush the monster that is Bolshevik atheism, and those who imagine the *Führer* to be the Anti-Christ in disguise, wrapping himself in a bastardized symbol of the Cross."

"Both sides must still view him as an art thief. Yet they all remain silent," Martin replied.

Parker continued as though he hadn't heard Martin. "Any Vatican position must consider the fact that Italy is Hitler's ally.

The very survival of the Vatican depends, obviously, on Mussolini's good will and, by proxy, Hitler's."

"Both respect Swiss neutrality. Even Hitler wouldn't offend all of Bavaria by invading the Vatican, physically or symbolically," Martin said, not particularly caring if Elliott took offense at his amateur policy analysis.

Elliott Parker cleared his throat. "In any case, staunch Catholics that they are, the fathers are both touchy on the subject of Pius's behavior toward Hitler. So let's not bring it up. Okay?"

"Fine by me." Again Martin, while keeping a straight face, wanted to laugh. *Staunch Catholic* indeed. Martin knew no one more constant in his Catholic faith than Professor Elliott George Parker.

Father Troquier and Father Theodosius Roskosz, each wearing a black, ankle-length cassock, rose from the steps of the chapel to greet them as Martin and Elliott approached. "Gentlemen, welcome to Georgetown," Father Roskosz said in a voice that startled Martin. The priest's high pitch failed to go with his tall, barrel-chested build, his large head with its scarred face masked by a thick, salt-and-pepper beard. *Paul Bunyan with a Judy Garland voice*, Martin thought, just as he accepted the man's crushing handshake.

Father Troquier's parts, by contrast, were all of a harmonious whole. The pale delicate features struck Martin as almost porcelain-esque, blues eyes that sparkled, a sheen to his slicked black hair, a fragile handshake that was not quite effeminate, a soft, mellow voice resonating with nasal French tones that seemed to echo as though his sinuses were catacombs full of whispers.

Yet Martin knew Father Troquier's surface mousiness belied a steely determination to make his influence count inside the corridors of Washington on the subject of urging America to join directly the war against Fascism, while he actively solicited contributions across America and Canada via mail and telephone, money intended to aid the French Resistance.

"It's good to see you again, Professor Wynerson. I'm pleased you take a keen interest in our cause," Troquier said as he gestured for Martin to seat himself on the granite steps.

"And I to see you, Father." Martin touched the stone block with a palm, realized it was not as cold as he had anticipated, and sat, wondering what Elliott might have said to make the father mis-suppose a keenness for any of the padre's causes.

Elliott Parker seated himself on the bottom step and pulled out a pack of Lucky Strikes, offering one to each of the priests. Father Roskosz accepted one and Parker handed him a pack of matches.

As he struck a match, Roskosz said to Martin, "Wynerson. Are you Jewish?"

"Minnesota Lutheran."

Roskosz inhaled deeply from the cigarette. "Ah, yes. Ancestors from the northern side of the Baltic."

Martin nodded. "My great-grandparents came from Norköping, just south of Stockholm."

"The Swedes are playing a cagey game with the Germans, a game of acting as an innocent neutral," Father Troquier said in a tone that made clear he took less than a neutral view toward the matter.

"So far it has kept them from being occupied," Martin rejoined.

Father Troquier shrugged. "The Swedes, like the Finns, are sandwich meat between two slabs of rye bread, the Germans and the Russians. Sooner or later --." The priest bit his left index finger to finish making his point.

Elliott Parker broke the moment of tension by saying, "Now that we've established Martin's ethnicity, gentlemen, let us proceed to exchange our little secrets about what we think our common enemy is up to. Jean-Marcel, let's start with you."

"Göring has made several more visits to the Jeu de Paume. Mostly looking for Cranachs, as always. Would you believe that Fat Herman actually pays for what he steals? And often a fair price!" Looking at Martin, he added, "Not that the seller has a choice whether to sell, of course."

Martin said only, "I assume you mean the Jeu de Paume Museum and not the hotel of that name."

The Frenchman laughed. "The museum barely has space for everything the Germans have brought there, let alone the tiny hotel. Truckloads daily. Truckloads!"

Elliott asked, "Do we know yet where they are sending the art works after they catalog them at the Jeu de Paume?"

Troquier's eyes brightened. "Indeed! Now we do. In fact --." He paused and looked askance at Martin.

Elliott Parker, interpreting the look, said, "If I didn't trust Martin to keep our secrets, I would not have brought him."

The French priest sighed. "Very well." He lowered his voice and paused again for dramatic effect. "This is my most savory morsel of news. The Resistance has managed to place an informer on the French staff at the Louvre, aiding the *Sonderstabe Bildende Kunst.*" Again looking to Martin, he said, "That means --"

"I speak German," Martin said. "The Special Staff for Pictorial Art is part of the *Einstab Reichsleiter Rosenberg,* the ERR."

"Very good! But do you know it is run de facto by Göring, not Rosenberg?" Troquier added in an attempt to regain the upper conversational hand.

Hoping to keep the Frenchman on track, Elliott Parker asked, "Has your informant yet learned where any of the stolen French art is being taken?"

"She has!" he shouted. But Troquier's look of triumph vanished quickly as he apparently wished he hadn't revealed the gender of the French spy.

"Go on," Parker urged.

"We clearly do not know all the locations yet, but would you believe one of the primary repositories for now is Mad Ludwig's architectural abomination at Neuschwanstein?"

"That place has less room than the Jeu de Paume hotel," Martin said jokingly. But from the look the French priest gave him Father Troquier was not amused.

"Anything else?" Parker asked.

"*Mon Dieu*! Is that not enough?"

"That is excellent, Jean-Marcel," Parker replied. Then he nodded toward Father Roskosz.

"Barring a miracle --, " the Polish priest crossed himself, " – the Germans will overrun Leningrad within the next few days. Our observers in Königsburg tell us the SS is already sending trainloads of art work back to Germany from the Baltic states. And now ERR men are finishing up their work in Riga and moving to join General von Leeb's Army Group North to direct the dismantling of the Hermitage, the czars' palaces, and whatever else they deem worth saving before Hitler carries out his promise to erase Leningrad from the face of the earth."

Dumbfounded, Martin asked, "Is he serious?"

"Hitler?" Elliott said. "I'm sure he means it."

Father Roskosz gently lay a hand on Elliott's arm. "I'm afraid you know the man who has been placed in charge of the Leningrad ERR."

Parker looked perplexed, but only momentarily. "You mean –

Roskosz nodded. "Rainer Zeitz. Or rather, *Sturmbahnführer* Zeitz."

While Elliott Parker took a turn at sighing, Martin asked, "Is he the Rainer who is the son of the gallery owner we spent time with in Munich on our trip to Germany in 1937? Werner Zeitz?"

"The same," Parker said. "Werner fled to London during the Christmas holidays in '38. Rainer not only stayed in Germany, but – as Father Theodosius has just said – he joined the SS just before Hitler invaded Poland."

Martin nodded. "During that evening we spent with the Zeitzes Rainer made clear he was a Nazi sympathizer. So he joined the SS. Oh my!"

"At least the Germans had sense enough to put his art expertise to good use instead of sending him off to become cannon fodder," Elliott said.

It was Father Roskosz's turn not to be amused. He said acidly, "They'll dumb him down until he wishes he were cannon fodder. An educated Nazi stands out like a sore thumb. Those at the top are all failures and dilettantes who can't abide anyone who becomes serious, let alone successful, in a profession. I'm sure that accounts for part of their grievance against Jews. Rainer Zeitz, no doubt, has learned that already or he wouldn't be a *Kunstverschaffner* whistling at the gates of Leningrad."

Kunstverschaffner. Martin turned the word over in his mind. Sounds better than *Sturmbahnführer*, he decided. Then Martin let his thoughts wander back to that summer evening in 1937. Dinner for five in a small, private room at the Hotel Kempinski on Maximilianstrasse, hosted by Werner Zeitz, who, though merely the owner of a tiny Munich gallery, *Das Altes Kunstörtchen*, The Little Old Art Place, was known and respected throughout Europe as both a knowledgeable historian and a candid judge of contemporary art trends. Famous artists vied to have Werner Zeitz exhibit their works; buyers and dealers flocked to his gallery to witness his selections. The old man – in his late sixties, Rainer being somewhat of an afterthought – conducted his gallery showings much like the orchestra conductor he resembled: white hair combed back in a lionesque pompadour, broad shoulders atop a ramrod-straight spine, piercing blue eyes, and a bass voice like a kettle drum.

Martin and Elliott were also joined that evening by Werner's son, Rainer, and Werner's niece, Anna. Anna Stahlinger. Unforgettable Anna. Werner's sister's daughter. Anna's mother had married Felix Stahlinger, director of the Stuttgart city art museum.

Martin stopped to calculate. In 1937 Rainer was twenty-five years old; Anna twenty-three.

"Your German is very good, Herr Wynerson," Anna had said after Martin had ordered *Jaegerschniztel mit Rotkohl und Spaetzele*. "A bit of an Austrian touch to your pronunciation, but here in Bavaria that is acceptable."

"I would have thought it acceptable in all of Germany now that Herr Hitler is Chancellor," Martin remembered saying. "But, yes, my teacher in Minnesota grew up in Vienna."

Anna had laughed a dainty laugh, though little else was dainty about her, Martin remembered. Not that she was dumpling-shaped. Far from it. Anna was tall for a woman -- and solid, with shoulder-length blonde hair. Neither plump nor thin. Built like an alpine skier Martin thought before finding out that she was exactly that. "I'm afraid Viennese scarcely consider themselves Austrians, Herr Wynerson. They deem themselves much too sophisticated and look down their noses at the rest of their countrymen, much the same way Parisians hold all other Frenchmen in contempt. How lucky you are to live in America, where, I'm told, all men are truly equal."

Martin chuckled. "Not quite. Tell any New York City dweller that any American living west of the Hudson is his equal and you will receive a very rude reply indeed. By the way, you're English is excellent also. Have you been to America?"

When Anna replied, "I learned my English here in Munich from a woman who grew up in Chicago," Martin felt himself beguiled by the young woman's charm, wit, and loveliness and wished he could stay in Munich longer, get to know her better. The longing he felt, he had to admit, was driven as much by hormones as by any sense of intellectual like-mindedness.

Rainer, by contrast, failed the most crucial of Martin's tests for abiding friendship. Rainer's only appeal was that he reminded Martin of several of his best Minnesota male friends. But the similarity was only physical. The Nordic look. Several inches over six feet tall, Rainer tended to stoop slightly. Hawk-faced and barely containing a pent-up energy -- anger directed toward his father, Martin first guessed, and later confirmed -- Rainer reminded Martin of a bird of prey about to spring from a high branch toward an unsuspecting ground squirrel. Yet, from that day's conversations, Werner's son was, in Martin's judgment, intellectually a rooster in eagle's feathers, a sophist and perhaps a clever opportunist – making him an imposing figure in physical stature only. A tall man with a dwarfish character. Thus, over the course of the evening, although Martin found himself awed by Rainer's depth as an art historian, Rainer Zeitz seemed to take no more than a perverse pleasure from knowing so much, rather than reveal a deeply felt love for art. Martin thought him akin to a skillful magician, a showoff amused by his ability to toy with and to dazzle an audience, but also keenly aware his talent was, if not shallow, at least unserious. Martin felt no empathy with such a flippant attitude. And, while resentment toward an antagonistic father was a perspective Martin knew all too well and shared, Martin expected more, a great deal more, from the son of a man who represented the very core of European art respectability, understanding, and advancement.

"I prefer the American style of university education, Herr Wynerson, and wish I had had the opportunity to study art in your country," Werner's son had confided to him over dessert. "Under the German lecture system bright students are not permitted the luxury of responding to this or that tiresome point made by any given stern and stodgy old professor." Rainer glanced sideways toward his father as he spoke.

Werner picked up on his son's implication. "Pay him no mind, Herr Wynerson. Rainer was still wearing short pants and taking naps when he began to believe he knew more about everything than his elders know. Such an attitude is amusing when spoken by a four-year-old. But in a man of Rainer's age? Well --."

Martin replied, "At least your son has shown the good judgment to follow in your footsteps. My father – a bricklayer – expected me to become a physician or a lawyer."

"My son only pretends to follow me in my profession. His appreciation of art and my own are worlds apart," Werner said with a touch of melancholy.

"Nonsense, Father. We both worship the same pantheon of artistic deities."

"Up to a point, yes," Werner allowed. "But after that --."

"What point is that?" Martin asked.

Werner said, "The rise of Bismarck. For all my son's complaints about the rigidity and lack of freedom in the German university system, my son has the soul of a Prussian."

"He means I prefer order to chaos," Rainer said. "Prefer rules to anarchy, whether in government or art."

"Oh, yes. Indeed you do," Werner said, raising his voice and point a finger at his son. "And you believe your failed artist, the

Austrian corporal, Chancellor Shickelgruber, will restore order to the world of art by declaring heretics and casting their works into the fires of hell."

"No, Father. I believe Herr Hitler is merely bringing to light the more obvious deficiencies of those artists who presume to foist upon the serious adult world their canvasses covered with the fantasies and nightmares of imbecile children."

To that Werner merely snorted.

Rainer turned to Elliott, who had been listening intently to the father-son exchange. "You have written a famous article on this very subject, Herr Professor Parker. Do you not agree that, using your analogy, just as the noun is at the very heart of language, giving language its substance quite literally, so, too, is realism the substance, the proper subject of, art?"

"I did say that, but I was making a historical point. My use of *proper subject* in that article is intended to be descriptive, not prescriptive."

Rainer came back with, "But you also urged art critics to keep in mind Plato's admonition that the role of philosophers is to keep the poets in check, and, by extension, artists. Now I ask you, who in this century has kept the artists in check? The answer – until now – is: no one."

Exuding sarcasm, Werner said, "My son, alas, wishes to believe with a faith that indeed surpasseth all understanding that this pompous gang of thugs now in charge of Germany ranks as philosopher-kings. Such blindness! But what can a father tell a son? Because they trick themselves up in fancy uniforms and control the sources of information, we must not merely salute them, but deem them to be the wisest of the wise as well. They wish to equate modern art with chaos, the Third Reich with unqualified orderliness. What foolishness! No, worse. Dangerous foolishness."

Elliott spoke directly to Rainer. "One of the most serious failings of Plato's *Republic*, as I see it, is that he seems to have left no room for a Plato to develop, let alone his very own hero, Socrates. Who will play the role of Plato in the Third Reich?"

"No one," Werner said loudly as he passed out glasses of port. "Trust me. The second coming of a Plato in this country under these hoodlums will be as welcome as the Second Coming of Christ in the story of the Grand Inquisitor that Ivan tells Alyosha in *The Brothers Karamozov*. Christ is not welcome back at all. Rather, he is a serious inconvenience who needs to be put to death again so that the Catholic Church can carry on with its business of manipulating the masses."

A long silence prevailed. Martin could see that both Elliott and Rainer were made uncomfortable by the old man's comparison. So he intervened by asking Rainer, "As both a student of -- and admirer of -- the works of Franz Marc, I would like for you to explain to me why his paintings have ended up in an exhibition labeled Degenerate Art."

Rainer tensed and looked away for a moment before composing himself and saying, "Franz Marc's inclusion in that collection is a mistake. A serious mistake. And the Reich has acknowledged as much by removing his works."

"One work only! *Der Turm der blauen Pferde*, The Tower of the Blue Horses," Werner interrupted loudly. "And then only under pressure from the Army Officer Corps. Four more Marcs remain in the exhibition."

Rainer replied, almost in a whisper, "It is a beginning."

Anna broke her silence to diffuse the tension. "Enough *Kunstpolitik* for a while, gentlemen. May I propose a toast to our pair of indomitable guests?"

All four men reached for their port glasses.

"To America and all its grand achievements! We Germans envy you and salute you!"

"Amen!" shouted Werner.

"Agreed," said Rainer.

"We thank you, Anna," Elliott said, clinking his glass against hers.

Martin nodded his acknowledgement.

"And now," Anna said, "I would like to invite both of our American guests to join me tomorrow on a trip to Garmisch-Partenkirchen to view our wondrous Alps."

And so, on his final day in Bavaria, Martin had gone by train to the site of the 1936 Winter Olympics, lunched at the luxury hotel Partenkirchen Hof, and hiked across meadows side by side with Anna to view Germany's highest peak, Der Zugspitz, while Elliott decided to remain in Garmisch, complaining of breathlessness due to the altitude.

On the return hike Martin and Anna stopped beside a small, clear stream to eat cheese and apples. Finished eating, Martin lay on his back to watch the clouds, then rolled onto his side to gaze dreamily at the still-snowcapped-in-early-August mountain peaks. Then, of a sudden, he sprung to his feet and broke out into a chorus of *Fröliche Wandersman*, happy wanderer that he was at that moment. When he stumbled over forgotten words to the third verse Anna finished the song for him, then clapped and laughed.

In a lower meadow they stopped to look up at the ski slopes. "Do you ski?" Anna asked.

"Yes. Cross-country skiing is very popular in Minnesota. Unfortunately we don't have any mountains there, just low hills. So alpine skiing is not possible. How about you?"

"Yes, I ski."

"Did you come up here to watch the '36 Winter Olympics?" Martin asked.

Anna nodded. "I was in them. One of eighty women to compete."

"Which events?"

"Alpine skiing."

"Did you win a medal?"

"No, but my teammate Cristina Cranz did. The gold medal! I was not in top form." Anna pointed to the two-inch scar across her left cheek.

"What happened?"

"I fell in a practice run six weeks prior to the games. The cut on my face was nothing compared to the bruises on my arms and legs. I managed to compete, but not well."

"I thought you might have earned your scar in a duel," Martin jested.

"I do fence, but not especially well. Not at an Olympic level."

"Do you intend to try to compete in the next Olympics?"

"Now that they might be held in Switzerland, yes. Did you hear that the Japanese have decided not to host the 1940 Winter Games now that they have gone to war with China again?"

Martin realized that, since leaving the States, world news had passed him by. "So Switzerland has agreed to host the Games?"

"Only if they get their way on the matter of ski instructors not being classified as professionals and thus ineligible for the

Games. Otherwise --." She shrugged. "Too bad. St. Moritz is such a lovely venue. Have you been to Switzerland?"

Martin said he had not.

"So many fine mountains. Too bad it is populated with such boring people."

Martin thought to himself the latter can't be said of Germany.

Back in Munich that evening Anna took Martin to the Hofbräuhaus, where they spent two hours dancing polkas to sounds of an oom-pah-pah band dressed in *lederhosen*. Martin surprised Anna with his polka skills. "I learned early. Everyone in Minnesota does polka. My partner when I was a young school boy was Roberta Loftsgaard, who lived next door. You remind me of her."

"Is that good?"

"Very. Roberta was wonderful." Martin thought better of mentioning that he had also been forced by his father to take accordion lessons, which he abandoned after the fourth session. In doing so Martin allowed his father to chalk up yet another disappointment in his son.

As the train for Bremerhaven pulled out of Munich with Elliott Parker already dozing in the seat next to him, Martin replayed the previous day in his mind and decided that, eerie though it was to travel cautiously through such a repressive country as 1937 Germany, yesterday had been one of the cheeriest, most pleasant days of his life.

The reverie of that trip faded and, refocusing on the current conversation, he heard Father Troquier ask Elliott, "What is the latest news from *Grauergeist?*"

Gray Ghost? Martin didn't understand and his puzzlement prompted Elliott to explain. "That's the code name of my primary contact in Switzerland. Because he slips back and forth across the Swiss/German border, he insists on keeping his identity secret to everyone but me."

Martin thought: That explains how he was among the first outsiders to know so many of the details about the infamous Fischer Gallery auction in the Grand Hotel National in Lucerne at the end of June, 1939, when more than a hundred works from the Degenerate Art Exhibition were sold off to an audience that included many international celebrities. Those works, he reminded himself, included pieces by Franz Marc and Paul Klee.

Elliott had written him a long letter explaining those events and assured Martin that the Harvard Group was already busy tracking each of the works -- and their new owners, many of whom were Americans.

The insider details of that auction must have been passed along to Elliott's group by *Grauergeist*, whoever he is. Also perhaps from the same source who had told Elliott about a Berlin event ordered by Joseph Goebbels: the burning of more than four thousand works of art in the courtyard of the Berlin Fire Department's headquarters.

Elliott continued, directing his remarks to the fathers. "*Grauergeist* confirms the use of Neuschwanstein Castle as a major repository. In addition, he has also heard the same rumors that are being passed to Otto Benesch, namely that Hitler intends to use salt mines in the Salzkammergut mountain range as an even larger storage area because of his Linz Plan."

Otto Benesch was an Austrian art historian, now a refugee working with Elliott's Harvard Group. The Linz Plan, Martin knew, was Hitler's dream to build an art museum on a truly grand scale in the Austrian city of Linz, the *Führer's* birthplace, and fill it, in part, with old --- and approved – masterpieces taken from wherever agents of the Reich could get them and by whatever means.

Father Roskosz asked, "What word from Werner Zeitz? Is he still in London?"

"Yes. He's helping the British in any capacity they allow him. But I'm afraid he's lost all contact with those who remained behind in Munich. He's appealing to the Vatican to help him, but I'm afraid his hopes on that count are higher than is warranted," Elliott said solemnly. "Werner's attitude toward the church doesn't exactly inspire the Vatican to want to help him."

Martin spoke. "Anna Stahlinger. Any word on where she is? How she is?"

Elliott hesitated, then answered. "None at all, Martin, I'm sorry to say."

With no further information to exchange, the men shook hands all around, Elliott promising the two padres he would keep in touch by mail and telephone until the next time he came to Washington. On the walk back toward the taxi stand Elliott asked Martin, "Refreshing to know so much or simply frustrating?"

"I just wish there was something we could do about all this, more than just talk about it," Martin said.

"I agree. But, without a quiver full of thunderbolts, we're left to whimper and snivel, which is far from satisfying. Yet, for whatever good it may eventually prove, we are keeping careful track of the damage," Elliott said.

"Do you think we'll be drawn into the war?" Martin said, as Elliott hailed a cab. "I mean really into it, not just Lend-Lease and yelling across the Atlantic for the Brits to keep a stiff upper lip?"

"I certainly hope so," Parker said firmly. "And none too soon."

4

Wednesday
December 10, 1941
Schloss Königsberg
Königsberg, East Prussia

Dear Cousin Anna,

I write to you with much good news.

After some early indecision, I chose to bring the dismantled Amber Room slabs to Königsberg by railway. Though I feared some group of Bolshevik or Polish partisans would cause a catastrophe by blowing up the train, both *Wehrmacht* and *Kriegsmarine* engineers assured me that floating the crates down the Baltic promised at least equal, perhaps greater, danger than using the otherwise empty railcars that brought troops and supplies to the front. Some of the lesser items from Catherine Palace are coming to Königsberg by truck convoys even though many train cars remain empty. I'm sure the reason is that the *Wehrmacht* wishes to demonstrate to the SS who is who. No matter to me. I just laugh. Let them play their games.

Once Leningrad is captured and I have a look at the contents of the Hermitage, I may wish then to return the works from there on barges. That brings me to the sad point of saying no one knows when Leningrad will fall. No one will even venture a prediction.

The *Führer's* plan now, I'm told, is to lay siege to Leningrad, to starve its inhabitants into surrender. Our army, from the generals on down, were not particularly pleased at the prospect of spending the entire winter camped before the city's gates. I must admit I am glad I am not required to do so.

Not that Königsberg's climate offers any improvement over Leningrad's at the moment. Because my work has kept me camped here inside the castle night after night, I now know how I would capture the city of Königsberg, if I were a general of an opposing army. I would surround the city, force everyone to retreat into this impregnable fortress, then wait for all of them to die of pneumonia. So easy! So guaranteed!

I must tell you about my *Hauptscharführer,* Karl Vollmer. During the unloading of the Amber Room crates, after we moved the rail cars to a siding, some idiot failed to set the brakes properly, the cars began to roll, knocked Karl down and onto the tracks. A wheel ran over his right arm and I am sad to say the arm could not be saved.

But Karl is strong! Never demoralized. Never!

The surgeon was taken aback when he sensed I was more distressed and outraged at Karl's misfortune than the victim himself. In any case, Karl is resting in the local military hospital, more comfortable by far at the moment than I, who must sleep in this windowless dungeon of a castle.

More good news: When Karl is released from the hospital I have arranged for him to take a long recuperation leave and I am sending him to his mother's family in Estonia. He has several aunts, uncles, and cousins in the town of Virtsu, on the Gulf of Riga. Virtsu is directly across from the two large islands, Saaremaa and Hiiumaa, which are now being reinforced heavily with shore-to-sea batteries. (The safer to travel between the Fatherland and Leningrad, once the latter is in German hands, of course.)

The official purpose of Karl's trip to Estonia is to serve as a recruiter for the new Waffen-SS divisions Berlin has approved. These new divisions will consists *entirely* of *Folksdeutscher*. Himmler, with the *Führer's* approval, thought this would be an excellent way for the Baltic countries to show their thanks for our liberating them. However, I'm not sure whether Karl will impress them or intimidate them when they see his empty sleeve.

In response to the postscript question you posed in your last letter, yes, I'm dismayed that I did not make up with my father before he left Munich. I know. Making up requires two parties, but I should have been the one to make the first move, to extend my apologies, be the first to admit I should have tried harder to see things from his point of view.

Even now I think of him often, and rather fondly for the most part, wishing – hoping the Luftwaffe brings him no harm, even as I equally hope for our airmen's success in bringing the English to their knees. Now that the *Führer* has declared war on the Americans as well, perhaps Father will move to New York City or Washington or somewhere he thinks he can be useful in their cause. Not that I suppose he can be useful, but I will feel better in regard to his safety. I understand that the older of the two American art professors who visited us the summer the *Entartete Kunst* exhibition took place in Munich, Professor Parker, is part of a group of art historians whose job is to follow all aspects of what they maliciously refer to as German *Kunstraub*. Art theft indeed! A pox on them! But there I go, damning Father again by extension.

All the more fortuitous that Karl is able to make the kind of reconnaissance we discussed when last I was home. And on that subject I have great news! After I finish setting up the remainder of the exhibition here – the Amber Room ranks foremost, but is far from the only showpiece – I am allowed a lengthy leave to return to Munich, though I must go by way of Berlin in order to drop off the enormous stacks of paperwork that necessarily accompany these projects. But still, I will be home again! And soon!!

Fondly,
Cousin Rainer

_____

Wednesday
December 10, 1941
George Washington University
Washington, D.C.

Dearest Maddy,

We're at war!! Can you believe it? How shocking! But only in the way it has begun for us. The years of ambiguity about isolationism are over; the multitude of diplomatic shell games has come to an end. Uncertainty has been hanging over us like Grandma Helga's broken chandelier.

Now that we are officially at war, here's my plan. I intend to apply to the university for a leave of absence in order to enlist. However, there's no guarantee the university will grant me such an open-ended leave. If not, then I'll have a serious choice to make. I can't quite picture myself in uniform, let alone engaging in combat. Yet, I consider enlisting to be my duty. I'm sure that is one issue on which Father and I can agree. Perhaps the only one.

I would appreciate your candid opinion as well on this matter.

I am saddened that I won't be able to come home for the holidays this year. I doubt if I could find an empty train seat, even if I had planned to come home. Washington is such a madhouse these past couple of days. I swear the population has quintupled since Sunday.

Did you listen to President Roosevelt's speech to Congress? How inspiring! I'm certainly glad he's on our side. But then when I was in Germany in 1937 I listened on the radio to Adolf Hitler, listened with a group of German students at the University of Leipzig. The man is truly mesmerizing in his knack for touching just the right nerves, stirring up resentments, appealing to Germans' vilest instincts. The students went crazy with applause, time and time again. All the while Elliott Parker and I listened we were unconditionally appalled, though we dared not say so, of course.

On a cheerier subject, I have just this morning posted a small boxful of gifts to you and the rest of the family. You needn't worry that I'll be alone on either Christmas Eve or The Day itself. I received more invitations than I could accept.

I'm writing to you from my office here at the university. I've just finished putting together the final exam for my Twentieth Century Art in Europe course.

I know my students will have some difficulty focusing on exams, but I've tried to make several of the essay questions they may choose among pertinent to current political events. Many of my male students have already indicated they intend to go from their last finals directly to one of the many military recruiting locations in the immediate D.C. area.

Keep me well posted on what the other boys in our family of military age plan to do, Cousin Armen, Cousin Will, and Cousin Jack. Maybe Will will get his chance to act out his Viking seaman fantasies, don his armor and stand at the bow of a battleship waving a sword.

I hope I can be of some use, some way, in helping recover the art the Germans have pilfered. From all the news Professor Parker forwards to me, a vast army will be necessary to search for the many thousands of missing works. I had best not get my hopes up too much, however, lest my wartime role end up being peeling potatoes in the galley of Cousin Will's battleship – bound for Japan. Only time will determine my role. Time and some Army paper-pusher. But, before I start feeling sorry for myself prematurely and read like a sniveler who has nothing going for him, I'd best wrap this up.

It's late, an icy wind is blowing down the Potomac, and I'm almost certain I've missed the last bus to Arlington. Oh well, the long walk will do me good, give me time to think this war business through more thoroughly, convince myself any service toward smashing the Germans and the Japs is honorable.

Remember that you are in my thoughts daily and, busy as I am and happy as I am with my position here, I miss you, miss Minnesota, miss Mom and, yes, I even miss The Old Man, ill-tempered, hard-headed, unforgiving creature that he is. I still love him. Somehow, someway I really do.

Love you even more! And miss you terribly. Write soon, think of me always.

The best brother you've ever had!
Martin

5

Monday
January 19, 1942
Restaurant Stag and Pheasant
Berlin

Rainer pushed his dumplings aside, tasted a mushroom, then began carving his slab of venison. A momentary twinge of guilt made him pause. The Waffen-SS soldiers freezing in the trenches outside Leningrad would kill me if they knew I was so well-fed, drinking French wine, sleeping under eiderdown. But his moment of sensitivity quickly subsided. I was not so foolish as to become a soldier, he reminded himself, and continued eating.

Just as he began to rend his second dumpling a man appeared beside his table and asked, "*Sturmbannführer* Zeitz?"

Rainer continued to poke his knife blade into the dumpling. "Yes," he said impatiently, refusing to looking up.

"*Reichsmarshall* Göring requests you be his guest tomorrow after lunchtime at Karinhall. He will provide a car to take you there. Pick-up time will occur here at precisely noon."

Setting aside his utensils and looking up, Rainer recognized the man as Fritz Görnnert, the chief of Section One of Göring's huge staff. He was a former Brownshirt and now was the *Reichsmarshall*'s primary link to Martin Bormann, the *Führer*'s private secretary. Rainer did not like the man and felt no need to be civil to him. "I already have a ticket on the morning train to Munich."

Though his pass for leave from the front was open-ended, Rainer worried -- irrationally, he knew -- that he could be recalled at any moment, ordered to return to the miserable conditions the German Army currently endured in its winter *sitzkrieg* stand-off against the Red Army.

Only returned to Berlin a few days earlier from Königsburg in order to brief his superiors on his successful efforts at Tallin and Pushkin, Rainer wondered how Göring had managed to find him so quickly. Rosenberg, he decided. The art commission for whom he labored, though officially attached to the SS, was in fact independent. And, despite the commission's being called *Einsatz* Rosenberg, everyone understood that Herman Göring's sense of acquisitiveness, superior to all other members', was the key factor propelling Rainer's unit to rapacious aspirations. Someone on the committee would have told the head of the Luftwaffe where to find him.

"The *Reichsmarshall* insists," Gönnert said politely enough, though the undercurrent in his look spoke other that politeness.

Rainer sipped at his Bordeaux, rolled it on his tongue, closed his eyes, then swallowed. When at last he opened his eyes he announced, "Tomorrow. Karinhall. Very well."

———

Monday
January 19, 1942
Smith Hall of Art
George Washington University

Martin shuffled his lecture notes on the lectern as he waited for his diminished class, now mostly female, to assemble. Fall semester's weeks leading to final exams had been discombobulating. Pearl Harbor, followed by Hitler's declaration of war on the United States.

Loose talk already drifted on the wind to the effect that the university's administration was thinking of combining some classes, canceling others. Not only had many male students already withdrawn from the university in order to enlist in the armed forces, but many faculty and staff of military age had begun to petition for leaves of absence in order to do the same, Martin among them.

A young woman entered the class room and took a seat in the front row. Martin saw that she had been crying, her eyes still swollen though her tears had dried. Martin looked at his seating chart before saying, "Something the matter, Miss Jensen?"

She looked and snuffled. "I just said goodbye to both my brothers at the train station. They are off to boot camp somewhere in South Carolina." Pride clearly mingled with apprehension.

Martin spoke to the positive aspect. "I'm sure you're very pleased with their sense of duty."

Miss Jensen pulled a handkerchief from her small handbag. "I am now, but what... what if –." She bit her lip. " -- if they get killed?"

Martin had no easy answer to that question. War is hell, General Sherman had declared. And Martin was sure the coming conflict would reveal that the man who burned Atlanta might well have understated his case.

Miss Jensen suddenly burst out saying, "I feel so helpless! My brothers are going off to war and here I sit, safe and sound, studying about a bunch of dusty old paintings. What could be more detached from the real world where people are bent on killing each other?"

Another student, a middle-aged man whose name Martin could not remember, limped into the classroom with the aid of a cane, overheard the young woman's outburst, and now stood beside Miss Jensen. "A subtext to this war, ma'am, is a war of artistic ideals -- whose canvasses live and whose don't. And who decides those fates. Men will die over that issue. Not nearly as many as will have died in jungles and on beachheads, but art will take its toll, too, in this war." The man looked to Martin. "Am I correct, Professor Wynerson?"

Martin thought of his trip to Munich nearly four years earlier. Yes. In Europe art had become a major focus of the Nazis' effort to twist the Continental vision of what counts as superior civilization to its own demented perspective.

Yet he doubted Miss Jensen was quite ready for someone to suggest she envision her brothers on a skirmish line of pawns in a deadly battle of contending views of what constituted great art. Oil on canvas is not nearly as tangible as blood on sand.

Martin nodded his assent to the man with the cane, who now slumped into the half-desk next to Miss Jensen. He then added, "Men are not going to be rising from their trenches and advancing toward enemy lines in the names of Rodin, Rembrandt, Vermeer, Picasso, and Michelangelo, unless those happen to be the surnames of the comrades beside them."

Miss Jensen sighed. "My brothers know nothing about art. And could not care less. If you asked them, neither of them would be willing to die to save a painting. Who would, in fact?"

"An interesting point," the cane-wielding man declared loudly. "Do you have an opinion on that, Professor Wynerson?"

Martin did. He judged, accurately he supposed, that many a man had donned a uniform in the name of an abstraction, often a fuzzy one. Fuzzy abstraction, that is, not a fuzzy uniform. How many rag-tag colonials fought the British as much in the name of Jefferson's lofty, yet hazy, "self-evident truths" as much as for just protecting their own local farms and villages? How many Civil-War-era farm boys between Maine and Missouri fought against slavery, without knowing a single slave? Fought for "one nation indivisible" without understanding what that really meant?

"Tell me, Miss Jensen. If under attack by our enemies, would your brothers fight to protect the Statue of Liberty? The Golden Gate Bridge? Mount Rushmore?"

"Of course!" she said.

"Those, too, are works of art. Architectural triumphs on a grander scale, in one sense at least, than any painting on canvas in a wooden frame. But the principle is the same."

"I see what you mean."

Martin hoped so. Two minutes until class time. The room began to fill, as much as it would. When the bell rang, Martin stepped to his podium and announced, "Today's topic is: Modern Art and the Nazi reaction to it."

Tuesday
January 20, 1942
Karinhall

Deer tracks crisscrossed the snow near where Rainer eased himself out of the black Mercedes that brought him from Berlin. He stared with a mixture of amusement and disdain at the pair of stone lions guarding the emblem of the Göring family crest. The more plebeian one's roots, the more bombastic one's efforts to mask them, Rainer thought, recalling the *Reichsmarshall's* paltry credentials to any claim to aristocracy. Yet here stood Göring's lavish mansion, a vast expanse of lodge and woods that might make Fredrick the Great envious.

Rainer could only surmise why Göring had invited him. The chill winter air made him shudder, yet he shed his great coat and handed it to his driver, a Luftwaffe *Leuntnant*. He then flicked lint, both real and imagined, from his SS officer's uniform and strode toward the woman waiting on the portico of the main entrance. She wore a gray woolen dress and loose matching shawl and introduced herself as Gisela Limberger, gave her title as that of Göring's private secretary. "Welcome, *Sturmbannführer*. The *Reichsmarshall* is pleased you are able to join him."

Her firm handshake from a callused hand reminded Rainer of the painstaking record-keeping for which she was noted. That Göring trusted his art ledgers to a woman floated as a wicked joke among those cynical Berliners who also loved to speculate on the *Reichsmarshall's* homosexuality. Among sophisticated Berlin circles, Frau Limberger, if not her master, merited respect.

No *Kinder, Kirche, Küche* for this woman. In that regard – and that regard only – did Frau Limberger remind Rainer of Anna.

"I'm pleased to be here," Rainer announced, granting the woman a slight, deferential head bow.

Inside, Frau Limberger led Rainer down a long, wide corridor, passing several large ornately decorated rooms full of sculptures, paintings, tapestries, and jeweled furniture. The rooms struck Rainer as more cluttered than decorated. Yet, as he passed the rooms, he recognized in every one, at least one, and often several, masterpieces. The whole, however, was clearly less than the sum of its many fine parts. Too much, too concentrated.

Rubens hung everywhere, emphasizing a theme of nudes -- known to be popular, not only with Göring, but with Rosenberg as well. Rainer wondered how well Frau Limberger took to the multitude of plump female nudes adorning the walls. If they embarrassed her, her demeanor failed to betray any sense of mortification. Finally she ushered him into a room, smaller than the others he had passed. If only because it was less cluttered, Rainer judged it more pleasing.

"Please wait here while I announce you to the *Reichsmarshall*. I'm afraid he is very busy today and can only spare you a short time. He has only just returned from seeing the *Führer* at Wolfshantz and now Herr Hitler has asked the *Reichsmarshall* to pay a visit to Mussolini. Poor man! So many duties!" And she left, closing the door behind her.

So this is Karinhall, Rainer mused while waiting for the number two man in the Reich to appear. His senses of fascination and deference competed with a sense of revulsion. An art museum with sleeping quarters, hunting grounds, and a kitchen, Rainer decided as he reflected on his brief glimpses into the rooms he had seen. Finally, the words that came to mind were *prunkthaft* and *grell*. Ostentatious and gauche. Garish excess. The place reminded him of the Victorian clutter he has seen on display in English exhibits representative of 19th century British upper-class decor. So much money; so little taste. Yet, Rainer reminded himself: *de gustibus non disputandum.* Or so those with little or no artistic discernment liked to claim.

The door opened and Frau Limberger preceded the corpulent *Reichmarshall*, dressed in a gold silk smoking jacket, into the room. She then closed the door behind her and stood in front of it, arms folded, as though she were Anubis, the jackel-headed god of the Egyptian dead.

Rainer rose and saluted.

Göring returned the salute and gestured for Rainer to retake his seat. The *Reichsmarshall* plopped his beefy self into a stuffed, leather-covered chair. "Ah, *Sturmbannführer* Zeitz. How good to see you again. My, how handsome you look in your uniform. Relax, please. We are informal here."

"Thank you, *Herr Reichsmarshall*." Rainer sat down tentatively.

"Tell me about Königsberg," Göring said. "I am told the exhibition there is excellent, thanks mostly to you."

"You are too kind, *Herr Reichsmarshall*."

"Not at all. I have just returned from Wolfschantz, where the *Führer* himself remarked how thrilled he was that the Amber Room has been restored to its Germanic heritage." He paused, then Göring smirked and giggled like a schoolgirl with a naughty secret. "I understand *Generaloberst* Kruger resented your presenting him with battlefield orders."

Careful what you say, Rainer told himself. "I merely explained to him I was an instrument for those who thought he would do well to reconsider his next day's tactics in attacking Pushkin."

"Of course. And you were correct to stand up to him. Field generals need to be put in their places now and then. A little battlefield success gives them faulty notions of infallibility."

"We both thought we were doing our duty to the best of our ability," Rainer said, not wishing to add to his apparent reputation as a brash challenger of the wisdom of generals.

"Your work, both at Pushkin and at Königsberg, deserves reward, *Sturmbannführer* Zeitz. Though yet unofficial, a promotion for you is in the works, I assure you. To *Standartenführer!*" Göring said, beaming at being the first to pass along such news.

"I am most appreciative, though, as I said, I was only doing my duty."

Göring shook his head wistfully. "How time passes. You were but a young lad the last time I saw you. And now look at you. So handsome! So dashing in your uniform."

Young lad. Rainer remembered the small Munich luncheon hosted by his father many, many years ago. That was the *only* time the *Reichsmarshall* had ever seen him. Göring had come to his father's gallery to consult on a pair of Klee paintings being offered for sale by a dealer in Lucerne. Afterward, at lunch in a private room at Restaurant Vogelsanger, Göring had drunk too much wine and become obnoxious toward a young female servant who found his efforts to reach under her skirt provoking. Rainer wondered how much sexual mistreatment the austere Frau Limberger was obliged to endure in order to preserve her role as *Kunstrechner*, tallier of Göring's treasures. Perhaps none. Rainer judged her unattractive. But that didn't mean the

Reichsmarshall did. Or maybe the Berlin rumors --. He flicked that thought away as though it were lint on his uniform.

"I remember your visit well, *Reichsmarshall*," Rainer replied diplomatically. "As I recall, your bid for a pair of Klees was successful."

"Thanks to your father. Unfortunately --." Göring decided not to finish his remark.

Unfortunately indeed, Rainer thought. Unfortunately Klee is out of fashion. Worse. Lumped with all the other art and artists who were rated degenerate not long after the Nazi Party came to power. "I understand, *Herr Reichsmarshall*. Times change."

Göring smiled, clearly grateful for Rainer's giving the remark a constructive twist. "Yes, yes! So they do, which is why I've invited you here. I have a very special favor to ask of you."

Rainer perked up. "A favor?" he said as neutrally as he could manage.

The *Reichsmarshall* withdrew a small pouch from his jacket, poured the contents into his left hand, then returned the empty pouch to the same jacket pocket.

As Göring rolled the pouch's contents in his left hand, Rainer stared and thought: Marbles? He continued to stare, all the while noticing that the *Reichsmarshall*, clearly stressed at the thought of asking a favor, began to relax. No. Not marbles. Diamonds. A pouch full of diamonds.

After sneaking a quick glance at Frau Limberger, the *Reichsmarshall* spoke. "I understand you manage a successful connection between Munich and Switzerland." Then he sat back, waited, rolled the diamonds faster between his fleshy palms.

A *successful connection*. Rainer had to decide quickly who was going to out-coy whom. The *Reichsmarshall* obviously knew a bit, perhaps a great deal, about Rainer's over-the-border links.

Rainer decided not to affirm or deny. He deflected the question by asking, "What is your interest in the Swiss, *Herr Reichsmarshall?*"

Göring stopped tumbling his diamonds. "Dealing in art, as you well know, is a complicated business."

Rainer nodded, reflecting on his father's lifetime as a dealer.

"I believe in offering a fair price for quality goods. My integrity throughout the European art world is well-known. I do not steal, I don't cheat."

But you are a cheapskate, Rainer mused, while masking his opinion with a faux-sincere nod. Fair price indeed. Tighter than bark on a linden. "The Swiss are trying to cheat you?" Rainer asked, knowing full well that was not the *Reichsmarshall's* point.

"No, no. It's just that --." He glanced at Frau Limberger, who stared back at him impassively.

"I have a dealing that needs to be... that I wish to be kept *so vertraulich wie möglich,* as confidential as possible." The diamonds moved more rapidly from hand to hand as he waited for Rainer's response.

"Confidential," Rainer repeated.

"As you probably are aware, for most of my dealings in Switzerland I deal directly with Gottlieb Reber or else have the director of my collection, Walter Hofer, make arrangements with him. But this matter now requires more discretion, you must understand. I have given some thought to using the diplomatic bag between Berlin and Bern for some future arrangements. However, in this instance even that method will not do." Göring stopped passing diamonds and sat as still as if he were a figure in a painting.

To Rainer the obvious question was: Why won't the diplomatic pouch serve your current intrigue? But the answer was already clear. The *Reichsmarshall* didn't care to have Germany's diplomats know about the transaction he was about to reveal. But reveal only if he sensed that Rainer was fully prepared to go along with this mysterious scheme. "I'm not sure I understand, *Herr Reichsmarshall.*"

Again, the diamonds moved, slowly, rhythmically. "You move art from Munich to Zurich, Basel, and beyond without the knowledge of Swiss customs, not so?" Göring said.

Brilliant, *Herr Reichsmarshall!* Draw me into your conspiracy with a simple observation that couples a hint that we share deceptive activities, with an implication that my continued success in such guile may depend on the grace of silence from the head of Luftwaffe. Neither admission nor denial served Rainer's interest. But he had to say something. "I've tried to do so a few times, not always successfully."

"But your methods have improved," Göring said, asserting hope as much as fact.

"It's a delicate and dangerous business. Success often depends on luck," Rainer said.

Frau Limberger spoke, catching Rainer off-guard. "But your success ranks well beyond luck, *Sturmbannführer.*" Clearly the *Reichsmarshall* allowed her more liberty and power than Rainer had imagined.

Rainer decided to try to stare her down. "Swiss customs is always a gamble and the gambler's fallacy applies. One success does not promise another."

Frau Limberger replied, "Your success, as I understand it, comes not from outwitting Swiss customs so much as bypassing them."

"The Swiss border is well-patrolled, Madam."

"And Swiss cheese has no holes," she replied.

Rainer looked to Göring, who was clearly amused at the SS-officer's discomfiture. "You have something in mind for me to do for you."

Göring nodded to Frau Limberger, who then walked to a sheet-covered object Rainer thought too awkwardly shaped for a piece of furniture. With a snatching motion she unveiled the mystery, revealing what appeared to be a set of unframed paintings.

"Go on, go on. Look at them," Göring urged. The *Reichsmarshall* slowly managed to raise his corpulence to a standing position, stumbled toward the paintings, let Frau Limberger steady him, then gestured for Rainer to join him in viewing the full set.

Rainer stepped to the collection and knelt down. Slowly the *Reichsmarshall* flipped each painting forward, giving Rainer a long, careful look at the entire collection.

One by one he examined each one, recognizing them all as having come from the Degenerate Art exhibition he had attended in Munich four and half years earlier. He knew the names of most of the painters. Some he had even met. He even recalled the names of several of the paintings. Vasilly Kandinsky's portfolio of twelve prints he called *Map of "Little Worlds"*, Laser Segall's *Two Phantoms*, Oskar Schlemmer's *Mural with Five Boys*, Erich Heckel's *Girl with a Rose*, Paul Klee's *Moon Over the City*, Ernst Ludwig Kirchner's *Male Nude*. And there were several paintings of female nudes, works by Christian Rohlfs, Max Pechstein, Karl Schmidt-Rottluff, Karl Hoffer.

Smiling to himself, Rainer though: Of course! These nudes are all much to skinny for the *Reichsmarshall's* taste. Rainer looked at Göring, raised an eyebrow, but said nothing.

Embarrassment made the *Reichsmarshall* blush as he stammered, "I prefer Ruben's style of women. Voluptuous, yes? Not these stick figures. But others will find them to their liking, I'm sure."

"No doubt," Rainer said. He looked at Frau Limberger and saw she was as impassive as a block of stone. No voluptuous, smiling mass of flesh was she.

"I know you are familiar with the artists," Göring said. "That is partly why I asked you here."

Partly. So why else? Rainer wondered.

Göring came immediately to his point. "I would like to exchange these for... for works more acceptable to display, more readily acknowledged as pieces of art cherished by our beloved German people. Do you understand me, *Sturmbannführer?*"

"Exchange them, *Herr Reichsmarshall?*"

"Yes, yes."

"With whom? And for what?"

"Swap them with a dealer who fancies them; trade them for some Crananchs. Can you do that?" Göring spread his arms wide. "Why do I even ask? Of course, you can."

Rainer rubbed his face slowly with his right palm, trying hard to look pensive and reflective. Finally, focusing on the *Reichsmarshall's* diamonds, he said, "I may be able to do it. But much time and expense will be required on my part."

Göring played vigorously with his glittering baubles as Rainer watched. "Yes, yes, of course. I do not expect you to perform this transaction for free."

Rainer sensed the *Reichsmarshall* was vulnerable, then also judged the moment would not last. "A commission, expenses, and a bonus."

Göring grasped his diamonds and held them fast. Frau Limberger edged forward in her chair. It was she who broke the tense silence. "A bonus, Herr Zeitz? We don't understand."

Rainer smiled and looked to the *Reichsmarshall*. "You may not understand, Frau Limberger, but I'm sure the *Reichsmarshall* grasps the concept entirely from having dealt in good faith with my father so often for so many years." Rainer looked to the *Reichsmarshall* for assurance and received it.

"Your father, in all cases, was an honorable man."

Good, Rainer thought. More than halfway home with my lie. "I shall want one of the paintings as compensation, in addition to my monetary commission."

Frau Limberger, who had seated herself next to Göring, slid forward on her chair, nearly rising. "That is unacceptable." She looked to the *Reichsmarshall* for reassurance. He did not return her look, instead fumbling once again with his handful of jewels.

"It's not as if I'm asking for a Rembrandt. These are condemned paintings, every one of them. Am I mistaken or are there those who matter who suppose these paintings --" Rainer gestured toward them, " -- no longer exist?" Both Göring and Frau Limberger understood perfectly whom Rainer meant by *those who matter*. The *Führer*, Himmler, Goebbels, Bormann primarily.

In a low, venomous tone Frau Limberger spat, "Blackmail!"

Rainer, though amused, forced himself to sound indignant. "Think of it as a small -- and just -- compensation for a hazardous undertaking."

"How hazardous can it be? You do it all the time," she shot back.

"If you are so confident in your knowledge of how it is done and how safe it is, why bother with me at all? Do it yourself," Rainer said, staring at the woman evenly.

Göring interceded. To his secretary, "The *Strumbannführer* is right. These are not ordinary works of art bound for an ordinary exchange." To Rainer, "I grant your request. Select one work to keep for yourself."

Frau Limberger held firm at the edge of her chair, not pleased, but knowing she had been defeated. "One painting only. I shall know if you attempt to cheat the *Reichsmarshall*."

"I understand, Frau Limberger," Rainer said, standing, bowing, reseating himself. "Your reputation is well known. All Berlin speaks of you." He had thought to say *All Berlin speaks well of you*, but decided to let ambiguity prevail.

Göring sat down and clapped. "How much better you go to Munich with these paintings than have to return to the Russian Front. I am sorry the Army is commanded by so many feckless oafs. Why, can you believe that when I was at Wolfschantz the *Führer* asked me to provide three million winter coats and blankets to the armies on the Russian Front?"

Rainer looked properly amazed.

"Yes! The Luftwaffe is providing winter salvation to the Army. Can you believe such nonsense?" Göring set his diamonds aside. He was comfortable in a stance of superiority now. "The Army will not dare to assault the Stalinists again until the Russian winter goes away. And by then, the clouds will part, at which moment my air force will clear a way for the Wehrmacht and Waffen-SS to march their way into Leningrad."

Hell will freeze over, Rainer thought, before your Stukas and Messerschmidts make life easy for German forces to take Leningrad. Then he realized that for the soldiers camped before the gates of Leningrad hell had already frozen over. Meanwhile, the Luftwaffe sat parked hundreds of kilometers from the front, the *Reichsmarshall*'s airmen waiting comfortably for winter to end.

"Which painting do you choose?" Frau Limberger inquired.

"I'll decide later," Rainer announced, though he knew his choice already. The Klee.

"I have records to keep," Frau Limberger said frostily.

"I will inform you. Or someone working with me in Munich will reveal my choice, should I be too busy dodging bullets on the Russian Front to facilitate your paper shuffling, Frau Limberger." He was damned if he was going to give her the satisfaction of knowing.

Her frost grew thicker.

Göring, failing to note the hostility of the exchange, said cheerily, "The choice is yours, yes, and take your time. Just be certain to let Frau Limberger know. Now as for the Russian Front, the Red Army will be in full retreat, I assure you. As soon as the weather clears long enough for my bombers to attack *en masse* you will have no bullets to dodge."

"The Army as a whole will be grateful... again, *Herr Reichsmarshall*. As will I," Rainer assured him.

Göring nodded vigorously. "And when we take Leningrad —" his eyes widened — "I want to be there at The Hermitage, be among the first to inspect its treasures."

Inspect. Of course. Rainer suppressed a sneer.

"With you at my side, naturally," Göring added, slapping a thigh.

Naturally. "I hope your wish comes true, *Herr Reichsmarshall*," Rainer said.

"More than a wish! We shall be there! Soon!"

Not if success depends on the Luftwaffe, Rainer thought, while saying, "I look forward to the moment."

"Until then, *Sturmbannführer*." Göring clapped, then slowly stood. The meeting was over.

Well, not quite.

Rainer said, "Before I leave may I be permitted a question that has been on my mind for some time now, *Herr Reichsmarschall?*"

Goring opened his arms again, a gesture of magnanimity. "Of course, of course."

"Franz Marc, from Munich. Do you recall the name?" Rainer asked.

"Most certainly I do. Would a soldier like me forget a man who was awarded the Iron Cross?" Göring said.

"My question is this. All of Marc's paintings from the traveling *Entartete Kunst* exhibit were eventually withdrawn and all of them sold at the Fischer Auction in Lucerne. All but one of them. The first of his paintings to be withdrawn, *The Tower of the Blue Horses*, was the only one not auctioned off in 1939. May I inquire what has happened to it?"

Göring smiled broadly and looked at Frau Limberger, who remained impassive. Again looking at Rainer, he said, "I'm quite surprised you have not discovered its whereabouts by yourself. After all," he gave a hearty laugh, "whenever you are in Berlin you probably walk past it at least once a day."

"Berlin?"

"On Prinz Albrecht Strasse, very close to SS Headquarters," Göring said, pleased with himself.

Rainer looked to Frau Limberger. With a smirk she said, "The Prussian Chamber of Deputies."

Rainer smiled and nodded. Yes, he couldn't help but walk past the building of gray limestone, with its Doric columns, on his way to do business with the SS bureaucracy. "Thank you. When I'm next in Berlin I shall stop to see it."

"You are fond of Franz Marc's work?" Frau Limberger asked.

"As you know, he was from Munich. My father knew him. Now many Munichers ask me about that painting, as if I should somehow know," avoiding a direct answer that might give the woman leverage on him. "I only wish to cease appearing so ignorant in front of my friends and fellow Munichers."

"Your father is in London now, is he not?" Göring asked.

"That's where he went when he left Munich. I haven't heard from him since then."

"He is a good man. I respect him greatly, if not always his opinions on art," Göring said, sounding sincere enough. "I hope no harm comes to him. When the English finally capitulate, I hope he sees fit to return to Munich."

Rainer decided to change the subject and asked, "When and if my father returns to Munich is up to him. As for getting these paintings to Munich, is that up to me?"

Frau Limberger spoke. "A Luftwaffe truck will deliver them to your father's gallery. Former gallery. It is empty and available is it not?"

Rainer thought, she knows perfectly well the gallery is boarded up.

"The truck leaves tonight. Do you wish to accompany the truck or use your morning train ticket?"

"Better that I not cancel my train plans. When may I expect the truck to arrive?"

"Two days," Frau Limberger said. "How long for you to complete the exchange?"

"I don't know. Swiss dealers have the advantage. I must keep the collection in Munich until a bargain is reached. And that makes me ask: What happens if other Germans discover the paintings in my possession?"

"Under no circumstances will you implicate the *Reichsmarshall*," Frau Limberger said harshly.

"Does that include you?" Rainer asked softly.

Göring dropped his bag of diamonds onto the floor. "Discretion! You must maintain discretion! Two paintings. Take two if you must."

Rainer looked at Frau Limberger and caught her ice thawing and refreezing. She was clearly not used to finding herself in such an awkward, powerless situation. "One painting will do, *Herr Reichsmarshall*. Only one." Rainer knew that, unlike the *Reichsmarshall*, Frau Limberger remained more to be feared than pitied.

6

Tuesday
February 3, 1942
Smith Hall of Art
George Washington University
Washington, D.C.

Dear Sis,

Great news! The Army Air Corps wants me and I report for basic training in South Carolina in ten days. Imagine me – a flyboy. A pilot.

Kemper Sloane, from the University of Virginia, will be taking over my classes. Having failed his Navy physical due a lame back from a childhood injury [He fell out of a tree chasing a raccoon!], Kempah (as we call him) is resigned to sitting out the war stateside in civilian clothes. "You Yanks just pretend y'all are marchin' through Georgia," he jokes.

Only I'll be flyin'!

Kemp has even asked if he can take over my apartment. Small as mine is, his, north of Union Station, is even smaller. He says he doesn't mind the extra travel distance. I've mentioned his desire to my landlady, who seems agreeable, though she intimated she would, of course, have to raise the rent. Of course!! Apartments are indeed becoming dear around D.C. Even the University may begin renting dorm space to non-students, given the sudden drop in enrollment.

Has food inflation ballooned yet in Minnesota? Today I paid a nickel for a single orange, a dime for two bananas. Next, I suppose, milk and bread will become dear. The price of war. Soldiers must be fed. Rationing next? No doubt.

The atmosphere in our capital is absolutely electric! So much going on – well above the normal din, as I told you in an earlier letter. In a way, I'll miss being here at the heart of planning and command. Yet, Sis, I truly do long to be on the front line of battle. My brief trip to Berlin in 1937 convinced me the Nazis are a danger to the whole world, an evil to be stamped out even though the cost may prove steep. I not only heard danger in their talk, I saw malevolence in their eyes. Poison exudes from their very pores. They must be stopped.

That they avidly destroy magnificent art because such art does not suit their vision of The World marks them as demons from hell, I say, though others may not derive that conclusion from such behavior.

As you can readily conclude, Maddy, I am pumped up to go to war, to learn to fly, and, yes, to slay Nazis. Once again I pray I do not end up in the Pacific, even though the Japs are surely an equal form of vermin. I know it's the same war, but the Germans offend me more personally, just as, I am certain, our neighbor Clyde Loftsgaard hates the Japs more from the anguish of Clyde Jr.'s dying aboard the Oklahoma at Pearl Harbor. Poor Roberta! Her younger brother dead. He meant so very, very much to her.

Anyway, the trains from D.C. to Spartansburg, South Caroina take only a day or less. I have no idea how much, or little, time I'll have to write you during basic training, but count on hearing from me just as soon as I am able to write. Assure the entire family they have my love and are in my thoughts often. Even father.

Love, Martin

Tuesday
February 3, 1942
Wasterkingen, Switzerland
German/Swiss border

Alternately sipping from his mug of hot apple cider and nibbling on a slab of fresh *Bauernbrot* slathered with marmalade, Rainer sat with his elbows on Hanni Kalmbach's kitchen table and watched her knead dough. From her oven came the smell of more fresh bread baking.

"Are you sure I cannot cut you another slice of cheese, Herr Zeitz?" she asked. "I would feel shamed if you leave my house hungry."

In Switzerland and wearing civilian clothes, he was Herr Zeitz, not *Standartenführer* Zeitz -- recently promoted from *Sturmbannführer*. "You are a magnanimous hostess, Frau Kalmbach, and I assure you I am fully satisfied with your most generous offerings. Your homemade bread and cider are both as fine as I have ever tasted."

"You are too kind." Hanni Kalmbach spoke in *Schwyzerdütsch*, which he could understand by listening carefully. At least it wasn't the damnable *Plattdeutsch* Karl Vollmer rattled off whenever he became highly stressed. Rainer himself had worked long and hard to rid himself of the lazy, mushy Bavarian accent he grew up speaking, with its *ish*'s in place of the hard *ick*'s of the Northerners. Although not as damning as he had heard British accents could be, German accents, too, gave away one's social standing and carefully spoken High German was obligatory in order to reach certain levels of society. A Berlin accent naturally was best, but Rainer had never quite mastered that degree of harshness, a guttural resonance sounding like a Doberman's throaty snarl, to pass himself as a haughty Brandenburger.

Rainer looked at his watch. Anna should have returned by now in the company of Frau Kalmbach's husband, Otto. The drive from the Eglisau train station to Wasterkingen was no more than five kilometers. And the last train of the evening would have arrived at Eglisau just over two hours ago. Unlikely a Swiss train would run late, especially one with such a short run. The distance from the Zurich Hauptbahnhof to Eglisau amounted to no more than 30 kilometers.

As a village of only thirty-seven citizens, Wasterkingen lacked phone service. On Rainer's first visit to Wasterkingen a year and a half earlier Frau Kalmbach had lamented that the nearest telephones were in Eglisau, bemoaned the fact that she must catch a ride there in order to phone her sister in Winterthur, then end up walking home most often because seldom was there motor traffic on the road from Eglisau to Wasterkingen, no one to offer her a ride.

Rainer had wondered at the time why she thought it necessary to place phone calls to her sister. Loneliness, most likely. Her husband and her two sons, Jurgen and Hans, worked the hay fields and fruit orchards from sunrise to sunset most days, while she tended to the cows, chickens, and goats, as well as baked bread to sell once a week in Eglisau, along with milk, eggs, and the sundry products of the pear and apple orchards.

Rainer still did not understand how Anna had managed to involve the family Kalmbach in their venture to move art from Germany to Switzerland, but she clearly had some hold on them – besides money. *Geld macht das perfect Schmieröl,* but Rainer suspected she used more than cash as a lubricant. A disincentive perhaps. A threat of some kind. Whatever it was, he didn't want to know.

The Kalmbach farm was perfect. A long way from Munich, but otherwise well situated, with large pear orchards forming part of the border and on the German side a seldom-used side road, more of a cart path, off the country road between the German villages of Dettighofen and Bühl, that passed within yards of the border fence. And an unused barn loft for storage.

Less than a kilometer east of Eglisau the Rhine River became the natural border between the Swiss and Germans. Flowing out of Lake Constance, the Rhine was too swift to risk a river crossing at night in a small skiff with such a valuable and temperamental cargo as paintings.

A week had passed since Anna had crossed into Wasterkingen on her way to find a buyer for Göring's lot of 'Degenerates". If not a buyer, then someone who could make an exchange: the Degenerates for two or three Cranachs. Why Cranachs enchanted the *Reichsmarshall* was something else Rainer did not know, did not want to know.

This was the night Anna had told Rainer to meet him at the Kalmbach farm to guide her back to Germany. Not that she needed him. In the past one or both of Otto Kalmbach's sons had led her through the pear orchard, across the fence, to a waiting truck parked on the cart path. But because this set of paintings was Rainer's *coup*, rather than works Anna herself had obtained, she thought it important than Rainer at least "put a toe across the border" as a way of participating more intimately in their joint intrigue.

Rainer had agreed and now here he was, sitting in a farmer's kitchen, whiling away more hours than he had planned, without so much as a newspaper to read, let alone a book. He cursed himself for not bring reading material. But then he hadn't expected Anna to be so tardy.

Strauss waltzes floated in the air, mixing with the smells of yeast, flour, and fruit. Poor reception made the violin sounds emanating from the corner radio sound as if the instruments had been tuned by a deaf man. Plus, Rainer opined, one Strauss piece sounds very much like any other, making the waltz hour seem like the Zurich station was playing a broken record with no one on hand in the studio to notice and fix the damned thing.

Suddenly, above the waltz music, came a knocking at the door. Alarmed, Frau Kalmbach looked at Rainer, who shook his head. "My Otto doesn't knock when he comes home," she said, her voice quavering. "Quickly. In there."

There was an unlit bedroom. After snatching up his greatcoat and fedora, he hastened in, leaving the door cracked just enough for him to see between the door and the frame. He watched as Frau Kalmbach dusted flour from her apron, nervously brushed at an imaginary out-of-place hair, then headed toward the front door. Halfway there she reversed herself, quickly snatching Rainer's cider mug and plate of bread, moving them to a sideboard.

"Gertrude! What are you doing here at this time of night?" Hanni Kalbach asked when she discovered who had been knocking on her door. "Come in. come in. I was just baking bread."

Rainer saw Gertrude, whoever she was, step inside. Older than Hanni – in her sixties perhaps – the gray-haired woman had a thin, weathered face and a crooked nose. She wore a coarse, heavy shawl, from under which she produced something that appeared to be a light bulb. But maybe not. He drew his Luger.

"I was hoping you might have another spare radio tube," he heard the woman say. "Another one of mine burned out. I know I still owe you one from two weeks ago, but I promise I will replace every one that I have borrowed just as soon as my pension check arrives." Gertrude's eyes darted about the interior house, as if radio tubes might be trying to hide themselves from her.

"I'm sorry. We have no more spares at the moment," Hanni told her. "I would invite you to stay for a cup of cider and some bread, but, as you can see, I am in the middle of my baking. And I must attend to my next batch of dough before it rises too much."

"Where is Otto?" Gertrude asked. Her eyes never stopped moving around the large room that served as both dining room and kitchen.

"Not back from town yet. He's late, but not yet late enough for me to worry."

"Is Otto's sister's step-daughter coming with him? Greta, yes?"

Rainer reminded himself that on Anna's forged Swiss papers she was 'Greta Riedel'.

The old woman was saying, "You know, Hanni, I spoke with her last week in Eglisau, while she waiting for the train. She's not Swiss, is she?" Gertrude smirked. "Of course, she's not. What a question! She speaks no Suisse-Deutsch. She's Bavarian, isn't she? She definitely has a Munich accent."

"She's from somewhere near Munich," Hanni allowed. "Augsberg, maybe. I'm not sure."

"Tell me again what it is she's doing in Switzerland?" Gertrude asked. "Is she an anti-Nazi on the run?"

"Please, Gertrude. Can't you see I'm busy? Why don't you ask her yourself, if you are so curious. She is kind enough to pay us visits. You know Otto and I are not the nosy kind," Hanni said firmly, leaving no doubt the latter character trait distinguished her and her husband from her unwanted visitor.

"Well! In my opinion one must do one's best to be informed, in case something happens," Gertrude said.

"In case what happens? What are you talking about?" Hanni asked, her voice rising.

"Because we live right next to the Germans, all kinds of schemes might be happening and we wouldn't know it unless we keep our eyes and ears open. Not so?"

"Take your foolish talk and go home. I have to think about putting food on my table and clothes on my family's backs without filling my head with worries about *schemes*. You listen to your radio much too much. Maybe it's good your tube went *kaput*. No more radio stories to fill your head with wild imaginings." Hanni opened the door and stood expectantly.

"I just hope this young woman is who and what she says she is. For your sake as well as hers," Gertrude said as she stood in the doorway.

"And what is that supposed to mean?" Hanni said.

"You know perfectly well what I mean, Hanni Kalmbach." And with that said, she made a dramatic turn and disappeared into the darkness.

When Rainer stepped back into the dining room he could see that Hanni was shaking. "Who is that dreadful hag?" he asked.

"Gertrude Forsch, the village gossip, as you might easily surmise. A busybody who minds everyone's affairs but her own. She lives alone and collects a small pension from the government. Her husband worked for the railroad and was killed in an avalanche near Andermatt. The roof over her head is in danger of collapse, we think. She eats only what she grows for herself, which can't be much. She owns one scrawny cow, a rooster and two hens. But no one feels sorry for her."

"Is she a danger to us?" If so, Rainer wanted to run after the old crone and strangle her.

"She has cried wolf so many times that no one listens to her tales of human conspiracies and ominous night creatures. No one lets children near her. But a danger to us? No. Whatever fantasy she weaves, no one will credit it for a single moment. In Eglisau she is known as the Witch of Wasterkingen. An ugly and tiresome joke."

Rainer felt relieved by Hanni's reassurances. He certainly didn't want to have to deal with the woman if doing so was in any way unnecessary. "Does she come here often?" he finally asked.

"Not often, though Otto insists once is too often. I believe I am the only person in Wasterkingen who will even open the door to her. But always I do not let her stay long, never invite her to sit for coffee and sweets. I tell myself it is best for me to hear her latest fairy-tale first, then pass it on to Otto, who can then warn everyone else."

"Has she ever gotten anyone into trouble?" Rainer asked.

"Oh, many times, but never for long. And never anything serious," Hanni insisted.

Rainer saw Hanni's look and realized he was still holding the Luger at his side.

Ten minutes later the door opened and Otto came in. "Herr Zeitz, are you ready to return across the border?" he said without so much as an hello.

Rainer put on his coat and hat and nodded. "Thank you again, Frau Kalmbach. I hope we don't cause you any trouble."

Otto asked Rainer, "What trouble are you talking about?"

Hanni spoke. "Gertrude Forsch was here, asking questions about Greta."

Otto nodded. "Yes, we saw here walking home as we drove back."

Hanni asked the question before Rainer could. "What kept you?"

"Gunter Schneider's truck broke an axle as he was crossing the bridge. He was hauling goats and many of us ended up chasing the poor, frightened creatures after they spilled out of the truck bed. Then I helped move his truck off the bridge and helped him find Urs Kimpel's son to fix his truck. Naturally Urs was in the *bierkeller* soaking his head in a liter of beer."

"Is Anna with you?" Rainer asked.

"Outside. She is eager to leave."

"I'm ready. Thank you again, Hanni."

"You are most welcome, Herr Zeitz," she replied, but her worried look told Rainer he was not entirely welcome.

As Otto closed the door behind them he said, "Do not worry about the widow Forsch. I will see that she does not become a bother to us."

"How will you do that?" Rainer said.

"Just leave her to me."

"Rainer! Come hold me. How I've missed you so," Anna called as she stepped out of the darkness into the light of Otto's lantern. She pulled him to her and hugged him tightly.

"Are you okay?" Rainer said.

"Yes. But very tired. My week has been very long and getting longer," she said.

Rainer saw that Anna's right coat sleeve was covered with blood. "Are you injured?"

"Among all the loose goats, the one I chose to chase down had apparently cut its hind leg when it jumped from the truck. When I finally cornered it I had to carry it back across the bridge," she said.

Rainer looked toward Otto, who shrugged and said nothing.

"Let's return to Germany." Anna gestured for Otto to lead the way.

Rainer followed Anna, who followed in Otto's footsteps through the thin covering of snow. As they reached the pear orchard Rainer could see, by the faint light of the lantern, deer tracks, reminding him of the tracks he had seen at Karinhall. Suddenly a hare flushed from behind a pear tree and leaped away ahead of them, through the orchard in the direction of the border fence.

Catching his hat on a tree branch, Rainer stopped momentarily to readjust the hat on his head. When he looked up he saw a pair of huge eyes, then watched as the owl swooped down, quickly and silently, in the direction the hare had run.

And then they were at the border fence. As he stepped through the opening in the wire, Rainer thought: The deer, the hare, and the owl know nothing of borders.

Otto bade them goodbye with a handshake, rather than words, leaving Rainer holding the lantern. For only a moment could Rainer hear Otto's footsteps as he crunched through the dry snow. Then silence. He knew that come sunrise the Kalmbach sons would obliterate any signs of human tracks near either side of the border fence. Looking up, Rainer could see Orion overhead and thought: What a strangely peaceful place to be at such a time.

"Come, Rainer. I am cold and tired, yet have much to tell," Anna said, tugging at his sleeve.

Parked in the trees near the road, a hundred yards on the German side of the border, sat the two-seater 1936 Wander Roadster Rainer's father left behind when Werner decamped for England. Germany, along with much of the rest of the world may still have been mired in a deep economic depression in 1936, but Europe's wealthiest class did not seem to take notice. Werner Zeitz's art gallery continued to thrive, allowing him to indulge himself in a car that, to Rainer's mind, was much too flashy, much too fast for a man Werner's age.

On reaching the roadster Rainer pulled his new briar from his coat pocket.

On seeing him reach for tobacco, Anna said, "I almost forgot." She pulled a small bag from her pocket and handed it to Rainer. "Here."

"Where did you find this?" Rainer looked admiringly at a pouch of Dunhill London.

"Same place I bought these." She showed him a pack of Lucky Strikes. "In Bern. American tobacco is readily available there."

"What were you doing in Bern?"

"On my way to Geneva."

Rainer did a double take. "Why did you need to go all the way to Geneva?"

"Start the car and I'll tell you. I'm cold."

Rainer drove slowly, driving east several kilometers before turning northwest on a main road that followed the Wutach

River upstream. Their destination was the town of Singen, seventy kilometers from Wasterkingen. The only way to reach Singen without re-crossing into Switzerland was to make a three-quarter circle that circumvented the Swiss canton of Schaffhausen. In the winter of 1940 Anna and Rainer had rented a small warehouse in the industrial section of Singen to serve as a German-side safe haven for their planned *Kunstverkauf*, their art-selling expeditions into Switzerland. For overnight stays such as tonight's Anna had also purchased a small house between the Rhine and the criss-cross of railroad yards from a young widow whose Wehrmacht-officer husband had been killed in the early days of the invasion of Poland. Because Singen was an industrial town, both Anna and Rainer judged it large enough not to have their comings and goings, by either car or truck, attract attention akin to Frau Forsch's nosiness in Wasterkingen.

And, though no direct rail service existed between Singen and Munich, trains from Singen and Munich both ran to Stuttgart, Anna's home town, where she could store works of art in an annex to her father's museum.

"I've found a dealer to handle the *Reichsmarshall*'s paintings," Anna began, shortly after they were underway. "They deal exclusively with private collectors."

"They?" Rainer said.

"Have you ever heard of Nils and Sigrid Sundstrum?" she asked.

Rainer had to think for a moment. The names sounded vaguely familiar. "Swedish?"

"Yes. I thought you knew everyone in the art world."

"You flatter me," he said.

"All the better if even *you* haven't heard of them."

"Why didn't you simply go to one of the Swiss dealers? Or one of the several good German ones now parked in Bern, Basel, Zurich, or Lucerne?"

"Because they are all under surveillance," Anna said.

"How do you know this?"

Anna hesitated, then said, "Theodor Fischer warned me."

"Bah! Fischer is greedy. He wanted to make sure you would choose him."

"Maybe. But I thought it best to be safe. If we were going to offer the paintings at auction I most certainly would have chosen Fischer. As the biggest art auctioneer in Switzerland would he not have been able to fetch the best prices?"

"The *Reichsmarshall* was firm. A quiet trade. No publicity."

"Exactly," Anna said. "Which is why I ended up selecting--. Oops! You are still trying to remember them, yes?"

"I'm trying to figure out what Swedish art dealers are doing in Switzerland. Looking for bargains, just like everyone else, no doubt."

"Wrong. They are in Switzerland for a reason entirely unrelated to art."

"In that case, I give up. Who are these mysterious Sundstrums who have captured your icy heart?"

"They are physicians with the Red Cross in Geneva. They also own a small gallery in Stockholm."

"Now that you tell me this I think I met them once. In Berlin. Long ago," Rainer said. "I recall the names and I can picture them, but only vaguely."

"Both of them are quite tall and thin. Nils is very aristocratic-looking with a mustache and wire-framed glasses. And a

Roman nose. Sigrid stoops noticeably and has a slight deformity in her left hand."

"I do remember them. It was on my first visit to the Nierendorf Gallery. I forget now what the Nierendorf brothers were showing, but I remember a Swedish couple whom Father introduced to me. Your description matches what I remember. How did you find out about them?"

"Manfred Ohlmaier."

"The textile industrialist in Wintertur? I've met him. He had several dealings with my father, who never liked him."

Anna said, "Werner never likes anybody who is rich. He once told me he had never met a wealthy person who had an adequate appreciate for art."

"Yes, and that includes Manfred Ohlmaier. My father once said of the man that he only buys paintings to demonstrate to his friends how much money he can afford to spend."

"He should have been contented to take the man's money."

"No, no, no. You know my father. Always 'It's the principle, Rainer. The principle!'"

"I remember."

"How do you come to know Ohlmaier?"

"His son, Klaus, was a volunteer assistant coach for the Swiss ski team in the '36 Olympics. Manfred paid for a portion of the Swiss team's expenses. So he was there to see what his money bought him. As for Klaus, besides the role of coach at Garmisch, he was quite busy misbehaving himself with women. And I have photos to prove it. Lots of photos. And Manfred knows I have them. So he was quite willing to pass along the names of the Sundstrums after he allowed that he didn't think he could easily find any Cranachs on his own. He himself uses the good doctors."

"So they are interested in making a trade?"

"Very much so. And they know someone who owns two Cranachs. Lucas, the Elder."

"Perfect."

Anna nodded. "Better yet," she continued, "I offered the Sundrstrums only Göring's skinny nudes. Not the whole group. Don't worry. Göring will never know. Or Frau Limberger."

Rainer hoped she was right. Frau Limberger was not one to take such a deception lightly.

"Another reason for choosing the Sundstrums. Not only do they work exclusively with private parties, to be safe they don't deal with any Germans, Swiss, or Austrians. The Sundstrums don't like Nazis."

"If that is so, why are they willing to deal with you?"

"I told them I was merely a *Folkdeutscher* from Latvia – Riga, to be more precise -- and that the only thing I liked about Nazis is that they rid my homeland of the Bolsheviks."

"And they are naïve enough to believe this?" Rainer asked, incredulous.

"They are Swedes. They can't tell a Bavarian from a Frieslander. Besides, I did my best to sound like Karl's mother. Riga isn't so far from Virtsu. And speaking of Karl, when does he return from his rehabilitation and recruiting time in Estonia?"

"Berlin is permitting him to remain in Estonia until I am called to return to Leningrad. Then he will rejoin me."

"You need to contact him immediately. Our enterprise is now going to have need of him," Anna said.

"How so?"

When Anna explained her plans to Rainer, he took his hands off the steering wheel long enough to clap, before saying, "You are so clever, Cousin Anna. So very, very clever."

7

Wednesday
August 9, 1942
Ellington Field
Houston, Texas

"She's all yours, Cowboy. Show me what you can do," Martin's flight instructor shouted from the rear cockpit of the single-engine AT-6 used for advanced training. Luckily, Martin had been warned about Jerry Basswick, whose reputation had earned him the epithet – behind his back, of course – of Jerry the Wicked Bastard, for his fiendish behavior toward cadets arriving at Ellington for Advanced Pilot Training. Not that all the advance preparation in the world prepares a cadet to be left entirely to his own devices the first time in the cockpit of a new aircraft, Martin reminded himself. Still, it was better than being caught completely unprepared.

After six weeks of basic training – no flying – in San Antonio, he had gone for nine weeks of Primary Pilot training in

Sweetwater, followed by nine more weeks of Basic Pilot Training in Greensville. Martin figured he had already logged more than 30,000 miles of flying time without ever leaving the state of Texas.

"Let's go, Wynerson. What's the holdup?"

Okay, Mister Wicked Bastard. Here we go! Martin checked his flap settings again, 15 degrees, then eased the throttle out. And suddenly they were rolling down the runway. Fifteen minutes later, having reached an altitude of ten thousand feet on a heading of two-seven-oh degrees, due west toward San Antonio, Martin began staring at the huge thunderhead looming before him.

"Hold your course, Wynerson. You're soon gonna find out what its like to ride a Brahma."

Martin didn't care for the undertone of cruelty in the instructor's voice. "You want me to try to climb above it, sir?"

"Hell, no. Maintain your altitude."

From out of the corner of his right eye Martin spotted what appeared to be a Piper Cub at two o'clock, a thousand or more feet below the AT-6. He pointed toward the smaller plane, in case Basswick hadn't seen it yet. About then the AT-6 began to bounce and buck more than slightly.

"Basswick called out gleefully, "That little fucker is losing ground. The Little Piper that can't." Then he shouted, "Hang in there, Little Fucker!" and cackled. Just then the Piper banked, made a tight one-eighty turn, and darted away on its newly found tailwind. "That'll teach him to try to piss into a hurricane."

The AT-6 bucked more severely and its right wing dipped. Martin fought the stick to hold his course.

"Show this little bitch who's boss, Wynerson. Don't let her slap you around."

"I'm trying, you asshole!" Martin swore under his breath.

"You want to go home to your mommy, Wynerson? Is that what you're thinking? Well, just pretend your momma's in Corpus Christi. And take us down to two thousand feet while you're counting your worry beads."

Martin found the temptation to go into a nose dive to achieve the lower altitude almost irresistible. Unfamiliarity with the aircraft's recovery capability made him refrain. I'm not suicidal for chrissake! he wanted to scream. He had taken both the PT-19 trainers at Sweetwater and the BT-13s at Greenville into many a precipitous decent, but only in the latter days of each nine-week program. On his first flying day in Advanced he wasn't going to make a fool of himself. Or a corpse.

With visibility zero, light became dimmer and dimmer on the descent through the thunderstorm. A sudden updraft made Martin's stomach feel like he was on the elevator at the First National Bank of Minneapolis. From all sides the winds ripped, twisted, and hammered the plane until he was sure it would crumple like a tin can under the heel of his father's work boot. All the while, Basswick kept shouting, "Yee hah! Ride 'em, Cowboy!" The man was insane. How had the Army allowed this sado-masochist to become a teacher of budding airmen? Was he a closet Nazi? Born Gerhard von Bassenberg perhaps?

In near blackness rain began to pelt the canopy. Rain came so hard Martin was certain Texas rain gods armed themselves with fifty-caliber machine guns. The sound of the rain unnerved Martin more than buffeting from the winds. At last the altimeter indicated two thousand feet.

"Take her lower, Wynerson."

"How low, sir?"

"Till you can see where the fuck you're going."

Martin complied. But at one thousand feet visibility remained zero.

"Lower, Wynerson," Basswick said in a deep, quiet voice. Quiet for him.

The change from Bassick's previous shouting and cackling suddenly gave Martin the creeps. Tilting the stick forward, Martin headed for five hundred feet. But once there the plane might just as well have been a toy plane forgotten on a child's closet shelf. Blackness still surrounded them and Martin remembered one of the instructors at Sweetwater telling a story about a storm his father had driven their car through in western New Mexico that hugged the ground so closely his father had had to pull off the highway. Rain descended like driven spikes and Martin's instructor then, a large and seemingly fearless man, said that in that moment, as a young child, he had hunkered down into a fetal position in the back seat of his parent's car because it was as if it were midnight at noon.

Not until lower than the altimeter would register did Martin hear the Wicked Bastard say, "Okay level off and look for a place to land." Good, Martin thought. And if necessary, I'll walk back to Houston.

"Pay attention to those telephone wires up ahead. Hit those and you'll flip us like a flapjack. Then some runny-nosed lieutenant will have to watch your mother cry when he hands her the folded flag from off your coffin."

Who'll hand the flag to *your* mother? Martin wondered. Christ! I bet you don't even have a mother. Spawn of the devil! Yes, that's what Basswick is.

As he flew well clear of the row of telephone lines, below them and perpendicular to their make-shift flight path, Martin heard his instructor call out, "That road's surface looks hard enough to make a landing. Circle around and put this hunk of metal down."

And us with it, Martin thought. He accelerated slightly and listened as the 600 horsepower Pratt & Whitney engine seemed to relish the added exertion. He maneuvered the plane into a low bank left and began a slight ascent, continuing to bank until he lined himself up with the two-lane road.

A minute later he adjusted the flaps into landing position, then slowly eased the aircraft down, down, down until its wheels hit the highway with a thud, thud, thud. Or is that rain pounding hard against the canopy? He thought. No, I came in hard, rather than the light-as-a-feather touch I always strive for. At least the backseat bastard hadn't yelled at him.

Then Martin saw the series of deep potholes with a pair of planks bridging them and only a pair of sawhorses for warning barricades. His first thought was to gun the engine and take off again before he hit the mess. But it's waaaaay too late for that, he realized. Instead, he braked and tried to steer left of what appeared as a gaping abyss. To his right a sign read: Breslau -- 1 mile. Suddenly he felt the plane overcorrect to the left. And then he saw the telephone pole.

He woke lying on his back and felt a gawdawful itch in his left leg just below the knee. When he reached to scratch he touched something soft and smooth. Silky smooth. The satin binding of a blanket, binding of the kind his mother said he always caressed as a child lying in his crib just before he fell asleep.

Then he heard voices. A woman's; then a man's. They were both speaking English but with heavy German accents. The sign. Breslau. How did I get to Germany? Am I a POW? Was I right? Basswick really is Nazi? A spy who made me fly into the thunderstorm because the clouds held some secret, magic passageway to Germany. And the Wicked Bastard himself must have parachuted out just before I landed, because he never so much as said, "*Ficken Sie sich, Herr Wynerson! Du bist ein Idiot!*" as I was bringing the AT-6 in for its unscheduled landing.

"Ach so! I see my patient is awake," said the same woman's voice he had heard moments earlier. "And how are we this fine day?" she pronounced *we* and *this* as *vee* and *zis*.

"*Wo bin ich?*" Martin asked.

"Well! You speak German. *Zehr gut!*"

Martin felt the itch again in his leg and leaned forward to see a thick cast from his thigh to his ankle. "Where am I?" he repeated.

"Hallettsville, if you must know. And my name is Ehrentraut Meinke, but you may call me Nurse Betty. You are in the Hallettsville Hospital. We aren't much, but we are the closest medical facility to where you crumpled up your airplane."

Nurse Betty was a ruddy-cheeked dumpling of a woman, reminding Martin of his Aunt Florence. "Where is Hallettsville?"

"Where US Highway 90 and US 77 cross. Now do you know any more?"

"Texas?"

"Where else?"

"One of the last things I remember before… before what?" Martin had to concentrate hard. "—Before I saw… oh, god! A telephone pole."

"Yes, you crashed on Texas State Road 957 between our town and Breslau."

"That's it. Breslau. That's the sign I saw. *One mile* it said. What day is it?"

"Friday. You have been here since Wednesday afternoon."

"How did I get here?"

"Fortunate for you, *ja*, that a rancher saw your plane try to land on the road. He was out searching for stray calves lost in the storm."

"A rancher was out in that storm?"

"A better question is why *you* were out in that storm."

"Just learning to fly, I guess."

"Here is our doctor. He will tell you what shape he finds you in," Nurse Betty said and stood aside.

"I am Doctor Gerber. "

As he reached to shake the doctor's hand, Martin saw a short, balding man whose yellow bow tie hung at an odd angle from a shirt badly in need of some starch and a good pressing. "Hi, Doc."

"Well, young man. How do you feel?" *Vell, yunk mahn.*

"I don't feel much of anything – except for an itch under my cast."

"You are being given a bit of morphine. Just a bit," the doctor said. "Your leg is broken. Also a couple ribs are cracked. Later the nurse will show you your face in a mirror. Not very handsome at the moment, I'm afraid."

Martin then realized how tightly taped his torso felt. Luckily that didn't itch. As for his face, well, he could tell people back home he had picked up a few battle scars even before going overseas. Yes, I'm still in Texas he reminded himself. "You speak German, correct?" he asked of the doctor.

"I do."

"Both you and the nurse."

"This part of Texas has many German-American communities. Lots of Czechs, too, in this area."

"*Danke sehr*. All of you helped me."

"Don't be so eager to thank me. Your leg was broken in several places and I'm afraid it may never return to normal." The doctor held up his hands, palms out. "Believe me when I say I did the best I could. But the people who used crowbars to pry you out of your cockpit added to your injuries. They couldn't help but bend and twist you a bit. They, too, did their very best, I'm sure."

"How soon will I be able to return to flight school?" Martin asked.

The doctor shook his head slowly. "In the most recent movies the nasty Germans say to recently captured British prisoners of war, 'For you the war is over'." *Zee var ist oh-fer.* "I'm afraid I must say that to you also."

Martin allowed himself a moment of self-pity, then remembered his instructor. "There was another man in the plane with me."

"Ah, yes," Doctor Gerber sighed. "You are luckier than your flight instructor."

"How much luckier," Martin asked, his throat tightening.

"At least you are still alive," the doctor said. "Mister Basswick died from his injuries. Much internal bleeding. There was nothing I could do to save him. I'm sorry."

Sorry. Yes. It's proper to feel sorrow at a man's death, Martin told himself. Even Jerry Basswick's death. Martin closed his eyes and tried to picture a fuzz-faced lieutenant handing Basswick's mother a folded American flag at his graveside, but the images wouldn't come into focus. Surely I was wrong and he does have a mother, Martin thought, just as he saw Nurse Betty reload his IV bottle with the morphine that would ease him back into an itchless sleep.

Wednesday
August 9, 1942
Dynamo Stadium
Kiev, Republic of the Ukraine

"*Verdammt!*"

Karl Vollmer pounded his fist on his knee as the Ukrainian soccer team scored another goal against the Luftwaffe all-star team just minutes before halftime, making the score 3-1 in favor of the Ukrainians.

Sitting beside Karl, Rainer Zeitz was quietly amused by his *Hauptscharführer's* discomfiture. Not only Karl's, but that of the entire large gathering of German military and SS present to watch the mighty German team defeat a rag-tag collection of Slav players, many of them only recently released from German POW camps.

When summer first arrived in Kiev several bored German officers recently posted to the city and environs had formed an *ad hoc* soccer league made up of players and teams from various German army units, as well as soldiers from the Hungarian and Rumanian divisions attached to Army Group South. The organizers were surprised when a local baker asked if the league would allow a Ukrainian team to participate. The Germans had agreed, all the better to demonstrate Aryan superiority to the *Untermenschen* of Kiev.

At the same time Karl was damning the German team's misfortunes, the inhabitants of Kiev -- who filled most of the stadium -- screamed and cheered, many standing and shaking their fists in the air.

"We should have taken them all out to the ravine. Every last one of them. Maybe we still will," Karl said, a mix of anger and glee in his voice.

Rainer had heard the rumor, repeated by SS soldiers assigned to work in the museum with him, that SS squads had 'eliminated' as many as a hundred thousand locals in a ravine outside the city. If so, he did not care to confirm such a story. It has nothing to do with me, he reminded himself. Karl probably knows more than he is telling. He also understands that I do not appreciate listening to such shameful tales. Besides, the number of killings, if they happened, must be greatly exaggerated. The Reich cannot have a successful *Ostarbeiter* policy if it systematically kills off the very people it plans to use as laborers.

Minutes later Rainer saw a company of SS, each man with a leashed guard dog, gathering at one end of the stadium. As the halftime gun sounded he realized the soldiers and their dogs were not there to guard anything or anyone. And, when the SS directed their dogs to charge into the crowd of joyful fans, he stood and told Karl he intended to take a walk.

"Want me to join you?" Karl asked.

"Unless you'd prefer to stay and watch the mayhem across the way."

"What is going on over there?" Karl said when he, too, saw the SS with their dogs.

"Unable to put the *Untermenschen* in their places on the playing field, we will do so wherever else we can," Rainer said and walked away. *In their places.* Maybe the rumor about the ravine is true.

From Karl's look Rainer decided Karl was unsure whether Rainer's remark was serious or a piece of sarcasm. Karl said only, "I'll stay. The second half will be better."

Karl had rejoined Rainer in late May, meeting him in Kracow, Poland, which lay on a line between Berlin and Kiev. Before then Karl had left Estonia and returned home for a bit of leave in Schleswig-Holstein. While visiting family near Kiel Karl had agreed to do the favor Rainer asked by making certain everything was in place to implement Anna's plan to move art that she and Rainer captured – *procured* was Rainer's preferred description -- to Karl's grandfather's farm near the village of Todendorf, on the Baltic coast. Rather than move art to the Sundstrums in Geneva, they would store it at the farm until it was safe to move it across the Baltic Sea directly to Sweden.

When Karl's grandfather Wilhelm died, Karl's younger sister Berta moved there from Kiel and hired a neighboring farmer to tend the milk herd. But when the neighbor's sons were called into the army the work became too much for the neighbor. So Berta sold the herd and moved back to Kiel. And now the farm lay abandoned, which suited Anna's and Rainer's needs perfectly.

Better yet, Karl's grandmother, Ilsa, proved such a shrew in her lifetime, complementing her husband's reputation for cruelty, that most neighbors in surrounding towns and villages towns deemed the farm hexed and gave it a very wide berth.

Anna had agreed to pay Karl for the use of his grandfather's farm, offering a thousand marks a month as rent. In private Rainer had told Anna he thought such a sum excessive, but she had insisted. How she possessed that much money was a mystery to Rainer and, though curious, he was content to let it remain so.

Away from the rest of the glum-looking German spectators, Rainer lit his pipe and strolled outside the stadium, wondering whether to return for the second half or go back to his work quarters, a cramped room on the second floor of the Museum of Western and Oriental Art, to try again to make arrangements to transport the museum's inventory to Königsberg. He had never been an avid soccer fan, cared very little for sports of any kind. He left sports enthusiasm to cousin Anna, though Anna would not have enjoyed being here. She hated Russians. Hated Bolsheviks really and she made no distinction between Russians and Ukrainians. She would have laughed, Rainer mused, at the thought of Ukrainians actually welcoming the Germans as their saviors from Stalinist oppression. "More fools them," Anna would have sneered. And the sight of so many -- so many beautiful -- Orthodox churches would certainly enrage Anna. Who knows how crazy she might become at seeing St. Andrew's Cathedral, on its hill, looking over the entire city? Rainer thought.

Why Anna hated Slavs -- *Schwachkopfen*, blockheads, she called them -- so intensely Rainer was not quite sure. Perhaps the young man in the Institute of Art she fell in love with while she was a student at Philipps-Universität in Marberg had soured her. She dismissed him from her life when she discovered he was not only an avid Communist, but also one quarter Jewish. But before finding out his flaws, she had been truly and deeply smitten by the fellow's wit, charm, looks, and brilliance.

No. Though an avid soccer fan herself, Anna would not like Kiev or its inhabitants, however ardent her competitive athletic and political fires burned. At the moment, Rainer reminded himself, more serious competition was occurring in Kiev, serious to the point that he was thinking of asking Berlin for help in dealing with the issue. Two issues really.

First, was the matter of the *Ostarbeiter*, Ukrainian workers being sent to Germany to work as slave labor. The Grand Plan was to ship them back by the tens of thousands. So far the reality was that only a few thousand had been sent, mostly young women intended to serve as housemaids, supposedly in aid of German women in the *Küche* raising *Kinder*. In any case, trains packed with *Ostarbeiter* were trains unavailable for transporting art work.

Regarding the second, and more serious issue, Rainer had already drafted a letter of complaint, his grievance focusing on two matters he considered totally unacceptable. One was the matter of wholesale destruction of Russian art by Army Group South. Bad enough in itself, but worse was the fact that such behavior was not only condoned but encouraged by the army group's top officers.

Field Marshal von Richenau had been the initial instigator, though thankfully he had died back in January, dying from his own stupidity, Rainer reminded himself. Why would anyone choose to maintain his physical fitness by running several kilometers daily in temperatures averaging minus twenty degrees Fahrenheit? God or the Fates had toyed with the field marshal, perhaps to teach others a lesson. A heart attack after one of his runs had not killed him, but his medical evacuation airplane crashed when trying to land in Leipzig, putting an end to his nonsense. It had been the field marshal, back in November, who had declared no Russian art worth saving and his successor so far had made no effort to alter that additional piece of von Reichenau's *Dummheit*.

Rainer agreed that few, if any, of Kiev's treasures matched the prizes waiting in Leningrad. And what was going on in the north anyway? Why hadn't the Luftwaffe succeeded in bombing that city into surrendering by now? Must the army suffer through yet another miserable winter, continuing to lay siege? How I long to leave this miserable place and walk the halls and galleries of The Hermitage.

Besides the contention of save-or-destroy Kiev's vast artistic offerings, the issue remained among those who favored saving them of whether to keep all salvaged art *in* the Ukraine or return most or all of it to Germany. The *Führer* seemed to favor the former option, as part of his *Lebensraum* plan of repopulating the Ukraine with German settlers. Local art to amuse these emigrants apparently was deemed better than no art at all. Yet no German wielding any power in the captured realm appeared to agree with Hitler. Rather, they all refused to acknowledge he held such a view, given that such a notion was incompatible with their rapacious designs.

All of them -- *Reichsleiter* Heinrch Himmler, *Reichskommisar* Koch, von Kundberg's *Sonderkommandos*, Rosensberg's ERR units, Göring, and even private German construction contractors hired by the Reich to assist the army's engineers -- felt they had license to loot and pillage whatever the Wehrmacht failed to destroy. Himmler had even ordered the Waffen-SS Division Viking to assist the archeological wing of the SS -- headed by *Sturmbannführer* Jankuhn, a professor from Kiel for whom Rainer held no affection, to aid "by any means necessary" the returning of booty to Himmler himself.

That is why Rainer decided he needed to reflect more on whom he might approach – via an urgent, private letter – to bring a halt to both the widespread destruction of Ukrainian art and the plundering of what survived. No less than Order and Discipline themselves were at stake. Something must be done.

Back at the museum entrance, following his walk from the stadium, he decided to cross the street and sit a while in Schevchenka Park, the better to reflect on the content and potential recipient of his letter. As he stood at the curb a motorcycle slowed and the rider hailed him. When the man removed his goggles Rainer recognized him as Kurt Schnelker, one of several Waffen-SS *Kriegsberichter*, war correspondents attached to SS army units, he had met since arriving in Kiev. Most of them spent much of their time milling around the local command posts of the army and Luftwaffe. If Rainer recalled correctly, Schnelker was a frequent contributor to *Der Beobachter Zeitung*, the influential Berlin newspaper dominated by Doktor Goebbels himself.

"Good afternoon, *Standartenführer*! Why are you not at the Battle of Kiev?" Schnelker asked, laughing.

"I watched the first half," Rainer said.

"I know. I saw you leave. No stomach for defeat, eh?"

"Perhaps the second half will go better."

"Indeed! And perhaps hell will freeze over by morning."

"Where is your faith?" Rainer said.

"Faith is difficult to maintain when the team you root for cheats unmercifully, with the aid of German referees, and still cannot muster the resources to win."

"The game has clearly restored the morale, if not the faith, of the citizens of Kiev," Rainer allowed.

"So it has. Or rather, did for a short while. Our dogs finally muted their enthusiasm -- but only slightly."

"They are not my dogs."

"Tell the crowd that," Schnelker said.

Rainer shrugged. "So why did you leave the game?"

"I have a deadline to meet. I must set the scene for the German people. And then tomorrow write up the results, including all the play-by-play details."

"A bit difficult if you're not there."

"Not at all. Before I go to bed I will have heard the game recapped, moment by moment, more times than I will be able to bear. My duller-witted colleagues will see to that."

"And how will you explain a German defeat, if that is the outcome?" Rainer asked, not daring to smile at the thought.

The newsman threw back his head and cackled loudly, then said, "If we lose then the game does not exist. Never happened. The column I am about to submit will turn to ashes. Literally."

"Bad news becomes no news."

"I will write an alternate column, some vague piece about the partisan uprisings in the northern Ukrainian woods and how our valiant German soldiers are crushing them under their collective heel. Unless, of course, I can think of a better topic."

Rainer's mind lit up. "Can you spare me a few minutes. Perhaps I can offer you a more immediate, more local subject of interest."

"Of course." The newsman dismounted his cycle and parked it on the grass.

"Let's cross to the park and sit," Rainer suggested.

As the two men crossed Terenschenkivska Street Kurt Schnelker said, "Oh, before I forget. Are you doing anything important the next few days?" Following Rainer's glare, he went on, "I mean really important? Anything that can't wait a few days or... or be done by your trusted aide?"

"Why do you ask?" Rainer gestured toward a bench in the park.

As they both seated themselves on a splintered bench, reporter Schnelker said, "Several of us are cycling down to Odessa in the morning. I invite you to join us. Ride in my side-car with me. We'll see what's occurring on the shore of the Black Sea, perhaps take a stroll or two on the sands. Maybe even treat ourselves to a swim."

Rainer recalled the summers of his youth, when his parents and Anna's took them on holiday to the Baltic shore. "Sounds splendid. I do have one important task to complete, but Karl can finish up for me. Yes! I would be delighted to join you. Odessa also has a Museum of Western and Oriental Art. Mining its contents will serve as an adequate justification for my taking leave of Kiev for several days."

"So what topic do you wish to recommend to me?" Schnelker asked.

Rainer spent the next half hour repeating every point he had made in his as-yet unaddressed letter outlining the confusing and conflicting policies toward confiscated art assets within Army Group South's zone of control.

Kurt Schnelker listened quietly and attentively, but made no commitment after Rainer had finished. "Because this matter is ongoing, I detect no urgency. So let me think about it. By the time we return from Odessa I'll have reflected on it sufficiently to make a recommendation to you how to proceed. Who knows? By then I may decide to carry your case directly to Minister Goebbels, leaving out all references to *Reichsleiter* Himmler, of course."

Of course. Bad news becomes no news. Rainer felt dismayed that Kurt lacked his own sense of urgency regarding the matters, but still, if Herr Goebbels himself decided to espouse his causes, then waiting would be worth it.

"I'll pick you up across the street at 6:00 a.m. We have six cycles. Another BMW like this one and four DKW's. Don't ask how we got them. Just enjoy the ride. And pack lightly. Whatever we lack we'll buy in Odessa." That said, Schnelker fired up the BMW's engine and was off.

In the corridor outside Rainer's work space two SS corporals sat at a pair of low desks as they bent forward cataloging several stacks of paintings, all still in their frames.

One corporal looked up and asked, "How is the soccer match going?"

"Not well." Rainer told him the halftime score.

The second corporal looked up and nearly shouted, "The great German team will emerge victorious in the end!"

"For the sake of the Ukrainian team, we had better hope so," Rainer muttered.

"I have heard rumors the Ukrainian players are all spies," the first corporal said.

"The Gestapo will have them confessing, if they are," said the second earnestly.

And even if they aren't, Rainer supposed.

Late into the evening Karl Vollmer helped Rainer finish packing the pair of crates containing several Rubens, Breugels, van Ruisdaels, and dozens of engravings by Lucas Cranach. One crate, containing the Rubens and Cranachs, was destined for Karinhall, a surprise gift for Reichsmarshall Goring. Once he had delivered the first crate, Karl would transport the second crate to his grandfather's farmhouse near Todendorf. Already Rainer began to imagine Frau Limberger's look of astonishment when Karl presented her with "mementos rescued from the people of Kiev", as his brief note to the *Reichsmarshall* would read.

The space allotted him on a rail car added belatedly to an Ostarbeiter Express bound for Dresden would barely hold both crates, each of them large. But he didn't want to risk sending them separately. He wanted Karl to accompany both containers every meter of the way to their final destinations.

Rainer had already convinced himself he was not guilty of the slightest hypocrisy from this endeavor. *My* motives are pure, he reassured himself. I am rescuing works from among the finest artists of Europe, saving them from a people who cannot possibly appreciate them. Well, perhaps Cranach does not deserve to be counted among "the finest", but that is a minor point.

One foot resting on his small duffle, Rainer stood curbside still wearing yesterday's uniform, having slept in it. No sense in putting on a clean uniform for the hot, dusty ride to Odessa. I can bath and change when we get there, maybe even scrub off the filth of Kiev in the waters of the Black Sea. Won't that be delightful!

Sharply at six o'clock Kurt Schnelker and ten of his fellow SS *Kriegsberichter* turned off Tolstoy Avenue onto Tereschenkivska and stopped in front of Rainer, puffs of exhaust from their engines swirling in low clouds that made the rising sun turn brindle.

"Climb in! Adventure awaits us!" Kurt called over of the sound of the motorcycles, sounding as though he had benefited from a better night's sleep than Rainer.

After squeezing himself into the sidecar and donning the goggles Kurt handed him, Rainer nodded that he was ready and Kurt set off in the lead, the five other cycles following close behind. They had not gone far before Rainer was reminded of the long, uncomfortable trip nearly a year earlier when he and Karl had set out in another BMW with sidecar and crossed the Russian wasteland between Narva and Gatchina Palace. His estimate, from looking at a map the night before, was that Kiev to Odessa was at least twice that distance. But maybe the road is better, he told himself before realizing such a fortuitous circumstance was highly unlikely.

"Have you been to Odessa before?" Rainer shouted at Kurt.

"No. Have you?"

Rainer shook his head. At least he had something to look forward to now. The waters of the Black Sea were surely warmer than the perpetually chilly waters of the Baltic. And now that forward elements of Army Group South had taken Kharkov and Rostov and were driving on Stalingrad, Odessa should be safe enough.

"We are getting out of Kiev at a good time," Kurt said. "The natives are delirious and I'm afraid that, dogs or no dogs, they are going to prove unruly for a day or two. At least until the *Reich-scommissar* reestablishes Aryan superiority."

"Because of the game?" Rainer said.

"Of course. To keep a man down you must keep him stripped of his pride," Kurt screamed over the roar of the accelerating motorcycle.

Ah, yes. The soccer game. Karl had returned to the museum bitter and surly. Each team had scored twice in the second half, making the final score 5-3 in favor of the Ukrainians.

"Dumb luck. That's all. No other way to explain our losing to a bunch of *Nichtswissers*," Karl had said.

"How can they be know-nothings?" Rainer had chided. "They know enough to beat a German all-star team."

"Luck. That's all it was," Karl had insisted.

Rainer had decided further teasing was not a wise course.

Instead, Rainer called out to Kurt, "Want to change your mind and stay here? Some good stories may pop up."

"To hell with good stories. I want to sit on a sandy beach and dream of consuming vast quantities of food and wine. *Good* food and wine. Not army swill."

Rainer nodded in full agreement with that sentiment, then, after trying to adjust himself in the sidecar to get more comfortable, he gave up, sighed, and decided to focus on the scenery, such as it was.

Despite the fierce battles fought recently, Kiev was far from a total blight. Its woods and sprawling parks reminded him of Berlin. But only in that respect. And Rainer judged the multitude of Orthodox churches, with their fine sets of spires, to be really quite splendid, even if the rites conducted beneath them were misguided.

He had not bothered to examine any maps of the terrain between Kiev and Odessa, though he did recall hearing Karl explain to one of the corporals clerking for them that the pine forests extend some way south of the city.

Their motorcycle caravan had the broad boulevard leading toward the Holosiyivsky Forest, as he recalled Karl had called it, to themselves. Few Ukrainians had permission to drive private vehicles and thus far they had encountered no German military cars, trucks, or other motorcycles even though the sun was now high in the morning sky.

Finally it occurred to Rainer that he had seen no civilian pedestrians either. No doubt they had all stayed up half the night in celebration of their hollow soccer triumph and were now passed out, exhausted -- drunk on phantom glory.

Sudden he heard familiar sounds that froze his spine: the staccato of automatic weapons firing. Somewhere ahead of them. Off to the left. We're under attack! And the next thing he knew his face and goggles were spattered with something so thick he could not see. Before he could pull off his goggles something bounced hard against his left side and, in the instant more it took him to fling aside his goggles, he saw that Kurt had fallen – or been knocked – from his seat and was being dragged along, Kurt's pant leg snagged in the footrest.

Helpless either to climb from the sidecar or to aid Kurt, Rainer watched the speeding motorcycle arc slowly to the right, hit the boulevard curb, bounce wildly, and continue on, before hitting a tree root, tipping the sidecar, snapping the tie arms and sending Rainer, still trapped in the capsule, sliding toward a huge pine tree. Rainer squeezed his eyes tightly shut, ducked his head, and braced himself for a nasty impact.

When Rainer opened his eyes again he looked to find the source of the cigarette smoke he smelled. Karl Vollmer sat beside him, holding a half-smoked Eckstein.

"Where am I"

Karl offered him a drag from the cigarette. "Still in Kiev. Army hospital."

"What day is it?'

"Same day as you crashed. Almost midnight. You've been here since this morning."

"How am I?" Rainer felt nothing.

"Alive, which is more than is so for most of your fellow travelers."

He re-closed his eyes and again saw Kurt being trapped between the bike and the sidecar. "Kurt is dead, I suppose."

"Before he hit the ground, the ambulance driver said."

"Lucky him."

Karl nodded. "Yes. I saw what was left of him."

"Partisans?"

"The Gestapo doesn't think so. Locals, most likely. Soccer fans. The game has jacked up their courage. The day has been full of similar incidents all over the city. The Army is bringing in several companies and a few dozen panzers to deal with the situation."

Rainer tried to reach for Karl's cigarette when he finally felt pain. His entire right side suddenly burned. Nor, even with great effort, could he extend his arm far enough to come even close to Karl, who finally put the butt to Rainer's lips.

"Your clavicle is broken. Plus your wrist, two ribs, and your hip. Not to mention your right knee is damaged. You and your sidecar really hammered that poor tree."

"No bullet holes?"

"Kurt proved to be an effective shield. Not to mention the fact that you and Kurt were farthest to the right. Or so the military police captain judged when he tried to reconstruct the shooting scene. Two or three submachine guns fired from a low fence between two houses. They could see you coming for a long time and they had the discipline to hold their fire until they could not miss. Maybe they were partisans. Or, more likely, POWs recently released from camps – like most of their soccer team." Karl took away the half cigarette, crushed it out on the floor, and lit a fresh one for Rainer, putting it in Rainer's left hand.

"Looks like I will be riding with you back to Berlin," Rainer said, managing a wan smile.

Karl shook his head. "The doctor says you will be placed on a train full of wounded, but not until you have healed some. Meanwhile, the *Ostarbeiter* train our crates were to be part of left on time this afternoon."

Rainer flinched.

Karl made a calming gesture with is hand. "Don't worry. The crates remain in the museum cellar. Using your name and rank, I arranged a place for our goods on a train leaving tomorrow morning. With your permission, both the boxes and I will be on that train."

With a sigh of relief Rainer nodded, then handed Karl the unfinished cigarette and fell back into a long, deep sleep.

8

Friday
Christmas Eve, 1942
Kochel am See
Lake Kochel, Upper Bavaria

"Go on. Open it," Rainer coaxed.

Lili Kraegler, Rainer's young cook and housemaid, held the small packet in both hands at her waist, staring at it in the firelight, eyes wide, while Rainer sat in his father's overstuffed chair and sipped at a small brandy. Lili looked at Rainer and smiled. "It's really for me?"

"Yes. For you. Only for you. Unless, of course, you choose to share it with someone."

She pulled one end of the decorative ribbon binding the gift, then dropped the ribbon and carefully unfolded the wrapping. "Oh, Herr Zeitz, it's beautiful."

"Unplug the stopper and share the scent with me. I hope you like it. The clerk at the shop in Munich assured me you would," Rainer lied. The single ounce of Guerlain perfume in its Baccarat crystal bottle had belonged to his late mother, a gift from Werner on some very special occasion or other. Her birthday or perhaps a wedding anniversary. But Maria had squirreled away unopened the richly scented water in its expensive container. Just prior to his leaving for Kiev Rainer had found it in a trunk full of his mother's belongings that Werner had stored in the attic of their home in the Munich district of Schwabing. He remembered it when he returned home and thought that someone ought to enjoy it. Lili came immediately to mind.

Lili gave a gentle tug on the bottle top, then lifted the crystal stopper to her nose and broke into a broad grin. "Oooooh, so delightful. So delicate. Are you sure it's for me?"

"For no one else. Come. Bring it closer. Let me savor this delicacy."

The twenty-year-old daughter of the caretakers of his father's lakeside chalet walked to Rainer, standing between him and the fire, and held out the stopper.

"No, no. Dab some on your wrist. That is how I've seen other women test perfumes. You must find out if it is compatible with your own dainty, feminine scent."

Lili did as she was told, holding out her wrist for Rainer to sniff.

He took her arm and gently tugged her a step closer, putting his nose to her perfumed wrist as he stepped forward. "Divine. I think the maker must have had you in mind when he created this potion."

"Oh, Herr Zeitz, you are too kind."

"I would offer you a brandy and invite you to sit with me by the fire, but I know you are eager to go home. Christmas Eve is a time for families."

"Thank you, Herr Zeitz. Yes, my parents wait for me. But I feel so sad that you will be here all alone. I wish you would reconsider my parents' invitation to join us."

"I am not alone. I have my brandy and a good fire." Rainer patted his belly. "And I am full of the fine meal you fixed for me."

"When the war is over you should take a wife, Herr Zeitz. Marry a woman who would fix you fine meals every night of your life."

"Do you know any such woman you might recommend to me?"

Lili blushed. "I am too young for you?"

"No, but you are deserving of a better man, someone who can take care of you in elegant style."

"Such as buying me costly perfume?"

"There is more to life than fancy desserts, Lili. By the way, your chocolate torte was magnificent. According to my father, I am little more than a *Luftmensch*. And my cousin Anna claims *Aus Dem Leben Eines Taugenichts* could as well be a story about me."

"But you are not a good-for-nothing, Herr Zeitz. You are an important and wonderful man."

"Who, but for his father's success would not have a pot to piss in, excuse my language."

"I will still be here when the war is over, Herr Zeitz." She made a half turn and gave Rainer a coy look. "In case you should change you mind."

"Thank you, Lili. I shall keep that in mind. Now run along and give my best wishes again to both your parents for a merry Christmas. I shall see you all again tomorrow evening after dinner. I'm sorry your brother cannot be here to share your holidays."

"Good night, Herr Zeitz. Sleep well." Lili curtsied and walked away slowly, twirling one of her blonde pigtails.

She has a fine figure, Rainer thought, picturing Lili first as he had seen her two days earlier, dressed in her brown and navy blue *Bund Deutscher Mädel* uniform, then as a nude framed in a painting. She is neither as stout as a Rubens figure nor skinny as one of Mueller's stick-shaped women.

Yes, a fine figure, but not exactly a fine mind. She's too simple a girl for me, Rainer decided. Of good character, brought up well. But now, at age twenty, Lili was a member of the League of German Maidens' *Glaube und Schönheit*, Faith and Beauty, organization within the BDM, whose purpose was to train German women of marriageable age in the domestic arts.

Rainer thought, I don't want a *Kinder, Kirche, Küche* woman. So then, what kind of woman do I wish for? A *Weltbürgerin*, to start with. A woman of the world. *Kosmopolitisch*. And... a woman made of Marc Antony's "sterner stuff". A woman such as... such as Anna.

Thinking of Anna made him wonder if Anna had taken his refusal to join her and her parents in Stuttgart for the holidays as a slight. If so, too bad. He had a reasonable enough excuse: his injuries still required him to immerse himself in the sulphur and iodine waters of the Bad; to soak his mending bones and drain the cares of war from his psyche. Besides, Bernhard and Magda Stahlinger were not his idea of the kind of people with whom to celebrate anything, let alone Christmas. Anna's father possessed an accountant's mind, even measuring the success of his museum's exhibitions only by how many visitors each attracted. Quantity over quality. And her mother was a chronic whiner, even in her prayers, according to Anna. "God must put fingers in His ears and roll His eyes whenever He sees Mutti clasp her hands together and bow her head," Anna had once told him.

Much as he disliked his aunt and uncle, Rainer had bought them Christmas gifts. When at last the army doctors in Kiev decided in late September that he was fit enough to travel, he found room on a train bound for Munich by way of Budapest. And, when the train arrived in the Hungarian capital, Rainer had granted himself a two-day shopping leave, planning well ahead for Christmas, before continuing on to Munich.

Wandering the market streets, he had managed well, still relying on a cane, which was certainly better than the damned crutches he had started out using once he was well enough to stand and walk. He judged he was no more adept at moving about on crutches than were the soldiers who had lost a leg, an entire ward full of them on the ground floor beneath him at the Kiev hospital.

Rainer thought of Lili's slightly older brother, Rudi, who was a gunner with a panzer division in Norway. How lucky Rudi was! There were worse places a German soldier could spend Christmas than in Norway. Far worse. Leningrad was still under siege and Rainer wondered what equipment *Reichsmarshall* Göring was called upon to supply to the army *this* winter. Three million little silver tubes of frost salve?

In Egypt Rommel's Afrika Corps now found itself in hellbent retreat, following its inability to crush the British at El Alamein. And worst of all, Army Group South's 6th Army found itself encircled at Stalingrad. Three hundred thousand men, a thousand panzers. Whispered rumors leaking back from the Eastern

Front told of temperatures at Stalingrad dropping lower than -20 degrees Fahrenheit; 6th Army's bread ration dropping to 50 grams per day per man; soldiers not only eating their horses but later digging up the frozen bones in search of overlooked scraps.

From his limited experience, he judged it worse to see crippled and lifeless soldiers brought back from the front lines than it had been to stand close enough to hear gunfire and shelling, as he had when confronting General Kruger on the outskirts of Pushkin.

Pangs of guilt made Rainer shudder as he moved his chair nearer the fire and reflected on the plateful of roast beef, the pile of potatoes and onions, accompanied by a liter of beer, and then the enormous wedge of cake washed down with real coffee. To forget the war's horrors, those he could imagine in Stalingrad and those he had seen firsthand in Kiev, Rainer reminded himself of his shopping successes as he added another small log to the fire and poured himself two fingers more of brandy.

During Anna's last visit Rainer had shown her the gifts he had bought her parents, asking at the same time that she help him wrap them. He was clumsy at his very best. With his entire right side still under repair he was sure to make a botch of folding corners and tying ribbons.

For Magda he had found a handmade silver bracelet in Budapest; for Bernhard, a small set of centuries-old gold coins. That they were genuine Rainer was nearly certain; that they were a personal family heirloom the seller was willing to part with cheaply in order to pay for his children's medical needs, Rainer doubted very much. He was aware black markets in Budapest, as elsewhere, teemed with valuables confiscated from Jews being sent to Himmler's camps.

After Anna had helped him with wrapping, he presented her with the gift he had chosen for her, one he had made a special trip by train to Salzburg to purchase. When Anna opened the box she immediately gave him a sideways grin, knowing the gift was in part a private joke. But a set of Austrian-made Riedel crystal goblets were nothing to sneer at, joke or not. Rainer knew she had suspected a trick of some sort when the attached card read: "for Greta Riedel", her pseudonym when in Switzerland.

"I have something for you that I think will complement the crystal quite nicely," Anna had said. She had gone outside to her car, which was by then covered with freshly fallen snow. From a window Rainer had watched her heft a wood case from the trunk. If he judged correctly she had brought him a case of wine.

"My God! How could you afford this?" Rainer had said, dumbfound by such serendipity when he lifted the lid. Twelve bottles of 1934 Chataeu Latour Pauillac. "This costs the world, Anna."

"Only half the world. Actually it's a gift to both of us from Herr Ohlmaier. So six bottles are mine. And here is your real gift from me." She held out a velvety box that fit in Rainer's palm.

Rainer opened it carefully, finding inside a Rolex watch described as *for military officers*. "It's quite handsome!"

"I thought you'd like it."

Rainer bussed Anna on a cheek. "So this is what cost you half the world."

"I was with a banker in Bern. Because I knew several of his dirty little secrets, he took me to a jeweler on whom this banker could tell some tales. As a result I paid considerably less than I might have otherwise."

"Still, I am impressed by your choice. Thank you so much."

"And I thank you," Anna had said. Pointing to the wine and the crystal, she said, "Let us drink a toast to ourselves."

Warmed by the fire and brandy, Rainer reminded himself that day after tomorrow, the 26th, Anna would return to Switzerland to bargain with the Sundstrums on a price for delivering the second crate of paintings Karl had taken from Kiev to the farm near Todendorf. The day after New Year's Rainer was again to pick up Anna at the Kalmbach house in Wasterkingen.

Karl had come to the chalet a week earlier to report that the second crate was now safely locked away in the cellar of the farmhouse outside of Todendorf. Frau Limburger had indeed been astonished when Karl appeared unannounced at Karinhall to present the *Herr Reichsmarshall* with the assortment of paintings, etchings, and drawings from Kiev. Though Göring himself was not present to accept the crate full of booty, he had sent a two-sentence note of thanks to Rainer two weeks later, which is more thanks than Karl got from Frau Limberger. Her astonishment had not turned into gratitude, but then Rainer had already warned Karl that butter would not melt in that witch's mouth. Karl had laughed when told that by Rainer, but he was not laughing when he told his own story. With Rainer's permission, Karl had gone to spend the holidays with his own family, traveling to the thick fogs and cold mists of the Baltic coast.

Rainer worried for Karl's safety, despite urging the *Hauptscharführer* to go. Already the Allies had bombed Lübeck and he had no doubt Kiel would be a leading target, given its prominence as a primary launching point for U-boats operating against North Atlantic convoys. My God! German cities are now being bombed, Rainer thought with disgust. Another of *Reichsmarshall* Göring's failures, along with the Luftwaffe's inability to provide supply relief to the poor bastards trapped in Stalingrad. The reason Anna had to delay seeing the Sundstrums so long, he reminded himself, is that the good doctors are now busy visiting German camps full of Allied POWs. That thought brought him back to Göring. The Luftwaffe was making the Allies pay a heavy toll for their bombing of the Fatherland. But still they come. The *Reichsmarshall*, for all his boasts, has not been able to stop them.

As he sat swirling the dregs of his brandy, while staring into the fire and thinking of his father in London, he heard a knock at his door. When he opened it there stood Johan and Hildegard Kraegler. "Come in, come in. Such a pleasant surprise."

Hildegard spoke first. "When Lili came home and said you still refused to join us for Christmas dinner we decided to make one more effort to persuade you to join us tonight or at the very least tomorrow for dinner."

Johan nodded. "You can't eat leftovers on such a day!"

"But what fine leftovers they are," Rainer said, ushering the pair in and closing the door behind them. "Please. Take off your coats and sit by the fire. How thoughtful of you both to walk such a long way. And through such snow."

"We also wish to thank you again for the precious gifts you brought us. You are so thoughtful," Johan said.

"We open all our gifts on Christmas Eve, you know. We started doing that when Rudi was very young. Such an impatient child!" Hildegard said with more pride than dismay.

"And naturally my wife gave in to his little tantrums. So indulgent she was," Johan explained.

"But not his father," Hildegard said in a mocking tone, shaking her head.

Rainer took their coats. "I'm sure you wish Rudi could be with you. This war is such a hardship on parents." The thought made Rainer think of his own father.

"Rudi is where he needs to be," Johan said pridefully.

"He could be worse places," Hildegard said, echoing Rainer's own earlier thoughts.

On a brighter note, Hildegard said, "Oh, Herr Zeitz, you should have seen the glow on Lili's face when she showed us the perfume you gave her. So thrilled. I cannot begin to tell you how much it means to her."

"I am thrilled for myself," Johan said, extending his hand to shake Rainer's. "Where did you discover such a find? Such a bottle of wine must be nearly as rare as a golden egg."

"Not quite, Johan." The six-year-old bottle of Scharzhofberg Auslese Riesling was indeed pricy, even though he bought it from a wine dealer who had done business with his father for nearly three decades. But he decided that Johan and Hildegard deserved the very best. They had served as caretakers of the Zeitz chalet at least since the time of Rudi's childhood tantrums. And as always, including Rainer's return in October, never was there a speck of dust in sight whenever any one of the Zietz family came to stay at the chalet, summer or winter.

No such claim could be made for the summer house in Schleswig-Holstein belonging to Werner's and Magda's brother, Rolf, who always insisted Rainer's and Anna's parents bring the children to laze on the Baltic seashore for a week, but never could find the time to bring his own family to Bavaria. As Rainer remembered it, Magda and his mother always spent the first day of the family holiday ridding the cottage of cobwebs, mouse shit, and small dead bats.

"You are deserving of special rewards for all your kindnesses and hard work on my behalf," Rainer told them.

"Already I have cookies and fudge piled high on the platter you brought me, Herr Zeitz," Hildegard said, adding quickly, "With a linen cloth between the plate and the confections."

Rainer had congratulated himself on finding a superb Herend porcelain platter during his shopping spree in Budapest, knowing the Hungarian-made china was nearly as prized as that of Meissen.

"I thought of you the instant I saw it," Rainer said truthfully. "I told myself 'How grand that will look in Hilda Kraegler's dining room'."

Seating them in chairs by the fire, Rainer again offered them drinks. "Some mulled wine? Hot chocolate? Beer? Brandy?"

Both Kraeglers turned him down politely. Then for half an hour the three of them relaxed by the fire and reminisced about events remembered from the many years of Rainer's and Anna's visits to Lake Kochel.

Such simple, yet enduring memories! Rainer, Rudi, and Anna each rowing a dingy far out into the lake to try to catch a pair of wild geese, Anna coming the closest as she left the two boys far behind; the time Rudi twisted his ankle on a hike on the side of nearby Mt. Herzogstand and had to be carried down, Rainer and Anna taking turns carrying him on their shoulders; the newly-born pair of fox kits Rainer found one morning barking their faint little barks from the wood-pile. More recently – My God, has it been more than seven years? -- during the summers of 1934 and 1935 Anna had both begged and bribed Rainer and Rudi to race Star-class sailboats with her on nearby Lake Wachsel in the expectation she could qualify for the 1936 Olympic competition to he held at Kiel. Rudi dashed her hopes by the end of that second summer, proving himself a far better sailor than either Rainer or Anna.

At last the Kraeglers said they were pleased to share Rainer's company but were weary and had best leave before Lili worried for their safety. They invited him again for Christmas dinner, which he again refused, then thanked him a final time and were gone.

Alone again, Rainer thought of his father, far away in enemy London. He walked to his bedroom and retrieved the special gift he had bought for his father, thinking that someday, when the war was finally over, he would see old Werner again and present him with the bottle of 1927 Pierre Ferrand cognac that he knew his father would relish.

He placed the bottle on the fireplace mantel, poured himself just a splash more of the nondescript brandy he was drinking that evening, then raised his snifter in salute toward the nobler cognac. "To your health and safety, Father! May we both live to sit here by this fire again and drink this fine Pierre together."

Friday
Christmas Eve, 1942
Blackduck Lake, Minnesota

Martin stood sipping eggnog at a bedroom window of the family cabin while he watched the last group of men leave the lake, their lanterns and flashlights glowing eerily as they trudged across the ice in the gathering darkness. Martin found fishing through a hole cut into lake ice to be an occasionally amusing way to achieve quiet contemplation while freezing one's ass off, but, to vast numbers of Minnesotans more hardy than he was, ice-fishing was an obsession. More *fool*hardy than he, he decided.

The cabin was one of three that sat side by side, the other two belonging to Martin's uncles. His father, Torvik, and Tor's two brothers, Lars and Stepan, had built all three cabins by themselves about the time Martin was in kindergarten. Well, not quite by themselves. Martin clearly remembered he had been given the job of passing out nails from the bin in the back of Uncle Stepan's pickup truck. And though they were called cabins, each unit was a two-story house, the upper floor of each being a bathroom and a sleeping loft filled with bunk beds.

Although the family came to Blackduck Lake in all seasons, Martin preferred the cabin and the lake in summer, when the lady slippers were in full bloom, the walleye, blue gills, and crappie were biting, and sundown always brought the haunting call of a loon.

While Martin sought solitude in the main floor bedroom, the rest of his family were in the main room of the cabin. Some, Maddy among them, were adding last-minute decorative trimmings to the blue spruce Christmas tree, the rest eating popcorn and kibitzing. All of them were listening on the radio to the choir of St. Olaf's College as the recorded version of its annual Christmas Season Concert began.

Feeling restless, Martin wandered into the kitchen, opened another beer, then stepped out onto the back porch to savor the final pinkish rays of daylight tinting the clouds. Despite the comforting tranquility that came with his being surrounded with family, Martin struggled with an uneasy sense of his place in the world. Or rather, lack of place. Serious place. The world was at war and his inability to be a participant ate at his self-esteem.

Although the military hearing that followed the airplane crash and the death of Lieutenant Basswick had exonerated him from nearly all responsibility for the loss of the aircraft and the death of his instructor, Martin chafed at the part of the committee's findings that attempted to minimize the Wicked Bastard's culpability. More than a dozen other cadets had testified to Jerry Basswick's reckless sense of invulnerability, one even invoking the *There are no old, bold pilots* axiom. But the committee officers preferred the *Speak no ill of the dead* principle, leaving Martin awash in more guilt than he knew he deserved.

Following his hospitalization at Fort Sam Houston and the hearings in Houston, Martin had been transferred to Williams Field in Arizona for the second phase of his recuperation. There he had performed light duty, shuffling papers in quantities only the Army could create.

And now, home on holiday leave, he felt even more out of place than he had felt languishing in the desert. He desperately wanted to *doooooo* something to right the wrongs of the world, 'take arms against a sea of troubles', as he liked to think of himself *doooooing*, not wasting away in Minnesota, even if it was Christmas time and these were the people he was closest to on earth.

"Martin?"

He turned and saw Maddy standing at the kitchen door.

"Come join us. Or, at the very least, come in out of the cold. The choir is on."

The choir. There was no other choir, of course. Maddy had sung in the St. Olaf Choir, following her freshman stint in the Manitou Chorus. Good old St. Olaf's. Hail to thee, my alma mater, Martin mused. But to hell with the choir. The world was in flames and singing praises to a Saviour who hadn't saved much of anything, to Martin's mind, was a form of blasphemy.

"Please, come in and join the family," she added. "You'll catch pneumonia."

Martin swore if he was tortured one more time by *Beautiful Saviour*, the choir's signature piece, he would starting running across the lake screaming like a madman. Catching pneumonia would pale compared to the frothing-at-the-mouth show he would put on.

"I'll be right in," he finally said. Instead, he stepped off the porch and prodded the ground with his cane to determine how much new snow had fallen that day. Although he had become used to walking with the cane, he loathed it, thinking himself a cripple and an old man before his time.

Join the family. Martin already felt as though he was joined to all of them like so many sets of interlocking Siamese twins. Had there ever been Siamese octuplets? Because gas rationing had begun on December 1st, the family had come up from Minneapolis in three cars instead of the usual five. Martin had convinced himself that, once they were all shoehorned in, they would never all get back out again short of dropping a stick of dynamite into the back seat of each vehicle.

"You're being overdramatic," Maddy had told him. Still, by the time they had reached Bemidji he was ready to tell Aunt Eva, sitting next to him, that she needed to lose thirty pounds, preferably more. For the sake of what little civility he had remaining by the time the trip ended, he kept his silence. No use having everyone annoyed with him for the rest of their time together.

Martin had no sooner reentered the living room than a loud knocking at the front door drew everyone's attention. When Maddy opened the door she warmly welcomed two people, a willowy blonde she greeted as "Brigit" and a young man in Navy umiform -- more of a boy, Martin thought – whom Maddy called "Einar".

By the time Maddy had introduced the pair to everyone present, making a point to leave Martin for last, he decided, Martin knew that Einar had just finished Signal Corps training near San Diego and when he returned there after Christmas leave he was to ship out on a cruiser bound for somewhere in the Pacific. Most of the Pacific action right now is on New Guinea and in the Solomons, mainly Guadalcanal, Martin reminded himself.

Einar's older sister, Brigit, Martin heard Maddy tell everyone, had been a classmate of hers at St. Olaf's, like her a member of the choir, where they had first met. And now Brigit was finishing a masters degree in music at Bemidji State and had already accepted a high school teaching position for next year in a school district outside St. Cloud.

Maddy told everyone that she had asked Brigit and Einar to join the family for Christmas Eve and Christmas because their own parents had to make an sudden trip to Milwaukee because one of their uncles was on his deathbed; that Brigit's last final exam happened too late for her to go with her folks and that Einar had come home to an empty house in Mankato so he decided to come north to join Brigit.

"Brigit, Einar. This is my older brother, Martin. Martin, Brigit and Einar Olson from Mankato. They are --."

"Yes. I've heard you explain their circumstances. How do both of you do?"

"Pleased to meet you finally, Martin," Brigit gushed. "Maddy has told me sooo much about you."

As Einar shook Martin's hand he remarked, "I hear you were in a serious airplane crash."

Martin nodded and added, "I was not only in a crash, I was the pilot who crashed the plane."

Brigit gasped. "Oh no! Maddy didn't tell me that."

"Were you flying solo?" Einar asked.

"I had a flight instructor sitting behind me."

"What happened?" Einar said.

"We tried to fly through a Texas-sized thunderstorm, got tossed around like a rag doll, then I tried to land on an empty country road that turned out to be under repair. Full of deep chuckholes. But by the time I saw them --." Martin shrugged.

"Was you instructor badly hurt?" Brigit asked.

"He bled to death before help arrived."

Another gasp from Brigit.

"It gets you out of the war," Einar said.

"Unfortunately."

"You mean --." Brigit stumbled for words.

"I wanted to go. Still do."

Einar gave Martin a thumbs up, but Brigit looked puzzled.

Maddy intervened. "No more talk of the war. This is Christmas Eve. Martin, please offer our guests some refreshment while Mother, Aunt Eva, Aunt Kristina, and I set the table and finish fixing dinner."

At dinner and for the rest of the evening Martin found himself never more than an arm's length from Brigit, with Maddy keeping them close, as if she were a seasoned sheep dog. Not that Martin was averse to Brigit. She was polite, self-assured, and revealed an intelligent curiosity. Her "Please", "Thank you", and "You're welcome" came naturally. She already had plans to organize an annual Minnesota-wide high school choir competition. And, during dessert, she asked, "Why does an art professor want to be an airplane pilot? Aren't you afraid you might bomb the very art works you love?"

""I try not to think about that," Martin said lamely and changed the subject, asking her about her current studies.

Brigit said her masters degree research on choral music was leading her to create a book of Michael Praetorius arrangements suited to a small town school or church choir, many of them even suitable for as few as two or three voices.

She had laughed, playfully rather than derisively, when Martin sang the first few lines of "*Es ist ein Ros Entsprungen*", after which Martin pointed toward his mother and told Brigit, "She reminded me every chance she got, when I was a kid, that I couldn't carry a tune in a bushel basket."

"Still can't," his mother, Lisbet, said, with Martin's father nodding in agreement.

Brigit had leaned close and whispered, "I think you did quite well," offering the first and only false flattery Martin detected from her the entire evening.

By midnight only Martin and Maddy remained in the living room. Tor and Lisbet had gone off to bed and Maddy had shown Einar and Brigit to their bunk beds upstairs before returning to be with Martin.

Curled up on the couch, her head in Martin's lap, with only dying embers lighting the room, Maddy asked, "So what do you think?"

"About what?"

Maddy nudged him. "You know."

"I think you should stop playing Maddy the Matchmaker."

Maddy popped up. "Don't you like her?"

"What's not to like?"

"Well, then?"

"Madeleine, Brigit already has a job lined up in St. Cloud come autumn. And for all I know I may find myself stationed in the Aleutians next week, in charge of keeping toilet seats warm in Dutch Harbor."

"Oh, Martin. You have a Ph.D.. The Army wouldn't do that."

Martin had deliberately neglected to tell Maddy about his first day at basic training in Spartanburg. The drill sergeant had asked each new recruit in the platoon to state his highest level of education. Martin, with his degree from Chicago, possessed far more formal education than anyone else. As a consequence, the drill sergeant – on whole a fair and decent man, Martin decided after he had finished training – appointed Martin to latrine-swabbing duty for the first ten days of boot camp.

"Indeed they might, Maddy. In any case, this is no time for me to be thinking even remotely of marriage, which is what I assume you have in mind for me."

"But Brigit would be so perfect for you."

"I love it when you act as if you know more about what's best for me than I do."

"Sometimes I'm sure I do," Maddy said.

"And what about you? Have Mom and Dad warned you yet that it won't be long until you'll reach the age when people start to give you the look that says, 'What's wrong with that young woman that she hasn't found a husband yet?'"

Maddy laughed. "Actually, Brigit's parents are the ones who have given her that caution."

"Well, trust me. You're next."

"I have miles to go before I sleep… with a husband."

"Very witty. But seriously, are *you* on the lookout?"

"No more than you."

"Then why pick on me? Did I drag some bowlegged, rodeo-addled cowboy back with me from Arizona and coax you sit in his lap so he could whisper in your ear about what a fine calf roper he is?"

Maddy arched her eyebrows. "That might have been interesting."

"Your bringing Brigit here has also been interesting. But please don't repeat your effort."

"I only want what's best for you, Martin."

"And you know best. Right?"

"Sometimes, maybe."

"I'm sure Brigit will make some man a fine wife. But I'm not that man. Okay?"

"Okay."

"Now tell me what you did to soften Dad up before I arrived," Martin said.

"He mellowed on his own. After your plane crash I overheard him tell Mother how he wasn't sure he could live with himself if you had died. He broke down and cried on Mom's shoulder. It's true. I swear."

Martin sat quietly for a long time and Maddy snuggled her head back into his lap. Barely above a whisper, Martin said, "You realize, don't you Maddy, we could have done worse in our choice of parents. A whole lot worse."

When Maddy finally fell asleep Martin eased away, covered her with a blanket, then slipped into the kitchen to finish wrapping the gifts he had bought during a long weekend leave at the Grand Canyon. He tried this best to stick to the family rule regarding Christmas gifts for each other: Something to wear, something to read, something to play with.

For Maddy he had brought back a squash blossom necklace, silverstudded with pieces of turquoise, a book about the history of Southwest Indian tribes, and a Hopi Kachina doll. For Mother, a blanket woven by a Navajo, a cookbook full of native Southwest Indian recipes, and a miniature cactus growing in a clay pot. For Torvik he had decided on a pair of moccasins lined with sheep wool, a subscription to *Arizona Highways,* and a bola tie made of leather, silver, and a piece of rock from the Petri-fied Forest. For the rest of the family, aunts, uncles, and cousins, he had bought jams and candies made from prickly pear cactus fruit. Martin was sure that for Minnesotans his little treasures would seem as exotic as the souvenirs Marco Polo had brought back to Italy from China.

As he finished wrapping his last gift he looked up to see his father, dressed in his pajamas, standing at the door from the living room.

"I didn't mean to interrupt," he said softly. "I just came out for a glass of water. For some reason eggnog makes me thirsty."

"I'm just finishing, Dad. I'm about to head off to bed."

"Is that Maddy on the couch?"

Martin nodded.

Tor opened a cupboard and took out a glass, filled it from a pitcher from the refrigerator, took a sip, then set the glass down. As Martin stood watching him his father took a tentative step toward him, hesitated, then walked to Martin and embraced him in a bear hug. "It's good to have you home, Son. Really, really good."

And with only Maddy listening from the couch, as she revealed to her brother days later, Martin and his father shared a good cry together.

9

Monday
January 11, 1943
Edgerton, Ohio

The train had stopped in the middle of nowhere and Martin looked at his watch, not that time mattered at the moment. His schedule was in the hands of the New York Central Railroad. Just then a conductor came down the aisle, explaining to passengers there had been a report of a delivery truck stalled on the tracks just a few miles ahead.

Martin had a flashback of his plane touching down on the deserted Texas backroad. Deserted except for a series of barricaded potholes. He pictured the train's engineer suddenly seeing the truck and the feeling of abject helplessness he would experience before slamming into it.

A woman somewhere behind him asked the conductor, "Are we still in Indiana?"

The conductor replied, "No, ma'am. We are a few miles into Ohio."

Peering out the window, Martin stared up at the small town's water tower, which read in huge letters: EDGERTON, OHIO. Looking back, he saw that the woman who had asked the question was sitting on the same side of the train he was. Still a long way to New York City, Martin thought. And then on to Washington.

Between Christmas and New Years Day Martin had been informed by the Army that, although he had not finished flight training, his rank was no longer in limbo. He was officially promoted to second lieutenant. He was meeting Elliott in New York City and together they would take a train to Washington, where they would arrive in time for the formal dedication on Friday of the just-finished military command building called the Pentagon.

Better still, Martin would take possession briefly of an office somewhere in the sprawling new complex. And several mores pluses. Professor Parker had arranged for Martin to begin adjunct teaching at Georgetown University, starting immediately, courtesy of Fathers Troquier and Roskosz. Only one class, but still --. Plus, Martin was to become a staff member of Elliott's Harvard Group, which soon would be taken over by the Army and was going to be called the American Commission for the Protection and Salvage of Artistic and Historic Monuments in War Areas. Thankfully, that title would be shortened, unofficially, to The Roberts Commission, after its chairman, Supreme Court Justice Owen Roberts. Part of the Commission, the one to which Martin was being assigned, was to be called the Monuments, Fine Arts, and Archives group, MFA&A for short. The Robert Commission, Elliott told Martin, would be working out of the National Gallery and the co-director of the Commission would be David Finley, director of the National Gallery.

Listening to Elliott tell him all this news over the telephone, Martin had been overwhelmed. Elliott had already lined up an apartment for Martin, although Martin would have to share the apartment with another young staff member by the name of David Fox, son of a family friend and a graduate of Yale with a degree in art history.

So much happened so fast Martin had scarcely been able to digest all the news, but he needn't have worried that he might forget pieces of his new good fortune. The next day an Army officer, a captain no less, showed up at the cabin to present him with a sealed packet reiterating everything Elliott had told him on the telephone.

Even Torvik had been impressed that an Army captain would come all the way from Washington to the woods of Minnesota to deliver an official set of military instructions to his son.

"You must be more important than I gave you credit for," Martin's father had said, no doubt supposing he had given Martin a fine compliment. Martin had smiled and thanked his old man. He tries, Martin conceded. Part of Tor's *trying*, in more ways than one, had been to ask Martin what he thought of Brigit. The question had been accompanied by a knowing look. At least he had not been as direct as, "About time you were thinking about getting married, isn't it, son?"

Brigit Olson. Martin tried to imagine himself married to her, but could not picture himself coming home every night and sitting down to dinner to discuss choir music, unruly students, and – eventually, inevitably – their own passel of homegrown urchins. In fact, he could not quite imagine himself married to any woman.

Well, no. There was one woman. Ellen Nordholm. But now, and forever, Ellen would occupy a special cell in Martin's imaginary dungeon for people who had treated him shoddily. He had begun dating Ellen when both of them were sophomores at St. Olaf's College. During their junior year they both elected to live off campus and they moved into apartment houses on the same block, two miles from campus. Because he had worked weekends and summers all through high school for Dr. Winters, the neighborhood veterinarian, Martin had been able to buy a car, a used Ford, at the same time he moved off campus. Throughout their junior year Ellen had relied on Martin for a ride to and from campus each school day. Then, on the final day of final exams that spring semester, as Martin was dropping her off at her apartment, Ellen announced that she thought it best if they stopped seeing each other. Martin had been so stunned he remembered just sitting slumped over the steering wheel long after Ellen had retreated into her apartment house without so much as saying, "It's been good to know you."

Martin's phone calls to Ellen at her home in St. Paul either went unanswered or were answered by her mother, who always told Martin, "I'm afraid you'll have to discuss your relationship with Ellen directly with her." But Ellen was never home. Then two weeks after classes ended Martin found out from one of Ellen's housemates that Ellen had been dating a senior on the basketball team since mid-semester.

How blind and stupid can a guy be? he continued to ask himself – even now. She used me. I turned into nothing more than her chauffeur. No. She turned me into her chauffeur without telling me. Dumping me would have been too inconvenient for her, until I was no longer of *any* use to her. For that I'll never forgive her.

The last Martin had heard, Ellen Nordholm was teaching at an elementary school in St. Paul. He hoped she was more direct and honest with her pupils than she had been with him, but somehow he didn't think she would be.

Elementary school. Outside the train a dozen young boys were playing by a roadside. Martin wondered why none of them were in school on a Monday before realizing the time difference between Chicago and Ohio meant school was probably over for the day.

One boy caught his attention. The lad looked more shabbily dressed than the others. His jacket appeared ripped in several places. Martin counted seven small holes in one rubber boot, three in the other. Shreds of material hung from his pants at both knees. And worst of all, among the dozen boys only this child wore no hat. Yet he clearly was not ashamed. He played with as much vigor and enthusiasm as the others. And none of the others, as Martin watched, took notice, let alone made mention, of the poor kid's grim attire.

The youngster made Martin think back to his own youth. The boys' ages, he guessed, ran from eight to twelve or thirteen. Junior High boys. When Martin attended Wenceslaus Junior High a young lad his age named Jakob Stellhorn also went there. Jakob lived over one block from him and stood a year behind him in school. Jakob's parents were poor. As Martin could best recall, Mister Stellhorn worked as a custodian at an elementary school somewhere in Minneapolis and Mrs. Stellhorn stayed at home to tend Jakob's three younger siblings. Mister Stellhorn's mother also lived in the small, single-story house on Delaware Avenue.

To his embarrassment now, Martin recalled that it was his mother who coined the word "Jakey" to describe Martin at those times when his appearance dissatisfied her. "Go ask your father to help you retie your tie. And for God's sake tuck in your shirt, Martin. You look Jakey," she would say as he stood for his weekly pre-church inspection. Worse, a sure sign that he was in need of one or more new items of clothing or a new pair of shoes, or that in choosing a shirt to wear with a certain pair of pants Martin had misjudged and failed to coordinate his wardrobe, his mother would tsk-tsk, shake her head solemnly, and proclaim, "No, Martin. That simply will not do. You look like a Stellhorn." To *look like a Stellhorn* was Mother's ultimate fashion rebuff. Harsher than disheveled, scruffy, or unkempt. A sloven among slovens. I wonder what ever became of Jake Stellhorn, Martin thought, and his heart went out to the Jakey-looking kid outside his train window.

The boys were hard at play, crouching down in the drainage ditches that paralleled the gravel road, six on each side. Each lad held a length of board hewn in the shape of a rifle. Two-by-fours, Martin guessed. Hunkered down on snowy grass, in turn one boy from each side of the road raised himself on one knee and fired a pretend volley across the road.

They are too young to have learned about places like Antietam and Verdun, Martin knew. He wondered how a junior high history teacher broached the subject of tens of thousands of men killing each other at close range in the name of this or that lofty-sounding cause. How *he* first came to learn about such events he could not begin to recall. Maybe from reading one of Uncle Stepan's shelves full of dime novels or from comic books. He could remember his junior high history teacher well enough. Agnes Emenhiser, a kindly, yet no-nonsense, woman who knew her subject and expected you to learn the wisdom she imparted. But, try as he might, he could not recall a single detail from his yearlong stint in Mrs. Emenhiser's class.

The train started to creep forward, leaving the young boys and their snowy battlefield behind. As Martin settled back in his train seat again the battle at Verdun reminded him of something -- a phantom hovering at the murky edge of his consciousness. Then the ghost came into focus. It belonged to Franz Marc.

Co-founder of *Der Blauer Ritter*, The Blue Rider Group, Marc had died at Verdun, shot off his horse a quarter of a century earlier. Horses. He heard the Germans still used them to pull supply wagons. Martin could not quite reconcile the concept of the new Nazi war tactic, the *blitzkrieg*, with its wide swath of steel behemoths racing across France, across Russia, across North Africa, with the notion that the whole speeding enterprise was being followed by teams of horses pulling carts full of food and ammunition.

Thoughts of Franz Marc caused Martin to wonder what had become of Marc's *Der Turm der blauen Pferde*. He told himself to remember to ask Elliott. He was sure Professor Parker remained in touch with Werner Zeitz. And he recalled clearly, even though five and a half years had passed, that Werner had said *The Tower of Blue Horses* had been removed from the *Entartete Kunst* exhibition, following a demand from the German Officers Guild.

But what happened to it then? Werner had not said and Martin had been too much in awe of the old man to ask. The thought that it might have been destroyed by now caused Martin to feel as despondent as he did whenever he thought about Ellen Nordholm. And just as bitter. Thinking of Marc's great work smashed or burned made him want more than ever to be flying in the first wave of bombers destined to level Berlin. He must remember to ask Elliott to ask Werner Zeitz what he knew of the Marc painting.

And whatever became of Werner's repulsive son, Rainer, Martin wondered. Probably working for that glib ogre of a propaganda minister, Josesph Goebbels, attempting to justify Nazi policies to the world.

Then there was Anna. What would she be doing? She definitely was not the *Kinder, Kirche, Kuche* type. As Martin closed his eyes and thought back on his day in the Alps with Anna Stahlinger the train was reaching full speed again. Soon the rhythmic *clackty-clack* made him begin to nod. Then, with a pastel vision of Anna dancing carefree across a meadow full of edelweiss, he fell asleep.

Monday
January 11, 1943
Wasterkingen, Switzerland

"She didn't tell you?"

Rainer was again sitting in Frau Kalmbach's kitchen waiting for Anna. Sipping homemade hot chocolate, Rainer had asked Hanni Kalmbach if Frau Gertrude Forsch had been nosing around still and asking questioning about *Greta*. "Tell me what?"

"When were you here last? A year ago?"

"Approximately."

Hanni removed three loaves of *Bauernbrot* from her oven, then took off her apron and sat down across from Rainer. "Frau Forsch was found dead near the bank of the Rhine three, maybe four, days after you were here. Some boys hiking along the river's edge near the border fence found her body. Frozen stiff and her throat had been cut. The Zuricher Kanton Polizei investigated, with Otto's help. But they came to no conclusions. Otto suspects a *Flussrauber*, a river robber. With the war on we hear stories all the time about men putting boats in the water below the falls and floating goods downriver. Why they bother, I do not know. The land fence is easy to cross, as you well know."

"What was Frau Forsch doing down by the river?" Rainer asked.

Hanni shrugged. "Who knows? Maybe she was killed elsewhere. The police checked out her house but found nothing. It had not been broken into, nothing damaged, nothing stolen that anyone could tell."

"And she had no family?"

"No. We buried her in the Eglisau cemetery. Otto put her house up for sale, but no one would buy it. Haunted, everyone thinks. So we finally sold all her animals and belongings at public auction and we all use her house as a public warehouse."

Rainer could still picture the Witch of Wasterkingen as if it were only yesterday, remembering that he had watched her from behind the bedroom door. Then he wondered if Otto might have killed the old woman, thinking he was doing us all a big favor. Perhaps his helping the *Polizei* amounted to helping misdirect their investigation. But why dwell on it, he asked himself. The woman was dead and Wasterkingen was well rid of her.

On Frau Kalmbach's radio German Propaganda Minister Joseph Goebbels had started to speak. She actually listens to this stuff? Rainer thought. Maybe it's the only station she receives, although Wasterkingen is less than forty kilometers from Zurich.

Rainer decided he should not be so uncharitable to Minister Goebbels. After all, it was he who initiated action against those Germans in Kiev who were destroying so many Ukrainian works of art or else stealing them for purely personal gain.

Rainer had listened spellbound to *that* Goebbels speech. Goebbels spoke then almost as if he were reading the letter Rainer had shown to Kurt Schnelker in Kiev the day of the fateful soccer game. The soccer game. Karl had been prescient about the post-game outcome. The Gestapo had indeed tortured and killed the winning Ukrainian team, accusing them all of being spies for Stalin. If Kurt Schnelker had in fact forwarded Rainer's ideas to the Propaganda Minister, no credit had come Rainer's way. Perhaps the *Kriegsberichter* had forwarded the accusations to Goebbels and claimed them as his own. Or maybe the fault lay with Goebbels himself. I'll never know, Rainer mused. In any case, the important thing is that action was taken. Goebbels had even gone farther than Rainer and called the Kiev abuses *war crimes*, not that he had heard of anyone's being punished yet.

Wishing now that Hanni Kalmbach would find a station playing a set of boring Strauss waltzes, Rainer finished his hot chocolate, tuned out Goebbels, and began thinking more about his half of the equation of dealing with the Sundstrums. As soon as he returned to Berlin he needed to contact the *Kriegsmarine*.

Under the guise of examining the feasibility of using barges and ships to move art collected in the East from the collecting point at Königsburg back to Germany, he should have little difficulty acquiring information of the frequency and patterns of all gunboat patrols between Königsburg and Kiel, as well as getting a copy of the most recent charts showing all the minefields in the Baltic between the two cities. Karl's older brother, Klaus – much too old to serve in the military -- still maintained his fishing boat at Laboe, on the outer edge of Kiel Inlet, and continued to fish the Baltic with his two teenage sons serving as deckhands. All we need from the Sundstrums is a declaration of when and where to make a landing in the south of Sweden, just in case a crossing became necessary soon. Rainer, however, was counting on Anna to persuade the Sundstrums to wait, perhaps even until the war was over.

Unlike Anna, the Sundstrums were showing impatience. The trade for the Cranachs a year earlier had whetted their appetites. To keep them partially satisfied Anna had made several small trades and sales, nothing of significance, although just before Rainer had left for Kiev Anna had asked him if he would mind letting go of the Klee. When he told her he refused to part with it she had given him a puzzled look, but had not argued the point. Nor berated him.

For Anna, the reason for her and Rainer's clandestine art dealings was to serve two long-term purposes, one longer than the other. The shorter goal was to help finance Adolf Hitler's eventual replacement, to buy the German Chancellory through bribes and whatever other means were necessary to insure the next *Führer* was an ardent, arch-conservative Catholic, preferably a Bavarian, but in any case one who promised to restore Catholicism to primacy throughout the new German empire. The second goal, an extension of the first, was to extinguish both the Lutheran and the Russian Orthodox Churches and their entire priesthoods within German-held territories.

A third goal, which Anna left to others to implement, was to see that the next pope openly supported the first two goals. The current pope, Pacelli, was a cautious vacillator, refusing to give open support to the Nazis on the slim off-chance the Allies might actually win the war.

Why Hitler, Goebbels, and all the other feckless dilettantes at the top of the Nazi pyramid wasted so much energy railing against the Jews eluded Anna. Jews were a negligible lot compared with Lutherans and the hordes whose allegiance to the Eastern Church remained steadfast, though currently submerged, hidden from Stalin's steely eyes. Anna did not share the Nazi hierarchy's *Judenbesessenheit,* obsession with Jews. Yes, they were Christ-killers and deserved punishment, 'sins of the fathers' and all that. But to let them become all-consuming was self-defeating, draining the Reich of energies that sorely needed to be directed elsewhere.

Rainer viewed Anna's intensity on these issues with a quietly bemused detachment. Yes, he agreed Germany was blaming Jews for things they were not responsible for and that made for a dangerous blindness. He reminded himself that von Manstein's effort to break the Russian stranglehold at Stalingrad had failed. Hoth's panzer spearhead had been beaten back. So? Blame the Jews? Better to blame Göring. And the *Führer.* Did the Jews stop Rommel in Egypt? Was our failure to cross the Channel and smash the English because of some huge Jewish conspiracy? Hardly. To think so was what the English philosopher Bentham would have called "nonsense on stilts".

No longer a man of faith himself, Rainer went along with Anna's intrigues because they suited his sense of iconoclasm. The one issue on which Rainer and his father seemed to agree was their contempt for the Church, though neither was willing to express disdain openly. While still in Germany, Werner had even continued going to mass regularly, behavior Rainer deemed hypocritical. Anna, Werner joked behind her back, was a more ardent and orthodox Catholic than the Pope had even been. Thus her scorn toward both Hitler and Pius XII.

A second and more compelling reason Rainer was willing to play Anna's art-theft game was the knowledge that not all their ill-gotten gains would be directed toward political and theological machinations. Rainer saw profit for himself, something to offset the humiliation of wearing an SS uniform and obeying the orders of too many witless men. Rainer estimated he could siphon off a few bundles for himself from Anna's growing stash of Deutschmarks, cherrypick a handful of paintings he fancied, and, if all went well, perhaps someday even hold a position of high authority in the next chancellor's regime. Anna, he imagined, fancied herself the *eminence gris* to the next chancellor, given that she was ineligible to be elected Pope Anna I.

Anna's disappointment with Reich leadership began, as Deiter recalled, near the end of 1935, when Himmler began his *Lebensborn,* Spring of Life, program, where women, married or not, were encouraged to produce pure-born Aryan children of SS men. Himmler even provided nursing homes for such women, the first one being at Steinhöring, near Munich. The mothers could then opt either to keep their babies or put them up for adoption. What set Anna's teeth on edge was Himmler's proclamation that only one hundred percent Nazi, non-Catholic families were eligible to adopt such children. *Non-Catholic!*

Rainer recalled Anna's rage. He had never before seen her so irate. He was afraid she would do herself so much harm, pacing floors and pounding furniture and walls, that she would end up unable to compete in the upcoming Olympics, due to begin in early February.

Not long after the Olympics Rainer found out for the first time about *Die Draufgänger,* the Daredevils. Anna's political group had adopted the name from the German women's alpine ski team, who had chosen that nickname for themselves during the Olympics. This was the secret organization that had dedicated itself to goals of replacing Hitler, wiping out the Lutheran and Russian Orthodox churches, and helping elect an even more compliant pope. Reluctantly, Anna had revealed her membership in the group to Rainer because, as she had explained, no single person alone could hope to achieve such seemingly impossible goals. And she did not want Rainer to think her *eine Verrückte,* a kook.

Although she would not reveal the names of many of the members of *Die Draufgänger,* she did go so far as to tell Rainer the co-leaders were Heinz Sachler, whom Rainer knew as the son of Ferdinand Sachler, head of the giant Stuttgart firm Sachler Optical, and Hans Meinermann, a bishop from a diocese just north of Leipzig. Heinz Sachler had been one of Anna's friends since childhood.

As a lapsed Catholic, Rainer was not eligible for membership, Anna had explained. But he could serve in an adjunct capacity because his skills as an art historian would prove useful. When Rainer failed to be impressed by such flattery, Anna modified her pitch and told Rainer *Die Draugänger* judged his aid necessary, rather than merely useful.

Rainer found this amusing, in so far as Anna, in explaining her opposition to, yet fondness for, Adolf Hitler, had told him that Hitler, though ultimately unsatisfactory, was a historical necessity.

"Now you sound like a Marxist!" Rainer had chided.

"A Hegelian, perhaps, but never a Marxist," she had rejoined.

Ever since that exchange Rainer had come to think of himself as *Die Draufgänger's* historical necessity.

Shortly after 6 p.m. Otto and Anna came through the front door. Stomping the snow from his boots, Otto grumbled, "A wind is blowing up the Rhine that would turn milk to ice before it could come out of the cow."

"Let's go, Rainer, before the weather worsens and we're stuck here, " Anna said clutching her arms to her chest and shivering.

"Won't you stay for a cup of hot chocolate, dear?" Hanni asked.

"Thank you, but no. We must be leaving."

Rainer fetched his coat and hat, pulled on his overshoes, and raised himself with his cane. As he walked toward the door, just before he passed Otto, he asked Anna, "Why didn't you tell me about Frau Forsch?" As he spoke to Anna, he watched Otto's face. Rainer was sure Otto's naturally ruddy, and now wind-burned, face turned a several shades paler.

Anna replied, "I didn't think her worth mentioning."

"Someone who might have betrayed us isn't worth mentioning?" Rainer said.

"She knew nothing."

"But suspected much."

"I also failed to tell you that my family dentist in Stuttgart was arrested by the Gestapo for imbedding a cynanide capsule in the filling of someone suspected of sabotaging his own factory assembly line. Danger is everywhere. I'm afraid that, beneath the starch of your SS uniform, lurks a spongy, even panicky, soul. So as not to sound alarmist myself, the better to keep you from melting like butter in an oven, I often spare you such ugly details as the murder of Frau Forsch."

"Let's go," Rainer said between clenched teeth. Turning to the Kalmbachs he gave a slight bow and said, in a cheery tone, "Thank you again for your hospitality."

By now Anna knew the way back across the border without a need for Otto to lead them. Outside, Anna said, "I'm sorry, Cousin. I didn't mean to show you any disrespect in front of them. I am tired. I apologize."

"Spongy soul that I am, I absorb your apology, Cousin."

They walked in silence the remainder of the way to the car. Then Anna reached in her pocket and pulled out a small packet. "Here. I bought this for you in Bern."

Rainer waited until they were both inside the car, away from the penetrating wind, and opened the small package. Pipe tobacco. He read the label: Balkan Sobranie.

Anna explained her choice. "Sorry, but no Dunhill London was available. The tobacconist assured me this is also very good and quite similar to the British cut."

"Thank you." He pulled back a corner and sniffed the packet, identifying Turkish *yenidje* as one component of the blend. "I'll save it, if you don't mind."

"Suit yourself, but I need one of these." Anna lit up a Lucky Strike.

"So what did our business partners in Geneva have to say?" Rainer asked.

"The prospect of Breugels and Van Ruisdales excites them, but I told them they must be patient. Someone may be watching them."

"Who?"

"A nurse at the Red Cross in Geneva is working for a new American organization called OSS. I don't know what the letters stand for, but they are apparently something like the German *Abwehr*. Intelligence-gathering, as well as engaging in grimy little escapades to try to be a nuisance to the Reich."

"Spies!" Rainer spat.

"More or less."

"So how did you find this out?"

"Remember Giesela Englebrecht?'

"No."

"She was a member of the Swiss ski team. We have kept in contact and remain friends."

"So how did she find out?"

"She works for somebody. She won't say for whom."

"Maybe she's a spy for the Swiss government and is engaging in a grimy little escapade to deceive you."

Anna shook her head. "What does the Swiss government have to gain by having her tell me lies?"

"Since when does anyone know what makes the Swiss do anything?"

"Whether her story is true or false, I used it to our advantage, telling the Sundstrums to keep watch on her and using Giesela as sufficient justification for our continued waiting, for not moving our stash across the *Ostsee* in haste."

"That's good."

"When Frau Sundstrum attempted to use the fact they may be watched as a lever to try to up their commission fee, I turned it back on them by saying that maybe it is time for me to seek out a safer alternative, such as my making an approach to one or more Swiss bankers in Zurich."

"And how did the good doctors take that?" Rainer asked, smiling.

"Herr Sundstrum, who is clearly the weaker of the pair, clutched his chest as if he might be having a little heart attack. Frau Sundstrum merely narrowed her eyes and said, 'I see'."

As Rainer turned right on the road that followed the Wutach River, he said, "I hope you were bluffing. We don't need any more people, Swiss, German, or any other nationality knowing our scheme."

Anna laughed derisively. "You know me better than that, Cousin. Inviting a Swiss banker to purchase a Breugel or a Van Ruisdale is like offering caviar to one of Frau Kalmbach's swine."

10

Tuesday
August 3, 1943
Prussian Hall of Deputies
Prinz Albrecht Strasse
Berlin

Rainer stood motionless, staring at Franz Marc's four blue horses stacked in front of a rainbow. A voice from behind him broke his reverie. "Is there something I can help you with, *Standartenführer?*" He turned to see a short, sparrow-faced man wearing a baggy brown suit staring up at him.

"I am Rudolf Petschke, unofficial caretaker of this building. Seldom does an SS officer come to linger in my hallways. So I was wondering if perhaps you are looking for something you can't find?"

"No, Herr Petschke, I have found what I am looking for."

A look of dread came over the man's face. "You... you don't intend to remove this painting do you?"

"Why might I do such a thing?"

"Because --. No. It's nothing. Nothing. Do what you must."

"Are you fond of the painting, Herr Petschke?"

The man stared down at his shoes for a moment. Then with a hang-dog face, he looked at Rainer. "In some ways I am. We all are, I mean. It's just that --."

"Just what?"

"It's so big and looks so perfect for the space. We would have difficulty finding another work of similar size to replace it."

"Do you know anything about the painter of this piece?" Rainer asked.

The man gave a tentative nod. "He was killed at Verdun and awarded the Iron Cross."

"Anything else?"

"No." Rudolf Petschke's eyes betrayed him.

"You must guard such a painting with great care, Herr Petschke, painted, as it was, by a German war hero."

"Yes, yes, *Standartenführer*. I agree completely."

"By the way, who is the official caretaker of the building?"

"The Berlin *Polizei*. Little real business is conducted here. We are no more than a historical afterthought these days." The man frowned. "I should not be saying *no more than*." He looked about furtively, as if checking for ghosts. "The great Bismarck once walked these halls, you know."

"I know, which is why I say again, guard these halls in the name of such heroes as Bismarck and Franz Marc."

Rainer laughed to himself when the wimpy little man started to brace and salute. He half expected the gnome to clack his heels and shout "*Zu Befehl!*" As ordered. Thankfully, he spared Rainer those theatrics.

"Are you a horseman, *Standartenführer*?"

"A rider? No." Only twice in his life had Rainer even been close enough to touch a horse. Once, after a train ride from Munich to Vienna with his father, Rainer had been permitted to visit the stables of the Lippazaners at the Spanish Riding School, to step inside a stall and caress a flank of one of the magnificent beasts. And there was the time when Karl's grandfather had allowed Anna and him to enter his pasture and feed sweets to his pair of Brabants, the Belgian draft horses he used to pull his plow through the rocky fields before planting potatoes between the Ostsee and the inland moors.

Rainer turned back to the painting, but, when he failed to hear the man's footsteps receding, he turned back to see Herr Petschke still standing there. "What now?"

"Did you hear the good news?"

"What news is that?"

"American B-24 bombers tried to destroy the oil fields at Ploesti but were blown out of the sky by our anti-aircraft guns. The news is all over Berlin and people are rejoicing."

Yes, Rainer had heard that news. What he had not heard was how much damage the Americans had inflicted, despite their heavy losses. Considerable, he supposed. Otherwise, Herr Goebbels would also be broadcasting that news across the city loudly enough for even the dead to hear. Nor had Berlin's official news agency, *Das Neue Berlin*, made many remarks about Allied successes in overrunning Sicily; whether the Russians had yet retaken Kharkov. And, regarding Mussolini's dismissal, Berlin's attitude amounted to: Benito who?

Rainer hoped he would not be asked, let alone ordered, to return to Kiev. That city was hell enough even when the Army controlled it – to the extent that it ever did control it. Disorder then, disorder now. And soon? Panic. He assured himself he did not want to be in the middle of chaos.

No. He decided his best immediate course of action would be to revisit Rostock, Lübeck, and Kiel. Although stalemate continued at Leningrad, while Army Group Center and Army Group South mixed retreat with failed counterattacks, he presumed the Red Army had plans to try to dislodge the German divisions on their right flank as well.

Best re-examine our Baltic ports and quietly make tentative preparations to move the stockpiles of art works, including the Amber Room, out of Königsberg. Quietly because words such a *retreat, withdrawl, retrench*, even the phrase *create a new defensive line*, were anathema to the *Führer*. Sufficiently so that a man could get himself executed if Hitler even so much as supposed that man entertained such a notion, let alone spoke it.

Naturally, if one were traveling from Lübeck to Kiel, one might take a brief, short diversion a kilometer or so off the coastal road to inspect an old, abandoned farm house while one was checking to see that the vital lighthouse at Todendorf was in good working order.

Saturday
August 6, 1943
Stuyvesant, New York

"Very peaceful out here, isn't it?"

Martin was looking across the Hudson River from the rear terrace of Elliott Parker's home. His wife's home actually. The sun sat atop the rich green forests of the Catskills, beyond the river's west bank. The voice behind him belonged to Elliott's wife, Katherine. Martin turned and nodded. "Everything about your home is beautiful and peaceful. And dinner, by the way, was superb."

His hostess gestured to him with her small glass of port. "Thank you for the compliments. I'll pass along your dinner praise to my cook, Mrs. Kramer. Father stole her from one of the Roosevelts. One of his few victories over them. Did Elliott explain to you that my grandfather built this house for my father and my father's new bride?"

"No. He's told me none of its history."

"Grandpa worried about my father's health. Perhaps you've heard of my father. Bradley Winthrop Vanderhagen?"

Martin shook his head. "Sorry."

Katherine Parker, with her wavy, shoulder-length brown hair, hazel eyes, thin face to go with her slender form – curvaceous in a long, hip-hugging white dress with small, navy blue polka dots -- looked as if she could have modeled for the cover of any one of several glamour magazines Martin had gawked at in D.C.'s Union Station while waiting to board the train to New York City. "Brad ran one of the biggest banks in upstate New York. He was known as the Duke of Albany and most people refer to this place as Vanderhagen Castle." She paused. "Or The Mausoleum, depending on whether you liked my father or not. His arch enemy was Franklin Delano Roosevelt. My father always referred to FDR as 'That Man'."

Martin smiled. "On the ride up we passed Hyde Park. It can't be more than… what? Fifty, sixty miles downriver?"

"Forty-nine point four," she said with a grin. "Anyway, the purpose of this sprawling acreage was to give my father a place to unwind each weekend, after five hard days of railing against *That*

Man and all he stands for. It didn't work. Poor Old Bradley died of a heart attack shortly before his fiftieth birthday. I'm sure the Roosevelts drank champagne the night they heard that news."

She paused, remembering, and Martin waited quietly.

Finally, her gaze refocused. "Anyway, I inherited everything. Mother died when I was young."

"You're still young," Martin said, meaning it.

"Thank you. Shall I say *younger* then? In any case, here we are. Or rather, here I am much of the time, while Ellliott is off doing his --."

"Patriotic duty?"

"Yes. For lack of anything better to call it. But here I am, doing my duty."

"It's a lovely place to be stationed."

"I like it. Not for its looks especially, but for its location."

"The place is definitely a castle. Built to withstand a siege," Martin said.

"And many a siege it's been under," she said, laughing. "It's built of foot-thick limestone. Beford limestone I believe it's called. From quarries in Beford, Indiana if I remember hearing Daddy correctly as he explained it to guests time and again. The limestone comes from the same place as the stone used to build many of the famous places in Washington, I'm told."

"I like it better here. Or at least I like its location better," Martin said.

"The limestone's wonderful. Luckily we have lots of windows to open in the summer and a fireplace in almost every room to get us through the nasty winters."

A boy burst through the French doors and rushed to wrap his arms around his mother's waist. "Guess what, Mom?"

While hugging the child, Katherine Parker said to Martin, "Excuse my son's discourtesy, Mister Wynerson." To her son, "Now, Selby. Before I play 'Guess what, Mom?' with you, let me introduce you to one of your father's most promising colleagues. This is Mister Martin Wynerson. Martin, this my eight-year-old son, Selby."

Selby held out his hand. "I'm sorry, sir. I didn't mean to be rude."

Martin shook the young man's hand. "You weren't rude. You were merely exhibiting the uncontained enthusiasm of a child with exciting news to share with his mother."

Selby bowed his head and muttered sheepishly, "Naw. I was rude. I'm sorry."

Martin acknowledge the apology with a nod. "Is it all right if I listen? Or would you prefer to have her guess in private?"

The child's eyes brightened. "You can play, too, if you want."

Katherine Parker said, "Now, let me see. You and Spencer --." She turned to Martin. "Spencer is Selby's best friend. Same age. Lives just down the road." Back to Selby. "Jack took both of you to Saratoga National Park for the day. So that must mean you both saw the ghosts of British redcoats marching in formation."

"Oh, Mom. Spencer and I aren't that dumb."

"Not dumb. Imaginitive," she said.

"Guess again. Something real."

"Perhaps Mister Wynerson should take a turn at guessing." Selby looked at Martin. "Go ahead."

Martin stroked his chin before saying, "You went fishing in the river and caught the biggest catfish ever caught in these parts."

"Wow! You're close. Well, sort of."

Mrs. Parker's voice took on a reproaching tone. "You didn't drag any tadpoles or frogs back into this house, did you, young man?"

"Aw, Mom. Only a couple. And they're special. Spencer's dad said so."

"What makes them so special?" she said.

"Because Spencer and I caught 'em!"

"Selby, you know how much I loath slimy little critters. Why don't you take your frogs back to the river, where I'm sure they'll be ever so much happier."

"Aw, Mom."

A stern look from Mother.

"Okay. But first can I ask Mister Wynerson a question?"

"*May* I ask," Mrs. Parker corrected.

A nod. "May I?"

"That's up to Mister Wynerson."

Martin said, "Ask away."

"Are you Canadian? 'Cause you talk like one. We sometimes get Canadian visitors around here."

"No, Selby, but you're close. I'm from Minnesota." Martin had worked hard in recent years to minimize his accent, not wanting to sound like yet another Skanderhoovian -- dumb Oles, as they were known in some parts of the Midwest – and not wanting to listen to Lars-and-Lena jokes he'd already heard a thousand times.

Selby pointed to Martin's cane. "Why do you walk with a cane? You're not *that* old."

"Selby James Parker."

The boy knew he had committed some social blunder as soon as he heard his middle name. "I was just asking, Mom."

"It's quite all right, Mrs. Parker," Martin said soothingly. "I don't mind." To Selby, "Almost exactly a year ago I was injured in an airplane accident. I haven't quite fully recovered yet."

Katherine Parker added, "Mister Wynerson was the pilot of a plane that crashed. His injuries were very, very serious."

Selby's face lit up. "Did a Kraut or Jap shoot you down?"

"Selby James!"

"Well?" The boy stared earnestly at Martin.

"I'm afraid it wasn't that dramatic, Selby. I got caught in a nasty thunderstorm and tried to make a forced landing on a highway. But the highway was being repaired and, when I swerved the plane to avoid some deep chuckholes, I ended up smashing into a telephone pole."

"Wow! You're lucky you weren't killed," the boy said.

"Indeed I was lucky. Very lucky." Martin saw no pointing in noting that his instructor was not so lucky as he noticed the boy's mother holding her breath, expecting Martin to add that ugly footnote.

"Will you ever fly again?" Selby asked.

"No. I'm told my flying days are over."

"Aw, gee. That's too bad. We need lots of good pilots to bomb the beejeezus out of the Japs and the Krauts."

"Selby Parker, you are excused from civilized company until you gain better control of your mouth."

"What'd I say, Mom? I've heard Dad say *beejeezus* plenty of times."

"We'll talk about it later. Run along and tell your father about your frog-catching endeavors. I'm sure he will be more thrilled than I am."

Martin empathized with Selby. Even though he could not recall his own eighth year, he assumed it must have been similar. Trying to live up to parents' expectations is not easy. "He strikes me as a very fine young boy, Mrs. Parker."

"Oh, he is. He's a splendid child. The trick is to keep him that way."

Katherine Parker excused herself to mingle with other guests. Martin decided to remain on the terrace and watch the sun's last rays lose their color. The day before he and David Fox had taken trains from Washington to New York City, then from there to the town of Hudson, where Elliott had picked them up for the fifteen-minute ride to their overnight quarters in the village of Kinderhook, not far from Stuyvesant. In all, Elliott had invited a dozen art historians to his home for the weekend and had arranged guest quarters for all of them at nearby inns.

The Van Schaack House, where Martin and David were staying, was an elegant inn whose guests had included John Jay, Aaron Burr, Washington Irving, and the eighth president of the United States, Martin Van Buren, whom Martin learned from the innkeeper had been born in Kinderhook and whose father ran a local tavern that was part of the Van Buren home.

The purpose of Elliott's invitation was to say farewell to his fellow art historians; to announce to his guests, in his parlor just prior to dinner, that he was bound for Switzerland, the length of his stay there undetermined.

"Until we've won this damned war and set things right afterwards," he said.

Martin had glanced quickly at Katherine Parker, who had stood stoically at the side of the room, her arms folded. He thought he saw a brief quivering at the corners of her mouth as Elliott's words emerged. Her eyes had remained fixed on her husband, unblinking. When Carter Powell, from Columbia University, had asked how Elliott planned to get into Switzerland, given that the country's borders were closed, Elliott gave Carter a wink and claimed, "I've been assured by General Donovan that will not be a problem." At that remark Katherine Parker abruptly left the room.

General Donovan, Martin had heard in Washington, was the head of a new intelligence-collecting organization called the Office of Strategic Services. OSS for short. Martin knew nothing about the group, but had heard unconfirmed rumors that MFA&A teams would be working closely with OSS.

David Fox joined Martin on the terrace and took out a pack of Camels. Twilight had turned to darkness and the flame from Fox's match, then the glow of burning tobacco, was all the light they had. From afar Martin could hear the croaks from frogs young Selby and his friend had failed to snare. Or perhaps the two boys had done as Katherine had implored Selby to do, release the slippery little creatures and what Martin was listening to was the froggy equivalent of the *Hallelujah Chorus.*

"Hard to stand here in this regal setting and imagine war is being waged on the other sides of the world," Fox said. "We should be thankful, Martin, that we have two big oceans to protect us."

Martin imagined himself standing in a backyard in Minneapolis watching wave upon wave of Heinkels and Junkers, lit up by search lights and bursts of anti-aircraft shells, before saying, "Yes, we should."

David Fox was shorter than Martin, with broad shoulders and thick forearms. His round face should have a corncob pipe sticking out of it, Martin had thought the first time he met his roommate. He looks like he stepped out of a Popeye cartoon. In fact, David Fox was, like Popeye, a "sailor man", though, unlike the comic book character, Fox was an officer, an ensign. An ultra-fastidious ensign, who always looked like a model on a Navy recruiting poster, all sharp and spit-polished in his Navy dress whites. Why David was not serving in a combat position puzzled him from the first day he met Fox. Rumors floated about that many Catholic graduates from Yale were being issued special dispensations, being invited to serve in various intelligence branches rather than face the prospect of serving in combat positions. He had yet to find anyone who could verify that rumor and he was too inhibited to ask David to confirm or deny such a bold claim.

"I'd give anything to be going with Elliott. Wouldn't you?" Fox said, after blowing smoke out over the terrace railing.

"Maybe not anything, but I'd give a lot," Martin replied, wondering if he'd give up the company of a woman such as Katherine Parker. If married to her, I'd opt to stay behind, thank you, Martin thought before flushing the wayward notion from his mind. But others replaced it quickly. He found himself comparing Katherine with Brigit Olson and decided Brigit came in second. A distant second. And Katherine's my age, too, he reminded himself. "Stop it, Martin!" he scolded himself silently. Or was that his mother's voice rattling in his head? Yes. Then his mother's reprimand was replaced by Katherine's whispering in his ear as they lay beside each other on a four-poster bed. "Don't stop now, Martin," she was saying. Sweet Jesus, Wynerson! Get hold of yourself. Katherine's voice faded and now he was hearing Martin Luther's words, spoken by Pastor Aalgaard in catechism class. *Esto peccator et pecca fortiter.* Be a sinner and sin vigorously. But what is the rest? Martin thought hard before the second part came back to him. *But even more vigorously believe and delight in Christ who is victor over sin, death, and the world.*

I, too, am a victor over death, Martin reminded himself by tapping his weaker leg with his cane. Over sin? Well... so far.

Monday
August 8, 1943
Todendorf
Schleswig-Holstein

"We should walk down to the beach to eat." Karl Vollmer pointed toward the water.

"What's wrong with sitting out here in the *Biergarten?*" Rainer asking, holding blood sausages in one hand, a bottle of Riesling in the other.

"We are bad for business," Karl explained. "Our SS uniforms make everyone suppose we are here to eavesdrop on them."

Conversation in Zum Alten Fritz's *Biergarten* had indeed ceased, even though every table but one was occupied by two to four locals, there to enjoy lunch on the cloudless summer day. Although no one was staring at Karl and him, Rainer finally sensed that every patron was acutely aware of the SS men's presence.

"To the beach then," Rainer said at last, speaking a bit louder than necessary for Karl to hear him. "Is one beer for you enough?" Rainer had decided not to try the beer from the nearby Kiel *Brauerei*, despite Karl's recommendation. The Riesling he chose instead came from a small winery whose vintage he had sampled before on a trip with his father to the Mosel Valley.

Knowing their uniforms looked out of place on the beach's white sand, Rainer ignored the families and hikers strolling past them. No question they were conspicuous. When people saw them they were given a very wide berth, except for the child whose ball escaped him and rolled in their direction. When Karl stood and fetched the ball for the child the young boy froze in his tracks, staring intently at Karl's empty, pinned up right sleeve.

A man, presumably the boy's father, came running up and took the child by an arm and moved the boy behind him. "I am terribly sorry. We did not mean to bother you."

Karl kneeled and held out the ball. "It's quite all right. Children and balls usually manage to become separated from each other often. Is he your son?"

The man hesitated, then nodded.

"What is his name?"

Dread cross the man's face. "Please. We've done nothing wrong."

Rainer stood and brushed sand from his trousers. The man stiffened. "My *Hauptscharführer* and I are fond of children. You son is a handsome lad. We mean no harm. Please continue your game. If you like we will move further down the beach so you can have our place here."

Karl tossed the ball back toward the boy. The father picked it up while continuing to shield his son. "Thank you, but we must be going." Keeping himself between the boy and the SS men, the father herded his son back toward the rest of his family, a woman and two young girls, all of whom who had watched with growing trepidation, Rainer noticed.

"We are more bother here than we are worth, Karl. Come. Let's drive to the farm."

"They take us for Gestapo," Karl, said and finished his beer. He dropped the bottle on the beach.

"Nothing we could say would convince them we are harmless," Rainer said, retrieving the bottle and placing in the sack with his half-finished bottle of wine. "Don't you think it odd that our own people fear us more than we are feared by the people of Kiev, for example." He knew they both remembered the day of, and the days following, the epic soccer match.

"Better to be feared than loved, don't you think?" Karl said.

"I wouldn't know," Rainer said as he started back toward Todendorf.

Rainer took extra caution driving on the road leading to the farmhouse driveway. Until all conversation at the tavern ceased, the main topic of discussion had been a local farmer who had been blown to bits, along with his horses, when his plow blade apparently hit an unexploded bomb while he was turning over the rocky sod of his potato field.

No one had any doubts that many more such bombs lay strewn, and often buried, all across Schleswig-Holstein. Lately Königsberg had been receiving a great deal of attention from Allied bombers. And, because the neck of the Jutland Peninsula was the path of least German land mass to cross, most Allied bombers, no matter what their target in northern Germany, elected to return to England by flying just off the southern Baltic coast. To lighten their return loads Allied bombers often jettisoned their bombs when a mission was cancelled; dumped them when they could not find their target; dropped them too late for Kiel when their bombardiers found themselves harassed or frightened by flak or Messerschmidts, too soon for Lübeck. The farmer mourned by those gathered at Zum Alten Fritz was not the first local to die by tripping off an unexploded bomb. Nor, Rainer knew, would he be the last. He did, however, wish very much that neither he nor Karl become lamented by Zum Alten Fritz's patrons.

The farm house stood in a state of disrepair, its timber facings in need of paint, the roof beginning to sag, a window pane cracked. Weeds grew everywhere. But Karl insisted that the building remained structurally sound, erected on a solid foundation with a dry cellar. Following a careful inspection of the exterior and surrounding grounds, neither Karl nor Rainer detected any signs of intruders.

The outside doors leading to the cellar creaked from years of rust. Karl noted he thought it best not to oil the hinges, lest some nosy person suppose a reason existed why unused doors failed to stick and squeak. The concrete walls of the cellar showed stress cracks, but Karl assured Rainer they were nothing serious. Black pitch, the kind Karl's brother used to stop small leaks in the hull of his fishing boat, Karl explained, highlighted the ubiquitous cracks.

"Here is the best part," Karl said proudly as he peeled back two wooden facing panels to reveal a locked wooden door. It's bottom began fifty centimeters above the cellar floor.

"A vault?" Rainer said.

Karl nodded. "I suppose one could call it that. Yes. Inside it's big as a bank vault. *Luftdicht,* as well. Air-tight." Karl loosened a panel to the right of one of those he had separated from the wall.

After swinging the heavy door open he reached inside the vault, withdrew a kerosene lantern, struck a match against the concrete wall, and lit the lamp. "Come. If we're lucky we won't find too many cobwebs."

Once Karl had climbed inside the vault Rainer followed. The room was three times bigger than he had imagined. Karl had not exaggerated.

"Sorry. Not room enough to stand up, especially for someone as tall as you," Karl said.

Taking the lantern from Karl, Rainer shone it around and estimated the room to be seven meters long by five meters wide by slightly less than two meters high. "What is it's real purpose?"

Karl pointed to a pair of large crocks, each capped with a wooden lid. Then he walked over, pull one of the lids up with great effort, and stuck his head down into the crock for an instant. "Only a faint lingering odor." He recapped the crock. "These each hold twenty liters of liquid, but their purpose is to hold sauerkraut while it is fermenting. The seal on the lid is quite good. And the reason the room is as near to airtight as my grandfather could make it is because even the most devoted sauerkraut lover does not wish his entire house to smell always of fermenting cabbage."

"My God! How much sauerkraut did he make at one time?"

"The room is so big because my grandfather also used it to store wine and my grandmother used it to store other pickled vegetables. A partition used to run down the middle to contain the smell of the sauerkraut. Sauerkraut-flavored wines are not very tasty. And occasionally Grandfather made his own beer." Karl made a face. "It wasn't very good. Horrible in fact."

Rainer nodded. "This whole room is as solid as an air raid bunker. Anna will definitely approve of this."

Karl gave him a quizzical look. "She already has."

Rainer looked dumbfounded.

"Yes. She was here for a day during the time you were last in Königsberg. June. Or was it late May? In any case, she checked everything out for herself. And, yes, she did approve. I'm surprised she didn't tell you."

Rainer, too, was surprised. And dismayed -- again. Anna had kept another piece of news from him. He remembered writing to her, telling her the dates he would be in Königsberg to carry out his plan to evaluate the feasibility of moving artifacts by sea from the Königsberg collecting point back *closer to the German people*, as he had put it to anyone who asked, not *farther from the danger of advancing Russian lines*, which is what he meant. And Karl was correct. He had traveled to Königsberg during the first week of June. I must ask her why she failed to tell me. And... and not allow her to wave me off dismissively with "For the same reason I didn't tell you about --."

With that Rainer put his exasperation out of mind. Together he and Karl checked and rechecked the waterproof sheathing each painting stored in the vault was encased in. Rainer declined Karl's offer to unwrap each item.

"I trust you," he said. As an afterthought he appended, "And Anna."

"At least please examine my ledgers. They are completely in order," Karl said, handing over his inventory log of the vault's contents.

"I'm sure your papers are in order. I have no doubt you would make even Frau Limberger proud."

Karl winced. "That dreadful woman. No. I'm sure she would manage to find some fault with my accounting. She reminds me of the nuns who taught me in my *Grundschule*. Lucky for me I now have only one set of knuckles to rap with a ruler," he said as he set the lamp down for a moment and wiggled his fingers.

After leaving the room and its camouflage just as they had found it, they exited the cellar and stood facing what had once been a field of alfalfa but now yielded only a crop of thorny weeds mingled among wild grasses. A westerly from off the North Sea suddenly freshened, blowing Karl's peak cap off his head. Rainer pinned the cap with the tip of his cane before the cap could blow away.

Rainer again stared out at the fields, now overgrown with gorse, and tried to imagine happy peasants, as perhaps painted by Pieter Breugel, swinging hand scythes and singing to themselves. Instead, all he pictured were dour, stooped *Ostarbeiter* guarded by grim-faced SS men bearing whips and truncheons and he quickly looked away, forcing himself to focus elsewhere.

A pair of starlings sat and sang on a fence post. That was a good sign. But on the roof a stork's nest sat empty, perhaps abandoned. And Rainer remembered seeing no signs of mice or bats in the cellar, unlike what his mother always found at Uncle Rolf's cottage, which was not all that far away.

"I am puzzled why no one comes here and tries to steal things." Rainer pointed to a perfectly respectable pair of wooden chairs on the front porch.

Karl chuckled. "I'm sure the *Grauergeist* chases away anyone who dares to come here. His spirit is very powerful and nasty."

Rainer laughed softly. "Ah, yes. *Der Grauergeist.*"

"You laugh, but many people from these parts take him seriously," Karl said.

"Him? Why not a her or an it?"

"Whatever the spirit may be, the terror *Grauergeist* provokes is real."

"*Mein Sohn, es ist ein Nebelstreif*," Rainer quoted from Goethe's *Erlkönig*.

"No simple streak of fog would induce the horror locals feel when they talk of *Der Grauergeist*," Karl said, looking all about him furtively.

"Perhaps your grandfather himself is the gray ghost," Rainer suggested.

Karl scowled. "Come. Let's leave. Even I am feeling spooked and I have spent my entire life coming to this place."

Rainer was not about to argue with a haunted man. They had finished their examination of the site and judged it safe, except for perhaps a direct hit by an Allied bomb. Rainer imagined that in all likelihood even a very big bomb might not carry enough explosive to penetrate the meter-thick walls of Karl's grandfather's sauerkraut vault.

Monday
August 8, 1943
National Gallery
Washington, D. C.

"What are you up to, Wynerson?" David Fox, munching an apple, peered over Martin's shoulder as he sat on the grass beneath a shade tree in the rear of the National Gallery.

"I'm composing a note to Mrs. Parker, thanking her for the marvelous weekend."

"A thank-you note? Written just to Mrs. Parker? Not Elliott, too?"

"You know perfectly well that Elliott is leaving this afternoon to begin his journey to Switzerland," Martin said, covering his half-finished letter so that David could not read it.

"Are you sure it's only a thank-you note? Looks to me like you're already on your second page. I'm mean, how many lines does it take to say 'Thank you'?"

"I enjoy writing letters."

"Especially to lovely ladies, eh?"

"It doesn't hurt."

"So what do you really think of Mrs. Katherine Parker, Martin?"

"She struck me as a splendid woman."

Fox mimiced Martin. "'She struck me as a splendid woman.' A splendid woman whose husband just happens to be leaving her for only God knows how long."

"So?"

Fox sat down beside Martin, still trying to catch a glimpse of what he had written. "Come on, Martin. Say it."

"Say what?"

"Say that you've got the hots for Mrs. Katherine Parker of Stuyvesant, New York."

"I do not."

"Liar."

"Tell me what you think of her, David?"

"That's it. Get me to confess first. Well, okay. I think she's one damned fine-looking woman and I wouldn't mind... well, use your imagination."

Martin winced and rolled his eyes. "I think you should amend your remark to say 'one damned fine-looking married woman'."

"Whose husband just happens to be leaving her for blah, blah, blah."

"During which time I'm sure she'll be dutifully faithful to him," Martin said.

This time Fox mimicked Martin by rolling his eyes and wincing. "You're something else, Wynerson. Tell me this. Have you imagined yourself lusting after her?"

Martin did not like the direction the conversation was taking, yet he felt trapped. "Who wouldn't?"

"Well, then? What's to slow you down, let alone stop you?"

"Excuse me, but there's a world of difference between thinking about... well, you know. Between thinking and doing."

"No, no, no. If it's a mortal sin even to think it, what's the point in settling for nothing but the fantasy?"

"That's a bunch of Jesuitical bullshit, David."

Fox flinched. "You're not Catholic."

"No, I'm Norwegian Lutheran."

"Should have figured you for a heretic with a first name of Martin. But, may I remind you, in the True Religion the intent to do evil is as much a sin as committing the act."

"Well then, Foxy, if I ever decide I want to drown you in the Potomac for being a smartass, I'll just go right ahead and do it."

Fox grinned. "Might as well. Might as well be damned for a murderer as damned for a dreamer."

Martin returned to writing his letter and David Fox lay down on his back, hands under his head, and closed his eyes.

After rereading what he already written, Martin decided his tone was quite appropriate, his sentiments neither coy nor sappy. He had never deemed himself a flirtatious sort of fellow, though he was certain a bit of boldness with women had its proper time and place. This letter was not such a place.

"Plan to visit her?"

Martin looked at Fox, whose eyes remained closed, but his grin spread from ear to ear. "I hadn't thought of it."

"Think of it. I can tell you made quite an impression on her. Mister Martin Pure-As-Freshly-Fallen-Snow Wynerson. She was smitten by your innocence and baby-faced charm. Christ! I bet you're still a virgin, eh, Martin?"

The answer to that, Martin told himself, was none of David Fox's business. Nor anyone else's. He thought back on the summer following his senior year at St. Olaf's, the backcountry canoe trips, the nights alone in the tent with curious and eager Maddy in out-of-the-way campgrounds, then quickly purged his mind of those sweet memories.

"Your silence speaks volumes, Martin," Fox said, barely above a whisper.

"Think what you will of me, David. I've no intention of commenting on my sex life. Or lack of same."

"I bet Mrs. Parker could teach you a thing or three about how the birds and the bees make little birds and little bees."

"I'm not interested in making little birds or little bees, Mister Fox."

"Sweet music, then."

"Nor that."

"The man that hath no --."

"May we change the subject, please? Just lie there with your eyes closed and pretend Mrs. Parker is teaching anything you still need to be taught and allow me to finish my letter to her."

"Want me to finish it for you?"

"I can just imagine."

"No. That's your problem, Wynerson. Too little imagination. You simply can't picture yourself up there in Stuyvesant in that sprawling house, alone with the woman of your dreams."

"Don't forget the kid."

"You think she couldn't pack his bag and send him over the river and through the woods to grandma's house just like that?" Fox snapped his fingers.

"I don't know. I don't care to find out."

"Well, shit. If that's your attitude, put in a good word to her for your good buddy, David Fox. Tell what a magnificent rogue I would be; what a satisfying bedroom playmate I promise to be."

"Best you write your own letter, if those are the sentiments you wish to pass along to her," Martin said.

"I'm afraid I'm a better stud than I am a scribe."

"Too bad. But I refuse to pimp for you."

"You're no fun, Martin. No damned fun at all. Just a stick in the Potomac mud."

"And so I shall remain."

David Fox stood and held out his apple core. "I was only teasing you, Martin. See? The apple of discord is eaten." And with that he gave his apple a toss and together they watched it splatter against the rear wall of the National Gallery.

11

Friday
December 24, 1943
Munich

The Hauptbahnhof smelled of human sweat and urine. Even thick tobacco smoke, floating like a Baltic fog through the station, failed to mask the odors of human excretions. Where are all these people going? It's Christmas Eve. Why are they not home with family, an annoyed Rainer wondered. Then he supposed: Delayed, like me. Trains no longer run on time, thanks to Allied bombers.

The increasing frequency and intensity of Allied bombing was the reason Rainer had come to Bavaria. Now considered fully rehabilitated from his injuries, he no longer had to endure paper-pushing and political-infighting at SS headquarters, such tedium relieved only by too infrequent local trips to assess how far the various art-collecting points' efforts to log their inventories trailed the accelerating accumulation of works being trucked in. In every case any likelihood of catching up seemed hopeless.

And now a subtle shift had begun. Without conceding that Allied bombing had become worrisome to the point of near-panic, Himmler, Göring, Goebbels, and perhaps even the *Führer* himself – along with his toady, Bormann – were asking, through quiet back channels, for search-and-assess investigations to find more secure storage sites for the growing stockpiles of art. And, because most of the finest works were destined for the yet-to-be-built *Führer* museum in Austria, the most immediate and intense searches had been ordered to be carried out in Bavaria and Austria. The most likely candidates to examine, Rainer had been told, were mines, along with monasteries and castles capable of withstanding the force of the bomb the Allies called a 'blockbuster". Already the collection filling Mad Ludwig's monstrosity at Neuschwanstein was being prepared for evacuation.

The bus to Schwabing was standing room only and, had Rainer not been exhausted already, as well as running later than he had promised Anna, he might have walked, dragging his suitcase on the ground behind him. Instead, he endured the elbowing and a closeness to other passengers that made the train depot smell like a rose garden by comparison. Foreboding not only hung in the air but clung to people's faces. *Gemütlichkeit* had given way to *Mürrischkeit*, sullenness. The same with travelers in Berlin, as well as those in Leipzig who had waited in the station for trains some thought might never come. The collective *Weltanschauung* had began with El Alamein, then hardened like concrete after *Feldmarschall* Paulus's surrender at Stalingrad. Not even the Pollyannas at SS headquarters had proven immune, although only men's looks betrayed their thoughts. No one ever spoke of any shift in attitude, either in himself or in others, lest he be accused of defeatism and frog-marched to a secluded courtyard and stood before a firing squad.

Rainer smelled cabbage cooking as he entered his father's house. He found Anna standing at the stove, attentive to preparing a meal.

"Aren't you going to greet me?" Rainer said wearily.

Startled, Anna dropped her wooden spoon. "My God! You look like shit."

"Thank you, Cousin. I actually feel much worse than that."

"Where's your cane?"

"I don't need it any longer, although it would have been handy to use on several people who annoyed me at the Leipzig train station."

"That's wonderful news!" Anna said and softly applauded.

"What time is it?" Rainer asked. "Someone stole my watch in Leipzig."

"Half past six. I was about to give up on you," Anna said.

"That makes two of us. As I said when I phoned you from Nuremberg, I left Berlin yesterday morning. The trains are a mess. Friday's bombing attack on Berlin did considerable damage, including destroying part of the Tiergarten. Not as much as the huge mid-November raid, but still --. Then I had to wait in Leipzig for hours. Same thing in Nuremberg. The train was suppose to pull out shortly after my call to you. It was another hour after that."

Anna nodded sympathetically.

"I brought you a Christmas present." Rainer handed her a small box.

"Too small to be crystal, unless it's perfume like you gave Lili last year."

"How do you know what I gave Lili, if anything?"

"One of my magic powers."

"No. It's not perfume."

"Then what?"

"Open it and see for yourself."

Anna worked the box open. Inside was a smaller box, this one made of velvet. When she opened it she gasped. "You didn't?", she snapped, glaring at Rainer.

"Of course not. I wouldn't steal from *that*. What do you take me for? An unprincipled robber?"

"Never!" Anna carefully lifted the amber broach and matching earrings from the velvet box. "Where then?"

"I actually paid for them. With my very own money. A while back on one of my many trips to Königsberg."

"Very lovely. Thank you."

"You're welcome. You may try them on later. What are you cooking?" Rainer said.

"I bought a piece of veal on the black market. All I have to go with it is cabbage and turnips. But I found a prize Gewürztraminer in the cellar."

"I'm hungry, but I could also sleep for a week. You'd think a train would be a decent place to get some sleep, but no. Too many people. Too many children."

"Sit down and tell me all about it. Kick your boots off. I'll pour you some Spanish sherry I traded for." Anna poured her cousin a small glass of pale sherry, then poured another for herself. "*Heilige Abend*, Rainer!" she said sarcastically. Holy evening.

Rainer raised his sherry glass in a half-hearted response, then drank it down in one gulp, actually relishing the burning sensation it left in his throat. "I sent Karl to the farmhouse again. The U-boat pens at Kiel took some nasty bombing a week ago Monday. I want to be convinced again that the sauerkraut vault has not been reduced to a pile of rubble."

"Are you disappointed the Russians have retaken Kiev?" Anna asked.

"They are welcome to it."

While Rainer went to wash up Anna dished up supper. When he returned she waved for him to come to the table. "Speaking of the sauerkraut vault, as you call it, I have some excellent news." She uncorked the wine and generously filled two glasses.

Rainer sat and helped himself to a slice of veal. "Well? Tell me your news."

"First, I have a new job."

"What kind of new job?" The last Rainer knew Anna had been working at the Haus der Deutscher Kunst helping set up exhibits.

"At the Führerbau." She sat back and let the news sink in.

"In what capacity?"

"I'm an assistant to the man in charge of inventory, Herr Schmidt, who also loans me to the man who oversees security, *Hauptsturmführer* Becker."

"A mere captain?"

"Not a very bright one at that. Before long I'm sure he'll find himself at the Russian front, though I'll do my best to keep him at his present post. I already have figured out a couple of ways to alter the inventory and move pieces to the old gallery."

Rainer nodded approvingly.

"The second and third pieces of news go together. Most of the paintings being brought to the Führerbau are destined for Hitler's glorious new art museum in Linz, if he ever gets to build it. So the works that are arriving are among the very best, of course. Do you recall the Schloss Collection?"

"This is all old news to me, Anna. Himmler wanted to involve me with the Schloss business from the very beginning, meaning he wanted me to be in charge of tracking down the Schloss children. I reminded him I was not a police detective, though I didn't dare add that I had no interest in hunting French Jews. The politics involved with the Schloss Collection has been worse than anything I encountered in Kiev. But now I understand the air has cleared and the collection is in Munich. But while it was going on I would have been a fool to have anything to do with it. I was running out of excuses when suddenly Himmler came to his senses momentarily and sent a couple of his toadies to accompany Rosenburg to Paris. Last I heard, Göring's man at ERR, Bruno Lohse, was dealing with the Munich end, but I still managed to keep my distance."

Anna nodded. "Two hundred thirty works from the Schloss arrived at the Führerbau from Jeu de Paume at the end of last month. Most of the collection."

"But not all," Rainer said.

"Not all were selected for shipment, but also some were pilfered along the way."

"Of course. A side story you may not be aware of, but will enjoy, is that Lohse offered a pair of Rembrandts from the Schloss to the *Reichsmarshall*. He turned them down."

"I can't believe that," Anna said.

"It's true. Rumor is that Walter Hofer, who oversees the collections at Karinhall intervened. As you know, Lohse and Hofer hate each other."

Anna sneered. "You mean nominally oversees. I thought you said Frau Limberger actually is in charge of the collection. Perhaps Fat Herman is simply afraid to try to insert his own greed into a collection prized by the *Führer*. The *Reichsmarshall* has moved steadily up the *Führer's Scheissliste* this past year."

"You mean Herr Maier?" Rainer said.

Anna smiled and nodded, recalling that several months earlier Göring had boasted publicly, "If so much as a single Allied bomber reaches the Ruhr, you may call me Maier." These days, Rainer thought in disgust, Allied bombers devastated the industrial heart of Germany routinely, with all too little interdiction by the Luftwaffe.

"Guess who has been put in charge of the inventory of the Schloss paintings?" she said.

"No. You can't be that lucky."

"Luck has nothing to do with it. I may be new, but I am already the best and everyone knows it."

"But not everyone likes it, I'm sure."

"I don't care. Imagine, Rainer! A room full of Schloss pieces in our possession!"

"Anna! Give yourself some time before you do anything spectacular. I would not care for either or both of us to end up with our heads beneath a guillotine blade. Besides, now I must figure out a way to transport any appropriated goods by some means other than railway. Every major junction between Munich and Hamburg is a pile of twisted metal."

"I've already figured out how to move all the pieces that fail to appear on the Führerbau inventory."

"By magic, no doubt."

Anna ate a bite of veal and shook her head. "So many trucks arrive at the Führerbau that, at any given time, two or three break down and need to go in for repairs. Sometimes such repairs take weeks. Parts are scarce and trucks at the battlefronts have priority. A truck could vanish from there for a month and nobody would notice. No one from Herr Becker on down keeps very close track of the truck count – except me."

They ate in silence for several minutes, until Anna said, "You seem preoccupied. What is troubling you?"

Rainer paused, then asked, "Do you think Otto Kalmbach killed Frau Forsch? The matter has troubled me for some time."

"I assure you he did not."

"How can you be sure?"

Anna set her fork down. "Because I killed Frau Forsch."

Rainer pushed his plate away. "I was hoping you would tell me Otto did it." He shrugged. "But I don't know why I asked. I'm not sure I would have believed you if you had told me he did do it. The blood from the runaway goat. You made that up?"

"No. That happened."

"Do you have regrets?"

"About the goat?"

"You know what I mean."

"None at all."

"Did Otto refuse?"

"I didn't even ask him. I knew what had to be done. And once I decided it was necessary, I would not delegate such a task. I did ask him to take her body elsewhere. Let her be found some distance from the village. And I asked him to misdirect the police. But ask him to kill her? No. That was my job and I did it."

"I see."

"Dear Cousin, I truly hope so." She walked around the table and kissed him on his forehead, then put her arms around him. "You're wondering why you had to ask to find out the truth."

"Yes."

"Because I know how much you hate to know the grimy details of our business. I thought I was sparing you. But here, all this time you have been agonizing. I'm so terribly sorry."

"You're right. I thought I didn't want to know. But it has eaten at me for a long time."

"Are you displeased with me, my sweet cousin?"

"No. I guess that I am --."

Anna kneeled beside him. "Go on."

"I am embarrassed for myself for being so squeamish. You know, when Frau Forsch left the house that night I was tempted to run after her myself and choke her to death."

"You see, Rainer? We think alike, you and I. Only --."

"Only you do not dance from one foot to the other, play Prince Hamlet," Rainer said, stroking her face gently.

"I do what must be done."

"And speaking of our business, how are our friends in Geneva holding up?" Rainer asked.

"Impatient, but understanding. I take them a few baubles now and then to prevent them from forgetting us. By the way,

I picked up another pouch of Sobranie for you in Bern." Anna seemed relieved the subject had changed.

"I thank you."

"I have something else for which you will thank me even more." Anna threw her arms around Rainer's neck. "I have a very special present for you this Christmas Eve. I've been saving it. You may have it after we clean up from our dinner."

"A present?"

"After you enjoy a warm bath and shave."

"Will you give me a hint?"

"Better still. I'll tell you. You may have me. Surely you are not too exhausted to make love to Anna."

Rainer broke her grasp and stood. "I thought you were still entertaining that young assistant curator at Haus der Kunst. Isn't he your latest?"

Anna made a face. "One week. Only one week, but it seemed like a month. What a bore Herr Pitzer was. His bedroom skills are less than those of a river carp. No charm; no talent; no more Anna."

"No replacement? You're in Bern so often, it seems. Perhaps a watchmaker or a Swiss bureaucrat in a gray suit? Or how about Captain Becker?"

"All the studs are in the military. The real men are all on the front lines. As for the Swiss, the men are such little trolls. And the worst trolls live in Bern. Well, no. The next to worst. The very worst live in their steel vaults underground on Zuricher Bahnhofstrasse."

Rainer laughed. "Otto Kalmbach is hardly a troll. And I judge his sons look virile enough."

"Farm boys? I'd sooner hump a fence post."

"What about some of the young men on the Swiss ski team?"

"Same thing." Anna tapped the side of her head. "No subtlety, no carnal sophisitication. Rutting with most men is so boring because they are little more than grunting animals. Exchanges of just the right erotic whispers and knowing looks are half the pleasure, not so? And so few men possess such talents."

"Have you tried other women?" Rainer said.

"A few times – for novelty. But I find I prefer the whispers of an imaginative man."

Rainer pulled her close and whispered, "So you are reduced to sleeping with your cousin. Poor, poor Anna."

She whispered back, "Lucky, lucky Rainer."

Friday
December 24, 1943
Meridian Hill District
Washington, D. C.

Dear Maddy,

I know. I wrote you only two weeks ago, but, because I can't be with you and the family for the holidays, I want you to know I am thinking of all of you, especially you, on this holiest of nights.

A short while ago, when I switched on the radio, I found a Maryland radio station that, as I was turning the dial, announced, "And now from Northfield, Minnesota, an hour of Christmas carols from the world-renowned St. Olaf's College choir, under the direction of Olaf C. Christiansen." Hearing those words made me tingle all over. I take it Olaf has taken over the choir from his father, Melius. Anyway, I'm listening as I write. (Don't remind me. I bad-mouthed the choir for so many years.)

My weekend trip to New York City, the day after I mailed you my card, letter, and presents, went off splendidly. I met Katherine at Karl Nierendorf's gallery and we spent most of Saturday shopping for her son, parents, and friends. NYC is such a marvelous place. That night we stayed at a small hotel just off Park Avenue called the Old Briar Club. The owner is a friend of her late father. On Sunday we strolled through Central Park, cold as it was. Then we caught a matinee movie – *Casablanca* at one of the second-run theaters on Eighth Avenue -- before I had to put Katherine back on the train for Hudson. I watched the train depart and thought of myself as Rick putting Ilsa on the airplane, only I intended to see Katherine again. After moping and aimlessly wandering the streets of New York, I finally put myself on a train to D.C.

My roommate, David, took off for Boston last Saturday to spend ten days with his family there. I was glad to see him gone for a while. His teasing me about spending time with Katherine had become tiresome. He's jealous, purely and simply. I'm hoping he takes up again with an old girlfriend of his he met while she was attending Boston College. Maybe she can calm his raging hormones.

Work at the gallery is going well. Word has filtered in from Switzerland – from Elliott via his informant who uses the code name *Grauergeist*, I think – that Munich is a major holding point for art works intended for the ostentatious art museum Hitler plans to build in his home town of Linz, Austria. If so, I hope to go to Munich again when the war is won and marvel at Hitler's collection before helping return every piece of it to its rightful owner.

One of the National Gallery's officers, Huntington Cairns, told me he had word that the old man in Munich I told you about, Werner Zeitz, a gallery owner with whom Elliott Parker and I had dinner one evening and who now lives in London, is not in very good health. The British climate apparently does not agree with him, although "Hunt", as he prefers to be called, said he thinks mostly what ails Werner is homesickness and being sick of the war and what it is doing to his beloved Germany. That and thinking of his only son, Rainer, serving in the SS and supervising the movement of some of the art the Nazis have looted from occupied countries.

Our work here at MFA&A is directed toward eventually recovering every last piece of such art and returning every work to its former owner. A immense task, I know, but one I look forward to taking part in with every fiber of my being. Speaking of my fibers, I'm getting stronger by the month. I'm no longer wobbly and creaky as Uncle Stephan's old wheelbarrow. I've promised myself that come summer I'm going to walk to the near bank of the Potomac some evening and see if I can't hurl my blasted cane to the far shore.

Once again, give my love to all. I think of you all daily. But especially you, dear sister.

Happy, Happy New Year !!!
Martin

P.S. The choir is about to render *Beautiful Saviour*. You know my attitude toward that piece. I may have altered my general opinion about the choir, but I still hate its signature song. So, as I end this letter, I am also tuning the radio to a different station.

Wednesday
January 6, 1944
Hohnstorf, on the Elbe River
65 kilometers east of Hamburg

"Yes, the bridge is sound. My daughter rode her bicycle across it only yesterday," a butcher in the town of Lüneburg had assured Rainer. A bicycle proves the soundness of a bridge, Rainer mused. *Sancta simplicitas!*

"How far yet?"

"Another twenty-two kilometers," the butcher had said, handing over the sausages Rainer had purchased while inquiring about the road ahead. Seven hundred kilometers already. In how long? Rainer looked at his new watch, another treat from Anna's shopping in Bern. Four o'clock. Nearly dark. Thirty-three hours. That comes to what? Scarcely more than twenty kilometers per hour. How dispiriting!

He sat in his Mercedes truck at the northern edge of Hohnstorf and stared ahead at the bridge over the Elbe. How many more liters of coffee must I drink before I allow myself more than an hour's sleep? Don't think about sleep. Just continue to concentrate on the immediate task.

He climbed out of the truck and relieved himself against the right rear tires before compulsively rechecking his cargo. The eighteen pieces Anna had thus far filched from the Schloss Collection still lay hidden in back of the pallets stacked with wooden crates marked *Geheimnis: Kriegsmarine*. The crates contained ordinary truck batteries from the BMW plant in Munich, but the manifest Rainer carried with him listed them as batteries especially designed for the new super U-boats ready to be launched at Kiel against Allied shipping. No such U-boats existed. Yet, in these dark days with the Allies gaining the advantage at nearly every turn, every disheartened German wanted desperately to believe the *Führer* was preparing to unleash a full arsenal of revolutionary weapons that would remind the rest of the world of the Fatherland's scientific and engineering genius.

So Anna's magical fingers had been busy at more than pilfering works of art from Hitler's Führerbau in the days between Christmas and New Year's. She commandeered both a truck and fuel coupons from the art-collecting motor pool, batteries and blank invoices from BMW. For the latter items she used blackmail against a Schwabing neighbor she knew in BMW's accounting office who had been forging dummy invoices on her own, collecting from the Reichsbank, and pocketing the money.

The idea of inventing supernatural U-boats and such boats' need for magical batteries belonged to Anna as well.

Unfortunately Anna possessed no magic wand to make Rainer, the truck, the batteries, and the Schloss paintings arrive magically and instantly in Kiel. Nor dared she take leave from her duties at the Führerbau to accompany him, to provide driving relief. Nor did she deem enrolling anyone else to serve that purpose an intelligent option. In the end, Rainer thought it unwise as well. *In the end,* meaning when he had finally given up trying to debate the subject with Anna. Sitting in Hohnstorf, waiting for other heavy trucks to come along in order to assure him the bridge was indeed as sturdy as locals had promised, Rainer wished he had been more persuasive. Driving itself had not been tedious. An adventure, rather, as he took lesser roads and avoided completely passing through, or even near, cities he knew lay in ruins, such as Nuremburg, and major railroad intersections, such as as Würzburg. More than once he had taken a wrong route and had to retrace his path. But the most stressful moments were always those when he was obliged to step down from the truck to deal with other Germans. To buy food, to buy diesel fuel, to ask directions, and, as in Lüneburg, to inquire about road or bridge conditions ahead of him.

His long, slow journey had taken him from Munich to Ingolstadt, then up the Altmühl River Valley to Ansbach, where he had taken his first brief rest. Then he drove west of Nuremburg northward to the medieval city of Bamberg, where he had rested four hours in the shadow of St. Martin's Cathedral, from where he could see the four steeples of the Kaiserdom.

The name St. Martin's had brought to memory the American he had met, courtesy of his father, before the war. Rainer wondered what might have become of the man and hoped he was not now a pilot of one of the bombers wreaking havoc on German cities. How ironic that would be, Rainer mused. An art historian specializing in twentieth century art, utilizing the most modern of weapons, unleashing them onto art galleries, many of which were – no, had been -- repositories of much of the world's best known modern art.

His only threatening encounter on the trip, so far, Rainer recalled thankfully as he watched a pair of trucks cross the Elbe bridge toward him, had come from a pair of Jesuit priests who had emerged from St. Martin's to question his presence and threaten to call authorities unless he moved on immediately. What provoked them he did not stay to ask. It was not as if his lone truck sitting there was going to provoke an Allied air attack on the city. In fact, Bamberg had been truly blessed, its medieval ambience unblemished by contemporary warfare. But then the town possessed no war industry to attract Allied attention.

Everyone else he had talked with along his way thus far had proven extraordinarily friendly, if not downright obsequious. Although he usually detested fawning, he discovered that he welcomed the many instances of "How may we be of help, *Standartenführer?*" and "Is there anything further we can do to assist you, *Standartenführer?*"

Rainer started the truck engine and edged forward toward the bridge. To his left, downriver, lay what was left of Hamburg. In late June and into August the Allies had loosed incendiary bombs on the city. The ensuing firestorm, which had lasted for weeks, killed more than forty thousand inhabitants, not that the survivors needed such a statistic to assure them catastrophic losses had occurred. How ironic, Rainer thought, that the Allies convince themselves that only wicked Germans are capable of the destruction of tens of thousands of noncombatants.

Beyond the Elbe lay the port city of Lübeck, one of the early casualties of Allied bombing. Rainer remembered that in response to the first bombing of Lűbeck, Göring retaliated with what he called the Baedeker Blitz, the bombing of the British cities of Exeter, Norwich, and Bath. His choice of those cities was, he said, because, like Lűbeck, they were beautiful. He wasted planes, men, and bombs on targets of no military value. The *Führer* should have dismissed him then and spared the Fatherland any more of Fat Herman's foolishness.

Rainer finally rested on the outskirts of Lűbeck while he decided which route to Todendorf would be safest. Remembering the farmer whose plow had tripped an unexploded bomb, he worried that he might better wait for daylight before proceeding. But so near the coast, so near operational centers of the *Kriegsmarine*, he feared he might be pressing his luck to linger about and risk being stopped by someone who knew no super U-boats existed, no boats existed that required his load of ordinary truck batteries. So, weary and hungry, he pressed on.

———————

Wednesday
January 6, 1944
Washington, D. C.

"Another love letter from Katherine?"

Martin looked up from his desk to see David Fox peering over his shoulder. He hastily covered his mail. "From my sister," he said gruffly.

"I've seen your sister's handwriting. Doesn't look like Madeleine's script to me."

"Maybe she hurt her hand."

"Oh yeah? Read me the passage where she tells you she hurt her hand."

"Am I nosy about your mail, David?"

"No. But my mail is utterly boring. Yours isn't."

"How would you know?"

"Because you tell me. When you get a letter and don't pass along anything about its contents, I figure it must be from Mrs. Parker."

"So what's the harm in her writing to me?" Martin asked, still shielding the letter.

"Harm? Did I say anything about harm?"

"Do I tease you about letters you get from Bertina?" Martin said, referring to the girl David claimed to have spent much of his Christmas leave with in Boston.

"You can't tease me about Boston Berty because she doesn't write me letters. I told you she's engaged and lives with her mother. How would it look if her mother caught her writing love letters to another Navy man while her financè is in the Pacific getting shot at by the Japs?"

"Katherine and I are just friends. Can't you and Berty correspond as *just friends?*"

"Just friends, my ass. Come on, Wynerson. Give me some credit."

"For what? Being a snoop and a rumor monger?"

"Man, if you're not boffing the Queen of Stuyvesant, New York, you're a bigger fool than I can imagine. You're not Catholic, for chrissake. I didn't know Lutherans took vows of celibacy."

Martin shrugged. "Don't you have work to do?"

"I can take a hint. Just one question before I go back to my own desk."

Martin gave Fox the evil eye.

David pointed to Martin's letter. "The letter smells of perfume, but I don't recall your sending perfume to your sister for Christmas. On the other hand --."

"Get out of here," Martin said, making a fist in a mock-threat gesture.

So what if the letter is from Katherine? So what if she tinged it with a dab of the perfume I bought for her in New York City? She's nobody else's business but mine.

Martin hunkered down to his current assignment, studying maps of Bavaria and Austria to try to pinpoint potential sites where the Nazis could harbor their stolen art, places better protected from the destruction the Allied air forces were inflicting on German cities. Information filtering back from sources such as Fathers Troquier and Roskosz -- via their contacts and Elliott's informant known as *Grauergeist* -- all suggested the Germans were in a state of alarm just short of panic, scrambling to shift their vast quantities of plunder to rural locales, places akin to Neuschwanstein Castle, which now, in the wake of the Luftwaffe's weaknesses, seemed all too vulnerable. Martin knew he had to pinpoint sanctuaries that were not only rural but substantial -- both in size and in the security they offered against air attacks.

For some time the Allies had known about Hitler's grand plan to build a museum in Linz, a place to show off the best of the Old Masters from Western Europe. It made sense to Martin that the Nazis would chose places in the Bavarian and Austrian Alps to hide such works. The Alps provided the best cover, given its frequent cloud cover, nasty winds and weather, and deep valleys. But what would protect the art from Alpine weather? The answers, Martin decided, were simple enough: mines and monasteries. The Alps were rife with both. Mines were a given. And most monasteries were as much fortress as minster, originally built as defensive bastions.

The Alps made Martin think again of Anna Stahlinger and that glorious afternoon he had spent romping across alpine meadows and lunching beside a brook gurgling with summer snow melt. Well, maybe not romping, he decided. Tripping? No. Gamboling? No. Lambs gambol. Bounding? Deer bound. The perfect word escaped him. But he recalled that, by whatever name, there had been a spring in his step. And that bounce had returned. His eyes weary from staring at his maps and noting the locations of potential hiding places, Martin finally cleared his desk and reopened his letter from Katherine.

Thursday
January 7, 1944
Todendorf
Schleswig-Holstein

"I suppose I could steal a propeller blade from another boat. I've looked all along the waterfront on both sides of the inlet. All the boats too damaged to float have already been stripped for their parts."

Rainer sat slumped in a chair on the front porch of the farm-house. Karl sat in the other chair. Karl's older brother, Klaus, sat on the porch steps and told how Allied air attacks on Kiel on Monday and Tuesday had scored multiple successes, but many bombs had also gone wildly astray, including one that destroyed a boat moored less than twenty meters from his own boat. The explosion had done minor damage to Klaus's boat above the water line, but had also ripped loose the mooring lines of the boat in between Klaus's and the shattered boat, forcing it to rotate, its stern backing into Klaus's stern, breaking his boat's rudder and bending the propeller shaft and the blades.

Exhausted from his trip, Rainer had slept in his uniform. At sunrise he had risen, bathed, shaved, and put on a clean uniform, while Karl had made a simple breakfast of cucumbers and sour cream, a hardboiled egg, and weak tea. Just as Rainer was feeling revitalized, Klaus had arrived with the bad news about his boat.

"Any other boats available?" Rainer asked as he toyed ner-vously with his pipe.

"A man does not loan out his boat, even to his closest friends," Klaus said solemnly.

Karl said, "Then maybe we should steal a whole boat instead of just a propeller."

Klaus looked at Karl as though his little brother had sug-gested stealing infants from their mothers' arms.

"Well then, what do you suggest?" Karl snapped at his brother.

Klaus had an answer. "I know of a boat we might be able to buy."

"Buy?" Karl shrieked. "Are you a manager of a local Reichs-bank when you are not playing at being a poor fisherman?"

Klaus looked to Rainer.

"How much does a boat cost?" Rainer had no idea about fishing boat prices.

"She doesn't want money."

Karl, still irritated, said, "She? A woman owns a boat?"

"Only by default," Klaus said. "All three of her sons are dead. Max died at Kursk; Wilhelm in Sicily; Emil... well --." Klaus bowed his head.

"Well what?" Karl demanded.

Klaus whispered, "Stalingrad."

Karl's tone softened. "Frau Bettinger. She is a good woman. So were all her sons."

"What does she want, if not money?" Rainer said.

"Someone to move her and her belongings to Braunschweig. She has a sister there. She says Kiel no longer holds any meaning for her," Klaus said. He looked directly at Rainer for a moment, then looked toward Rainer's truck, then back at Rainer.

"You have made her an offer already?" Rainer said.

"That is not my place... unless you want me to be the one to talk to her again."

Karl spoke. "I know her boat. It's a good one." Looking at Klaus, he said, "It's even a better one for our purposes."

Klaus nodded to Rainer in agreement.

"What's to say this boat won't suffer the same fate as yours?" Rainer asked Klaus.

"I could move it, but then questions will be asked. That my boat is damaged comes only from a freak combination of bad luck and an Allied pilot's stupidity. One bomb strays into our marina."

Rainer knew about luck. He thought again of Kurt Schnelker and the motor bike in Kiev. One hail of bullets; he is dead and I am not. "Very well. Tell this woman to have her belongings ready for us to pick up on Sunday morning."

Klaus frowned. "She's a deeply religious person."

Rainer looked at Karl, who gave a single nod. "Very well then. Sunday afternoon. No later." How many prayers did she say for her sons, begging God to protect them? Too few, clearly. Not that more would have helped. God has turned His back on this war. Shut His ears, closed His eyes, Rainer decided.

12

Sunday
May 14, 1944
Upper Saranac Lake
New York

Martin shielded his eyes from the lake's glare as he opened the bedroom curtains. Behind him on the bed Katherine Parker stirred. "Come look, Kath. A pair of mallards and a brood of seven chicks. They're swimming along near the shore, single file, except for papa. He's out ahead. Probably looking for predators."

Katherine pulled on a robe and walked to the window.

Martin pointed and said, "How'd you like to have septuplets?"

Katherine laughed and shook her head. "Sometimes Selby is more than I can handle. What time is it? God, I slept like a log."

"Don't know, but the sun's been up for hours," Martin said, kissing her gently on a cheek. "What time do we need to leave?"

"No hurry. Mid-afternoon. We can lollygag until then. The last train from Hudson doesn't leave until after eight tonight," Katherine said. "How long did it take us to drive up. Four hours?"

"About that," Martin said.

"We have the whole morning to enjoy ourselves. Come back to bed and help me lollygag."

This trip to see Katherine was Martin's fourth since the weekend in mid-December when she had met him in New York City. On each trip she been waiting for him in her car outside the Hudson train depot. Each time she had driven him to a different trysting spot, every one of them far enough from Stuyvesant that she felt certain no one would recognize her. To his MFA&A superiors Martin had always given the reason for needing to be away from D.C. to be that of additional consulting with Karl Nierendorf in New York City.

The first three times Martin had come, Katherine had asked her parents to take care of Selby, her excuse being that she needed to go to New York City for one reason or another. This time Selby had gone off to Boston with his friend Spencer, whose father was treating the boys to a Red Sox series with the Detroit Tigers -- one game on Saturday, a double-header on Sunday. And this time, instead of taking Martin to a hotel, she had brought him to her summer cabin, although in Martin's mind a lakefront house with six bedrooms and four baths qualified as something a bit classier than a summer cabin.

Martin described for her his own family's side-by-side cabins at Blackduck Lake, told her how much he loved every moment of the times he had spent there through the years.

"We have a couple canoes down at the boathouse. I've seldom gone out in one myself. Elliott is not a fan of the outdoors. I love being on the water. Shall we go out? You can show me how it's done," she said after they had finished both their lollygagging and breakfast.

"I'd love to. My sister, Maddy, and I used to canoe every-where all summer long, every summer."

"You can tell me all about your sister and about your summer adventures together."

So, as they glided south along the western shore of the lake, Martin told Katherine of his youth in Minnesota, how the land and lakes there compared with the Adirondacks, and spoke with deep-felt love about his younger sister, Madeleine, though care-ful to omit the naughty secret he and Madeleine shared.

"She sounds so grand, Martin. I'm sorry my parents saw fit to raise me as an only child, even though I suppose I'm going to share that fault. Elliott and I have no plans for further chil-dren. I'm sure I'd be a better person for having had a sibling." As another pair of mallards and their chicks waded ashore nearby, Katherine pointed. "Or even six. My parents could have afforded a dozen of us. Financially at least. Emotionally… well, I'm afraid I gave them serious pause."

"How so?" Martin asked as he continued making slow, rhythmic J-strokes.

"I gather I was quite a hellion."

"Was?"

"Okay. Am."

"I thought good Catholics are supposed to have big families."

"A great many American Catholics take exception to that notion."

"How did you meet Elliott?" Martin felt nervous raising the subject of her husband. Elliott Parker had barely been mentioned in all their previous assignations. But his ghost was always lurk-ing. So he might as well bring him into the open.

"At Yale. My cousin Emory was a classmate of Elliott's. Emory invited me to go along for his tenth class reunion. I was a senior at Vassar at the time and Poughkeepsie is only seventy miles from New Haven."

"Vassar. Wow!"

"Vassar was an easy choice. Fifty-five miles from home; seventy miles from New York City. I had the best of three worlds. My father would have preferred my going to Holy Cross, but he didn't insist. Mother went to Smith and she thought any one of the Seven Sisters would be acceptable."

"Was it love at first sight?" Martin asked.

"I think it might have been for Elliott."

"But not you."

"No. Eleven years' age difference seemed an impossible gulf at the time. Sometimes it still does."

"But you love him."

"I suppose I do. He's a comfort… when he's here. Which isn't often, even when he is. Do you know what I mean?"

"Not exactly."

Katherine remained silent for a few moments, searching for the right words, then said, "He's so detached. His mind is always elsewhere. Mostly on his work, I guess. I can't really tell. And he won't say." More silence. "He seldom consults me about anything. Just announces. Decrees, out of the blue. Like that time back… whenever it was that you went with him to Germany."

"Nineteen thirty-seven."

"Okay. He just came home one day and told me he was going."

"How did you react?" Martin asked.

"I shrugged. I was used to such behavior by then. But I didn't like it. I mean, he was saying 'Goodbye. See you in a few weeks.' Then poof! He was gone."

"What about this time? When he left for Switzerland."

"He obviously didn't just walk out the door. After all, we had a big send-off party. You were there. You saw."

"Yes. I saw you. You walked out on his speech. Clearly displeased, as I recall."

"As *you* recall. My reaction is certainly not something Ellliott recalled."

"Yet, you say you still love him."

"What else can I say? He's my husband; the father of my darling son; an art-world hero. What more can I ask of a man?"

Martin stopped paddling and directed the canoe toward a green, shaded spot on shore.

Katherine looked back. "I'm sorry. That was unkind. To you, as well as to Elliott."

Ashore, Katherine and Martin lay on a blanket, eating cheeseburgers Martin had cooked. Meat, except for steaks and choice roast cuts, had gone off the rationing list at the first of the month. As they ate, they watched a pair of squirrels scramble among the branches of nearby Balsam firs. They limited their conversation to small talk about the weather and how the changing of the seasons alter the landscape at their respective summer lakes.

Eventually Katherine asked, "What about you, Martin? What does life hold in store for you after this wretched war ends?"

Martin lay back, hands folded under his head, gazing up at the sky. "I guess I'll go back to teaching at George Washington. Get married, have a kid or two. If I have a son I'll go to baseball games with him, teach him how to handle a canoe, pitch a tent, start a fire from scratch."

"And your daughter? What will you share with her?"

"I guess I'll attend her piano recitals, watch her perform ballet, sing opera. Whatever she wants."

"And what will your children's mother be like?"

Martin closed his eyes and pondered, before saying, "Someone like you."

"I'm flattered, Martin. Really, I am. But no two women are alike. Haven't you figured that out yet?"

"I guess I haven't," he said.

"You can't go through life looking for my twin. You'll never find her."

"Then I'll settle for a close approximation."

"You hardly know me, Martin."

"I like everything I do know."

Katherine curled up next to him and rested her head on his chest. "In another life, perhaps we'll meet as college freshmen. We'll split the geographic difference. Ohio. Or Michigan maybe. Somewhere."

"You *are* a dreamer."

"Maybe."

"I guess we need dreams to smooth the sharp edges of reality," Katherine said. Then, "God, listen to me. Spouting pop philosophy. Who am I to talk about sharp edges? I was born with an entire set of silver in my mouth and grew up thinking the world is always served on a silver platter, along with tea cakes and sherry, delivered at half past three every afternoon."

"Feel guilty for being spoiled?" Martin asked.

"I didn't exactly choose to be born to the manor. But if I could have chosen, I certainly wouldn't have changed very much about my life."

"Very much."

In a soft, languid voice, barely audible, Katherine said, "Let's not discuss the what-might-have-beens any more. It's a commonplace that the longer one lives the more regrets one has. There'll be time enough near the end of the road to revisit them all, wade into a tear-filled pool of self-pity, rewrite the stories of our lives and make them lead toward happier endings."

Martin raised himself onto an elbow and wiped a tear from the corner of Katherine's eye. "I bet you write poetry when no one is looking."

Katherine sat bolt upright. "God, no! The ink would never dry. I'd be such a sappy sentimentalist. I lack the cold, steely eye of an Emily Dickinson. So best I simply sit beside a lake and babble my silly notions to a handsome young man who makes me smile and makes all my doubts and disappointments drift away like campfire smoke on a lazy summer night."

Martin kissed her cheek and tried to pull her back down.

Katherine resisted, standing up instead. "Come. We must go. Otherwise, you'll miss the train." And suddenly the spell was broken.

Sunday
May 14, 1944
Mariastern-Gwissen Monastery
Hohenweiler, Austria

Rainer emerged from the musty, dank underground of the Cistercian Abbey and filled his lungs with the fresh air. The Bodensee lay just a few kilometers to the east and he hoped he had time to spend part of the afternoon at Lindau and gaze at the lake. But first he had to finish his unpleasant business with the damned Trappists.

"The first trucks will arrive no later than Friday. Make sure your cellars are prepared to receive our crates."

Father Berthold stood beside him, shaking his head. A tall, gaunt, pasty-fleshed man who spent half his time looking heavenward, Father Berthold, Rainer thought, might have stepped from the canvas of El Greco. His dusty white robe added to the effect. "I have yet to understand the need for this inconvenience. Surely you have other places, locations not so remote, not so... so dedicated to the sanctity of spiritual matters, Herr Zeitz?"

"*Standartenführer* Zeitz, *Father* Berthold," Rainer said harshly. "If you expect *me* to defer to *you* because you trick yourself out in a holy robe and title, you are mistaken. I, too, have a title and wear a costume. And, in this instance, you will defer to me because of them."

"But why? We have nothing to do with the war that rages elsewhere."

"Damned if you don't! Tens of thousands of faithful Catholic young Austrian men are fighting in an effort to crush the atheist Bolsheviks and their Jewish allies. What will happen if those men fail and Russian tanks come rolling up to the gates of your abbey?" Rainer then mimicked the priest's voice. "We have nothing to do with the war."

"I will pray for our soldiers."

"Have you prayed for them already?"

"Yes, but I will pray harder."

"Good. Very good. God, it appears, is getting very deaf in His old age. Although it is clear someone is getting through to Him. Did you know that yesterday the patriarch of the Russian Orthodox Church died?"

Father Berthold simply stared at Rainer.

"It's true. God has killed a heretic."

"I will pray for his soul."

"You needn't bother. Use your time more wisely. Clean out your cellars." Rainer thought to himself, Anna should be here. She would tell this fool what she thought about his wanting to pray for a Russian Orthodox soul.

"What does storing works of art in our cellars have to do with stopping the Russians?" Father Bertold asked.

"Sale of such art will finance the Reich's war effort," Rainer said confidently, even though he knew his claim was at best a half-truth.

"I need to consult with the Vatican first to see what the Holy Father thinks," Father Berthold said.

"Pius has already spoken. His silence on all matters harmful to the Reich speaks volumes. There is no need for you to give him an opportunity to contradict himself."

"I don't like it. It goes against everything I believe."

"Nonsense. Your beliefs are as flexible as the cords that tie your robe. I have no time to play scholastic games with you. The trucks are coming; you will prepare your cellars to receive as many crates as we decide to send here."

Father Berthold wrung his hands. "Have you heard what the Allies are doing in Italy?"

"Trying to figure out how to break through the Gothic Line. *Feldmarschall* Kesselring is too much for them."

The monk shook his head emphatically. "No. I mean that they have begun to bomb the abbey at Monte Cassino."

Rainer threw his head back and laughed loudly. "So that is why you are shitting your pants over our bringing a few paintings to your cellar. You needn't worry. This place holds no strategic value. That is why we've chosen it."

"What about the railroad?"

The train from Munich to Lindau was still running, Rainer reminded himself. "Hope the Allied bombers are accurate. Better yet, pray for their accuracy. Meanwhile, get your fellow monks to make room for what my trucks are bringing."

Father Berthold bowed his head in resignation.

Rainer filled his pipe and waved for Karl to bring the car up from where he had been waiting. The monk continued to stand next to Rainer, looking expectant. "Something else?" Rainer finally asked as he struck a match.

"How long?"

"How long until what?"

Father Berthold shook his head. "How long will you require the use of our cellars?"

"Until we don't."

"The war is going badly," the priest said.

"I thought the war has nothing to do with you. Yet you know recent details about the situation in Italy. Do you know the Russians are pushing us back in the East?"

Father Berthold said he did. "And soon the British and the Americans will come from the West, will they not?"

"Rommel will push them back into the sea," Rainer said firmly.

The old monk winced. "The way he did in North Africa."

Rainer drew on his pipe. "Do you have friends in Switzerland, Father?"

"No."

"Good. Keep it that way." Karl stopped the Horch and started to get out. Rainer motioned for him to remain at the wheel. "Friday, Father Berthold. Be ready for us."

Father Berthold turned and walked away slowly, hands folded, head bowed in prayer.

Rainer felt weary and rode in silence as Karl drove toward Lindau. He marveled at how well Karl could shift gear with the stump of his right arm while he steered with his left hand. Karl loved to drive and Rainer continued to let him.

He closed his eyes and made himself forget the war, put its changing fortunes for the Reich out of his mind. He had made two more trips between Munich and Todendorf, each trip in a truck carrying two dozen paintings taken from the Schloss collection, including a Cranach, a Breugel, a van Dyke, and a pair by Frans Hals. Both trips had gone smoothly, in part because Karl had come along to help share the driving burden.

Frau Bettinger's outrageous behavior had leavened the first return trip back toward Munich, though Karl and Klaus failed to share his sense of comic relief at the old crone's antics. She had proven as difficult to satisfy as a boot camp drill instructor, bellowing orders and issuing complaints, finding all manner of fault with Karl, Klaus, and himself. "Be more careful with that table. That belonged to my great-grandmother." "*Schnell! Schnell!* At the pace you are moving my sister in Braunschweig will have two more birthdays before I see her." "No, no, no. Those chairs cannot be stacked that way. Have you never moved furniture before?" And on and on.

Rainer wondered, too, why Anna had not considered this area near the abbey, where Germany, Switzerland, and Austria meet, to store the works destined for the Sundstrums. Lindau and Bregenz were much closer to Munich than Wasterkingen and Zurich. Surely in either Lindau or Bregenz lived a war widow eager to sell her home. Except for the railroad, as Father Berthold pointed out, the area held no military value for either side. Too far from anything. Perhaps also, she had been unable to find a local equivalent to Otto Kalmbach, who, according to his cousin, was as avaricious as any Zurich banker.

But even greed has its limits, as Anna discovered six weeks earlier when the Allies bombed the small Swiss city of Schaff-hausen, equidistant from Wasterkingen and Singen. The dead numbered somewhere between fifty and hundred. The Allies apologized immediately, of course, claiming they had made a mistake. But Otto Kalmbach had taken the bombing personally, telling Anna he was certain the Allies meant to punish him for helping her and Rainer. Rainer had laughed until he hurt when Anna told him of Otto's mixture of fear and astonishment that the Allies had found him out. Rainer's own opinion was that, although Otto was not the intended target, Schaffhausen had been no mistake. The Allies would not have known, or cared, about Otto Kalmbach, but they surely knew and cared that Swiss munitions for German use were being manufactured in Schaff-hausen.

In any case, Otto refused to cooperate any longer—at any price -- and Anna needed to find another safe crossing point into Switzerland in order to continue to maintain the Sund-strums' interest by providing them with small, but immediate gratifications, while the ultimate trophies, the contents of the sauerkraut vault, remained in Todendorf, circumstances as yet too dangerous to transport them to Sweden.

Maybe she hadn't looked hard enough along this end of the Bodensee, Rainer surmised. Greed is hardly an exotic trait. In any event, she has never mentioned this end of the Bodensee as a possibility, Rainer thought. But then she seldom tells me anything unless I ask. And even then --.

But now it might be necessary. Perhaps he could even take a short time to inquire discreetly, he thought. Anna at the moment was busy arranging for the transportation of the entire art-work horde being held at the Führerbau from Munich to the safety of the salt mines located in the Salzkammergut Mountains southeast of Salzburg. Well, the transportation of those works other than the ones for which she was stealthily making alternate arrangements.

On the two previous trips between Munich and the sauerkraut cellar, the "special batteries" camouflaging the paintings were simply dumped in a field after the paintings had been unloaded. The vault held room for many more paintings, but the boat Klaus had purchased from Frau Bettinger – she had demanded money after all – had been bought with money from one of Anna's private accounts and was now problematic. Too small for the growing number of art works. And Rainer dreaded the thought of two Baltic crossings. But the thought of leaving any prize paintings behind, especially his Klee, dismayed him equally. He would have to give more thought to a solution. Maybe buy another boat. He didn't know. Still plenty of time to plan, he told himself. Or was there?

Rainer let his mind wander to less vexing matters as Karl slowed for other traffic upon nearing Bregenz. Anna should have been here to lecture Father Berthold. She would have done a better job of it than I did. I wonder if she's heard the news of Patriarch Sergei's death. That will excite her.

∫

13

Friday
September 1, 1944
Stuyvesant, New York

Speaking English in his thick Berlin accent, Karl Nierendorf was holding forth as he stood in the middle of a group of Katherine Parker's guests. "Zey can bomb Churmany till hell turns to ice but zey vill neither veaken ze people's morale nor slow ze factory production. Dis I can assure you. Did zee English melt like butter ven zee Luftwaffe bombed zeyr cities? Vee must hammer, hammer, hammer on zee ground till vee are standing on Prinz Albrecht Strasse."

Martin leaned against the archway between the parlor and the dining room, watching and listening, sipping wine, wondering if he had made a mistake by accepting Katherine's Labor Day weekend invitation. At least this time his claim to be consulting with Karl Nierendorf was true. After his train ride from Washington to New York City, he had ridden to Stuyvesant with Karl in the back seat of Max Hepperschorn's stylish Duisenburg, with Max at the wheel. Max, too, was a former gallery owner from Dresden who had closed shop, emigrated, and now was now working as a docent at the Metropolitan Museum and living off his considerable savings, carried out of Germany wrapped in a suitcase otherwise full of dirty clothes. Max hoped to return to Germany after the war and now his chances for doing so sooner than later were looking up.

Martin was still feeling residual excitement from the Allies liberating Paris. Was that only a week ago today? Did D-Day happen less than three months ago? For Martin the summer seemed to have lasted a year. His exhilaration stemmed from two sources. First, he hoped the Nazi's hasty evacuation of the French capital had forced them to leave behind at least some of their booty. Second, with the fall of Paris David Fox suddenly had become busy helping Father Troquier at Georgetown. So busy that he had to reverse his acceptance and send regrets to Katherine that, alas, he would be unable to attend her weekend gathering in Stuyvesant. Alas, indeed! Martin had barely been able to mask his *Schadenfreude* when David told him the "unfortunate" news.

By Martin's count the invited guests who did manage to attend numbered at least forty and he wondered if he would even get so much as a minute alone with Katherine, whose mother seemed to follow her everywhere like a nervous pup while Katherine played her demanding role of attentive hostess.

Suddenly he felt a light touch on his arm and when he turned Katherine was there.

"I asked Max to take Mother for a spin in his fancy automobile. He was more than glad to do something to get away for a while. I think Mister Nierendorf wears him down. And Mother, of course, was thrilled."

"I think she wears you down," Martin said.

"Thank God she hasn't invited herself to move in with me. Luckily she has a large circle of friends in Albany. Sooner than later one of us would kill the other. Anyway, later let's try to plan at least a few minutes alone. I'll make an excuse for you to stay when it's time for Max and Karl to return to the inn and offer to drive you back myself. I've received another letter from Elliott. I can't believe he's been gone a year already."

"Does it seem longer or shorter than that?" Martin asked.

"Sometimes one; sometimes the other. Anyway, the letter is several weeks old. He says he planned to get it to me by using the diplomatic pouch of one of the neutral countries, Portugal or Sweden. If that didn't work, he says he has contacts at the Red Cross in Geneva."

Martin waited for her to continue.

In a low voice she said, "I just want to be near you. To have you hold me. To be alone with you. To hear you whisper sweet endearments in my ear. Elliott's letters are so… so formal. It's like he's writing a report to some bureaucrat in Washington. Well, no. That's unfair. He's not that reserved. But he could share a lot more of himself than he does." Just then her son, Selby, entered the room and came running to her.

"Mom, Mom. Mrs. Kramer said I could have a small helping of the dessert she's made, if it's okay with you. I'm to be her official dessert tester."

"Promise me it won't spoil your dinner," Katherine said.

"I promise."

"Then tell Mrs. Kramer it's all right with me. By the way, do you remember Mister Wynerson?" Katherine gestured toward Martin.

"You're the guy who crashed his airplane. Where's your cane?"

"I no longer need it."

"Does that mean you can fly again?"

"No. I'm afraid not."

"Why not?"

"The Army Air Force probably thinks I'd ruin another of their expensive airplanes."

"That's not fair."

"No. But I don't mind. I have important things to do here."

"In Stuyvesant?"

"In Washington."

"Do you ever go to any Senators' ball games?"

"No. I'm a Cubs fan and I understand you're a Red Sox fan. How are they doing?"

"Aw, they lost Wednesday to the Yankees and fell back into fourth place, four games out."

"Are you a ballplayer?" Martin said.

Selby stared at his shoes. "Dad used to play catch with me, but now --."

"Would you like to play some catch now?" Selby looked at Katherine, who smiled and nodded her assent. "After you test Mrs. Kramer's dessert, of course."

Selby's face brightened. "Sure. Is it okay, Mom? He can use Dad's glove. I know where it is."

"Yes, you may. I have to tend to my other guests, but you two run along." To Martin, "Thank you. See you later." Then, in a whisper, "And again after that."

––––––––––

Friday
September 1, 1944
Königsburg, East Prussia

"I appreciate your concerns, *Standartenführer* Zeitz, but I still think transporting the Amber Room crates by rail is safer."

Rainer stood in the chill basement of Königsburg Castle as he and Museum Director Alfred Rohde watched SS men nail shut the last of the twenty-nine crates containing the Amber Room panels. The smells of mold and mildew mixed with the odor from the director's perspiration. Despite the cold air, the man's shirt was soaked and he repeatedly mopped his forehead with a handkerchief. He sweats from fear. Certainly not from overexertion, Rainer knew.

Panic, better than mere fear, described Herr Doktor Rohde's state of mind, Rainer decided. Yes, the British had bombed Königsburg in August, but by now that hardly distinguished it from other strategic German cities. Rainer had been in Munich when the distress call from Rohde came. You must see to the Amber Room immediately! One might have thought enemy tanks were rolling into the city even as he spoke.

However, Rainer had decided to acquiesce in the director's pleas, hollow as they were. Otherwise, Berlin was ready to send him to Vienna in order to find out why the monastery at nearby Mauerbach was incapable of handling all the works of art left behind by Viennese Jews when they departed for the relocation camps.

Who was Berlin trying to fool? Left behind? Departed? Relocation camps? Are they too embarrassed to speak forthrightly to one of their own SS officers? And I already know why Mauerbach is inadequate – without ever having seen the monastic castle. The place was not designed for the purpose of holding treasures belonging to two hundred thousand people.

Rainer's plan for moving the dismantled Amber Room contents by boat from Konigsburg to one or another isolated beach on Germany's Baltic Coast was hardly foolproof. But he believed his strategy offered better odds than Rohde's idea of loading the crates onto a train bound for Berlin and hoping for the best. Rodhe dreaded the notion of the amber panels ending up at the bottom of the sea, put there either by Allied bombs or by an accident of striking a submerged German sea mine.

"Few mines float on the surface, *Herr Doktor*. And the barges I plan to use have extremely shallow drafts. The barges will be towed by tugboats using long towing cables. One of those boats will strike any mines in the path I propose. And that path takes the entire convoy, barges, tugs, and gunboat escorts, well off the coast, which will also rule out attacks from enemy bombers. The Allies follow the coast line and their targets are port cities. My plan is to land the barges here." He had unfurled a map of the Baltic coast and his finger came down near the lighthouse at Todendorf.

Rainer delighted in the fact that his plan would place the Amber Room panels so close to the sauerkraut vault. And though he realized that Anna, too, would savor such an exquisite irony, he took added satisfaction in knowing he had not shared his plan with Anna. He had no doubt she would immediately start scheming to find a way to hijack the entire shipment, not that the twenty-nine crates would all fit into Karl's cellar vault, even if the vault were otherwise empty.

"Have you heard about what is happening in Warsaw?" Rohde asked Rainer, his voice tense.

"I've heard. Don't let it bother you. The SS will crush the upstarts." Maybe the *Herr Direktor* fears the Poles more than the British, Rainer thought. With the Red Army now practically camped on the banks of the Vistula, the Polish Home Army suddenly has found its backbone and was trying to take over Warsaw from the small German garrison.

"But what if the Poles here in Königsburg decide to try to imitate their comrades in Warsaw?" Rohde asked.

"Close your gates and lock them. Was this castle not built for exactly such a purpose?" Rainer said.

"But --."

"But nothing."

"What if the Russians come to their aid?"

"It won't happen. The Bolsheviks will be pleased to watch Poles and Germans kill each other."

"How can you be so sure?"

"It's Stalin's way. He will treat Poland no differently than he has treated the Baltic republics."

"You think the war is over, *Standartenführer?*" Rohde's failed attempt to hold Rainer's gaze gave away his own sense of defeat.

"Not at all," Rainer lied. "But Poland will once again become a nasty battleground. At this very moment the *Führer* is developing secret weapons of great magnitude."

"Do you think they will be enough?" Rohde asked expectantly.

"I do. Are you not aware of the rocket miracles we have rained on the English from Pennemünde? All we need to do is make more such weapons and turn them eastward. And that is only the beginning." Rainer tried his best to sound convincing, even though he did not believe such miracles would save the Reich.

Doktor Rohde gestured toward the crates of amber. "Shall I move these now?"

Rainer shook his head. "Berlin would frown on such a show of alarm. And right now Himmler would not be pleased to think that, while he is putting down the uprising in Warsaw, you assume the cause here is hopeless enough to order a retreat."

Rohde shuddered. "I see what you mean. Thank you, *Standartenführer*."

From Rohde's current state of mind, Rainer concluded he should press his advantage. In for one lie, in for a dozen, he decided. "Berlin fully backs my plan for moving the amber. For now I would do nothing about these. Let them lie here. They are safe enough. This cellar is impregnable. But when the time comes to move them – if it comes – think about putting them to sea. I would not want to be wearing your shoes if you sent them by rail and they failed to arrive."

Before Rainer's eyes the man seemed to shrink to the size of a field mouse. In the spirit of self-preservation, however, Rohde asked, "And if they fail to arrive by sea?"

Rainer raised himself to full height, sighed deeply, and solemnly announced, "The final decision is yours, *Herr Doktor*."

14

Thursday
December 14, 1944
Washington, D.C.

Union Station bustled with soldiers, sailors, and civilian Christmas-season travelers, most bearing bags full of gifts in addition to their luggage. As the train from Chicago slowed to a stop Martin walked along the platform until he saw Maddy bouncing in her seat and waving excitedly. Minutes later he helped her from the train, taking her shopping bag in one hand, Maddy's right arm in his other. After standing aside to allow passengers behind her to disembark, he gave her a bear hug while kissing her on the side of her neck.

"Martin! Don't squeeze the stuffing out of me," she squealed.

"What stuffing? You're skinny as a curling broom."

"Oh, I am not. Before I left home I ate enough of Mother's Christmas cookies to stoke a pregnant polar bear sow."

"You look great. Let's split the difference and leave it at that. Come along. We'll head for the cab stand, or would you rather have some lunch first?"

"I'm starved. Mother packed me enough box lunches to feed an army, but the trip was so boring I ate everything by the time the train was half way across Pennsylvania. One snow-covered cornfield looks pretty much like any other."

"Didn't you bring along anything to read?" Martin asked as they walked toward the exit.

"I tried to read *Gone With The Wind*, but I kept stopping to fantasize myself as Scarlett falling into the arms of Clark Gable."

"And then what?"

"And then the infant across the aisle would scream again and I made myself think of something else before Clark turned me into the mother of a house full of screaming babies."

"Poor you, Dear Sis." Martin held open one of the doors facing Columbia Monument and they both felt the blast from a cold wind.

"Poor me, for sure. I was hoping it would be warmer here than back home."

"It probably is," Martin said. "I know a diner up Massachusetts Avenue just past the Government Printing Office a couple blocks. The food isn't too bad and not too expensive. No lutefisk, no lefsa, no krumkaker, but I'm sure you can find something edible."

Maddy made a face and stuck out her tongue.

Over vegetable soup and onion bread Maddy told Martin, "I think I've met the man I'm going to marry."

"Clark Gable?"

Maddy laughed and shook her head.

"Does he speak Swedish?"

"No. That's always been optional. You know that."

"Can he polka?"

"He can polka in a closet," Maddy said with a sly grin.

"That's not optional, I'm sure."

A wider grin.

"So tell me all his lesser virtues," Martin said.

Maddy rattled off her new beau's *bona fides*. "His name is Ray Gillingham. Raymond Gillingham. He's a pilot. He's from Milwaukee. He graduated from University of Wisconsin with a degree in math and I met him at a USO dance in St. Paul. He was on leave and visiting his sister who lives in St. Paul. He had been flying submarine patrols from a base in Greenland and was headed for the Pacific, but he couldn't tell me where."

"So why Ray out of all the guys at the USO dance?" Martin asked.

"He invited me to dance. And later he invited me again… and again and again and again."

"And you accepted and accepted and accepted."

"He's handsome and he makes me laugh. He wants to get an advanced degree and become a college math professor when the war is over. I've met his sister and she's a doll."

"A doll. Meaning?"

"You'd like her. Her name is Clara, she's two years older than Ray and she's not married."

"Interesting, but don't start up trying to play matchmaker again. Okay?"

"She'd be perfect for you, Martin."

"Still imagine you're a better judge of who's perfect for me than I am, do you?"

Maddy's shoulders slumped. "Are you still seeing that married woman?"

"Her name is Katherine. So use it. And yes, I am. On rare occasions."

"Am I interfering by coming here? Be honest."

"No, you are not. Katherine is busy preparing to spend the holidays with her family. Mother, son, aunts, uncles, and so on. Just like we do."

"Used to," Maddy corrected. "Christmas hasn't been the same when you've not been there to celebrate with us."

"I understand. This war can't last too much longer. Then I'll be able to return home – to my real home – on Christmas breaks."

"I'm looking forward that. And I know everybody back home will be thrilled as well. Promise?"

"I promise."

After a pause Madeleine asked, "Did you make it to New York City to shop with Katherine?"

"No. We'd planned to meet there again, but her son had chicken pox. So we won't be seeing each other until long after the holidays are over."

"Do you love her?"

"I like her a lot. We've become very close friends."

"Just friends?"

"Well --."

"Where will it lead, Martin?"

"Nowhere. When the war ends that will be that. But we both know how it is. Right now we're just two lonely people who've found some good, but temporary, companionship."

"You can both just walk away from your relationship some-day?" Maddy asked, looking at Martin sideways.

"We tell ourselves we can."

"Does she still love her husband?"

Martin stared up at the ceiling. "I'm not sure how much she ever loved him."

"Then why'd she marry him?"

"It was easier than not marrying him, she says."

"For better or worse," Maddy said sarcastically.

Martin looked back at Maddy. "In poker there's a saying. You play the hand you're dealt."

Maddy came back with, "I don't know all *that* much about poker, but isn't there another saying, muttered by those who lost the hand they were dealt? Deal, cry the losers? Do you think that someday she'll want a redeal?"

Martin shook his head slowly. "She's Catholic, Maddy. Divorce is out of the question."

"Then my suggestion is this: Next chance you get, come home to meet Raymond's sister."

Following a short cab trip to the Meridian Hill district, Martin led Maddy to his apartment. "Not much, but it's half mine."

After a quick survey, Maddy proclaimed, "It's bigger than I imagined. I pictured you holed up in a place the size of a dormitory room at St. Olaf."

"Sometimes it seems even smaller than that. Luckily, David and I don't keep the same hours. He's a night owl and usually works at the National Gallery until well past midnight. Sometimes I'm leaving for work just as he arrives here."

"You said he was going to be out of town all the time I'm here?" Maddy said, plopping herself on the couch and testing its softness by pressing the seat cushion.

"He has a new girlfriend. A woman who teaches German at the University of Maryland over in College Park. She's from Virginia and invited him to her home in Richmond to meet her parents."

"Uh-oh. Watch out!"

"I've met her. She oozes charm like a maple tree oozes sap. Good-looking, too. I don't know what she sees in David."

"Maybe she's just using him to get her hooks into you," Maddy surmised.

"Not my type. Besides, I already know German."

"Does she *versteh Blutshuld*?"

Martin's look darkened. "Stop it. Stop right there." *Blutshuld.* Literally, blood guilt. But in German it also meant *incest.*

"I'm sorry."

"I hope so."

"I mean it."

"That reminds me. You may sleep on David's bed. I have his permission."

Maddy made a pouty face.

"Don't even think it, Madeleine."

"Why not?'

"Close your eyes and think of Raymond."

"I'd rather close my eyes and think of tents, canoes, and sleeping bags." Pause. "And us."

"That was long ago and far away."

"But now is now and here we are. Together. Alone. And with no one else to cling to but each other. Raymond and Katherine are worlds and worlds away." Maddy wrapped her arms around Martin, stood on tiptoes, and whispered, "*Bruderlust*, my dear brother. *Bruderlust*."

December 14, 1944
Kochel am See
Lake Kochel, Upper Bavaria

Rainer stood at an upper-story window of his father's chalet and watched two pairs of headlights approach. Snow was falling and the tires of both autos struggled for traction. The front car exhibited less sideways slippage than the car behind it and Rainer assumed Anna was at the wheel of that vehicle. Behind her came the Sundstrums, whom he looked forward to meeting again. Intimate business partners, he understood, ought not remain strangers, lest they distrust one another more than business partners should. He knew it was more difficult to loath a man or woman one had dealt with face-to-face. A simple reason Nazis hated Jews so readily, Rainer believed, was that rarely, if ever, had a member of the Party ever known a Jew personally. Soon he would find out if his tolerance for Swedes improved with additional contact. He doubted it.

Minutes later Rainer extended his hand to the pair of Swedish physicians. "Welcome to Kochel am See. I am pleased to meet you both again."

"Likewise, Herr Zeitz," Nils Sundstrum said, shaking Rainer's hand.

"A pleasure," his wife, Sigrid, said with a slight, quick bow of her head.

For the meeting Rainer wore a wool sweater and wool knickers that ended just below the knees and long wool socks. He looked like a skier, rather than an SS officer, which was his intention.

"Anna, take their coats and show them the fire while I pour brandies," Rainer said. His recollection of the couple put them younger than they now looked, but then Rainer realized the turbulent times had aged most people he knew, accelerated facial lines, gray hair, sharpened signs of *Weltschmertz* on every face he encountered these days.

Nils Sundstrum reminded him of a mortician he knew in Munich -- tall, quiet, solemn, with a face that looked as though it would be at peace with corpses, hardly a welcome countenance in a physician. By contrast, his wife had small, dark, darting eyes that went with her general appearance of nervousness, as if she were a mouse creeping through an alley full of cats.

Brandy in hand and seated by the fire, Herr Sundstrum gestured with his brandy snifter, "A charming place you have here. Cozy, peaceful, remote."

"My father purchased the chalet back in the early 20's, following an injury to his back. A small spa is not far from here and he believed mineral baths would cure his aches."

Nils Sundstrum eschewed small talk and came to the point. "Fräulein Riedel assures us you are now fully prepared to move your collection of paintings from Germany to Sweden."

Rainer blinked and shifted in his chair. He was unused to hearing Anna referred to as Fräulein Riedel and reminded himself not to slip and call her anything other than Greta. "Yes, I am prepared – when the time is auspicious."

Herr Sundstrum took a sip and brandy before smiling and saying, "And when do your chicken entrails tell you that time will be?"

"Soon."

Frau Sundstrum nodded. "The vise is closing."

Rainer pictured a mouse surrounded by cats prepared to pounce. "I have no illusions."

"But he dare not speak them," Anna intruded. "Public expressions of defeat are dealt with swiftly and harshly."

Nils Strundstrum nodded. "We know. We have seen enough examples in our travels throughout Germany." He nodded to his wife, who stood and held out a packet for Rainer.

"With Greta's help we have prepared these," Sigrid said.

Rainer accepted the packet and opened it. Inside were several documents, a pair of Swiss passports on top. When Rainer opened the first passport he saw a photo of himself, one taken just before the war had begun. The name on the passport was Helmut Spühler; the address was a street in Wintertur. The second passport showed Karl Vollmer, now Max Edelman from Aarau. Besides the passports, the packet contained letters of introduction, each signed by a different member of the International Red Cross executive committee in Geneva, a map of Germany and Austria showing POW camps, and sets of instructions on the duties of Red Cross workers in the field and how they were to conduct themselves with those running the camps.

"Everything is genuine, except for the passports, of course," Nils Sundstrum said.

"And if we are challenged?" Rainer asked. "Neither Karl nor I sound Swiss, although where we will be they think everybody south of Frankfurt talks as if they have marbles in their mouths."

"A phone call to Geneva will settle the matter. Anyone on the executive committee will vouch for you."

"Anyone?"

Both Nils and his wife nodded.

Rainer looked at Anna, who smiled and gave him a reassuring nod. So. The rumors that the executive committee of the IRC is under the control of the Reich are not merely rumors after all.

"When you arrive in Sweden you may also use our names," Sigrid Sundstrum said.

"But not before then, I take it," Rainer said.

"If asked, you may say you know us, but do not ask anyone to contact us for verification," Nils said.

Rainer wanted to ask: Why not? But the answer was simple enough. The Sundstrums themselves might, at that moment, be on Reich soil and even the best forged documents sometimes do not stand up to scrutiny. The Gestapo may act like brutal thugs, but not all of them were stupid animals.

The last set of documents were survey charts of the southern Swedish coastline, depths marked at hundred-meter intervals and out to depths of twenty meters.

"I strongly urge you not to carry the charts on your persons or in your vehicle," Nils said.

"They would be difficult to explain," Rainer allowed.

"Nor did we dare mark your landing spot."

"Which is?"

"East of Ystad there is a lighthouse. Just west of the lighthouse a little-used road comes down to the sea at a tiny village called Löderups. As you can see, the water is shallow for many meters out from the beach, but it is the best we can do. You make contact in the village. Do not try to take any of the valuables ashore on your own. Your contact is at the village tavern, whose owners are named Ivar and Olga Pedderson. They own a sea-rescue motor launch big enough to bring the goods ashore in no more than two trips. You must, of course, drop anchor after dark and row ashore. If you arrive in the middle of the night and the tavern is closed, they live upstairs. Go to the rear and up the stairs. Carry something blue and green and alternately hold the colors up to your lamp. Otherwise, they may shoot you for burglars."

"And from Löderups?" Rainer said.

"The Peddersons will see that the paintings are moved to Stockholm. For you and Herr Vollmer I have arranged transportation to, and accommodations in, Stockholm. I hope that suits you," Nils said.

Rainer looked to Anna, who gave him a single nod. "Payment?"

"That is the second reason we are here. To settle that matter," Sigrid said.

The tricky part, Rainer knew. Naturally, Rainer and Anna did not want to surrender the paintings until payment to them was secured; the Sundstrums did not want to part with money until the paintings were safely under their control.

Anna stood. "I have what I believe is a solution to everyone's unspoken anxieties on the matter of making an exchange of such magnitude."

Nils spoke. "Until now we have worked together successfully without cheating one another."

"But this trade represents a different magnitude," Anna said.

"Agreed," Sigrid said, unable to mask her edginess.

"So what I propose is that we settle with one another by degrees. That is, an installment sale."

"Surely you don't propose more than one boat trip between Germany and Sweden. That is far too much of a risk," Nils said.

"No. One boat trip. All the paintings. But the installments involve something else. Something new and perhaps of equal value to the entire set of paintings."

Even Rainer's jaw dropped. This was all news to him, too.

Anna opened an envelope of her own. "Consider this a down payment."

She handed the contents to Nils, who looked at it carefully before passing it to his wife.

"I don't understand," Sigrid said.

Anna explained. "On Adolf Hitler's fiftieth birthday, in nineteen thirty-nine, a group of German industrialists paid Frau Winifred Wagner one million Deutschmarks for several of her husband's original scores so they could present them to the *Führer* as a gift. Only a few weeks ago Frau Wagner petitioned the *Führer* to transfer the scores from Munich back to Bayreuth for safekeeping. I am told the *Führer* laughed and told Frau Wagner that he had in mind a much safer place to store them. He meant the salt mines at Alt Aussee in Austria." Anna allowed herself a brief chuckle. "I'm afraid it will be Frau Wagner who has the last laugh."

"You stole this from Adolf Hitler?" Sigrid asked, her face a mixture of astonishment and terror.

"The scores were stashed in a tiny room at the Führerbau. You need not worry. The container they were in remains locked and they are all accounted for on the inventory of items that have already arrived safely at Alt Aussee."

"But--." Frau Sundstrum's hands trembled and her voice quavered. No other words formed.

"You would rather I made arrangements with another dealer?" Anna said coldly.

Frau Sundstrum looked to her husband.

"How many scores do you have?" Nils asked.

"The one you are looking at is *Reinzi*. I also have *Die Feen*, *Die Liebesverbot*, *Das Reingold*, and *Die Valkure*. Besides those, I possess what I believe is an orchestral sketch, an original also, of *Die Fliegende Hollander*."

"May I see the score?" Rainer asked as he stood and walked toward the Sundstrums.

Nils held out the manuscript.

While Rainer studied his newly found asset, Anna explained her plan for making exchanges. "You may take this score with you as a down payment. When Rainer hands over the paintings to the Peddersons in Löderups, they will present Rainer with a receipt for half our agreed upon price for the paintings *and* for the five Wagner scores plus orchestral sketch, which, by the way, will cost *you* only half a million Deutschmarks. A bargain, yes? And the payment will be in American dollars, as we agreed before regarding the paintings alone."

Nils Sudstrum nodded. "Enskilda Bank's main branch in Stockholm, correct?"

Anna continued. "Correct. And the balance you owe us you may make in five more deposits, each ten percent of the total price, the first payment to be made one week following the arrival of the paintings in Sweden. Then four more payments one week apart, always on Friday. The Monday following each of those payments you will receive one more Wagner score. If payment is not made, the score will not be delivered. Do you agree to these terms?"

Nils looked to his wife, who hesitated.

"Is there a problem?" Anna said.

"No," Nils said firmly.

"Good. Here is the account into which you will transfer the funds." Anna handed him a slip of paper.

Nils looked at the slip, then looked again at the Wagner score.

"Authenticate it, by all means. If you dare." Anna handed him the envelope from which she had taken the score.

"We will trust you," Nils said.

Anna laughed. "Honor among thieves. Is that not the saying?" Neither Sundstrum seemed to find any humor in her remark.

"We must be going. But first, one small detail." Looking at Rainer, he asked, "How will we know when to make the first deposit? How are we to anticipate your arrival in Löderups?"

Anna answered. "Someone on the Geneva executive committee will contact you and pass along a message from Helmut Spühler saying he needs to speak with one of you regarding a certain medical procedure for British POWs interred at Stalag Luft I in Barth. Once you receive this message from Geneva you will have forty-eight hours to make the deposit. Do not worry. The call will not reach you on a Thursday or a Friday."

Five minutes later Rainer stood with Anna as they watched the tail lights of the Sundstrums' car disappear quickly amid a flurry of snowflakes. "I don't like them," he said softly.

"I was sure you would not find them congenial, but, after all, they are scarcely regular dinner guests," Anna said.

"What if I said I don't trust them?"

"I would say you are probably right not to do so, which is why I set up the arrangements that we all just agreed to."

"You made it too easy for them to make off with the paintings. And they didn't seem very enthusiastic about your Wagner *coup*."

"They were trying extra hard not to reveal their eagerness. But trust me. They are as greedy as anyone else. Perhaps more so. The numbers were running furiously through their heads and they both liked what they calculated. A private collector will pay them more than our great industrialists paid Frau Wagner."

Rainer frowned. "Then why didn't you set a higher price on the musical scores?"

"Because I lied about the scores being worth as much or more than the paintings. And I'm supposing the Sundstrums thought I was either lying or am stupid regarding how much the paintings will bring. No matter. They were stuck agreeing to the terms because they know how fat the scores will make their own bank account. So they will pay us for the paintings in the way I asked them to pay in order for them to get their greedy hands on the Wagner scores."

"Clever as always," Rainer said, turning from the window. "But I'm surprised the Sundstrums gave you no argument about the price. And, at any price, how can you suppose they can find such a sum of money?"

"Easy. They have already approached at least two Zuricher bankers that I know of, and perhaps more than the two. I can just see the little Bahnhofstrasse trolls in their three-piece suits fighting over who will provide the Sundstrum's financial backing. It will be like watching goats butting heads during rutting season."

"I would have thought they might approach Swedish bankers," Rainer said.

Anna nodded. "Maybe so, but, unlike in Switzerland, I have little knowledge of what goes on in Sweden."

Rainer finished his brandy and asked, "Why did you bring them here? You have handled everything that transpired prior to this evening tonight from Geneva."

"They insisted on meeting you in person again. Berlin, years ago, was... well, Berlin years ago. You saw what an apprehensive little mouse Frau Sundstrum is. They wanted to put a face to your name. Clearly, you were forgettable long ago."

"They had my photo," Rainer said, waving a hand toward the packet containing his fake passport.

"A photo was not enough."

"I'd hate to be the patient when Frau Sundstrum holds a scalpel in her hand."

"I don't think she performs surgery," Anna said.

Rainer laughed. "No doubt there are countless men still alive who might not be alive if she were a surgeon."

"She and her husband serve our purposes. You need not embrace them. Or see them ever again, for that matter, I suppose."

Rainer placed his brandy snifter on the fireplace mantel and put his arms around Anna. "May I embrace you, Cousin?"

"Certainly."

"Do you plan to stay or do you intend to leave me by myself for the evening?"

"I thought you would be entertaining Lili Kraegler every night while you are here."

Rainer sighed. "I thought about how rude I was to her last year this time and had indeed thought to make it up to her. But the little slut out-trumped me. She's joined the Lebensborn at Steinhoring and is waiting to give birth to a blond, blue-eyed little *Strassenkind*. "

"Who is the father? Or does she know?" Anna asked.

"Johan Kraegler told me Lili invited some *SS Obersturmführer* from Munich to visit her several times in late spring. His name is Erich Harzner. I know him from the SS *Junkerschule*. He's a *Scheisskopf.*"

Anna snuggled close to her cousin. "Poor Rainer. You should have taken Lili when she offered herself. She could have given the Reich a colonel's son instead of one fathered by a lowly lieutenant. When is her child due?"

"Some time in February, according to Johan."

"Maybe you should come back in April and have her for yourself – before Herr Harzner comes to impregnate her again. You wouldn't want the lieutenant to receive a paycheck as large as yours before long would you?" Anna chided, knowing how much Rainer detested Himmler's policy of increasing the pay of an SS officer every time such an officer successfully fathered an *Echtdeutsch* child.

"I'm sure that by April I will have other things on my mind. More important matters."

Anna laughed. "What could be more important than fathering another soldier for the Reich?"

"Very amusing. By April there may not be a Reich."

"Such blasphemy, dear cousin! What happened to *Loyal to Death*?"

"Ask Himmler. It's his motto."

"In the end I am willing to bet Himmler will show no more loyalty to the Reich or to the *Führer* than anyone else. It will be every man for himself."

"What about women?" Rainer asked puckishly.

"You know where my loyalties reside," she said.

Rainer tapped her chest. "With Anna Stahlinger."

She kissed Rainer on his mouth, then stepped back and whispered, "Take me to bed and I will show you how unselfish I can be."

Thursday
February 15, 1945
National Gallery
Washington, D.C.

The tall, angular man at the lectern, though a civilian, wore the uniform of a lieutenant colonel in the Army. The rank, Martin had been told, was deemed *simulated* rather than *honorary*. Whatever the jargon behind his appointment, John Nicholas Brown was now going to be MFA&A's cultural advisor to General Eisenhower's staff and in charge of setting up procedures and policies for art restoration in Europe.

Martin already knew Brown was well-suited to the job. Not because he was one of the richest men in America, which he was, but due to the fact that he was an avid amateur art historian and had, in fact, participated in the restoration of Hagia Sophia, the Temple of Holy Wisdom in Istanbul. Following that experience, Brown had used his wealth to start up the Byzantine Institute of America.

Now, before heading off to London, he had come to summarize the activities of MFA&A in Italy, as well as the organization's successes in France since the Normandy landings. That done, he opened the meeting to questions.

A captain asked, "Why so many delays and obstacles? It's as if some of our own people don't want us to succeed."

"You're quite right, Captain. It does seem that way. In fact, it *is* that way, but I can't come right out and say so – to certain people, that is. Among us are a great many Philistines who don't deem our job very important." He paused to smile. "Now if someone stole the heirlooms from one such Philistine's grandmother living in Iowa, you can bet he'd be on the streets of Oskaloosa, immediately forming up a *posse comitatus* to chase the culprits down."

Martin raised his hand.

Brown looked at the seating chart in front of him. "Lieutenant Wynerson?"

"How soon before those of us sitting here get into the action?"

John Nicholas Brown locked his hands behind him and began to pace. Finally, he stopped and turned to his audience. "I don't know. It depends." Pause. "Depends on what? On whom? The answer lies with many people. As you surely have surmised by now, from living in the very bowels of politics at its best and worst, even so great a crusade, as Ike calls it, is scarcely free from disagreements. The War Department has its share of poppinjays, some of whom believe our group should be considered either a low priority or no priority at all. Without wanting to strut too much, I can only tell you, Lieutenant, that much depends on the success I achieve – or don't achieve – in London."

Martin stood and said, "We all wish you much success, Colonel," after which the entire room burst into applause.

15

Friday
February 16, 1945
Washington, D.C.

"Stop being silly."

Martin winced at Katherine's jibe in response to his suggesting they might want to take separate cabs to Katherine's hotel. As they walked toward the cab stand outside Union Station Martin muttered, "I should never have told you about Maddy's way of putting me in my place."

"Oh, stop being so sensitive, Martin." She paused. "And stop being silly."

Martin groaned.

"For God's sake, between my getting off the train and here, how many hundreds of people have seen us together already? How odd would it look to anyone who was watching us -- and nobody is -- for us to walk arm in arm all this way and then to part as though we hardly knew each other?"

"You're right."

Still uncomfortable after their shared taxi ride, Martin waited while Katherine Parker filled out the registration form at the front desk of the Hotel Lombardy. He had chosen the Lombardy because he was familiar with it. George Washington University's administration kept a block of rooms reserved there, some for visiting scholars, others to accommodate interviewees for faculty positions.

When she finished, Katherine waved off the bellboy but tipped him anyway, then looked to Martin, who carried her suitcase to the elevator. Inside the elevator she kissed Martin's cheek before saying, "I'm ecstatic to be here. You don't know how much I've missed you."

"I hope Selby won't be too disappointed … or too curious," Martin said as the elevator creaked and groaned.

"Selby was actually looking forward to having my sister and her daughter come to stay at our house for a few days. You've met Estelle haven't you? And Vivian? Vivian's the same age as Selby and they get along surprisingly well."

"You spoken of your sister, but I have yet to meet her," Martin said.

"You'd like her. She's always so cheerful. Anyway, Estelle was thrilled to be able to get away from Syracuse. Estelle's husband, Robert, is away in the Pacific somewhere. Robert's an orthopedic surgeon stationed on a hospital ship. So Estelle and Vivian moved in with Robert's mother."

"Did she or Selby believe your story?"

The elevator stopped and Martin led the way to Katherine's room. Inside, Katherine said, "Selby did. I think Estelle suspects there is more to my coming here than to see if I can find out firsthand more news about Elliott. She didn't exactly say anything, but I could tell. My sister and I have always been close and have shared most of our secrets." She looked at Martin's doubtful stare and repeated. "Most. You are not for sharing."

"Are you hungry? I didn't think to ask, I've been so amazed that you're actually here," Martin stammered.

"Hungry for you," Katherine said, putting her arms around Martin.

"Dinner and a movie first? Or later?"

"Later."

The movie came before dinner. They saw July Garland in the recent release of *Meet Me in St. Louis*, playing at the Trans-Lux Theatre on Fourteenth Street, a block from the White House. Afterwards they walked the long block to the dining room of the Hay-Adam Hotel, where the cost of dinner there strained Martin's meager resources. Later he and Katherine stood in the cold outside the hotel staring across Lafayette Park toward the White House.

In a playful mood despite the freezing weather, Katherine asked, "Shall we go across and see if the President is up for listening to our advice on how to conduct the war?"

Martin pulled his coat tighter around his neck. "He seems to be doing very nicely without our wisdom. Besides –." Martin lowered his voice as he leaned in closer to Katherine. "Besides, rumor is that he's not at home, that he's off somewhere at a conference with Churchill and Stalin so that they can hammer out the details of how the world will look after the war. But even

FDR's being out of town, let alone out of the country, is supposed to be a state secret. So don't tell anyone I told you." Then Martin added, "You're not an Axis spy I hope."

"Vat vould make you tink zat I am zum kind uf Nazi spy, Herr Wynerson?"

"Certainly not your Hudson River accent."

"Okay then. I promise not to tell Berlin or Tokyo. Let's go. I'm cold. Besides, I don't suppose Eleanor would be interested in your ideas about which Picasso or Rembrandt would look good in the Lincoln bedroom nor my opinions about how better to decorate the East Room."

"No, I suppose not."

Back in their room at the Lombardy Katherine sat on the edge of the bed and kicked off her shoes. "The war will be over soon, Martin. Don't you think?"

"It looks that way."

"What then?"

"I'm almost certain I'll be going to Europe, perhaps to join Elliott."

"I meant: What about us?"

"I don't know. It's going to be very difficult."

"Do you mean for you? Or for me?"

"Me for sure. What about you?"

Katherine bowed her head and nodded.

Martin sat on the bed beside her. "I wish we'd met long ago."

Katherine put her head on his shoulder. "Me, too. Except --."

"Except?"

"I wouldn't trade having Selby for anything else in the whole world."

Unable to think of a fitting response, Martin remained silent and held Katherine tighter.

"When you come back from Europe… what then?" she finally asked.

"I don't know. To start I'll probably return to teaching at GWU, although what I would really like is to go to Minnesota, maybe teach at a small school there. Saint Olaf's, Gustavus Adolphus, Carleton, Macalester. Or some place like them."

Katherine wiped away her tears and sat up straight. "Haven't you heard the song from World War I? 'How ya gonna keep 'em down on the farm after they've see Paree?'"

Martin laughed. "Yes, I've heard it, but I don't believe it. Minneapolis isn't exactly the farm and Washington isn't Paris, or so I suppose, having never been to Paris."

"Don't you like living in Washington?" she said.

"No. But I can see why a lot of people enjoy it, thrive on the close proximity to so much power."

"I understand that. The politics in Albany was my father's meat and drink. In fact, for ever so long I was a snob who thought there was no life worth living west of the Hudson."

"And now."

"You're from way west of the Hudson and you have a life that is definitely worth living."

"I don't know. I'm pretty boring most of the time."

"Oh, stop it. Don't be so self-deprecating."

"Maybe you can come to Minnesota some day and see for yourself firsthand that indeed people between the Hudson River and the Red River are lively, interesting people. At least many of them are. As for Beyond the Red River… well, I'm not sure. For me that's *terra incognita*. 'Here be Dragons', says my map."

"You're so funny."

"Funny hah-hah? Or funny weird?"

"Mostly hah-hah."

"What about you after all this is over, whatever *all this* eventually comes to?" Martin asked.

"Back to being a dutiful wife. Probably even a faithful wife again."

"Happily ever after? Do you think Elliott is sitting over there in Bern wearing blinders while all those Swiss milk maidens strut up and down Upgefuck Me Strasse, flaunting their pails of cream?"

"What Elliott does is his business; what I do is mine."

Martin lay back on the bed, closed his eyes, and quoted from memory.

Wem Gott will rechte Gunst erweisen,
Den shickt er in die weite Welt,
Dem will er seine Wunder weisen
In Feld und Wald und Strom und Feld.

"It sounds lovely. What does it mean?" Katherine asked, as she curled upon the bed next to Martin.

"It's from a novelette titled *Aus dem Leben eines Taugenichts* by a fellow named Joseph von Eichendorff. The title translates to *From the Life of a Good-for-Nothing*. The poem stanza translates roughly to mean: To whomever God shows favor, God sends that person into the wide world. To him – or her, I suppose – He will show His wonders, show them in fields and forests and streams."

"But not in the big cities," Katherine countered.

Martin poked her in her ribs. "Stop acting silly."

Katherine poked back. "I thought that phrase irritates you."

"I only pretend it irritates me."

"You're not a very good pretender."

"I'm not?"

Katherine shook her head. "You vould make a terrible spy, Herr Wynerson. You vould be caught in a zekund."

"Zen I von't try zat, ja?"

"Stop acting silly." Then Katherine turned serious. "Do you think someday we'll part like Bogart and Bergman? You'll put me on a plane and never see me again?"

Martin told her about the time in New York City when he imagined just that as he watched her train pull out of the station.

"'We'll always have each other.' Isn't that the line?" she asked.

"Not quite. 'We'll always have Paris' is the correct line." Martin sighed. "I dread the idea that we'll always be friends." When Katherine scowled, he said. "No wait. What I mean is, just friends. I'll go nuts if I have to spend the rest of my life only seeing you at weekend parties, seeing you and having to pretend.... pretend we're just casual acquaintances. 'How are you, Mrs. Parker? Good to see you again, Mrs. Parker. Lovely weather we're having, Mrs. Parker.'"

"I know. I dread that, too, but –."

"But what?"

"I won't leave Elliott. Well, he's not exactly here to leave, but you know what I mean." She looked away for a moment, then said, "What I really mean is, I won't leave Selby and I won't leave him fatherless. So what does that leave? Oh, that sounds stupid. Too many senses of leave. What remains is what I want to say."

"We'll always have Paris?"

"Stop it. I'm serious. I'm more than serious. I'm terrified. No, I don't want 'Hello, Mister Wynerson. Yes, the weather's been magnificent lately, Mister Wynerson. May I ask the maid to refresh your drink, Mister Wynerson?'"

"I wish I were the boy next door and you were Judy Garland. That worked out better than Bogart and Bergman," Martin said.

"Yes, but we're pretenders in a different script, Martin, and I'm afraid there is no happily-ever-after ending."

"Then let's continue ad-libbing more script and maybe we'll never get to the end."

The next day Martin took Katherine to the National Gallery. "Have you been here before?" he asked her.

"Only once. Elliott brought me here several years ago."

Martin hoped she would not notice how much the collections had changed. When the war began many of the most prized and valuable paintings had been quietly removed and taken to the Biltmore Estate in Asheville, North Carolina for safekeeping; lesser paintings were hung in their stead and galleries rearranged to mask the removals. Patrons and visitors were fed a sequence of fibs and obfuscations meant to disguise the real reasons for many famous and popular works' absence.

That many of the National Gallery's works were stashed for the war's duration remained classified, so Martin couldn't share the state secret with Katherine. "Let me show you where I work. Or did work," Martin said, taking Katherine by an elbow and leading her down a flight of stairs to his former work space.

"Did?"

"Until recently my assignment was to pinpoint likely places in Bavaria and north central Austria where the Nazis would cache their massive art collections, as the Allied vise squeezed them – the Nazis, that is – into a smaller and smaller space." Martin unfolded his large map and showed Katherine his markings. "Monasteries and salt mines are favored. Your husband, by the way, is responsible for pinpointing the Nazi's most important site, a huge salt mine in Austria, southeast of Salzburg. It's called Alt Aussee.'

"How did Elliott find it?" Katherine asked.

"Actually *he* didn't, but his primary German spy gave him the name and location."

"Elliott is working with a German spy?" Katherine's look of astonishment unnerved Martin for a moment.

"It's top secret. Don't tell anyone. Even me," Martin said, grinning. "Not a spy exactly. More of a collaborator. Your husband has managed to convince a German art expert to work with us, to feed us information about the flow of art the Nazis have looted. Elliott's *coup* is really quite spectacular." Martin took a deep breath. "I'm not supposed to be telling you this, so please don't speak of it to anyone."

"I've seen the poster. *Keep mum. She's not so dumb.*"

"Assure me again. You're not a German spy are you, Katherine?" Martin said, feigning shock.

"The last time I looked I wasn't."

"Whew!"

"How did Elliott manage such a *coup*, as you call it?" Katherine asked.

"Nobody knows, but the information he's getting is genuine. We know nothing about the collaborator, other than his code name is *Grauergeist*. But we've cross-referenced his information with several other sources and everything he feeds us is accurate. Well, I shouldn't say us. Elliott is the hero here. The sole hero."

"My God, Martin. I thought my husband was just an art professor. Now you tell me he's some sort of … what are they called? Spymasters?"

"I'm not sure working with one collaborator makes him a spymaster. Control officer is the more usual term we use."

"So. When you go overseas what will be your duties? Dealing with art or with spies?"

"Some of each. Because I speak fluent German I've been shifted to what is being called 'Special Operations'. That means I will be interrogating all kinds of people regarding what they know about missing works of art. I'm told I may find myself questioning SS generals at one moment and museum janitors the next. I must assume no one placed in front of me for interrogation is ignorant of what happened. The scale of art theft has been so vast that no one within territories at one time held by the Reich can be uninformed. Everybody knows something."

"But some know more than others," Katherine said.

"Definitely! And those are the ones we'll be –" Martin held out both hands and slowly made them into tight fists.

———————

Friday
February 16, 1945
Berlin

An icy northwesterly wind prompted Rainer to adjust the collar of his greatcoat tighter around his neck as he and Karl descended the steps of SS headquarters. As they reached the bottom step a Mercedes stopped in front of them and a man of Rainer's rank emerged from the rear seat. Sour-faced, looking drained, his eyes sunken, the man nonetheless straightened himself when he saw Rainer and extended his right arm briskly. Rainer and Karl were both slow to react, but finally each slowly responded, raising their own right arms, each muttering a tepid *"Heil Hitler"*. The other's man's eyes narrowed and he started to speak, but apparently thought better of it and continued on past them up the steps.

As they crossed Niederkirchner Strasse toward Potsdam Platz Karl looked over his shoulder before saying, "I don't like that man."

"Him or his work?" Rainer asked.

"Neither. I'd go mad if I had to serve under him."

"Many men have indeed gone mad carrying out Colonel Eichmann's orders."

"I've heard the stories," Karl said glumly.

"The stories you haven't heard about him are even grimmer."

"Then spare me."

Minutes later Rainer and Karl, each bending forward against the cutting headwind, reached the protection of the Prussian Chamber of Deputies. Staring up at the massive, grayish green columns, Karl allowed, "This is an ugly building but at least it serves as a good shield against the wind."

Rainer smiled. "I know. You would prefer to think of the Prussians legislating beneath a thatched roof, with cows, goats, chickens, and pigs grunting, braying, and squawking beneath them on the ground floor."

"Since when has sitting in a fancy building improved men's governing?" Karl asked.

"Political architecture must project power, Karl."

"Grandeur isn't power."

"But it is the necessary face of power."

"Or so politicians imagine."

"No, Karl. So we *all* imagine. Try to picture the *Führer's* Nuremburg rallies held on a hillside among vineyards instead of in a grand stadium. Not the same."

"Christ spoke to the multitudes from a hillside," Karl pointed out.

"Yes. And Jesus Christ became simply another failed politician. Just one more Jewish troublemaker – one who was disposed of easily."

Karl stared at Rainer in disbelief.

"It's true. Think about it. He died a failure. Success has come to those who figured out how to use him as a symbol of power, a symbol like this building. A grand edifice to mask peasant ideas. Buildings are important political tools, Karl. Thus buildings like this; thus great cathedrals."

Karl snorted. "Greek columns in Berlin. They're ugly."

"The eye of the beholder, Karl. To many people the Christian cross is merely an unimaginitive symbol of mass Roman terror;

to Christians it is a symbol of beauty, and even more powerful than their architecture. Choosing the cross as their symbol is Christianity's crowning genius because its clever misuse as an ultimate gesture of sacrificial martyrdom alone resurrected an otherwise failed Christ. Without it, Christians would be one more long-forgotten cult, remembered as an historical footnote only for having entertained blood-thirsty Roman crowds.

"Certainly their theology hasn't made them a power to be reckoned with, because it isn't worth the scrolls its scribbled on. Utterly selfish and mean-spirited. Not that I think selfishness entirely immoral. But to make an eternal reward depend on one's assenting to a precise set of confusing propostions? How preposterous! And perpetual torture for all those who fail to assent – fail regarding even *one* of their claims? Heretics and infidels *all* up in flames. Christians would burn us all for the slightest misstep. And that, my dear Karl, makes Eichmann's burning Jews seem like a small sideshow by comparison."

Karl Vollmer stood listening blankly at his *Standartenführ's* malicious soliloquy, not comprehending. Nor wanting to.

Inside the Chamber of Deputies, Rainer paused, looked around, then proceeded down the corridor to his left until he came to the Marc painting. From behind him he heard Karl whisper, "You're going to find a way to take it, aren't you?"

"Eventually. Yes."

"It's too big."

"Too big to hide under my greatcoat? Yes. It measures 200cm by 130cm."

"How?" Karl asked.

Just then another voice. "Ah, Colonel Zeitz. Back again to admire *The Tower*."

Rainer turned. "I see you've kept it safe for me, Herr Petschke."

The security man gave an of-course shrug. "You're not going to take it from me, are you?"

Karl flinched, alarmed.

Calmly, Rainer said, "I don't think the *Führer* has a place for it in Linz. So far as I know, no one else covets it either. So I leave it in your good hands, Herr Petschke. Guard it well, as you have done thus far."

"Thank you, Colonel."

"Any further word on your youngest son?"

The security man lowered his gaze and shook his head slowly. "You are kind to ask."

On his previous visit Rainer had learned that Petschke's twenty-year-old son, Horst, came up missing during the Wehrmacht's December counter-offensive against the Americans in the Ardennes. A gunner on one of Sepp Dietrich's panzers, the young man was not among the dead crew found in the burned out Tiger tank. "With luck he will turn up among the wounded or captured."

Rudolph Petschke nodded, but it was clear to Rainer that the man was doubtful any such luck would touch his son. "So many have died, Colonel. So many."

And for what? you are thinking. Rainer stepped forward and put his hand on the man's shoulder. "You can be proud of your son, I'm sure."

"Pride. Yes. I have that. It's something." He turned and walked away slowly, head still bowed.

When the security man was out of sight Karl sighed in relief. "I thought he had overheard us."

"Perhaps he did, but he wouldn't have figured out what we really meant. Herr Petschke merely supposes I am as fanatical about saving paintings as Eichmann is about exterminating Jews."

"Aren't you?" Karl said, smirking.

"Occasionally. The man is right. Pride."

Monday
February 19, 1945
Washington, D.C.

The weekend passed quickly for Martin. On Saturday, after lolling in bed until nearly ten o'clock, he and Katherine had walked to Woolworth's. There they competed to buy as many quality gifts for each other as the agreed-upon maximum of three dollars each allowed. By the time Martin had selected half a dozen lace doilies, a bud vase, and a pair of candleholders Katherine came up to him and declared herself the winner of their contest, having bought a picture frame, a pair of salt & pepper shakers, a rooster coffee cup, and a new wallet – with sixty-three cents left over. Martin had conceded with reluctance, given that the loser, by agreement, had to buy two blue-plate specials at the lunch counter.

Saturday night they had taken a taxi to the Georgetown University gymnasium, where the USO had hired a local swing band to provide dance music courtesy of Duke Ellington, Glen Miller, and Tommy Dorsey hits. Martin's agile footwork had surprised Katherine. "In Minnesota it's polka, polka, polka from the time you're four years old," he explained when she asked the source of his nimbleness.

Sunday they made love until noon, then ordered room service. Afterwards they strolled the entire length of the Mall from the Washington Monument to the Lincoln Memorial and back, holding hands and kissing frequently in the thin shade of winter-barren cherry trees.

"Sometimes I wish this war would never end," she had said to him as they stood staring up at the chiseled statue of the man who had welded the fractures along the Mason-Dixon Line, though it was a salvation of unity achieved as much by grapeshot as by reason. Lucky for the losers, Martin reminded himself, because they had failed miserably to calculate the slippery slope toward total anarchy embedded in their separatist logic.

"Come on, Katherine. You don't really wish for a second that the war should never end and neither does anyone else."

"You're right. What I meant was: I wish *we* would never end."

"We won't."

"We will. In all in the important senses."

Katherine decided to stay until Tuesday, saying she wanted to visit a pair of long-time girlfriends while Martin went to work. She thought it best not to introduce them to Martin, who said he understood. So Martin was sitting at his basement table, examining reconnaissance photos of the Austrian Abbey at Hohenweiler when he heard a familiar voice behind him.

"May I interrupt you, Martin?" Father Troquier asked.

Martin turned. "Of course, Father. You're always welcome. How good to see you again."

"The Germans are moving underground and south, not so?"

"Their Alpine Redoubt."

"Rats abandoning a sinking ship."

"Except in Berlin."

"Ah, yes. The rat captain will not abandon his bridge," Troquier opined.

"I'd love to be in the vanguard that marches into Berlin," Martin allowed.

"Alas, your mother didn't suckle you in Siberia."

Martin closed his eyes for a moment, reopened them, and said, "I wouldn't want to be a German in Berlin when the Russians arrive."

"Stop feeling sorry for Berliners. The Russians will give them all exactly what they deserve."

"The Russians will brutalize them; crush them like so many fire ants."

Father Troquier smiled. "Yes, they will."

"You approve."

"I believe the American phrase is: Hanging's too good for them."

Martin nodded, slightly embarrassed.

"Christianity sanctions -- no revels in -- perpetual torture, but perpetual torture is too good for Nazis. We must invent a nastier end for them than eternity in hell."

"What can be worse than perpetual torture?" Martin asked.

"Physical agonies are nothing compared to horrors of the imagination. The history of Christian punishment against heretics, even during the Inquisition, is simple-minded compared with all the iron-fisted possibilities available. The Church has never been brutal enough. The only good German is a screaming German."

Martin winced.

"You talk of fire ants. Yes. Stake every German out on a hill of fire ants. Tie them all up and toss them into rooms full of hungry rats. Bury them alive."

"You risk becoming as evil as they are," Martin said.

Troquier bristled. "No! They have earned the hell I wish on them. Earned it in spades, as you Americans say."

Martin shook his head. "I'm sorry, but I don't share your sense of justice, Father."

The priest gestured toward an empty chair next to Martin, then sat down. In his soft voice he asked Martin, "You have a sister?"

Martin nodded.

"You parents are alive?"

Another nod.

"German soldiers raped my younger sister; made my parents watch. Afterwards, the German officer in charge cut all their throats."

"Who lived to tell?"

"My crippled older sister. The Germans let her live so she could spread the word about what happens to members of the Resistance."

"I'm sorry," Martin mumbled.

"Don't be. My family was defiant to the end."

"Still, how devastating for you."

"Yes and no. During the First World War the English playwright Bernard Shaw penned a line in his play *Heartbreak House:*

Courage will not save you, but it will show that your souls are still alive."

"I understand," Martin whispered.

Father Troquier scooted his chair closer to Martin. "So tell me, Martin. Are you really up to the task of interrogating Germans?"

"I think so. My training has been quite thorough."

Troquier laughed. "Convince me you can break men and women well-practiced at lying to you with straight faces."

"I will assume all of them are lying all of the time until convinced otherwise."

Troquier nodded. "A start. But these people are all accomplished liars. They've done nothing else for years. They even lie to themselves convincingly."

"So I've been told."

Troquier removed a cigarette from his cassock and lit it without asking Martin's permission. After inhaling, he blew smoke into Martin's face. "They will show you nothing but contempt."

Martin reached out, gently took the cigarette away, crushed it in his hand, then crumbled the tobacco onto the priest's lap. With a fixed stare, he said, "So I've been told."

Troquier gave him an appreciative smile, before saying, "You'll do well with the Germans, but what about closer to home?"

"Meaning?"

"I hope you've figured out that Katherine Parker is merely using you."

Martin struggled not to explode. "Using me?"

"To avenge herself for her husband's affairs in Switzerland."

Martin stared blankly at the priest.

"Yes. An important part of Elliott's assignment in Bern is to seduce women in order to pry information from them that might be useful to the Allied cause. I'm told he's been quite successful at that particular task. A young secretary at the Swiss Foreign Office has been especially forthcoming."

"And Katherine knows?" Martin asked in a low voice.

"Yes. Of course. He tells her." Troquier lit another cigarette. "There have been others. Elliott G. Parker, I'm told, is considered quite a lady's man among Swiss Misses."

"You make it sound as though they are lined up to bed him," Martin said.

"Perhaps they are."

Martin bristled at the priest's smirk. "How do you know so much?"

Troquier stared at the ash on his cigarette. "I'm sure you have already concluded that I am more than a mere art professor and priest, *Monsieur*."

"What more?"

"Specifically, I cannot say. But you may surmise."

Art professor, priest, and an insufferably pretentious prick, Martin thought.

"So what leads you to suppose Katherine Parker is merely using me?"

"She has said so."

Martin suddenly felt numb. "To you?"

"Of course not. I am not her confessor. I apologize that I am not allowed to reveal my sources, but trust me."

Sources. Plural. He's bluffing. No, worse. He's lying. "Suppose I tell you that Katherine and I are nothing more than good friends?"

"Hotel receipts and a portfolio of photographs do more than suggest otherwise."

Bastard! "Where do you get off collecting --?"

Troquier held up a hand to silence Martin. "In time of war no one's behavior is exempt from scrutiny."

Spying on anybody, any time is okay in the name of national security. How close we've come to mirroring Nazi Germany, Martin thought. Wanting ever so much to give Father Troquier a "*Sieg Heil*" salute, Martin refrained. "So you've been spying on me at Elliott's request?"

"Not at all."

"On his wife?"

"No. Things simply came to my attention."

"And you avidly pursued them."

"Reluctantly."

Martin gave the priest his best you're-a-bald-faced-liar look.

Troquier held up both hands, as if in surrender. "Please, understand my position, Martin. Information came to me that Katherine Parker had made you her lover. As a priest, my duty is to condemn such behavior as a mortal sin against God's commandments. On the other hand, as a Frenchman --." He gave Martin a classic Gallic shrug. " -- I understand."

"But still feel obliged to pass along your... observations."

Troquier nodded.. "I care for your safety. So I think it my duty to warn you."

"Against what?"

"You work for Elliott. Important work. Your work is vital to the outcome of the war. The outcome of the post-war. Don't let Elliott down, your country down."

The priest spelled out his implications. That his affair with Katherine distracted from the war effort in three ways: (1) by siphoning off security personnel to follow him and Elliott's wife when they might be engaged in tracking real enemies of the state; (2) his dalliances might have interfered with Martin's concentration on his war work, (3) that knowledge of his wife's retaliation may have hampered Elliott's own best efforts at achieving maximum results from his Swiss sexual entrapments.

"For want of a nail," Martin whispered when the priest finished. "Nazis conquer the world, thanks to Hudson River socialite's seducing a Minnesota hick."

"You underestimate yourself, Martin."

"And you've blown all of this entirely out of proportion."

"Have I?"

"Yes. Now please leave. You're interfering with my concentration on my war work."

Troquier stood.

"I can't believe you actually had Katherine and me followed."

Troquier gave Martin another Gallic shrug. "If you and Katherine sleep with each other, perhaps next one or both of you will be seduced by German spies."

"You're sick."

"No. Cautious."

"Sick."

"Reflect carefully on what I've said, Martin. But wait until the shock has worn off. You'll see more clearly then."

"I'm sure I will."

Martin waited until the priest had gone to snap a pencil in two and hurl it at the door, hitting an incoming corporal.

The corporal smiled. "Bull's eye, Lieutenant. Or am I not the intended target?"

Martin made a face, then shook his head. "Sorry."

The corporal jerked a thumb in the direction of the departed priest. "Surely you're not angry at the padre. I thought he was your friend."

Nodding, Martin said, "You are correct. He was."

In their hotel room that night Katherine Parker sat in a winged chair beside their bed and toyed with her nightgown. Martin sprawled on the bed and stared at the ceiling. "Troquier is a bastard," she said sharply. "Not that that is news to anyone." She giggled. "He's even a bastard literally, according to rumor. In any case, he's carried on that tradition in high fashion."

Martin raised himself on an elbow and looked at Katherine. "Really?"

"Two children by two different women. Maybe more. The man is shameless," she said.

"Do you know about what happened to his family in France?" Martin said.

"I've heard the rumors. I'm not sure but what he didn't invent the tale in order to make himself pitiable, all the easier to pull off some of his seamier stunts, like throwing our liaison in your face."

"So what about us?" Martin said, getting to the point of his petulance. "Now that we've been exposed."

"Do you want it... us... to be over?"

"No."

"Nor I." She reached out and stroked Martin's face. "I mean that."

"Do you think Father Troquier has told Elliott?"

"He wouldn't dare."

"Why not?"

"He just wouldn't. Trust me."

"Did you know about Elliott's affairs?"

"Yes. Elliott told me. Confessed in a letter."

"Were you shocked?"

"Shocked? No. Dismayed? Yes. Especially the way he went about it. His letter dripped with guilt. You'd think he was talking to a priest in a confessional. But he penned his own absolution. Duty, duty, duty, in one of those close-your-eyes-and-think-of-England kinds of explanations for why he was doing what he was doing."

"Did you believe him?" Martin asked.

"Not for a second." She grinned. "Well, maybe for one whole second, but not for two."

"Not duty then?"

"Duty? Bah! Yes, he was fucking some high level secretary in the Swiss Foreign Office. Pumping her for information, as I like to imagine. But I scarcely believe he found the project distasteful. Pump, pump, pump." She stood and began thrusting her hips obscenely.

"You're angry with him."

"Of course, I am. Whether for God and country or any other high-minded reason, the breaking of the monogamous pact in marriage is the greatest betrayal a husband or wife can commit."

"Then why us?"

"Perhaps the bastard priest is right after all. 'Revenge is mine' sayeth Katherine Parker."

"So where do we go from here?" Martin said.

"That's easy. I go back to New York; you go back to hunting Nazi art caches."

"You know what I mean."

"Remember? You're suppose to say something along the line of 'We'll always have Paris'."

"Okay. We'll always have Lake Saranac," Martin said, trying to imitate Bogart.

Katherine smiled. "Yes, we will."

"Somehow I don't feel any better."

Katherine then slid onto the bed beside Martin. "This is not the end of us. You don't want that; I don't want it. Leave Troquier to me."

"He's a powerful man."

"Only in a twisted way. One reason he's not back in France is that even the French Resistance can't trust him entirely. He knows a great deal, but he talks too freely. I know how to put him in his place."

"How?"

"Father Roskosz."

"How so?"

"The Pole is as conservative as Troquier is licentious. If Father Theodosius were pope, we'd all be burned as heretics, anti-Nazi or not. The Poles trust no one and rightfully so. The whole world is out to get them."

"Now wait. The British were willing to go to war for them after Hitler invaded them," Martin responded.

"Only for their own selfish reasons, or so the Poles assume," Katherine said.

"So how will Father Roskosz contain Troquier?"

"The same way any dog owner reins in an over-exuberant dog. Jerk on his chain until he sits."

Martin shook his head. "The relationship between the two men hasn't struck me as that of dog-owner to high-spirited puppy."

"Believe me. When Father Roskosz says 'Heel', Jean-Pierre Troquier obeys."

"Lucky us. Or so I hope."

In a corner of a noisy, jam-packed Union Station Martin stood with his back to a pillar, his eyes closed, his arms embracing Katherine. "You'll come back?" he whispered.

"I promise," she whispered back and kissed him hard on the lips.

"Well, well, well," came a familiar voice. "Sweet sorrow made to taste even sweeter."

They broke their clutch and turned to see David Fox grinning at them, his duffle bag slung over his right arm, a folded newspaper in his left hand, his Navy dress hat cocked jauntily at an angle. He had obviously just stepped off the inbound train from New York, the train Katherine would board soon for the trip back home.

"Weren't you due in yesterday?" Martin said. "I missed you at work this morning."

"Delays, delays," Fox shrugged. "But nothing so worthy of delay as a beautiful woman to cuddle. Hello, Mrs. Parker. I'd ask how you are, but that is evident."

"Hello, David," Katherine said, dabbing at her lips with an index finger.

Fox stepped closer and peered at her. "No smudges, Ma'am." Pointing to Martin's cheek, he said, "Can't say the same for you, Martin."

Martin started to wipe his cheek, but Katherine beat him to it. "I'm about to see Katherine off. Same train you arrived on apparently."

To Martin Fox said, "Can't convince her to stay? Too bad." To Katherine, "Washington is such a fabulous town. Did you get to see much of it?"

"Quite a lot, actually," she said.

"I'm sure Martin was a great guide. He's learned a great deal since coming here from the Great North Woods. Haven't you, Martin?"

"More than you imagine, David," Martin said, trying to minimize sounding scornful.

"I assume you've kept up with the latest war news," Fox said.

"Which news?" Martin and Katherine spoke simultaneously.

"Today's news. We've reach the Rhine; the Russians have reached the Oder; fires are raging in Dresden worthy of hell itself. We hit Dresden just like we did Hamburg."

"The war will soon be over," Katherine said.

"I hope so. How about you two?" Fox gave them an exaggerated wink.

"Whatever brings my husband home," Katherine said solemnly.

"Don't know about that. I'm under the impression Martin and I will be joining Elliott as soon as the fighting stops. Maybe sooner, eh Martin?"

"Maybe."

"You do still want to go, don't you, ol' buddy? The fix isn't in for you to stay behind, is it?"

"I'll be right there with you," Martin assured him.

"Great! Need someone I can trust to cover my backside." With a shoulder-shift Fox readjusted his duffle and said, "Must run along. It's been an exhausting weekend for me, too. See you later, Martin. Hope your trip home is uneventful, Mrs. Parker." Turning on a heel, he trudged off.

Martin and Katherine watched him until he disappeared into the crowd.

"Can you handle him, too?" Martin asked when she turned back to face him.

"I don't know." She tried to mask her angst but failed. "Can you?"

16

Thursday
March 8, 1945
Schloß Ziethen

Rainer's summons to a private audience with Heinrich Himmler came unexpectedly. Karl drove a Kugelwagon to Orienburg, then turned toward the town of Kremmen in the Brandenburg countryside and soon found Ziethen Castle.

The *Reichsleiter* kept Rainer waiting for half an hour before receiving him. A *Herrenhaus*, a manor house, in the style of the English, Himmler's retreat was inordinately drafty, Rainer thought. No wonder Himmler always looks so pale and sickly. Finally, a maid ushered him into a large office, where the head of SS sat on the edge of a desk with a broken chair turned upside down on top of it. Blinking as though his pince-nez glasses were ill-fitted to him, Himmler surveyed *Standartenführer* Zeitz as if he were a curious piece of sculpture. The rhythmic tap of the man's riding crop against his palm was the only sound in the room.

From years of listening to others' stories, Rainer was well aware of the sadistic little games Himmler liked to play with his subordinates. But he gave the *Reichsleiter* no cause to stretch out the ordeal. He stood at attention, eyes fixed on a spider crawling along the top of a dust-covered filing cabinet. The tapping of the crop reminded Rainer of *Feldmarschall* Göring, sifting his bagful of diamonds from one hand to the other.

Finally Himmler asked, "What do you think of the idea of moving some of our works of art, some of our most important German cultural treasures, to Sweden for safe keeping?"

Is this a trap? Rainer wondered. "I think it highly dangerous," he finally allowed.

"More dangerous than leaving them here in the Fatherland?" Himmler snapped back loudly.

"Mines provide excellent shelter."

"But what good are mines if the Allies are camped at all the entrances?"

"The Allies also control the airspace above the Baltic," Rainer said.

Himmler smiled. "But they won't shoot at what they can't see. U-boats are what I have in mind. Tell me such a plan will work."

Rainer gave Himmler a well-perhaps look. "What will the Swedes say?"

"I am dealing with them already."

Ah, yes, Rainer thought. Rumors circled in Berlin that Himmler had been making unofficial peace overtures to the Allies via the Swedes, was in contact with Count Bernadotte, nephew of King Gustav V, and also vice-chairman of the Swedish Red Cross. The latter fact made Rainer again suspicious. Had the Sundstrums betrayed him? "How do the Swedes intend to treat German-owned works of art once they land on Swedish soil?"

"They will recognize their Reich ownership and hold them for safekeeping."

Fact? Or wishful thinking? No matter, Rainer decided – except in the case of those paintings I possess. "Are you dealing with the Swedish government or with private Swedes?" Rainer asked.

"Officials at the highest level."

"And my role?"

Himmler stood and began to pace, now slapping the crop against a knee. "I want you to go to Kiel, Lübeck and Rostock. Make certain each port can handle shipments from Berlin as quickly as possible. Leave immediately. Time is vital."

"How am I to deal with the *Kriegsmarine*?" Rainer asked.

Himmler walked to the desk, withdrew a folder from a side drawer, and handed the folder to Rainer. The folder was marked *Streng Geheim*. Top Secret.

No wonder he chose to see me here, rather than in Berlin, Rainer mused.

"Even *Grossadmiral* Rader cannot countermand these orders," Himmler shouted as he slapped the folder with his riding crop, nearly knocking the folder from Rainer's hand.

But the realities of the war may be sufficient to countermand them, Rainer thought. Allied bombing had severely crippled the three major Baltic seaports. Where am I going to find idle

U-boats? he wondered. Still, this assignment can serve my own purpose, he decided.

"I shall leave for Kiel immediately," Rainer announced and snapped off a smart "*Heil Hitler.*"

"I want to hear from you within five days – in person, *Standartenführer*. And I want assurances that my plan will succeed."

"Yes, *Reichsleiter*. I shall find a way."

Himmler let out a sigh. "I knew I could count on you. You have always succeeded in these matters when others have failed."

In more ways than you will ever know, Rainer thought, and quickly took his leave.

Thursday
March 8, 1945
Washington, D.C.

"You're too modest, Herr Schmidt. Your position in Dusseldorf consisted, not of being a reference librarian at the city library, but, rather of serving as one of the primary curators of the Dusseldorf Museum of Art, not so?"

"No, no, no. You clearly have me confused with someone else," the small, gray-haired man across the interrogation table from Martin Wynerson insisted.

"Ah! Someone else. Yes, perhaps I have you confused with a man named Gerhard Roegner. Do you know a man by that name?" Martin asked.

The small man shrugged. "The name is not familiar to me."

Martin opened a manila file folder and made a show of rummaging through it. "Um. Here it is. Let me acquaint you with Herr Roegner. I just happen to have a set of photos of the man, excellent photos taken of him by one of his colleagues." Martin turned the photos and pushed them toward the man. "Tell me, Herr Schmidt. Do you have a twin brother?"

"Excellent, excellent, Martin. Perfect, in fact." The praise came from Edgar Weiss, a Jew who had served with the Weimar government and whose brother owned an art gallery in Essen that had been shut by the Nazis in 1936. Weiss now hired himself out to MFA&A as advisor on interrogation techniques. He also had been an interrogator in the German Army in World War I.

"Thank you, Eric. You may go," Weiss said to the man who had played the role of Gerhard Roegner.

Alone with Martin, Weiss admonished, "Never forget, Martin, that the men you will be dealing with are not only accomplished liars, but often pathological liars. They will deny everything you throw at them to the bitter end."

"And what constitutes *the bitter end*, Herr Weiss?"

"You throw them in a cell, then throw away the key."

Martin nodded, from respect more than understanding. "Does incarceration get them to tell the truth?" Martin asked.

Weiss sighed. "Seldom, in my experience. With the high-end Nazis expect very little. True believers are always tough to crack. Whatever they believe in. They tend to stick together; always assume the gods will intervene on their behalf; never recognize failure. For them total collapse is deemed a mere temporary setback."

Martin nodded that he understood.

"But when you are dealing with those who simply have been swept up in events that overwhelm them, events they have little personal stake in, then your chances of breaking their wills increase significantly. Such people will frequently respond to hard-edged sympathy toward their plights. Make them aware they are helpless, their fate hopeless unless they cooperate. A gentle reminder that the gods have abandoned them and you are their only hope can sometimes turn the weakest among them. One the other hand, giving them no sympathy whatsoever and instead reminding them, if applicable, that circumstances warrant their being shot often works just as well. What one man will grab at, considering it the last straw of his salvation, will stiffen another man's sagging spine. Only experience, I'm afraid, will teach you to smell out what will break a man – giving him a small sense of hope or giving him a sense of no hope at all.

On the walk back to his apartment, Martin pondered his own sense of weakness. Edgar Weiss had now served as his mentor for three weeks and, though Edgar had offered Martin nothing but encouragement, Martin remembered vividly his first meeting with Weiss.

"Are you tough enough to succeed at this assignment, Herr Wynerson?"

"I think I am, sir."

"You think? Just give me yes or no."

"Yes."

"Your background tells me otherwise."

Friday
March 9, 1945
Oranienburg
Ruppiner Kanal

Worried about Allied attack fighters, Karl had talked Rainer into taking a pair of motorcycles rather than a car. Now Karl signaled to Rainer that he had to stop to pee.

"Too much coffee, Karl?" Rainer asked.

"When was the last time we had coffee?" Karl muttered as he unzipped his trousers and let a stream of piss pour down toward the canal.

"The same morning we had real butter and marmalade on our toast," Rainer answered.

"Humph! That was so long ago I don't remember."

"Hey! You uncivilized bastard! If I want to shower under a waterfall, I'll pick my own waterfall, thank you very much." The voice came from a woman standing on a barge moored under the bridge.

Karl and Rainer both had to lean over the bridge railing to see her shaking her fist at them.

"I bet my piss is cleaner than that sewer scum you're floating on," Karl shouted down to her.

Rainer put his hand on Karl's shoulder. "Ease up." To the woman he called out, "I apologize for my uncouth friend." He saw that she was dressed in rags, a filthy yellow bandana on her head. Whether she was young or old, he could only guess. The war had ravaged most young German women's looks, try as they might to preserve their youthful appearance.

She shouted back, "If you're so full of piss, go aim it at the Russians. Or are you running away from them, too?"

"We are on Reich business," Karl said sharply.

"Liar! You're cowards, running away. I've seen dozens just like you for days now. Saving yourselves and leaving good German women to be raped and murdered by Russian soldiers. You have no shame, no pride, no honor. The rats that live on my barge have more courage and principle than the likes of you."

"Watch your tongue, woman," Karl shouted angrily.

"Why should I? What will you do? Shoot me? Go on. Shoot. Do me a favor. Spare me a Russian dick up my ass, then a Russian bullet through my brain."

"Come, Karl. You only fuel her bitterness."

"She called us cowards!"

"And nothing we can do or say will alter her opinion. Let angry women vent – but from afar."

They stopped to rest and refuel in Wittenburg, eating crusty sandwiches of cheese and liverwurst Karl had requisitioned from the commissary in Berlin. From his saddlebag Karl produced a bottle of Riesling.

Dropping wearily to the ground under the shade of a roadside elm tree, Rainer said, "Oh ho! What kitchen corporal did you steal that from?"

"Black market. A pair of *Hauptsturmführers* named Schlee and Uhlmann, both in Klinghoffer's group. They claim they can provide anything anyone wants. I don't know how, but --"

"Who cares? Open the bottle and hope they didn't sell you vinegar."

Karl feigned feeling insulted.

"Or maybe your own piss!" Rainer said.

"No. The barge woman is drinking that."

"I feel sorry for her."

Karl gave Rainer a puzzled look.

"No. Not for that reason. I'm saddened to know she's right. The Russians will rape her. Then, if she's lucky, they'll kill her."

"I hope you're wrong," Karl said glumly. After opening the wine and pronouncing it drinkable, he said, "I still think this trip of ours is a clever trap set up by Herr Himmler."

"You worry too much, Karl. I happen to know that Himmler's aide, *Oberstgruppenführer* Wolff, has made a secret visit to Bern, where he tried to arrange a separate peace with the British and Americans – on *Reichsleiter* Himmler's behalf."

"Can Himmler do that?" Karl asked, after swallowing a mouthful of wine.

"Not without the *Führer's* permission, which I doubt he has."

"How do you find such things out?" Karl asked.

"Anna."

"How does Anna come to know such things?" Karl asked.

"Anna knows everything, dear Karl. Anna could set God Himself straight on things she knows that God has yet to discover."

Karl crossed himself at Rainer's blasphemy.

"Anna claims to be privy to every whisper in Bern. And, closer to the truth, is that it is the Swiss who know everything. No doubt when we get to heaven, Karl, we'll discover God is a Swiss bureaucrat and His son is a banker."

Karl gave no indication of being amused. "So how does an unofficial inquiry by Himmler to the Western Allies mean the *Reichsleiter* is not setting us up?"

"Himmler is looking for a way out. For himself. Sooner than later Himmler himself will be one of those the barge woman sees crossing over her bridge, fleeing Berlin, fleeing the Fatherland. Oh yes, Himmler plans for us to move his private art collection for him. But trust me. Himmler himself won't be far behind us, if the art transfer is successful."

"So taking his art to Sweden is a test."

Rainer nodded. "I think so."

"What about our own art works?" Karl said.

"Too dangerous now. We must be more patient than Himmler. After all, I don't think the *Kriegsmarine* will permit us a U-boat for our own purposes. And a surface crossing now would be suicide. Do you think Schlee and Uhlmann can provide us with a U-boat?"

Karl laughed.

Rainer took the wine bottle from Karl. "You said they could procure anything. Maybe they have a U-boat hidden in the Ruppiner Kanal, submerged beneath the angry woman's barge."

Karl grabbed back the Riesling. "Too much wine for you."

"Perhaps we could crawl into the bottle, when it's empty, and float to Sweden."

"You're mad, not drunk," Karl said.

"Only the mad will survive the coming days, Karl. And not *all* of them."

"Do we really have to return to Berlin? Can't we simply disappear? Hide out at the farm?"

"Yes, we will disappear and hide at the farm. But we must return to Berlin first. Himmler has not set a trap for us, but that doesn't mean he trusts us. I'm sure our moves are being monitored. Loosely perhaps, but monitored. If we fail to show up in Kiel, other SS will hunt us down. The same if we fail to return to Berlin. But don't worry. I have plans. Complicated. Too unwieldy maybe. But our plight is beyond anything simple or simplistic."

Suddenly Karl jumped to his feet. "Listen! Come! Farther away from the road." He grabbed Rainer by the tunic collar and began pulling.

"What is it?"

"Allied fighters. Flying low."

Rainer listened and heard the engines, several of them, humming like a swarm of bees. Then a different sound, soft, staccato, followed by explosions somewhere in the direction of the road toward Kiel. He and Karl both flattened themselves on the ground until the air was still.

Karl was the first to sit up. "Aren't you glad we ride the bikes? In a car, we would --." He shook his head, thinking the remainder of his remark too obvious to bother uttering.

The strafing took Rainer's thoughts back to being shot off the motorcycle in Kiev. Instinctively he touched his old wound. "Yes, the bikes were a good idea, Karl." This time. But not always.

"And your own bike, even. Better than a ride in a sidecar, like the trip from Tallin to Gatchina Palace, eh?"

"Yes. Better." Humor him now, Rainer thought. Little does he know what is in store for him on his return trip from Kiel to Berlin.

Friday
March 9, 1945
New York City
Grand Central Station

After hugging Martin tightly, clinging to him, Katherine let go at last and took a step backward, holding out both trembling hands. "Look at me. I'm like an alcoholic at last call ordering up a final drink. I had to see you, Martin. I want one for the road."

Martin pulled her to him. "I know. I understand. I'm here. I'm yours."

"I'm sorry you had to come here to New York, but I just couldn't bring myself to go to Washington."

"Have you avenged yourself on Father Troquier yet?" Martin asked as the walked down the concourse toward taxi row.

"I turned the tables on the bastard. I told Father Roskosz that I heard on good authority that Marcel Troquier has been sleeping with several women, one of whom is a suspected Nazi sympathizer."

"Is that true?"

"The former, yes; the latter, no. At least not that I know of. But Father Roskosz won't care. Simply hearing that Troquier has broken the vows of celibacy was sufficient to anger pious old Theodosius."

"Will Roskosz confront him?"

"Oh, I'm sure he will."

"Troquier will immediately suspect you are the source," Martin said.

"I know. And I don't care."

"Can Father Troquier get back at you in any way?"

"Oh, I suppose he could send one of his French-American friends to garrot me, but he won't."

Martin touched his own neck instinctively.

"Father Roskosz assured me he intended to warn Troquier to take no reprisals, unless he wanted to find himself whisked off to Europe to make a solo parachute jump into the middle of the German lines on behalf of The Resistance."

Martin stopped walking. "Father Roskosz could pull off such a threat?"

Katherine shrugged. "I have no idea. I'm hoping Marcel Troquier has no idea either. And doesn't care to find out."

Martin said, "By the way, David Fox hasn't teased me unmercifully, as I expected him to do. And that makes me suspicious of him. Not to mention I think he either has been following me or having me followed by one of his friends. I'm reasonably certain both he and his friend shadowed me all the way from my apartment to Union Station."

"Shadowed. God, Martin. This is America, not Occupied France. Marcel Troquier and David Fox are supposed to be on our side."

"Anxieties run deep, even with the war nearing an end."

"Jealousies, too," Katherine added. "Come on. I'm starving."

17

Saturday
March 10, 1945
SS Garrison Headquarters
Kiel, Schleswig-Holstein

Karl Vollmer stared at the list Rainer had just handed him. Six hundred cartons of cigarettes, one hundred tins of Danish ham, five hundred tins of sardines, twenty cases of white wine, twenty of red; fifty cases of beer from the Kieler Brewery, two hundred pounds of potatoes, a hundred pounds of cabbage. "Where am I going to find *any* of these items? And why?"

"Why? Because back in Berlin these items soon will prove as valuable as gold bullion in the Reichsbank."

Rainer handed him a second list. "These people will provide the items."

"Who are they?"

"People whose loyalty to the Reich has been less than outstanding," Rainer explained with understatement.

"Why haven't they been arrested already?" Karl wondered aloud.

"Because neither Himmler nor anyone else in authority has found them out."

"Then --."

Rainer held up a hand. "This list comes from Anna. Guard it carefully."

"How does *she* know?" Karl asked, before remembering: Anna knows more than God, Rainer had said.

"I don't question Anna's methods of coming by such information. And she assures me we can trust it."

Karl stared at the addresses. They were scattered all over Schleswig-Holstein. "I will need a convoy of trucks and a month's time to go to all these places."

"I've requisitioned one truck. It's waiting outside. Meet me here Monday at 6 pm – with everything."

"Not the farm? But --." Rainer's look told Karl arguing was pointless.

"No arguing, Karl. Neither of us must go anywhere near the farm."

"But we must return to Berlin? Why not hide out here for a while?"

"Because, to repeat, I assume Himmler is having us shadowed. If anyone asks what you're doing, tell them you are gathering supplies in support of a special secret miracle-weapons mission. That will impress people. We must return to Berlin because Hans Frank is expecting to meet me. He'll be not only curious but enraged if I fail to show up."

"I thought you disliked Frank," Karl said glumly.

"I do. But he says he's bringing me something to take care of for him, some special item from Krakow. I imagine it's a painting he's stolen that he wants me to hide for him. Now go. We haven't much time."

"*Zu befehl*," Karl muttered, resigned. "Am I allowed help in gathering these items? I can't carry cases of beer and sacks of potatoes."

"I'm sure the people on your list will gladly help you," Rainer said.

"Do you really expect them to cooperate?" Karl said, incredulous.

"Approach them politely. Your SS uniform will naturally frighten them, but explain that, in exchange for the goods you want, the SS offers a forty-eight-hour escape amnesty for them and their families."

"They won't believe me."

"They'll want to believe you, despite everything else they think. A glimmer of hope is better than no hope at all."

"But if they refuse to cooperate?" Karl asked.

"Shoot them. Meanwhile, I'm off to see a man about a milk cow."

Karl felt a sudden itching in the part of his right arm that was missing. Never a good omen, he knew.

Saturday
March 10, 1945
New York City

In an indulgent frame of mind, Katherine had booked a room for the weekend at The Carlyle. "I don't want what may be our final fling to occur in a flop house, Martin dear," served as her explanation when Martin stood agog in the hotel lobby.

The night had been long and frenzied, a may-never-see-you-again passion sustaining their love-making well past the state of mutual exhaustion. Now Martin found himself being seated by the maitre d' – or the *Herr Ober*, as he was called at Lüchow's. The day was sunny and crisp, springtime in the air. So they walked the several blocks south from The Carlyle, off Central Park between Fifth Avenue and Park Avenue, to the popular German restaurant on East 14th Street. America may have been at war with Germany, but New Yorkers had never been at war with Lüchow's.

"Is this your idea of rubbing Father Troquier's nose in his suspicion that you hang out with Nazis?" Martin asked as he thumbed through the menu.

"Sort of. Let him eat Black Forest cake." Katherine giggled and then pointed at various works of art hanging in the New Room. "Recognize any of these?"

"Some," Martin allowed. "That one over there, the man with the game bag, is by one of Rubens' students, a fellow named Frans Snyders. The oil at the far end? I have no idea."

"I do, but only because Herr Lüchow himself told me," Katherine said slyly.

"Friends with the owner, are you?"

"Not really. I've met him at a charity event or two. First name is August. Charming man. Very dedicated to his customers. I came here once after a charity auction and he was kind enough to invite me to join him."

"So. The painting?"

" It's called *October – The Potato Gathering* and the painter's name is Auguste Hagborg. Herr Lüchow bought the painting because it happened to fit the space at the end of this room."

"Good a reason as any; better than most," Martin said.

"I'll be quiet so you can scan the menu," Katherine said.

"What do you recommend?"

"One of everything."

"Wish I could. What are you going to order?"

Katherine reached over and turned the page of Martin's menu. "There." And pointed to the middle of the page.

Martin read: Filet mignon of venison, hunter style.

"And you?" Katherine said.

"Pheasant with pineapple kraut sounds intriguing."

"I hear it's very good. But let's ask an expert." Katherine gestured for Martin to look up.

A familiar voice addressed them both. In thick German, Martin heard, "Good evening. What a pleasant surprise to see the two of you together." The voice belonged to Karl Niedendorf.

Martin rose and shook the gallery owner's hand. "Delighted to see you, Herr Niedendorf. Delighted indeed!" Martin proclaimed while thinking otherwise.

"Won't you join us, Karl?" Katherine asked.

"I'm sorry. I can't, much as I'd love to. I'm meeting a pair of potential buyers, patrons of a Cleveland museum. Are you in the city for long? If so, I'd love to take you both to dinner some evening soon."

Katherine spoke before Martin could. "Martin's only here for the weekend, Karl, but I accept."

Martin shot her a look.

"I wish you'd given me warning of your arrival, Martin," Nierendorf said. "I would gladly have rearranged my schedule. Your companionship rates top priority with me, you know."

"*Danke*, Herr Nierendorf, but the purpose of my visit here is classified. So I was not permitted to warn anyone."

Nierdendorf looked doubtful. "But Katherine knew?"

"Washington invited Katherine to join me so I could have a cover, make it appear I was here on a strictly social occasion."

"Bah! They should have invited both of us, to make your visit seem to be a strictly social occasion , as you call it."

"Yes, well –" Martin gave an exaggerated shrug, " – my superiors rarely seek my opinion."

"I understand completely. Well, it is a pleasure to see you both. Soon this damnable war will be over. Then no more skulking around, eh? We will all get together to celebrate the end to Hitler and his thugs."

"Indeed, Herr Nierendorf. I look forward to your company at that celebration," Martin said.

The gallery owner changed the subject. "When you visited Berlin before the war, Herr Wynerson, by chance did this charming lady's husband treat you to the culinary delights of the Stag and Pheasant?"

Martin smiled. "Indeed he did. It was one of the most memorable feasts I experienced while in Germany."

"The food here is nearly as exquisite." Nierendorf shook Martin's hand vigorously, then bent over to kiss Katherine on the cheek. Straightening himself, he said to Martin, "May I suggest the pheasant and pineapple kraut. Mmmm. Superb!"

With that he bowed and left.

When Nierendorf was out of sight Katherine took Martin's hands in her own. "Ah, Washington! The great, mysterious secret-mission man. Quick thinking, Martin."

"He nearly had me in a corner."

"Of your own making."

"Is Karl one of the German spies Father Troquier is so worried about?"

"Are you serious?" Katherine said.

"Maybe. He'd be perfect. A well-known anti-Nazi exile."

"At least he's not in jail. Or worse, in one of those dreadful camps Roosevelt has thrown every Japanese-American into." A waiter came and Katherine ordered a bottle of Gerwürtztrauminer to start.

Martin nodded his assent before adding, "The President would have to put barbed wire around the entire state of Texas in order to incarcerate every German- and Italian-American."

"Maybe that's not such a bad idea ," Katherine said, smiling. "Barbed wire around Texas, I mean."

"Oh, Texas isn't that bad a place, Katherine. That's where I learned to fly."

"And looked what happened to you."

"Remember the Alamo, and all that!" Martin said.

"Bah! The Alamo," Katherine sneered. "The fight for Texas independence was nothing but a blatant land-grab, commerce masquerading as principle. If Mexico ever wants to reclaim Texas, they won't get any argument from me."

Martin was not used to the company of a woman willing to express her political opinions, let alone express unusual opinions forcefully. But he decided he liked the idea. Still, he suddenly found himself looking around to see if anyone at nearby tables was listening.

Saturday
March 10, 1945
U-Boat Base Konrad
Kiel

"May I remind you, *Standartenführer,* a war is going on."

"Yes, *Fregattenkapitän,* I do need to be reminded. My many duties do not include keeping myself aware that a war still goes on. The last time I bothered to check into the matter German forces rumbled toward the gates of Moscow and Britain stood poised to capitulate. In Berlin we have heard very little since then to contradict the claim that a German victory is imminent."

"I see. Yes. You *are* from Berlin." As lead naval staff officer of U-Boat operations Günther Hessler cut an imposing figure, standing with Rainer beneath the concrete bunker that was now part of the Deutsche Werke drydock system. The foremost legend in all the U-Boat service, having been part of the most successful patrol of the entire war against Allied shipping as captain of U-107, Hessler looked too young, too aristocratic, too handsome and agreeable to have swum with the sharks. But so he had. And later, his celebrity assured, he had, for good measure, married *Grossadmiral* Dönitz's daughter.

"But not *of* Berlin, *Herr Fregattenkapitän.*"

"Yet, you are here on behalf of the *Reichsleiter.* And you want to borrow a submarine."

"If you can possibly spare one," Rainer said softly.

"And if I can't? What then?"

"I am to insist."

"Insist. Yes. I am sure you are the insisting type. Well then, what about one of those?"

Hessler pointed to a row of what Rainer could think of only in terms of their looking like baby whales. Or large sardines.

"What are they?" Rainer asked.

"We call them *Seehunden*, sea dogs. They are midget submarines. Crews of two."

Rainer shook his head. "I'm afraid I would need at least a dozen. Perhaps twice that number."

"Where is it you are going again?" Hessler said, fishing.

"Classified, as I already announced," Rainer said.

"Classified. Of course."

"And the cargo?"

"Also classified."

"I suppose I could let you have – sorry, loan you – a *Schulboot*, one of our training boats. However, better for your purposes – whatever they are – might be a *Milchkuh.*"

Rainer feigned ignorance. "A milk cow?"

"Looks like a pregnant whale. Used to carry fuel to our wolf packs. We have one that has not been on patrol yet. We could cut a passageway into the fuel-carrying tank for you to use as a cargo hold for... for your classified cargo."

"That sounds promising."

"Not much call for long-range fueling runs any longer, now that we are no longer --."

"At the gates of Moscow?" Rainer filled in.

Hessler gave Rainer an appreciative smile. "Exactly."

18

Tuesday
March 13, 1945
Ahrenshoop
Mecklenburg Bay

The beach at the artist colony was deserted as Rainer stood at the
end of Weg zum Hohen Ufer and looked westward across the
breakwater toward the setting sun. He had parked his motorcycle next to the bicycle stand on a side street leading to the beach.
As the sun sank toward the bay he walked slowly northward
along the beach, his destination the pink, thatched-roof home
of Oskar Lohnes, long-time friend of his father, Werner, and
notoriously successful art forger.

As he trudged through ankle-deep sand Rainer remembered
days as a teenager when he and his father would leave the rest
of the family at the rental cottage at Hohenfelde, Werner at the
wheel of the family car, and make the half-day trip to Ahrenshoop, north of Rostock, to visit Werner's many artist friends

who made the colony their permanent home. While the men drank and chatted in the Namenlos Café -- part of the Fischerwiege Hotel, set atop a low sand dune surrounded by trees – Rainer would be allowed to go bike-riding along the coastline with Oskar's son, Jürgen.

In the distance Rainer saw a truck lumbering northward slowly along Dorfstrasse, making him think of Karl. His aide has surprised – no, amazed – him by returning from the impossible quest Rainer had sent him on, not only with everything on the list, but by coming back several hours early.

"I only had to threaten one man. Everyone else shuddered at the sight of me. No one wanted to die with --." Karl suddenly looked away.

"—With the end of the war so near?" Rainer finished.

Karl had peered about furtively to see if anyone was listening, then nodded.

"I'm sure most of them were practicing their English when you knocked at their doors," Rainer suggested.

Karl laughed. "I think most of them were praying."

"Yes. Praying that the British reach them before the Russians do."

"Perhaps."

"Wouldn't you?" Rainer asked.

Karl tapped his uniform. "A British bullet probably feels the same as a Russian bullet."

"No doubt. Same with hangman's ropes."

Karl winced.

"Don't worry, my friend. We will experience neither. I promise you."

The look Karl gave his superior lacked reassurance. "Do you still want me to drive these…" he gestured toward the truck, "… to Berlin?"

"Yes. But I want you to wait until dark, wait until the sky is free from Allied strafing."

"Thank you, *Standartenführer.*"

"And you know where to deliver everything?"

"The Stag and Pheasant restaurant, beside the Havel and across from Pfaueninsel."

"Yes. And make delivery only to the owner, Fritz Priebe, or his son, Horst."

As Rainer anticipated, the tavern went silent the moment he stepped inside. Odors of stale beer and smoke made him cough. But at least in Ahrenshoop the war had clearly not disrupted the availability of beer or tobacco. As he walked toward the bar he caught the scent of fresh beer, saw several patrons smoking.

All eyes turned from his gaze, including those of the bartender, a haggard-looking, buxom redhead wearing a filthy barmaid's outfit. Rainer noticed several of her teeth were missing. He removed his cap and placed it on the bar. "I'm looking for Oskar Lohnes. He's not at his house." He spoke loudly to no one in particular. The silence that followed was eerie. Turning to face the crowded tables, he let his gaze pass slowly over every face, but he recognized no one.

"Oskar Lohnes? Anyone know where I can find him?"

No response from anyone.

"Then I'll go back to his house and wait," Rainer said, turning back to retrieve his hat.

From the back came, "Oskar is dead."

Rainer weaved his way through the tables to confront the man who had spoken. "How did he die? And when?"

"Last year. He stumbled home drunk and someone found him the next day, dead in front of his house," said the middle-aged man, the three remaining fingers on his right hand crippled.

"He's buried in the local cemetery then?"

The man gave a curt nod.

"Come then. Show me his grave."

Terror filled the man's eyes and he shrank back. "I...I don't know which marker belongs to Oskar."

"Then we'll look together," Rainer said.

"No!"

"Why not?"

The man shook his head, saying nothing.

Rainer looked to the man sitting next to him, an older man smoking a pipe. "Perhaps you can show me Oskar's grave."

The man stared down at the table.

Rainer pounded a fist on the table. "Enough lies! My father is Werner Zeitz, an art gallery owner from Munich and a close friend of Oskar Lohnes. For many years my father brought me here each summer – before the war. Maybe some of you remember my father, if not me. I am here to see Oskar as a friend, not as a feared or hated SS officer. And I am going to see Oskar, whether he is dead or alive. And someone in this room is going to take me to him."

Looking around the room, Rainer spotted a young woman rise slowly. She might have been pretty once, but now, as she stood facing Rainer, he saw that she was gaunt, hollow-eyed, almost lifeless.

"I will take you to Oskar," she said in a raspy voice. "But first you must answer my questions."

Rainer walked closer to her. "Ask."

"What is the name of Oskar's son?"

Rainer gave the girl a flinty look. "His name is Jürgen. About my age. He and I used to sail on the bay while Oskar and father drank and talked in this very tavern. What is your second question?"

"Jürgen has a prominent birthmark. Anyone who knows him well knows where it is and what it looks like. Can you identify it?"

"You must mean the sausage-shaped wine stain on the right side of his lower back. Here." Rainer pointed to the spot on his own hip. "Your final question."

"Oskar's wife. Can you describe her?"

"No. And neither can you. We are both too young. Frau Lohnes died giving birth to Jürgen, after which Oskar burned every photo and painting of his wife that he could lay his hands on. Or so my father has told me."

The young woman looked around the room, stopping to stare into the eyes of several of the elder patrons.

"Well? Do I pass?" Rainer asked.

"Not yet. Who is Oskar's favorite painter?"

"You mean besides himself?"

The girl smiled. "Besides."

"He has two favorites. Karl Schmidt-Rottluff and Emil Nolde."

"Why are they his favorites?"

Rainer looked about the room and saw all eyes now on him. "Schmidt-Rottluff because of his politics, as much as for the quality of his works. Nolde because he is from Schleswig, near where Oskar himself grew up. And because Oskar has always been able to paint expert forgeries of Herr Nolde's works."

Rainer watched as several patrons gave each other knowing looks.

The girl quickly downed the dregs from her beer glass. "Come. Oskar is ill, but I will take you to him."

———————

Tuesday
March 13, 1945
Washington, D.C.

"Chasing down members of the *Bundt* camped out along the Hudson, Martin?" David Fox whispered as he passed Martin carrying several large map rolls under one arm.

Martin looked up from his desk, set his magnifying glass down, and said, "No. Were you?"

"Not me. I don't have any leave to spare. So how's Katherine Parker?"

"Busy with charity work," Martin said warily.

"Are you one of her charity cases?"

"Do I look like a charity case?"

"Definitely not. But I bet she made time for you anyway."

"And who or what did you make time for while I was gone?" Martin asked.

"I spent most of my time with Father Troquier, going over lists of French works he's especially interested in seeing recovered. And that reminds me, Father Roskosz asked me to send you around to see him. Sooner is better, if I understood him correctly. He has Wednesday mornings free and will be at his small townhouse in Glover Park. Here is the address. Nine o'clock. Don't be late. You know how he is about punctuality."

"Did he say what he wanted?" Martin inquired, hoping it had nothing to do with Katherine.

"He didn't say, but I'm sure you can guess," Fox said.

"Can I?"

"Stop acting coy, Martin. Everyone knows about your little flare-up with Father Troquier. And now that Roskosz has kicked Marcel's butt, he probably wants to give you a blow-by-blow account."

Marcel, is it, Martin thought. What a cozy pair they have turned out to be.

Tuesday
March 13, 1945
Ahrenshoop

The girl told Rainer her name was Thelda Eggert and that she had moved Oskar in with her after her parents had gone to Rostock in December hoping to learn the fate of her brother, who was an infantryman serving in Yugoslavia and had not written home in several months. Both parents died during an Allied bombing raid, leaving her alone. She still knew nothing of her brother.

Oskar's eyesight was failing and he suffered coughing spells. As she lit a fire under a pot of tea she explained to Rainer that she thought Oskar's house too draughty, too cold, too dank for her to accept Oskar's invitation that she move in with him. Together they agreed they would both be better off if he came to live with her. She would cook for him as best she could, given the limits of food available; he would provide companionship to her, relieve her of the feelings of loneliness she suffered with her family gone.

Rainer followed the girl into a room lit only by fire and saw a figure wrapped in a heavy blanket sat in a rocking chair close to the hearth. To Rainer the entire room felt oppressively warm.

"Oskar dear, I've brought someone home with me who asked to see you." She spoke to him as though he were a child. The man kept rocking as though he had not heard her.

Thelda turned to Rainer and whispered, "He doesn't hear well either. You'll have to speak loudly."

Rainer nodded and followed her as she pulled a pair of straight-back woven chairs beside the old man.

Old man. He's fifty-eight, Rainer reminded himself. Yet he looks to be a man of eighty, he thought, as Oskar continued to stare at into the crackling fire, not even acknowledging Thelda's presence.

"Oskar?" Thelda said loudly as she sat and leaned toward him.

"I hear you," he said, his lips scarcely moving. "Who have you brought?"

Thelda gestured for Rainer to sit. ""Do you remember Werner Zeitz?"

"He turned his head toward her. "Of course, I remember. Has Werner come to see me?"

"His son is here. Rainer."

"Ah, yes. Tall, handsome Rainer. Bright young man. Where is he?"

"On your left side."

Only when Oskar turned toward him did Rainer realize he scarcely recognized the man. Sunken eyes, ghostly pale flesh, a nearly vacant stare. Gone was the ruddiness, the grin, the twinkle in the eyes, that revealed what Werner called *Die Lebensglut des Kunstler*, the painter's ardor for life. But Oskar's glow was now gone. Not even a flicker, or so much as a dying ember. All that remained were ashes. Or so Rainer judged.

"You are Rainer Zeitz? The lad who used to play with my Jürgen?"

"I am. The very same."

"No. None of us are the same. What is that you're wearing?"

"A uniform."

"Yes. I can see that. But not *feldgrau*."

"No."

Oskar then looked into Rainer's eyes. "How is your father?"

Rainer reached forward and took Oskar's clammy hands into his own. "I'm sorry, but I don't know. I haven't seen him or heard from him since... since the war began."

"Munich. Is he still there?"

Rainer shook his head. "He left Munich and went to London."

Oskar looked puzzled. "London?"

"Yes. London."

Oskar's eyes widened. "He made enemies, yes?"

"He did not share the political views of –"

"Of the Nazis," Oskar finished.

"Yes," Rainer said, embarrassed.

"And what of his gallery?"

"Closed."

"Burned out?"

"No. It's still there. Boarded up."

"And what of you?"

"I stayed."

"So I see. But what have you done with yourself?"

Rainer watched as the old man's eyes bore in on him. "I work to recover works of art stolen from us by the Russians."

The old man said nothing for a while, then finally mumbled, "I see."

Thelda's kettle whistled and she stood. "You will have tea, won't you, Herr Zeitz?"

Rainer nodded.

"We have no sugar."

"Without will be fine." When she was gone Rainer asked, "What can you tell me about Jürgen?"

"He is a fine young man. Not the accomplished artist I hoped for, but he has an appreciation for the world of paint on canvas, even though he lacks the talent to make a serious contribution of his own."

"Where is he now?" Rainer asked.

"A soldier. A *Leuntnant* in the Wehrmacht."

"Where is he posted?"

"Somewhere in Norway."

Thank God, Rainer thought. Lucky Jürgen. The Allied vice closes on Germany, yet the *Führer* refuses to bring home the fourteen divisions sitting in Norway waiting for an Allied landing that will never occur.

Thelda served tea, wrapping Oskar's cup in a piece of cloth before handing it to him. The old man took a sip and immediately began to cough. Rainer seized the cup from Oskar's hands as the cup began to tilt.

"Sorry," Oskar said when his coughing spell ended. "My hands aren't as steady as they used to be."

Thelda added, "Nor are your lungs. May I put a poultice on your chest?"

"No, no, no. I will be all right," Oskar said. Turning to Rainer, he said, "Sometimes she makes too much fuss over me."

"She cares about you, Oskar."

"I know, I know. But I resent the indignity of being made to feel as helpless as a newborn infant. I still have my pride, you know."

"Yes, I can see that," Rainer said and found his opening. "Speaking of your pride, Oskar, are you still the best art forger north of Berlin?"

Oskar gestured that he wished to have his tea cup returned to him. Rainer obliged him. "North of Berlin? Is that all you can credit me with?"

"I was testing the level of your pride," Rainer said.

"Pride is all I have left. But a man can't paint with pride alone. Look at these hands." He held his cup in front of him with both hands, each one trembling. He took a sip of tea, then looked at Rainer. "But tremors are the least of my problems. I'm dying, Son of Werner. I'm dying."

Rainer looked at Thelda, who nodded.

Oskar said, "The *alte Hexe*, the old witch who lives among the trees in the Darß, brought her pair of Dachshunds to smell me out last week. She came back the next day and said the dogs told her my insides were starting to decay, so quickly in fact that nothing could be done."

"A *Hexe*," Rainer repeated. "Have you consulted a doctor?"

Thelda laughed and Oskar shook his head.

"We have no doctors. No one has doctors. They've all been taken by the Army," Thelda said.

"Except for Herr Doktor Salzkotten," Oskar reminded her.

"Oh, yes. I forgot," Thelda said. "Our seventy-year-old local physician hanged himself last month before the Gestapo could arrest him. Doktor Salzkotten, according to rumors, provided poison to his grandson in Berlin, who intended somehow to slip the poison into the *Führer*'s tea or coffee. Now how preposterous is that? Somebody in Ahrenshoop had to have made up the story and told the Gestapo in Rostock, who were stupid enough to believe it."

Rainer asked, "Why would someone make up such a tale?"

Oskar answered. "Fritz Salzkotten spoke his mind too freely. Tell him, Thelda."

"One day in the tavern I heard the doctor tell Herr Breckler that someone ought consider putting the *Führer* into a permanent state of sleep and that he, the doctor, knew exactly how to do it. Herr Breckler said nothing, even though I'm certain he was in sympathy with such an idea, because just then Frau Arnstorf walked by their table and gave them a stern look. I'm convinced Frau Arnstorf overheard the doctor and reported him to the Gestapo. Whether she or the Gestapo made up the story of his giving poison to his son, I don't know."

"I'm sorry you are dying, Oskar. I've come for your help. I hope you are up to it," Rainer said.

"Help with what?" Oskar said.

"Removing more paintings from Germany before the Russians get them."

"Whose paintings?"

"The works of great German artists."

Oskar Lohnes sat quietly for several moments, staring into his tea cup, before saying, "Did you know that not long ago Karl Schmidt-Rottluff bought a painting from Ernst Wilhelm Nay?"

"Yes. I knew that, Oskar. Karl Schmidt is a generous man. Poor Nay has been living in total isolation in Berlin. He was short of money and Karl helped him out, even though Karl has cut himself off from the world, staying in Pomerania."

Oskar looked puzzled. "I thought Karl had an apartment in Berlin."

"He did. It was bombed out nearly two years ago."

"How sad."

"Will you help me, Oskar?" Rainer said, pleading.

"What can a man in my condition do?"

"Two things. First, I asked about your forgery skills, not because I want you to forge anything. Rather, I want you to help me determine whether a painting I bring you is a forgery or not. Can you do that?"

Oskar looked up. "Who is the artist?"

"Franz Marc."

Slowly a smile came to Oskar Lohnes' face. "I never forged a Marc, but I'm sure I could recognize if someone else did. I am familiar with his style, know his techniques. Bold, but simple. Now Kandinsky, on the other hand --. I would never even consider trying to fake a Kandinsky." He paused and looked puzzled. "I thought all of Marc's works were destroyed with the *Entartete Kunst* purge."

"You'd be surprised how many have survived. And where they are. And who owns them," Rainer said.

"Very little surprises me anymore."

"If I bring you the painting will you be able to examine it?"

"If the worms inside me haven't devoured my guts before then. Yes. Which work is it?"

"*The Tower of the Blue Horses.*"

"It's huge," Oskar said, holding out his arms. "Where did you find it?"

"In Berlin."

"They're all *Heuchlern*, are they? Every last one of them."

"Hypocrites? Yes, Oskar. Every single one of them." Including me, Rainer thought.

"And the second thing you want from me?" When Rainer had finished explaining what else he wanted, Oskar turned to Thelda and asked, "Can we do that?"

Thelda replied, "I'll find a way."

19

Wednesday
March, 14, 1945
Washington, D.C.

Dearest Maddy,

My bedside clock reads well after midnight and I can't sleep. So, rather than lie in bed listening to things go bump in the night, I decided to write you. I've been negligent, I know, in not writing you more often. No excuses.

I haven't forgotten you. In fact, I think of you more and more, now that spring has arrived. Just yesterday I saw a pair of mallards land on the Tidal Basin near the Jefferson Memorial and immediately thought how often we sat on the shore of Blackduck Lake at sundown, watching and listening for loons.

My days are busy, but my nights are ever so lonely. I do wish you were here to snuggle up beside me, fill me in on all the goings-on back home. Maybe we could even read poetry to each other like we used to. Can you still remember all the lines to "Who Killed Cock Robin?" Remember how I used to try to switch a word on you and you would always catch me? How about James Whitcomb Riley's "Little Orphant Annie"? The gobblins will get you if you don't watch out? And how I tried to help you with your German with *Wer reitet so schwer durch Nacht und Wind* --? Remember how we used to argue whose poem was scarier, Goethe's or Riley's? And after you read me R. W. Service's "Cremation of Sam McGee" I swore to you I'd never go ice-fishing again. Yet, there we were, the very next month, out on the lake, lines in the water, shivering as we sipped mulled cider in Dad's little-red-barn-on-skids.

God, how I long for those days. Or ones just like them.

Folks in Washington are all business these days. I swear, the nearer to the end of this war we get, the more frantic and crabby most of my colleagues get. And oh! The distrust. Why, you'd hardly realize we are all on the same side. I've heard plenty of rumors to the effect that in Germany everybody spies on everybody else. Neighbor on neighbor; children on their parents. Well, let me tell you: in that respect Nazi Germany differs very little from what goes on right here in Washington. The loose-lips principle has everyone on edge, looking over his shoulder, cocking an ear to the conversations of passersby, looking over other people's – often total strangers' – shoulders. It's not healthy, Maddy. The atmosphere is truly poisonous with mistrust. And I resent everybody's trying to justify their intruding into my private life in the name of national security.

I have a meeting this morning with Father Roskosz. I can't recall if you met him when you were here. He teaches at Georgetown. Polish. Art historian. Staunch, conservative Catholic. But a decent man, from what I've been able to judge. Unlike one of his colleagues, Father Troquier. That man is creepy as a spider, in several senses of *creepy*. I have no doubt the man's name will come up in our conversation and I intend to share my darkest suspicions about Marcel Troquier with Father Roskosz. Oops! There I go, sounding like one of *them*.

I worry, too, about my apartment mate, David Fox. If I may make a clever remark, the man has been acting foxy with me lately, sniffing about in my personal business.

How hopeful I am that, once we set off to Europe, we can all put this political-intrigue stuff behind us and concentrate on catching Nazis and other art thieves. There are plenty to catch. So we will have no business setting snares for each other.

Still no date has been set for our departure. I am hoping that, once Munich is safely under Allied control, we will be on our way. We dare not lose time. I am ready. Too ready and eager, perhaps. Maybe that accounts, in part at least, for why I can't sleep lately.

Enough ink spent on whining and sniveling. But I am truly homesick for people I love and trust. Above all others, you!

All my deepest love,
Martin

Wednesday
March 14, 1945
Ahrenshoop

Rainer spent the night with Oskar and Thelda, sharing a meal of watery potato soup, augmented by a few spears of wild asparagus gathered by Thelda from behind nearby dunes. So meager was Thelda's larder, Rainer felt guilty for not thinking to pack a saddlebag with foodstuffs from Karl's roundup. He slept on the floor near the fireplace, although Thelda had banked the fire to conserve precious firewood.

During supper Thelda had explained to Rainer, "We have plenty of boats to choose from. Fuel is the problem. Civilian supplies of petrol and diesel are both scarce as doctors. The Army takes it all. I'll have to bicycle the thirty kilometers to Rostock to steal enough to get you from here to Kiel. I can bring the fuel back in beer barrels on a horse cart."

"Take Wilhelm Stetter and Otto with you," Oskar had said to Thelda. To Rainer, "Wounded veterans. Neither a friend of the Nazis. They can be trusted."

Thelda said, "No. Men are too conspicuous, even sagging cripples. I'll take Otto's sisters."

Rainer had hesitated involving Thelda and other women in his dangerous plans. Am I too chivalrous? he wondered. But then he thought of Anna and acquiesced.

After a breakfast of peeled cucumbers and ersatz coffee, Rainer repeated his plans – such as they were – then bade farewell to Thelda and Oskar. As he set out through a chill fog back to his motorcycle, he thought about fuel and how he had taken the vital liquid so much for granted, even though he was aware how important a role oil had played in Germany's military strategy in Africa, the Caucusus, Romania, and elsewhere.

Astraddle his motorcycle, Rainer was about to kick-start the engine when he saw two men walking toward him out of the morning mists. From their black leather trenchcoats and fedoras worn low he knew they were Gestapo. He dismounted the bike.

"Herr Zeitz?" the shorter of the two asked when they arrived in front of him.

"*Standartenführer* Zeitz," Rainer corrected.

"We are from Gestapo headquarters in Rostock and we would like to ask you a few questions," the taller man said. His egg-shaped head, wire-framed glasses, and pencil mustache reminded Rainer of Heinrich Himmler on stork's legs.

"What sort of questions?"

The short man's eyes narrowed. "To begin with, what are you doing in Ahrenshoop?"

"What? You know my name but don't know why I am here? How shameful of you, gentlemen."

Neither man showed any sense of shame. "Your purpose," repeated the short man.

Rainer snorted. "Actually, it is none of your business, which is why you haven't found out already. Isn't that right?"

"Everything is our business, Herr Zeitz," said the taller man.

Rainer ignored the slight. "Wrong, gentlemen. My business is not your business."

"You spent the night at the house of Oskar Lohnes."

"So I did. And perhaps if you had crept a little closer and listened through the keyhole you would know what I am doing in Ahrenshoop."

Neither man said anything.

"You know my name. Do you know my position within the SS?"

The short man. "You are a *Kunstverschaffner*."

"Very good. And what do you know of the history of this town we stand in?"

"An artist colony."

"Right again. Now add one plus one."

The tall man. "What does Oskar Lohnes have to do with your being here?"

"Gentlemen, must I remind you that I operate under higher authority than you? First of all, I am here under top secret orders from *Reichsleiter* Himmler himself. Second, I do all my work under the auspices of a *Führervorbehalt*."

"Oskar Lohnes is under watch because he may be disloyal to the Reich," the short man said. "Now I repeat, what were you doing in the house where he is staying?"

Rainer remounted the motorcycle to make himself appear more at ease. "Very well, gentlemen. I will share my mission with you, but only because I now realize you can be of great assistance to me."

The two Gestapo men looked at one another, dubious.

Rainer explained. "Oskar is helping me and his appearance of disloyalty is deliberate. His knowledge of what goes on in Ahrenshoop is unsurpassed. And what he is helping me with is this: To be on the lookout for art thieves passing this way. As I'm sure you know many Germans have given up on hopes of victory over the Allies and are attempting to flee the Fatherland. And many of those cowards intend to take with them valuables belonging to the Reich. Right now Berlin is teeming with thieves intent on escaping to Sweden with works of art, not only belonging to the Reich, but destined for the *Führer*'s grand art museum to be built in Linz. We must stop them. Do you not agree?"

Neither Gestapo agent moved or spoke.

Rainer scowled. "Come, gentlemen. Do not bring your own loyalty into question."

Finally, the taller man grudgingly conceded Rainer's points thus far. "Go on."

"Any thieves coming this way Oskar will find out about and inform me. And Berlin-to-Rostock is one of the routes of choice by any knowledgeable thief. Good boats remain available in Rostock. Fuel, too, can be found by those who know how to find it. Other routes are possible, but this will be one of the main routes, I am certain."

The Gestapo pair said nothing.

"Already we hear rumors of a major movement of stolen art heading this way, works enough to fill a boat of some size. The means by which the Gestapo can help me is by seeing to it that an armed launch, fully fueled, is manned and at the ready, moored between Ahrenshoop and the lighthouse up north at the end of the Darß Forest, and ready to intercept any thieves attempting to make the crossing to Sweden, to arrest such thieves and confiscate their cargo."

"Very interesting, *Standartenführer*, but tell us why you were in Rostock examining the submarine pens for their fitness," the short man said, smirking.

Rainer mulled how much to tell before saying, "A U-boat is coming from Kiel to Rostock to take on a special mission. A secret mission. You may contact *Fregattenkapitän* Günter Hessler at the *Kriegsmarine*'s operational headquarters, if you doubt me."

Short Man sneered. "Perhaps that mission is to carry away Reich's art to Sweden." Turning to the tall man, he said, "What do you think?"

Rainer spoke before the tall man could respond to his companion. "Excellent thought! Go the nearest telephone and call Walter Schellenberg and announce to him that his boss, *Reichsleiter* Himmler, is in a conspiracy with the *Kriegsmarine* to use a U-boat to steal precious Reich's assets and that you know this because in Rostock you overheard an SS *Standartenführer* examining the U-boat pens and now he declares that a U-boat is coming from Kiel to Rostock on an unexplained mission. Do that and see just how quickly both of you find yourselves back in Rostock, standing in front of a firing squad."

The color drained from the faces of both Gestapo agents.

"Well?" Rainer said.

Finally Tall Man managed to ask in a tremulous voice, "What is the U-boat coming to Rostock for?"

"Ask one of your superiors to ask the *Reichsleiter*. I am not at liberty to discuss its mission with you. Even the *Kriegsmarine* doesn't know. Now if there is nothing else, I suggest you return quickly to Rostock. I return to Berlin tomorrow, where one of my first duties will be to see if you have posted a launch at the tip of this peninsula."

The two Gestapo men looked at each other, frustrated and beaten. Each gave Rainer a curt nod and turned to go. "Wait," Rainer called out. "I need your names, please. Write them down for me. I don't trust having to describe each of you to *Reichsleiter* Himmler. I may fail to portray you precisely enough and end up getting one of your colleagues in trouble."

The short man pulled a small notebook from beneath his coat, scribbled a pair of names, then handed the page to Rainer.

"Which one of you is Herman Lang?"

"I am," said Tall Man.

Rainer said, "Thank you," as he kicked his bike's start pedal. When the two men turned to leave he put the cycle into gear and roared past them, heading north.

Two kilometers from Ahrenshooop the road turns east, away from the beaches, and follows the edge of the Darß Forest until it turns north again and passes through a corner of the forest between the villages of Wieck and Prerow. With dense, low forest on either side of him, Rainer slowed, then turned off the road, cut the motorcycle's engine, and pushed it through ankle-high grass to a thicket of gorse. Fog still hung low in the mid-morning air. After checking to see that his bike was not visible from the road, he returned to the trees near the road, crouched and listened. Minutes later he heard the sound of an auto engine coming from the south. Then the car flashed by and he felt reasonably certain the driver of the car was Pieter Steffens. Beside him in the Horch sat his partner, Herman Lang. Pushing his bike back onto the road, he started the engine and sped south back to Ahrenshoop to warn Thelda and Oskar to expect a visit from the Gestapo and to explain what their narrative to the Gestapo must be.

Wednesday
March 14, 1945
Washington, D.C.

Theodosius Roskosz's pale yellow row house sat on 39th Street, three blocks west of the National Cathedral. The sun had already burned away the low, thin overcast, making the mid-morning bright. Yet the paint on the priest's house seemed to dull as the sunlight intensified. Martin knew because he had stood on the curve where Watson Place turned in Garfield and stared nervously northward up 39th Street, working up his courage.

When Father Roskosz opened his door he was not wearing his customary cassock, but instead had donned denim trousers and a red plaid shirt made of wool. Paul Bunyan lives! flashed through Martin's mind as he stared, mouth agape, at the barrel-chested giant of a priest. Only an axe and a blue ox were missing to complete the theatrical appearance. Then came the high-pitched voice and the cartoon apparition suddenly lost its credence.

"Come in, Mister Wynerson. Come in. Welcome to my modest home."

And modest it was. Martin imagined this was what a monk's cell in a monastery must look like. The living room floor was bare, the furniture stark, consisting of a seedy-looking couch, its fabric worn smooth in several spots, and a pair of straight-back wooden chairs, unpadded, a Spanish Colonial coffee table sprawling before the couch. Beside the window hung a wooden crucifix. Above the couch a framed print of Botticelli's *Madonna and Child*. Opposite the couch a photo of Pius XII, in white miter and cape, gazed down from the balcony of St. Peter's.

"Please be seated," Roskosz said, gesturing for Martin to take a seat on the sofa. "Make yourself comfortable. I'll return in a moment with refreshments for us both."

On the coffee table lay an immense Bible, beautifully bound, with gilt-edged pages. The book's spine looked so delicate Martin decided against opening it for fear it might break. He ran a palm along the spine and judged it to be more substantial than it first appeared. So he gently raised the cover and stared down at a title page. The scrolling was ornate. Polish, maybe?

Father Roskosz returned, bearing a large wooden tray on which perched a small silver coffee urn, two large mugs, and a plate of savory-looking pastries, jam oozing from their middles.

"Ah, I see you've taken an interest in my Bible," the priest said as he sat the tray down beside the holy text.

"It's magnificent!" Martin said. "Tell me about it."

"I shall. But first, eat." The priest poured coffee into the mugs. "Cream? Sugar?"

"Neither."

Roskosz then handed Martin a napkin and pointed to the pastries. "They're called *paczkis*." He pronounced the word *poonch-kees.* ""They're a Fat Tuesday tradition with us Poles. The filling is apricot. Go ahead. Try one. Eat several, in fact."

Martin noted Fat Tuesday was long past. In fact, Easter was coming soon. April 1 this year. Same as April's Fool's Day. He picked up a *paczki*, examined, then tasted it. "Wow! Excellent. Did you make these yourself?"

Roskosz shook his head. "Bakery in Georgetown. They deliver."

"A Polish bakery so close?" Martin said.

"Unfortunately not. Italian. But they make a passable *paczki.*"

"Tell me about the Bible," Martin said, nodding toward the book as he filled his mouth with pastry.

Father Roskosz picked up the Bible and held in on his lap as though it were a sleeping infant. He carefully opened the book to somewhere in the middle then slowly turned the book so Martin could see the text.

"A Polish edition, as I'm sure you have guessed by now. This is a hundred-and-thirty-year-old copy of the translation done by a Jesuit named Jacob Wujek in 1593. He lived in Kracow. His was not the first Polish translation, but it was immediately praised by Pope Clement III and is still considered a classic. This copy has been in my family for several generations. It was a gift from my father upon my ordination."

"What a wonderful treasure!" Martin said.

"Yes. I hold it extremely dear," the priest said as he closed the book and returned it to the coffee table. "More coffee? Another *paczki?*"

"The pastry is delicious, but no. Thank you."

"Treasures are the main reason I invited you to see me, Martin. I have a favor to ask of you."

Uh-oh. Here it comes. Stay away from Katherine Parker. Elliott's treasure. Martin braced himself for a polite lecture on morals.

Instead, the Pole spoken passionately of riches closer to his own heart. "The treasures I am about to speak of are the works of art stolen from my native land by the Germans. The numbers are vast. However, we Poles know, from too much experience, that our concerns will become... what is the American expression? Lost in the shuffle?"

Martin nodded. "Yes. I understand."

"I am aware your posting will be in Munich, where you will interview people brought in from Bavaria and western Austria. Many of these works I am about to name may well have been destined for Hitler's grand museum in Linz."

Father Roskosz handed Martin a hand-written list, on which he had named *Saint Anne* (Veit Stoss carving), Jozef Chelmonski's *Adoration on Good Friday*, *Madonna and Child with Angels* by Lorenzo di Credi.

The priest said, "These are the three that are most likely to turn up in Austria or Bavaria, I believe. I am especially concerned about the Chelmonski because it once resided in the Poznan Museum, where my brother was a curator."

"I promise to keep watch for all three," Martin said.

Roskosz hesitated as if about to say something, then deciding against it. Finally, with a sigh, he said, "Among the rumors I hear is that one of the German cardinals has been abetting the Nazis in both hiding and transporting works taken from Poland."

"Which cardinal?" Martin said.

"I cannot – rather, will not -- say. I have no evidence, only rumors. But I assure you, I will never speak to that man again, in this life or the next."

Martin stared at the list for a moment before saying, "Withholding his name does not help your cause, Father Theo."

"On the other hand, maligning a man without proof does not help maintain the peace in my soul."

"I understand."

After helping himself to another *paczki*, the priest said, "I hope the Holy Father forgives the German Church, because I cannot. I am glad I do not wear his shoes. It takes much praying and reflecting to be pope these days."

As well as a great deal of silence on many subjects, Martin thought to himself. The choice was not between Bolshevism and Nazism, but too often Pius behaved as if only by tolerating Hitler could Stalin be thwarted. "Perhaps, someday when you are pope, Father Theo --."

Father Roskosz laughed and held up his half-eaten pastry. "Maybe one of these *paczkis* has a chance to become pope. I do not."

When Martin gave him a puzzled look, the priest added, "They are made by Italians. I am not."

Roskosz smiled at his little joke, but behind the smile Martin thought he detected a trace of bitterness. Martin gave an I-wouldn't-know shrug. "You can always hope."

The two men sat in silence for several awkward moments, then Father Theo said, "Speaking of maligning without proof, I have only Father Troquier's word that our mutual friend, Katherine Parker, has acted adulterously with you."

So. It has been on his mind. And now he wants me to indict Katherine – and myself -- for the sake of his soul's peace, among other reasons. "Am I in the confessional, Father?"

"No. You are not Catholic. But I assure you my discretion is absolute."

"Unlike a certain Frenchman you could name."

"Unlike."

Unable to look Roskosz in the eye, Martin stared at the diminished plate of pastries, then asked, "What is the correct phrasing? Bless me, Father, for I have sinned?"

"That will do. And if we were in the confessional, I would now propose a penance," the priest said.

"So what would you have me do? Theoretically, of course, given that we are not in the confessional."

"Stop seeing her, Martin. Oh, I know that what you do seems harmless enough now. But even in your Lutheran world sins have a way of catching up with you."

Martin finally looked up at Father Roskosz. "Go and sin no more?"

The priest nodded.

"But Luther urged, '*Esto peccator et pecca fortiter*'."

"Now really, Martin. Do you truly believe that being a sinner and sinning vigorously will make you more worthy of God's grace?"

"What grace?" Martin said, with an anger that surprised even him. "Where's God's grace to let such a war as this one we're in happen?"

"The war is horrible, yes. I do not pretend to understand the how nor the why of it. I pray daily for that understanding, to understand why God has chosen such a horrific means to achieve His ends. What I can see and understand is that Katherine Parker's behavior with you does not contribute to a better world. The only outcome can be pain and sorrow."

Martin felt numb. The priest's remark contained too many grains of truth. Pain and sorrow may not be the only result, but --. But what?

"Katherine is a good woman; you are a good man. Don't sully your characters any more than either of you have done already."

Sully? When was the last time I heard that word used? It's so archaic. But then so is Father Theo. A genuine throwback to an earlier, simpler time, Martin thought. "You spoken with Katherine about this?"

"No. We spoke, as you know, but not about this. I preferred to confront you instead."

"Thanks."

"I'll speak with her on this matter, if you like."

"I'd rather you wouldn't."

"As you wish."

"The issue will be moot soon anyway," Martin reminded the priest.

"I am hoping that is the case."

"Your continued discretion?"

Roskosz nodded. "You may count on that."

Martin took a sip of cold coffee, then stood and waved the list of art works. "You may count on my vigilance in looking for these."

"I'm sure I can, Martin."

After shaking Father Roskosz's hand, Martin left quickly. As he passed the National Cathedral, he stared up, nearly tripped on a broken piece of sidewalk, then straightened his shoulders and picked up his pace. Damn you, Father Theo. I don't need your divine, meddlesome intervention.

19

Thursday
March 15, 1945
Gestapo headquarters
Berlin

Other, more urgent priorities! The officious desk dragon guarding the gate to Himmler's office refused to say what those new priorities might be, but Rainer could guess. The *Reichsleiter* was now too busy plotting how to save himself, with or without his precious art works. Very well, Rainer thought. I will take my cue from Himmler and do the same for myself.

He had reached the stairwell and was standing aside for a courier who ascended the marble steps two at a time when Rainer heard a voice behind him.

"*Standartenführer* Zeitz! Can you spare me a few moments?"

Rainer turned and recognized the tall, handsome figure of Walter Schellenberg, second only to Himmler in the Gestapo hierarchy, beckoning him from the doorway of a nearby office.

Schellenberg was not a man to trifle with, being the man credited by most with bringing down Admiral Carnaris, former head the *Abwehr*, German Intelligence. Carnaris was now a prisoner in the camp at Flossenbürg, just north of Munich, where he was to be hanged for treason, another plotter against the *Führer*'s life.

Once in front of Schellenberg, Rainer snapped off a sharp *Heil Hitler* salute and followed the man into the office, where he took an offered seat. The Gestapo man eased himself into the swivel chair behind a large desk.

"So, Zeitz, you've been stirring up sand fleas in Ahrenshoop, I'm told."

"That is correct. Part of my duties," Rainer said. "And what duties are those?"

"Preventing art works belonging to the Reich from being whisked away to Sweden."

Schellenberg gave him a dark look.

"Unauthorized works, moving illegally," Rainer added.

"Sweden. Yes. I see. Why Sweden, do you think?"

"Fewer difficulties at the moment than other directions," Rainer said cautiously.

After staring at the ceiling -- for dramatic effect, Rainer surmised – Schellenberg said, "Yes, definitely. I agree. Does the *Reichslieter* know about this?"

Cagey bastard, Rainer thought. "Surely in your many discussions with the *Reichsleiter* regarding Sweden the topic has come up, has it not?"

Rainer was aware, from the SS rumor mill, that Schellenberg himself was the force driving Himmler to initiate contacts with

Sweden's Count Bernadotte, contacts aimed at trying to arrange a separate peace between Germany and the Western Allies. Now was the time to hint that he knew about such efforts. Schellenberg showed no signs of either surprise or irritation. He was too good for that, Rainer decided.

"You are quite perceptive, Zeitz. But explain to me what your presence in Ahrenshoop has to do with the matter."

Still being cagey. "I judged that, as a famous artists' colony, Ahrenshoop would be a magnet for information about the illegal activities I wish to stop. Perhaps even a magnet for the clandestine art itself."

"Do you wish me to infiltrate the colony? I agree the place is a ripe source of information, but surely you cannot trust anyone there to provide you with reliable intelligence."

"I trust Oskar Lohnes, whom I'm sure your two men from Rostock interviewed."

"Lohnes is a friend of your father, not so?" Schellenberg said, his eyes narrowing almost imperceptibly.

"A friend of mine as well."

"Your father fled to England, did he not?"

That's it. Put me in my place without discrediting me entirely, Rainer thought. "My father fled; Oskar did not. Friends can have their differences." Think of your long-time, horse-riding companion, Admiral Carnaris, Rainer wanted to say, but knew better.

"I suppose that can be so. In any case, I think your suspicions of art fleeing to Sweden are accurate and I applaud your plan to place a small gunboat at the headland of the Darß. I have seen to that order myself."

"Thank you," Rainer said.

Schellenberg stood and offered his hand across the desk. "Carry on, *Standartenführer*."

"I shall," Rainer said.

"And keep me informed."

Another "I shall."

As he exited the office and headed again toward the stairwell, Rainer wondered: Why doesn't Herr Schellenberg have *other, more urgent priorities?* Perhaps because he knows something Himmler doesn't.

Thursday
March 15, 1945
Washington, D.C.

My dear Katherine,

A brief note only, lest I give the Devil time to read my thoughts. He's watching and listening, I've decided. Or at least his minions are.

I paid a visit to Father Roskosz yesterday. The purpose of his invitation ostensibly was to ask me to keep my eyes open for paintings and sculptures especially dear to him, works heisted by the Germans from Poland. But before we finished he brought up our relationship, as told to him by Marcel Troquier.

The good padre's judgment on us, passed along free of any hellfire-and-damnation sermonizing, is, quite simply: End our relationship now. Sin no more. I took his pronouncement to be closer to friendly advice than to a Church edict, but what do I, a Lutheran and hence a heretic, know?

Father Theo promised me, us, something akin to the sanctity of the confessional, his guarantee not to tattle. But I have no idea what his churchly obligations commit him to. And he made clear that, above all, his concern is for the peace of his own soul, not the peace of ours.

I have no clue what he will do if we continue to thumb our noses at him, at everyone. I would greatly appreciate your thoughts on the dilemma we find ourselves confronting. I don't want to give you up, yet I don't want the power of the Church to come raining down on you either. I have little to fear from these people who disapprove of our bond, but I will lose sleep thinking about what harm devils in robes and uniforms may bring to you.

Write to me soon. Please.

My continued love,
Martin

Tuesday
March 20, 1945
Restaurant Stag and Pheasant
Berlin

When Karl Vollmer and Rainer entered the dining room from the kitchen, the room was vacant except for its sullen owner. Fritz Priebe, though a superb chef, was also a lamentable alcoholic, and he now sulked alone at a corner table, a nearly empty bottle of red wine in front of him. The pair of SS men ignored him, taking seats at the table farthest from the drunken man.

"I want you to take half of the supplies still here over to the island," Rainer said to his aide as he tore the seal from the neck of a bottle of wine. The island he referred to was *Pfaueninsel,* Peacock Island, in the middle of the River Havel. In more glorious days Joseph Goebbels had used the lovely island, with its little castles and English-style gardens, to entertain lavishly.

"So we're staying," Karl said glumly.

"We may have no choice." Rainer loosened the thin wires of the hood, which he then tossed aside. Holding the cork in place with a thumb, he twisted the bottle slowly lest he pop the cork, rather than allow it to ease away from the bottle.

"What makes you think the Russians won't swarm the island and find us?" Karl asked as Rainer poured champagne into the pair of flutes Karl had set before them.

"No one to rape; nothing there worth stealing."

"But they'll have to look to find that out."

Rainer sipped from his flute. "The Russians have been studying maps of Berlin since Stalingrad, reading all about the city. My guess is that by now they've even given all the sewer rats Russian names. They'll know the island is not worth their bother."

Karl drained his wine in a single swallow. "I hope you're right. Otherwise --."

They both knew that *otherwise* was too vile to contemplate. Even so, Rainer tried to make light, saying, "Otherwise, Karl, we both may find ourselves perched beside the Volga, listening to balalaikas entertain us."

Karl spat on the floor. "The Russians are criminal monsters. Spawn of the devil."

Rainer countered, "In *Twilight of the Idols* Nietzsche remarks, 'Evil men have no songs. How is it, then, the Russians have songs?'"

Karl snorted contemptuously.

Rainer changed the subject. "Now tell me again, Karl, how glad you are that you gathered up our magnificent stockpile in Schleswig-Holstein." Rainer removed a folded sheet of paper from his tunic and waved it in front of his aide.

"Am I free to say what I am thinking?" Karl asked.

Rainer looked over at the restaurant owner, now seemingly passed out, his head on the table. "Go on. But speak softly."

"You are right. *Der Führer* is mad and I'm sorry no one has succeeded in --." With his index finger Karl made a slicing motion in front of his throat. He then tapped the paper Rainer held.

The paper was a flier handed to Karl by a Hitler Youth that morning as Karl had made a reconnaissance trip to nearby Potsdam on the restaurant owner's bicycle in search of barrels in which to store reserves of fresh water. Dated the day before, the leaflet announced a scorched-earth proclamation issued by Adolf Hitler: On all warfronts food and buildings are to be destroyed without exception.

"Insane!" Karl proclaimed. "Food and buildings! Yes, I am now glad I took food from all those traitors."

"*Götterdämmerung!*" Rainer said.

"Twilight of the Fools, too, I hope," Karl muttered.

Rainer sighed. "I can't imagine frontline officers heeding this piece of *Scheiss*." Then he remembered his confrontation with General Kruger as the panzer commander advanced toward Leningrad, prepared to destroy everything in his path.

"Would you, if you were one of his generals?" Karl asked.

"Certainly not."

"At the risk of being shot?" Karl pressed.

Rainer ran a finger around the rim of his wine flute while he considered his answer. At last he said, "Perhaps not," Rainer said. "At least I'm pleased to know you approve my requisitioning all these provisions, *Hauptsturmführer*."

Karl grunted, then said, "I just hope we live to eat them."

Rainer watched Karl re-cork the wine bottle. "I have no idea how long my meeting with Hans Frank will be," he said.

"Don't let him bully you," Karl said. "He's no longer the Governor of Poland."

Rainer laughed. "He's little more than a fugitive on the run. I will have an advantage, whatever he wants from me."

Karl asked, "Why does he choose you? I thought his lackey, Mühlmann, would be the one he'd want to salt away his booty."

"You're behind times, Karl. Since last we dealt with Herr Frank he has a new art advisor, someone named Wilhelm Ernst von Palezieux. Never met him and probably never will. The illustrious governor fled Kracow hastily with only a small entourage. I am guessing he fled with more paintings than human companions. In any case, I cannot wait to see what he brought with him."

"I'll be back from the island by the time you return," Karl said. "What about our drunken friend?"

Rainer looked toward the restaurant's owner before lowering his voice and saying, "Give him more wine. Keep him drunk. I'd hate to have to dump him into the river for knowing too much, because then I'd have to rely on your cooking again."

Tuesday
March 20, 1945
Washington, D.C.

Martin sat on the steps of the Lincoln Memorial feeling sorry for himself. As Easter approached he had no plans for spending the holiday with anyone. He had yet to hear from Katherine; he felt enormously homesick; and even the weather, sunny and balmy on the day before the spring solstice, failed to correspond with his melancholy disposition.

"Hey, Mister?"

Martin turned to see a young girl, perhaps seven or eight, holding a camera out toward him.

"Will you please take a picture of me and my mom standing in front of President Lincoln?"

Martin forced a smile. No point dragging a pretty little girl into his gloominess. "Sure." And he accepted the camera.

The girl, wearing a yellow dress with a white bow and Buster Brown shoes, announced, "We're from Pennsylvania and there's no school this week."

"Where in Pennsylvania?" Martin asked.

"Biglerville. That's near Gettysburg."

"No wonder you want your picture taken with President Lincoln. I bet you know all about him."

"Yep. I do."

"Where's your mother?"

The girl pointed up the steps toward a woman who, damn it, reminded him of Katherine. "There she is. The lady in the blue dress and white gloves."

With a winning smile, too, Martin thought. "And what's your name?" Martin asked the girl.

"I'm Priscilla. And my mom's name is Rebecca."

Martin stood and watched the woman named Rebecca descend the steps toward him.

"Do you mind, sir? I hope we haven't interrupted you."

"My pleasure, ma'am."

The camera was a Baby Brownie, New York World's Fair edition, sold only at the World's Fair, as Martin remembered. He asked Priscilla about it.

"My daddy bought it there when he took us. Or so Mommy tells me. I was too young to remember."

Martin ventured, "Where is your daddy?"

Priscilla's eyes brightened. "My daddy's in Africa bombing Germans." She grinned.

"He's a pilot?" Martin asked.

"Yeaaaah! He flies a B… B --." She looked toward her mother.

"A B-24," Rebecca said.

Martin knelt down to Priscilla's level. "How do you know your daddy's in Africa? That's supposed to be a very big secret."

Priscilla jumped up and down and clapped her hands. "I know, I know. I know because Mommy and Daddy fooled everybody. Tell him how, Mommy."

Rebecca blushed. "Promise not to tell?"

Martin nodded.

Priscilla said, "You're not a G-man, are you?"

"No. I'm not a G-man, young lady."

"Then tell him, Mom."

With a mixture of embarrassment and pride Priscilla's mother explained. "Roger and I worked out an elaborate code. First, when he shipped out overseas he sent me a torn dollar bill. The bill was torn on the lower right side, which meant he was going to Africa. Then in his letters home he used a code we had created. The code told us he was flying a B-24, flying from a base somewhere in Tunisia."

Martin laughed. "So much for all the money the government spends on black ink and censors."

"Will you take our picture now, Mister? Mommy and I have lots of places to go yet today."

"Priscilla!"

"Sorry, Mom. Sorry, Mister."

Martin said, "That's okay. I wouldn't want you to miss anything while you're here." With a waggle of his fingers Martin positioned the two women so that Father Abraham's imposing countenance appeared between them, then held his breath, pressed the tiny button, and listened for the click.

"There. The two of you are immortalized in the company of Mister Lincoln."

"Thank you ever so much," Rebecca said as she took the camera from Martin. "You're very kind."

"My pleasure," Martin said.

"Come along, Priscilla. I hear the Smithsonian calling us."

"You do? Okay. Goodbye, Mister."

"Goodbye, Priscilla. Goodbye Priscilla's mother," Martin called as the two receded down the steps of the memorial. And, like a dash of cold water in his face, Martin's loneliness returned. Rebecca. Rebecca who? An attractive woman for sure. And no doubt lonely. Perhaps together we could --. Well, for a little while, anyway. Then Martin brought himself up short. Stop it, Wynerson. She's a married woman. Married with a child. He sighed and reminded himself: Yes. And so is Katherine Parker.

Friday
March 21, 1945
Berlin

"So who is she?" Karl Vollmer asked, staring at the painting Rainer had returned with late the previous evening.

"The title is *Portrait of a Young Man*," Rainer said.

"Looks like a woman to me," Karl said. He twisted the key on a tin of ham, peeled back the lid, and shook the ham onto a plate. After scraping away the jellied coating, he cut off a slice and passed a slice to Rainer.

"Long hair for men was in fashion during Raphael's time," Rainer explained as he poked the ham slice with a fork.

Karl spat. "If it is a male, he's a prissy *Schwul.*" A homosexual.

Rainer shook his head dismissively and waved his wine glass, requesting a refill, which Karl obliged.

The two men sat in one of the small bedrooms on the level above the Stag and Pheasant's dining room. Rainer had sent Fritz, temporarily sober, out to neighboring restaurants, most of which were also closed permanently, to trade food stocks for cigarettes with an admonition that he expected fierce bargaining – along with a strict accounting when the innkeeper returned.

After treating himself to a generous top-off of Fritz's best white Burgundy, Karl made himself comfortable again and said, "Tell me about Governor Frank. You scarcely spoke a word about him last night, you were so enchanted with his gift to you." Karl gestured toward the famous Raphael.

"Herr Frank was pompous as ever. Despite his being an obvious fugitive scrambling out of Kracow ahead of the Wehrmacht's retreat, he swears eternal allegiance to the *Führer* and claims he truly believes miracles will yet happen to end the Allies' successes and save the Reich."

"Of course," Karl said sarcastically.

"The painting is one of many he personally took from the Czartoryski Museum in Kracow. But, in his haste to decamp Kracow, it is one of only a handful he found himself able to bring with him."

"Poor fellow," Karl said.

"In any case, knowing the value of this particular painting, he insists I must find a secure hiding place for it. Then, when the fortunes of the Reich have turned again and victory is in sight, he will retrieve it from me and pay me generously for my efforts."

Karl laughed. "And you said, '*Ja, ja, ja*, Herr Governor.'"

"Something like that. Yes."

In a more serious tone Karl asked, "What *are* you going to do with it?"

"I don't quite know. Eventually, of course, we'll take it to the farm. But between now and then --." Rainer shrugged. "It won't be easy."

"All the more reason to get out of Berlin quickly. I don't like the idea of hanging around here. It's not safe. And I don't mean just the Russians."

"I know what you mean," Rainer said. "The latest joke is the *Volksturm*. Whoever thought of organizing the old and the lame into a militia capable of defending Berlin has an odd notion of *able-bodied*. You should have seen the clusters of old men marching rank and file in through the streets. Dozens of companies, hundreds of men, all carrying rakes, shovels, hoes, whatever else they could muster from the rubble."

Karl shook his head. "Same thing with gangs of Hitler Youth around here. Boys so young they should be home so their mothers could mop the snot off their little pink noses. Instead these urchins are digging foxholes and shoveling rocks to build strong points. I saw one boy carrying a *Panzerfaust* that is longer than he is tall. Who are we that we send children to man machine guns?" He held up the remaining ham by way of offering Rainer more.

"No, thank you. By the way, our plans to grab the Marc painting and make for the farm have been thwarted. See. I told you laying in all these stores would prove necessary."

Karl groaned. "What now?"

"Thuringa. The Werra District. The *Führer* has finally allowed Berlin museums to evacuate their works to the mines southwest of Erfurt."

"Does that make the *Führer* a defeatist?" Karl whispered.

"It proves he does have moments of sanity."

"Why Thuringia?"

"Churchill, Stalin, and Roosevelt met at Yalta to cut Germany into pieces after they win the war. The *Führer* somehow learned that the mines near Merkers fall just inside the American sector."

"When do we leave?"

"Tomorrow. Several convoys have already left Berlin. But the Culture Minister, a man named Rust, says it may be another week or so before everything is out of the city. I can't believe they've waited so long. Nor can I fathom why anyone would think storing works of art in the lower levels of the zoo's *Flak* towers was a good idea."

"So what is our job?" Karl asked.

""Observe. Intimidate, if necessary. Jurisdictional squabbles are already rife. Politics *über alles*."

"As usual."

"So let's decide where to hide the Raphael. I don't want to take it with us to Thuringa," Rainer said.

"Why don't we simply pretend to go to Thuringa, but head for the farm instead?"

"Because we are not going alone. A detachment of Waffen-SS will accompany us – for our protection."

"For our protection," Karl muttered contemptuously.

21

Easter Sunday
April 1, 1945
Washington, D.C.

"Wait! I've changed my mind," Martin shouted to the cab driver and rapped on the passenger-side window. The driver nodded and jerked a thumb in the direction of the backseat.

Until now attending Easter services at Georgetown Lutheran Church seemed like a good idea. But, as he watched families dressed in their finery strolling hand-in-hand toward the entrance of D.C.'s oldest Lutheran church, with its grand stone façade, Martin could not bring himself to join them.

"Take me back," he said to the driver as he settled into the rear seat of the taxi. On the return ride toward his apartment Martin took out the terse note that had finally arrived from Katherine.

Martin,

After much thought and agonizing, I now firmly believe we must do as Father Roskosz urges. Painful as I know it will be for both of us, I am certain that putting an end to our relationship will prove best for both of us in the long run.

I will truly miss you,
Katherine

Not even *Dear* Martin. *Painful as I know it will be.* Is that a quote from Father Theo? Close enough. "Damn you, damn you, damn you!"

"Something wrong, Mister?" the cabbie called out.

"Sorry. Just muttering to myself."

"I do that a lot myself," the cabbie said.

Martin crushed the note into a ball then instantly regretted his action and tried to iron out the page, pressing his palm against his thigh. He then folded the wrinkled sheet and stuffed it into the shirt pocket of his dress uniform.

David Fox had left town for the weekend, off to North Carolina with an office-pool tart who had promised to introduce him to the delights of sweet-potato pie.

After changing into casual civilian clothes Martin made himself a ham sandwich and opened a bottle of Pabst. Turning on the Magnavox, Martin learned that the U.S. 3rd Army was driving deep into Hessen and Thuringa, closing in on the city of Erfurt and preparing to capture the mining districts along the Werra River.

Oh, to be in Germany! Oh, to be anywhere but here, he thought. His Easter feast consumed, Martin turned off the radio and plopped himself on the sofa, where, to thoughts of sharing a sleeping bag with Maddy in some remote canoeing camp in northern Minnesota, Martin fell asleep.

Thursday
April 5, 1945
Lake Havel
Berlin

The thumping sound of Karl's footsteps coming up the stairway distracted Rainer from staring once again at the Raphael painting. When Karl entered the bedroom in the restaurant loft he handed Rainer a folded sheet of paper before announcing, "Our friends were only able provide us with Russian uniforms. They have no British uniforms, officers or otherwise." Karl held up a pair of brown uniforms with red epaulets. "I hope you don't mind, but I promoted myself to captain. You are still a colonel."

"How much?" Rainer asked. The SS officers running a black market from within SS Headquarters were known to be hard-nosed bargainers.

"They wanted two hundred cartons of cigarettes," Karl said.

"Thieves!"

Karl grinned. "I didn't say that to them – after all, they are officers and I am not – but we agreed on one hundred twenty-five."

354 | Jeff Ridenour

Rainer nodded, pleased. "Did you try yours on?"

"Yes. It's a bit snug, but tailoring was not included in the price. Your trousers may be a bit short. Russian officers are apparently all short and stout these days."

"I'll try it on later," Rainer said and opened the sheet of paper. "Shit! What does Schellenberg want now?"

"*Feldmarschall* Göring's head on a platter, from the talk among my level of SS at headquarters. Maybe he wants you to be the one to bring it to him."

Rainer snickered. "I'm probably the only one left in an SS uniform who can get close enough to Fat Herman to do the job."

Karl said, "To get close enough to him now you'll have to make your way through an army of Luftwaffe toadies at Karinhall."

Rainer said, "I heard he's moving his Karinhall collections to Upper Bavaria. If he heads there, too, Schellenberg can find someone else to do his dirty work."

"Another delay, in any case," Karl said.

Rainer looked again at the Rafael. Won't Anna be proud of me?

Karl sat down in the room's only other chair. "Would you like to know the latest news from Thuringia?"

"Let me guess. The Americans have already run up their flag in Erfurt."

"Nearly so. Kassel and Gotha have fallen. And… are you ready for this?" Karl said playfully.

"I'm ready to believe almost anything."

"The *Amis* have found the salt mine at Merkers."

"The gold."

Karl nodded. "Yes. The gold."

Rainer winced. "That means all our work, everybody's work, in Thuringia was to make life easier for the Americans."

"It appears so."

Rainer was not surprised. He had thought the entire enterprise a fool's errand from the beginning. Hiding Berlin museum paintings in the potassium and salt mines was not a bad idea, except for the fact they lay directly in the path of the U.S. 3rd Army, which was advancing at full speed north from Bavaria and west from the Rhineland. That the Americans were coming turned out to be of little concern to the men in charge of the mines and the convoys. More important to them was whose valuables deserved to be placed in what mines ahead of which other valuables. As it turned out, the most prized mine, at Merkers, ended up protecting almost no art works at all because the Reichsbank had decided to move its entire reserve of gold, silver, and currency from Berlin to that mine, which left almost no room for art storage. And now nearly all the Reich's monetary assets were in the hands of the Allies. What *were* they thinking? Rainer wondered. Folly, madness, imbecility! Panic has destroyed even bright men's reason.

"When does Schellenberg wish to see me?" Rainer said, staring again at the piece of paper. "This doesn't say."

"Right away," Karl said.

Rainer stood. He slipped the pair of Russian uniforms under the mattress, then lifted the mattress again and slid the Raphael between them. Taking the painting with him to Thuringia was one thing. There he could explain it away as simply one more painting to be hidden. But Schellenberg would know better. Few details escaped Himmler's second-in-command.

"Let's go," he said to Karl and muttered a prayer to no deity in particular that the Raphael would still be there when he returned.

Thursday
April 5, 1945
National Gallery
Washington, D.C.

Word of the Thuringian finds by Patton's 3rd Army spread quickly among MFA&A personnel. Their collective hope was that such an impressive discovery would boost the status of restoration in the eyes of the Army. John Nicholas Brown's earlier assessment had proved prescient. Army brass on the ground in Europe did not give the proverbial rat's ass about art salvation. As too many generals saw their task, killing German soldiers -- preferably from afar with tanks, artillery, and airplanes -- was not just the main job of Americans in Germany, it was their only job.

Maybe rescuing art isn't all that important, Martin reflected as he left the gallery for the long walk home. Perhaps I – all of us at MFA&A – have overestimated our worth. At the moment nothing seemed much worthwhile to him. I've reached a nadir, he realized. No Maddy, no Katherine, no grand voyage to Europe yet in sight.

He stopped for a sandwich and coffee at a corner delicatessen. Sitting at a corner table in the otherwise empty restaurant, he asked himself who, besides a handful of snobs, truly gave a shit whether the works of Rembrandt and Picasso hung on gallery walls, sat boxed in chilly salt mines, or went up in flames as hordes of fiends danced about the pyre waving their swastikas? If asked, how many people knew a Rubens from the Rueben sandwich he was eating? Or, worse, cared? Damned few, he supposed. Whether that meant too damned few, he wasn't sure at the moment.

While asking for a refill on coffee, he picked up the *Washington Post* and thumbed his way to the movie section. Nothing appealed to him. But then on the wall he saw a Red Cross poster advertising a pair of John Wayne movies at their local headquarters on E. Street. *Flying Tigers* and *Fighting Seabees*. The price of admission was to sign a pledge to donate a pint of blood. In Martin's current mood he thought: they're welcome to every drop I have.

Thursday
April 5, 1945
Gestapo Headquarters
Berlin

Sitting at his desk, feet propped up, *Obergruppenführer* Walter Schellenberg struck Rainer as disproportionately calm in light of the scarcely veiled pandemonium occurring elsewhere in the building. But then Schellenberg, Rainer was certain, knew secrets no one else knew, not ever Himmler.

"Sit, Zeitz, sit. Ignore what's going on out there." A vague wave toward the door.

Rainer declined the offer of a cigarette, removed his cap, and sat.

"Sorry about sending you off to Thuringia. Not my idea. I'm sure you did your best."

"I tried."

"I now have a more productive task for you to carry out," Schellenberg said, then lit up a cigarette and took several puffs. He stared for a long time at his burning cigarette, seeming to be totally engrossed.

Rainer tried not to squirm.

Finally, Schellenberg crushed out the cigarette and slowly lit another. After inhaling from the new cigarette and blowing smoke out through his nose, he said, "When I was a student at the University of Bonn, early on I took a seminar in metaphysics from a Jew named Jacob Blumberg. One afternoon when I arrived at class he was already in the room, sitting as I am, smoking a cigarette and staring out the window. No acknowledgement that any students were present. Fifteen minutes later he was still smoking and staring out the window. Finally, in disgust, I stood to leave. As I scooped up my books and walked toward the door, he turned to me and said, 'What's the matter, Herr Schellenberg? Don't you enjoy studying metaphysics?'"

Rainer managed a wan smile.

"What petty little games we sometimes play, eh? Toying with one another's minds?"

Such as now, Rainer thought.

"Get to the point, you are thinking, yes?"

"You seem to be in no hurry, *Obergruppenführer*."

"I am not, but everybody else is. So what is my problem, you wonder?"

"Do you have a problem?" Rainer asked.

"You play the game well, Zeitz."

"Are we playing a game?"

"See? A clever one, you are."

"If you say so."

"I do. I do."

"I'm always pleased to accept a compliment, especially from someone more clever than I."

Schellenberg gave Rainer a smile, then said, "The reason I wanted you here is this. I want you to escort *Reichsleiter* Himmler's collection of... well, you know. Escort the convoy of trucks taking his goods to Rostock to meet the U-boat coming from Kiel. Packing is nearly completed. You have only to act as escort." He paused. "Well, no. I want you to remain with the cargo until it is all safely on board the U-boat."

Rainer nodded. Another caretaker mission. He wondered if he would have time to fetch the Raphael and steal the Marc.

"I make this added offer," Schellenberg said. "You and your aide, Vollmer, may accompany the U-boat to Sweden. What do you think?"

What is *he* thinking? Rainer asked himself. "I have much work remaining here, *Obergruppenführer*. I prefer to stay."

Schellenberg's eyes narrowed. "Zeitz, if I thought for a moment you felt the slightest twinge of loyalty to anyone or anything other than yourself and your own selfish ends, I'd have you marched outside to the courtyard and shot."

"Excuse me?" Rainer stammered.

"Games, Zeitz. Games!"

"Am I missing something?" Rainer asked.

"Not for a moment and you know it. I offer you Sweden and you turn me down. Why?"

Rainer thought carefully before answering. "You know my father fled to London before the war began. He believed I should have joined him. I would not want to do anything to reinforce his adverse opinion of me, such as fleeing now like a coward."

"You can do better than that, *Standartenführer*. You don't give a shit what your father thinks of you."

"Every son cares what his father thinks of him."

"Nonsense. Try again."

"Okay. I don't believe a U-boat will succeed in crossing safely to Sweden. I'd prefer not to drown."

"That's better. I still don't believe you, but I cannot argue with a man who has a premonition."

Spoken by a man with ample experience, Rainer thought. Himmler, according to stories now elevated to the status of legends, sees more omens than the most superstitious medieval peasant ever imagined.

"When you reach Rostock you will remain there until the U-boat sails. Then you may return to Berlin."

If there still is a Berlin, Rainer left unsaid.

"One more thing," Schellenberg said. "You do know that your cousin Anna Stahlinger is in Switzerland, don't you? When the Americans were about to capture Munich she headed south to Austria, then crossed over to Switzerland. She's in Bern, working with the Americans."

"Americans?"

"She's not a traitor. She's actually working for me." Pause. "Something I'm sure you don't know, but may as well learn now, is that the Americans, though officially allies of the Russians, don't trust the man they call Uncle Joe. They want to know as much about him as they can learn. And who better to help them than us? So Anna works in the office of a man named Allen Dulles, America's chief spy in Switzerland. She fell into the job, so to speak, by way of these." He reached into a desk drawer. "I'm certain these will interest you."

Rainer accepted a sealed envelope.

"It came by way of --. Oh, never mind how it got here."

When Rainer opened the envelope he found himself staring at photos of a nude Anna, in bed with a man he failed to recognize. Or did he?

"His name is Elliott Parker. Officially he is an art professor, part of an American unit assigned to recover and return stolen art from territories the Americans have taken back. Unofficially he works for Dulles, whose group is known by the initials OSS. Anna's art expertise came in handy in allowing her to get to know Herr Parker. But, as you can see, other talents allowed her to get to know him even better."

"So I see," Rainer muttered, trying to conceal his annoyance with his cousin.

"I want you to go directly from here to Schloß Ziethen, and from there to Rostock. I shall be in touch with you while you are in Rostock." That said, Schellenberg gave Rainer a dismissive wave.

Rainer left SS headquarters, found Karl, and filled his aide in on the latest set of frustrations facing them.

Saturday
April 7, 1945
Washington, D.C.

At last! A letter from Maddy. Martin had left work early, his eyes blurry and his head aching from staring at maps. Now, a beer in hand and a plate of stale oatmeal cookies in front of him, he read.

Dear Martin,

Sorry to be tardy with my Easter letter. My annual spring cold hit me later and harder than usual. I scarcely enjoyed the grand feast Mother put on for everybody. But I shouldn't complain. Dad's left arm is in a sling. He fell off a ladder while climbing down from checking the cottage roof for leaks. I do believe he suffered more pain from embarrassment than from the fracture to his ulna.

Easter, alas, is nearly as much an ode to gluttony as Thanksgiving. Praise be rationing is mostly over. Again,

Dad drove down to Iowa to pick up a ham. Yummy! Wish you'd been here to share.

Mostly I just want you to know how much we all miss you. I almost can't bear the thought that soon you'll be heading across the sea for who knows how long. I know you are ever so eager to go and that makes the idea a little less painful for me. But not much. I know how much your going means to you, wanting to feel you're finally going to make a useful contribution to making things right again over there.

But the increased distance will only make it worse for me. Actually, not the distance directly, but the added slowness of the mail because of it. Hah! I should talk. Look how desultory I've been while you're still stateside. Like that word? *Desultory*? I found it in the dictionary while I was looking up *desuetude*, a word I heard a professor at UM use during a lecture I went to on literary trends in the twentieth century. I decided I'd try to work it into the next letter I wrote you. *Desultory*, that is. But, come to think of it, I found a way to work *desuetude* in as well. Sort of.

Mom is going to see Doc Leonard next week. Do you remember Mrs. Pengilly, who lives down on the corner? Well, she's been diagnosed with sugar diabetes and is now going up and down the block telling everybody who will listen to her everything she knows – or thinks she knows – about the disease.

The upshot is: Mom is worried she might have it. No good reason for her to think so, other than the bee that fat, strudel-munching biddy put in her bonnet. She doesn't have one single symptom, Martin. Not one. But she says she ought to have a check-up, just in case.

Jeez! I'm sorry. Re-reading this, I sound more like a hospital nurse passing along my ward's patient charts to you. Overall, we're all pretty darned healthy. And safe. Thank God for safe. I think of all the pitiable folks living in all the world's war zones and count myself lucky. Count all of us here at home very lucky.

Confession, Martin. The glass cover on the photo of you I keep next to me when I write is now so smeared with lipstick that I have to fetch some cleaner and a cloth so I can recognize you again. Yes, it's a conceit that I put on lipstick before I sit down to write you. But you do like me to wear it when --. Well, you know when. Oooo! I'm all tingly just thinking about it. About you and me – together.

Stop, Maddy, I'm telling myself. I remind myself I could fall over dead from the excitement. Then Mom would walk in, find me dead, read my letter, fall over from shock, after which I'd die of embarrassment if I weren't dead already.

I can hear you now, mimicking me. "Stop being silly, Maddy Wynerson," you are saying. And stop I shall. Stop writing, that is. Not stop thinking about you; not stop loving you. Never! Never! Never!

Your dear, dearer, dearest (yet only!!!) sister,
Madeleine

22

Friday
April 13, 1945
Washington, D.C.

During a midday break Martin meandered outside the National Gallery and stood at the corner of 7th Street and Constitution Avenue. Little traffic moved through the usually busy intersection. Pedestrians walked with their heads down. The scene reminded Martin of the muffled silence common to Washington on the day after a mid-winter snowstorm. But this was spring. The sun was shining; the weather was warm. Instead, this was the day after news arrived from Georgia than President Roosevelt had died. The effect on the city – no doubt the nation – was numbing.

The basement of the gallery had been abuzz all morning, everyone speculating on what the consequences of the president's death might be. Upon first hearing the news Martin found himself straining to remember the name of the vice-president. Then he overheard someone mumble the name *Truman*. Harry? Yes, that was it. Harry Truman. Definitely a man without distinction. Intelligence? Good judgment? Common sense? The ability to rise to the stature to which events had now elevated him? "Let's hide and watch," Maddy often liked to say.

Meanwhile, here I sit, damn it.

"Hey, Martin. Have you heard the good news?" David Fox popped into the room doing a clumsy Fred Astaire imitation.

Only someone like Fox would think the president's death good news, Martin thought. He truly is a rotten character.

"We've been assigned. At last! New York departure date of May One. Munich here we come!"

"You not just making this up?"

"Hell, no! Go upstairs. Ask anybody," Fox said, all smiles.

Just then a clerk named Jamison walked in.

Martin said, "Hey, Jaimie. Have we really been given a ship-out date?"

The clerk, "Fox is lying, if he told you that."

Martin glared at Fox, who in turn glared at Jamison.

Then Jamison recanted. He grinned at Fox. "Gotcha, Foxie." To Martin, "'Tis true, Lieutenant. You and Br'er Fox here sail for London from New York City on the first day of May. Congratulations."

Martin mentally mumbled a half-hearted apology to Fox for thinking so badly of him, then turned his mind to Katherine, wondering if he should invite her to see him off.

———————

Thursday
April 19, 1945
Rostock, Germany

Rainer had now spent two weeks in Rostock and the only vessels belonging to the *Kriegsmarine* that showed up were ships from convoys bringing wounded soldiers home, along with panicked refugees from the East, fleeing ahead of the Red Army's advance. No U-boats.

This day three more ships arrived and the streets of the city were again choked with dirty, hungry wretches, many carrying their few remaining possessions on their backs. As he had when other ships full of these pitiful creatures showed up in the port, Rainer doubled the number of guards protecting the five-truck convoy filled with Himmler's pilfered art works.

Little of Rostock, as far as Rainer had been able to determine, was left standing. Because of the Heinkel aircraft factories, the Allies had made Rostock a premier target. So that Rainer and his entourage could have living quarters, local SS had cleared tenants from one of the few buildings immediately south of the Stein Tor judged still structurally sound. In a park across from the railroad station the trucks were parked, circled like covered wagons in a Hollywood western.

Though trains no longer ran, throngs of refugees continually milled about the Bahnhof, apparently expecting miracles in the form of untwisted tracks, workable engines, and comfortable coaches to speed them away, take them to where people wore clean clothes, ate bread free from insects, slept in soft beds through quiet nights, and awoke not having to face yet another war to end all wars.

Rainer stepped out into the morning sunlight and checked his bearings, looking for the steeple of St. Mary's Church, built in the 13th century. If one wanted to witness a miracle incarnate, one need look no farther than the church. Nearly bombed to oblivion as Rostock had been, St. Mary's still stood, unscathed.

Not daring to leave the city since arriving for fear of not being present to greet the milk-cow U-boat, Rainer had sent Karl to Ahrenshoop to determine the status of the boat Thelda was going to capture and hide. Karl returned saying he had been unable to find Thelda but left a message with Oskar Lohnes for her to get in touch with Rainer. Karl's opinion regarding Oskar's health was not reassuring. Nor was he pleased to hear from Oskar that the Gestapo had not only made inquiries about Thelda but apparently also was having her followed.

Karl had gone to Ahrenshoop on the 9th. No word had come from Thelda until the 17th, two days ago. Her message had been simple and delivered by a bearded, one-legged veteran: Thursday, 10 a.m., north side of Marienkirche, St. Mary's. Signed: T.

After shooing away a beggar who wanted to shine his boots with a dirty rag, Rainer turned and saw a pair of girls -- one a teenager, the other younger -- blocking his way. Both wore *Jungmadel* uniforms, the collars and cuffs of each in need of mending.

"*Wie heissen Sie, bitte?*" the older girl asked.

"My name? Or my rank?"

"Ihr Name, bitte."

Well, they're only girls, Rainer thought. Indulge them. "My name is Zeitz. Rainer Zeitz."

The younger girl looked at the older one, who nodded. Then the younger girl thrust a small piece of paper at Rainer.

"What is this?"

"Take it, please," the older girl said.

Rainer obeyed. Then he watched as the two girls turned and ran off, disappearing into a horde of refugees pushing and jostling one another as they made their way toward the train station. When he unfolded the paper it read: Change. Cemetery next to Old Marketplace on Altschmiedestrasse. Go to the *Stadtmauer* behind cemetery. Same time. Signed: T

A member of the merchant-driven Hanseatic League formed in the 13th century, Rostock was once a walled city. Several sections of the old wall, the *Stadtmauer*, still stood.

After asking directions from a local policeman, Rainer walked the four blocks leading to Der Alte Markt, zig-zagged his way through the cemetery, and waited, leaning against the chill stone blocks of the ancient wall.

His watch read ten minutes after ten when he saw a one-legged soldier dressed in the *feldgrau* of the Wehrmacht coming toward him on a pair of crutches. He was not the same soldier who had presented him with Thelda's note two days earlier, unless the man had shaved his beard in the meantime.

Only when the soldier stopped in front of him and took off a grimy field cap did Rainer realize it was Thelda.

"How better to blend in than to be a crippled soldier, eh?" she said.

Rainer nodded. "They're everywhere."

"Uncomfortable but effective, yes?" she said. "My leg hurts from being doubled so long."

"How is Oskar?" Rainer asked.

"Not well, but I can't get medicines. Wine is the only sedative I have to give him."

"And the boat?"

"No one told you?"

"Told me what?"

"The boat blew up," Thelda said.

"Blew up?"

"But not the boat you want," she said, teasingly. "Truly? You didn't hear?"

Rainer looked at her. "No."

"We captured the Gestapo launch. Don't ask who *we* consists of. The launch is hidden in the Darß Forest just south of the lighthouse. The propeller broke while we were moving it. Not knowing where to find any spare parts, we stole a prop from a boat here in Rostock.

Rainer frowned.

"The boat's crew are dead and well-buried. To cover the absence of boat and crew we blew up a small fishing boat a few hundred yards off the lighthouse. Several witnesses will swear the boat must have hit a mine and sunk. At this point no one is likely to send down a diver to check the wreckage. To find your boat, start at the end of the lighthouse road, step off one hundred sixty paces, then turn right and go into the woods to a tree with a pair of railroad spikes driven into its trunk at knee-level. Go right again, this time one hundred paces and you will find the boat. It's actually not far from the beach, but this is the best way to find it."

"How much help will Karl and I need to launch it?" Rainer asked.

"Moving it took four of us, using pole skids and a tractor. Find me when you are ready and I will help."

"That may be a while. You are kind to help. I am grateful, even though at the moment I have no way to show my gratitude."

"I don't care about your gratitude, *Standartenführer*. For that matter, I don't care about you. You are nothing to me."

"Then why --?"

"Because of Oskar's respect for your father; because of their long-time friendship. That is why I do this. Oskar says your father is not to be held accountable for his son's turning out to be a Nazi and a fool."

"Oskar's right. Tell him I said so. Now go. I will show up again in Ahrenshoop, but likely not very soon."

"Why? Why not leave now?"

"I can't."

"What prevents you?"

"A painting in Berlin."

Thelda scoffed, "News this morning is that the Russians have bridged the Oder just south of Stettin. In only a few days Russian soldiers will be standing here where we are standing. No painting is worth risking your life for. By the time you return to Berlin the painting will surely be gone. For that matter, Berlin will be gone – and you with it."

"Perhaps, but I must try."

"You are more than a fool, Herr Zeitz. You are mad."

Rainer shrugged. "In a world gone mad."

Thelda held out her hand. "I wish you much luck, for you will need all you can find. Luck is all you have."

"I've made plans."

"Explain that to the Russians when they arrive."

Rainer shook the young woman's hand. "Thank you for your good wishes for me."

Thelda nodded, then gestured toward nearby gravestones. "Just remember, Herr Zeitz, that eventually the lucky and the unlucky end up the same. Sooner or later everybody's luck runs out. It's only a matter of time."

"The difference between sooner and later is what distinguishes us from them," Rainer said, with a sweeping move of an arm in the direction of the rows of markers.

"Then I shall count on seeing you later," she said, snapped off a smart salute, turned, and hobbled away.

———————

Thursday
April 19, 1945
National Gallery
Washington, D.C.

David Fox entered the map room and turned the air blue with his cursing. Fists clenched, he pounded on his desk, sending a protractor, compass, and several pencils onto the floor.

"Get turned down for a date, David?" Martin asked.

"You obviously haven't heard the news."

"I rarely do until you bless me with tidings of comfort and joy. I take it this news isn't so cheery. Something Harry Truman did? I know you don't like him."

"I wish it were Ol' Harry S. Then at least I'd know who to throw rocks at."

"Whom, David. Whom."

"Whom shazoom. Our departure date has been postponed."

Fox was genuinely angry. No feigning it. So he can't be putting me on, Martin decided. "Postponed for how long?"

"Until at least the first of June. One whole fucking month."

With a deep sigh, Martin exhaled an audible, "Shit!"

"Exactly, " Fox said.

"Any reason given?"

"Politics. Army politics. Apparently Third Army doesn't want MFA&A to use the most logical building in Munich for us to do our business. They want the Führerbau for their own headquarters. So there's a big squabble about that. And then – get this – Third Army claims there's not enough housing to provide us with adequate quarters. Munich is just a pile of rubble, you know." His began to shout. "Well, what about tents? Give us a couple of tents, for chrissake. We'll even build our own latrine."

"And it's going to take an entire month or more to resolve this?" Martin said.

"Patton can move his armor a hundred miles a day, but it's going to take his staff a whole month to find quarters for a handful of us. Rotten bureaucratic bastards!" Fox pounded his desk again.

"Meanwhile we're just supposed to sit here on our thumbs?" Martin said.

Fox made fists with his thumbs jutting up. "I know where I'd like to put my thumbs and it ain't in no Christmas pie."

"Who do we see about getting leave? I'm not sitting here marking the days off by scratching chalk marks on the wall," Martin said.

"Ask Captain Timberlake. He's the one who gave me the news."

"What about you?"

"Me? Fuck it. If the Fräuleins have to wait a while longer to get their hands on me, I'll just have to plow my way through another company's worth of women over at the Pentagon."

Lucky you, Martin thought. But what am I going to do? No Katherine to go to. However, just maybe --.

Friday
April 20, 1945
Rostock, Germany

As Rainer sat in his undershirt and held out a foot for Karl to ease a boot onto it, the door to their small room opened and Walter Schellenberg strode in with Heinrich Himmler right behind him. Karl dropped the boot and stood to attention, his left arm extended but no "Heil Hitler" came from his lips. Rainer remained seated, an act of insubordination neither of his superiors seemed to take offense at.

"Leave us, *Hauptscharführer*," Schellenberg said quietly.

Karl saluted again, looked at Rainer, who nodded, then left, closing the door behind him.

"A brandy, gentlemen?" Rainer asked, pointing toward a bottle of V.S.O.P on a shelf.

"No, thank you, Zeitz," Schellenberg said. Himmler shook his head.

Bootless, Rainer walked across the room to a closet and retrieved his tunic. After buttoning all its buttons he turned to the two men, either of whom he had expected to say something by then, and said, "Oughtn't you both be in Berlin with the *Führer*, wishing him a most enjoyable birthday? Today is his 60th, is it not?"

Schellenberg grimaced. "You know us both better than that by now."

"Ah! Let me guess. You've come to board the U-boat that will arrive any minute now and whisk you away to Stockholm."

"Tread carefully, Zeitz. I could still have you shot, you realize," Schellenberg said.

"Then tell me why you are here."

Himmler spoke for the first time. "We are on our way to Lübeck."

"Is that where our U-boat intends to dock?" Rainer said.

"The Swedish legation is there," Himmler said.

"Count Bernadotte," Rainer said.

Himmler continued. "We're certain Count Bernadotte can persuade the British and the Americans to make
peace with us, then join us in a common stance against the
Bolsheviks."

Rainer looked toward Schellenberg to see if he was party
to such a lunatic fantasy. The *Obergruppenführer* nodded
solemnly.

"Am I to join you?" Rainer said.

Schellenberg said, "No. You are to leave here for Karinhall
immediately."

"Karinhall?"

"That weasel Göring has already sent several trainloads of
works from his collections south to the Obersalzberg. I want you
to intervene, to stop him from sending any more."

"But aren't they safer there? And why send me to stop him?
The Russians will be there quickly enough. If they've crossed the
River Oder, they'll be there soon."

"Actually not," Schellenberg said. "General Rokossovsky is
heading directly for here on a broad front, while General Zhukov aims directly for Berlin. In between? Nothing."

"So, assuming I make it as far as Karinhall, what do I do
when I get there? I understand the *Reichsmarschall* has surrounded himself with a phalanx of Luftwaffe men."

"Göring knows you. You've worked with him before," Himmler said. "He'll let you through."

Rainer held his palms out. "Okay. I get through. How do I
stop him from doing anything he chooses to do?"

"Arrest him," Himmler said sharply. Sounding like Hitler,
Himmler said, "He's a traitor. Shoot him if you must!"

Rainer had to force back a laugh. Through the years Hitler often has referred to Himmler as "der treue Heinrich", Rainer reminded himself. But the man now on his way to sell out the *Führer* calls Göring a traitor.

"You need to prevent him from removing any more art from Karinhall," Schellenberg said, sounding far more reasonable than Himmler.

"Prevent him for how long?" Rainer asked.

"Until the British and Americans arrive to relieve you," Himmler shouted, almost shrieking.

"Take your detachment of troops with you. I'll arrange to have the convoy guarded," Schellenberg said.

As if it matters, Rainer thought. "When do I leave?"

"Immediately. Before Göring can do more harm," Himmler insisted.

More harm. Yes, shipping a bunch of second-rate art work south constitutes more harm than anything you do or have done, Rainer thought angrily.

"By the way, Zeitz, what was your final decision regarding the Amber Room?" Schellenberg asked.

"My final decision was to let Rohde make the final decision. No. *Let* is too strong. He insisted, so I gave him two choices: ship it by rail or ship it by barge. Knowing Rohde as I do, I suspect he did neither."

"Then the Russians have it back," Schellenberg sighed.

"Or no one has it. Maybe the Russians blew up the castle, not knowing what lay in the basement," Rainer surmised.

Schellenberg smiled a small, tight smile. "I think Rohde himself might have blown up the castle."

"Before or after he removed the crates of amber?"

Schellenberg shrugged. "*Auf Wiedersehen*, Zeitz. Good luck with Göring."

Rainer walked to the door, opened it, and shouted, "Karl, come help with my boots. The *Reichsleiter* and *Obergruppenführer* are leaving." Then he stood aside and watched the men depart, no one saying anything.

As Karl entered the room Rainer saw Schellenberg turn, give Karl a fixed gaze and start to speak. But then Himmler's second clearly thought better of it, spun on a heel, and walked briskly to catch up with Himmler.

Friday
April 20, 1945
Washington, D.C.

"You're calling long distance, Martin? How extravagant! What's the matter?" Maddy said from the Minneapolis end of the phone line.

"Nothing's the matter. Well, I mean I'm not sick or hurt or anything. I'm calling because I want to see you."

"See me? I thought you were leaving for Europe in a few days."

"I am, but --." Martin explained the snafu without using the word. Maddy knew the word and also understood that the 'fu' did not stand for *fouled up*. Though scarcely a prig, Maddy disdained the "unnecessary use of vulgar slang". In her case, *unnecessary use* was a redundancy.

"Yes! I'd love to see you. Will you be coming home?" Maddy said.

"I'd rather spend time with just you, Sis. Just the two of us. I've arranged seven days' leave."

No response.

"Maddy?"

"I'm hardly reluctant, Martin. My mind is racing, trying to figure out how to go about it. What to tell Mom and Dad. What to say to my boss at the library."

"I'll pay for your ticket, Maddy. I'll even meet you more than halfway. How about Chicago? I can catch an overnight train and so can you. Only a couple hours difference in arrival times. I've checked the schedules."

"My God, Martin you are --. I was going to say *scheming*, but *efficient* is more accurate."

"Then your answer is yes?"

"Of course, it is. Just tell me when. I'll figure out everything I need to do and say on this end."

"God, Maddy. I can hardly wait. This is going to be great."

"It will indeed, my precious brother. You can't begin to imagine how much I miss you, dream about you. Want you."

"Yes I can, because I share the same longings, the same fantasies."

"Stop it, Martin! You're making me want to stick my tongue all the way through the telephone line to kiss you."

"Just stick it as far as Chicago. I'll stick mine out to meet it there."

"Oooo! I feel so deliciously wicked," Maddy said. "I can hardly wait."

"Naughty, not wicked," Martin corrected and explained the details of his plan for their clandestine rendezvous.

23

Saturday
April 21, 1945
Lower Pomerania
Ten kilometers from Karinhall

"Do you suppose Frau Limberger is still keeping tally of Herr Göring's collections?" Karl asked as he steered the Kugelwagen down the tree-lined road toward the *Reichsmarschall's* estate.

"If not in person, her ghost is no doubt still in charge," Rainer allowed.

"Having met her, I fear even more meeting her ghost," Karl joked.

"I agree. The ghost of Frau Limberger will scare any man shitless."

"After all the crummy food we endured in Rostock, that would be almost welcome."

"On that topic, I wonder what the Austrian corporal dined on for his birthday yesterday?" Rainer asked.

"What do you think?"

"Perhaps his chef prepared Beluga caviar and steamed sturgeon in honor of the imminent arrival of a host of Russian guests, eh?"

"No. Instead, I think Herr Schikelgruber would order up borscht and carp heads," Karl said, using the surname Adolf Hitler was born with.

"No, no. That would be disrespectful. After all, if Fredrick the Great could present the Amber Room to a czar, the least Herr Hitler can do, by way of welcome, is to serve up the culinary treasures of Berlin. From the dead animals at the Tiergarten he could present seared trunk of elephant, fried hide of hippo, burnt hair of monkey, and the scorched manes of lions. After all, Hitler holds Stalin in at least as much esteem as he holds the leader of any of several African tribal chiefs."

Karl slowed the car when ahead he saw a roadblock. At least it was a German blockade, not a Russian one. "So soon?"

"They're not Luftwaffe, Karl."

"So I see. Waffen-SS, I think." As they approached the blockade, Karl said, "I see some Wiking Division patches. They are not even German."

"At least they're not Russians," Rainer said evenly.

A major stepped out from behind the sawhorse barricade and approached the Kugelwagon. He studied Rainer carefully before saying, "What is your purpose in driving on this road?"

Rainer saw no point in telling him such a purpose was none of his business. "I am on my way to see *Reichsmarschall* Göring."

"Why so?" the major said.

"By order of *Reichsleiter* Himmler I am to secure the *Reichsmarshall's* art collection, to see that no more of his works are removed from Karinhall."

"The *Reichsmarshall* has already left his estate," the major declared.

"Even so, I am to see that none of his belongings follow him," Rainer said.

The major shook his head. "No longer. The *Führer* has other plans for you."

"In addition to orders from the *Reichsleiter*, I possess a *Führervorbehalt.*"

The major smiled. "My orders, too, come from the *Führer* and take precedence over yours. Stopping Zhukov from reaching Berlin, you must agree, is more important than stopping the *Reichsmarschall's* art works from reaching Bavaria."

"Of course, I agree," Rainer said. "But my aide and I are of no use fighting the Russians. We would prove more hindrance than help. So, if you please, stand aside and allow me to carry out my orders. And I wish you luck fulfilling yours."

"I cannot allow you to pass, *Standartenführer.* My orders permit of no exceptions."

"You obviously made an exception for *Reichsmarschall* Göring," Rainer pointed out.

"You are not a *Reichsmarschall.*"

"But I am the stand-in for *Reichsleiter* Himmler and his deputy," Rainer countered, hoping Himmler and Schellenberg had not already been arrested for treasonous acts.

"Enough!" the major said. "You and your aide are not exempt. You must come with us."

Rainer climbed from the Kugelwagon. "I demand to speak with your commanding officer."

The major laughed. "General Steiner has more important things to do than listen to your quibblings."

"Felix Steiner?"

"Yes. Don't tell me you know him personally."

"Only by reputation," Rainer said. "The only Waffen-SS general respected by Wehrmacht officers."

"Good. Then I hope you will serve under him proudly, but serve under him you will, proud or not." The major then gestured for a squad of soldiers to step forward. The men lowered their automatic weapons as the did so.

Rainer looked at Karl, who gestured for him to get back into the car. As Rainer opened the car door, Karl said, "Like our choice between Russians and British. We can go long and be shot in the front by Russians or try to flee and be shot in the back by our own soldiers. Either way --."

"You're right," Rainer said. "At least for now."

Saturday
April 21, 1945
Union Station
Chicago

From a distance Martin recognized the back of Maddy's red hat as she sat on a bench in the middle of the Great Hall. Her hat, with its black veil, had been his gift to her on her twenty-second birthday, along with a pair of white gloves.

Despite crowd noise reverberating through the cavernous hall, Martin crept on tip-toe until he stood behind his sister. Then he cupped in hands to his mouth and said, "Paging Miss Madeleine Wynerson. Paging a Madeleine Wynerson."

Maddy flinched and knocked her hat off as she turned. "Oh, Martin. You can be so --."

"So silly," he finished as he took her in his arms and lifted her over the bench.

"Martin! People are watching!"

"Let 'em watch." He spun her around to face him and kissed her, keeping his lips against hers as he pulled her down in order for him to retrieve her hat.

"Oh, Martin, I'm so excited to see you! But, please. Behave yourself. Save your antics for when we're... well, when we're --."

"Alone."

"Yes!"

"Then let me take your luggage and let's get out of here so we can --."

"Be alone!" Maddy swooned.

"God. I thought Mom and Dad bought you a new suitcase when you finished library school," Martin said as he stared in mock-disgust at the worn and faded box with a broken claps that Maddy had brought.

"They did, but I preferred to bring this one. It reminds me of --."

"I know what it reminds you of." Visions of a previous escape to Chicago flashed through Martin's mind, his and Maddy's very first non-tent-camping peccadillo away from home. "Did you pack the same items?" Martin remembered the sexy underwear and night-gown Maddy had surprised him with and still wondered how she had bought them, brought them home, and packed them without their nosy mother's discovering Maddy's flimsy, naughty little secrets.

"You'll see."

"I hope so."

"Where are we staying? Same place?"

Martin nodded as the exited the train station. "The Inn at Lincoln Park."

"At least it has nostalgia going for it," Maddy said snidely.

"It was the best I could do on such short notice," Martin explained. "I know. The rooms are small, the bathrooms smaller. Everything is poorly lit. But --."

"But we'll be too busy to notice. Right?"

"I hope so."

"Stop repeating yourself, Martin."

"Yes, ma'am."

In the taxi to the hotel Martin asked, "What did Mom and Dad say when you told them."

"They're disappointed they couldn't come along," with a broad grin.

"Actually, I'm kind of sorry I can't see them. I do miss them. Even Dad."

"You're kind of sorry," Maddy teased.

"Well… yes, I am."

"But not *that* sorry, right?"

Martin gave his sister a tight hug. "Not *that* sorry. No."

Sunday
April 22, 1945
Oranienburg
15 kilometers north of Berlin

"Don't tell anyone you speak Russian," Rainer said to Karl as they crouched beside an abandoned panzer with its left tread untracked. "*Leuntnant* Hochhalter may decide to send us out on forward patrol if he finds out."

"Why not tell him? Staying here is surely going to get us killed. Look at who we are surrounded by. Old men, boys, the wounded. And do you suppose those sailors and paratroopers over there –" he pointed to several dozen men in uniform who lay prone, lining the east bank of the Havel-Oder Kanal, smoking, chatting, or simply staring " – have ever seen combat?"

Since their conscription into combat service Karl and Rainer together had determined General Steiner's so-called Army Group consisted of no more than pathetic remnants of several SS divisions, Prinz Eugen, Nordland, Wallonien, Wiking, Nederland -- all comprised of *Aüslander*, foreigners – and a chilling mixture of Hitler Youth and *Volkssturm*.

Initially, not even the major who had "enlisted" them could explain to Rainer where General Steiner's "Army Group" was located. Information delivered to the major was confusing, the major admitted. First reports placed Group Steiner in Eberswalde; later accounts put the phantom army closer to Oranienburg. So the major had split the difference and moved toward Klosterfelde, where he simply guessed and turned left toward Oranienburg. Or maybe, Rainer surmised, he turned left because left was west, away from the Russian advance.

Only now, from *Leuntnant* Hochhalter, the commander of their ragtag unit, they learned that sizeable and heavily armed Russian units were both north and west of them and straddled the canal, cutting "Army Group Steiner" off from its hoped-for support, Field Marshal Hasso von Manteufel's Third Panzer Army.

"Perhaps you're right, Karl. Volunteering for a forward patrol would be safer, if only marginally."

Just then their lieutenant came down the line. "Prepare to move out. We're to follow the canal south, become part of the right wing defending the canal. The center will form at Oranienburg. And God help those on the left."

"*Leuntnant*, I have something important to tell you," Karl said as the officer walked by.

"Later. Move. The only important thing you can tell me now is that you are willing to help that group of wounded men over there to try to keep up with the rest of us." The lieutenant waved toward a cluster of men, most of whom struggled to their feet by means of crutches.

Sunday
April 22, 1945
Chicago

As they lay in bed, Maddy gently ran the tip of her index finger up and down the middle of Martin's bare chest. "You're not getting over her, are you?" she said.

"I'm trying."

She bent forward and kissed him lightly on his cheek. "Well, you're simply going to have to try harder, Brother dear. Look. She's married, she has a son, she has standing in a lah-dee-dah community. That's quite a lot to hang on to. So... given the choice, her decision was pretty obvious, Martin. Kiss *your* tush goodbye. How do you say *trifle* in German?"

Martin forced a smile. *"Bloß eine Kleinigkeit.* A mere little thing."

"That's you to Katherine Parker."

"You're right, Sis. That's all I am; all I was."

"It's not the end of the world, Martin."

A grin. "It's not?"

"As we just proved."

"So we did."

"You and Katherine will always have Paris. Well… at least Lake Sodomy, or wherever it was."

Martin gave Maddy a mock scowl. "Saranac."

"If you say so. Anyway, chalk her up to experience, Martin. You are much better, you know."

"At what?" he asked slyly.

"At talking about other women when you're in bed with me."

"That's all?"

"No. But don't press your luck by asking for a rave review."

"Okay. Let's get dressed and get out of this dark cave. See Chicago. Find someplace great to eat. No more talk about Katherine. I promise."

Monday
April 23, 1945
Havel-Order Canal Bridge
Hennigsdorf, Germany

"Hurry up, you bastards!"

From his prone position beside the canal Rainer watched Lieutenant Hochhalter raise himself on one knee and shake his fist toward the German sappers placing explosive charges beneath the bridge.

Russian infantry – from the Forty-Seventh Army, Karl had determined – already had made two assaults on the bridge. Now, from the increasing *pings* of bullets ricocheting off bridge girders, disabled tanks, and the abandoned German mobile artillery known as *Jadgpanzers*, the Russians were about to launch a third attempt.

Flattening himself, the lieutenant said, "We're lucky. They obviously want to capture the bridge intact. Otherwise, they'd have blown us all to hell by now with artillery and Stalin organs."

"How comforting," Rainer said in reply. "Here. Trade me. I'm pulling rank for just this moment." He pushed his Mauser 98K field rifle toward the lieutenant and, in return, relieved the lieutenant of his MP 38 machine pistol.

"Eager to kill more Russians faster, eh?" the lieutenant said.

"Karl, with his arm and a half, is a better marksman with the Mauser than I am. I haven't fired one since *Junkerschule*."

The lieutenant turned toward the bridge just as the sappers raced away from it. "Cowards! They didn't even wire those charges."

Karl shouted, "No time now. Here come the Cossacks."

"Cossacks hell," *Leutnant* Hochhalter sneered. "They're Siberian monkeys, which is why Zhukov wastes them so freely instead of precious artillery shells."

Some hundred meters beyond the far side of the canal Russian soldiers suddenly stood *en masse* and charged the bridge.

"We won't stop this one," the lieutenant judged. "Time to give up the bridge. Live to fight another round." He stood and shouted down the line of cowering German soldiers. "Fall back! Fall back!" Then, as he waved his rifle over his head, pointing the barrel of it rearward, a bullet struck him in a thigh, and, as he dropped his rifle to grab his wound, another bullet struck the side of his face.

Rainer watched, as the lieutenant, as if a figure caught on slow-motion film, pitched forward down the canal bank. "After him, Karl. Let's go. We'll never make it trying to retreat across open ground." Rolling over the embankment, Rainer saw Karl scrambling ahead of him, trying to catch the lieutenant before the wounded officer fell into the water.

Gunfire from the advancing Russians intensified as Rainer reached the lip of the canal. He eased himself over when he saw a barge just below him, the long boat moored fast against the canal wall. Karl already had boarded the barge and sat with the lieutenant cradled in his arms. Rainer dropped onto the boat and knelt beside the two men.

"So much for the lieutenant's luck," Karl said, his black tunic now smeared with blood. "Let's get below before the Russians see us."

Rainer nodded, then reached out to close the lieutenant's eyes.

Karl rolled the officer from his lap and crossed himself before scampering into down the steps of the companionway into the galley. Rainer followed. Moments later they heard shouts, in Russian, coming from the far side of the canal, soon accompanied by bullets raking the port side of the barge, causing both men to drop flat against the galley deck.

Beside him Rainer felt an arm. A cold arm. "Karl?" he whispered.

"Over here," Karl whispered back from his other side, and somewhere ahead of him. Forcing himself to look, Rainer recognized the yellow bandana belonging to the woman who weeks earlier had cursed at Karl for pissing into the canal. Until then Rainer had not even realized this was the same bridge he and Karl had crossed with their motorcycles on their way to Kiel.

"Karl."

"Yes?"

"Crawl this way."

Outside, Russian voices grew louder and more numerous.

"They're crossing the bridge," Karl whispered. "We need to hide ourselves better."

"I know. But come look."

Karl scooted to Rainer, pulling himself on his elbows.

"Recognize her?"

Karl nodded. "At least she won't have to worry that the Russians will rape her." Suddenly Karl raised his head, leaned on his armless elbow, and cocked his head.

"What is it?" Rainer asked.

"Take cover. Grenade."

Both men scrambled to shield themselves. Rainer rolled under a bunk and pulled a wooden bench tight against him. Before burying his face in his hands he saw Karl topple a table, turn it toward the rear hatch , then try to burrow under the dead woman.

Moments later came a *thud, thud, thud*, followed by a deafening explosion. Even with his face buried, Rainer saw the galley light up, felt the heat, heard wood splinter and glass shatter. Then he could no longer even hear the pulse pounding in his ears. He waited, expecting his life to drain from him. God! My head is going to explode, he told himself. He wiggled his fingers and felt nothing. I'm paralyzed, was his next thought. He tried to move but could not so much as raise his head away from his hands. What a way to die! Maybe this is how the barge woman died. Slowly, face down on the deck of this filthy, rotten barge.

"Karl?" he tried whispering, but couldn't tell if any sound emerged from his mouth.

His world was completely black when Rainer regained consciousness. He thought he heard sounds but perhaps I'm only imagining them, he decided. Still, the creaking noises, real or not, remained persistent, rhythmic even. I think I recognize those sounds. He realized his head no longer hurt and he searched his memory. Yes. Sounds of a boat rocking. The sounds he heard when he woke once as a teenager on Karl's brother's boat and discovered the boat had returned from the sea and was now moored alongside a pier in the Kieler Fiord. I'm on a barge and it is rocking against the side of the canal. I'm alive. Unless hell mirrors life.

"Karl?" Whispered. No answer, so he waited a while. Then, louder, "Karl?"

"I'm here, *Standartenführer*. I'm trying to find matches to light the candle I found."

"What about the Russians?"

"They've moved on. At least for now. Others will surely follow, but perhaps not until daylight."

"I'm glad you're alive," Rainer said.

"So am I. Glad for both of us. We may not think so when the sun comes up, but for now let us be thankful."

"Is the woman still here?" Rainer asked.

"I dragged her out and put her overboard. Same with the lieutenant. We may be here for some time," Karl said.

"How did the woman die?"

"Bullet. Probably from a ricochet. Or maybe she died from fright before the bullet found her."

"Are you injured?"

"Not badly. The woman made a good shield. One small shard of shrapnel near my crotch. Lucky me. It missed my balls. If I still had my right forearm it would have ripped into that and no doubt a surgeon would want to amputate it."

"I'm glad you can laugh at such misfortune," Rainer said.

"Telling little jokes on ourselves may be all that keeps us from wanting to drown ourselves in the canal. We are not in very jolly circumstances, you realize. Alive? Yes. Safe? Far from it. We are now surrounded by Russians who may prefer cutting our balls off to shooting us."

"Go back to telling funny jokes," Rainer said.

"Okay. Do you know how I knew you were still alive after the grenade went off?"

"How?'

"You snored louder than usual."

"I never knew I snored. Why did you not inform me years ago?"

"Because until now you have always outranked me."

"Until now?"

"I found a Russian general's uniform neatly folded under the bunk over here on my side."

"Well then, *zu befehl, Herr General.*"

"I'm only joking again. As long as we remain on this barge, we are both lower than the lowest private. We are Russian prisoners, without yet having to raise our hands above our heads and march toward a gulag."

"Then we must find a way off before more Russians come along."

Karl snorted. "Yes, of course. But where do we go. And how?"

"A plan is forming in my aching head. It will form more quickly – and more clearly – if I have something to eat. That is your task. Find something to nourish us."

"I already have. The barge woman may have been a surly old crone, as well as a filthy one, but she kept a good food store on board. Some of it survived the grenade blast. But I have yet to find a means by which she lit a fire. As soon as I do, I will show you. Then feed you."

"Let me help you," Rainer said, but when he tried to raise himself up on his knees he collapsed.

Monday
April 23, 1945
Chicago

"What about us, Martin?"

While eating a late breakfast at a small diner on Michigan Avenue, biding their time until the Chicago Art Institute opened, Madeleine told Martin that her hoped-for future husband, Ray Gillingham, had been killed when his B-29 crash-landed on its return from a raid over Japan.

Martin had expressed all the proper sentiments. And now he felt sorry for his sister. What an injustice! So few eligible men had come her way. So few suitable eligible men. What heartbreak she must feel, he thought. "What do you mean? Us?" Martin jabbed his fork repeatedly into a soggy waffle he had no intention of finishing.

"I mean, when you return from Europe can we --." Maddy looked away from her brother.

"Can we what?"

"Stop acting obtuse. I mean, can we stop having these sneak-off-to-Chicago weekends and live together openly?" Then she added, "As openly as we dare, that is. I've decided I want to spent my life with you."

"I hadn't thought about it, to tell the truth."

"I figured as much. Well, I'm asking you to think about it now."

Martin set his fork down. "You want me to move back to Minnesota?"

"Anywhere, Martin. I'm sure I can find a librarian position anywhere you choose to live."

"Us? Together? What will people say?"

"That's just it. I can't say that I don't care what people say. Or think. And obviously you care. We'll just have to be...well –."

"Discreet?" Martin offered.

"To say the least. We wouldn't even have to live in the same house. Or even next door. The same side of the same town will suit me."

"Will I then have to do my own laundry?"

Maddy slowly, silently mouthed, "Stop being silly."

"Stop avoiding the issue, is what you mean."

"That's usually the case when you say something silly."

"People can be put in jail for being *blutschülderisch*, you know," Martin said.

Then he looked around to see if anyone at another table might be watching.

"Jail? Don't be silly. We're not going to jail. Is that what really bothers you? Fear? Guilt maybe?"

"No. Neither of those. But we simply can't stop being cautious, Sis."

"I understand that. But we can't throw our lives away based on a dread of imaginary spies peeking in our bedroom window."

"Katherine and I had real spies."

"So you've told me."

"Can't dismiss that prospect out of hand."

"No, but we can deal with it without spending the rest of our lives slipping away to cheap hotels."

"I agree."

"And I'm not about to dump you, Martin, because of worries about my community-standing. I love you and want to be with you always. No one else, nothing else, matters to me as much as you do."

He reached across the table and took his sister's hands in his. "And you mean everything to me, Madeleine Wynerson. Everything."

"Everything important," she corrected. "I know your fling with Katherine was just that. She was as much a toy to you as you were for her. I'm sure all your sweet, whispered endearments to her amounted to no more than the usual man-in-bed mind-fuck blather."

"Maddy!" Martin's jaw dropped and again he scanned the small restaurant for eavesdroppers.

"Sorry, Martin. But did I get your attention?"

"You have my full attention."

"Good. When you come back I want you to find a position that suits you. If George Washington is where you want to return, that's fine with me. Plenty of librarian jobs will be available. If you prefer somewhere else, that's fine, too. Just let me know and

I'll pack my bags. I'll wait tables in Des Moines, if I have to, just to be near you."

Just then their waitress came. "Will there be anything else, folks?'

Martin could not resist. "Do you know of any waitress jobs available in Des Moines?"

The waitress gave Martin a puzzled look. "That in Iowa?"

Martin nodded.

"That where you're from?" she said.

"Not yet."

24

Wednesday
April 25, 1945
Havel-Oder Kanal

Finding a rudderless skiff proved serendipitous. Karl had snagged the small boat as it drifted with the canal's southerly current, drifted amid other flotsam, much of which consisted of bloated corpses, soldiers mostly, both Russian and German, but also several civilians.

Rainer's plan to float the barge down the canal, tying it up during the day, turned out to be unworkable when Karl discovered the barge was firmly wedged between the side of the canal and another, partially sunken barge on the port side.

"It would be easier simply to walk downstream on top of corpses," Karl had pointed out grimly.

Rainer had estimated the distance from the bridge to the Stag and Pheasant, via the canal, to be about twenty kilometers.

Trying to cover such a distance by following the canal-side path left them far too exposed to Russian patrols.

After Karl decided the skiff was structurally sound – seaworthy, *seetüchtig*, scarcely seeming appropriate -- they had loaded it with all the useable foodstuffs they found on the barge. When they had climbed the canal bank in search of their weapons they found none, but Karl had discovered a loaded army-issue Walther P38 on the barge. How the barge woman had come by the pistol permitted Karl several minutes of ribald speculation, until Rainer cut him off.

"*Machts nichts*," Rainer had said. "Just make sure it fires properly." After a look from Karl, he added, "Without actually firing it, of course."

"Then lend me your tin of machine oil, *bitte*," Karl sneered.

"Try cooking fat."

"I already did."

Karl also loaded a canvas rain tarp into the skiff to cover themselves when they tied up and hid during the daylight hours. He gathered water from the canteens of German soldiers who died in the retreat from the canal.

"Don't plan to shit while the sun is up," Karl had teased Rainer.

"I can manage," Rainer had said. "But can you go from sunrise to sundown without pissing?"

Karl had then produced a pair of rusty tin cans, presenting one to Rainer.

"You think of everything," Rainer had said admiringly.

"Not quite. I found no books for you to read, arranged no orchestra to entertain you."

Now, two days later, their skiff had drifted fifteen kilometers – through tiny Tegeler See, past Spandau, just into Wannsee. Another five kilometers to go, by Rainer's estimate. Despite a favorable current, debris, in the forms of wrecked barges, corpses, and the discards from two armies engaged in close, bitter combat, had made maneuvering down the canal slow work.

At dusk Karl freed the skiff's hemp painter from its mooring, a separated tread belonging to a crippled panzer that lay on its side atop the canal bank as though it were a wounded elephant escaped from the Tiergarten.

Though the sun had set, the sky continued to glow burnt orange and Rainer remarked, "You were wrong, Karl, when you said you were unable to provide an orchestra." Fierce artillery exchanges had filled the daylight hours and continued on now, unabated. To the west raging fires in the center of Berlin flickered and glowed eerily, reflecting off a low cloud cover. Adding to the sense of dissonance was the fact that, despite the presence of two armies totaling more than a million men between them, plus more than a million Berliners trapped between those armies, not another living soul was either visible or audible as Karl poled the skiff out into the current.

"Wagner himself should be here, conducting the Berlin symphony," Karl said.

"Our little trip here is not exactly equivalent to Siegfried's Rhine Journey," Rainer joked lamely as he relieved himself over the side of the skiff. "And we are not returning any magic gold to the care of the Rhine maidens."

"Do paintings count?" Karl asked.

"Perhaps they do. But are we not the thieves, rather than the redeemers?"

"What is Wagner's phrase for the thief?" Karl paused. "He who –."

Rainer finished, " – is willing to renounce love forever," referring to the mortal in Wagner's Ring cycle who brings down a curse on gods and men alike by stealing the sacred gold of the Rhine.

Gesturing for Rainer to help him roll up one of the canvas coverings, Karl said, "Surely that is not us."

"No. You are right." But, Rainer thought, perhaps *he* is a *she* in this case, Anna stealing the sacred paintings of Europa.

Sunday
April 29, 1945
Washington, D.C.

"Your sister, Madeleine, right?"

Martin nodded, staring warily as David Fox held the framed photo Martin had placed on his bedside table in their apartment that morning.

Fox let out a long, roguish whistle. "She's changed a lot since the last time I saw her. Changed much for the better, I hasten to add. Quite a looker. How old is she now?"

"Still four years younger than I am," Martin said petulantly.

"Married?"

"No."

"But has a boyfriend, right?"

"Sort of," Martin obfuscated.

"Bet she gives a dynamite blowjob."

"David! How rude! Disgusting."

"Well? Does she?"

"How would I know?" Martin lied. "Knock it off."

"Oh, come on, Martin. By the time nearly every teenage girl with a slightly older brother graduates from high school she's invited her big brother to help her out by giving her a bit of practice and experience before she goes out on real dates with strange guys."

"You have a truly sordid mind, David."

"Thank you."

"I don't want to hear your crap."

"No lie. This isn't crap. Scouts' honor, God's truth, and all that."

Martin rolled his eyes, but sat.

Fox explained, "In my junior year at Our Lady of Mount Carmel High School in Boston Jimmy Brennan invited Chris Haggerty and me to his house one afternoon and hid us in his bedroom closet, which happened to have a pair of tiny peep-holes in the door. From inside the closet Chris and I watched Jimmy's fifteen-year-old sister, Mary, get down on her knees and do Jimmy in such exquisite fashion that I knew right away she'd taken plenty of cigar-smoking lessons already. I could hardly believe my eyes. His sister, Mary. Miss Prissy Goody Two Shoes. Holier-than-thou, angelic Mary turns out to be a bj queen."

"And from this one peeping-Tom episode you indict all younger sisters?" Martin said.

"You bet! If Virgin Mary Brennan turns out be an avid covert cocksucker, then they all are. Fess up, Martin. Your sister learned fellatio kneeling and praying at the altar of Lord Martin himself."

"I can't believe how depraved you are even to suggest such a thing," Martin replied, hoping he did not appear as disingenuous as he felt.

"Sure you can. Haven't I given you plenty of confirmation already? Want more proof? I can give you Chris Haggerty's address and phone number. He's 4-F; works for the Post Office in Quincy. He'll cheerfully confirm my story."

"Spies everywhere," Martin muttered.

"What's that?" Fox asked, leaning closer to Martin.

"I said 'Spies'."

25

Tuesday
May 8, 1945
Berlin

As he unbuttoned his Russian captain's tunic, Karl Vollmer explained to Rainer, "*Generaloberst* Jodl signed an unconditional surrender document yesterday in France. For the Russian's benefit the ceremony is being repeated today here in Karlshorst. General Zhukov and the other Russian generals will be there."

"Karlshorst? Maybe we should attend," Rainer said slyly.

"Go if you like. I've had enough adventure for one day," Karl said and slipped on a grimy, too-big civilian shirt he had traded for with an old man in Potsdam trying to sell a pair of worn-out shoes. The cost: two cigarettes.

Ten days had passed since Karl and Rainer arrived in their wooden skiff at the shoreline near the Stag and Pheasant restaurant. Since then they had kept themselves hidden on the second floor, except for a night trip on the skiff to Pfaueninsel to check their hidden stores.

The restaurant's owner, Fritz Priebe, and his son were both gone when they arrived. And, if they had gone for good, the pair had taken little if anything with them when they departed.

Rainer, having peeled open a can of sardines, handed the oily tin to Karl, who, in turn, dangled a slippery fish in front of the gray tabby that had made itself their permanent guest after finding an empty sardine can in the trash barrel behind the restaurant on the second day after their arrival.

"Ah, Karl, the world is truly upside down. While every citizen of Berlin roams the streets in search of a stale crust of bread, our little four-legged *Grauergeist* need only sit at your feet and smile in order to be rewarded with a handsome piece of fish."

"And while those citizens scavenge, you sit with your feet propped up and admire your Raphael. This mongrel is not the only decadent creature in the room," Karl replied.

Indeed! Rainer thought, not only pleased, but thankful and surprised that he had not fallen victim to an art thief. "Decadence to those clever enough to find it, eh, my self-indulgent little kitty?" To Karl, "*Sauve qui peut.*"

Karl snapped back, "Does 'Every man for himself' include children?"

"No, it certainly does not."

"I hope not. Snot-nosed Hitler Youth running from the Russians are not quite the same as seasoned Napoleonic Guards fleeing the field at Waterloo."

"Nor I do include women," Rainer said. "I'm afraid that for the women of Berlin their ordeal has only begun."

"And for many their ordeal is already over. Would you like me to recount the number of women I saw on my outing, women who had been raped and murdered, their throats cut, lying on the bloodied steps of their apartments?"

"Spare me."

"I thought so."

"What news of our glorious leaders?" Rainer asked.

"Rumor is the *Führer* shot himself last week, after marrying that empty-headed woman, Eva Braun. Double suicide in his bunker. The Goebbelses poisoned themselves and their children."

Rainer poured himself and Karl each a small glass of wine. "So. Hitler expected fourteen-year-old boys to stand and face the Russians, but for himself? He takes the coward's exit." All too vividly, Rainer recalled watching a pair of SS men hang a Hitler Youth from a Henningsdorf bridge girder because the boy refused to advance as part of an idiotic counter-attack against the Russians. This is what we have come to, he thought.

"Did you say something?" Karl asked, shooing the cat away.

"No. In your street-scouting did you hear anything about Himmler or Schellenberg?"

"No. I doubt if either of them returned to Berlin."

"What about Göring?"

"Only that the *Amis* are looking for him, searching the areas around Berchtesgaden."

"News of anyone else?" Rainer said, sipping wine.

"Bormann has vanished," Karl said, referring to, Martin Bormann, Hitler's private secretary and long-time, intimate advisor.

Rainer laughed. "I'm not certain that Bormann ever really existed. More likely he has simply been a figment of everyone's imagination. So, now that the imaginations have been destroyed, *poof!* Gone."

"But not forgotten. The Allies are aggressively looking for him," Karl said.

"Tell me, Karl. How does one chase a clever fairy?"

"Not easily. Perhaps we should turn ourselves into fairies."

"No. For the present we will remain here, occasionally turning ourselves into Russian officers."

Wednesday
May 9, 1945
Washington, D.C.

Dear Maddy,

Did you dance in the streets to celebrate V-E Day yesterday? Although I didn't dance, several of us from the Gallery milled among the crowd at Union Station and hoisted a beer (or three) in honor of our troops' successes.

Yet, despite our official victory, no word yet on when our little gang sails for London. Soon, I hope, or else I'm likely to begin strangling people for lack of anything else useful to do.

My first victim will be David Fox. No sooner had I put up your photo (on the stand next to my pillow!!!) than he scooped it up and began casting aspersions regarding your sexual predilections. He was ever so crude. Simple ghastly! And my insisting that he stop merely served to egg him on. The cad! Later he tried to apologize, but I am convinced that his groveling lacked sincerity. Dastardly fellow!

Listen to me. *Dastardly*. I've been reading too many issues of *Dime Detective*, *Black Mask*, and *Detective Fiction Weekly*. But then I have little else to occupy my time, except to look forward into the hazy future, wishing fervently to replace Edward R. Murrow, to be the one who announces to you "This is London", or else to look back at our all-too-short time together in Chicago. But, oh what a time it was!

Your letter arrived Monday and I am pleased to read that you thought our days (and nights!) together made you wish they'd never end. I've been giving this latter notion considerable thought, doing so from the moment I left Chicago. Most of the paperback novels I'd chosen to read on the train ride back proved tiresome and predictable. The only one I finished was Raymond Chandler's *The High Window*, about a precious gold coin that disappears. The plot twists and turns based on lots of dark family secrets.

Thought of you instead. Well, no. I thought of us and our dark family secret. And thought about how we should carry on. Oops! I mean *carry on* in the sense of getting on with our post-war lives, not in the sense of noisy hand-wringing. I definitely don't want those two senses to merge for us.

One of my colleagues here at MFA&A, a relaxed character named Bud Chavais, can't praise his home town of Santa Maria, California enough. The climate, he says, would satisfy Goldilocks. Not too hot, not too cold; not too wet, not too dry. He claims his folks grow enough citrus right in their own back yard to have oranges for breakfast every day of the year and put a slice of lemon in their ice tea any time they choose. And just down the road farmers grow hundreds of acres of strawberries all year round. And his town is only a few miles from the ocean!

I think that when this war is over we should hang red-bandana bindles over our shoulders and set out for this paradise by the sea. What do you think? Just imagine. No snow to shovel, no mosquitoes to swat. Hallelujah! Give the notion some thought. (Look on your map. Santa Maria lies northwest of Santa Barbara some seventy miles, along a major north-south highway Bud calls El Camino Real, the King's Highway, and just west of a little set of mountains called the Cuyamas, which he pronounces Koo-AHM-eez.)

Don't worry about what we might do to put food on our table – short of stealing oranges, lemons, and strawberries. You can start a bookstore and I can start an art gallery. And if one or both of those enterprises fails to catch on, well… we can set up a fruit and vegetable stand, sell off all of our purloined produce to passersby along the King's Highway. We'll manage somehow.

Food for thought anyway. (He wrote, making a sophomoric joke.)

And don't worry. I promise I'll only strangle people in my dreams. I want to go to Europe too badly to do something foolish enough that I find myself staring out from behind the bars of a military stockade.

Want to go to California too badly, too!! And we'd better plan to take the train, not walk like penniless hobos. I'm not sure my bum leg is up to hoisting the rest of me up and over the Rockies. Come to think of it, hobos also ride trains across the country. So the train it will be. And these detective fiction magazines I've become addicted to had better find some better writers, because California is a lot further away than Chicago and I'll need something to read in between those times we're bouncing together on a bed of hay inside a boxcar.

Time isn't moving fast enough, Maddy. I want to be there, there, and everywhere – except here, sitting on my thumb and watching the rest of the world go by.

I'll write more the very instant I know more.

Your favorite brother,
Martin P. Wynerson
Lieutenant, US Army

Thursday
May 31, 1945
Berlin

When he heard brakes squeal Rainer pulled back an edge of the heavy blackout curtains that still covered the bedroom window above the Stag and Pheasant. Two trucks had stopped. Russian trucks. So he fetched a Schmeisser from beneath his bed, inserted a full magazine, checked the door lock, then returned to the window. Only then did he see Karl sitting behind the steering wheel of the second truck, a butter-colored vehicle with words stenciled in Cyrillic on the side. Then, from the passenger side of the forward truck *Hauptsturmführer* Wolfgang Schlee emerged, wearing a Russian uniform. Good, Rainer thought. Karl not only found the black market dealer but managed to strike a deal.

Karl climbed down from the truck cab and began gesturing to two other men accompanying Schlee, posting them as guards, apparently telling them who and what to watch for. Rainer clucked in amazement at how adaptable Karl Vollmer was, and more versatile with one and a half arms than most men were with two.

Hearing his fellow Germans start up the stairs, Rainer put away the submachine gun Karl had bought from a street urchin for five cigarettes, unlocked the door, and self-consciously rechecked to assure himself the Raphael lay safely buried between the mattress and springs of his twin bed.

Karl came bursting through the door in fine spirits, saying, "*Standartenführer*, look who I found doing business no more than two blocks from General Zhukov's headquarters."

Though holding a lower rank than Rainer, Wolfgang Schlee merely tipped his cap informally after entering the room. "Zeitz, you're out of uniform! What would the *Reichsleiter* say?" Schlee barked playfully.

"Karl informs me that *Reichsleiter* Himmler is past caring that I am out of uniform."

Schlee laughed loudly. "Indeed! Ten days ago at Lüneburg. Swallowed cyanide while some British doctor was examining him. No more putting up with his diatribes and nonsense."

"What of Schellenberg?" Rainer asked.

A shrug from Schlee. "Captured. The Allies will probably hang him on the same scaffold they build for Göring."

Ah, yes. The fate of Fat Herman will surely be the gallows, Rainer agreed.

"You're not hiding Bormann, are you?" Rainer asked Schlee.

"Ha! If I knew where to find him, I'd ask him to hide me. The man is more elusive than one of Werner Heisenberg's electrons."

Rainer reminded himself that before the war Wolfgang Schlee had taught physics at a Gymnasium near Dortmund. "So what have you brought me? And at what price?"

"You're not even going to offer me a glass of wine before we discuss the deal? How rude, *Standartenführer*. I know enough about you to declare with a high degree of certainty -- certainty, that is, not certitude – that somewhere you harbor several vintages, any one of which would make the Hapsburgs proud, perhaps even envious."

"You give me too much credit, Schlee. After all, we just lost a war."

"No, no. That collection of criminals –" he waved in the general direction of central Berlin " – lost our war for us. We didn't lose it."

"Whoever the losers, they drank up the ship's full complement of wine before going down with the ship."

"Shall I search that lifeboat you have moored down at the lakeside?" Schlee asked, smiling.

"No need. For my friends I managed to smuggle a few bottles ashore," Rainer replied, maintaining the metaphor.

"Good. Let's drink."

"Red or white?"" Rainer asked.

A shrug. "As long as it's not green," Schlee said.

Rainer retrieved a bottle of Rhone from the closet and poured three glasses.

As he poured, Schlee said, "Now the French can go back to making great wine, doing what they do best, and do it with smiles on their faces instead of bayonets up their asses."

Rainer handed the *Hauptsturmführer* and Karl each a glass of wine. "Whom do you toast these days?" Rainer asked Schlee.

"I drink to my best customers," Schlee said, hoisting his glass and nodding a salute.

"And what have we bought?" Rainer asked.

Schlee gestured toward the window. "I assume you peeked outside already. The second truck, the creamy one, is now yours. It's a ZIS-5 with plenty of kilometers on it, but it runs well, and I changed the oil filter today. Your *Hauptscharführer* watched me. The tank is full and, on our way here, I pointed out two Russian refueling depots."

"How much?" Rainer said.

"A hundred cartons of cigarettes. Plus some extras at no charge."

"Extras?"

"Show him," Schlee said to Karl. As Karl reached into a canvas sack, Schlee went on. "Head and neck bandages. And an eye patch. Wear them when you go out. Wear them for two reasons. Disguise is the first. Finding and arresting SS officers of your rank is a high priority among all the Allies. Second, because you don't speak Russian the bandages will explain why you can't speak at all or hear well. If some Russian asshole thrusts a piece of paper in front of you and expects you to read it, that is your problem. Two eye patches will make you look conspicuous."

Rainer spoke. "On the subject of conspicuous, don't you think a cream-colored truck is a bit much?"

Schlee agreed. "That's why you'll appreciate it. First, you'll be able to find it easier because it stands out. And two, because it stands out, no one will steal it."

"What does the signage say on the side of the truck?" Rainer asked.

Karl said, "Defend the city of Lenin."

Rainer looked at Schlee.

The black marketer laughed again. "A touch of irony, Zeitz. No extra charge."

Not amused, Rainer said, "I left before the siege began."

"Yes, yes. And everybody knows how successful you were at doing your part. Stealing the Amber Room, for god's sake. Made you famous."

"I didn't steal it. I merely repossessed it."

"I understand. Gift of Fredrick the Great to Peter the Great. And now back again. But try telling that to the Russians."

"Not if I can help it."

"Exactly. And to help even more along that line –" Schlee reached inside his tunic and removed a pair of leather wallets "—I had these made for you and your aide." He handed one to Karl, one to Rainer. "Russian identities. You, Zeitz, are now Colonel Viktor Churansky from… the city of Lenin. And Karl here is Captain Gennady Skolov from Narva, Estonia, which helps explain his Baltic Russian and accent. You will both recognize your photos. They're from the Leipzigerstrasse archives, and doctored only a little."

"How much for these?"

"*Gratis*, Zeitz, *gratis*. I only play the role of highwayman when doing business with *Untermenschen*."

Rainer forced a smile. "Thank you."

Friday
June 1, 1945
Washington, D.C.

Martin sat alone in his apartment, having decided not to go to work at the National Gallery until after lunch. Then he could work late into the evening, compiling notes with fewer interruptions. At least Memorial Day was over. He had enjoyed the ride to Arlington Cemetery with other MFA&A men and women, dutifully paid his respects to the dead, new and old, afterwards wandering the streets of the Capitol, feeling lonely and frustrated, unfulfilled in so many ways.

In years past the holiday had meant Martin would listen to the last hour of the Indy 500 being broadcast. For years he had thrilled to the legendary voice of Graham McNamme, making Martin almost believe himself sitting in the grandstand somewhere near the starting line. Then, in 1935, CBS took over from NBC and Ted Husing's reportage lacked the drama, the immediacy, the color and flavor that McNamme had brought to the race. And now, since the start of the war, the race had not been held. Martin realized that, with rubber and gasoline rationed, holding the event would be in bad taste, not to mention the strain on fans' purse strings and consciences, burning fuel and rubber to attend a spectacle that would expend even more just to entertain them.

No mail delivered on the holiday either. But now Martin sat expectantly, hoping today would be the day another letter from Madeleine would arrive. But, just as a watched pot is never supposed to boil, so, too, apparently a watched mailbox would never be filled. But then, just before noon, Martin saw the postman walking up the sidewalk to his apartment.

And – yes!!! – a letter from Maddy.

Dearest Brother Martin,

California sounds wonderful! Wish we could leave immediately. I'm serious! I haven't looked forward to anything with so much enthusiasm in a looooong time. (My trip to Chicago to see you exempted, of course.)

I've even begun doing research on California, wanting to know everything about the climate, the people, the agriculture, the economy. Just everything!!

And... if I may be bold enough to make a suggestion: How about Santa Barbara instead of Santa Maria? Here's why. I've learned that just last year the University of California opened a new campus – at Santa Barbara. And... it's practically right on the beach. A university, naturally, means a library and an art history department. We won't have to sell vegetables! Except on weekends. What do you think? About UCSB, not selling veggies on weekends, Mister Silly.

I've been to the lake with the folks, but it's just not the same without you there with us. With me. Will I miss the loons? *Ja*, sure. You betcha! But California has birds, too. Seagulls and sandpipers, I know.

Dad spent most of his time at the cabin doing his usual repair-the-ravages-of-winter puttering. Mom just stands around and shakes her head a lot. I think she realizes the place simply isn't the same without lots of kids around.

What do you think about our building a summer cabin in the Sierra Nevada mountains? Actually, that's redundant, I've learned. *Sierra Nevada*, in Spanish, means *snowy mountains*. But you probably know that already. Anyway, do you think a get-away cabin is a good idea?

Right now I'm busy trying to learn all about what people wear in California. Clearly not parkas and snow boots and wool mittens and long underwear. Except

maybe up by our cabin in the Sierras during the win-
tertime. They don't wear much near and on the beaches.
Not that they cavort naked. No such luck. But much of
the year they're nearly so. At least that's what I've read.
Oh, I can hardly wait to go there, to be there. Before I
start becoming too saggy and flabby to look present-
able in public in a bathing suit, let alone my birthday
suit.

While you're away finishing up winning the war,
I'll continue to read, and read, and read all about sunny
Southern California. Then, when you return, we can sit
down together and begin to make real plans. Oh, I'm so
excited I can scarcely hang on to my pen.

> Write soon. Tell me what you think.
> Love,
> Maddy

As Martin re-read his sister's letter for as third time, David
Fox came bursting into the apartment.

"Thought I'd find you here. Guess what? We've got a firm
date, Martin. A firm date! Did you hear me?"

"I heard. Is this another joke? Yours or the brass's?"

"Scout's honor. Firm. As in f-i-r-m. Our boat sails from New
York City on June 27th."

"The 27th? That is a joke. Jeezus. That's almost another month.
The thieves will all be gone by then, vanished to… who knows
where. But you can bet they won't be hanging around Munich or
Salzburg," Martin said glumly.

"The brass says otherwise. They claim that the longer we wait -- up to a point -- the more rats we'll have to grill," Fox said.

"How do they figure that?"

"Food. Shelter. Shoes, shirts, pants, and hats. German citizens are desperate for any and all of those things. And they'll gladly trade information for necessities, including info about where the art works have gone. Brass says hundreds of thousands of Germans are lacking basic survival goods. Cities and roads are clogged with these folks. DPs they're calling them. Displaced Persons. And a lot of them are either art thieves or else people who know who and where the art thieves are."

"The twenty-seventh?"

"God's truth, Martin."

Martin stood and pointed an index finger at David Fox. "If you're lying to me, I swear I'm going to kill you."

26

Sunday
June 3, 1945
Potsdamer Platz
Berlin

Karl Vollmer parked the truck a block from the Platz. The route getting there had, by necessity, been circuitous, given that only a few major streets in central Berlin were passable, the rest still blocked by the detritus of war. The effects of Allied bombing paled compared with the consequences of savage, street-by-street tank and artillery exchanges. Combined, the results had flattened much of the city.

Now, swathed in all his head-damaged-colonel bandages, Rainer stood where Ebertstrasse entered the Platz and stared at the destruction. Karl stood behind him, eyes searching, a Walther hidden in his empty sleeve.

"The silence is unnerving, Karl."

"Loosen the wrappings from around your ears."

"No. That's not it. Listen. What do you hear?"

"Rats scurrying everywhere. I can't see any, but I hear them."

Across the plaza, where Stresemannstrasse began, Rainer watched two small children scuttle across a pile of rubble on all fours as though they were a pair of crabs.

"This place used to be so alive. Now look at it," Rainer said softly.

"Göring's palace remains standing," Karl muttered, stepping forward and nodding west up Leipzigerstrasse toward the Luftfahrtsministerium.

"Proof of the Luftwaffe's prowess at defending the Fatherland, yes?" Rainer said snidely.

"Proof that the *Reichsmarschall* built a better building than he built an air force."

"The Marc painting. You're certain it's still in the Chamber?" Rainer said.

"I looked at it briefly yesterday. Not only does it remain hanging, but, unlike many other things inside, no harm has come to it."

A Russian GAZ Jeep came down the street and stopped in front of the Prussian Chamber of Deputies. An officer stepped from the passenger side, then the Jeep drove on.

"Who is that?" Rainer asked.

"Major Ivan Ristov. He's in charge of the guards detachment for the Chamber and several other buildings," Karl said.

"What do we know of Major Ristov?"

Karl cleared his throat. "Not much yet. But Joachim Uhlmann says he is working on finding the major's weakness."

"Uhlmann. Is there anything Schlee and Uhlmann can't do?"

"Chase the Russians back to Moscow," Karl deadpanned.

"Yes, well --." Rainer let his thought evaporate as he watched a young woman wearing an ankle-length coat and blue bandana and pushing a wheelbarrow come into view. She stopped beside the tall pile of rubble where earlier he had watched the pair of children climb across. Slowly, and with great selectivity, she began loading the wheelbarrow with bricks chosen from the pile.

"Is this how Germans will rebuild Germany, Karl? One brick at a time?"

"No. Look at her. Look at everyone we see – except ourselves. She is weak, frail, maybe even sick. She'll die before she builds anything."

"Does that make you feel guilty, *Hauptscharführer?*"

"If I let guilt over the consequences of this war rack me, *Standartenführer*, I would have killed myself long ago."

"You feel no guilt at all?

"I didn't mean that. I said I don't let my guilt torment me."

"Good, because the Allies will gladly do that for you. For them it will not be enough that those in God's grace have achieved the salvation of surviving this war. Like the good Christians they are, they will now want those fallen from grace to suffer."

"The Russians are not Christians," Karl said.

"No. Not formally. But even the most callous heathens among them have been infected with the poison spread by the moral imposter from Galilee."

"Have you given up on the Church?"

Rainer laughed a small laugh. "No. That was not necessary. It is the Church that has abandoned us all."

"Then where do we turn?"

"Karl, if I knew that I would climb to the top of that heap of boards and bricks where the woman now carefully weighs the qualities of each brick as if she were God judging souls and I would shout out my creed. But who would listen?"

"I might."

"Thank you. But, unable to feed Berlin by magically multiplying our little cache of sardines and hams, unable to heal the blind, unhang the hanged, I'm afraid I would be a prophet without honor, as the saying goes."

"Maybe if you had a mighty symbol."

Rainer's eyes brightened. "Yes! But it can't be a cross. That has been taken." He paused for dramatic effect. "How about a twisted cross? But, no. The swastika also belongs to others."

Before Rainer could continue his mockery Karl pointed to the Chamber of Deputies building, where Major Ristov emerged. "He's coming our way."

The two men watched, Karl fingering the trigger of his hidden Walther, Rainer adjusting his bandages. Halfway across the plaza the Russian major stopped, turned, and walked toward the lone woman, who was still sorting bricks. When he reached her the major spoke to her, making hand gestures that suggested his German was less than fluent.

The woman kept her head bowed, not speaking. Suddenly the major tore away the woman's bandana, tossed it on the rubble, then tipped the woman's face up with his fingertips. After he spoke to her again she nodded and dropped her hands, which, from the moment the major arrived, she had balled into fists at her chest. Then the major locked one of her elbows with his own and, together, they stepped toward the Chamber building. With another quick move the major released the woman's arm, walked back to the wheelbarrow, and dumped the bricks. Then he returned to the woman and led her slowly into the building.

Subdued and silent, Rainer and Karl observed all this. Once the woman and the major disappeared into the Chamber of Deputies, Karl said, "It's not the first time for her. The fact that she's still alive --."

Rainer nodded. "At least we've discovered one of the major's weaknesses."

Sunday
June 3, 1945
Washington, D.C.

Martin sat alone in his apartment. David Fox had left early, telling Martin at breakfast he had a date with a cute blonde. This, after coming home well after midnight, stumbling about the apartment, making enough noise to wake Martin, who got up only to find Fox passed out on the couch and reeking of beer and cheap perfume.

Now that the reality of his going to Europe began to set in Martin felt overwhelmed. News from MFA&A members already there gave Martin the willies. His task ahead seemed not only daunting, but impossible. From his readings, Martin judged that not a single painting, piece of sculpture, manuscript, tapestry, musical score, or any other work of art from a Nazi-occupied territory remained in its original location, every one of them carted away.

We'll never find them all, he thought. That was a given. Half maybe? How much had been destroyed? And of that, how much intentionally? How much merely as collateral damage, caught between two clashing armies? Thousands of years of precious treasures burned to ashes, ground to pebbles, splinters, and confetti, blown to smithereens. Dust to dust, ashes to ashes. Martin wondered if he would show up merely to help preside over a cultural funeral.

He turned his mind momentarily away from thought of confronting a debacle too immense to comprehend fully and thumbed through his most recent research, an exercise deliberately intended to forget about art briefly. Even though the war in Asia raged on, secrecy rules had loosened and he had managed to trace the whereabouts of his P-38 squadron, the group of fly boys from Ellington Field in Houston who had survived Texas without lasting injuries and gone on to join the war as genuine mission-logging pilots. They were now members of the 26th Photographic Reconnaissance Squadron, a group that had begun their overseas duty in Sydney and Brisbane, Australia, then moved northward to New Guinea, stopping at places with exotic names, such as Dobodura, Port Moresby, Nadzab, and Hollandia, before spending six months on the tiny island of Biak, off the northeast coast of New Guinea, flying over targets in the Philippines before and after the bombers made their runs. In the aftermath of MacArthur's landings, the 26th was now stationed at Lingayen on the island of Luzon and Martin pictured himself lying in the sun beneath a coconut palm, sipping milk from a coconut he had cracked open with the butt of his .45 revolver. Except that he learned from letters passed along from his former buddies' wives that most of the pilots of the 26th had – illegally – discarded their army-issue .45s in favor of long-barreled .22s. Less kick; more accuracy. So Martin pictured himself shooting a coconut, afterward drinking from a straw pushed into the bullet hole.

Then he remembered the little girl at the Lincoln memorial who handed him a Brownie camera and asked him to snap a photo of her and her mother. Priscilla. Yes. That was the girl's name. And her father, she said, was a pilot of a B-24 bomber flying out of Africa. Lucky him! Well… except he has a wife and child back home pining for him. It ain't all peaches and cream, he reminded himself. Or pineapples and coconut milk.

Martin looked at the wall clock. Almost noon. Jeez, where has the morning gone, he wondered. If someone were to show up at my door, he'd think I was the one who was hung over.

He decided he needed to respond to Maddy's last letter. He had an hour and a half before the "swing and sway" music of Sammy Kaye's orchestra began on its regularly scheduled Sunday Serenade program out of Cleveland. Fetching paper and pen, Martin sat down at the kitchen table and gave the contents of his letter more thought before he started to write.

Santa Barbara. A new university. He could buy Maddy a wedding ring and they could pose as Mister and Mrs. Martin Wynerson. Own their own home. Spanish style, of course, with a red tile roof. He could teach art history; she could… well, do whatever university librarians do. Sort books on Plato from books on Pluto, he guessed. Maybe Maddy could even become the art history librarian and fill the stacks with the finest collection on art history west of… west of Chicago. And we could sit on the beach and eat oranges all weekend long – every weekend.

Why, I wouldn't even have to shoot an orange before we savored its sweet succulence, he reminded himself.

Wednesday
June 27, 1945
Berlin

Shameless beggar that she was, the gray cat purred and rubbed against Karl's legs the moment he returned to the upstairs bedroom above the restaurant. "No treats, Sweet *Kätchen*. Go finish the food I left for you," he said, nudging the furry beast away. "Don't you realize children in Berlin are starving?"

"Don't remind us," Rainer said, his feet propped up on the footboard of one of the beds while he sipped from a bottle of beer. "What news? Aside from starving children."

"Truman is coming to see us. Stalin, too! Churchill is doubtful. How is that for news?" Karl said, sitting on the other bed to remove his boots.

"Coming where?"

"Here. Potsdam. A Big Three Conference, they call it. Similar to one they held in Tehran back near the end of 1943."

"Why is Churchill doubtful?" Rainer asked.

"British election. Some fellow named Clement Atlee is expected to defeat him and become the new prime minister."

Rainer laughed. "What a bunch of ungrateful little shits the British are! A nation of shopkeepers indeed! They represent the folly of democracy better than any nation, Karl. Simpletons permitted to decide great matters of state. Too bad their navy is so large and spirited. Otherwise, they're scarcely distinguishable from the French."

"The French make good wine," Karl pointed out.

"Ah, yes. You are right. And the British have given the world what? Gin and Scotch."

"Swill. Both of them," Karl said.

"So when is this conference to be held in our neighborhood?" Rainer asked as he drained his beer.

"It begins on July 17th."

"That's too long to wait."

"But preparations are already starting. The Russians will be busy, especially their guard units, because they are taking the role of official host."

"Sooner is better then," Rainer said.

"Schlee and Uhlmann filled me in on Major Ristov. They say that offering to buy him women won't work because he boasts he can have all the German women he wants for free."

"What then?"

"The usual. Cigarettes, liquor, non-perishable food. But especially cigarettes. They remain the primary alternative to cash in this city."

Rainer sat quietly for several moments before asking, "Who will approach Major Ristov?"

"I will have to do that," Karl said in a tone suggesting the notion did not exactly thrill him. "Schlee and Uhlmann say that is our risk."

"Do either of the *Hauptsturmführer*s know why we wish to speak with, deal with, the Russian major?"

Karl shrugged. "For now they only guess. But they're not dumb. You know that. Ristov guards paintings; you collect paintings."

"Collect. Thank you. I'm sure that is not Schlee's term for what I do. Did."

"No." Karl let it go at that.

"So what else did our friends, the black marketers, say?"

"They said that they will guarantee Ristov will not double-cross us."

"And how will they achieve that?"

Another shrug from Karl. "They wouldn't say."

"Can we trust *them* not to double-cross us?"

"I think so. They want whatever is left in our cache when we leave, whatever we won't be taking with us."

"Did you tell them we intended to leave some of our goods behind?" Rainer said.

"I hinted as much."

"Do we dare double-cross them?"

Karl shook his head. "That's not worth the risk. But, for safety's sake, I believe we should make them go to a third party in order to be told the whereabouts of the goods we leave behind."

"A third party. Who might that be? Stalin? Truman? Churchill? This new fellow, Atlee? No, because they won't be here yet," Rainer joked.

"I was trying to think of someone while I was driving back from seeing the *Hauptsturmführer*. No one came to mind *until* --."

"Until when?" Rainer asked, taking his feet off the bed and leaning forward in his chair.

"Until I happened to stop by the field hospital at the east end of the Tiergarten, across from the Kaiser Wilhelm Memorial Church. Or rather, what remains of the church, which is almost nothing. I was looking for fresh bandages for your head and neck. Inside one of the tents I found someone you know. Two someones actually. The hospital is being run by the Red Cross. Does that give you a hint?"

Rainer needed no time to think. "The Sundstrums are here in Berlin?"

"Unless there happens to be another husband and wife pair with that surname who also happen to be physicians working for the Red Cross."

Wednesday
June 27, 1945
New York City

Martin stood on the waterfront and watched giant cranes hoist rope nets filled with crates of supplies urgently needed by the British. He was aware that, even for the victors, the near future promised little except more of the same. German submarine wolf packs had sent more than ships filled with American-made weaponry to the bottom of the North Atlantic. British victory gardens had served better at nourishing souls than sustaining bodies. Nor was commercial agriculture enough. And international trade in any form was impossible for an island surrounded by long, gray metal sharks.

American rationing, Martin knew, was minimal compared to the austerities and sacrifices endured by British civilians. V-E Day had not changed that. So Martin recognized that he amounted to no more than an afterthought on a ship filled with food, clothing, and who knew what all else.

"Looks like the Brits won't have to eat their Gainsboroughs and Constables after all, eh Martin," David Fox said as he stood with one foot on his duffle bag and watched several longshoremen unload crates from a truck bed and stack them on the wharf. "Or smoke sheep shit," he added pointedly when Martin failed to respond.

Finally Martin said, "And what do you suppose the Germans will eat when all they have left are paintings and sculptures buried in their mines?"

"Nothing I'd like better than to swat some snot-nosed little Kraut turd I caught trying to munch on the corner of an Edvard Munch painting."

"Let them eat *lederhosen, ja?*" Martin said contemptuously, even while enjoying Fox's word play.

"Let 'em eat their own shit," Fox snapped.

"There is some shit I will not eat," Martin replied softly.

"What?"

"Paraphrase from a line in an e. e. cummings poem. *I Sing of Olaf.*"

"Swedish?"

"American. *More brave than me, more blond than you.*"

"Anybody's more blond than me."

Martin nodded. "Keep that in mind when you're in Munich."

"What's that supposed to mean?"

"I mean don't provoke people unnecessarily. The war may be over but that doesn't mean every form of hostility has ended."

"I know that," Fox said. "But speaking of provoking people unnecessarily, as you call it, is she coming to see you off?"

Martin avoided Fox's leer, but he knew it was there. Martin knew Fox didn't have to spell out who he meant by *she.* He meant

Katherine. And Fox knew that Martin knew. "No. I haven't even heard from her since –"

Suddenly Fox was looking past Martin and waving his arms. "It's Karl Nierendorf, come to see us off."

But when Martin turned he scarcely saw the art dealer. Instead, his gazed fixed on the woman with him. It was *her*.

Karl Nierendorf was all smiles, handshakes, and hugs. "David, Martin, I couldn't let the two of you sail off to the Continent without saying thank you, goodbye, and good luck." Zank you, gutbye, gutluck.

"Hello, David. Hello, Martin," Katherine said, reserved. No bon voyage kisses. Not even a hug or a handshake.

"Thanks for coming, Mrs. Parker. It's good to see you, isn't it, Martin," Fox said, nudging an inert Martin. "Great to see you both."

"Yes. Thank you for coming," Martin said, though his look toward Katherine said otherwise.

Karl Nierendorf said, "Gentlemen, I apologize for not inviting you to join me sooner. I've been out of town, up in Albany actually, until this morning. But I heard you were coming and wanted very much to be here to wish you both well on your important tasks that lie ahead of you. And when I asked Mrs. Parker if she would be gracious enough to join me in seeing you off, she said she would be pleased and honored to be here. Didn't you, Katherine?"

Katherine smiled a gracious smile and said, "Elliott is depending very much on both of you. And until he can tell you so himself, I wanted to make sure you are aware how very, very much he trusts you and knows he can count on you."

What is this? Martin asked himself. Some generic graduation speech Karl asked her to prepare during the ride down from upstate? She's mouthing the words, but I'm far from sure she really means any of them. She could be dishing this pap out to anybody who happened to be standing here. The only reason she's here is because she was too polite to turn down Karl's invitation.

"We appreciate your letting us know, Mrs. Parker," Martin heard David Fox saying. "Don't we, Martin?"

That's it. Twist the knife, you bastard. "Yes. We appreciate it, Katherine." He had started to say "Mrs. Parker," but realized that would make everyone pause. Everyone present knew him well enough to know he was on a first-name basis with the woman. Was. Had been. Keep up appearances, Martin, he told himself. This won't last long. Then she'll be out of your life forever, just as she promised.

"Martin, may I speak to you alone for a moment?" Katherine was suddenly saying.

Yes, ma'am. He felt like a servant being asked to trudge off to a corner for a private rebuke. "Sure," he said neutrally.

"Excuse us, gentlemen," Katherine said, giving Nierendorf and Fox a quick smile before drawing Martin several paces away.

Martin gave the two men a beats-me shrug as he followed her.

"I apologize for this surprise, Martin," she began. "I didn't know about any of this until this morning when Karl stopped by the house."

"No need to apologize. I'm pleased you were willing to come." He wasn't sure he meant it.

"You don't act like you're very pleased."

"I thought I'd already seen you for the last time. Would never hear from you again. And I would have been right, wouldn't I?"

Katherine hesitated before saying, "Yes."

"Not all condemned men relish a temporary stay of execution."

"Is that how you look at my presence?" she said.

"How else?"

"If your mother were dying and you had a chance to see her one last time, wouldn't you leap at that opportunity?"

"Yes. But you're not my mother, you're not dying, and I'm not the one rushing to you. I haven't written, I haven't called, I haven't tried to see you, all out of respect for your wishes. And now you rub all that in my face." Martin watched Katherine's upper lip tremble, but he made no move toward her.

"Now I am sorry I came, Martin. This not how I wanted it to be."

"Sure it is. And I swear I've heard this somewhere before. Are you sure you didn't read the script from some Bette Davis movie where, dripping with sweet insincerities, she sees some hopelessly naïve schmuck off to war?"

Katherine took a step back. "I didn't expect so much bitterness from you."

"What did you expect instead?"

"I'm not sure. But not this."

"Want me to drop to my knees, kiss your feet, and thank you for all the wonderful times we had?"

Katherine's shoulders slumped. "You know I don't."

"Why did you have to come here? Damn it! When a movie says *The End*, you're supposed to get up and walk out of the theater, not leave, then return to your seat and demand a replay of the final scene."

"I still have all your letters," she said softly.

"Burn them."

"I treasure them too much."

"Burn them, damn you, and stop toying with me like this."

"Is that what you think now? That I'm toying with you?"

"I know you are. I may be bitter, but you are one nasty, sadistic tease. I bet you jumped at Karl's invitation, seized the chance to torture me one more time. The letters are your ropes, whip, and blindfold. You'll never burn them because you know that's what I want."

"I'm sorry, Martin. I truly am. I didn't want our relationship to come to this, to end like this."

"Spare me your tears. Once I board that ship I want never even to think of you again."

"Get thee behind me, Satan. Is that what you think?"

"Pretty much."

Just then Karl Nierendorf strode over to them. "Is everything all right?"

Katherine nodded as she dabbed at her eyes.

Martin said, "Parting can be very emotional, Karl. You know that. I'm sure when you took leave of Berlin you were deeply torn."

"I was certainly that," Nierendorf agreed.

"Goodbye, Martin," Katherine said, her voice firm.

"Goodbye, Katherine."

Karl put an arm around each of them. "Take heart, as you Americans say. This moment is not as though you will never see each other again, *ja?*"

27

Thursday
June 28, 1945
Tiergarten
Berlin

"Are your injuries real or are these bandages merely your cam-ouflage?"

"I'm perfectly healthy," Rainer said to Sigrid Sundstrum as she removed the swathing from around his neck.

"So I see. Certainly well-fed for a Berliner."

"I'm not a Berliner. I'm from Munich."

"So touchy!"

Nils Sundstrum stood beside them, alternately watching his wife work on Rainer and peeking out from the privacy curtain he and his wife had hastily put up once they realized who their "patient" was. "Speaking of Munich, your cousin, Anna, thinks you're dead."

"A reasonable assumption under the circumstances. So Anna is back in Munich?" Rainer said.

"No. She's still in Bern, working for some American civilians," Nils said, as his wife tossed away Rainer's filthy dressings with a look of disgust.

"Anna is a collaborator?" Or a German spy, he thought, remembering what Walter Schellenberg had said.

"I don't think so. Probably just using the Americans. They're a bit naïve, you know. Anna claims even their spies are insufficiently cynical. Much too trusting."

"Anna would know all about that," Rainer said with a mixture of pride and dismay. So it's likely she *is* working for Schellenberg. Was.

"Why are you still in Berlin?" Sigrid asked while she swabbed Rainer's neck with disinfectant.

"Berlin is safer that most places. Well, places I would have a reasonable chance of escaping to. You know what I mean. The moon is a bit far."

Nils asked, "What about the Red Cross papers we provided you with?"

"I still have them. I'm simply waiting for a more auspicious time to use them."

"Auspicious," Sigrid snorted. "For you there will be no such time. Get out while you still can. If you can. Every day Allied intelligence officers come snooping into all our tents."

"I'm leaving Berlin soon. I just wanted to confirm that our agreement still holds."

Rainer watched the pair of physicians look at one another.

"You have the paintings here in Berlin? You're mad," Nils whispered loudly.

"No. Not here. I'm not a total fool."

"You have means to move them to Sweden?" Sigrid asked.

"Yes."

"How soon?"

"Is there a rush?" Rainer said.

"Do you own a private U-boat?" Sigrid said with a touch of sarcasm.

"I almost had one for my own use."

"Almost. Too bad," Nils sighed.

Sigrid said, "Art hunters are prowling like hungry wolves. The Allies are searching; those people who helped the Nazis steal all these years now are looking out for themselves, stealing for themselves; those from whom you stole works are now here to get them back, with or without the help of the Allies."

"I stole nothing. Don't include me among the thieves."

Speechless at his cheeky claim, both doctors simply stared at Rainer.

"Well? Do you still intend to do business with me?"

Another exchange of looks between the Sundstrums before Nils said, "We do. Have you added to your inventory?"

"I've hardly had time," Rainer responded, hoping to deflect the issue without having to lie.

Nils fetched a pen and piece of paper from his black medical bag. "I'm going to write down the names and address of our two sons in Sweden, in case you successfully cross the Baltic before we have returned to our homeland. Anders lives in Stockholm, Lief in Malmö. Both are authorized to deal with you on behalf of Sigrid and myself." He wrote quickly, folded the slip of paper, and handed it to Rainer.

"Let me check outside before you leave," Sigrid said and slipped out past the isolation drape.

Less than a minute later she returned and spoke without drawing back the curtain. "It is safe to leave, but hurry."

Rainer slid off the wobbly, wooden operating table, shook Nils' hand, and said, "See you in Sweden."

As he stepped outside the huge white canvas tent, he heard Sigrid, behind him, say sharply, "Do not come back here again."

Tuesday
July 4, 1945
London

The green U.S. Army Chevrolet coupe crossed the Vauxhall Bridge and turned right on Milbank. From the cramped rear seat David Fox and Martin Wynerson stared out in wonder at the sights along the Thames.

"Won't be long now," said their driver, James Iverson, a member of London OSS. "The Tate's just ahead."

Both Martin and David were glad to be in London, even more glad to be off the ship. By the time the two men disembarked at Portsmouth Martin had mostly recovered from several days of queasiness. David had not. Martin marveled at his luck, supposing his torture mild, given that, prior to this Atlantic crossing, the largest boat he had ever been in was a canoe.

Although the weather was both mild and sunny, the smattering of Londoners Martin observed on the streets dressed as if rainfall were imminent. Perhaps it was.

As the car inched through afternoon traffic Martin noticed a woman standing on the pedestrian walk between the road and the river. She was remarkable, Martin thought, for carrying a baby in one arm and a placard in the other. Her poster read: *Mister Atlee, please.*

Martin bent forward and tapped the driver on a shoulder. "Is it true, Mister Iverson, that Prime Minister Churchill is likely to lose the election?"

"Yes. After the vote on Thursday good old Winston will find himself standing in one of the many unemployment lines you'll see if you're here long enough."

"How can the Brits be so thankless?" Martin asked.

"Apparently they consider Churchill a crisis-only manager. They waited long enough to bring him on. And now that the danger is past, they'll give him a thanks-and-goodbye salute."

"Voting with their middle fingers," Fox said grumpily, his eyes still bloodshot, but not from any hangover other than hanging over the ship's rail for half the width of the Atlantic.

"Democracy allows that," Iverson said.

"So Mister Atlee will be going to Potsdam?" Martin inquired.

Iverson nodding, his eyes fixed on traffic. "Where he'll be little more than a pupil expected to keep his mouth shut and pay attention."

"Pay attention to whom?" Fox asked. "Truman's been in office for how long? Less than three months? That leaves Uncle Joe to tutor the other two on the subject of how best to make the Germans grovel."

"I hear President Truman's a pretty good poker player," Iverson shouted over the sound of honking horns.

"He'd better be," Fox said. "Otherwise Stalin will chew up Harry the Haberdasher's fedora for lunch, then spit the pieces back to him."

Suddenly traffic jammed up to allow a convoy of American troops the right-of-way.

"Administrative units," Iverson explained. "They're the last to leave. That's why you won't hear any American bands playing *Yankee Doodle* today. The bands have all gone stateside already, along with everyone else except these guys."

"Nothing in the Army moves until the last piece of paper is filed in the proper drawer in triplicate," Fox said.

Iverson said, "I agree with you, Fox. The old saw that claims an army marches on its stomach isn't quite true. No army moves very far until the quartermaster files his requisition for food stores and the means to move them, and even then --." Iverson paused before adding, "Just got a letter from a college buddy of mine who flew twenty-five missions in the Pacific. He returned to the States on a boat from Brisbane to San Francisco. Took three weeks. And he claims the only thing anyone on the boat had to eat – passengers and crew for the entire three weeks -- was spaghetti noodles."

"Cooked, I hope," Fox said.

"After a while I doubt if that would make much difference," Martin said.

Iverson went on. "I figure the reason the German army got stopped at the gates of Moscow had nothing to do with the Russian winter. Instead, some idiot in the German quartermaster corps misread a frontline commissary sergeant's handwriting. The sergeant asked for ten trainloads of potatoes and end up with a freight car full of bridles and carp."

Martin had to think about that, then, after figuring out Iverson's remark, turned to Fox, who also looked puzzled. "Think, David. *Trainload of potatoes* is *Zugladung von Kartoffeln*; *bridles and carp* is *Zügeln und Karpfen*."

Fox called out, "Very nice, Mister Iverson. I like that. Might even be true."

"Thank you. Apocryphal, I'm sure, but funny anyway."

Several minutes later Iverson pulled the Chevy up at the taxi stand in front of a bombed out building. "I was asked to stop here to let you see what happened."

"So this is the Tate Gallery," Martin said, looking out the window in awe.

"What's left of it," Iverson said.

Fox peered, too, rubbing his eyes. "Everything inside got moved to Wales?"

"Good thing, huh?" Iverson said.

"Any plans to rebuild it?" Martin asked.

"Eventually," Iverson said as he made a u-turn and pulled back out into traffic.

After leaving the Tate he worked his way over to Grosvenor Place, where he continued north to Wellington Arch. After a right onto Piccadilly, he made a left onto New

Bond Street, soon stopping in the middle of a block of row merchants.

"This is it, gentlemen. You'll find Mister Parker waiting for you inside."

"Elliott Parker?" Martin said, climbing out. All he and David had been told was to expect "an art expert" to give them a briefing.

"Yes, sir," Iverson said, giving David Fox a hand as Fox exited unsteadily.

"Where are we?" Fox asked.

"Sotheby's. Just knock on that pair of double doors. I'll return later to pick you up," Iverson said and drove away.

"David, Martin, welcome to London." Elliott Parker sounded genuinely glad to see them. "I trust the boat ride over was not too excruciating."

After shaking Elliott's hand, Martin turned to his companion and asked, "Is it still excruciating, David, or is your agony reduced merely to being unbearable?"

Fox held out a limp hand for Elliott to shake and said, "I probably look worse than I feel. I've just about recovered, but a couple of days ago I was ready to throw myself over the side of the ship."

"You almost did," Martin said.

"I'm sorry you suffered, David. Would either of you gentlemen like a drink?" Elliott asked.

Both men passed.

"Then follow me. There is someone I want you both to meet, then we'll get right to work. Lunch will be brought in for us in about an hour," Parker said and led them through the dimly lit interior of the auction house.

In a better lit room directly behind the auctioneer's dais Martin saw an elderly man sitting at a table and was quite sure he knew the man from somewhere. Yes, now he recalled the face.

"Martin, you remember Werner Zeitz from Munich, I'm sure," Elliott Parker was saying as he led Martin to the table.

"Indeed, I do," Martin could say truthfully and held out his right hand. "I am very pleased to see you again, Herr Zeitz."

The old man shook Martin's hand from his sitting position. "Thank you, Herr Wynerson. Your visit to Munich with Herr Parker was the last good memory I have of the city I spent so many years in. Please forgive me for not rising to greet you. My legs have turned to rubber, my knees to concrete." He pointed to a pair of handsomely carved canes. "If it weren't for these, I would be forced to scoot about like a legless street beggar."

"I understand, Herr Zeitz. No need to apologize. Just the fact that you are here raises my spirits immensely."

Elliott intervened and introduced David Fox to Werner, who pumped David's hand and arm vigorously.

"*Fuchs, ja?*" Werner said, winking.

"*Ja,*" David said. "*Ein Fuchs.*"

Werner then launched into a popular German children's ditty. "*Fuchs, du hast die Gans gestohlen. Gib' sie wieder her –*"

To which David Fox gleefully added, "*Sonst soll dich der Jäger schiessen, mit dem Shiessgewehr.*"

All four men broke into laughter and clapped.

To Martin Werner Zeitz said, "I understand you have been collaborating with Karl Nierendorf."

"I have! What a brilliant and gracious man."

"I hear he even took time to see your ship off."

"Yes. That was very thoughtful of him." Martin thought he detected a sly exchange of looks between Elliott Parker and the old man, but perhaps he was imagining it.

"Werner has been in London since the end of 1938, where he has been invaluable in helping our cause, providing us with information we might not otherwise have been able to collect so early, if at all," Elliott explained. "In particular he has been helpful in sorting out the Nazis from the anti-Nazis among art dealers and artists, especially in Bavaria and Austria."

Werner Zeitz made a palms-up gesture of modesty.

Then, just as Elliott was about to continue, Martin clumsily interrupted. "Excuse me, but you have a son, Herr Zeitz. Rainer, yes?"

Furrows appeared on the old man's forehead and his eyes narrowed. "Yes," he said almost inaudibly.

"Do you know what has become of him?" Martin said.

Werner Zeitz looked up into Martin's eyes, stared for a moment, then said, "No. And what's worse, I don't care to know."

Perplexed, Martin looked at Elliott, who gave him a don't-pursue-it look.

But Werner continued. "I hope my son is dead, but if he's not – "he shrugged, " — he should be."

Martin suppressed a gasp, before recalling the unpleasant exchange between father and son eight years earlier. Their spat remained vivid in his memory for its being both surprising and disheartening.

Shifting to a subject Martin deemed more pleasant, he asked, "What of your niece, Anna, Herr Zeitz?"

Werner Zeitz looked at Elliott Parker again. And it was Elliott who answered Martin.

"You'll see her when you get to Munich. She's working with us. She obviously knows a great deal about Munich and the Munich art world. She's already proving invaluable."

Martin could scarcely contain his delight, but managed a polite, "I'm looking forward to seeing her again, to working with her," instead of *Yippee*!

"Let's get started with our work, gentlemen," Elliott said, playfully poking Martin to curb further fantasizing. "Martin, David, look to your left. We're about to play *ein kleines Spiel*, a little game."

Thursday
July 5, 1945
Berlin

Karl Vollmer shut off the ZIS's headlights a block from the Prussian Chamber of Deputies and edged the truck forward by the faint light emitting from the guard shack near the building's entrance. Looking at his watch, Karl said to Rainer, "I told you we'd be early."

"That's all right. Let's hope we can continue to trust Schlee and Uhlmann."

"And if we can't?"

"Then we must hope Major Ristov fears the consequences of coming this far before trying to betray us."

"Ristov doesn't strike me as a chess grandmaster," Karl said.

"Nor does he strike me that way. But surely even he can figure out his safest course is to take what we are offering him and keep his mouth shut."

Checking his side mirror, Karl said, "Here comes a truck pulling up behind us now."

As if given a signal, two guards emerged from the guard shack and started down the steps. Karl and Rainer each gripped his pistol a little tighter. From his passenger-side seat Rainer looked in his side mirror and saw a man step from the passenger side of the truck behind theirs. When the figure lit a cigarette Rainer recognized Major Ristov.

To Karl, Rainer said, "You watch the guards. I'll shoot the major if anything goes amiss."

Karl whispered, "*Zu befehl*", slid across to where Rainer had sat, and watched the two guards position themselves, side by side, rifle barrels lowered, to Rainer's left.

Compulsively, Rainer checked behind his seat to reassure himself the Raphael was where he had hidden it, then climbed down from the truck cab, and walked to Major Ristov, who saw Rainer's pistol, and reached for his own. But then Rainer holstered his and Ristov appeared to relax. In German, Rainer told the major the promised cigarettes, food, and liquor were in the back of the ZIS and Ristov removed a sheet of paper from his pocket, after informing Rainer that was his intention. Rainer stepped forward and recognized the page as the inventory list.

"I will check your goods against what you promised," Ristov said, speaking broken German. He then untied the canvas flaps at the ZIS's rear, took a flashlight from his pocket, and climbed into the truck bed.

At the sound of yet another vehicle approaching, Ristov turned and aimed his flashlight over the top of his own truck. Unable to see, he jumped to the ground and pushed past Rainer, who followed him. The third vehicle was an American-made Jeep with Russian markings and a fifty-caliber machine gun mounted on the rear seat. When the Jeep stopped behind Ristov's truck Major Ristov's flashlight illuminated Joachim Uhlmann behind the steering wheel, a soldier Rainer failed to recognize manning the machine gun.

"What is this?" Ristov demanded.

"Do you have insurance companies in Russia?" Rainer asked Ristov.

The major looked puzzled.

"*Versicherungsgesellschaft*, Major. This is my insurance company," Rainer said, pointing at the Jeep.

Ristov still looked baffled.

"*Schutz?*" Protection.

The major finally nodded, curling his lip, irritated. Ristov returned to Rainer's truck and climbed into the bed. Minutes later he emerged and acknowledged the inventory matched the agreed-upon terms.

Rainer then nodded to Joachim Uhlmann, who backed his Jeep up far enough for Major Ristov to turn his own truck around so that his and Rainer's trucks were bed to bed.

Again out of the truck, the major gestured for the two guards to begin transferring the goods, then motioned toward the Chamber of Deputies building and Rainer hastened up the steps, stopping only long enough to beckon Karl to join him.

Once inside the hall, Rainer slowed his pace, walking toward Franz Marc's masterpiece as though he were walking toward a church altar. Then he took a moment to gaze up at the Marc painting with a reverence he felt for few other objects – or people.

There will be time later to stand back and fully appreciate my prize, Rainer told himself. For now, get out! Leave Berlin before Ristov changes his mind, before someone less accommodating comes along to stop me, before -- ." With Karl's help Rainer lifted the painting from the wall, balancing its substantial weight carefully between them, and exited the Hall of Deputies, staggering only once as they descended the steps to the truck.

"Do you plan to leave Berlin?" Ristov asked Rainer after the painting had been secured in the back of the ZIS.

"Immediately," Rainer said. "You will never see me again."

"How, without papers?" the Russian asked, a trace of smugness in his question, Rainer thought.

"That, Major, is my problem."

"It may also be mine if you are caught."

"A risk we both take then."

"You must have papers to exit Berlin."

Rainer's turn to look smug. "I have papers."

Ristov looked dubious, but then looked over his shoulder at Joachim Uhlmann, looked back at Rainer, and nodded. "Before long that man… and his comrade… will need papers of their own."

"I'm sure they've thought of that already. Thank you, Major. Enjoy your loot." *While you can,* Rainer added silently as he saluted the man.

"Which way will you leave?" Ristov demanded gruffly.

"Into thin air," Rainer said.

The answer clearly did not suit the major, who repeated, "Which way?"

"Where all Germans want to go," Rainer lied. "To Switzerland, through Austria."

"*Guter Glück,*" the major wished him, ungrammatically.

Rainer smiled, made a slight bow, and answered politely, "*Vielen Dank,*" while at the same time he thought to himself, *You blockhead bastard!* He assumed Major Ristov harbored the Russian version of that contempt toward him.

Friday
July 6, 1945
Onboard a C-47
Over Belgium

Martin marveled that David Fox could sleep despite engine noise, plane vibration, and frequent stomach-in-your-throat turbulence. Martin found the plane ride more exasperating than the boat ride from New York to Portsmouth. But then he decided that, after being a pilot, however briefly, his lack of control over the plane constituted part of his annoyance and most of his anxiety. He tried to finish the novel he had started during the trans-Atlantic crossing, but finally gave up and closed his eyes, hoping his nascent headache would go away or at least diminish.

Soon he found his mind replaying Elliott Parker's "little game". On easels perched six paintings, most of which Martin thought he recognized when Elliott removed the sheet covering each one.

"David, Martin, what are we looking at?" Elliott had begun. "Come over. Take closer looks."

Fox approached a pair mounted side by side and said, "This one is obvious. It's Hogarth's portrait of his six servants. I'm guessing this one beside it is also a Hogarth."

"Very good," Elliott said. "Before either of you go any farther, let's focus on these two. Look at both of them carefully. By the way, to save time and explanation, all six of these are in Tate Gallery collections. The British government was kind enough to deliver them back to London on a temporary basis. Now go on. Take a few minutes to examine them."

"Are they forgeries?" Fox asked.

"You tell me, Mister Fox," Elliott said. "You've done a bit of research on Hogarth. Put it to use."

"David and Martin scrutinized both paintings closely, occasionally looking at one another. Martin knew he didn't want to embarrass himself by making a false claim and he was certain David didn't either.

Finally Elliott Parker announced, "Time's up. What are you verdicts? You first, David."

Fox made a face and offered, "They both look genuine to me."

"I agree," Martin said even though he wasn't sure. At least this way he shared equal disgrace if wrong.

Elliott turned to Werner Zeitz. "Are they right?"

Werner shook his head. "Both are fake. Very excellent fakes, to be sure, but the greatest forgery is still a forgery."

Fox shrugged.

Martin reexamined the paintings, then asked, "How should I have known?"

Elliott gave Martin a sympathetic smile. "Weeks of hard work. The man who did these is wasting away in jail. He's much too good to be doing forgeries, but he says they pay better. I'll come to that point shortly. First, let's look at the next pair." Both were familiar landscapes by John Constable. "Same issue, gentlemen. Real? Or fake?"

Martin and David took more time than on the previous pair, but in the end Martin allowed, even before asked, that he could not tell.

In an apparent attempt to one-up Martin, Fox declared, "This one on the left, *Flatford Mill*, is a fake."

"Correct, David," Elliott said. "Unfortunately so is the second one. But this time they were done by two different painters. Both in fact were sold at black market auctions. *The Mill Stream* sold in Manchester for forty pounds. *Flatford Mill* sold in London, where buyers should know better, and went for four thousand pounds – with serious bidding competition."

Elliott pulled the sheets from the final pair and announced, "To spare you both further trauma, I'll give you the answers regarding these two Turners. They're both fake also. When I said all six are in the Tate, I meant all six authentic paintings are in Tate collections. These last two are by the same forger and within the past year no fewer than three forgeries of each has sold, three here in England, the other three in Scotland. Of those six forgeries, four were resold within days of the original purchase. And each resale was for more than double the amount paid to the forger."

Elliott gestured for both men to take their seats. "So what are my points?"

"Buy directly from a forger," David said.

Elliott gave Fox a wan smile. "What else?"

"People are easily fooled," Martin said.

"Yes. Sometimes for good reason. Both of you are far more knowledgeable than most buyers, even wealthy, long-time collectors. Yet you were unable to tell real from fake. Now admittedly these six paintings are too well known for any collector to suppose they were available, above or below the table. And this is England."

Martin and David nodded.

"On the Continent matters are far different. Right now works of art are changing hands there faster than a con man moves peas in a shell game. And *shell game* is an apt metaphor. Unfortunately in the European markets at the moment most of what is being bought and sold is genuine. Forgeries are unnecessary."

More nods.

"A second point?" Elliott asked, then waited. When both Martin and David both hesitated, Parker walked to a corner and retrieved two more paintings, both small. "Look at these," he said and handed one to Martin, one to Fox.

"I don't recognize either one," Martin said.

David shook his head. "Me either."

"Nor should you. The artist is a nobody and his paintings, these and others, show neither skill nor imagination. But each sold for the equivalent of a thousand pounds because the artist was a clever hustler who convinced the buyers that these were works Hitler and Göring had once squabbled over, each prizing them for himself. Meanwhile, a block away from where these were sold a genuine Monet – since recovered – sold for what amounted to thirty pounds. The seller was not only stupid but desperate."

Werner Zeitz added, "Dozens of similar stories can be told."

"So my second point is this: Money is a driving force at the moment and pricing cuts both ways. Those still with ample means, and there are more than you might imagine, are paying exorbitant sums for essentially worthless pieces, while distraught sellers are willing to peddle Rembrandts for the price of a pair of shoes and a loaf of bread."

"Most sales are distress sales?" Martin asked.

"Indeed they are. It's a buyers' market at the moment," Elliott said. "But buyers and sellers will both be fearful. No one wants to get caught, but neither do sellers want to starve. Many buyers fear missing out on bargains. And who can blame them? Think, gentlemen. Wouldn't you follow the scent of Rembrandts selling for a tiny fraction of what they would go for under normal circumstances?"

"I would," Fox said shamelessly.

Martin wondered what he would do and was unable to give himself an honest answer.

"Keep in mind that the people we are bringing in for interrogation are already prime suspects, not random flotsam plucked from the streets. Every one of them will already have a history, none of them a very savory one. We are too few to nab every chance amateur who finds this or that Impressionist piece turn up on his doorstep and tries to peddle it in exchange for an overcoat or a pair of shoes. We are looking primarily for those who, in the past, have knowingly fenced, brokered, or directly sold works in quantity. By hammering them we break the chain."

"What if they don't break?" Martin asked tentatively.

"Hammer them harder," Werner Zeitz growled.

"Exactly," Elliott said. "Always look for a money trail. And in these tumultuous circumstances look for easily convertible assets, especially precious metals. Forget about occupation money, real or counterfeit, because the people you will be dealing with give it no value. Look for black market exchanges. Nearly every man, woman, and child in Germany is living from day to day. They are the sellers and want the basics. Food and clothing. Buyers will mostly be non-Germans. I encourage you, however, not to pause over a man's or woman's nationality. Give non-Germans no more quarter than you would a Nazi."

"Art for dollar's sake," David Fox observed.

"Yes," Elliott agreed. "We are not dealing with men – and women – who give a damn about art for its own sake. Certainly Germany's grand pillage was not motivated by aesthetic considerations. Art is simply one more commodity, although the rules of supply and demand are upside down. Even though there is a great deal of demand, suppliers, in most cases, are small-time, diffuse, and in no position to bargain. Even those whose motives are decent must be willing to pay dearly for their pleasures."

"You say look for a money trail, Elliott," Martin said. "But what do we do if we find one? We can't follow it very well when our charge is limited to interrogating."

"Follow it, Martin. Interpret your charge loosely. And –" Elliott paused before adding, "—if necessary, damn the niceties."

Werner stood and the others gave him their attention. "Many of the people you question will be urbane, educated, soft-spoken, witty, perhaps even charming. Let none of those traits disarm you. Their civility, however imposing, is but a thin crust, beneath which lies an assortment of truly heartless souls in league with the devil."

"Are there any good Germans, Herr Zeitz?" Martin asked.

"Not any more. All the good ones died fighting -- fighting the Reich, that is. The only ones left are either Nazis or else cowards like me."

Damn the niceties? Cowards like me? Are these the same two men I sat between in Munich eight years ago? What a telling effect the war has made on both Elliott and Werner. Well, perhaps on me, too, Martin thought. Then he turned his mind to three women – Katherine, Madeleine, and Anna – and tried to visualize just how much the war had altered their natures. Plenty in Katherine's case; more than a small bit in Maddy's. Anna's? He would soon find out.

At least Elliott had not asked him anything about Katherine. And David, bless his twisted soul, had not brought up her name. Maddy. I must write her a letter soon after we land, Martin told himself. I should have written her already.

With David Fox still sound asleep next to him, Martin turned his thoughts back to that day eight years earlier when he had frolicked across an alpine meadow in the breathtaking company of Anna Stahlinger. Filled with anticipation, Martin checked his watch, tried to estimate the remaining flight time to Munich, and, as his mind fogged over, he heard himself humming *Fröhliche Wandersman.*

28

Saturday
July 7, 1945
Ahrenshoop, Germany

"I know what you're thinking, Herr Zeitz," Oskar Lohnes said, collapsing back into his rocking chair, making the spindles squeak as he sat. To Thelda, "Another cup of tea, please." To Rainer, "You ask yourself whether you can trust the judgment of such a feeble, dying old man. Am I right?"

Rainer stood beside Oskar, balancing the frame of *The Tower of Blue Horses* on the lumpy mattress of Oskar's bed. "I value your opinion above all others, Herr Lohnes. If you tell me this painting is not a forgery, then I believe you."

"No. Comforting words, but your eyes betray you. I see better than you do. Do you know that? I have the eyes of that cat," he said. "Still." He pointed to the gray cat Karl cradled in his half arm, the cat Karl could not bring himself to leave in Berlin. "And my nose. It can still smell a forgery at twenty paces. Yes. I may be dying, but my vision and my instincts are still very much alive and well."

Rainer knew he would be obliged to arrange to have the painting examined by other experts in Sweden. His showing *The Tower* to Oskar was mostly a courtesy, a bow to Oskar's relationship with Werner, a gesture of appreciation to Oskar's hosting them, however shabby the hospitality. Real or forged, this was the painting he possessed, the painting he had risked his and Karl's lives to claim.

Thelda returned with a mug of tea. "Gentlemen, do you mind leaving Oskar to rest. This is more excitement than he has experienced since... since the Gestapo was here."

Outside, Rainer and Karl watched a late morning fog creep in, looked on in amusement as the cat pawed at the ribbons of mist streaming by. They had spent the previous night in Barth, stopping there for three reasons. Both were too tired to drive further; they feared more Russian patrols as they neared the Baltic; Rainer clung to his notion that they would require wearing British uniforms in order to land safely at a beach near Todendorf, because Germany east of Lübeck was the British Zone of Occupation.

Barth had been a prisoner-of-war camp right up until April, when, as the Russians approached, German personnel abandoned the camp, leaving several hundred mostly American POWs behind. But earlier in the war Stalag Luft I, as it was known, had been a detention camp for captured British airmen. Because of this Rainer had hoped to find British uniforms he and Karl could use. But their search of the vacant camp turned up none.

So they had spent their time waiting for darkness to fall, heating tinned ham over a poorly vented barracks stove and sleeping on bunks, covering themselves against the damp sea air with moth-eaten blankets that had been left behind when the Russians liberated the camp. Before morning Karl had announced how glad he was not to have had to suffer the miseries of being a POW in a German Stalag. His immediate anxiety, however, as he had revealed to Rainer only as they drove away from the camp, was that Rainer would want them to steal uniforms from prisoners buried outside the compound.

"My dear Karl, do you really suppose I would have asked you to dig up corpses and strip them of their uniforms?" Rainer said, as the two of them now stood outside Oskar Lohnes' thatched-roofed house. Karl placed the cat on a fender of the ZIS and lit up another of his wretched Eckstein cigarettes. Rainer tried his best to avoid the curls of smoke. He prided himself that he had not had a smoke in nearly two months. No pipe, no cigarettes. But then all available tobacco was now more wretched than when the war began. Waving off Karl's gesture, he chided himself for indulging in too much self-congratulation, asking himself: Does a farmer praise himself for not chewing horse droppings?

"How else will we get British uniforms?" Karl asked.

"I've given up the notion. You were right from the very start. We'll disguise ourselves as fishermen."

With disdain, Karl said, "*You* will disguise yourself as a fisherman. I *am* a fisherman."

Thelda stepped outside and announced, "I've prepared a small meal with the items you brought us. Come in and eat."

Last-minute bargaining with Schlee and Uhlmann yielded Rainer an additional supply of fresh food to bring on their journey, in exchange for revealing their cache of goods left behind on Pfaueninsel. The black marketers had also thrown in several small bundles of basic medical supplies, intended to serve as validation for their trek, should any Russians stop them. That had happened only once, at Neubrandenburg, forcing Rainer to swath his head and neck hastily in gauze. But the Russian officer in charge of the road block, after showing inordinate interest in the details of the paperwork Karl handed him, suddenly caught sight of the gray cat nestled in Karl's lap, and quickly lost interest in the his questioning, wanting to tickle and stroke the cat instead.

Past the blockade, Karl made a point of reminding Rainer, "See? You were so reluctant to let our little *Grauergeist* come along."

"And lucky for you, me, and the cat that the little beast chose not to treat the Russian's grimy fingers as though they were tinned sardines."

Knowing Thelda and Oskar would judge the tinned ham a glorious treat, neither Rainer nor Karl disparaged eating what had been their own staple for so many weeks, dreary though it had long since become to both of them. The fresh vegetables, courtesy of Schlee and Uhlmann, they all devoured eagerly.

After serving the modest meal, Thelda dished up small helpings for herself, sat, and explained, "The boat is still seaworthy. A nearby fisherman helped me caulk the hull seams with tar and oakum. So you shouldn't drown halfway across the bay. I estimate we've stolen enough fuel in recent weeks – the Russians are stupid and careless – to get you to Kiel. Or wherever your destination might be, short of there. We'll take care of disposing of your truck."

Oskar stopped eating long enough to ask, "Is the Raphael really a gift to you from Hans Frank?"

"It is," Rainer said, permitting himself a broad grin. "Only don't spread the word, because Herr Frank himself doesn't yet know of his generosity." Then Rainer sat back and told Oskar the story behind his possessing the Raphael.

———————

Sunday
July 8, 1945
Munich

Dear Maddy,

Greetings from Munich!

For all my many months of impatience wanting to get here, I almost wish I hadn't come. The Munich I experienced and fell in love with in 1937 is gone. In its place lies devastation well beyond anything I could have imagined. I'll spare you the grim details. Suffice to say the city has been bombed into oblivion. Yet people here assure me that, of the two declared purposes for inflicting such damage here and elsewhere, we (the Allies) accomplished neither. German war production failed to wither. Instead, war manufacturing increased. Nor did heavy bombing break the morale of the German population, although the latter point is difficult for me to verify. They are a broken people now. (Credit Karl Nierendorf with predicting our bombing efforts would fail.)

Elliott Parker surprised David Fox and me. He met us at Sotheby's in London and provided us with an excellent overview of the current situation on the Continent. I was delighted to see him again. He will be joining us again in a few days here in Munich, he says.

With him in London was a man I first met in 1937, Werner Zeitz, who ran a highly successful gallery in Munich. But his vocal opposition to Hitler led him to emigrate to London in 1938. Werner's son, by contrast, joined the SS and became an art procurer [*Kunstverschaffner*], someone who followed up German invasions by choosing which works of art were to be sent back to the Fatherland, certainly a morally ambiguous job. At least so for a man with a conscience. That is: Not merely saving art, but saving it for Nazis.

I met Werner's son in 1937 and I judged him to be a man without a conscience. So no doubt his task was easier than it would have been for many. On the other hand, conscience, as a mover and a guide, is much overrated.

You needn't remind me. Protestantism, especially our Lutheranism, places great faith in the power of an individual's conscience to direct a person's moral choices and religious understanding. I'm afraid, after seeing what I've seen since my arrival, I have a difficult time crediting that view. Men directed by their consciences could not have wrought the hell I am witnessing. Wrought. Listen to me. Do I sound as if I'm some Old Testament scold? Next I'll be proclaiming: Let there be light!

Soon David and I will be going to Austria for a week or so, first to Salzburg, then on to a small lake called Bad Aussee, where the Nazis cached thousands of art works deep inside a large salt mine. Joining us will be four men from a small group called the Art Looting Investigation Unit, a non-military wing of an organization called the OSS. I think I told you about the OSS. The head of it is a New York lawyer and Wall Street crazy named Bill Donavan. I met him once and decided I was glad he is on our side.

Also, David says Elliott Parker worked along side, maybe even with, the chief OSS man in Switzerland, somebody named Allen Dulles. I know nothing about him. I'm not even sure David was supposed to tell me as much as he did, but you've met David and know what a talker he is. And a show-off.

Because most of Munich has been flattened, David and I are staying in a make-shift tent camp near where our work headquarters building is. Ironically, the place where we work is called Der Führerbau due to the fact that, prior to the war, it was Hitler's office headquarters and most recently was a collection point for works of art destined for the grand museum Hitler intended to build in his hometown of Linz, Austria.

Sorry I didn't find (take?) time to write sooner. I have no idea how long mail takes to travel from here to Minneapolis-St. Paul. Not long, I hope.

Please keep me informed about everything good you discover about Santa Barbara. The more I consider the idea of our living there, the better I like it.

Hugs and a thousand kisses,
Martin

Tuesday
July 10, 1945
Lübeck Bay

Karl stood up in the boat and waved a dirty undershirt over his head and shouted, "Hey, you in the boat! Over here! Over here!"

After bidding farewell to Thelda and her friends who helped drag the launch out of the woods and down into the sea, Rainer and Karl had set a course from Ahrenshoop due west across Mecklenburger Bay toward the narrows of Fehmarn Sound, which fed into Hohwachter Bay and Todendorf. But four hours later, just before 4 a.m. by Rainer's watch, the boat's engine died.

No amount of cursing, praying, attempts at restarting, or kicking the engine's cowling had induced the machine to start up again. So, for a day and half they had been drifting south and sometimes west, driven by light northerly breezes. With no land in sight they were not sure of their position. Luckily, no patrol boats had appeared so far, either Russian or British, perhaps because the sea was now cluttered with bloated corpses, hundreds of them. The stench grew so bad that even Karl's furry *Grauergeist* refused to eat and buried its head in a spare blanket that lay in the boat's bow.

Then a small motorboat appeared off to the west, moving unhurried, with a single figure standing at the stern. As the boat came closer Rainer peered through binoculars and saw the figure was that of a young man who seemed to be slowing beside each corpse to prod it with a long pole. Finally the other boat came within hailing range, allowing Karl to wave and call out.

As the boat neared, it stopped dead in the water, though Rainer could hear its engine still running. "It's a boy," Rainer said to Karl. Fifteen or sixteen, the lad wore a heavy Wehrmacht jacket and a Greek fisherman's cap.

"What do you want?" the boy called out.

Karl shouted back, "Our engine died. We need to be towed to shore."

"Who are you?"

Karl looked to Rainer, who called back, "Refugees."

"From where?"

"Rostock," Rainer lied.

"Where are you headed?"

"Kiel."

As the boats drifted closer together the boy reached into his boat and pulled up a gun, which he aimed at them. "Why should I trust you?"

"Why should you not?" Rainer asked.

"Thieves, robbers, murderers are everywhere. Perhaps you want only to rob me."

Karl shouted back, "We mean you no harm. We only wish to get to shore to fix our engine. Look!" He held up the gray cat. "We mean no one any harm."

"I don't trust you," the boy said and made a prodding motion with his gun.

"Put that gun away," Karl said. The two boats were close enough now that Karl recognized the weapon as an army-issue Gew 98 from World War One. "You pull the trigger on that rifle and it will blow up in your face. Put it down."

"I'm leaving. I cannot help you."

Just then the engine on the boy's boat sputtered, sputtered again, then died.

Karl shouted, "Now you are no better off than we are. You need our help."

The boy quickly lay down his gun, reached behind him into the boat bottom and triumphantly raised a fuel can. "I am prepared," he shouted, voice full of spite.

Karl and Rainer watched helplessly as the boy refilled his tank. The boats had stopped drifting nearer one another and Rainer estimated the distance to be ten meters.

"I could shoot him," Karl said in a low voice to Rainer, "but we'd risk sparking his fuel and blowing us all up."

"Let's try to reason with him," Rainer said, doubting the likelihood of success.

They watched as the boy closed the cap on the fuel tank, set aside the now-empty fuel can, and restarted the engine.

All of a sudden the engine came to life and the boy's boat lurched forward, the motion knocking the boy off balance. As the boy fell, his boat came at the men's launch with its bow raised, slamming into their boat. Seeing it coming, Karl and Rainer both braced themselves, but the cat, surprised, let out a deafening yowl.

Karl jumped into the boy's boat, grabbing the rifle and tossing it overboard as he made his way to the engine and shut it off just as the boy stood up and jumped Karl from behind. Karl drove an elbow into the boy's ribs, knocking the boy down. Karl then turned and stomped on the boy's ankles before stepping forward to place a boot on the boy's chest.

"Don't kill me! Don't kill me! I will help you. Please!" the boy cried.

Rainer reached to pull the sides of both boats together, then used spare rope to raft the two to one another, all the while listening to the boy bleat and sob.

Finally Rainer boarded the boy's boat and motioned for Karl to help the boy sit up. "What is your name?" Rainer said, tipping the boy's face up to look into his own.

"Andreas."

"Well, Andreas, you must be more careful in the future. Always assure yourself the gear is in neutral before you start the engine." Rainer hoped talk of the future would reassure the boy.

"Yes, sir."

"How old are you?" Rainer asked.

"Fourteen. Almost fifteen."

"Were you in the Hitler Youth?"

Andreas nodded.

"Where is your home?"

The boy pointed west.

"What is over there?"

"Neustadt-in-Holstein."

Rainer looked at Karl. "Christ! We're almost at Lübeck."

"What are you doing out here alone?" Karl asked.

The boy slowly pulled up the left sleeve of his jacket to show the men the collection of watches affixed to his arm."

"You mean you're out here robbing corpses?" Karl snapped.

The boy lowered his eyes.

"Who are all these floaters? Where did they come from?" Rainer asked.

Andreas searched for his water bag, found it, took a sip, then began. "These bodies, most of them, come from the concentration camp at Nuengamme, near Hamburg. In May the SS marched the prisoners to Neustadt and loaded them on three old rusty ships. I heard neighbors whisper that the number of prisoners numbered ten thousand. I saw the ships because one of my Hitler Youth projects was to make a scrapbook about ships, mostly *Kriegsmarine* and Allied warships, but others, too. I made drawings and clipped news articles and photos."

"Go on," Rainer urged softly.

"The ships were the *Cap Arcona*, which used to be a luxury ship that took rich people form Hamburg to South America, the *Deutschland*, another liner, and *Theilbek*, a freighter. According to rumors we heard, many prisoners starved to death or were shot on the march from Neungamme. Those who survived were loaded onto the ships. The SS then planned to blow even more holes in the leaky hulls and let the prisoners all drown as the ships sank."

"The SS did this?" Rainer asked, gesturing to the sea filled with corpses.

Andreas laughed. "No. The British saved the SS the trouble. After the prisoners were on the ships, but before the SS could sink them, British Mosquito bombers flew over, saw the ships, and bombed them. It was the British who sank the ships."

Karl grabbed Andreas' arm. "And now you steal from the dead?" Aloud, Karl counted fourteen watches strapped to the boy's arm.

Rainer said, "Camp prisoners would not own watches."

"But the SS and ships' crews who were still onboard when the Mosquitoes attacked did. Very fine watches, some of them, as you can see for yourselves," Andreas said.

"What do you do with the watches?" Karl said.

"Trade them to the *Tommies* for chocolate."

"*Tommies*, you say? Are there many British near your home? Or where you launch your boat."

"Not now. The British want nothing to do with all these corpses. They don't go near the beaches."

"Good. You will take us where there are few British soldiers."

Andreas' eyes brightened. "May I keep the watches?"

"I should throw you overboard," Karl snarled.

"No! Please!"

"Be quiet," Rainer said to the boy. "You're going to guide us to shore and help us once we get there. How successfully you help us will determine whether we let you keep the watches,"

Rainer said. And whether you keep your life, Rainer thought, but didn't say

———————————

Wednesday
July 11, 1945
Munich

Even the grass in the English Garden seemed to Martin to be a paler shade of green than he remembered as he now sat where a noisy beer garden once had bustled with raucous patrons, where bar maids had clutched beer mugs the size of champagne magnums, and where an oom-pah band comprised of fat men wearing *lederhosen* and Tyrolean hats had played twenty variations of *Solang Der Alte Peter* and *In München Steht Ein Hofbräuhaus* until well after midnight.

Birds bathed in the muddy of waters of a dozen nearby bomb craters, unmindful of taller two-legged creatures meandering through the park in their ragged clothes, oblivious to the birds, as well as to anything else further away than their next footfall.

Anna Stahlinger sat on the grass beside Martin and nibbled on a slice of bread, part of a modest lunch she had packed in a small basket and brought with her after finally accepting Martin's invitation to get away from their work at the Führerbau for an hour or so. General Eisenhower's harsh order restricting Allied military personnel from fraternizing with Germans did not extend to socializing with fellow workers who just happened to hold German citizenship.

Anna's acceptance had to wait until she returned from a brief trip to the salt mine at Bad Aussee, where she helped take inventory, comparing what she could remember of the works stored in the Führerbau by the Nazis with works now discovered in the mine. Until now Martin had seen very little of Anna and each was eager to know of events in the other's lives since the summer of 1937.

"My parents died last year," she began. "My mother refused to leave Stuttgart, despite my father's pleading with her to move to Uncle Werner's chalet in the Alps. Allied bombing of Stuttgart was relentless. The ball bearing factory, so many rail yards, the metal works, you know. One night they waited too long before heading to the air raid shelter."

"I'm sorry," Martin said.

"Don't be. I never liked my mother. As for my father, he should have gone to the Alps, left her behind."

Martin thought of his contentious relationship with his own father, but knew he could never wish such a fate on Torvik. "I saw Werner in London."

"I supposed you would. Elliott said he was going to reintroduce you. How is he?"

"Not bad for a man his age, although he's bitter about his son. What do you know about Rainer?" Martin asked.

Anna shook her head. "Not much. Months have passed since I've heard from him. He joined the SS. Did you know?"

"Elliott told me."

"My cousin hurt himself while he was in Russia. Broke his leg in an ambush while he was on his way out of Kiev riding in the sidecar of a motorcycle. It could have been worse. His companion, who was driving, was killed. That reminds me, Elliott told me you were nearly killed in an airplane accident."

"My co-pilot was killed," Martin said. "I, too, ended up with just a broken leg."

"Just?"

"Well, my pride was wounded worse than my leg."

Anna continued. "I'm guessing Rainer is dead. His last posting was in Berlin and, from what I am told, Munich is a paradise compared with Berlin. Not many survived after the Russians arrived. Except for that traitorous coward Himmler, nearly all SS stayed and fought the Russians block by block, building by building. Do you know the SS motto?"

"*Meine Ehre Heist Treue*," Martin acknowledged. My Honor is Loyalty. But loyalty to whom? Martin wondered.

As if reading his mind, Anna said, "Loyalty to Hitler. Hitler only."

Mulling over the concept of loyalty, Martin decided to ask, "What made you decide to work for the Allies?" While waiting for an answer, he helped himself to a small piece of cheese in Anna's basket.

"Why? Two reasons. First, I hated Hitler and all the toadies he kept around him. Yes, I know. These days you'd be hard pressed to find a German who admits ever to liking a Nazi, let alone being one. But in my case it's true."

Martin said nothing.

"So, you might ask, why did I not join this or that anti-Hitler group? Yes?"

"Okay. Yes," Martin said.

"Because every single organization that formed to oppose Hitler consisted of failed men. Failed and... what is the English word for *schwach*?"

"Weak? Feckless?"

Anna nodded. "Feckless. I like that. Oh, don't get me wrong. Many of them were brave. But all failed. Even Field Marshal Rommel failed."

"So how did you contact Elliott Parker?" Martin said.

"I didn't. We met quite by accident. I was walking into the train station at Berne to catch a train for Geneva, where I thought perhaps I could find a job with the Red Cross. As I was going in Elliott was coming out. We didn't exactly bump into one another, but he saw me and remembered me. I missed my train but was glad I did. We found a quiet place to have coffee and talk. When he heard my circumstances he offered me a job working with him in Bern."

Feeling bold, Martin asked, "Do you have a boyfriend?"

Anna hesitated, then said, "No. Do you have a girlfriend in the States?"

"Too busy," Martin said cautiously.

"Tell me about your family."

So Martin narrated a brief history of the Wynersons, saving Maddy for last.

"What is it with men and their fathers?" Anna asked when he had finished.

"High expectations, I imagine. On both sons' and fathers' parts."

"There must be more."

If there was, Martin didn't know what it was. Or wasn't prepared to say. He wasn't sure he'd ever been entirely honest with himself on the subject of his father.

29

Saturday
July 14, 1945
Todendorf, Germany

"I must say, Karl, that was invigorating."

"A motorcycle would have been better," Karl said.

"No. Two motorcycles. I took my last ride in a sidecar long ago," Rainer said as the two of them dismounted the bicycles they had received from Andreas and his father in exchange for their boat and two tins of ham.

They scarcely longed for the boat, but they paid a price for giving up the hams in order to satisfy Andreas' father, who owned a small, shabby resort near the beach next to the Pelzerhaken lighthouse, just outside Neustadt-in-Holstein. Rainer allowed that, in the long absence of resort guests, adding an extra boat to his tiny fleet meant less to the man than the two tins of ham. But, because the bike ride of forty-odd kilometers had taken three days, rather than one and a half, as Karl had originally calculated, the two men found themselves short of food on the last night. Short, because they had elected to share the last tin of sardines with the furry *Grauergeist*. Thus, Rainer listened to Karl's stomach and mouth both grumble as they watched the cat feast.

The extra day and a half resulted from Karl's misremembering details from the only map they had, the one in his head. At least the trip was scenic, Rainer allowed, and almost free from British patrols. The only time they found themselves scrambling into the woods was near the village Altharmhorst, in the middle of what Holsteiners proudly called the *Holsteinische Schweiz*, Swiss Holstein, which Rainer dismissed as a bad joke, given the lake-dotted land was nearly as flat as a billiard table.

"I'll shelter the bikes from prying eyes," Rainer said, glad to be putting down the Raphael and the Marc, both made bulky by being wrapped in a heavy green waterproofing material Thelda claimed was developed by I.G. Farben especially for the *Kriegsmarine*. With Oskar Lohnes' help, Rainer had stripped the paintings from their frames and left the frames with Oskar for firewood. Thelda had helped him roll and wrap the canvases. And while Karl carried their food and the cat in a basket between his handle bars, Rainer had peddled and steered with both paintings balanced on his bars, no simple task, given the size of *The Tower of the Blue Horses*.

"Open our food cache in the cellar and fix us something good. I'm starved," Rainer called to Karl, who was already unlocking the front door to the farmhouse.

"How about a nice tin of ham?" Karl shouted back.

Next morning they were on the bikes again, having left the cat to guard the house. Their destination was the fishing harbor at Laboe, on Kiel Inlet, where Karl's brother, Klaus, kept his fishing boat. With the paintings safely locked in the hidden cellar vault, they took a direct route, less concerned about having to explain themselves, should they be stopped.

"I will never take sleeping in a soft, warm bed for granted again," Rainer told Karl as they peddled along. "Last night I slept better than I've slept in months. How about you?"

"The cat was restless. He kept me awake. I think he dreamed of a diet of mice instead of sardines," Karl said.

Three hours later the two of them stood on what was left of the pier where Klaus' half-sunken fishing boat rested on the bottom of the sad-looking marina. Klaus, whom they had surprised at his home in Brodersdorf, stood beside them.

"I salvaged what I could, but the boat is a loss. No one to help me salvage her, even if she were repairable," Klaus explained. "Look. The boat next to mine has barely been scratched."

"Can we take it?" Rainer asked, earning a glare from Klaus.

"I'm not a thief," he said.

"Can we buy it?" Rainer asked.

"With what?" Klaus said. But then added, "No. It's not for sale. The British have already claimed it."

"Claimed it?" Karl said.

"The British don't mind being thieves. Several *Tommie* army officers came two weeks ago to look at it, said they could make use of it, declared it off limits to anyone except themselves, and left. No one's seen them since, but no one wants to risk any British military wrath."

Rainer concealed his anxiety by joking, "The *Kriegsmarine* has no further use for its U-boats, but I don't think the Royal

Navy will permit us to borrow one. So we'll have to think of something else," Rainer said.

Monday
July 16, 1945
Munich

"Sit down, please, and state your name."

The woman flicked imaginary dust from the offered chair before she sat in it. "I am Maria Gottschalk."

"Do you know why you are here, Frau Gottschalk?" Martin asked politely.

"I do not. I have done nothing. The war is over, and now you Americans behave worse than the Gestapo."

Another defiant innocent, Martin thought, only slightly amused. He was becoming used to the steady parade of liars brought before him. Some of them were bold and clever, but most became tangled in a pathetic web of inconsistencies so quickly that he felt embarrassed for them. Some of them Anna would warn Martin about ahead of time. Others, she told him, were so incompetent at deception that she would wait until after he had interrogated them to fill him in on what she knew about them. She did this, she explained, just to see how quickly Martin could unmask them on his own. Frau Gottschalk fell into this category.

Martin glanced at his file on the woman. "What was you occupation during the war?"

"I was a bookkeeper for a clothing shop."

"Menninger's, yes?"

"*Ja.*"

"And how long did you work for Herr Menninger?"

"Oh, I don't recall exactly. So many, many years, it was."

"Ten? Twenty? Thirty years?"

A shrug. "Twenty some, I think. A long time."

"Any other jobs while you worked at the clothing store?"

"Oh, no. Herr Menninger's books were complicated. I had no time for other work."

"Tell me, Frau Gottschalk, do you remember your childhood very well? When you were a small girl growing up?"

She gave Martin a puzzled look, but answered, "Yes."

"Remember your wedding? Your husband? Times before the war?"

She hesitated, her eyes narrowing. "Yes."

"Then surely you remember working for Friedrich Stern?"

Alarm spread across her face. "Oh, yes. Herr Stern. That was for so short a time. You can forgive me for not recalling such a brief period."

"How brief a period, Frau Gottschalk?"

"A few months, perhaps. Maybe less."

"A few months? Think hard, if you will. How few?"

"I don't remember."

Martin stared at her, a deliberate, dispassionate look, neither cold nor warm.

"I don't remember."

"Perhaps my showing you ten years' worth of payroll records would aid your memory," Martin said. Thank God for the Nazi obsession with record-keeping, carefully preserving the paper documents even of those people they shipped off to be turned into ashes.

Frau Gottschalk stared back at him blankly.

"How old are you?"

A weak voice muttered, "Forty-four."

"So. You worked for Herr Stern for nearly a quarter of your life, yet you don't remember."

"The war. So distressing. It plays tricks on my memory."

Time to move on, Martin decided. "Tell me about the paintings we found in your house. Where did they come from?"

"Gifts from Herr Stern to me."

"Gifts? What was the occasion?"

"Many occasions. Tokens of appreciation for my loyalty," she said smugly.

Loyalty to someone she didn't recall working for, Martin wanted to point out, but didn't. No need to spit in her face gratuitously when she was well on her way toward convicting herself. Let the facts alone nail her.

"Bonuses then?" Martin asked.

"*Ja*! Bonuses."

"How much did Herr Stern pay you on a weekly basis?"

She looked at the ceiling as if searching for a number. "Only a few marks. Not much."

Martin half expected her to add that he was a tightwad, of course, because he was a Jew. "Yet he gave you tens of thousands of Reichsmarks' worth of bonuses."

"He did."

"Were you aware at the time Herr Stern was arrested by the Gestapo that those paintings you tell me were gifts given to you for your loyalty had in fact been sold to a buyer in Mainz and were going to be sent by train to that buyer?"

"That cannot be true! Those were gifts to me.'"

"I'm prepared to show you the invoices."

"Fakes! You have faked documents in order to entrap me! Those paintings were never going to be shipped."

"Why not?" Martin asked, already knowing the answer.

"Because --."

"How do you know they weren't leaving Munich?"

"Because Herr Stern promised them to me."

Martin folded his hands together on the interrogation table. Time for the dénouement. "You knew, Frau Gottschalk, because you were in the pay of the Gestapo to spy on Friedrich Stern. And the reason you knew the paintings would never leave Munich is because the buyer, Ernst Goldblatt, was also a Jew and to be arrested in Mainz at the same time the Gestapo came to arrest Herr Stern."

"No! Never did I spy for the Gestapo."

"I have witnesses, Frau Gottschalk. I have Gestapo payroll records," Martin said calmly. When she flinched, Martin realized it was not the first time someone sitting across from him showed more fear of the written word than spoken ones.

"They made me. The Gestapo promised to harm my family if I did not cooperate with them. You cannot understand what it is like to hear threats made against your children. I had no choice."

"And afterwards you stole the paintings for yourself."

"I didn't steal them. Yes, I took them home. But I took them to protect them. The Gestapo was going to board up the gallery. The paintings were not safe left there."

Enough, Martin decided. "And what did you do to try to protect Herr Stern?"

"Protect Herr Stern? I did nothing."

Martin stared at her in silence.

"You don't understand. He was a Jew."

Tuesday
July 17, 1945
Ahrenshoop, Germany

"What are you doing back here? Oskar's funeral was Friday."

Rainer had expected a more welcoming response from Thelda. "I'm sorry. I didn't even know."

"Then why are you here?"

"I need your help."

"You had all the help I can give."

"Please. May I come in?"

She stood back, holding the door wide open, but she did not look pleased. When she closed the door she motioned for Rainer to take a seat. "How did you get here? If you are returning the boat, I have no need for it. I don't want it."

"May I have some tea?"

Thelda lit a fire in the stove, filled a teapot, and put it on to boil. "How did you get here? Keep the boat. I have no use for it."

"Using extra food stuffs we had cached in... in Kiel, I bartered with Karl's brother for an old Opel flatbed truck. Klaus was kind enough to include enough petrol to get here. The truck is outside."

"Where is your friend?"

"I left him behind with the paintings in --."

"Kiel," Thelda said with a tone of contempt, making clear she knew he was fudging. "So why come back?"

"I need to find a way to get to Sweden." Rainer explained what had happened to Klaus' boat.

"Nice clothes, by the way. More becoming to you than the fisherman's garments you wore when you left. Where did you find them?"

"I had them stored in --."

"Yes, I know. Kiel." She gave him a I-know-you're-lying smile.

"How did you cross from the British Zone to the Russian Zone?"

"I'm a Red Cross representative. I have papers to prove it. Real papers."

"Phony name on them, of course."

"Well, yes. I am now Helmut Spühler."

"What about the launch you used to leave from here?"

Rainer told her about the boat's engine failure, their drifting into Lübeck Bay, about the grisly scene they had witnessed there, their encounter with Andreas and the subsequent trade of the boat for bicycles.

"After all that you choose to come all the way back here? I don't understand. Sweden, yes. I see that. To sell your stolen paintings. You can't sell them here. The Allies will find out before you can flee to Rome, or wherever people like you go so the pope can make you vanish."

"I thought someone here in Ahrenshoop might know a route from here to Stockholm. A way, a means."

Thelda glared at him. "Someone?"

"You."

The kettle whistled and she poured tea. Handing Rainer a mug, she said, "This is the best I can do for you. Weak tea."

"What's to become of you?" Rainer asked her.

"I was born here. Some day the people of Ahrenshoop will bury me near Oskar."

"And in the meantime?"

"Meantime? What does it matter?"

"You are too young to embrace such an attitude," Rainer said.

Thelda smiled a listless smile. "In my young life, Herr Zeitz, I have seen too much not to *embrace such an attitude*, as you kindly put it."

———

Wednesday
July 18, 1945
Munich

"So, David. Are you taking Fräulein Strumpet to a dance again?"

David Fox was grooming himself in front of the mirror in their tent, combing more oil into his wavy hair, slapping his face with a second dose of aftershave lotion. "Her surname is Strumpf and she's not a whore."

"She's merely appreciative of all the gifts you lavish on her," Martin said, lying on his cot, propped on one elbow, watching Fox preen. Frieda Strumpf worked in the basement of the Führerbau as a cataloger, the same job she had held under the Nazis, and David always managed to find several excuses a day to descend into the underground storerooms to verify the presence of this or that work of art. And Martin had to admit that, with some makeup, a new dress, and a pair of heels, Frieda Strumpf was definitely a stunning piece of sculpture.

"Exactly. And if she chooses to thank me from a supine position with her skirt hiked up, who am I to deny her show of gratitude?"

"Just a lonely GI."

"What about you, Wynerson? Why aren't you chasing any pussy?"

"Not interested."

"Listen. The male population around here has been decimated. These Munich Fräuleins are desperate. And believe me, they put out as well as any closet-polka Lena back in Minneapolis."

Martin regretted having shared his repertoire of Lars-and-Lena jokes with David.

"You're sister's not here, Martin. So she surely can't begrudge your treating yourself to a temporary alternative, can she?"

"Enough! I've told you before, leave my sister out of this."

"Okay. Okay." Fox took one final look at himself sideways in the mirror, adjusted his tie, threw Martin a farewell kiss, and was gone, the sound of his whistling *Swinging on a Star* fading into the distance.

Martin told himself he was not at all resentful of David's amorous triumph, despite the fact that for a while he had thought himself languishing on first base with Anna, but hoping to score. That he had Anna in mind as a *temporary alternative* was none of David's business.

Unfortunately, in the three weeks plus that he had been in Munich three lunchtime picnics were all Anna had allowed him. But then she refused any more of those innocent *treffs* – without explanation. The bitterness he felt when he finally discovered why left him feeling so ill, so shaken, he could barely rise from his cot for two days, canceling his schedule of interrogations and feeling worse for adding guilt to his sullen anguish. Anna, he learned by a chance, unwelcome encounter, was having a relationship with Elliott Parker.

Walking alone after dark toward one of the few hole-in-the-wall cafes open in Munich, Neff's, on Luisenstrasse between Königsplatz and what was left of the train station, Martin had crossed the street to avoid a small mountain of rubble ahead of him. No sooner was he on the other side than he saw a man and woman, walking in the same direction, arm in arm half a block ahead of him, the woman's head leaning on the man's shoulder.

When the couple reached Neff's, light from the café window illuminated the pair enough for Martin to recognize them as Anna and Elliott. Martin backed against the nearest wall and watched them enter the café. Re-crossing the street and standing in the darkest spot he could find yet still see into the café, Martin saw the café owner seat Anna and Elliott near the window.

He had waited and watched, feeling guilty, yet too absorbed and angry to quit his covert station.

During their meal Anna and Elliott frequently paused in their eating as Elliott squeezed, and twice kissed, Anna's hands. Even from his distant location Martin thought he could see a look bordering on veneration in Anna's expression as she conversed with Elliott. She certainly spoke with more animation and ardor, he realized, than she had ever displayed in his company.

The next day had begun Martin's two-day spell of illness. Even David Fox had sensed Martin's despair and kept his distance. Curled on his cot, Martin dreamed often of Maddy and thought to write her, but, in his state of gloom, he feared any letter he attempted would inevitably descend into self-pity and no amount of effort at limiting his text to frivolous reports on Munich weather, his interrogation work, and daily life in a foreign country would mask his senses of disillusionment and homesickness. Madeleine would read between the lines.

After returning to work, Martin found himself spending all his free time either sleeping or else wandering the streets of Munich, as pathetic and cataleptic as the nomads whose courses intersected his own.

Aside from his disinterest in drinking and socializing with other officers, Martin refused to go into any American officers' clubs after learning from one of his fellow MFA&A members, Eileen Becker, that Nazi-pilfered art work adorned the walls of every single club she had inspected in both Bavaria and Austria. Worse, if such were possible, Nazi thefts also hung in several American generals' and colonels' private offices she had been invited into. And worst of all – she nearly cried when telling Martin – was that, not only did these top-ranking officers know the works were stolen, they all made clear they intended to do nothing about it.

So, Martin chose to meander the streets of Munich, always alone and frequently after dark, despite several warnings from MPs that such behavior was dangerous in a city full of so many hungry and opportunistic wretches. In response Martin would show the MPs the service revolver he carried with him.

Thursday
July 19, 1945
Berlin

As Rainer neared Berlin, security was intense and traffic backed up for several hundred meters at a checkpoint outside Oranienburg. The Russians wanted no surprise incidents at the upcoming Potsdam Conference. Rainer spent the night parked in a forest near Gransee, sleeping seated, behind the steering wheel, a pistol on his lap. He, too, had wanted no surprises. Perhaps leaving Karl behind, guarding the farm, had been a mistake. But too late to worry about that now.

Before leaving Ahrenshoop Rainer had walked to the church-side graveyard where Oskar Lohnes was interred. He had no trouble locating Oskar's plot, with its freshly turned dirt and absence of the headstone Thelda had ordered. Oskar, she said, had chosen his own epitaph: *Unless there are sunsets to paint, I want no part of Heaven.*

As he waited for the line of vehicles to edge forward toward the Russian checkpoint, Rainer recalled how he had knelt at the foot of the grave and spoken to the old man as though he were still alive and rocking easily in his parlor chair. Having abandoned any belief in an afterlife, Rainer understood that he was talking only to himself. Still, he felt a need to carry out the pretense.

"I thank you for being such a close and abiding friend to my father, Oskar. You meant a great deal to him. He will grieve deeply when he knows you are gone."

He had picked up a fistful of sandy soil and let it slowly filter threw his fingers. "Painful though it is for me to concede the viewpoint to you and Werner, you and my father were correct from the beginning in your assessment of the consequences the Austrian corporal and his disciples would bring down on our nation. In my miscalculation, in my blindness, I have truly disgraced myself. Disgraced myself in such a way no apology is adequate. Cousin Anna was wrong to think we could simply wait them out, replace them with more serious men when they were gone. Dilettantes? Yes. But they were also serious men. Serious in a way only you foresaw. I remember once you shouted at my father, 'Werner, the most damning fact about these scoundrels is that they have no sense of humor. None! They are unremittingly humorless. And for that trait we shall all pay dearly.'"

For all *their* show of seriousness, the Russians manning the Oranienburg checkpoint took one look at Rainer's Red Cross documents, pointed at the official symbol, smiled, nodded, and waved him through toward Berlin, with a hearty, though oddly accented, "Welcome to Berlin, Comrade. Enjoy your stay." He assumed the men had required considerable coaching in courtesy and joviality, qualities that would surely evaporate the instant Atlee and Truman were airborne for London and Washington.

His window rolled up, Rainer waited until a hundred meters separated him from the checkpoint before looking in his rear-view mirror and shouting, "Fuck you, Comrades!"

The white medical tents at the eastern edge of the Tiergarten had been rearranged since Rainer had slipped into one of them to chat with the Sundstrums. So he stopped a passing nurse to ask the whereabouts of the Swedish couple, first showing her his Red Cross 'credentials'.

Frowning, she asked, "You've been away for some time, Herr Spühler?"

"Not only away, but out of touch. Small villages on the Baltic, in need of advice," Rainer replied, sensing there was something he was supposed to know but didn't.

"Both Nils and Sigrid are dead. The Sundstrums decided to take a much-needed break and flew home to Stockholm when a plane was available going that way. Only the plane apparently developed some kind of trouble before reaching Stockholm and crashed on the northern tip of Öland Island. There were no survivors."

"I'm terribly sorry to hear that," Rainer said, and meant it. "How tragic!"

"As yet Geneva has sent no one to replace them. We are dreadfully short of staff. You knew them well?"

"No, but I knew them and held a deep respect for them." As art fencers, Rainer thought silently, not as physicians. So. Another source of helping me find a route to Sweden is eliminated.

"Might you be able to make known to Geneva our acute shortage of medical personnel? Several times already I have carried out procedures well beyond my training. But what are we to do? Let people die?"

That is a matter of indifference to me, he thought. "I'll do what I can, but you are already well aware of how stubborn Geneva can be."

The nursed touched him on the arm. "I can see it in your face, Herr Spühler. You have persuasive powers others lack."

More fool you, woman. "I promise. I'll do my very best." Just leave me alone, he thought. Go away.

"I must be going, but tonight I will pray on your behalf that your appeal to Geneva will be successful."

Better yet, pray for me that I make it to Geneva.

From the canvas tents of the hospital grounds Rainer drove to Potsdamer Platz, slowing to stare at the Chamber of Deputies, but deciding against revisiting the scene of his crime. Maneuvering his Opel truck slowly amid streets still cluttered with rubble, past the remnants of once-solid, if not particularly handsome, buildings, avoiding pedestrians as oblivious as any soldiers he had seen since his mission to see General Kruger on the outskirts of Pushkin so many years earlier, he turned a corner and saw an old man offering to sell a bicycle to a young Russian soldier and suddenly wondered if perhaps he might find his black market friends, Wolfgang Schlee and Joachim Uhlmann. *They* just might be able to find me a spare submarine, he mused. Surely a boat of some kind. But he realized he had no clue where to begin to look for them. *Within two blocks of Zhukov's headquarters*, Karl had said. But that was several weeks ago, he reminded himself. They could have moved their secret workplace a dozen times since then – and probably had.

Nothing left but to leave Berlin, he decided. Head home. Or do I even have a place I can call home any longer? Driving southwest to circumvent the conference preparations in Potsdam, he headed toward the town of Erkner, where he passed through another Russian checkpoint, manned by yet another set of faux-cheery Slavs. From there, he made a quarter circle clockwise through the Brandenburg countryside before heading south toward Leipzig and on to his next destination: Munich.

30

Saturday
July 21, 1945
Munich

"I can't believe you allowed that bucket of *Scheiss* to go free," Anna screamed at Martin the moment she entered the room where Martin had recently finished an interrogation.

"Lack of evidence," Martin said.

"I have already told you, Herr Wynerson, that Georg Hoffmann is, and has been for some time, the biggest art thief in Munich. As one of the richest men in this city he can buy whatever pleases him. And, believe me, there is plenty of art in Bavaria that pleases him."

Two days earlier Anna had gone from calling him Martin to calling him Herr Wynerson. He wasn't sure exactly why, but he decided it didn't matter. Well, two could play that childish game. "There is a distinct difference, Fräulein Stahlinger, between what you believe to be the case and what no facts have yet established.

I need *Sicherheit*, not *Gewissenheit, ja*? Certainty, not certitude. *Versteh?*"

"Damn you. I have the proof. I told you."

"I know. The mysterious Wido Schliep in Hamburg."

"Yes. He knows all about Georg Hoffmann's dealings. Well, maybe not all, but enough to have him arrested."

"So bring him down from Hamburg to testify."

"You know I lack that power."

"As do I. I'm just a lowly interrogator, not a policeman. So I'm afraid that until he sits here in front of me and tells me his stories, he remains not only mysterious but also mythical. As in *erdichtet*, not *mythisch*. Invented."

"Wido is real and he knows Hoffmann possesses several Spanish Old Masters. Dutch, too. He has seen some of them even. And plenty more."

"Perhaps you can whisper into Elliott's ear to have Herr Schliep brought into custody, then transferred here. Maybe even kidnap the man. You know Elliott's motto: Damn the niceties."

Anna turned briskly and walked out, slamming the door behind her. Martin thought: If looks could kill --

---

Sunday
July 22, 1945
Munich

Munich had fared no better than Berlin and Rainer found he had to park on Leopold Strasse and walk several blocks east to the neighborhood in the Schwabing District where he grew up, where his father's house still partially stood. Entire blocks in between were now no more than piles of brick and stone. Where Werner had taken him for private piano lessons when he was seven years old, Fräulein Eisenfurth's basement flat on Schnorrstrasse, a single wall of the building remained upright. Fräulein Eisenfurth herself is surely dead, Rainer supposed. Though young and pretty, she suffered from a lung ailment that made her cough all through his lessons, cough so badly that Rainer finally told his father he no longer cared to listen to her rasping and wheezing.

Werner had concurred. So, for weeks afterward, Rainer silently thanked the deities of disease for giving the poor woman a malady that served as a convenient pretext for ending his own suffering at the keys of an instrument he had no desire to master. As he stared at the rubble where the flat used to be he took added satisfaction from supposing her piano was still there, somewhere beneath tons of brick, reduced now to nothing more than a mass of twisted wires and splinters.

Leaving Schwabing, he drove, as cleared streets permitted, to the damaged Alte Pinakothek Museum and parked across the street from the building. But before getting out to continue his assessment of the inner city, he popped a fedora on his head and bent the brim so his eyes were shaded, making the possibility someone might recognize him more remote. Satisfied, he walked east on Gabelsbergerstrasse two blocks to where his father's galley had been. The building was gone. But something caught his eye. Protruding from the bricks, a hand-written placard still nailed to a window frame read: *Judenliebhaber*. Jew lover.

He walked back to Luisenstrasse and turned south toward the Hauptbahnhof to check the train schedules, if there were any. Passing Café Neff, he quickly glanced through the window to see if he recognized any faces from days when he often whiled away afternoons there, sipping coffee and reading newspapers. He saw no one he knew.

He hoped at least some trains were running. Lost-in-a-crowd anonymity would better be achieved by taking a train across the Austrian and Swiss borders than being the sole occupant of a truck.

"Cigarettes?" an old woman asked him as he stood waiting for traffic to clear on Arnulfstrasse, across from the train station. Rainer looked at her out of a corner of his eye, wondering whether she was begging, buying, selling, or covertly sizing him up for something else.

"No."

"You don't smoke?"

"No."

"No need to be so curt. I was just asking."

"Ask someone else."

"Such a nice coat you are wearing. Would you like to sell it?"

Despite being summer, Rainer wore a knee-length all-leather coat, unbuttoned. Aware of being far better dressed than anyone other than American GIs, he knew his fake status as a Red Cross representative called for his looking equivalent to a prosperous Swiss businessman, despite the attention such misplaced stylishness would draw.

"So well fed, too," the woman said, reaching to pat Rainer's stomach before he grabbed her wrist. Jerking her hand away, she said, "Tell me where you dine so I can feast there, too."

"Go away. Please, just leave me alone." Traffic thinned and Rainer stepped off the curb toward the train station.

From behind him he heard the woman shout, "Go and sell what thou hast, and give to the poor, and thou shalt have treasure in Heaven."

"Crazy old crone," Rainer muttered. "Why should I wait for Heaven?"

A bomb crater lay where the station taxi stand used to bustle. Beside it a pair of MPs stood talking with a young man whose arm gestures and head shakes suggested to Rainer the man was adamantly denying knowledge of something. Rainer thought to veer away from the MPs, then decided such an abrupt change of direction might arouse their suspicions. So he walked straight at them, tipped his hat, and said, "Good afternoon, gentlemen," in English. Surely such behavior would disarm them, prevent them from wondering if he might be a cunning Nazi trying to slip past them in disguise.

No sooner had he passed them than he heard an American accent call out, "Sir, wait. *Halt, bitte.*"

Rainer stopped and turned slowly and saw one of the MPs beckon him. "Yes?"

The second MP dismissed the man he had been questioning. The man who was summoning Rainer said loudly, "This'll only take a sec, not that you're going to miss a train, however long it takes."

Rainer stepped over to where the two men stood. "How may I help you?"

"Y'all live here in Munich?"

"No. I'm Swiss. A Red Cross representative." He offered no papers, not wishing to appear too eager to prove who he was. He noticed the man whom the MPs had been speaking with, though told he was free to go, still lingered nearby. The man shot Rainer a disbelieving stare. But he said nothing. If the man was a local he would know Rainer's accent did not belong to any *Schweizer*. "How about you?" Rainer said. "Texas?"

"No, sir. Oklahoma."

"What can I do for you?"

The other MP said, "Beer. We're looking for some good German beer. Not this nickel-a-bottle swill they peddle at our PX. I realize we bombed the living shit out of you folks, but surely there's gotta be a brewery standing somewhere in these parts. Our flyboys ain't that accurate."

Rainer smiled and shrugged. "Sorry, gentlemen. I'm afraid I'm not much of a beer drinker. I suggest you try asking the owner of that café just up Luisenstrasse. Neff's. Or check with any local café. You'll find your answer in one of those, if anywhere."

"Thank you kindly, sir," Oklahoma said. "We 'ppreciate it."

Rainer glared at the loitering German and, in his sternest SS officer tone, said, "I suggest you disappear as quickly as you can, before I give these two men half a dozen reasons to arrest you for further questioning."

Instant fear crossed the man's face before he turned and ran.

Oklahoma whistled, then asked, "What'd y'all say to him?"

"I told him to get back to his wife before she finds herself a young, handsome, American boyfriend."

The MP slapped his thighs. "Yessiree! Ain't that the truth."

"Best of luck finding your beer," Rainer said and hastened into the train station, where he could breath normally again.

———————————

Sunday
July 25, 1945
Munich

Dear Maddy,

Bah! German women under forty, at least all the ones I've met so far, are insatiable, two-legged leeches. I understand that (1) most eligible men in their age group are either dead or maimed, and (2) most of them lack the means to support themselves, given few of them have ever held gainful employment. Still, the *Hausfraus* and *Fräuleins* of Munich give the concept of gold-digging a whole new dimension.

Poor David Fox dates a woman who is bleeding him dry. And even Elliott Parker, who ought to know better, has succumbed to the wiles of one of the most cunning sirens among these Bavarian equivalents to the Rhine maidens known as *Die Lorelei*. But, so far, yours truly has fended off all their tricks and charms. My key? Short of blindfolding myself and leashing myself to a Maypole, à la Odysseus, I simply avoid contact with them by staying away from their iniquitous gathering places, such as officers' clubs.

On the latter subject, allow me to fulminate for a paragraph or three.

I came here under the impression we Americans intended, as part of our crusade, to right the wrongs of Nazi art thievery; instead I watch as at least one American soldier per day is arrested for filching one or more works of art, most of them hoping to sneak their prizes home, treating them as though art is one more kind of war souvenir to which they are entitled. Ranking American officers need not stoop to such sneakiness. They simply appropriate art works and hang them in their offices, allowing the overflow to be hung openly in our officers' clubs.

And what is being done about such thefts among colonels and generals? Nothing. Nothing. Nothing. The works, as I say, are treated as no more than legitimate spoils of war. I'm ashamed – for the Army, for America. Suffice it to say, my expressions to others here of my disappointment at both the scale of the thefts by us and the extent of our indifference to such larceny has earned me both contempt and pity -- but no respect. I am merely thought to be naïve. Perhaps I am.

A little over a week ago I took a two-day trip to Salzburg, Austria, then beyond, into the mountains where the Germans had filled a huge salt mine with art loot. I went with an Army captain in charge of a convoy detailed to bring truckloads of the art back to Munich.

In a Jeep, the captain and I got well ahead of the convoy so we stopped at a small village for lunch while we waited for the trucks to catch up. The captain made the mistake, as it turned out, of engaging the inn keeper in a conversation about the war. The captain asked whether the inn keeper was relieved to have his country liberated from the influence and control of the Bavarian corporal and his minions.

Well. The inn keeper immediately burst into a tirade the likes of which I have seldom witnessed. He made clear to the captain that, for one thing, Hitler was not a Bavarian, but an Austrian. Clearly a point of pride with the man, not embarrassment. For another, he insisted Austrians welcomed the *Anschluss* and are deeply disappointed Germany did not win the war. Then the inn keeper added, gratuitously, that at least Hitler had rid Austria of its Jews. Unknown to the inn keeper, the captain's surname is Arnstein. We left abruptly, listening to the inn keeper continue to rant, even as we climbed back into our Jeep and rode away.

Yes, Maddy. I am disillusioned. Not about the Germans; I find I had few misconceptions about them. It's everyone else who baffles me. The lines between virtue and vice, right and wrong, the good guys and the bad guys have suddenly become indistinct, have even been erased in some areas.

Maybe I've led too sheltered a life. But, no. That's not the explanation. Nor do I think I've climbed up on some moral high-horse. If someone – several someones – hadn't judged worthwhile this job I and my fellow MF&A members are doing (*trying* to do), our unit would never have been organized, let alone sent here.

In any case, disheartened though I am, I will "soldier on". Wish I had a few bits of cheery news to end this piece with. Wait. I do. Re-reading what I wrote above, my train of thought leads me now from German women to German food. Thusly:

The worst German leech I've met is David Fox's *Busenfreundin*, bosom girlfriend. (Read into that as much as you like!!!) Frieda's an unappeasable little tart and David can't resist trying to satisfy her every whim. But Frieda has a handsome young nephew, Franzie, who is eight years old, and, as it turns out, is as eager to please us as David is keen to please Frieda. His notion of how to make us happy is to bring us these rich, indescribably delicious honey walnut tartlets, called, not surprisingly, *Hönigwalnusstörtchen*. (Obviously, *tart* led to *tartlets*.) Frieda says they are a Bavaria tradition, but Anna Stahlinger claims they originated in a hotel kitchen at St. Moritz in the Engadine Valley of Switzerland.

Anna, if you recall, is an alpine skier. Or was, before the war. Competed in the '36 Olympics at Garmisch-Partenkirchen. Because of her skiing, she's quite familiar with St. Moritz. So maybe she's right. Then again, she's also shamelessly insincere, willing to tell anybody anything, either to impress people or simply to get her way.

But now I've reverted to being negative again, when I actually meant to end on the high note [listen closely for Swiss yodeling in the background] of how delightful

Franzie is, how wonderful to have honey walnut tartlets delivered to our door. (Well, tent flap.)

When I asked Frieda where the tartlets come from, she said, "Don't ask." So I asked Franzie, who told me, "Aunt Frieda says I'm not to tell you." I do hope the charming lad isn't stealing them, for then I should have to park him in a church pew and ascend my pulpit.

It's late; I'm tired. More *wursts* to "grill" tomorrow. *Wursts* is the name David has given to the people we interrogate. We *are* making progress. Some people do confess – without our having to put their feet too far into the fire for too long à la the Spanish Inquisition. But the ugly bits of business I mention above put a stain on our victories, akin to someone's pissing on fresh snow. But triumph we shall, Sister Madeleine. I just hope I'm not too old a man by the time we've finished here. Santa Barbara beckons too strongly.

Love to all the family. Thoughts deeper than love to you.

> Your longing brother,
> Martin

Monday
July 26, 1945
Kochel am Se
Bavaria

"Poor Pierre! You've been unconscionably neglected. What's it been? Two and a half years?" Rainer blew dust from the neck of the cognac bottle and watched the dust settle back slowly onto the fireplace mantel. After lighting candles at either end of the mantel, he looked at the vintage date on the bottle of Ferrard. Nineteen-twenty-seven. Eighteen years. So very long go, he mused. An age of innocence by comparison.

Much as he wanted to uncork the brandy, doing so would break the promise he had made to himself. The cognac was a present to his father. Even so, he continued to stare at the bottle, trying to imagine its delicate flavor. He started to walk away, but stopped, turned, and said. "Stay where you are, Pierre. Before long Werner will decide he's drunk enough English gin, tea, and ale."

The chalet felt chill, even in mid-summer. Rainer brought in firewood and built a small fire, for nostalgia's sake as much as for the heat. For the first time in recent memory he did not sense threats all around him. He laid his pistol on the mantel, then kicked off his civilian shoes, laughing at himself as he did so, longing for the comfort of his SS boots. He pushed Werner's leather chair nearer to the fire, opened a bottle of Pinot Noir from the cellar, poured himself a glassful, then sat down to unwind. All that's missing, he told himself, is a collection of Hölderlin poems to read. Well, a meerschaum might be nice, too, but no. My smoking days are over.

He decided he would worry about food later. In his search through the chalet he had found a forgotten tin of Danish ham tucked behind a carton of unopened spices. The very sight of the ham set his stomach churning. I'd rather starve, he assured himself, and put the tin back where he had found it.

The drive from Munich to Kochel had been satisfyingly familiar, even though he would have preferred to ditch the truck in Munich and ride the train, taking the Munich-Innsbruck line as far as Tutzing before switching to the short commuter than ended in Kochel. But --

"Track repairs are running behind schedule," was the explanation a railway official gave Rainer when he asked about traveling by rail to Innsbruck or Salzburg. "Soon, we hope. The Americans have promised us." Soon, alas, was too late.

Trains to Austria were running, he had been assured. With a locomotive attached to each end, a train could run in both directions with no need of a switch yard. The German end of the Innsbruck line was at Penzberg; the Salzburg line at Rosenheim.

He had stopped at the Kraeglers, knowing Johan and Hildegard would never betray him. But they were not at home. Perhaps they're off visiting Lili and their grandchild. Let's see. How old is the child? Six or seven months by now, Rainer calculated.

Sipping wine and watching the fire, Rainer turned his mind toward his future. I'll never be safe again in Germany, he thought. Living in the United States would be divine, but that will never happen. Not like that clever wheedler von Braun and his engineering cronies. Build rockets and fire them at the British? Go to America. Steal paintings from the French and Russians in order to save them? Go to jail. One's continued usefulness to the war's victors dictates one's fate. Justice? She is unceremoniously thrown in jail with all the other useless figures, another casual victim of little, soon-forgotten hypoc-risies of war.

So, Rainer concluded, I have two choices: Switzerland and South America. No choice at all, really. Life in South America? Jungles? Monkeys? Spanish-speaking peasants coaxing burros to pull their drab possessions in broken-down carts? Or do they use llamas? No matter. But worse than the indigenous peasants would be the German-speaking émigrés. Fellow SS members, most of them. Stupid, sadistic thugs. Rainer tried to imagine himself discussing art and poetry with any of the SS men he knew in Berlin -- aside from Walter Schellenberg, who he knew had been captured. Talk about *Untermenschen!* I might as well try to debate themes in Goethe with the chimpanzees at the Tiergarten. Better to give me a dinner table with educated Jews in every chair.

No. The Andes are not the Alps. So Switzerland it must be. But what will I do? Perhaps I can give advice to all those bank-ers in Zurich with their new and vast private collections. In fact, maybe Anna and I won't need to take our cache to Sweden. How about having a consortium of Swiss bankers purchase a ship, fly a Swiss flag of convenience on it, sail it to Kiel, load our collection (except for the Marc and the Klee), and sail it back to... where? Lisbon? Yes, Lisbon. From there they could fly the cargo into Zurich.

The more he considered it, the more Rainer liked that idea. I'll suggest it to Anna when I get to Geneva, he decided.

Tuesday
July 27, 1945
Munich

The sign in the café window read: *Open and Welcome. Especially Americans.* Especially Americans? Who else, Martin wondered, possessed the wherewithal to pay for a restaurant meal? Martin followed Elliott, David, and Anna into the threadbare establishment called Bistro Rudolf, on Theatiner Strasse near Marienplatz. *Bistro*, for chrissakes, Martin thought. The war's over but the Germans are still stealing from the French.

Martin was in a foul mood. He would rather not have come along to this luncheon meeting, yet he could scarcely refuse Elliott's invitation, especially when he represented it in terms of a need to discuss some current issues more privately than a conference room at the Führerbau would permit. Martin could not quite fathom why Elliott had included Anna, other than to suppose he wanted merely to flaunt her as his personal war souvenir. Such a footing now evidently entitled her to share sensitive information.

A waiter, perhaps the owner, seated them at *the* window table. Eight tables, one window. None of the tables had a table cloth. Martin wondered where the few eateries now open in central Munich purchased their raw ingredients. On the black market, no doubt. Where else? Works of art, he reminded himself, were not the only commodities bought or bartered for in the ruins of back alleys and burned-out basements.

As if to confirm Martin's black-market suspicion, the only wine available was Hungarian. So they all ordered beer, local brewing of which no amount of bombing could apparently eradicate.

Beers served, Elliott shelved small talk and thanked everyone for the hard work done thus far. Then he said, "Allen Dulles has asked a favor of us." He looked at Martin. "By now I'm sure you've heard about this man."

Martin looked at David Fox, who avoided Martin's gaze. "Head of OSS in Bern?"

Elliott nodded. "Good. Now the favor Allen requests is that we report to him, immediately through me, any rumors popping up in our interrogations that link Swiss nationals to the dirty business we are all here to put an end to. Now I know such a procedure violates the guidelines we have all pledged to follow closely, but Allen has good reason for requesting an exception. His role in Bern is, as you might imagine, extremely sensitive. Much, if not all, his success depends in large part on the goodwill of the Swiss people, especially those in high places. Accordingly, he would prefer not to be blindsided by accusations against someone he does, or might have to, deal with. I agree with him that in this instance, sidestepping regulations is in the best interests of our government and of our purposes."

Martin said, "Report immediately, through you."

"Yes."

"Only to you?"

Elliott hesitated, but only for a moment. "Allen is in the best position to evaluate what comes your way, whatever form the narrative takes. Let's call these tidbits rumors, for lack of anything better. And rumors are best sat on until they undergo metamorphosis into something more substantial. So, to answer you question, Martin: Yes. Report them only to me."

So now I'm working for the OSS as much as for the MFA&A, Martin thought. Then wondered if he had been doing so all along and simply didn't know it. "Okay."

"David? Anna?"

Both nodded to Elliott.

"Next I'd like Anna to brief us on what's she's learned from her most recent excursions into Switzerland. In particular, now that the war is over, what has begun to emerge regarding Nazi infiltration of the Swiss government, particularly within the bureaucracy at Bern, and of the Red Cross in Geneva?"

So that's where she disappeared to while I was up at Bad Aussee, Martin thought.

Anna said, "The Swiss government is discovering that many of their agencies were filled with Nazi sympathizers or outright Nazis. Some had worked their ways into high places. Lucky for the Allies Nazi bureaucrats inside the Reich kept voluminous and precise records of who, in Switzerland, was working for them. Using these records, the Swiss, from embarrassment rather than from ideological differences, have begun to purge their ranks.

"Nazis inside the Red Cross have proven more difficult to ferret out, because no records pertaining to them have been found. They may not even exist, though I think they do. Probably still buried in Berlin. Even so, with the war over, an extraordinary number of people in Geneva have resigned.

The reason they all give is that the war has exhausted them and their mission is no longer as vital as it once was, which is hardly true. Two Red Cross administrators suspected by the Swiss of being Nazis were arrested and ended up confessing to the Swiss. They also named other names and admitted the real reason so many people were leaving is that, despite a lack of evidence naming them, they all assume proof will surface sooner than later. They hope to flee Switzerland before they are accused and apprehended."

"What about Red Cross involvement in stolen paintings?" Elliott asked.

"Surprisingly, nothing at all has turned up so far," Anna said.

"Surprising indeed!" Martin said. "Especially given the ease with which Red Cross personnel can cross back and forth among all the European countries. Well, except maybe the ones the Red Army now occupies."

"I understand and agree, Herr Wynerson," Anna said, nodding. "But if such activities have occurred, perhaps even continue to occur, I do not know about them, nor does anyone else I am in contact with in Switzerland know about them."

"But you will continue to pursue the matter, Fräulein Stahlinger?" Martin said.

"Naturally. Perhaps part of each of your interrogations could be directed along that line of inquiry," she said.

"Mine already are," Martin said. Turning to Fox, "David?"

"Yeah, yeah. Mine, too."

Tuesday
July 27, 1945
Mittenwald, Bavaria

The afternoon drive, twenty-five kilometers due south, from Kochel am See to Mittenwald, had taken Rainer past Walchensee. Despite the day's being warm and clear, with a gentle breeze blowing from the direction of pine-covered Herzogstand Mountain, he saw no sailboats on the lake where long ago he had sailed with Anna. Who had time for sailing now anyway? Who had any interest even? Sailing on alpine lakes presumed a carefree spirit. Germany had no spirit, carefree or otherwise, Rainer knew. Its collective soul was as dead as much of its population.

He parked the truck at the edge of the small village and walked to the train station, passing faded frescoes painted on the sides of houses, wall paintings that, once upon a time, brought people from around to the world to see Mittenwald, the town Goethe had christened a living picture book.

Rainer had decided that, if anyone asked what a Swiss citizen was doing in the village on foot, he would answer: A Red Cross colleague attached to Munich had driven him to Mittenwald. Together they had walked the streets and viewed the frescoes, then eaten lunch together before the colleague returned by car to Munich, leaving Rainer to travel on alone by train from Mittenwald to Geneva, via Innsbruck and Zurich.

Rainer bought a ticket for Innsbruck, where he would change for a train to Zurich. Mittenwald was also the *Grenzübergang*, border checkpoint, for rail passengers and Rainer joined the queue to pass through onto the railway platform. When it was his turn he calmly showed his fake Red Cross credentials, which a man dressed in a police uniform scrutinized carefully.

From talking with Schlee and Uhlmann, the black marketers in Berlin, Rainer had learned how quickly many men who had been city policemen in the Third Reich now were returning to their former posts. The Allies had underestimated the need for civilian population-control and were unable to administer such control without calling for local assistance everywhere. But now, returned to power, German police, in many cases, had become bullying tyrants. Rainer hoped that attitude had not spread as far as Mittenwald.

"You are Swiss?" the policeman asked as he stared at Rainer's papers.

"I am." Rainer noticed a pair of American MPs lingering nearby, but their attention was focused on passengers stepping off the train that had just arrived from Innsbruck.

"Your purpose for being in Germany, Herr Spühler?"

Rainer gave the man a look of incredulity. "People in Germany need our help," he said.

"Yes. Of course. Your work is most important."

"Thank you."

The policeman handed Rainer's papers to him. "You are cleared."

As he started to step onto the train platform someone from the arriving train yelled, "Herr Zeitz! Herr Zeitz! Hello! Hello!"

Rainer hesitated, trying to decide which way to walk. But, before he could take another step, Johan and Hildegard Kraegler's daughter, Lili, rushed up to him and threw her arms around him.

"Herr Zeitz, it's so very good to see you again. I'm glad you are alive. I've thought about you often and was always so worried." And she babbled on. "We've been to Innsbruck for an outing. We left our car here and took the train. It's been so long since we have had a day away from Kochel. And the weather is so beautiful. And the baby has behaved so well. He's such a beautiful child."

Out of breath, Lili paused and the German policeman put a hand on Rainer's shoulder. "You know this man, Fräulein?"

"Of course! I used to be his cook and housekeeper. His father's, too."

"And what did you call him?"

"Herr Zeitz! His name is Rainer Zeitz."

An out-of-breath Johan Kraegler staggered up behind Lili. "I'm sorry. So sorry," he said to Rainer. "I tried to stop her. I did. I tried." Behind him Hildegard Kraegler came up, pushing an infant's pram. She said nothing as she looked at Rainer, but he saw her eyes pleading for forgiveness. Then the baby began to cry and she gave her full attention to the infant.

The MPs now were watching and the policeman beckoned them to join him.

Lili became confused. "What's the matter? What's going on?" She turned to her father. "What have I done, Papa? Tell me what I have done?"

Before Johan could answer her, Rainer said, "It's all right, Lili. You've done nothing. Everything will be all right. Just a minor misunderstanding. That's all."

But Johan closed his eyes and slowly shook his head. Hildegard had picked up Lili's child and, holding him to her breast,
had managed to calm him. But Rainer saw that tears now formed
in her eyes.

Suddenly Lili screamed, "You can't arrest him! The war is
over. Don't you understand? The war is over."

31

Saturday
July 31, 1945
Munich

"We allow you to shave, you know," Martin said, after hearing the MP relock the cell door behind him. "With close supervision, of course."

Rainer sat on the edge of his bunk, picking idly at a corner of the flimsy mattress. "Why should you care? Unless getting me to shave is merely one small step in a process of getting me to cooperate with you more fully."

"You should know all about steps to encourage cooperation of prisoners," Martin said.

"I wore an SS uniform, but I was not SS."

"Save your sophistry for the prosecutors."

Rainer looked up for the first time and carefully scrutinized Martin, finally saying, "You look vaguely familiar to me."

"We've met," Martin said.

Rainer cocked his head and stared. "I can't recall. Surely not since --. Well, since things warmed up."

"You're right. Try 1937."

Rainer scowled, but then something triggered vague memories. "You and another man. Here in Munich. Dinner with my father."

"Yes. Go on."

"Art professors. Your name is... wait, it's coming to me. Yes, Wine-something-or-other. Weinstein, maybe?"

"Wynerson. Martin."

"Of course! Swedish, yes? I knew you couldn't be Jewish."

"Why not?"

"Just not."

Martin pulled up the lone chair in the cell and straddled it backwards. "Now that both of us know who I am, let's figure out how you came to be Helmut Spühler of the International Red Cross."

"I stole the man's identification, obviously," Rainer said.

"It has your photo on it."

Rainer shrugged. "When Himmler found out I had it he wanted to send me to Switzerland. So I had the SS documents unit in Berlin create an identical set of papers showing me as... who am I, again?"

"Helmut Spühler."

"Whoever he was. Or is."

"You knew Himmler?"

Rainer shook his head. "He knew me."

"How? Why?"

"I was famous. Surely you've found that out."

"Was?"

"The Reich is dead. My fame died with it."

"Famous for what?"

"My circus act."

"Which was?"

"Juggling."

Martin recalled his own 1937 metaphor for Rainer: a magician. "You were a *Kunstverschaffner*."

"Yes."

"And a very good one, I'm told."

Rainer smiled. "By whom?"

"Your cousin, Anna." Anna earlier admitted she had lied when she told Martin about knowing little or nothing about Rainer's locations or activities during the war. What else she had lied about remained to be determined - by Martin's interrogating her, if necessary, he told himself.

Rainer suddenly stood. "Where have you seen Anna?"

"Here. In Munich."

"What's she doing here?"

"Where did you expect her to be?"

Rainer hesitated, then said, "I had no idea. But Munich is certainly the last place I would have thought she would still be."

"Why is that?"

"Munich at the moment is a bit too messy for Cousin Anna's taste. I'd pictured her sitting on a beach near Lisbon."

"So you have been in Munich recently?"

"Of course. Last week. Perhaps you saw me. I walked through several neighborhoods."

"How did you get here?" Martin asked.

Rainer shrugged.

"A truck was found abandoned in Mittenwald. Opel. Flat-bed. Yours?"

Rainer calculated whether the truck could be traced back to Kiel and decided it couldn't. "Russian vehicles are so unreliable."

"You drove from Berlin?"

Rainer nodded. "I even stopped long enough to say hello to Uncle Joe and Comrades Harry and Clement."

"By the way, I saw your father in London earlier this month."

"He's well, I hope."

"He is. And he even shared with me his hope for you."

"And that is?"

"He fervently wishes you dead."

Rainer slumped back onto the bunk. "How disappointing."

"Is that all you have to say about it?"

"I actually miss the old man, despite our... differences. I've even left a gift for him on the fireplace mantel at the family cha-let in Kochel. A bottle of 1927 Pierre Ferrard cognac. My wish is that, when he returns, he will invite me to share it with him."

"You won't be drinking any cognac for a while," Martin said acidly.

"I'm sure your people have already searched the chalet thor-oughly. Tell whoever stole the cognac I want it back. Tell them they can keep whatever they emptied from the wine cellar."

"We're not thieves, "Martin snapped, instantly regretting having uttered such a blatant falsehood. "But I'll look into it."

"Am I permitted to see Anna?"

Martin thought about that. "I'll look into that, too."

"So what is the penalty for rescuing art from pig sties, cow pastures, lions' dens?"

"Is that what you suppose you did?" Martin said.

"Mostly."

"So you really do consider the people you invaded *Untermenschen*."

"Yes, most of them. But I also include a great many Germans in that category. And we mustn't forget Austrians. Oh, the Austrians! Don't get me started on them."

"Do you include the failed painter from Linz?"

"No. Not with the vast river of flotsam. No, no, no. Hitler stood in a category by himself. The Platonic Form of a man who stands on a high mountain top, yet is still surrounded by a thick, swirling... *Nebel der Unwissenheit.*"

"Fog of ignorance," Martin translated.

"A fog of his own making," Rainer mumbled. "To change the metaphor, he was a man who sometimes could not see a forest for the trees, for staring so intently at the bugs on the bark."

"Well. It's Saturday. I'll return on Monday and we'll talk of art. You will enlighten me on the whereabouts of these items you claim to have rescued from the unappreciative rabble."

"Not now? I was just beginning to enjoy our little *Treff.*"

"Monday."

Rainer stood again. "I see. Give me time to squirm and pace, allow me to remind myself how confined I am."

"The guards will bring you pen and paper. Even a squirrel has to pause sometimes to remember where he's hidden all his acorns."

Sunday
August 1, 1945
Munich

"So. How did you come to this?" Anna said, following what Rainer considered a tepid embrace from his cousin.

"It's a long story."

"Where is Karl?"

"With the paintings."

"So tell me this *long story* of yours." She sat down on the cell bunk next to Rainer and listened. When he finished she took his hands into hers. "Poor Rainer. So pitiable. But you must hold out. You must."

"Why are you here?" Rainer asked.

"To see you, of course."

"No. Why are you in Munich rather than Switzerland? And why are you working for the Americans?"

In a low voice, she said, "I'm not working for the Americans. I am only pretending to."

"And what exactly is the difference there?"

"All the better to protect myself, misdirect them, help us."

"Us? Good. Do something about getting me out of here. That clever bastard Wynerson intends to let the walls close in on me. I know it. He won't have to tease any information out of me. These walls will squeeze it out. Where are your friends in Stuttgart? Tell them to rescue me before --."

"Before what?"

"I'm not sure."

"So the Sundstrums are dead. Too bad."

"I'm sure they feel that way also."

"Stop it. Your endless sarcasm achieves nothing, except to --." Anna gestured vaguely around the jail cell.

"So. My sarcasm is what landed me here."

"You know what I mean."

"Do I?"

Anna embraced him tightly. "Oh, Cousin, now the Americans have us at each other's throats."

"Yes. Of course. The Americans are responsible."

"The paintings are still safe then?" Anna said.

"They are going nowhere. Can you memorize a pair of addresses? They belong to the Sundstrums' sons in Sweden. They, too, are dealers who can help us. If we can find a way to get the goods to Sweden."

"Go on. I'm ready," Anna said.

After Rainer gave her the addresses, he said, "In case we can't find a way to move the paintings across the Baltic, I have another idea." Rainer explained his idea regarding a boat trip to and from Lisbon, then the flight to Zurich.

"It's a possibility," Anna responded neutrally. "Sweden is closer, however, and we don't have to involve anyone else. Besides, Zurich bankers make my skin crawl."

"So find us a boat. But first, concentrate on getting me out of here."

Anna broke away and stood beneath the single barred cell window, high on a wall. "So when does Herr Wynerson return to interrogate you again?"

"Not again. He hasn't started. Yesterday was only to welcome me, cajole me a bit. But his sole purpose was to intimidate me without declaring 'I am here to intimidate you, Zeitz'. He said he will come back tomorrow."

"That means he won't," Anna said firmly.

"You are familiar with his tactics, I take it."

Anna nodded. "Tuesday. Late Tuesday he'll return."

"Thank you. That will help. Now tell me how you managed to impose yourself on Wynerson. Don't tell me you're fucking him."

Anna shook her head. "The other one. Elliott Parker. I met him in Bern. He was easy." Then she told Rainer about the events in her life since the last time, months earlier, that she had been with him.

When she finished Rainer smiled. "Spying, fucking, and living comfortably. How nice! Too bad for you the war ended, eh?"

Anna smiled back. "Nothing has ended. The geese continue to lay golden eggs."

"How soon before you can get me out of here? I mean it when I say the walls are beginning to edge closer to me."

"Stay calm. I'll see what I can do."

Rainer sighed a deep sigh. "Now you sound like Wynerson."

"I'll return tomorrow. With news, I hope."

A scoff from Rainer. "Tomorrow. Does that mean Tuesday? Late Tuesday?"

"I'm glad to see you still have a sense of humor," Anna said as she went to the cell door and signaled for the guard to let her out. "Keep it."

———

Saturday
August 8, 1945
Munich

An extended session with Rainer Zeitz had forced Martin to grab a quick lunch at the commissary. Even so, when he checked his watch he realized he was going to be several minutes late for his meeting. By the time he arrived at Elliott Parker's borrowed office on the second floor of the Führerbau, Elliott, David, and Anna were already there and waiting. Out of breath, Martin mumbled an insincere "Sorry" then took his seat between Anna and David.

"We half expected you not to show up at all," Elliott said without explanation.

Insult or compliment? Martin wondered, then decided he didn't care.

"I take it your morning interview with Colonel Zeitz went well?" Elliott said.

"Yes."

Elliott waited for a moment, obviously wanting Martin to expand. But then he proceeded. "Good. I want you to spend the afternoon writing up your notes and, while you're doing that, I want David to have a go at Zeitz."

"But I'm on the verge of a breakthrough. I think it would be a mistake to lose momentum with him. Especially now."

"Especially now?" Elliott said.

"Yes. Just before we broke for lunch Rainer announced that he wanted to offer me, us, a deal."

"What kind of deal?" Anna said.

"A trade. His freedom for two paintings."

David Fox laughed. "He's nuts. Let me at him."

Calmly, Elliott asked, "Which two paintings?"

"Franz Marc's *Tower of the Blue Horses* and Paul Klee's *Moon Over the City.*"

Elliott frowned. "Both those works were in the Degenerate Art exhibition."

Martin explained, "Yes, but the Marc, if you recall, was withdrawn after a protest by the Army Officers' Corps."

"I remember now," Elliott said. "Go on."

"Zeitz claims to know where both these paintings are and that he will lead us to them, provided that, once the paintings are in our possession, he is granted his freedom. Safe conduct to a neutral country."

"What balls!" David said. Then, looking past Martin to Anna, "Sorry, Fräulein. I forgot myself."

With an icy stare Anna retorted, "You often forget yourself. Too often."

Fox shrugged and slumped a bit lower in his chair.

"His offer is a bit one-sided," Elliott said.

"That's an understatement," Fox said, in an obvious effort to redeem his standing.

"I told him that," Martin said. "But I didn't reject it outright. It's a positive step as far as I'm concerned. Up until now he's been cagey and stubborn. I view this as a crack in his armor."

"You may be right," Elliott said. "You were certainly right not to piss on his notion."

That remark earned Elliott a reproachful glare from Anna. "Sorry."

"Men," was all Anna said.

"Okay, Martin. I want you to postpone the paperwork. Get back to him. Let him think a deal may be possible, but also make clear we want more. Much more. Leads on the missing Schloss's, for example. And the Amber Room. The Russians know we have him and are raising a storm. They're sending their own unit down from Berlin to question Zeitz. The Amber Room means a lot to them. Dulles sent word to Truman's staff to tell the Russians no, but apparently Stalin himself asked Truman about Zeitz. With the conference winding down up there one of Truman's aides, with good old Harry's consent, told the Russians okay. As a gesture of goodwill."

"Fuck goodwill; fuck the Russians," Fox blurted out, then hastily turned again to Anna. "Can't help it. Boston street talk. I've been a potty-mouth since I was a kid."

"Still shit your pants, too?" Anna said acidly.

The rebuke shut Fox up.

Elliott said, "If two works of art survived from the Degenerate exhibition, there's an excellent chance others avoided the fire as well. Martin, I want to know."

"Yes, sir."

A knock came at the door.

"Come in," Elliott said loudly.

The MP captain in charge of detainee security, a man named Morris, stepped into the room. "Mister Parker, I have some very unfortunate news for all of you, I'm afraid."

"What is it, Captain?" Elliott said.

"Mister Zeitz is dead, sir."

Confused, Elliott asked, "Werner Zeitz?"

"No, sir. The prisoner. Colonel Zeitz."

Anna stood up, knocking her chair over. "Nooooooo!"

Sunday
August 9, 1945
Munich

Dear Maddy,

Disaster struck here yesterday and I must write you lest I allow my emotions to unravel. No, I've not been harmed. Physically I'm okay -- except for the churning in my guts. I scarcely slept last night. Composing a letter to you is the only ointment that ever works to sooth the aches and pains in my soul.

Just over a week ago an important SS officer was caught as he tried to cross the border into Austria. His importance was due to his being what the Germans called a *Kunstverschaffner*, an art procurer. That job meant he trailed behind a German army as it invaded in order to select works of art in just-captured territory and send those art works back to Germany. Having held such a position made this man extraordinarily knowledgeable regarding the whereabouts of currently missing art that I am trying to recover.

The man's name was Rainer Zeitz. I actually met him in 1937, along with is father and cousin, when I was in

Munich. His father, Werner, was an important man in the German art scene, having owned a prestigious gallery in Munich. Werner, by the way, finally closed his gallery in 1938 and emigrated to London. I met him again during my brief stop-over there on my way to Munich.

Assigned to interrogate Colonel Zeitz, I had been making good progress with him. When I first met him in 1937 I judged him just another typical Nazi in his political beliefs. Rainer had an interest in art, just like his father. But not the same *love of* art. I thought him a pretentious and humorless dilettante. But this past week, I must admit, my opinion of the man softened. The more we talked, the more amiable and likeable he became. And, despite his best efforts to uphold a contemptuous, dismissive posture toward the whole world of art and artists, I began to sense a passion and respect for art in him that, until our conversations, I would not have dared credit to him.

Now suddenly he's dead. Cyanide poisoning. Yesterday.

I spent the entire morning in his cell with him. We talked and joked and shared opinions on a wide range of painting styles and artists. All part of my interrogation method, moving forward by indirection. And it was working. I was on the verge of getting him to divulge a great deal of important information. He had already provided me with lots of juicy hints and a few scraps of solid information that I intend to follow up on. Then I leave his cell, eat lunch, go to a meeting, and suddenly the meeting is interrupted with the information that the man is dead.

Two army physicians examined the body. They both swear Rainer was examined thoroughly the day he first was brought to Munich and no cyanide capsules were found. Doctors are twitchy about that issue ever since Heinrich Himmler killed himself back in May by biting into a capsule of cyanide hidden in a tooth, even as a British Army physician was examining him.

So now a debate goes on whether Rainer killed himself or was murdered. His lunch plate, half eaten, lay strewn across the floor of his cell when a guard came to check on him and found him dead. Neither doctor, naturally, wants to accept blame for allowing a cyanide capsule implant to have slipped by them undetected. I share the view that he was murdered.

Though I am obviously not trained in such matters, I do believe I would have sensed any suicidal tendency in the man. And I did not. Yes, he was sullen over the fact he had been caught, as well as despondent over being confined to a jail cell, but in no way did he appear to me sufficiently distraught to want to kill himself. Quite the contrary, because, when he made an offer to exchange information for his freedom, in order not to discourage him, I deceived him into believing such a trade might be possible. And, no, I'm certain he did not recognize my tactic to be simply a ploy to keep him talking.

So that is my disaster story for this week. It looks as though I'll have a new one to tell when next I write.

(Soon, I promise.) Tomorrow I leave for Salzburg. A pair of inventories, taken a week apart, reveal several important paintings have either been stolen or otherwise misplaced. Several Austrian civilians employed by the Army are being frog-marched down to Salzburg so I may have the pleasure of their company as they sit across an interrogation table from me. David Fox is already in Salzburg.

So many mine helpers are being brought down that two of us will be needed to question them. Anna Stahlinger, Rainer's cousin who now works for us here in Munich as an inventory specialist, took the most recent inventory and reported the discrepancy.

Why no Americans at the mine are being brought in eludes me. Politics, surely. At least half of the thievery going on across Germany and Austria, both at mine sites and art collecting points such as ours in Munich, has been committed by American soldiers. Oh, well. I've given up fighting that battle. If one or more of the Austrians did it, I'll unmask him or them. If American GIs did it, the pilfering is someone else's problem.

Poor Anna! I have been on the outs with her almost from the time I arrived here. Unable to figure out her animosity toward me, I let it go and ignored her. (David Fox, I might mention, is at the very top of her shit-list apparently.) But now, with the death of her cousin, to whom she was very close, she's put her hostilities on a back burner and has been willing to accept what crumbs of aid, comfort, and sympathy I have been able to provide. At first I thought that, because she's German, she hated all Americans for what we did to her country. But she's never shown the slightest resentment toward Elliott. So that's not it. Anyway, her mood has swung between being hysterical, screaming and crying, and turning catatonic, sitting among us, yet acting as if she can neither speak nor hear.

I'm certainly glad, relieved, I have not experienced a loss such as hers, losing someone so near and dear. I can't begin to imagine her pain.

Sorry to burden you, dear sister, with a tiresome tale of all my woes. I hope you understand how much my writing you helps uncork the bottles filled with my pent-up fears, worries, and uncertainties. And I trust you read my letters in that spirit. I try not to be exasperating, but I know at times I am. Patience, please. I beg you.

Until I'm in your arms again –

Your most loving brother,
Martin

Wednesday
August 12, 1945
Salzburg, Austria

"You Americans think yourselves so virtuous as to put God Himself to shame. Well, let me assure you, there are many among you who are not quite so perfect."

The man's name was Gunter Fassholzer. Forty-six and unremittingly irascible, until brought to the mines he had worked as chief groundskeeper at one of the former summer palaces of the Austrian emperors at Bad Ischl, a small city down the valley from Bad Aussee.

Martin felt exhausted and was glad this day of interviews was nearly complete. Herr Fassholzer was his last interrogation. He would be glad to return to Munich in the morning. What pains in the ass these Austrian outlanders are. Smug bastards, every one of them. And they all have the audacity to accuse Americans of being self-righteous.

"Arrogant fuckers!" was what David Fox had called them over dinner the night before. "They're all in on it, I'm sure. They've cooked up this pack of lies collectively and, by God, they intend to stick to their bullshit story."

Martin doubted a conspiracy among the workers at the mine, but paintings were indeed missing. No inventory mistakes, Anna had assured them. And Martin knew the paintings hadn't donned boots, walked out of the mine, and taken off down a mountain trail on their own, whistling and yodeling.

Fox had fumed, "I hope Harry the Haberdasher still has another bomb or two up his sleeve. We can drop it on these Janus-faced, puffed-up little shits; blow 'em out from under their jaunty Tyrolean caps. Assholes! Give me a guy in jackboots any day."

Martin, along with all his colleagues, had been stunned to hear about the powerful secret weapon the United States had used against Japan on Sunday. A single bomb had wiped out an entire city of one hundred thousand people, the rumor claimed.

534 | Jeff Ridenour

How chilling, Martin thought, and in no way wished President Truman would authorize the use of such a bludgeon against the Austrians, no matter how vile, stupid, vicious, and haughty they might be.

"So tell me, Herr Fassholzer, how do paintings vanish from the mine?" Martin asked, already knowing the answer he was about to hear.

"You steal them."

"I do?"

"You know who I mean. Your very own soldiers."

"I see. And you don't help them in any way?" Pretend to concede his point partially and maybe he'll bend a little, too.

Gunter seemed taken aback by Martin's implication. But then indignation returned. "Help them? You think they need help?"

"It would make it easier for them, wouldn't it? You yourself have assured me of the difficulty in removing anything from the mine without someone's noticing."

"Yes, but no."

Martin gave the man his oh-come-now look. "Who better to ease that difficulty?"

"Other soldiers."

"A soldiers' conspiracy."

"*Ja!*"

"Can you name any names?'

"I know nothing."

"But wait. You just told me it was a conspiracy consisting of American soldiers."

"I only do my own job at the mine. I see nothing else."

"Do you mean to tell me that a man who oversees the grounds of an emperor's palace, who must know every shrub, every blade of grass, every tree, and who must know when each must be watered, when each must be trimmed, is so unobservant that he now claims he works all day and sees nothing?"

"That is correct."

"Of course, you talk among yourselves, you and your fellow workers. And none of you see anything?"

"Nothing."

"Then I'm going to recommend you all be fired, Herr Fassholzer. Blind men make for risky employees. Too risky. You all must be dismissed. Immediately."

"No! You can't do that. I have children to feed. We all have families."

"I understand. And I have paintings to find. So let's help each other." Martin watched the man stare at his fingernails and waited. After a long minute, Martin said, "Well? Can we help one another?"

Stammering in a barely audible voice, Gunter said, "I...I must talk with the others."

"Good. It's late. We are both weary. Go home. Or wherever you go at night and, yes, talk with your comrades. See what you can do for me. And if you can help me, I assure you I will help you all keep your jobs at the mine."

Martin watched the Austrian slink out the door of the small bookstore on Franz Josef Strasse the MFA&A had requisitioned for their ad hoc interviews with the mine employees. *My staying over another day will be worth everybody's time if that cranky bastard can convince his fellow mine workers to come clean,*

Martin thought. I don't expect them to implicate themselves, even if they're guilty. But I do think it far too strange that no American GIs from the mine have been brought in for questioning. Of course, they would all point fingers at the Austrians. But conflicting accusations are better than no accusations at all. No Americans suspected. Fassholzer's right. We're not that perfect. Somebody in khaki knows something.

Just then a man in khaki stepped in. Sergeant Benjamin Pettijohn, an MP and the man who found Rainer Zeitz dead in his cell. "Ensign Fox finished up half an hour ago, sir. He said he was heading back to your hotel and would wait for you there so you wouldn't have to eat dinner alone."

"Thank you, Sergeant. I'm leaving. But before I do, may I ask you something? Off the record? I know you've already been grilled till you're well done about Colonel Zeitz, but I want you to go beyond the facts you presented and form an opinion about how and why it happened."

"The docs say somebody slipped cyanide into his potato soup. I watched the guards deliver his lunch. I know it wasn't them and it wasn't me."

"Where would cyanide come from?"

"I overheard the docs talking about how German medical people had been busy during the war working on all kinds of new-fangled drugs. Experimenting on --." The sergeant swallowed hard and looked away.

"On what?"

Sergeant Pettijohn shook his head. "Human guinea pigs, sir. People in the camps. I gather cyanide capsules and other poisons can be gotten pretty easily in Germany, sir."

Martin didn't want to think just then about the horrors that occurred in death camps. Focus on Rainer Zeitz, he told himself. "Did you see the soup ladled up?"

"No, sir. Kitchen staff only are permitted in the kitchen."

"So how did the cyanide or whatever it was find its way into his soup? Was the stock pot checked?"

"Absolutely. No cyanide there. Lots of people had potato soup for lunch, including me."

"Was the tray in any way identified as going to Colonel Zeitz?" Martin asked.

"Yes, sir. The standard slip with the prisoner's name and items circled that were supposed to be on the tray."

"How long between the time the tray was placed where your guards could pick it up and the time they actually did pick it up?"

"Now there's a problem. The kitchen staff say one of them, a private by the name of Wilson, placed the tray at the pick-up window around noon. That's the best private Wilson can swear to. *Around noon.* My boys were running a bit late. Had a problem with another prisoner. They both claim it may have been as late as five, six, even seven minutes after the hour when they fetched up the tray and took it to Colonel Zeitz."

"Plenty of time for somebody to walk by on your side of the window and slip poison into the soup."

"Definitely, sir."

"Anyone seen in the vicinity outside the kitchen? That is, besides your guards and the kitchen staff?"

"According to my guards, only Mister Parker, Ensign Fox, and Miss Stahlinger. But they were all together, on their way to some meeting or other."

"Has this issue been discussed already with the people investigating Colonel Zeitz's death? Am I walking over ground already covered?" Martin said.

"I'm afraid you are, sir. The boys in Munich know about the time gap. And they say they're working on it."

"Who are *they*?"

"Mister Parker, mostly."

"Thank you, Sergeant."

"You're welcome. And good night, sir."

The six-hundred-year old building where Martin and David Fox were staying, Gasthaus zur Goldenen Ente, stood in a narrow alley near the center of Salzburg's Altstadt, only a few short blocks from the interrogation site. When Martin stepped outside, darkness had long since fallen. Out of habit under such conditions, Martin compulsively touched his holster. Reassured of the presence of his revolver, he started to walk briskly toward the hotel, suddenly realizing he was famished.

Salzburgers, he had noticed, closed up early in the old section of the city. As he walked alone he told himself he might well be in Munich, except for the fact that most buildings in Salzburg were still standing. Somewhere out of the darkness he heard strains of a Strauss waltz and identified it as *Artist's Life*, agreeable sounds from a scratchy phonograph coming though an open window on a pleasant evening. Martin began to hum with the waltz. He was within two blocks of the hotel, the music fading, when he became aware someone was now walking behind him, another pair of footsteps falling on the cobblestones not quite in sync with is own.

At the next corner he stopped under the streetlamp and turned. The person behind him continued toward him, stopping at the edge of the light's penumbra. Only then did Martin see the revolver pointed at him. "I don't understand. What are you doing?"

Martin saw the muzzle flash from the gun, felt the sledge-hammer impact on his chest. He staggered backward, trying to stay upright. His eyes were already too unfocused from the violent chest pain to see the next two flashes, both of which hammered him lower and made his knees buckle. A fourth shot, aimed at his forehead, guaranteed he was dead before his face hit the cobblestones. His killer then lifted his wallet, stripped out the cash, dropped the wallet into a nearby window box full of flowers, and walked off into the shadows.

BOOK TWO

Sins of the Fathers

Summer, 1992

32

Monday
June 8, 1992
Santa Barbara, California

As the United Airlines flight from LAX descended into Santa Barbara, Selby Parker looked out his portside window at the UCSB campus perched on a set of high cliffs overlooking the ocean beach and thought to himself: So that is where Madeleine Wynerson spent thirty-two years toiling among musty stacks of unread books, while writing unread letters to my father.

Her house, a small bungalow, lay on the far of side of Highway 101 from the airport on a cul-de-sac off Cathedral Oaks Boulevard. The grass had been recently mowed, the ornamental shrubs across the front of the house were neatly trimmed. At age seventy-nine, Madeleine had either a high school neighbor or Mexican landscaping crew keep her yard tidy, Selby supposed.

She answered the door almost before he rang the buzzer, impatient after more than forty years of waiting. "Mister Parker?"

Selby shook her hand, noting a firm grip for someone of her age and delicacy. She was not what he had envisioned. She had scarcely a wrinkle in her face or hands; her blue eyes were clear and bright; her voice strong. She stood straight and only her hair gave away her age, though even there strands of blonde still mingled with the gray. Her outfit matched: navy blue blouse, long skirt, Mary Jane shoes. Had Selby not known she was waiting eagerly to talk with him, he might have supposed she was on her way to a country club for an afternoon of bridge.

"Do come in. You can't begin to imagine how overjoyed I am that you are here," she said as she stood aside to welcome him into her home.

Selby could scarcely credit his eyes when he stepped into Madeleine's parlor. It was as if he were walking onto a movie set for a 1940's mystery. Then, like a dash of cold water to his face, he realized that was exactly what he had stepped into, only it was not a movie. The last time he had seen so many doilies, photos in sepia, fringed throw rugs, and furniture of solid oak was in his parents' home in the Hudson River Valley, when he was still a youth – in the 1940s. The only things missing to complete the portrait were a steam radiator on one side of the couch and sounds of Jack Benny upbraiding his servant, Rochester, coming from a Crosley radio on the other side.

Madeleine offered Selby a chair. She sat across from him on a button-tufted love seat that Selby imagined might have been purchased new by Eleanor Roosevelt. Between them on an Art Deco coffee table sat a pitcher of lemonade and a plate of cookies.

"Much as I know I should avoid asking -- the gift-horse-in-the-mouth principle, you understand -- I can't help asking why you are here. Don't get me wrong. I'm so grateful I could cry. In fact, I did cry myself to sleep last night. But I'm also very confused."

Selby nodded. "I understand perfectly. I'm afraid I was all too terse when I phoned you, Miss Wynerson."

"Please call me Maddy. Everyone else does."

"All right, Maddy. I thought it better to explain myself face-to-face. Having never met you, not knowing you, I didn't feel comfortable talking about some of these things to a voice I couldn't put a face to."

"Yes. I know what you mean, Mister Parker."

"How about Selby?"

She looked at him tentatively, before saying, "Okay." Then she folded her hands in her lap and sat with an expectant look, as though she were a polite young child in a classroom who had just been told it was story time.

"My father died last month," he began, to which Maddy said nothing and showed no emotion. "He was ninety-two."

"As old as the years," Maddy said. "Martin would be eighty-three."

"When I was going through my father's effects – his papers, old photos, a trunk full of keepsakes – I came across all the letters you sent him over the past forty-five years. All sixty-two of them."

Madeleine's eyes widened. "I had no idea. I never heard from him, you understand. Not even once. But obviously that didn't stop me from writing him, often at first, then dwindling down to once a year. My annual plea."

"I took the liberty to read your letters."

"You did?"

"All of them." However, one fact Selby intended never to reveal to her was that her father clearly had not read any of them, because none of the envelopes had ever been opened until he, Selby, opened them. They were bundled chronologically by decade, each bundle neatly tied, bound with Christmas ribbon, as though perhaps Elliott had made an annual holiday ritual of fastening the year's harvest of Madeleine missives together to place in the trunk. But it was also clear from this systematic assembly that, early on, he had decided not to read them, no matter how many she sent him.

So why had he even bothered to keep them at all? Any of them? Selby had no idea. Well, he reminded himself several times since finding them, he did know because, next to the bundles of letters from Madeleine, Selby had found a second set of letters. These were loose inside a shoe box and in no particular order. Each letter, twenty-two in all, remained inside its envelope. Each envelope bore one of two postmarks, New York City or Washington, D.C., and the postmark dates ranged from early 1941 to early 1945. Inside each envelope was a love letter from Martin Wynerson to Katherine Parker, Selby's mother, who died in 1977 of breast cancer.

Selby supposed Elliott came across the letters when he sorted through Katherine's effects after she died. He remembered offering to help sort out her belongings but Elliott had insisted on culling them on his own. That Elliott had turned sour for several days after that still stuck in Selby's memory. At the time Selby was sure something untoward had popped up, but he had never been sure what it was until he discovered Martin's love letters.

"I don't know what my father thought all those years, Maddy. I have no clue why he failed to respond to you," Selby fudged. Elliott took his stance on refusing to answer Maddy more than thirty years before Selby found the telling letters. "I believe the least he owed you was an explanation of why he might have been convinced there was little he could do to aid you."

"The least," Maddy repeated softly.

"You went to Salzburg yourself in 1946, correct?" Selby said.

"I did. The police there told me the same story the men from Washington told me when they came to our house in Minneapolis to tell me and my parents that Martin was dead. They said he was shot at night on a street corner while walking to his hotel. A common street robber killed him and took his wallet, stole his money. The police found his wallet in a nearby flower box."

"Do you have reason to doubt their conclusion?"

Madeleine avoided Selby's gaze. "Not exactly. Nothing concrete. But, besides writing to your father, I wrote to a Mister David Fox, who was Martin's co-worker, roommate, and sometime friend, both in Washington and in Munich. I wrote him at the same time I wrote my first letter to your father. My letter to Mister Fox apparently took several months to catch up with him. At least that is what he claimed, along with saying he was responding promptly upon receiving it. Anyway, Mister Fox held to the view that Austrian workers employed by the U.S. Army at Bad Aussee were responsible for killing Martin. Are you familiar with what I am talking about?"

Selby nodded. "The salt mine there served as a huge repository for Nazi art looted from all over Europe. I've read that a considerable amount of art theft occurred at the mine even after the mine was discovered and taken over by the Americans."

Madeleine suddenly stood. "Come with me, please. I'll show you the primary reason I doubt both the police account and Mister Fox's suspicion."

Selby followed her down a dimly lit hallway. Passing the kitchen, Selby noted a chrome dining table that could easily have come straight from the set of Ozzie and Harriet. At the end of the hall she opened a door, where he followed her into a bedroom.

The room instantly reminded Selby of a quintessential 1930-40's young man's bedroom, conserved with all the homey touches of a young, lonely mother or perhaps a widowed housewife. The walls were hung with photos of Martin, photos that showed him aging from smiling birthday toddler to serious Europe-bound lieutenant. In one large picture, centrally hung, Martin kneeled on the engine cowling of a P-38, adjusting his parachute pack preparatory to climbing into the plane's cockpit.

As Selby took a closer look at that photo, Madeleine explained, "Martin loved being a pilot." Then she told the story of the crash landing that ended Martin's flying days.

Selby was aware of the flying accident. He decided to wait a bit before telling her how he knew.

Reminders of a life too short engulfed the bedroom. A fishing pole and tackle box, a rusting bicycle with both tires deflated, a baseball mitt holding a baseball with mud scuffs and frazzled threads, an RCA Victor phonograph with its lid up and a vinyl LP on the spindle. Selby looked in and saw the LP was The

Andrew Sisters with the Glen Miller Orchestra, recorded at the 1939 World's Fair in New York. He even recognized some of the cuts: "Begin the Beguine", "Beer Barrel Polka", "Bei Mir Bist Du Schön".

"Martin loved the Andrew sisters," Maddy said when she saw Selby staring at the album. "They're from Minnesota, don'tcha know?"

"I bet you still remember the lyrics to most of the songs on the album," Selby said.

Maddy blushed and nodded. "I used to sing in the choir at St. Olaf's. But Martin couldn't carry a tune in --."

"In the proverbial bushel basket?"

"Even a wheelbarrow," she said, giggling like a pre-teen.

"Even if he couldn't sing, Martin was pretty special, wasn't he?"

"The most important man in my life."

Obviously, Selby thought. Then he decided to ask, "Did you ever marry?"

With no hesitation, Madeleine said, "No. We only planned to pretend we were married once we moved here." When she realized she had misunderstood Selby's question she tried to recover by saying, "Oh, you mean another man. No. Never. That would have been a betrayal of Martin's memory."

As she spoke, her voice trembling with emotion, Selby looked out a corner of one eye at the double bed covered with a quilt edged with satin binding, similar to one he slept under as a child. In a flash unworthy of a gentleman, Selby pictured a nightgown-clad skeleton lying on one half of the bed, while clinging to the pillow on the other half was a single strand of gray hair, reminiscent of Faulkner's "A Rose for Emily".

"How about you?" Madeleine asked.

"Me?"

"Marry?"

"No. My career was not very compatible with a successful marriage," he said.

"You followed in your father's footsteps," Maddy said with just a hint of reproach.

"My mother was a saint, I guess. And saints are rare. I lacked the patience to go looking for a saint of my own." A saint who had a dalliance with your brother, Selby thought, before pushing that image back into the dark corner of his mind from whence it had strayed, though it stayed long enough for Selby to wonder if the affair constituted infidelity toward Maddy by Martin.

"Here it is. What I want to show you," she said. From a dresser drawer she lifted out an envelope as though she were handling a tiny bird with a broken wing, cupping it in the palm of her hand, fearful of dropping it. "Martin's last letter to me." Slowly, gingerly she held it forth for Selby to accept.

"Are you sure?" Selby asked.

Her eyes brightened and she gave a quick nod. "I'm sure."

Selby found the room oppressive, thinking it had not known fresh air for years, and said, "May I take this back to the parlor? I'd prefer to sit while I read it."

"Of course."

Selby returned to the side chair and sat down. With much care he eased the letter from the yellowed envelope. He feared the letter itself might crumble to dust when he unfolded the pages, but it didn't. The pages merely crackled. He read the letter quickly, then returned to the first page and re-read it with more deliberation. Martin's penmanship had been bold and precise; no squinting or guessing required. When he finished the second reading Selby looked to Madeleine, who sat poised on the edge of the loveseat in anticipation of his reaction, and said, "This is a good beginning in my getting to know Martin." In fact, Selby knew, the real *good beginning* occurred when he read Martin's letters to Katherine.

Maddy nodded, approvingly. "Yes. It's too bad you never met Martin. You'd have liked him."

Selby cautiously slid the letter back into its envelope and returned it to Maddy. "Actually, I did meet your brother."

"You did?" she said excitedly.

"Twice, in fact, that I remember. The first time I was eight years old." Selby had performed the calculation on the plane ride between JFK and LAX. "My parents used to throw big parties at their estate on the Upper Hudson, at Stuyvesant. I met your brother at one of those parties. I remember he walked with a cane because of the flying accident. Then about a year later he came to another party and we ended up playing catch in the backyard, with him using my dad's battered old baseball glove, similar to the one I just saw in the bedroom."

"Yes, Martin loved baseball, too."

Selby decided the time had come to nudge her back on track. "I believe your purpose in showing me Martin's last letter was to suggest another reason why you doubt the Salzburg police's conclusion and David Fox's opinion about Martin's death."

"Yes. The business with the Nazi colonel who died. I knew my brother well enough to read between the lines of his letters. That killing made him worried for his own safety. As he says, he was having discussions about many important paintings that were missing. "

Selby took a cookie from the plate and began nibbling.

"There is another man I contacted, a man whose name Mister Fox gave me. The man's name is Benjamin Pettijohn and he lives in Pittsburgh. I took a train to see him when I still lived in Minneapolis. He was a sergeant of guards with the Military Police. Mister Pettijohn confirmed that Martin had severely riled the mine workers, made them mad enough to want to kill him. But Mister Pettijohn doesn't believe they did."

"So what is his theory?" Selby asked.

"He thinks the Russians killed Martin."

Selby tried not to wince. Jesus, he thought. Just when the Cold War ends this woman comes along and stirs the pot over the time when it all began.

Madeleine said, "Colonel Zeitz died on a Saturday. Martin wrote his last letter to me on Sunday. Sergeant Pettijohn says a team of Russian interrogators arrived Monday afternoon, which is why Martin fails to mention the Russians in his letter. You might have noticed the letter was postmarked that Monday."

Selby had missed that detail, but didn't say so.

"Anyway, the sergeant claims that when the Russians were told Colonel Zeitz was dead, they first demanded to see the body, then they insisted on an autopsy with two of their own pathologists from Moscow flown in to assist. He says the Russians were shown the body, but their request to be present at an autopsy was denied. They were furious, he says, and threatened repercussions. They accused the American staff in Munich of a premeditated cover-up of what all Zeitz had told Martin and made clear they believed the Americans had murdered Zeitz to keep him from spilling the beans to anyone else."

"Spilling the beans," Selby repeated.

"That was Sergeant Pettijohn's exact phrase," she said.

"So the sergeant thinks part of the Russian's retaliation was to murder Martin?" Selby said. He didn't want to tell her that made no sense, but it didn't.

"Yes."

"What would they gain?" Selby asked. "Better to kidnap him and make him talk."

Madeleine gasped. "I didn't think of that."

"I wonder why Sergeant Pettijohn didn't either." Selby thought: Not that Russians always acted rationally. God knows, they didn't. But rarely did they do something stupid that went against their clear self-interest. Maybe this had been one those rare occasions when they did. But better not to jump to that conclusion. More than one man has died mistaking Russians for bigger fools than they really are.

"I'm not sure the sergeant was entirely clear-headed when it came to Russians. He said that, after Munich, he spent three years in Berlin and had to deal with Russians constantly. He had nothing good to say about them."

Selby could relate to Berlin and dealing with Russians there. He understood the sergeant's attitude. Most Americans who served in Berlin during the Cold War shared it. But Selby reminded himself he dared not let that fact cloud his opinion that, in the matter of Martin Wynerson's death, the Russians were probably blameless.

"Are you aware of anything or anyone else that might have worried Martin?" Selby asked.

"He writes about being upset with American officers who fill their personal offices, as well as officers' clubs, with many of the very art works he was trying to restore to their rightful owners. But he mentions no one in particular, although I'm sure he rubbed some people the wrong way. Martin has a way of.... I'm sorry, *had* a way of speaking his mind on subjects he felt very strongly about."

And we all know what happens to outspoken subordinates, Selby thought but left unsaid. Yes, she had a point. But a general observation hardly constitutes a smoking gun. "Nothing more specific? In earlier letters he didn't mention anyone specific he had annoyed – or worse?"

"I'm afraid not."

"Too bad."

"But don't you agree there are possibilities pointing in other directions," Maddy said.

"Yes." Including one I've failed to mention, Selby thought. The one foremost in my own mind. And the principal reason I am here. If I thought disgruntled Austrian mine workers, mistrustful and exasperated Russians, or some two-faced American general were behind Martin's death, I wouldn't be here. But the possibility my father knew he had been made a cuckold by Lieutenant Martin P. Wynerson is another matter. Austrian miners, Russian interrogators, and high-ranking American officers would have provided more than ample sources of misdirection for investigators, professional and amateur.

"How do you begin then?" she asked seriously.

Selby glanced at his watch. "We'll start by my taking you to dinner. You can tell me more about what you know of how Martin became a protégé of my father. I know very little about how they linked up." In the trunk, along with the two sets of letters, Selby had found a copy of Martin's Ph.D. dissertation. The thesis' title, *The Metaphysical Underpinnings of German Expressionism: Kant, Kandinsky, Klee, & Kokoschka*, by itself had cowed Selby. After reading only a couple of pages, he capitulated, although on his way to the airport to fly to see Madeleine, Selby had dropped the dissertation off with Alastair Stiles, a New York University art historian Selby knew who had become an expert on Elliott's academic publications. Professor Stiles had agreed to read the thesis and provide Selby with a summary.

On the way to the restaurant Maddy had chosen she told Selby more than he really cared to know about Martin's early life, winters spent reluctantly ice-fishing with his father, and about summers at Blackduck Lake with her. Through his sister's eyes Martin's youth had been one endless string of fun-filled pastimes. Her recounting their canoe trips together in the north woods came across as though they were a pair of devout pilgrims on a holy quest. Selby sensed the *joie de vivre* radiating through her voice as she spoke of nights spent staring in wonder at the Northern Lights and knew there had been something extraordinarily special between the two of them on those particular trips.

Selby was surprised to learn Dutch Garden specialized in German food and that Maddy ate there often, declaring it her favorite Santa Barbara restaurant "because Martin would have loved it."

"Clement Moore at the University of Chicago was Martin's dissertation advisor and had also been a classmate of your father's at Yale," Maddy began, once they had ordered food and drink. "Professor Moore sent a copy of Martin's thesis to your father, thinking it might interest him and it did. Your father invited Martin to join him that same summer Martin got his Ph.D. They went to Germany for several weeks before Martin started his teaching job at George Washington University in Washington, D.C.."

"What came next?" Selby asked.

"Martin only mentioned your father one other time, as best I recall. Once before the war started, that is. Just a one-line mention that your father was keeping in touch now and then. I think he might have said your father put in a good word for him with a man named Karl Nierendorf, a German émigré who ran an art gallery in New York City and had hundreds and hundreds of paintings by Paul Klee. Martin, I remember, went to New York a few times to help Mister Nierendorf."

Selby made notes as she talked. "Then the war began."

"Only in Europe," she reminded him. "I remember Martin writing to say your father had come to Washington and invited him to a meeting with two art professors who maintained contacts with people whose countries the Germans had conquered." Maddy suddenly looked all around her. Then, in a low voice, said, "Lots of real Germans eat here, don'tcha know."

Selby nodded and winked. "I'm sure they do. But that war is over."

"I know. But I've heard it said that people in Europe have long memories."

Selby gave her a patronizing smile. "I think we're safe in talking about World War II."

Over an excellent meal Selby listened to Maddy tell what she knew of Martin's life stateside from 1941 until he sailed for Europe in June of 1945. That she made no mention of Katherine Parker did not surprise Selby. He imagined she knew very little and what she did know she no doubt judged unladylike to bring up.

When dessert arrived Selby asked, "What about you? How did you spend the war years?"

"Life went on at the University of Minnesota. Well, sort of. Physically fit men of service age left. Women, too, actually. At least a few. I didn't volunteer for WACS or WAVES or anything like that. I went with Mother to be a USO hostess on lots of weekends. I even gave polka lessons to soldiers who didn't know a polka from a minuet. Mother also helped out at the local hospital. I was once asked if I wanted to work as a riveter at the airplane factory in St. Paul. I turned down that offer, but maybe I should have taken it. Who knows? Maybe I would have been the one on that famous Rosie the Riveter poster."

"I take it you didn't get to see much of Martin."

"Not after his leg healed and he went to Washington to join the MFA&A. Once, when his trip to Europe got delayed, we each took a train to Chicago and spent a few days together. We --. Well, we just had a great time together. In fact,--"

"What?"

Tears came. "That was the very last time I saw him."

33

Wednesday
June 10, 1992
New York City

After taking Madeleine home, Selby had remained in Santa Barbara overnight, staying at the small, ten-room Harbor House Inn, downtown near the beach. In the morning he met Maddy for breakfast at a Denny's, where he pledged the equivalent of Scout's Honor to do his best to search for evidence refuting the official account of Martin's murder.

"Mister Parker, I truly am appreciative beyond my repeated expressions of gratitude. I mean it when I say this means so very much to me," she had told Selby as her handshake lingered when they said their goodbyes.

On the return flight to JFK, when not trying to nap, Selby listened to his conscience wrestle with itself. So what was I supposed to tell this woman? I can't tell her I'll take on a cause my father refused with the hope I can exonerate him. But that's what

I'm doing. I don't want so much to know who killed Martin as I want to prove my father had no hand in the young man's death.

At least I'm still committed. If, after speaking to Maddy, I judged Martin to be less than the decent character I thought him to be before I flew to Santa Barbara, I might have had second thoughts. But, from all I know so far, Martin Wynerson is the kind of man I approve of sharing my mother's company. Sharing her bed is an issue I'm not quite ready to dwell on, he added while reflecting.

Selby's own misty recollections of Martin consisted of a few brief, but heartwarming experiences, his clearest memories consisting of the man who stepped away from making cocktail conversation with boring adults in order to play catch; a pilot who had barely escaped death in a plane crash yet wanted fervently to fly again. What wasn't to admire?

And his letters to Katherine, though sophomorically mushy by Selby's worldly standards, nonetheless revealed a man of wit and intelligence, not too full of himself, and with a passion for Katherine ranking several notches above simple lust.

Associate Professor Alastair Stiles was a Yalie and the grandson of Morton Davenport, who was a colleague of Elliott's at Brown University and, before that, Elliott's classmate at Yale. At fifty-six – only one year younger than Selby – Alastair had always seemed much older to Selby, owing to the man's hair having turned white before he was thirty-five. Like Selby, Alastair had disappointed his family elders by choosing Princeton over Yale. And at Princeton both had been members of the University Cottage Club, the closest organization Princeton had resembling Yale's Skull and Bones.

"Your trip to California wasn't a bust, I hope," Stiles said when Selby sat down in the professor's cluttered office.

"No. It went better than I expected." Alastair Stiles was a man Selby could, and had, trusted over the forty-odd years they had known each other. When he had dropped off Martin's dissertation for Stiles to read, Selby had provided him with some of the background behind his trip, omitting only the letters *d'affaire*.

"So she isn't a nut case," Stiles said, with his usual, calculated use of blue-collar phrasing.

Selby shook his head in mock-dismay, before saying, "Yes and no." Selby related his experiences with Madeleine, including a detailed description of the room she devoted exclusively to Martin-memorabilia.

Alastair listened patiently, but when Selby finished he said, "She's a nut case."

Selby sighed. "But a quiet one. Persistent, obsessive, call her what you want – except for a *nut case*. Think of her akin to someone whose brother is MIA in Vietnam. She wants closure and hasn't got it."

Stiles scowled.

Selby said, "Yes, I know. There were thousands more MIAs in World War II, compared with Vietnam. The difference is that most people with family members missing in action from that war suffered their fates more stoically. Madeleine is an exception to that era's bear-your-grief-in-silence attitude."

"Is she a whiner and a sniveler like so many members of these current MIA organizations?" Stiles asked.

"Not at all."

"So tell me this: Why did she choose to badger your father instead of her congressman?"

"I can't quite answer that yet. I'm hoping you can give me more insight into why Elliott chose to mentor this particular fellow."

"Because he knew his shit better than most people coming out of art-history programs at that time. Points for your father. I read Wynerson's dissertation and it's damned good. Not brilliant, but close. How'd your father get hold of it?"

Selby explained.

"God bless the Good Old Boys, eh, Sel? Where would we be without 'em," Stiles said. "These days it's hard to convince these aspiring kids from the proletariat that *legacy* is a vital sub-species of *noblesse oblige*."

Selby winced and rolled his eyes. Likeable as he was, Alastair Stiles was a shameless snob, a trait Selby attributed to his having a half-British mother. "I know Martin went to Germany with my father in 1937. Then he tried to become a pilot when the war started, but crashed his trainer, spent a long time in rehab, finally ending up joining the MFA&A. How he and my father kept in touch in between the summer of 1937 and the summer of 1945 is fuzzy."

"I did a bit of checking on my own about that," Stiles said. "By the time he graduated from Chicago and before he went to Germany with Elliott, he had landed a professorship at George Washington. And while there, with your father's influence, he picked up a consulting job - back when consulting wasn't quite so flossy a station – with a prominent gallery owner at the time here in New York City. Karl Nierendorf was the man's name."

"I'm slightly familiar with the name," Selby said. "Madeleine mentioned him, too. A German émigré who set up a gallery in New York City. Owned lots of Klees."

"I'm sure you met him at one or more of the huge parties my dad says your parents used to host," Stiles said.

"Probably, but Martin is one of the few people I remember distinctly from those days," Selby said.

"There were actually two Nierendorfs, Karl and Joseph. They started galleries in Germany back in the 1920's. In 1936 Karl comes to America and opens a gallery in New York City, while Joseph remains in Berlin and manages their gallery there until he is called into the German army. In 1947 Karl dies intestate. So, with only German heirs, the gallery here is closed and is confiscated by the state of New York. In 1948 the Guggenheim buys Karl's entire estate, including more than 150 works by Klee. The price? Seventy-two grand. A steal – so to speak. Karl's German heirs get nothing."

"Lucky Guggenheim," Selby said.

"Luck, I'm sure, had little to do with it. Anyway, Joseph survives his stint in the Wehrmacht and plans, with the help of his wife and using her bookstore, to start another gallery in 1949. Instead, he dies. But the dream doesn't. In 1955 Joseph's stepson opens the gallery with the help of his future wife. That Gallery is still there today."

"So? I'm interested in Wynerson, not the Nierendorfs," Selby said.

"I know, I know. However, that little spiel was not one of my rudderless drifts you find so distracting. I do have a point."

"Which is?"

"The subject of art consulting. The present-day Galerie Nierendorf in Berlin is currently working with a consultant who may be able to help you with the business of Wynerson's being offered a deal by that Nazi colonel. She, too, is an expert on German Expressionist painters, The Blue Rider Group in particular. And her interest in missing paintings is a good deal more than merely professional."

"How so?"

"I'm getting there. Her grandparents were killed in a plane crash at the end of the war. They were both physicians working for the Red Cross in Berlin. They were Swedes and their flight crashed when they were taking leave, flying home to Stockholm from Berlin. Posthumously, they were accused by the Allies of fencing stolen art, dealing the goods out of their warehouse in Stockholm. The granddaughter – her name's Ingrid Sundstrum – is an art professor at Lund University, in the city of Lund, just northeast of Malmö, across the narrows from Copenhagen."

"I know it," Selby said. "It's one of the older and larger research universities in Europe."

Stiles nodded. "One of Miss Sundstrum's obsessive endeavors has been to try to clear her grandparents' names, prove the Allies' accusations unfounded. She's in Berlin and she knows a lot about where the art-thief skeletons are hidden."

"So to speak," Selby added.

"The Nazi colonel, you say, was in Berlin about the same time Marc's *Tower of the Blue Horses* vanished. Well, the doctors Sundtrum were there, too. But when the wreckage of their plane was searched – it crashed on a big island – no paintings were found onboard, stolen or otherwise. Still, the granddaughter, I think, will be worth... what do the Germans call them?"

"A little *Treff*," Selby said.

"Just like the old days, eh, Sel?" Alastair said, smiling.

"Just like the old days," Selby repeated, without any inclination to smile.

"Before you leave, I have to ask you something."

"Sure. Ask."

"You father and Wynerson were working together when Wynerson died, right?"

"Yes."

Alastair Stiles hesitated, then looked away.

"What is it?" Selby asked,

"I'm loathe to bring this up, but I think it may be something you need to know."

"So quit hemming and hawing. Tell me."

"Okay. When I read Wynerson's thesis certain phrases, sentences, and ideas kept leaping off the pages at me. I swore I had seen them elsewhere. So I went digging and I was right. I found identical wording and concepts in two of your father's publications."

"Are you saying Martin Wynerson plagiarized my father? That makes no sense. Elliott wouldn't have touched him with a ten-foot pole if that were true. And I know Elliott read the thesis," Selby said.

Stiles stared at his fingernails as he shook his head and said, "Just the opposite. Elliott stole from Wynerson. The passages I found were in two papers your dad published a couple years after his reading of Wynerson's dissertation."

"No question?"

"Sorry. His borrowing is rather blatant."

Selby muttered, "I wonder if Martin knew."

"*De mortuis nihil nisi bonum* and all that, Sel, but –."

"No, Alastair. I'm glad you told me. You're right. It may prove important."

———————

Thursday
June 11, 1992
Langley, Virginia

"Well, looks who's back. Busman's holiday, Mister Parker?"

"Your irresistible charm, Lois," Selby said as he passed Miss Garner, Lewellyn Champion's office administrator.

"He's expecting you."

Selby felt awkward returning to Langley. Over Christmas dinner in 1989, shortly after the Berlin Wall came down and the Soviet Union struck its colors, Selby had been helping his father, by then severely crippled with arthritis, cut up the food on his plate, when, out of the blue, Elliott had said, "About time you quit, isn't it, Son?"

"I'm not finished yet," Selby remembering saying, gesturing with his fork at a slice of ham.

"Not my food. You know what I'm talking about."

Elliott's ninety-year-old body might have been broken and dying, but his mind had managed to resist decay. His wits were sharp as ever, though spiraling into a well of cantankerous self-pity more and more frequently. Selby had not understood why so much bitterness. Elliott's life had been longer and fuller than most. Maybe that wasn't enough.

In any case, until then Selby had given no thought to quitting the CIA. The Cold War was over in form only. Churchill's

Iron Curtain may have been ripped from its rod, but a gossamer veil had replaced it, still effectively masking the intentions, if not the activities, behind it.

Then, without warning, the choice was not entirely his. Younger men, those with Koolaid still in their veins, but steeped in the nuances of computer gadgetry and cyberspace, were determined to drive from the temple all those for whom intelligence-gathering methods depended on land lines, shoe leather, and back-alley whispers. Selby and the rest of the Old Guard stood as much chance against the New Wave as Tennyson's Light Brigade had stood against Russian artillery in the Crimea. Selby fought in the internecine trench warfare that ensued, but, after a year in constant retreat, waved his white flag and walked, a viable pension and a health-care COBRA in his pocket.

Lewellyn Champion still hung on, despite the Director's shifting him laterally so often – from center, to guard, to tackle, to tight end – that he now held the position of water boy watching from the sidelines, an aging gofer performing trivial tasks. Selby told himself as he took the seat across from his former colleague, at least my favors will give him something useful to do.

"Long time, no pee, buddy," Champion said.

Selby shrugged. "That's what happens when you spend a lifetime trying to piss up a rope, Lew."

"Pretty cynical for you."

"Well, when I left here I finally stopped trying to keep my middle finger down. I need some help. I'm here hat in hand."

"Let me guess. George Schulz and Brent Scowcroft sent you to ask for help digging up dirt on Governor Clinton. Or if they didn't send you, some of your Upper Hudson country club Republican friends sent you."

"Domestic politics bore me, Lew. You're thinking of my maternal grandfather's trying to hire Pinkerton types to unearth skeletons buried in FDR's backyard. From what I hear Clinton is perfectly capable on his own of tying his dick around his neck in the form of a hangman's noose. Nor am I any fan of the President's. As far as I'm concerned, your and my father's alma mater owes the entire world a profound apology for handing both Bush and his namesake son degrees when neither one of them can speak English any better than a dull-witted twelve-year-old."

"I'll phone the Yale trustees as soon as you leave and tell them you said so."

"More likely, you'll phone the White House."

"Not if I want to keep my job," Champion said.

"I thought they collected dirt they can fling back later, if necessary."

"They do, but you never quite know what will amuse them and what won't. So Br'er Fox, he lay low."

Selby made a general waving motion toward the ceiling by way of asking silently if Champion thought his office might be bugged.

"You promise you're not nursing some political grudge? 'Tis the season."

"Nope."

"Grudges die hard, I'm finding out."

Selby laughed. "You know, Lew, someone said the same thing to me just the other day. In a different context, but otherwise the same. It was out in California."

"Come on, Sel. Californians don't have time for grudges, let alone long ones. They're too busy growing and smoking dope. The Golden State has become The Mellow Yellow State."

"It seems old stereotypes die as slowly as old grudges. On both coasts. No, this was a seventy-nine-year-old librarian. She's the reason I'm here."

Champion shook his head. "Then how may I help you?"

Selby explained that he was hoping to find out if David Fox and Benjamin Pettijohn were, either of them, still alive. And, if so, where?

"That's it?"

Selby nodded, then, grinning, looked up at the ceiling again, as if looking for wires.

"That should not be a problem. How many days ago did you want it?"

"Take your time, Lew. I know it's precious," Selby said, wondering, but not caring, how Champion would take the remark. "After forty-six years, what's a few more days?"

Champion appeared not to notice the dig at his fall from significance. "David Fox. Same David Fox as our own guy back in... when was the Prague debacle?"

"Seventy-two. The same."

"You were the one who rescued him, as I recall."

"I merely found him. He rescued himself."

"I remember. There was some dispute about his story."

"A lot of dispute," Selby said.

"Mind if I ask why you want these guys?"

"The librarian's brother was murdered in 1945. She refuses to accept the official explanation."

"Colonel Mustard in the library with the candlestick doesn't cut it for her?"

"Nope."

"What if these two guys are both sleeping with Jimmy Hoffa?"

"Then I'll want to see photos of their corpses, along with their dental x-rays."

"Fox should be easy, if he's still around. Took a disability, didn't he?"

"Yes. A bonus. He was ready to retire anyway. Prague was supposed to be his last hurrah." Selby snickered. "It was, only not the way he intended."

"These guys didn't kill the brother, I hope?"

"Probably not. But I'm hoping they know enough to be able to help exonerate someone who is high on the list of suspects."

"Who's that?"

"My father."

Tuesday
June 16, 1992
Gloucester, Massachusetts

The two-hundred-mile drive from Stuyvesant to Gloucester took four hours. After cruising I-90 through the Berkshires Selby watched heavy traffic bring him to a crawl as he passed through Springfield and Worcester, then skirted Boston. He ate a late lunch near the waterfront before rechecking his local map and driving the ten short blocks for his 3 p.m. meeting.

David Fox's house sat on a corner lot facing Eastern Avenue. The house was unpretentious, a small, two-story Victorian with a wrap-around porch and a white picket fence. A middle-aged woman opened the door, introduced herself as Fox's visiting nurse, and said she was just leaving.

"Selby Parker, I'll be damned. How long has it been?" David Fox said as he pumped Selby hand.

"Twenty years next month."

"How's your dad?"

"He died a few weeks ago."

"Aw, Jeez. I'm sorry to hear that. He was a fine man. I've always had nothing but the greatest respect for him. Someone from the Company should have let me know."

"He was ninety-two and hadn't been well for the last couple of years."

Fox shook his head solemnly, but then perked up. "Look at me. Eighty-four and still not only kickin' but managing to get by on my own. I shop, I cook, I go to Red Sox games. I don't drive, but public transportation is good in this town. The nurse? She comes by a couple times a week to see if I still have a pulse."

"You look good, David. The wound ever bother you?" Selby said, hoping a little flattery might help his memory when they got around to testing it. In fact, Selby barely recognized Fox. He'd grown a thick beard and his hair was long and unkempt. Deep wrinkles made his forehead look like a freshly harrowed corn field.

"Naw. No more than if I had some arthritis down there in the leg."

Prague. 1972. Ivan Andrevitch Shamlikov, a top Russian nuclear submarine engineer turned defector, had sat on ice too long in Washington waiting to have his credentials confirmed, so that, when he was cleared to tattle, he refused. He said he would open up only after he spoke to his older brother, Mikhail, and would then try to persuade him to defect as well. David Fox arranged a *Treff* between the two brothers in Prague, where Mikhail, a naval architect, would spend his summer holiday. Despite his age, David insisted he be the one to accompany Ivan, given Ivan had been his "puppy" from the time the engineer's defection was conceived. His request, after rattling around the upper chambers at Langley, was approved.

The date of the Prague meeting was set to coincide with the Bobby Fischer-Boris Spassky match in Reykjavik. Some unknown sage high up at Langley declared the Russians would be totally distracted by the Cold War clash in Iceland. As it turned out, Fischer's pummeling Spassky must have forced the Russians to wince and look away for a moment and when they did they detected a pair of Russian engineers and their American watch-dog fleeing Prague toward the Austrian border and gave chase.

Neither engineer was ever heard from again. David Fox turned up two days later in Passau, Germany, reported to local authorities by the crewmen who found him in a laundry-room closet on one of the lower decks of a cruise boat that regularly plied the Danube between Passau and Vienna. He had suffered gunshot wounds to his right calf and thigh.

Selby, who had been waiting in Linz, Austria for the three men to arrive there, rushed to Passau and managed to cover up the entire episode, funneling CIA largesse into numerous local pockets in order to do so.

No heads rolled directly at Langley because of the catastrophe, but an irrepressible rumor held that the Director invited at least two middle-level, no-name administrators to put in for immediate, early retirement. David Fox skated out the doors with a fat, wounded-in-action disability payout, despite noisy controversy from several quarters that the whole episode smacked of too much incompetence to credit the explanation that Fox was simply a bungler. But suspicions among a few at Langley that Fox himself had been turned by the Russians some time in the past never gained traction.

As Fox directed Selby to a seat near the living room fireplace Selby stopped to look at the 8x10 photo on the mantel.

"How about that, eh?" Fox said.

Indeed! How about that, Selby thought. A presidential face, no doubt an official White House photo, smiled at him. Handwritten at an angle near the bottom read: *Sincere Thanks for Your Heroic Effort! Warm Wishes, Richard M. Nixon.* Never before had Selby associated either *sincere* or *warm* with Nixon, but then neither had he ever botched an attempted defection, let alone a burglary. Maybe Colson and Liddy had identical photos resting on their fireplace mantels.

"So you're here about Martin Wynerson. Well, you came to the right guy, because we were close. While we were with MFA&A we shared an office in the basement of the National Gallery, as well as shared an apartment in D.C.. We didn't share any women though."

Selby saw Fox look at him carefully, perhaps looking for a sign Selby might know about Martin and Katherine, but Selby did his best not to indicate Fox had struck a nerve.

So Fox continued. "Later we sailed off to Europe together, where we met your dad in London, and later in Munich. Even though Elliott was OSS by then, OSS and MFA&A co-operated fully in art-recovery operations, especially in interrogations."

"You were both in Salzburg when Martin was murdered," Selby said.

"Yes. Another batch of paintings had vanished from the salt mine at Bad Aussee. We were sent to grill the Austrians who were supposed to be helping sort out all the works the Nazis had stored there. Some help."

"Martin's sister, Madeleine, says she wrote to you, asking if you agreed with the Salzburg police determination that a street burglar robbed and killed Martin and that you wrote back telling her you thought one of the mine workers was guilty."

Fox snapped his fingers in recognition. "Madeleine. That's her name. I couldn't remember it. Yeah. I remember. Jeez, that was what?… a year or two after Martin died that I wrote back to her. Don't know why her letter took so long finding me. I was still in Germany. Didn't leave until early '49. I wrote her because, even though I never met her, I felt like I knew her. Sort of. Martin was always talking about her. Maddy, he called her. Not long before we left for Germany Martin put up a photo of her in our apartment, one she had sent him in the mail. Nice-looking woman. Too classy for me. I liked 'em slutty back then."

"Tell me more about the mine workers," Selby said.

"After Martin was killed I interviewed all of the mine workers all over again. I put their feet to the fire, so to speak. There are limits, unfortunately, to how far we were allowed to go to extract information from people like them. Not like to today, I understand."

People like them? Selby thought. "Extract."

"Hell, yes. It was like pulling teeth."

"Any one of them in particular trigger your suspicions?" Selby said.

"Yeah. A snide piece of work named Gunter Somebody-or-Other. I can't remember his last name. He claimed Martin threatened to get them all shit-canned unless they came up with names of whoever was pilfering from the mine."

"And after your interrogations?"

"Nothing. Zilch. The police refused to do any follow-up."

"What was my father's reaction?"

"Elliott? Hum. Let me think. Pissed probably. We all hated the police. German and Austrian. Pompous, officious bastards. There was a difference, though. The German police loved nothing better than to pick on poor, defenseless Germans. Harass their own kind. Whereas the Austrian cops would go to any length to lie, cheat, and otherwise deceive us about anything any Austrian citizen did or was accused of doing. That's why I refused to believe their phantom robber bullshit."

"Think hard. How did my father react?"

Selby watched as Fox stared toward the fireplace mantel, which Selby found discouraging. Nixon could have given the Salzburg police lessons on lying, cheating, and deceiving. He certainly didn't want David Fox picking up Nixon vibes before answering the question. Selby thought: Who was it – Hunter S. Thompson maybe? – who once wrote that Nixon 'speaks for the werewolf in us'?

"Elliott was dismayed that he had no official standing with the Austrian police. I'm pretty sure he said he needed to take up the matter with US Army folks in Munich. The Army could put the squeeze on both the police and the mine workers. In fact, as I recall, the Army did make the same threat to the mine workers that Martin had made."

"Then what?" Selby said.

Fox held out his hands. "Then nothing. Lots of posturing, lots of paper shuffling. Before long things got dropped."

"Did Elliott share your view about mine workers' killing Martin?"

"Oh, definitely. Nothing else made nearly as much sense."

"What about Russians?"

"What about them?"

"I understand the Russians learned that you were holding Colonel Zeitz and also knew Zeitz had been talking to Martin about some of his war prizes. They had to have gone bonkers when they found out Zeitz had been poisoned. Could they have blamed Martin?" Selby said.

"Even if they did, why kill him? I mean, that left Martin as the only one who might know what they wanted to know. Their trying to kidnap him makes more sense."

Indeed, Selby thought. "Was there any evidence they tried? Was Martin killed in a struggle?"

"No. Martin was shot facing whoever killed him, but his gun wasn't drawn. Martin always carried his service revolver when he walked alone. He started that in Munich."

"He faced his killer?"

"Yeah. The cops figure he heard someone behind him and turned just in time to get shot. No. Forget the Russians. You and I both know they're not that dumb. Especially me." Fox tapped his right leg.

Selby nodded.

"Whose cockeyed notion blames the Russians?" Fox asked.

"Lewellyn Champion suggested it when I was getting your number and address from him," Selby lied, not wishing to reveal the name of his next interviewee.

Fox laughed so hard the effort provoked a coughing spasm. "Good old Lew. Still thinking with his head up his ass. Forever in the dark. I'm surprised he's still there. You're gone, I take it."

"I'm gone."

"Take an ER?" Early retirement.

"Yes."

Fox coughed again, pounding his chest until the wheezing stopped. "All the good guys quit or get fired. Now all Langley is left with is a bunch of KGB moles spying on each other."

"Something you know that the rest of us don't?" Selby said.

"Naw. I'm just guessing. But with dumb fucks like Lew the Champ pulling so many levers, you got to suppose it's happened. We both agree. The Russians aren't so stupid. Can you think of any place easier to infiltrate? Where else has gullibility been institutionalized? Ingrained to the bone? Made sacred? Well, besides J. Edgar's Fools-and-Boors Institute? That's a given. But I'm talking serious government-intelligence enterprises, not that overrated sandbox for retards."

"Lew's not as important as he used to be," Selby said with understatement.

"Good. That's good. He belongs back on his farm in Indiana, playing with corncobs. But the only way to get Lew out of Langley is to get Bush out of the White House. Christ, Bush was Director for a year. You'd think he could see through Lew's crap. Maybe if Clinton gets elected he will finish cleaning the shit out of the Langley stables." Deep sigh, more coughing. "Or maybe he won't."

"Anything else you can remember about Martin's death that might help?" Selby said.

"Help do what? That happened a thousand years ago, Selby. Back when bearded barbarians and yellow hordes swept across Europe and Asia, when Attila and Genghis breathed fire. The principals are all gone."

"You're still here. Shopping, cooking, going to Red Sox games."

"Not many of us left." Fox walked to the mantel to knock on wood.

"I know."

"So who else you going to see about this? Anybody I know?" Fox said.

Need-to-know remained a principle deeply ingrained in Selby. "I don't know yet. I haven't exactly been systematic. You came to mind. I asked Lew. I'm here on what looks like a go-home-empty-handed fishing trip."

"Well, you can tell Martin's sister you tried. That's more than a lot of guys would do."

34

Monday
June 22, 1945
Upper St. Clair
Pennsylvania

Benjamin Pettijohn turned out to be alive, but not well. Yet, he cheerfully agreed to meet with Selby and gave him directions to reach his daughter's house from the Pittsburgh airport. On Sunday morning Selby decided the time saved from the combination of flights from Albany to Pittsburgh, via Washington, D.C., versus driving was not worth the added aggravation. So he packed quickly and set out immediately for the 9-hour car trip. After a night in a Hyatt near the airport, he showed up refreshed for his late morning get-together with the former MP sergeant.

"Some place, huh?" Pettijohn said, after their initial introductions. "My daughter and her husband have both done well for themselves. Linda is a hospital administrator at Mercy Hospital and Joe is a dean at Robber-Baron University." When

Selby raised a puzzled eyebrow, Pettijohn clarified. "Carnegie-Mellon."

The three-story home, Selby judged, was one of the larger ones in a new, posh subdivision. "Very nice," Selby remarked as Pettijohn led him through the house to a deck with a sweeping view of the sprawling back yards of several neighbors.

"You talking about the weather?"

"The house and its lovely grounds," Selby said.

"Beats my having to spend my remaining days in a nursing home, let me tell you. I got my own apartment up on the top floor and an electric stairway lift to get me there."

Selby recalled his own father's difficulties moving about the Hudson River estate during Elliott's final illness-racked years. "Your daughter and son-in-law are very thoughtful."

"Yes, they are. But, more importantly, they can afford to be. Lots of parents have thoughtful children, but few of them can keep their parents in this kind of style. I'm a very lucky man." After showing Selby to an Adirondack chair and pouring each of them a glass of iced tea, Pettijohn said, "I'll be right back."

When he returned he had a portable oxygen tank slung over one arm and carried a cardboard box under the other. As he sat down next to Selby he plunked the box onto the glass patio table and gestured toward the oxygen tank. "Sometimes luck isn't quite enough."

"I understand you worked in the steel mills much of your life," Selby said, his knowledge courtesy of Lew Champion.

"As long as they lasted. Then I went to work for Allegheny County." He patted his chest. "Steel mills are mighty tough on the lungs. Not that I'm complaining, mind you. Christ! I could have been a coal miner."

"Let's talk about Martin Wynerson," Selby said after Pettijohn made himself comfortable in his chair.

"His sister send you?"

Selby grinned. "Sort of."

"I figured. Lordy, she came here decades ago. I could tell then she was as tenacious as God makes 'em."

"She is persistent."

"So after all these years and years she finally enlisted you."

"I volunteered, actually."

"I'm sort of surprised your daddy never followed up on Martin's death as much as I thought he might."

Or ought, Selby added silently, figuring that was what the man really meant to say. That makes two of us, he thought. "Tell me who you think killed Martin and why."

"Let me start out by telling you who didn't kill him. Those Austrian mine workers."

"Why not?" Selby said.

"Because they pretty much knew Martin's threat was idle. Sure, they got themselves worked up. Nobody enjoys a threat. But they also cooled down mighty quickly."

"Why idle?"

"Think about it. They did. There was limited labor in the mine area and the Army couldn't easily import outsiders. And they had worker solidarity on that issue. I know how important that is. I'm a union man. Plus, they were clear in their own minds that they weren't stealing – well, much. Hell, everybody was pilfering, including Americans. But at issue was big-time theft. The

Austrians were sure it wasn't them, but they had no idea who it was or how it was being done. They also recognized that they were prime suspects, but --. Here's an important point. Those men knew from the start they would be prime suspects. They knew that well before Martin Wynerson was shot."

"Martin's sister says you suspected the Russians," Selby said.

"I did. I do. The Russians were just as mad or madder than the Austrian mine workers. They were sure the whole point of Colonel Zeitz's death was to thwart them." Pettijohn paused. "Listen to me. Thwart. I've been listening to my son-in-law too much."

"So you think the Russians killed Martin in retaliation for Colonel Zeitz's death?"

"I do."

"Why wouldn't they try to kidnap him instead? That makes more sense to me."

"Maybe they did try. Things go wrong sometimes, you know."

Selby smiled a tight smile and nodded. Thinking of David Fox's Prague fiasco, he said, "Yes, things can go wrong."

"Murphy's Law, right?" Pettijohn said.

Indeed. "So how did the Russians react to Martin's death? Or did they?"

"Oh, they were indignant all over again. 'Now you've killed both men who knew where the Amber Room is hidden,' they said. They swore it was an American conspiracy to keep them in the dark."

"What made you not believe them?"

Pettijohn thought for a moment. "What's that phrase my daughter uses? They protesteth too much? They left in a big hurry, too. Claimed they had to hurry back to Berlin to tell Uncle Joe what a bunch of untrustworthy bastards we Amerikanskis were, so Joe could rag on Harry."

"Nothing more concrete?" Selby asked.

Pettijohn tapped the side of his head. "I know the Russians. I was in Berlin when they cut the city off. Berlin Airlift and all that hoopla. They're cut-throat sons of bitches."

Selby felt dismay. All the old man could offer him was a politically colored generalization about Russians. Nothing concrete.

"Hey, I damned near forgot my box here," Pettijohn said, interrupting Selby's silent lament. "Pictures from my days in Munich. Kept 'em boxed up all these years, but, after you called to say you were coming, I dug through my old albums and sorted these out. I used to be a camera nut. Took my Brownie everywhere. If you'd seen me back then you'd swear my camera was glued to my hands."

Selby patiently allowed the former sergeant to show him the photos. From Salzburg he recognized the Hohensalzburg Fortress, bridges over the Salzach River, the house where Mozart was born, shots of Residenz Platz. Then, in Munich, Selby saw the Führerbau, scenes from the English Garden, other shots where the only thing recognizable was the devastation. Then, at last, came photos with people in them.

"That's Martin and me," Pettijohn said proudly. "David Fox took it."

In the next pair of photos Selby recognized David and Martin, handsome men in their mid-thirties, grinning in front of a fountain, wearing their smart dress uniforms.

Then Pettijohn handed a photo to Selby with five people in it. Selby recognized Martin, David Fox, and his own father, wearing finely-tailored civilian clothes. "Who are the two women?"

"The one on the left we all called Fräulein Strumpet. Her last name was Strumpf or something like that. I don't remember her first name. Look on the back. Some of these have the names on the back."

Selby turned the photo over. "Frieda Strumpf. You were right."

"Good for me, 'cause I've got to tell you, more and more of the ol' Rolodex cards in my head are showin' blank when I roll my eyeballs inward to check 'em."

"Why Fräulein Strumpet?" Selby asked. "Was she a whore?"

"That was the name Martin gave her. Then we all started using it. She was David Fox's girlfriend. And a first-class, triple A, five-star gold digger she was, too. And probably a whore, too. She and the other girl were German workers at the Führerbau. Helped with inventory. Besides being a greedy little leach, Miss Strumpet was lazy as hell. I'd have fired her in a minute. But as long as she was washing Ensign Fox's socks I kept my mouth shut. We never called her that to her face or where Mister Fox could hear us, but he found out anyway and got real pissed. Lucky for me and my men he took out most of his irritation on Lieutenant Wynerson. Fox loved to dish out crap, play pranks, rib people, and make snide sexual chatter, but he never cared a bit to be on the receiving end."

"Who was Anna Stahlinger?"

"Like I said, she was a local who helped out with inventory."

"Lazy?"

"Oh, no. Just the opposite. Turns out she was also a cousin to Colonel Zeitz. Can't quite recall the exact connection. I think maybe Miss Anna's mother was a sister to the colonel's father."

"A cousin, eh?" Perhaps a cousin the colonel might confide in, Selby thought. "Was she ever permitted to see the colonel?"

"Oh, yes. She was authorized to visit the colonel in his cell any time she wanted to."

"Who authorized that?"

"Your father. He explained to me that he was hoping he might whisper things to her that he wouldn't think of divulging to Lieutenant Wynerson."

"And did he?"

"Not that I am aware of," Pettijohn said.

"So, if the Russians killed Wynerson, who do you think killed Colonel Zeitz?"

"My prime suspect there is Colonel Zeitz himself. He kept telling Lieutenant Wynerson that he felt the walls closing in on him. Told me the same thing more than once."

"Was Colonel Zeitz a wimp?"

"Oh no, sir. He was tough – mostly. He told me a few stories. One about how he got injured in Russia while riding in the side-car of a motorcycle. The driver was killed and the colonel walked with a cane for a year. And about how he fought the Russians at Berlin and had a grenade blow up just a few feet from him, nearly killing him."

"But you think he committed suicide."

"I've always been of two minds about how he died. But even the doctors who examined his body couldn't agree."

Selby said, "If the colonel didn't kill himself, who's your next favorite?"

"I wish I had one. Everyone who had any contact with the colonel at all was thoroughly questioned. Even me and my men," Pettijohn said.

"Who conducted the interrogations?"

"Your father and David Fox."

"Not Martin Wynerson?"

"No."

"Why not?"

"He and Fox got sent off to Salzburg."

"But before they went Fox interviewed people about Colonel Zeitz's death?"

"Before and after."

"But not Martin? He didn't interview anybody about the colonel's death?"

"No, sir. Not at all."

"Did that strike you as odd?" Selby asked.

"Yes. A bit. But it wasn't my business to question who was doing the questioning." Pettijohn paused, then added, "And not doing it."

"Who interviewed Fräulein Stahlinger? Can you recall?"

"Your father."

"Did he say if she told him anything useful?"

"Not to me."

Selby paused and stared out across the neatly mowed lawns while he thought. Finally he asked, "Do you think it's just possible the same person or persons killed both Colonel Zeitz and Lieutenant Wynerson?"

"Why? Because of their discussions?"

Selby nodded.

"Colonel Zeitz certainly knew one hell of a lot."

"Who would want to shut him up?"

"No one at the Führerbau. We were all working to get people like him to tell us everything they knew."

"An outsider then? How did an outsider get to the Colonel?"

"I have no idea. It's always haunted me that someone did get by my security. After all, it was my job to protect the colonel as much as to keep him locked up. And I failed."

"What happened to Frieda and Anna?"

"I don't understand. You mean when the Americans left?"

"Yes."

"I have no idea. My MP unit was transferred to Berlin just before Christmas of 1945. They were both still working at the Führerbau when I left Munich."

"Whose girlfriend was Anna?" Selby asked, then watched Benjamin Pettijohn bite his lip hard enough to leave a mark. "What's the matter?"

"Nothing's the matter. It's just that --."

"Was she yours?"

Pettijohn bristled. "Definitely not. No, sir." Then he softened. "Not that I would have bounced her off my cot for eating strudel, mind you. She was a looker... in a tough sort of way. Handsome, rather than cute, if you know what I mean. The athletic type. If fact I once heard someone say she competed in the winter Olympics before the war. Some type of skiing."

"You didn't answer my question," Selby said.

Pettijohn nodded sheepishly. "I know."

"Answer me, please. It may be important."

"Well, sir, she was sort of... sort of --."

"Sort of what? Why are you waffling?"

"I'm sorry, but I don't want to hurt your feelings if I can help it."

Why Selby had not seen it coming he later could not explain to himself, other than to admit he did not want to see it coming.

"Miss Anna and your father were what in genteel circles used to be called an item. We all knew your father was a married man, but at the same time everybody clearly understood that Miss Anna and Mister Parker were --." He could not bring himself to get the word out.

"Lovers?"

Pettijohn nodded. "It was war time, you must understand. I mean, even Ike had his lady driver."

Even Ike. Selby thought. I guess that made it okay for lesser men, except that good old Ike had also imposed a no-fraternization-with-Germans policy. But apparently exceptions were tolerated and hired help was fair game.

"It wasn't like she was some slut your father picked up, Mister Parker. Their relationship was not the same as Lieutenant Fox's with Fräulein Strumpet."

"Why is that?" Selby said sullenly.

"Miss Anna came with him from Switzerland."

"What do you mean?"

"I mean Miss Anna spent much of the war living and working in Bern with your father."

Tuesday
June 23, 1992
Sacred Heart Cemetery
Stottville, New York

Selby knelt and placed a single rose on his mother's grave. Grass had begun to grow on his father's grave -- next to Katherine's -- along with a couple of weeds, which he plucked and tossed aside. He mused at how young shoots of grass came up more easily than his youthful memories of Elliott came back to him. Maybe because he had so few. Elliott had been an absentee father. No, that was not entirely fair. Just mostly. When Elliott was still stateside, Katherine had chosen, willfully many would have said, to remain a truant wife. She had refused to follow her husband from Brown to Cornell to Harvard, disdainful of the role of academic wife. Her Stuyvesant estate was home to her, wherever her husband wandered. So Selby had grown up essentially without a father.

His best memories of those early years were the trips with his mother to Washington and London. Looking back now, he still relished his first sighting of a row of double-decker buses at Trafalgar Square; savored his astonishment at the life-like figures in Madame Tussaud's Waxworks, characters he had, until then, only read about and imagined.

After the war he had never understood why he and his mother had always met Elliott in London, but had never crossed over to the Continent, where Elliott actually worked. Only much later did he learn that the family of an active CIA field operative was forbidden to set foot on continental Europe, lest one or more members of the family fall prey to a Russian intrigue.

In death Katherine and Elliott would spend more time in close proximity than they had ever spent in life. Perhaps it's better this way, Selby thought, never quite able to figure out why they had wed in the first place. But, he asked himself, what child is ever fully capable of understanding the attraction that resulted in that child's parents' becoming more than two people passing by one another in their lives' courses.

Now Selby suddenly found himself wondering if Katherine knew about Madeleine's letters to Elliott. He wondered how Katherine reacted to news of Martin's death; wondered what she asked Elliott about it, if anything; wondered if Elliott even told her about Martin's dying. No way of knowing now, Selby lamented. They are lost answers. Lost forever. He certainly didn't recall his mother's ever mentioning Martin's death.

Having lingered long enough to be respectful, Selby drove the few miles back to the estate at Stuyvesant. The estate, he had already decided, would be his home. Even before his father died he decided to hang on to the estate, mostly out of sentimentality. But sentimentality, he finally came to realize, is more than the sum of its sappy and irrational parts. Having roots, even if some of the roots have borne leafy weeds, is central to maintaining a sense of who you are. So, after considerable reflection, he decided he wanted to make his mother's home his permanent home.

When Elliott had taken ill and was no longer capable of caring for himself, Selby had built a large caretaker cottage out by the apple orchard, then hired a live-in family to attend to both Elliott and the estate. Like Ben Pettijohn's daughter, Selby wanted nothing to do with nursing homes. And now that Elliott was gone, he had invited the caretaker family to stay on. They were good people in Selby's judgment and they accepted his offer, pleased not to have to move and seek other employment. Income from the family trust would allow Selby to continue to pay them the same annual salary, plus provide them free rent and a car. That they now had one less burden to care for was simply a bonus.

A phone message from Benjamin Pettijohn awaited Selby at the house. It said simply: Please call.

"Amazing what a few drops of Doctor Jack will do to lubricate the ol' memory gears," Pettijohn began when Selby returned the phone call. "I apologize for not having given any thought to Colonel Zeitz, because I thought when you showed up that you were only interested in Martin Wynerson. Now what I recall may not be important, but I do recollect a couple of facts about when Colonel Zeitz was arrested, facts we tried to use to trace his comings and goings. "

"Go ahead," Selby said.

Following the sound of Pettijohn's sucking oxygen, he said, "First, we found a truck, an old Opel, if I recall correctly, that we figured Zeitz had abandoned in the village of Mittenwald, where he was arrested trying to board a train for Austria. We never figured out where he got it originally, but we finally recognized that the truck had been in or near Berlin because it had passed through a Russian security roadblock there. Taped on one of the truck fenders was a little sticker stamp the Russians issued during the Potsdam Conference to prove the vehicle had passed through a checkpoint."

"So Zeitz had probably been in Berlin," Selby said.

"Well, at least the truck had been. Him, too, unless he picked the truck up somewhere between Berlin and Mittenwald."

"You said you remembered a couple of facts."

"Right. Colonel Zeitz had actually made it through the train station's border customs checkpoint at Mittenwald before he was recognized because he had some really good identification papers on him showing he was a Red Cross agent from Geneva. In fact, his papers were not just good forgeries. After some of our intelligence folks in Munich examined them, they declared his papers to be genuine."

"Then how was he found out?" Selby asked.

"Some family getting off a train coming in from Austria recognized him. A young woman ran up to him, shouting his real name. The family owned a house near his father's chalet in some small town not far from Mittenwald. When the name the woman was shouting didn't match the name on his papers the customs officer ordered him detained."

"So where did his Swiss identification come from?" Selby said.

"I don't think we ever found out. Then once he was dead, nobody seemed to care."

Nobody seemed to care, Selby repeated to himself silently. I wonder why not?

After thanking Ben Pettijohn for his call, Selby wondered if perhaps he owed the former sergeant a bottle of Jack Daniels. He finally decided that yes, he owed him, but also best not to send him any. That was no doubt illegal anyway. Also, maybe Ben dispensed those *few drops* of medicinal whiskey to himself without his daughter's knowledge or approval.

Later, when Selby had made notes on his visit to Ben Petti-john, he placed a phone call to David Fox, then waited while Fox took a several moments to sort through his memories, apparently having long since forgotten the names Frieda Strumpf and Anna Stahlinger. Given Ben Pettijohn's remark that Fox had always taken serious umbrage at Frieda Strumpf's being called *Fraulein Strumpet*, Selby decided against reminding Fox of the pet name in the hope it might aid his recollection.

Finally, Fox said, "It's coming back to me. We're talking forty-plus years, you must remember."

"I understand," Selby said. As time goes by, not only is a sigh just a sigh, but a fuck is apparently just a fuck you can no longer put a name or a face to.

"Frieda and Anna. Yeah. They were just a couple of local girls who helped us out at the Führerbau. Inventory stuff, I think. Why do you ask? How'd you even come up with their names?"

Based on need-to-know, he didn't want Fox to know he had seen Ben Pettijohn. So Selby fibbed just a tad. "I found some additional photos in my dad's attic. One of them was a photo of you, him, and two young women. All four names are printed on the back of the photo."

"Can't remember much about either one of them," Fox said.

"Have any idea what happened to them?" Selby said.

"As far as I recall, which isn't much, they were both still working for MFA&A when I left Munich."

"If anything else about either of them occurs to you, please given a call, will you?"

"Sure, sure. Will do."

Maybe he will, Selby told himself after hanging up. Like Ben Pettijohn's, maybe David Fox's Munich memories needed to marinate for a while. I wonder if I should send a bottle of booze to Fox, Selby thought. He's accountable to no one. He can sit in his parlor and toast Dick Nixon until the bottle is empty. Then maybe he'll recall that Frieda Strumpf and Anna Stahlinger were more than just a pair of local inventory helpers. Or perhaps he doesn't want to remember anything else about them.

35

Wednesday
July 1, 1992
Berlin

Although the U.S. embassy perched conspicuously in the middle of the city on Neustädtische Kirchstrasse, the Consular Section lay hidden away on Clayallee, in the Dahlem district. Less than a year had passed since Berlin once again became Germany's national capital, following a bitter parliamentary debate. Berlin had prevailed over Bonn, though barely, primarily because many Germans thought Bonn unworthy, considered it the trifle John Le Carrè regarded it to be when he titled a novel set there, *A Small Town in Germany*. America had played it safe, maintaining its official embassy in Bonn, while proclaiming "one embassy, two locations".

Many foreign embassies continued to search for prize space in Berlin, so that staffs, and consequently service, at many legations remained less than satisfactory. As far as Selby was concerned the

Americans had always run a half-assed German operation, even in Bonn, the ambassadorship invariably going to a backslapping political hack. So he had low expectations when he walked into the Consular Section and asked to see Alec Marsden.

"I'm sorry, sir. Mister Marsden is currently unavailable. And even under normal circumstances he does not meet with walk-in citizens," said a young woman Selby did not recognize.

Despite her effort to project steadfast adherence to the policy she had been trained to declare, Selby detected a hesitancy that told him she was feeding him a falsehood. "Tell Alec this is not a normal circumstance."

"Sir, I just told you Mister Marsden is not here for me to convey your message. Would you care to leave your name? I'll pass it along when Mister Marsden returns."

"Okay. My name is Selby Parker. S-e-l-b-y. Tell Alec I want to buy his patent formula for turning turnip leaves into premium beer. He'll understand." Selby waited while she wrote down his message, shaking her head in this-guy's-crazy fashion as she wrote.

Just as she finished scribbling a buzzer went off on her telephone. She answered, turned tight-lipped and sour, nodded, hung up, then glared at Selby. "Mister Marsden just returned and says he'll see you."

Selby waved at the mini-camera mounted high in a far corner of the office, then said to the young receptionist, "Alec and I are long-time friends. You were just doing your job."

"Are you as big an asshole as he is?" she said, pointing toward a far door.

"Depends. I try not to be."

She continued to glare. "Turnip leaves. Is that the best you can do?"

"Okay. I'm an asshole, too. Alec owes you a lunch."

"Like hell. You owe me a lunch."

At forty-four Alec Marsden stood as one of the younger of the Company's Old Guard. He was proving effective at bridging the gap between the e-mail and the snail-mail crowds. Hence his high-level, low-profile Berlin posting.

As Selby was closing the door behind him, Alec Marsden rose from his desk chair and said, "How short a time has it been since you assured me that seeing Berlin in your rearview mirror constituted your happiest moment since watching Nixon's resignation speech?"

Selby shrugged, then shook Marsden's hand and sat down in the offered seat. "Yeah, well, when's the last time you saw a fly take off from a shit pile and not come back?"

"You back onboard? If so, no one's bothered to tell me."

"No. Out is out. By the way —" Selby gestured with a thumb toward the door he just came through. " – Grim Grom's daughter out there called you an asshole. A big asshole. You put up with that kind of insubordination?" Selby grinned as he spoke.

"The meek have gone elsewhere. They have not inherited reception desks. Miss Ballbuster is a whole lot tamer than some in our system. She's new, but she's learning. Her no-nonsense approach will pay off in the long run."

"What long run?" Selby said. "The Wall is down. Doesn't everybody get to go home soon?"

"The Wall may be down but the game continues. It's like tennis without a net," Marsden said.

Selby gave him a faux-scowl. "I thought Germany was supposed to turn into one big Love Fest."

Marsden gave Selby a what-can-I-say gesture. "Nobody to love. I defy you to go outside and find anyone – and I mean anyone – within a thousand miles of here who admits to being, or having ever been, a member of the dreaded Communist Party. Lenin? Stalin? Ulbrecht? Who are they? Every god-fearing one of them will tell you the same story: From the day they were born, their sainted mothers held them in one arm and suckled them, while, with her free hand, Momma read them the works of Jefferson, Madison, Lincoln, et al.. An unshakeable Demokratski every one."

"So pack up and go home," Selby said.

"To paraphrase Abe Lincoln, calling yourself a believer in constitutional democracy doesn't make you one. Now why are you here?"

"I've become a foot soldier in an older war."

"Vietnam?"

"The Big One."

Marsden gave a low whistle. "Whose side are you on?"

"The good guys, only --."

"Only what?"

"I'm running into a problem trying to figure out exactly who all the good guys are. Or were," Selby said.

Alec Marsden propped his feet up on his desk. "Tell me about it. I've got time. The Cold War's over. Everybody says so. Tune me in to your war."

For the next twenty minutes Selby chronicled the relevant pieces of the lives of Rainer Zeitz, Martin Wynerson, and the attendant cast in their mini-drama, a play that failed to qualify even as a minor tragedy, given the unheroic, mostly pathetic natures of the *dramatis personae*. One player's part Selby deliberately scaled back in the telling – his father's role.

When Selby finished Alec Marsden asked, "Why am I privileged to hear this tale of woe? Murders with possible ripple effects."

"I'd like your help."

Marsden smirked. "My little black accounting book shows I don't owe you any favors."

"True. And you also keep a separate book registering your colleagues' peccadilloes, including mine, that we'd all prefer Langley never know about."

"I do?"

Selby nodded. "But I bet your black book cataloging those matters is much thinner than mine."

"And all this time I thought you were one man who rose above blackmail."

"I do. I simply ask you to reexamine your accounting book for possible errors. Perhaps you do owe me one or two small favors after all," Selby said. "Think back to Vienna, 1981. Two young boys playing in the street."

"Perhaps I do at that."

"And perhaps one or more of the notations in my book of sins needs to be corrected. Careful as I am, a misattribution or two just might have occurred."

"What's the favor?"

"Trace a pair of women as far as you can. Their names are Frieda Strumpf and Anna Stahlinger."

"That's it?"

"For now."

"Did your father look into this at all?"

"Elliott didn't come up with anything," Selby said ambiguously.

"Selby Parker, living the American male fantasy – Lone Cowboy."

"I don't own a white hat."

"No black mask either. And where's your guitar? Your famous horse? No Tonto, no Gabby Hayes, no Pat Butram. You've come to the Deutschland stage without your props."

"I never heard John Wayne sing 'I'm Back in the Saddle Again'," Selby pointed out.

"You're not John Wayne."

"So I'm not."

"I'll do your favor, chase your women. Just watch yourself so you come back to collect on it. Where can I find you?"

"I don't know. I'll call you."

Selby took the U-Bahn from the Dahlem District to Budapester Strasse, then walked the rest of the way to 9 Hardenbergstrasse, the site of Galerie Nierendorf. Ingrid Sundstrum was waiting for him.

"Pleased to meet you, Mister Parker," she said in a soft-as-fresh-snow Scandinavian accent.

She was blue-eyed, but not very blonde. Sandy hair tied back in a bun. Peach cheeks and half-glasses in black frames. Selby thought she looked too young to be a professor, though he knew she had turned thirty in April.

They walked south down Knesebeck Strasse and ordered lunch at Savigny Café, sitting down amid a well-heeled crowd Selby thought much too grand for him, but Ingrid appeared comfortable there.

"So how may I help you exactly? You teased me just enough in your phone calls to intrigue me."

Selby summarized the stories of the men who brought him there, again omitting his father.

"And you believe the Marc and Klee paintings may have played a role in the deaths of Lieutenant Wynerson and Colonel Zeitz, correct?"

"Yes. Sergeant Pettijohn knows very little about art, but he recalled one particular session when Wynerson was supposed to be interrogating Zeitz. He says he recalls it so clearly because Lieutenant Wynerson was acting totally out of character, laughing and joking with the colonel. Even the colonel was not his usual glum self. Both seemed to be having an animated conversation and thoroughly enjoying themselves and each other's company. So he listened in from outside the cell door. He says he distinctly remembers the names of Marc and Klee, wondering to himself who these fellows were that made both the lieutenant and the colonel forget themselves. Only later did the sergeant discover Marc and Klee were famous painters."

"Go on," Ingrid said, appearing to be captivated.

"Martin Wynerson apparently told my father and others that Zeitz wanted to make a deal, trading his knowledge of the whereabouts of the Klee and Marc paintings for his freedom.

Such a deal was out of the question, but at the time of Zeitz's death, Wynerson was still stringing the colonel along."

"Stringing him along? That's an Americanism for what exactly?"

"Letting the colonel believe such a deal was possible, even though it wasn't."

"So this offer of a trade, you think, may have prompted someone to kill them?" Ingrid said.

"It's quite possible, assuming that Colonel Zeitz hadn't simply invented his story in the hope it might give him an opportunity to escape jail."

"No, no. You may be on to something." She let Selby ponder that remark while she toyed with her coffee cup, tracing and retracing the rim, not looking at Selby.

Finally Selby said, "Tell me why."

"Marc's *Tower* was last seen hanging in central Berlin in early July of 1945. It hasn't been seen since. The timing is such that Colonel Zeitz could have been there at the same time, which means he could have known about its disappearance. Certainly, given his job description, he's an excellent candidate for having inside knowledge."

"Sergeant Pettijohn also told me that when Zeitz was captured he was thought to have abandoned a truck in Mittenwald. Maybe Zeitz himself took the painting and carried it with him, though the truck was empty. The first place everyone at the time thought to search was his father's chalet. It's near where Franz Marc spent some time. Kochel am See?"

"Yes. It's just south of Munich," Ingrid said.

"According to Pettijohn, they found evidence Zeitz had been there just before his capture. But no paintings turned up. And, given the distance between Berlin and the chalet, there are plenty of places he could have hidden it."

"Zeitz was from Munich, yes?"

"I'm thinking the same thing. In fact, Munich is my next stop. A person leaves traces of himself wherever he's grown up. I'm hoping that, even after fifty years, he's left some residue of his presence."

"Good luck on that count," she said.

Selby paused before bringing up what he guessed was going to be a touchy subject. Then finally said, "I understand your grandparents were also in Berlin during June and July of 1945."

Ingrid gave him a so-you-know-about-them look. "Yes. What about it?"

"When Colonel Zeitz was captured he was using genuine Red Cross identification, fobbing himself off as a Geneva representative," Selby said.

"How very interesting."

"Yes, isn't it?"

"Is this why you sought me out? Because of my grandparents?" she said crossly.

"Alastair Stiles said you are among the most knowledgeable art historians on the Blue Rider Group. But he also suggested you might take more than a professional interest in my project," Selby explained.

For several moments Ingrid's coffee cup became an even more intense object of concentration for her. At last she looked up. "My own interests would be two. First, to help find the missing paintings. To find them would be a grand triumph, for me personally and for the world of modern art."

"And the second reason?"

"To prove my grandparents had no dealings with, no connections of any kind, with Colonel Zeitz."

Selby thought of his own mission and of his father. "I understand both goals and would appreciate any help you can offer me."

Saturday
July 4, 1992
Munich

Selby sat lakeside at the Seehaus beer garden in the English
Garden and sipped a cold Paulaner while watching a group of
children, their bare feet dangling in the water, sit on the concrete
bank of Kleinhesselohe See and feed bread to a gaggle of raven-
ous ducks. Nearby, beneath one of the beer garden's fake boathouse pavilions, a brass band played "In Himmel Gibt's Kein
Bier." "*Und so wir trink es hier*," he sank softly.

Despite his outward *Gemütlichkeit*, Selby felt melancholy,
realizing that, although the beer hall – all of Munich, for that
matter -- teemed with jovial Americans, most on holiday, there
would be no fife-and-drum corps playing "Yankee Doodle
Dandy", no evening fireworks, no rows of stars and stripes snapping smartly in the Munich breezes. Fourth of July in Germany
commemorated nothing.

He was looking forward to seeing Ingrid Sundstrum again in
a week. She was eager to help and regretted the necessity of her
having several more days' work at Galerie Nierendorf in order to

finish the assignment she had taken on there. But after that she was free for the rest of the summer, as well as for the first term at Lund University, where she was on temporary leave from her lecture duties.

While in Berlin Selby had taken a room at the Hotel Art Nouveau, in the Savigny Platz District. The small hotel was just off Ku'damm on Leibnitzstrasse, not far from the Nierendorf gallery. Ingrid demonstrated her enthusiasm for Selby's company by inviting him to dinner that same evening. Her choice of restaurant had been Spree Athen, just down the street from his hotel. The restaurant was set up to look like a parlor in prewar Berlin, complete with a woman, accompanied by a piano, singing songs from the Marlene Dietrich and Lotte Lenya era. Selby thought the whole arrangement a bit much, except for the food, which was so-so – a harsh judgment, given that Selby hardly considered himself a gourmand. But the charm and intelligence of his hostess more than offset the blandness of the food and the peculiarity of the surroundings.

The next day he spent burrowing through various archival histories of the Third Reich before taking a night train to Munich. He knew that, once defeat became obvious even to the most dedicated Nazis – the Gestapo and SS – destroyed many of their records, lest the Allies find them and use them. Selby's expectations of finding anything helpful about Rainer Zeitz had been minimal and he was not disappointed in that regard.

After arriving in Munich, Selby walked through the neighborhoods that had been Rainer Zeitz's childhood home and the site of his father's successful art gallery. No cognitive vibrations had emanated from the walls, streets, or sidewalks. Many knocks on many doors turned up no one who recognized the surname Zeitz, let alone recalled anything about the family.

As Selby sat finishing his beer and wursts at the beer garden and watched the children cast bread upon the water, and watched lovers stroll by hand in hand, he reminded himself that, for today's citizens of Munich, World War II would seem almost as long ago as the Age of Dinosaurs. Even so, in the morning he planned to rent a car in order to visit Kochel am See. A small Franz Marc museum now stood just outside the village. Perhaps someone there might still be attuned to the Jurassic Age some still thought of as the 1940's.

"A message for you, Mister Parker," the concierge called out as he entered his hotel lobby.

Selby accepted the folded slip in puzzlement. Who knows I'm here? By *here* he meant the Hotel Forum am Westkreuz, a large, but quiet, complex well west of the inner city, conveniently across from an S-Bahn stop. He had not even told Ingrid where to reach him. But when he opened the note he found himself not entirely surprised. *Call me. Marsden.* And a number. The Company could never seem to find the moles nesting inside its own pockets, yet it could detect a chewed wad of gum stuck beneath a rock on the dark side of the moon.

"No point wasting your trip to Munich, Sel. I've got a piece of info you can play with down there, plus a couple more items," Alec Marsden said when Selby phoned him. "First, the Strumpf woman is long dead. Died back in early '46, according to Munich records. Amateur prostitute, though that hardly distinguished her from a lot of other women trying to survive in Munich at the end of the war. She ended up in a pauper's grave. Ho-hum. But --."

"But what? You waiting for a blare of trumpets?" Selby said.

"Okay. I'll do my own ta-daaaa! The woman had a nephew who lived with her before she died. Name of Franz. The kid was eight years old or so in '45. Makes him about your age. He's still alive. Lives in Landsberg, southwest of Munich. Hitler did some jail time there, as I recall."

And wrote *Mein Kampf* while there, Selby thought to himself.

"Anyway, I have an address for him."

Selby wrote the address.

"Second item. Anna Stahlinger. Vanished in the same time frame. Without a trace, as the saying goes. But I did turn up one bit of info you might relish. When she was working with your father in Bern her major assignment was to poke her nose into Swiss government bureaucracies looking for Nazis, of which she found quite a few apparently. But she also made regular trips to Geneva to try to identify Nazis working inside the Red Cross there. And she found plenty."

"So she, too, has a Red Cross connection," Selby said. Initiated by my father, went unsaid.

"Now, for the last bit of juiciness. You said that MP sergeant told you a couple of Russians went to Munich from Berlin and ended up raising holy hell when the colonel swallowed poison, right?"

"Yes."

"Well, the name of one of those two Russians was Konstantin Votichenko." Alec Marsden went silent, letting Selby absorb that insight.

"YV's father?" Selby finally said.

"Uncle."

"Interesting," Selby said slowly, his mind awhirl. "I wonder what YV might know?"

"Why don't you ask him?"

"He's in Munich?" Selby said.

"Hardly. He's retired like you, sitting at home in Leningrad, watching his grandkids grow up."

"St. Petersburg."

"Oh, yeah. Old habits die hard, huh? In any case, look him up. You're such good buddies and all."

"Am I permitted?"

"Why not? Cold War's over. Everybody says so. Door's open," Marsden said. "Call me when you get back."

Good buddies? Not exactly. Yevgeny Votichenko, my *bête noire* for how many years? From Krushchev to Gorbachev, Selby thought, the period between the two men representing the half-life of an imploding nucleus from that unstable element known as the Soviet Union.

It will be good to see YV again, Selby mused. What a novelty to see each others' full faces, engage in conversation, instead of peering at one another over the tops of newspapers while sitting on opposite sides of side-street cafés, waiting for the other to tip his hand.

But first things first.

———————

Sunday
July 5, 1992
Kochel am See
Bavaria

As Selby stood at the front door of the Kraegler chalet admiring the window boxes full of geraniums and petunias, he saw a face briefly peer out at him from behind lace curtains. Then the door opened and Selby explained who he was and why he was there. The man who greeted him was middle-aged, athletic-looking, very Nordic.

"Come in, please. I am Eric Kraegler."

A strong smell of camphor hit Selby when stepped into the foyer.

Kraegler apologized. "My mother suffers from a summer cold. I take her to the warm springs of the *Kurort* down by the lake every morning, but she still insists on rubbing her chest and throat with --." He waved both hands at the rank, invisible vapors wafting through the chalet.

"She's well enough to see me?" Selby asked, almost hoping the answer would be *No*.

"A guest in the form of a stranger will speed her recovery faster than all her ointments," the son insisted. "Wait here and I shall announce you." Moments later Eric returned and waved for Selby to follow him.

Lili Kraegler, by Selby's estimate, would be in her late six-ties. She looked older than that as she teetered rhythmically in a rocking chair, although all Selby could see was her face. Fore-head furrowed, face pasty, eyes watery, nose red. On her head she wore a knitted ski cap. From her shoulders to her waist she had wrapped herself in a crocheted shawl; from her lap to the floor she was bound in a heavy quilt. Only her labored breathing told Selby the mummy was alive.

Then she spoke, her raspy voice a young child's pitch, her Bavarian accent slushier than most. "Welcome, Herr Parker. My son says you wish to ask me things about long-ago times. I will remember for you what I can and promise not to make up things I can't remember. I am too old and too near the time when I must stand before Holy Mary for me to tell lies. Please be seated."

Her son fetched a chair and placed it beside the rocker, whispering to Selby, "Her hearing is not the best. But if you sit close and speak loudly, she will understand you."

Selby sat and tried his best to ignore the camphor. He simplified his story to the basics, ending by asking if Lili might know what happened to Anna Stahlinger.

"Only before the war did she come here often. By here I mean Kochel. I don't think she was ever in this house. Back then it was my parents' home. Papa was the caretaker for the Zeitz chalet. For them their chalet was a playhouse, a sometime thing. For us Kochel was our home." She smiled a wan smile at her son. "Is our home."

Selby nodded.

"I never cared for Anna. She was too close to Rainer. I think she may have even slept with him." Again she looked at her son. "I'm not always the stupid old fool you think I am. I know things."

"Mutti, I think no such thing of you."

She gave him a sideways look. "Of course, you don't. I am just being mean." Looking back at Selby, she said, "Much of the reason I disliked Anna was because I was jealous. I wanted to be the one to share his bed. Her incest had nothing to do with it. I would have resented any woman's claim on Rainer. But it was not to be. Not that I have regrets. After all, where would Eric be if I had married Rainer?" Yet another look at her son, this time sly, if not malicious, Selby thought.

"Do you know what became of Anna?" Selby asked.

"You mean after Rainer was poisoned?"

Selby nodded. "And beyond that."

She shook her head. "Even when Werner returned, she did not come to see him here. While he was still able he went to Munich to see her, but when he came back his heart was broken. He said Anna was not the same woman he knew before the war."

"How so?"

"So selfish, so greedy, so American." She smiled a fiendish smile. "Those were his exact words. Poor Werner. He died within a year of moving back to his chalet. A man's heart can only break so many times before it becomes unable to mend itself. He had no one left. I became his housekeeper that last year. My parents cared for Eric. And not once did Anna visit him. Worse, she did not even come to his funeral. In fact, Papa himself took the train to Munich to tell her Werner had died, tell her when and where his funeral would be. But when Papa came home he said he could not even find her."

"What year was that?" Selby said.

Lili closed her eyes, the tempo of her rocking unchanging. Finally, "Werner died in 1947. Or was it '48? No. 1947. Eric was not yet three."

"Do you know who your father talked to in Munich when he went looking for Anna?"

"The Americans, he said. He couldn't understand that because Werner had told Papa Anna was working for the Americans. But Papa said the Americans told him she had quit and vanished. I remember because at the time I thought to myself: Good. Maybe the Devil has taken her."

Or, Selby thought, someone else.

36

Monday
July 6, 1992
Landsberg am Lech
Bavaria

Selby thought Landsberg too lovely a medieval town, with its half-timber houses topped by red-tiled roofs, to be remembered now only for being the place where, from a jail cell, Adolf Hitler had discharged his bile onto paper and called it a political philosophy.

Arriving a bit early for his meeting with Franz Strumpf, Selby parked near the Rathaus on the Hauptplatz and strolled idly past tourist-enticing shops, waiting for the 6 p.m. closing time of the auto rental agency that Herr Strumpf managed.

When they met, Franz suggested they sit down for a beer and snacks at a nearby *Stube*. Selby readily agreed. Though only a couple years younger than Selby, Franz Stumpf appeared to Selby to be much older. Hard living? Hard drinking? Whatever the accounting, Selby had a there-but-for-the-grace-of moment as the two of them claimed a booth in the rear of Bayertor Keller, then ordered food and drink.

"Munich after the war. I was lucky," he began. "My Aunt Frieda had a job. Better yet, she had a job working for the Americans. My parents were both dead from the war, so I lived with her. Later, after she died, I was even luckier. I could easily have been sent to an orphanage, where the nuns would have beat me and the priests would have buggered me senseless. I'm told I was both cute and bright back then." He paused and gave Selby a but-look-at-me-now gesture. "A well-to-do, childless couple who lived on the Ammersee took me in. They raised dachshunds by the dozen and when I first arrived at their house I thought perhaps they had bought me to use as dog food. But I was wrong. They were good people, even though the *Amis* assured us all there was no such thing as a good German back then. In any case, the war hardly affected them. And they raised me as though I were simply one more cuddly little hound. And you know something? I am fifty-five years old and I have never been out of Bavaria. Here I rent cars to people who have been all over the world, some of them. But me? A homebody."

"Do you remember Anna Stahlinger?" Selby asked.

"Most definitely I remember *Tante* Anna. Not a real aunt, of course, but she encouraged me to call her that."

"What ever became of her? Do you recall?"

"She went away."

Selby waited while Franz gathered in his memories.

"Poof! Just like that. She left. I was heartbroken."

Selby continued to wait.

"She left just after Christmas of 1946. I remember distinctly because for Christmas Anna promised that in January she would take me to Garmisch and give me ski lessons. I was so thrilled. And then… no more Anna. She apologized to me and said she was helpless, that the Americans were sending her away."

"You're sure? Americans were sending her somewhere?"

"I'm sure because a few days later I got in deep trouble with Aunt Frieda about it."

"How so?" Selby said.

Franz smiled. "As much as my Aunt Frieda was a *Sheiss-mouth*, she expected me always to speak and behave as though I were the Holy Father himself. I believe it was the very day before Anna left us, though that doesn't matter, I overheard my Auntie shouting at her American boyfriend. And one of the things she said to him was, 'I can see clearly now that I, too, should have been fucking somebody else.' The shouting was because she was not going to get to go wherever Anna was going and she was not happy about it."

"Who was she shouting at?" Selby asked, even though he knew. And, indeed, Franz described David Fox perfectly.

"What got me in trouble was that later I asked Frieda why we didn't get to go away with Anna so I could still get my ski lessons. She said she had no answer to my question. But she assured me we were not going anywhere. Then I made the mistake of asking her, in the innocent way of a nine-year-old, 'Not even if you fuck somebody else?'"

Selby wondered how much guilelessness a nephew of Frieda Strumpf still possessed by then. Not much, he concluded. "Did you find out where Anna went off to?"

"No. And neither did Aunt Frieda, which angered her even more. She could not even write a letter to Anna, she complained. But the Americans were adamant. Anna was gone and that was the end of talking about her. Forget about her, the *Amis* said. *Kaput!*"

"What happened to your Aunt Frieda?" Selby said.

"Funny thing. Maybe she did fuck somebody who counted, because within a few days she, too, told me she was going away – to join Anna. Then she stunned me by telling me I was not allowed to go with her right away, but that she'd come back for me as soon as she could. She never came back and I ended up with the Schmidts."

"Who took care of you between the time Frieda left you and the Schmidts took you?" Selby asked.

"Anna's boss, Herr Parker. Same name as yours. But it was only for a few days."

Monday
July 13, 1992
St. Petersburg
Russia

Earlier in the day, when Selby found Ingrid Sundstrum, she was washing down a bagel with sparkling water in a lounge at Prague's Ruzyne Airport. Selby had ordered a beer and got a nasty look from his traveling partner, who, Selby guessed, was a strict adherent to the sun-must-be-over-a-local-yardarm principle, though he had no clue where he might find a yardarm in Prague by which to measure the sun's height. At 9:30 a.m. it would have to be a pretty short yardarm, he thought, but savored the beer anyway when the barmaid delivered it.

Ingrid's flight from Berlin had only taken an hour and she looked fresh. By contrast, Selby had been forced into taking a nine-hour ride on the *Nacht-Schnellzug* from Munich. And, despite his having a sleeper berth, despite the fact the express did not stop between Treuchtlingen and Prague, Selby felt as though he had been up the entire night.

Why no direct flights existed between Berlin and St. Petersburg or Munich and St. Petersburg baffled Selby. It was as if Russia wanted to continue to punish Germany. Frankfurt was the only German city offering service to St. Petersburg. Maybe the whole thing was Lufthansa's fault. In any case, he had booked himself and Ingrid on the two-and-a-half-hour Czech Airlines 737 flight leaving Prague at 11:30.

"So did you learn anything useful in Bavaria?" Ingrid said when Selby joined her.

"Yes. I learned that good guys can sometimes tell cruel lies."

Ingrid stared at him pensively. "This comes as a surprise to you after spending your career in the CIA?"

"I liked to think of myself as a Boy Scout."

"You were a Boy Scout?"

"No, but I could have been."

Ingrid laughed derisively. "In your business Scout's Honor doesn't mean much. You may imagine yourselves as cowboys, but none of you wear white hats."

"John Wayne never wore a white hat," Selby said lamely.

Ingrid shook her head. "Men and their cardboard heroes."

Selby had spared himself further embarrassment by filling Ingrid in on the particulars of his encounters in Bavaria.

"Which Americans do you suppose sent Anna away? And to where?" Ingrid asked when he finished.

"You forgot *why*. I don't know. Maybe my friend in St. Petersburg has some ideas." Actually Selby did have an idea regarding who. His father. But why?

Now, while waiting for their bags in St. Petersburg's Pulkove Airport, a dapper man in chauffeur's attire approached them and, in excellent English, asked, "Might you be Mister Selby Parker?"

Without acknowledging his name, Selby asked, "And you are?"

"My name is Sergei Stennvik. I work for Yevgeny Borisivitch. I am to escort you to his apartment."

"What is it you do for Mister Votichenko?" Selby said.

The man grinned. "Whatever he tells me to do. Come. I have a car waiting. I will speed you through the customs process. You need not wait in line with all the others."

So, Selby thought as he motioned a dubious Ingrid to follow him, even retired YV is still able to pull strings, jerk chains, move small, but otherwise intractable, mountains. Whatever metaphor for *quiet power* one chooses, Selby told himself, it applies to Yevgeny Votichenko, retired KGB man.

For thirty years Votichenko had belonged to Special Service II of the First Chief Directorate of the KGB -- the Committee for State Security. One of the primary duties of Special Service II was to undermine foreign intelligence services' effectiveness in countering activities of the KGB. Yevgeny had been one of their best, hence his assignment to Berlin, principally, but also wherever else Western intelligence attempted to peek under or over the Curtain that had become the Wall.

Yevgeny's apartment, Sergei explained as he drove, was in the heart of the city, close to the Russian Museum of Fine Arts, Philharmonic Hall, the National Public Library, a block off Nevsky Prospekt, on the corner of a pedestrian mall. When they arrived they had to climb a steep flight of stairs.

"Welcome to my humble abode," Votichenko said as he bowed and gestured for Ingrid and Selby to enter after Sergei opened the apartment door.

Having imagined all Russian apartments were drab, cramped, cookie-cutter rabbit warrens, Selby was surprised by the spaciousness of the place. Nor was it exactly humble. Neither was the man. He merely played the role, one among many.

Sixty-six and walking with a cane since tripping and falling down a flight of stairs in a London tube station in the mid-80's, Yevgeny Votichenko had remained otherwise healthy, fit even, despite his overindulgence in Turkish cigarettes and a fondness for good wines. A dapper dresser, he had turned the embarrassing tube station episode to his advantage soon after by sporting a golden-colored cane with an ornate handle hand-carved in the Black Forest.

The large living room contained Western furniture, both tasteful and expensive, and a pair of plush Oriental carpets. In a corner of the room Sergei began attending to a brass-colored samovar with porcelain handles, as Votichenko directed Selby and Ingrid to a couch.

Selby saw that Ingrid's nose had already begun to twitch from the redolent tobacco smell permeating the room. He wondered jut how sensitive she was, how long before she ran to the nearest window, flung it open, stuck her head out.

Taking a seat in an overstuffed chair opposite the couch, Yevgeny stroked his goatee and sized up Ingrid as though she were a figure in a particularly enchanting painting. "Tell me, Miss Sundstrum, how you came to be the accomplice to such an infamous scoundrel as Selby Parker."

Ingrid looked at Selby to see if he was going to take offense. When he laughed, she said, "Mister Parker has asked my help in pursuing a pair of lost paintings, whose recovery interests me very much. His own interest, that of determining who murdered an American military officer back in 1945, may be closely tied to the missing paintings in some as-yet-undetermined way."

Votichenko signaled for Sergei to serve tea, which he delivered in small clear glasses. "And you come to me because you think I may have knowledge of the deaths of SS Colonel Rainer Zeitz and of Lieutenant Martin Wynerson, based on the presence of my Uncle Konstantin Ivanovitch in Munich to interrogate Colonel Zeitz, correct?"

Ingrid looked again to Selby, who said, "You are uncommonly perceptive, Yevgeny Borisivitch."

Votichenko made a whisking, it's-nothing hand motion. "Amazing, isn't it, how easy it was for you to place a simple phone call to me; to board an airplane and fly here for this meeting. Four years ago that would not have been possible, eh?"

"The times, they are achangin'," Selby said. Then added, "Four years ago I could have saved the cost of both the phone call and the airfare. All I would have had to do was walk from my table at a café on the Ku'damm across the terrace to your table."

The Russian lifted his tea glass and toasted, "To simpler times."

"Can you help us, Mister Votichenko?" Ingrid said.

"Call me Yevgeny, please. Yes, I believe I can shed some small rays of light on parts of your mysteries."

Sergei returned to the room with a tray full of cheeses, breads, and cold cuts and placed them on the low coffee table in front of Selby and Ingrid. "*Zakuskis*," Sergei said.

"Appetizers," Yevgeny translated. "Literally *morsels*."

Ingrid looked to Selby, who nodded.

"You need not worry, Miss Sundstrum. I have no intent to poison you. We are all comrades now, eh?" Yevgeny said, laughing. "What better proof than my very own daughter, Nina, and her husband, Viktor Birgenev, both now attend graduate school in Boston. MIT."

"Engineers?" Selby asked.

"No, no, no. We have superb engineering schools here in Russia. At MIT they are working on degrees at the Sloan School of Management, hoping to learn how to become good capitalists."

Selby said, "You once assured me there was no such thing as a good capitalist."

"That's true. But soon there will be at least two, eh?"

Ingrid and Selby both helped themselves to the offered tidbits.

Votichenko nodded, pleased, and began his narrative.

"Uncle Konstantin and his comrade, Lev Greppov, did not kill the SS colonel, as some Americans in Munich at the time supposed. Nor did they kill the American lieutenant. My uncle kept a diary, and not just of the war years. He kept one his whole life, starting when he began his art studies at age fourteen. He gave me his set of diaries just before he died in 1983. I've read them all, several passages so many times the pages threaten to disintegrate at my touch. But in any case, Konstantin Ivanovitch discusses the accusations against him by the Americans and denies quite adamantly that either he or any other Russian so much as made an attempt to kill anyone involved in what he refers to as the Zeitz Affair."

The Russian paused to sip tea, then continued. "My uncle was actually very grateful to Colonel Zeitz. If it were not for those men the Germans called *Kunstverschaffneren*, Uncle Konstantin is certain he would have been sent to the front lines to become cannon fodder. Heroic cannon fodder, mind you, but cannon fodder nevertheless. Instead, he went off to Moscow, as did my parents. Lucky for them they and I did not have to endure the German siege, the infamous Nine Hundred Days.

"The samovar over there belonged to my grandmother. She was left behind in Leningrad, along with many others in my family. Few of them survived. My grandmother did not.

"But back to my uncle's luck. As it turned out, even Stalin went into a rage when he learned the Germans had dismantled the Amber Room and carted it back to Prussia. As part of his studies Uncle Konstantin had worked summers with the curators at Tsarkoye Selo, and so was most familiar with Catherine Palace and its Amber Room. Thus he was drafted into one of several art-recovery units hastily formed while the Germans were still advancing. By war's end he was in Berlin and Colonel Zeitz was at the very top of the list of Germans he was ordered to find."

Selby interrupted. "Does he conjecture who might have committed the murders?"

"He thinks the Americans killed the colonel, of course. He supposes Colonel Zeitz told the American lieutenant where to find several missing paintings, in particular where Franz Marc's *Tower of the Blue Horses* was hidden. Then he goes farther and thinks that, once several other Americans besides Lieutenant Wynerson also knew, one of them killed the lieutenant in order to race to the painting and steal it for himself."

"Does he name any names? Give any proof?" Selby said.

"No proof, but… he names your father as one of those most likely."

Selby nodded solemnly.

"Colonel Zeitz himself stole the Marc painting. So there is little doubt he was able to tell Lieutenant Wynerson where it could be found," Yevgeny said.

Ingrid, wide-eyed, said, "How did your uncle know that to be true?"

"Colonel Zeitz bribed the Soviet major in charge of security at the Prussian Chamber of Deputies. Food, wine, cigarettes. The major, a man by the name of Ivan Ristov, was not caught out on that event, but on another, whereupon he confessed to all his black market dealings with the Germans in the hope such openness might save him from a firing squad. It didn't."

"So Ristov looked the other way and Zeitz took the painting?" Ingrid said.

"Yes. Put it in a truck and drove away."

"I don't suppose your uncle mentions what kind of truck," Selby said.

"As a matter of fact, he does. He remembers because, in questioning Major Ristov, my uncle learned that Zeitz used a Russian military transport truck, a ZIS-5, with the phrase *Defend the City of Lenin* painted in large letters on its side. Uncle Konstantin found that highly amusing because of its irony."

"A ZIS, not an Opel?" Selby said.

"Correct. I know an abandoned Opel was found in Mittenwald when the colonel was captured, but my uncle is very clear about the make and model of the truck Zeitz used in his heist."

Ingrid asked, "Do you know if Major Ristov knew where Colonel Zeitz planned to take the painting?"

Votichenko shook his head. "Wearing a Russian uniform and using a Russian army vehicle, one must assume he would be obliged to stay within the boundaries of the Russian Zone."

Selby asked, "Anything in your uncle's diary about Colonel Zeitz's cousin, Anna Stahlinger?"

"Only that. She was his cousin. Oh, and that she was working for the Americans."

"He didn't try to question her?"

"He did, but was turned down. That, however, didn't distinguish her from anyone else. After the murder of Colonel Zeitz, if it was murder, the Americans tried to send my uncle and Comrade Greppov back to Berlin, saying they – the Americans – would allow no more questioning."

"So your uncle thinks Colonel Zeitz was murdered by Americans," Selby said.

"He didn't know, but he believed that to be the case. On the other hand, he claims even the doctors could not agree on suicide or murder."

Ingrid asked, "Did your uncle have any idea what became of Anna Stahlinger?"

"No. He returned to Berlin, then turned his mind to other matters." Votichenko held up a hand in a hold-on gesture. "If I may suggest something, I think your pursuit of the Stahlinger woman should become secondary to your looking for someone else. I'm surprised neither of you has asked about him."

"Who is that?" Selby said.

"Colonel Zeitz's aide, a man named Karl Vollmer. During the war they were inseparable. According to my uncle's research, Colonel Zeitz could not blow his nose or light a cigarette unless Herr Vollmer was present to hold the handkerchief or match. Yet, when Zeitz is captured, there is no sign of Vollmer. When my uncle asked the Americans about him he was told that Vollmer was dead, shot defending Berlin in the city's final days. My uncle did not believe that account."

"Why not?" Selby said.

"In my uncle's words, 'If you kill one Siamese twin, the other dies.' Besides, there is evidence Vollmer survived the fall of Berlin. Because Vollmer was present in Pushkin when Colonel Zeitz dismantled the Amber Room and took it in crates to Königsberg, my uncle decided to continue his search for Vollmer. It turns out Vollmer inherited a farm in Schleswig-Holstein, east of Kiel, and my father asked British permission to visit the farm. That part of Germany in late 1945 was part of the British Zone and the British turned down his request. But Uncle Konstantin arranged to have NKVD agents slip into the British Zone anyway and make cautious inquiries. The agents visited the farm and spoke to locals. The agents reported back that, although they did not find

Karl Vollmer, there was evidence at his farm that he, or someone, had been there recently. More importantly, several locals reported brief sightings of the man months after he allegedly died."

"So Vollmer never turned up?" Selby said.

"No. We cannot prove it but we suspect he joined the flow of SS members who found their way to Rome and then on to South America. Perhaps that is what became of Fräulein Stahlinger as well."

"That's possible," Selby allowed.

"In which case you must wonder whether she slipped off to Buenos Aires or Montevideo as a frightened Nazi or as an agent continuing to work for your father, hence pretending to be a frightened Nazi. Yes, my uncle was aware that she spent much of the war working for your father in Switzerland, which is why Uncle Konstantin was more interested in pursuing Herr Vollmer than Fräulein Stahlinger. Vollmer surely knew where Zeitz sent the Amber Room from Königsberg, whereas Zeitz's cousin probably did not."

"So this Karl Vollmer has, had, a farm in Schleswig-Holstein," Selby said.

"Yes. Near a village called Todendorf, on the Baltic. I'm not sure exactly where the farm is, but if you want to find it for yourselves, I'm sure someone local can help you. But before you consider that, there is another place you might wish to visit, another village on the Baltic called Ahrenshoop."

"I know the place. It's an artists' colony," Ingrid said.

"I was certain you were familiar with the place. The reason I suggest you go there is that Colonel Zeitz's father had friends there, my uncle learned. He also learned that, when Zeitz was a youth, his father took him for visits as part of their summer vacations. Uncle Konstantin himself went to the village, supposing it a likely place for Colonel Zeitz to visit. Plus, it is inside what was the Russian Zone of Occupation. Zeitz and Vollmer could easily take a Russian army truck there. And Uncle Konstantin wrote in his diary that he experienced what he judged to be a vast conspiracy of silence in Ahrenshoop."

Votichenko paused and shrugged. "I don't know what he expected. Of course, the Germans would hate any Russian back then, especially one who came asking questions about an SS officer. But --," Votichenko tapped his nose and looked at Ingrid, " – Konstantin Ivanovitch had a keen nose – just like Selby Parker and I eventually developed, for sensing the difference between silence based on ignorance and silence based on knowing a great deal. It is the difference between the look a man gives me that tells me *I know nothing* and the look that says *I know things you will never know.*

_____

Thursday
July 16, 1992
Berlin

"So how is YV enjoying his retirement?" Alec Marsden asked Selby as the two of them ate lunch at a bistro near the U.S. Legation. Selby had left Ingrid at the Galerie Nierendorf to attend to what she said was a minor, yet urgent, issue regarding a buyer from Brussels.

"Immensely," Selby said. "Ingrid and I stayed over an extra day, at YV's invitation and expense. He took us on an insider's tour of St. Petersburg and fed us as if he had every chef in the city at his disposal. The man is actually witty and charming. He delighted in showing off the city's treasures. And Ingrid, who had been there four or five times already, relished the opportunity to see things she had not been permitted to see before, especially at The Hermitage."

Alec snickered. "Who'd have thought Ol' Yevgeny was a charmer?"

"He also provided what may be some useful information." Selby repeated Votichenko's specifics gleaned from his uncle's diaries. "Will you pry open the lid again and see what more you can find out about Anna Stahlinger? See if Karl Vollmer's name pops out, too, will you?"

"Sure. This is even beginning to interest me, not that I give a shit about art. But missing persons vanishing with stolen goods are often the stuff of espionage, eh? Which spy stole what top-secret file and then disappeared into the ether?"

"Something like that," Selby allowed. "Check out the South American trails, via Rome and via Spain and Portugal. Somebody somewhere ought to have those files. Blow off the dust, if you can find them."

"When I find them," Alec corrected.

"By the way, YV had a question for me that I couldn't answer, so I said I'd ask you," Selby said.

"Ask."

"In what Yevgeny considers the CIA's ultimate achievement ever, he wants to know what the time frame was for the Company's recruiting Mikhail Gorbachev as its perfect and most successful mole."

"Gorby as a Company mole. That's funny as hell. Never thought about it. But I can see why he thinks that, now that I give it some thought. Do you suppose?"

"Who had either the balls or the brains to recruit him?" Selby said.

"Maybe he didn't need to be recruited," Marsden said, raising an eyebrow.

"So what do you think I ought to tell him?"

"Tell him Andrei Gromyko recruited him back in the '50s. That'll give him something to munch on for the rest of his retirement."

"We never grow up do we?" Selby said, "We're still just two gangs of schoolyard bullies swapping lies."

"Not to change the subject or anything, but I've got a question for you. And if you can't answer it, maybe Comrade Votichenko can."

"What's that?"

"After the sun goes down does Miss Sundstrum let her hair down? Take off those ridiculous glasses? Turn as steamy as a Swedish sauna?"

Selby chuckled. "You're going to have to ask Yevgeny."

"Because you don't know? Or won't tell?"

"A gentleman doesn't kiss and tell."

"Okay. I'll back off. But I'm still not sure why you're into this murder chase. I can't quite figure you for giving a damn. You don't even know any of the people involved."

Selby's look must have betrayed him.

Alec Marsden stared at him for several seconds, then said, "No. Come on. You can't believe your old man was mixed up in any of this sordidness."

"Can't I?"

"Look. I knew your dad. Not well, but I refuse to think he would involve himself in killing either Zeitz or Wynerson."

"Accomplice?"

"Jesus! So what are you out to prove? And don't give me any let-the-chips-fall-where-they-may horseshit."

"Why would I want to prove him guilty?" Selby said.

"I don't know. I spent my entire life hating my father. Even on the day he died I was still playing *gotcha*, always looking to put one more nail in his coffin, so to speak. He was a mean-spirited son-of-a-bitch. Everybody who knew him thought so. Yet, I spent my entire life with one eye looking for the next piece of validation to re-confirm that judgment, wanting to pile on proof so that the evidence bag would always outweigh the guilt I felt for loathing him."

"I never loathed my father," Selby said quietly. But the seeds of such an attitude may soon begin to sprout, he thought.

Saturday
July 18, 1992
Ahrenshoop
Mecklenburg-Pommerania

The door to the thatched-roof house opened slowly, revealing a woman with long white hair and sunken eyes in the middle of a gaunt, pasty face. She wore a checked plaid shirt and two sweaters, both unbuttoned. Her trousers were thick hiking knickers, her socks wool, her sheep-skin slippers came ankle-high.

"Thelda Eggert?" Selby asked.

"I might be. Who are you?"

Selby introduced himself and Ingrid, then said, "The man who runs the small library down by the Neues Kunsthaus sent us. He said his father had been friends with Werner Zeitz and a man named Oskar Lohnes; that you took care of Oskar for many years and might be able to provide us with some information regarding Werner Zeitz's son."

The woman stared back at Selby, unblinking and unmoving, for several moments, then said, "Come in."

Though the day was warm and sunny, a fire blazed in the fireplace. Selby and Ingrid both took offered seats and Thelda sat down after them, close to the fire. But as quickly as she sat she rose again. "I apologize. May I offer you tea?" When her guests declined she said, "If you'll excuse me, I will brew a pot for myself."

Looking around the small dark parlor, Selby imagined the witch's hut in the tale of Hansel & Gretel, only that hut lay deep in a forest and required following a trail of bread crumbs to find one's way out. Thelda's hut lay no more than two hundred yards from the sea, yet felt to Selby just as isolated as if it stood miles from anything or anyone. Sand dunes, covered with clumps of knee-high grass, shielded the hut from a view of the Baltic coastline, denied it line of sight to any other house in the village. Thelda Eggert lived alone in a crowd.

When she returned, teacup in hand, she sat again and said, "So you want to know about Rainer."

"Yes."

"But it's not really Rainer that interests you, is it? You are looking for the paintings."

Selby explained, "We are looking for the person who might have killed Colonel Zeitz and we are looking for the paintings he might have stolen."

"So. Someone killed him. I'm not surprised. How long ago?" Thelda said.

"August, 1945. Why aren't you surprised?"

"Back then people would kill you just to steal your boots. He had nice boots." Then she began to laugh. And laugh and laugh until she began to cry.

Ingrid started to speak, but Selby gently raised a hand to stop her. Ingrid pulled a handful of tissues form her purse and handed them to Thelda.

"Thank you," she said, dabbing at her eyes. Composing herself after sipping tea, she said, "Both paintings were special, too, of course. Those were why someone would kill him."

"He came here?" Ingrid asked.

"Oh, yes. Three times. The first time to arrange for help; the second to be helped, and the third time was to... I don't know. Just to say goodbye, I guess."

Ingrid said, "By both paintings you mean Franz Marc's *Tower of the Blue Horses* and Paul Klee's *Moon Over the City*, correct?"

"The Marc, yes. But the second painting was Raphael's *Portrait of a Young Man*."

Ingrid let out a "My God!" Then scooted her chair closer to Thelda. "Are you sure? It wasn't a Klee?"

Thelda turned quietly indignant. "I recognized your name, *Fräulein Professorin*, when Herr Parker introduced you. I understand you know a great deal about art, but so do I, having spent my entire life in this artists' colony and having known the artists who lived here and visited here. Rainer Zeitz had no painting by Paul Klee with him. He had the Marc and the Raphael. Both paintings were in this room and I was the one who removed them from their frames and wrapped them in waterproof material."

Ingrid looked at Selby. "The Raphael makes sense. The Nazi governor of Poland, Hans Frank, is believed to have stolen it from the Czartoryski collection in Kracow just before he fled Poland ahead of the Russians and returned to Germany. But, like the Marc, it vanished, never to be seen again. Frank, I'm sure, knew Zeitz, or at least knew of him. Maybe he gave the painting to Zeitz for safekeeping."

"Tell us why you waterproofed the paintings," Selby said to Thelda.

"They were going to take the paintings across the bay by boat," she said.

"Who are *they*?"

"Zeitz and his aide, Karl Vollmer."

"They had a boat?" Selby said.

Thelda laughed. "Yes. On his first visit Rainer asked me to find a boat for him. So I did. I stole a boat from the Gestapo and hid it at the edge of the Darß Forest, just north of here." She gestured northward.

"Where were they planning to go?"

"Originally we discussed Sweden, but finally Zeitz ruled that out – at least for a while. He and Vollmer were planning to go somewhere in Schleswig-Holstein, but he wouldn't tell me exactly where, although I overheard Vollmer mention having a brother living near Kiel."

"And they actually left here in the boat?"

"Yes. And made it safely, though not without much adventure. I know because some weeks later Rainer returned here – in a truck."

"How did he get here with the paintings?" Ingrid asked belatedly.

"In a Russian truck, which I disposed of after he left in the boat. The Russians themselves figured some of this out because a year or so after the war ended a pair of Russian Gestapo-types came here asking questions about Herr Zeitz. The Russians failed to mention that Rainer was already dead. What the Russians were chasing was their precious Amber Room. From us they got answers to nothing. Despite their threats, no one betrayed Herr Zeitz and the Russians finally went away."

"Anything else you can remember?" Selby said.

"Yes. Rainer was worried the Marc might be a forgery, but Oskar assured him it was not." Thelda smiled. "Oskar knew a great deal about forgeries."

"Having been an expert forger himself," Ingrid added.

"A good forgery requires more talent than most artists possess," Thelda said proudly.

"When Colonel Zeitz returned the last time was Karl Vollmer with him?" Selby said.

"No. He came alone, which was very odd because I knew Rainer did not especially like to drive."

"Did he mention Vollmer?"

"No. And I didn't ask."

37

Monday
July 20, 1992
Todendorf
Schleswig-Holstein

"What's wrong with this picture?" Selby asked Ingrid as they both stared at the skeleton lying on the floor of the hidden sauerkraut-fermenting crypt in the basement of the Vollmer farmhouse.

"Everything! It's awful," Ingrid whispered, as if perhaps she thought *Der Grauergeist* might be hovering nearby.

Selby focused his flashlight beam on the right sleeve of the skeleton's rotted jacket.

"There's no right hand," Ingrid gasped.

Selby reached forward and, with the butt of his flashlight, tapped the area where the radius and ulna bones should be, lying beneath the material.

"No forearm either. It's Karl Vollmer," Ingrid said and took hold of Selby's left arm.

"Likely so. Alas, poor Karl, we didn't know you."

"Stop making light. This is serious," Ingrid protested.

"I know it's serious. Sometimes a little black humor eases the tension."

"Not for me."

"Sorry." Selby shone his light around elsewhere. "Look. There's the screened vent to the outside. There's something behind the mesh." He duck-walked to the screen, Ingrid behind him, clutching his belt. "Looks like one of the other little critters you suggested. Whatever it was, it's claws are stuck in the screen. It was trying to get in."

"I recognize the skull type from studying animal anatomy for a charcoal-sketching class I once took. It's a cat," Ingrid said.

"A gray cat maybe. Look. Tufts of fur entangled in the mesh. Gray fur," Selby said.

"Maybe *Der Grauergeist* is, was, a cat," Ingrid suggested. "Then she saw something else that made her gasp. "Look!"

Selby turned to see her touching a back corner of one of the empty frames. He shined his light where she was brushing away dust with her gloved hand and read: Schloss.

"From the famous Schloss collection, many of which are still missing." Ingrid then briefly explained the nature and history Schloss Collection to Selby.

"So Colonel Zeitz was a very busy fellow," Selby said when Ingrid had finished.

"With a good eye for what was valuable," Ingrid said and began rubbing at the backs of other frames.

"Let's get out of this crypt," Selby said. I'm beginning to feel claustrophobic, not to mention dust-choked. We need to decide how we're going to handle this," he added, though he was already sure what he intended to do. And not do.

Once back in the main portion of the basement, Ingrid said, "How do we report a murder without getting ourselves in trouble for trespassing? Is that what you're thinking?"

"Not exactly. There will be no avoiding trouble if we report what we've seen."

"If? But --."

"No buts. German police are a humorless lot. Pious, officious prigs. We'll be swallowed by their bureaucracy."

"We can't just walk away," Ingrid said.

"No. First we replace the wall panels. Then we walk away."

They waited until they were seated in the restaurant of their Kiel hotel before discussing the possibilities regarding who had killed Karl Vollmer and had stolen Rainer Zeitz's cache of filched paintings. Ingrid had scarcely spoken a word since they left the Vollmer farm, spending most of the trip to Kiel glancing nervously out the sideview mirror in the expectation of a set of flashing lights from a car full of German *Polizei* suddenly appearing behind them.

To put her mind at ease as best he could Selby drove aimlessly through many of the narrow streets in Kiel's Altstadt for half an hour before finally ending up at the Kieler Bay Hotel on the west side of the long inlet that had made Kiel such an ideal port for Nazi U-boat flotillas. Even then Ingrid allowed that she half-expected a police reception committee to greet them at the hotel.

"Do you have any appetite?" Selby asked her when they were seated by a window with a view of the inlet.

"No, but I'd love a stiff drink. Make that two," she said. "And I'm almost sorry I don't smoke. Look at me." Palms down, she held out her trembling hands. "I'm not cut out for this spooky business. I don't see how you and Mister Votichenko could spend so many years doing all the things you did."

"Just a pair of fools who didn't know any better."

"I doubt that," Ingrid said, putting her hands back in her lap.

"As with any complicated dance, it's best to have a practiced partner," Selby said. Then, thinking back to David Fox in Prague, reminded himself that isn't always enough to prevent a pratfall.

"So who was our practiced partner today? Surely, I don't count."

"We had none today. So, yes, what we did was dicey. I'm sorry if I got you in deeper than you cared to go."

Ingrid said, "No one made me go over that fence, walk into that farmhouse. And I did end up learning a lot. We know a lot of excellent paintings that vanished during the war ended up stored in that basement vault. Finding that out was worth the risk."

"I'm glad you think so," Selby said as the waiter came and took their drink orders.

"So who was it?" Ingrid asked.

"Who killed Karl Vollmer and took the paintings?"

She nodded.

"Well, let's consider several possibilities. Obviously Rainer Zeitz is a prime candidate, if not *the* choice. He knew Karl, knew the farm, knew where the paintings were, we must assume, in order to offer a deal to Martin Wynerson. So if he shot Karl and decamped with the paintings and whatever else, where would he take them?"

Ingrid said, "Somewhere between Todendorf and Mitten-wald, a lot of territory."

"Yes. So let's consider the leading possibilities. First, Ahren-shoop. Rainer might well have taken the entire batch back to Thelda. He put a lot of trust in her on other matters. Two, Berlin. Possible, but unlikely, I think. Too dangerous. If he wanted them in Berlin, why take a boat across Mecklenburg Bay with two of the paintings, just to bring them back to Berlin?"

"That same reasoning rules out Ahrenshoop," Ingrid said.

"*Touché*. So maybe he took them south, say to Kochel. His father's chalet was searched, but then Konstantin Votichenko's men searched the Vollmer farmhouse and failed to find the vault. Or so Yevgeny says."

"Could he be lying? Or at least not have told us everything?" Ingrid said.

"I think he was misdirecting us about the Amber Room. I don't think those crates ever left Königsberg and the Russians know it. I think they dug out the castle and found the crates."

"Then why do they claim they still have no idea where the Amber Room is?"

"You have to know Russians. They still love to wallow in the self-pitying notion that the West has done them wrong. They act like minorities all over the world. They love the role of vic-tim and are constantly on the lookout for more evidence that they've been victimized. They're like Christians. Martyrdom becomes them. Absence of the Amber Room gives them one more opportunity to snivel. But Rainer Zeitz's paintings don't provide them a mud hole to wallow in. So Yevgeny had consider-ably less incentive to lie to us about the paintings."

"Except that, if his uncle's men did find them, the Russians would then have to explain why they failed to make that fact known and why they failed to try to return them to their rightful owners."

"There is that," Selby allowed. "Still, I'd like to think I have enough sense of Yevgeny Votichenko to be able to know when he's lying to me."

"Shall we go to Kochel and search the chalet for ourselves?" Ingrid said.

"It's a possibility. But perhaps, if it comes to that, I should go alone. You weren't exactly comfortable with our breaking into the farmhouse."

Ingrid grinned sheepishly. "Actually, I was thrilled with breaking in. It was the notion of getting caught that petrified me."

"Let's consider this question: Who else knew the paintings were at the farm? Besides Karl Vollmer, of course."

"You know, Herr Vollmer might have had too loose a tongue and someone he knew might have paid him a surprise visit," Ingrid said.

"True enough. Somebody sitting in Zum Alten Fritz could well be the culprit, except that the paintings are all still missing after nearly fifty years and somehow I can't imagine any of those grizzled old sots being able to keep his mouth shut for fifty minutes."

"There's that," Ingrid said, grinning. "Maybe one of them killed Vollmer, stole the paintings, then forgot what he did with them."

"Shall we return to the tavern and try jogging a few memories?" Selby said.

"With what?"

"Well, if the *in-vino-veritas* gambit fails we could always try beating it out of them."

Ingrid winced. "Stop it."

"Sorry," Selby said. "I think Wynerson is unlikely, but maybe he told someone else whatever Colonel Zeitz told him. The person he told then killed him and at some point went to Todendorf, killed Vollmer, and stolen the paintings."

"Wait. We are assuming whoever killed Karl Vollmer is the same person who took the paintings – and presumably at the same time, though not necessarily," Ingrid said.

The waiter delivered a bottle of wine and took their dinner orders.

"For now let's continue with that assumption – just to keep things simpler. A third suspect is Anna Stahlinger, who was allowed to visit her cousin in his cell. Colonel Zeitz could have told her."

"But maybe she knew all along. From what I've been reading and hearing, she might have had as many opportunities to steal works of art as the colonel," Ingrid said. "Maybe she and her cousin were both art thieves. And if that's the case, she may have feared her cousin had given away something that wasn't entirely his to give. In which case she killed Zeitz and Wynerson to protect her own interest," Ingrid speculated.

"And she killed Vollmer?" Selby said.

"Maybe. But Zeitz might have killed him before he went south, perhaps unwilling to trust his trusted aide with such a valuable stash."

"But Anna Stahlinger ends up with the cellar full of paintings."

"It's quite plausible, don't you think?" Ingrid said.

"Yes. But, for now, no more than plausible."

"So who else might fit the murderer/thief role?"

"David Fox, for one. And –."

"And. Say it."

"My father."

"No point in your dancing around the fact he may be involved. Isn't that possibility a driving force in your quest?" Ingrid said.

"It is."

"You know that Martin Wynerson could have told him the details of his conversation with Zeitz. For that matter, Anna could have told him. She worked for your father, too."

"Do you realize how difficult a time I'm having facing up to the possibility my father was a murderer, a thief, or both?"

"I do. Am I not in the same position with my grandparents? But in your case, perhaps your father was only an accomplice," Ingrid said.

"*Only.* Some comfort."

The first course arrived and both of them ate in silence for a while, savoring soup and fresh bread.

His soup bowl empty, Selby said, "Okay we've covered suspects. Let's think about the paintings. In conjunction with asking ourselves why they were stashed here – Todendorf, that is – ask yourself what you would do with them once you took them from the vault. Think like a thief in possession of many valuable paintings."

"I'd be so nervous, I'm not sure I would have the courage to move them," Ingrid said.

"Imagine a worse fear: leaving them where they are."

"I'd want the safest, easiest way I could think of."

"Which is?"

"In my case I'd take them home to Malmö and sit on them for a while. Maybe even a long while."

"And if you were Rainer? Take them home? To Munich? To Kochel am See?" Selby said.

"No. I don't think so. Too dangerous to move them that far."

"Sit on them?" Selby asked.

"That or –."

"Or what?"

"Or sit on them. Rather, have Karl Vollmer sit on them."

"Would you trust someone else to safeguard them?"

"Not anyone, but Zeitz and Vollmer were long-time friends. They'd been through the war together. Better to leave them here with a man you knew and trusted," Ingrid said.

"With such a valuable cache here, what would prompt Zeitz to leave it several hundred kilometers behind and head for Switzerland?"

"To arrange a transfer?"

"Good. With whom?"

Ingrid sighed. "He might have thought my grandparents were in Geneva."

"So you don't really think your grandparents were innocent of fencing art?"

"Maybe Zeitz was relying on rumors," she said defensively.

"Where do you suppose Zeitz acquired his Swiss Red Cross papers?"

"His cousin Anna?"

"Or maybe? Say it."

"My grandparents."

"Your grandparents were in Berlin. Zeitz passed through Berlin."

"That doesn't mean they met," Ingrid said.

"No. In fact, if they had, why would he continue south to look for them?"

"So either they didn't meet or he was looking for someone else."

"Who?" Selby asked.

"Cousin Anna?"

"She was in Munich."

"But did he know that?" Ingrid wondered.

The waiter returned. But, instead of bringing the next course, he handed Selby a cordless phone. "You are Herr Parker, *nicht wahr?*"

The caller was Alec Marsden. "Hope I caught you between courses, Selby."

"You mean you can't tell what I'm eating and when I raise my fork to my mouth?"

"Not quite. But I can tell you who you'd like to have for dessert."

Selby let that remark slide. "I trust you've found out something important."

"I'll let you decide that. All this relates to Anna Stahlinger. First, I find no evidence she used a Rome or Lisbon route to South America. In fact, there is no OSS record indicating she was helped to go anywhere. Second, we have no record that she was ever used as an agent in place, officially or unofficially. Her last pay period working for MFA&A was December, 1945."

Selby immediately recognized that date as coinciding with Franz Strumpf's story of Anna's telling him she would be unable to treat him to a promised Christmas-present ski lesson at Garmisch that same December.

Marsden continued. "Third, Anna did more for your father and the OSS than spy on Swiss bureaucrats in Bern, spy on the Red Cross in Geneva. She also made regular clandestine forays from Switzerland back into Germany. What her missions were is unclear. But between her and your father she used the code name *Grauergeist*."

Wednesday
July 22, 1992
Lund, Sweden

Before leaving Kiel Selby and Ingrid confirmed through local records and conversations that Karl Vollmer's brother, Klaus, had died in the summer of 1948, having become a loner alcoholic after losing his fishing boat to Allied bombing near the end of the war. After working as a hand on other boats, he tried to borrow against his third of the farm to buy his own boat, but was denied a loan. Karl refused to agree to sell the farm to help him and shortly afterward Klaus was found floating in the inlet near where, during the war, he had kept his boat moored. Fishermen who pulled his body from the water said he reeked of alcohol.

"That means Karl was still alive in early 1948. So Rainer Zeitz didn't kill him, obviously," Selby had told Ingrid.

"Yet Karl did sell the farm. Or someone sold it in his name," Ingrid pointed out.

Selby said, "We must consider the possibility now that the brother, Klaus, might have killed Karl. No doubt Karl's refusal to sell the farm pissed Klaus off. If he did kill Karl, he likely stole the paintings, too."

"Then someone killed Klaus?" Ingrid speculated.

"Someone who knew about the paintings and knew how to deal with them," Selby added. "Let's start with the folks who bought the Vollmer farm."

"You're thinking Klaus knew about the paintings but didn't move them?" Ingrid said.

"He was a fisherman with no boat. He needed help, he needed money," Selby said.

The name on the sale papers was Schlimmerfeld & Horne, which meant, whoever they were, they had owned the Vollmer farm from when Karl sold it in 1949 until the present. Or from when Klaus sold it, if he had killed Karl to get the farm. Before driving to Lübeck to return the rental car and catch a train for Malmö via Copenhagen Selby called Alec Marsden back to ask him to find out all he could about that company.

Now Ingrid had taken Selby to her faculty office at Lund University, where the Art History Department shared a building with the Department of Musicology. Her purpose was to re-examine her father's and grandparents old files of contacts, agreeing for the moment to allow the possibility that the Zeitz Cache, as they had come to call the missing sauerkraut-crypt paintings for short, had been brought to Sweden and that someone knowledgeable in Swedish art circles had served as an intermediary between whoever removed the paintings from Todendorf and wherever the paintings finally ended up.

Even as Ingrid was unlocking her file drawers Alec Marsden called Selby again, Selby's having given him Ingrid's office number. "First, the company," Marsden began. "Schlimmerfeld & Horne is a real estate division of Beckert, Braun and Speth. It's only property holding is the farm outside Todendorf. Beckert, Braun and Speth is a subdivision of Sieben Neckar Fabrik, headquartered in Stuttgart. And finally, Sieben Neckar is part of the Sachler Optical empire, owned by one Heinz Sachler. And guess who was one of Heinz's best boyhood buddies?"

"Otto von Bismark," Selby said mischievously.

"Bah! Sachler isn't nearly old enough. No. Hint: Sachler's been a life-long ski nut."

"*Fräulein Grauergeist*," Selby said in a whisper.

"Her name is even on the corporate papers for Schlimmerfeld & Horne. But the man I sent to poke around Stuttgart came up with something even better," Alec boasted. "Rather someone."

"Who?" Selby said.

"Anna Stahlinger herself."

Selby waited, but clearly Alec Marsden wanted to milk the moment for as much drama as he could squeeze from it. Finally Selby asked, "Where is she?"

"In a cemetery overlooking the Neckar River in a little gingerbread town outside Stuttgart. It's called Esslingen am Neckar. Heinz Sachler owns an estate nearby."

"Shit."

"Say what?"

"You heard me."

"End of your road?" Marsden said.

Selby sighed. "At least one of them. Any info how and when?"

"Her tombstone says February, 1949. Hospital records say she died of an aortic aneurysm. You know the Germans. They have medical records going back to the Teutonic Knights. Nobody is permitted to die until his or her paperwork is all *in Ordnung*."

"I understand, Alec. Thanks."

"Anyone else I can dig up for you?"

"Very funny. But, no. Not at the moment."

"Give me a call if you think of anything or anyone else."

Selby hung up the phone and saw Ingrid staring at him. "Anna is dead. Has been since '49."

"Oh."

"That about sums it up."

"You were pretty certain she was the one, weren't you?" Ingrid said.

"She ranked first, second, and third on my list."

"What now?"

Selby leaned back in Ingrid's desk chair and stared off blankly at Ingrid's bulletin board. "I don't know."

"Here are my files. Let's look at them somewhere else. If I stay here very long someone will want me to do something for him."

"Unlike me," Selby said.

"You I enjoy helping."

"Is that where your father fell?" Selby asked, pointing to a catwalk, as he and Ingrid sat in the vast storeroom of the small family gallery Ingrid still owned on Bergsgatan in central Malmö.

"Yes. He was working alone late at night when he slipped, tripped, stumbled, or something. No one has ever been sure whether he died instantly when he hit the floor or if he lay there half the night, still half alive."

"You were young when he fell."

"I was eleven years old."

"What's it like growing up without a father?" Selby said, although he had more than a passing acquaintance with the condition.

"My father became a more palpable presence dead than he ever was alive, despite, or maybe because of, our being close while he was alive. After his death I always felt as though he were hovering over my shoulder. Not in an intrusive way, mind you. Not looming. Just there. Watching out for me more than watching over me. Until I went to university I considered him in everything I did and thought."

"What would Daddy do?" Selby said.

"Yes. And you know what? Far more often than not I didn't know the answer. My father was a complex and often ambiguous man."

"I think I understand," Selby said. I understand all too well, he told himself.

"Even in college I went through phases when I feared I would never learn to think for myself."

"What of your mother?" Selby asked.

"I'm sorry to say I never cared much for my mother. She remarried. Too soon, I thought at the time. And too poorly. My step-father was a useless man, a fact we both recognized before she married him. They both died in an auto accident several years ago on the highway just this side of Halmstad. Hit head-on by a drunken minister whose car swerved into theirs."

"How sad," Selby said softly.

"So now I live by myself here in Malmö and hire a manager to run the gallery. We don't sell much but I have a good income from my inheritances, in addition to my university salary and consulting fees, such as from Galerie Nierendorf."

Selby gave her a look.

"Yes, part of my inheritance is from my grandparents but it's not ill-gotten wealth, not from paintings they allegedly fenced. They owned property around Stockholm. Anyway, I maintain the gallery here mostly out of respect for my father. His ghost still hangs about, but, I assure you, his is much more congenial than *Der Grauergeist*."

"And you had an uncle in Stockholm who worked with your grandparents," Selby said.

"Yes. Uncle Anders. He committed suicide in the early 50's, well before I was born. Father said Anders grew tired of Allied investigations accusing him of marketing stolen art work. His reputation and his business were ruined by the accusations, none of which anyone ever proved."

"Suppose the Zeitz Cache had been delivered to Sweden – some way, any way. What then? Who could deal with it? Successfully, that is." Selby watched Ingrid carefully, knowing he was treading on thin ice.

"That's just it! I can't believe anyone here would or even could manage to distribute such an incredible collection, whether singly or several at a time, without betraying himself."

"Plenty of Swiss succeeded," Selby reminded her.

"The Swiss! Bah! They hang on to their stolen goods, then think of themselves as doing the world a favor. Look at what they've done with Jews' assets placed in their trust."

"So you can think of no one?"

"No one," Ingrid said decisively.

38

Ingrid stood beside Selby as he stood staring fixedly at the head-stone bearing Anna Stahlinger's name. Finally she touched him lightly and said, "Something is bothering you, I can tell. Something beside the fact that she is dead."

Selby continued to stare for several moments before turning to Ingrid and whispering, "Harry Lime."

"I don't understand."

"Harry Lime. The sleazy black marketer in Graham Greene's *The Third Man*. Harry fakes his own death, funeral and all."

Ingrid said. "Yes. The movie. Orson Welles."

Selby nodded.

"You really think so?" Ingrid said.

"I'm willing to bet that if there's a body in this grave at all, it's the body of Frieda Strumpf," Selby said.

"What makes you think so?"

"Frieda made a scene about not getting to go wherever Anna was getting to go. Suddenly she's gone, too."

"They let her go with Anna. Surely you don't --."

"But they wouldn't let Franzie go with her."

A fearful look crossed Ingrid's face. "How cold."

"It's how I would have done it," Selby said.

"No!"

"If I were my father or David Fox or whoever arranged for Anna to disappear."

"I still don't understand why Anna had to go away," Ingrid said.

"Nor do I," Selby said. "Maybe she didn't have to. Maybe she just wanted to."

"And someone would kill Frieda Strumpf just to help Anna Stahlinger do what she wanted to do?"

"People have killed for less."

"But you're talking about your own father and one of his protégés."

"My father was in love with Anna. David Fox was tired of Frieda Strumpf."

"But --."

Selby removed a pair of fliers from his jacket pocket and handed them to Ingrid. "Tell me about this woman."

"Where did you get these?" Ingrid said.

"One is from your office bulletin board. The other one I found posted near the front door of your gallery. I didn't think you'd mind if I borrowed them."

"What do you want you want to know about her that isn't on the brochures?"

"Everything."

They began walking back toward their rental car at the edge of the cemetery.

"To begin, I've known Rosa Edelstein all my life. She's retired now, as you can read. Emeritus, art history, Levitz-Goldman University, near Boston. Her specialty is modern European art. She also branched out into Nordic art studies, which is why I saw her so much. She was a good friend of my father and she lectured regularly during summers at several Swedish universities. Now, even though she's retired, she still comes to speak. That's what the brochures are all about."

"She's German?" Selby asked.

"Yes, but she doesn't like to be thought of as German. She is a Jew who survived Dachau. She stills bears the prisoner identification number tattooed on her forearm."

Selby pointed to the photos of Rosa Edelstein on each brochure. "Do you know anything about these facial scars?"

"Dachau. Beatings. She doesn't like to talk about those days. They were horrible, worse than you can imagine."

"Few Holocaust survivors like to talk about *those days*," Selby added. "Overwhelming guilt at having survived when so many didn't is part of it."

"Why is it Rosa interests you?"

"Because I'm not sure she is who she says she is."

"An imposter? Hardly. As I say, I've known her all my life. What makes you think she's somebody else?"

"This particular scar." Selby tapped the left cheek of the woman whose photo appeared on the front of each brochure.

"Who do you think she is, if not Rosa Edelstein?"

"Anna Stahlinger."

Saturday
August 1, 1992
New York City

"You're lucky to find me here, Sel," Amanda Grady said as she ushered Ingrid and Selby into her Port Jefferson, Long Island apartment. "I'd planned to race in this weekend's regatta on the Sound, but my dog took ill and I decided to stay home and play nursemaid."

"Lucky me," Selby said as he looked at a bug-eyed King Charles spaniel lying on its side on a fancy doggie bed in a corner of the living room. No expert on dog health, Selby could readily tell the dog was out of sorts. "Tilly? Am I remembering correctly?"

The listless animal perked up slightly at the sound of her name.

"Yes. Tilly. Good memory. It's been a long while since you were last here. The vet says it's nothing to worry about. Don't know if that's good or bad."

"Why not?" Selby said.

"Remember the Scottish philosopher David Hume?" Amanda said.

"Vaguely."

"Once, when ill, Hume asked his family physician what the doctor thought was ailing him. The doctor told him it was nothing of any consequence. To which Hume is said to have replied, 'Too bad. I'd hate to think I died of something inconsequential.' And the very next day Hume was indeed dead."

Selby nodded appreciatively and watched Ingrid kneel to pet the ailing dog. "At least I don't have to chase you around the Sound. I get seasick easily."

"So you want me to run some aging projections on my software," Amanda said.

"Yes."

"Coffee, tea, brandy, a glass of wine?" Selby's hostess offered.

Ingrid shook her head.

"We just ate lunch, but thanks," Selby said and opened his briefcase.

At age forty-one Amanda Grady had already worked for NYPD, the FBI, and very briefly for the CIA, where Selby had met her when on the hunt for a suspected East German mole working in Bonn. Amanda had gone to college intending to become a rare bird, a female political cartoonist. So, to help with tuition while attending the University of Washington, she hired herself out part-time to the Seattle Police Department as a sketch artist. In her four years at UW Amanda's drawings had help identify criminals connected to more than three dozen cold-case files, including three murderers. Now she free-lanced for East Coast police departments, claiming that free-lance independence kept her from choking on the thick testosterone smog prevalent in most police and intelligence agencies. She also taught her trade part-time at nearby SUNY Stony Brook.

Knowing the photos from Ingrid's brochures would likely be inadequate for scanning and enlarging, Selby had called Ben Pettijohn and asked him to express mail, with a promise of reimbursement, his Anna photos to a post office box Selby had maintained over the years in Manhattan, the box's having proved useful for all those times Selby had CIA business in New York City, business often too rushed to allow him even a quick trip up the Hudson to Stuyvesant.

A second source of Anna photos came from the Olympic Museum at Olympic Park in Munich, where a helpful archivist named Hubert Weiss had cheerfully dug out musty photos from the '36 Winter Olympics at Garmisch, eventually finding some excellent facial shots of Anna Stahlinger and her ski-team companions, who called themselves *Die Draufgänger*, the Daredevils. One particularly fine shot, because it showed off Anna's scar, showed Anna hugging gold medalist Cristina Cranz.

On the Lufthansa flight from Munich to JFK Ingrid had compared the Anna/Rosa photos and insisted Rosa was not Anna. "The eyes, the hair. Totally different," she kept repeating to Selby.

"Hair, as you know, can easily be colored. And there are, were, plenty of blue-eyed European Jews." Selby knew, too, Ingrid was not ready to consider fully the implications of her father's close friendship with Rosa Edelstein. That he, of all people, might turn out to be Anna Stahlinger's covert art fencer was a notion Ingrid clearly was not yet ready to come to terms with.

Ingrid told Selby, "Regarding Jews. Anna is not Jewish, but Rosa is extraordinarily knowledgeable about European Jewish history. One time when I visited her at Levitz-Goldman she even took me to a lecture she gave at Brandeis' Tauber Institute for the Study of European Jewry. She talked in depth about Hitler's Madagascar Plan and the Wannsee Conference, things I'd never heard of."

"Her cousin was a member of the SS. She both worked for and spied on the Nazis. She lived in Munich part of the time. She would know these things without having to be a Jew."

"And why would she leave the scar? It's so obvious. If she's going to become a new person --."

"I don't know," Selby said. "Proof of Holocaust victimization, maybe. 'See what they did to me,' she can say."

Ingrid had sighed. "She once actually said that. How did you know?"

"I didn't. But why else would she not try to mask the scar?" Selby said.

To make the photo comparison fair Selby provided Amanda only pictures of young Anna, those provided by Ben Pettijohn and those from the Munich Olympic Park library.

"Keep in mind that what I do is as much art as science," Amanda reminded Selby and Ingrid.

"Is that what prosecutors tell jurors before your testify in court?" Selby said.

"You watch too much courtroom TV. My work isn't evidence, properly defined. Merely suggestive. Cops bring witnesses to me; prosecutors don't drag me into court."

"But your work sends people to jail," Selby said.

"It definitely helps. Sometimes."

Selby showed her the photos. "These were taken in 1936 and 1945." He pointed to Anna. "She was born in 1917, making her seventy-five years old now."

"You want to put an old lady in jail, Selby? Shame on you," Amanda said, as she led Selby and Ingrid to her bedroom office and set up her software on a desktop computer.

"She's likely involved in the murders of at least four people. No statute of limitations on murder. Plus, she's surely involved in the theft of dozens of major art works."

"But she looks to be the German equivalent of all-American. So innocent, so guileless," Amanda said.

"My father thought so, too."

Ingrid and Amanda both looked shocked, then looked away, embarrassed. Neither spoke.

Amanda first placed Ben Pettijohn's photo of Anna with David Fox, Frieda Strumpf, and Elliott Parker on her scanner, waited, then, with the photo loaded onto the computer, she began pecking and clicking. "I'm using the later photo first, because, even with it, we're talking forty-seven years between then and now. Obviously, the longer the time frame, the greater the changes, hence the greater likelihood of coming up off the mark. Sometimes way off."

Selby peeked at Ingrid, who gave him a smug, this-isn't-going-to-prove-you-are-right look. He shrugged. Maybe she's right, he thought.

"Does the scar stay?" Amanda asked.

"Yes."

As Selby watched, fascinated, he kept glancing at Ingrid, who was mesmerized by the transformations occurring on the screen.

"This is going to take a while," Amanda said. "It's not as slow as evolution, but it seems like it sometimes. Some folks who do this stuff can make greater leaps than I like to make."

"With equally good results?" Ingrid asked.

"Occasionally. A couple of guys in LA are really fast – and good. But most people end up having to backtrack, usually several times, and end up taking just as much, or more, time than I do. And frequently with less accuracy, when the sketch object is finally apprehended."

"Better help yourselves to coffee in the kitchen. I'm only into the 1960's. She wasn't a hippie, was she? That makes a difference. I did a woman once who went from looking like Ozzie and Harriet's daughter in 1955 to looking like Cher in 1965 and back to looking like Betty Crocker in 1975. I mean, that was the woman herself. I never came close to getting her right on my sketch pad."

"Did Ozzie and Harriet have a daughter?" Ingrid asked. "I don't remember one in the re-runs."

"No, but if they had, she would have looked like Annette Funicello."

Ingrid frowned. "How do you know that?"

Selby watched Amanda give Ingrid a strange look. "With this process I can work backwards, too. I started with Harriet Nelson and performed reverse aging on her until she was a teenager. She came out looking exactly like Little Miss Mouseketeer."

"Are you serious?" Ingrid said.

"I suggest you have Selby tell you the If-you-had-a-brother-would-he-like-borscht anecdote sometime," Amanda said.

Ingrid looked at Selby, who said, "Not now. And, yes, she's putting you on."

After that everyone remained silent and Selby fetched two coffees. Finally, several minutes later, Amanda declared, "There she is. Seventy-five years old, give or take a few minutes."

"You're sure?" Ingrid said.

"This is not mathematics, Miss Sundstrum. It's an inexact science," Amanda said icily.

Ingrid looked to Selby, who withdrew from his pocket the brochures bearing Rosa Edelstein's photos. Selby handed the fliers to Amanda.

"Not a ringer, but definitely a leaner," Amanda said.

Ingrid looked puzzled.

"Horseshoe talk for *very close, but not perfect*," Selby explained.

"Three, maybe four, clicks off," Amanda said and began altering the screen image slightly. Within seconds the screen resembled the brochure photos almost identically.

"Still have doubts?" Selby asked Ingrid.

"Yes. With this program you can turn a Rembrandt into a Picasso, I bet."

"I don't know about that, Miss Sundstrum. But with this program I've raised the dead and transformed a few pious church-goers into the closet-satans they turned out to be. It works very well and is getting better all the time. A good forensic anthropologist can take Selby's great grandfather's skull, scan it into a modification of this program, and come up with his likeness that you'd swear was cropped from a Civil War daguerreotype of the man."

"I need to think about this more. Thank you for your help," Ingrid said and walked back into the living room.

"Unhealthy skepticism," Amanda whispered to Selby when Ingrid was out of earshot.

"Comes from a lifetime partly filled with examining excellent forgeries," Selby said.

As their taxi crossed the Queensboro Bridge onto Manhattan Ingrid suddenly asked Selby, "Was Amanda ever your girlfriend?"

"No."

"She seems to know you well. It's obvious the two of you have spent time together."

"Professionally, yes." Selby looked at Ingrid, mildly astonished. "Besides, she's sixteen years younger than I am."

"You'd let that stop you?"

"Slow me down."

"You shouldn't let it."

"I don't want to be anybody's sugar daddy," Selby said and, in the rearview mirror, saw the driver's smirk.

"In Sweden sugar daddies are considered *chic*," Ingrid said.

"By whom?"

"Everybody."

"I'm not Swedish, as you've probably figured out by now," Selby muttered sourly.

"You could be."

"Honorary citizenship?"

Ingrid nodded, then giggled.

"Selvius Parkerson?" Selby said.

"*Ja*, sure," Ingrid said, laughing.

"Do you have a sugar daddy?" Selby asked.

"Not yet. I'm still looking," she said and gave Selby a sly look.

Alastair Stiles was just hanging up his telephone when Ingrid and Selby arrived his office in the James B. Duke House, on E. 78th Street in Upper Manhattan, home of NYU's Art History and Archeology Department. Seeing Ingrid and Selby, he rose from his chair and said, "Okay. We can go to dinner now. Robert will hand-deliver Rosa Edelstein's bio to us at the restaurant."

Selby became annoyed. "You're sending one of your grad students to the library to fetch the book tonight, then bring it to us?"

Stiles shrugged. "That's what graduate students are for."

Selby glared at his friend.

Stiles said, "Hey, when I was in grad school the Ol' Professor himself, my mentor Jack Overholt, explained to me that, in the Great Chain of Academic Being, graduate students are lower than whale shit and treated me accordingly. I try not to keep my students quite that low. On the other hand, I can't let them rise too far too quickly or they'll suffer the academic equivalent of nitrogen narcosis and oxygen toxicity. The bends."

Selby could only shake his head. Turning to Ingrid, he asked, "Is this how it is at your university?"

Ingrid looked sheepish, but nodded. "Students come, students go. Once in a while I remember one of their names."

"See?" Alastair said. "Now let's be going. I made reservations at Post House on 63rd Street. I'm in the mood for a good steak. And, as a bonus, Robert will get to see what possibilities come with tenure and promotion."

Ingrid looked at Selby, who explained, "Post House is outrageously expensive. But don't worry. Alastair's buying."

"I am?" Stiles said.

"You are," Selby assured him. "Possibilities. Tenure and promotion. Remember all that when the check is delivered."

Robert Stiles' student showed up just as salad was being served. The young man acted dutifully obsequious and very much impressed as he handed over Levitz-Goldman University's most recent faculty biography listings to Alastair.

"Good man, Robert. Now run along," Stiles said, dismissing the young man with scarcely a glance.

Why not *Good dog. Now back to your kennel*, Selby thought. Then sighed and recalled the 1960's radical, Alastair Stiles, champion of the classless society. Except in academia. Ah, how we grow up.

Selby's interest in the biography Alastair Stiles handed him lay in Rosa Edelstein's years before arriving at Levitz-Goldman. Her first university degree, according to what Levitz-Goldman published, had occurred at the Institute of Art History at Philipps-Universität in Marburg, Germany.

"I know it," Ingrid said when Selby asked her about it. "It houses one of the finest photographic archives of European art and architecture in the entire world."

"Rosa attended before the war. Degree granted in 1939. Same year Hitler invaded Poland. Anna Stahlinger would have been twenty-two," Selby said. "Rosa received her Ph.D. in 1953 from Georgetown University."

"Certainly respectable enough," Alastair said. "Still several highly regarded people in art history there." When Selby appeared to be distracted Stiles said, "If you're wondering why a Jew would enroll in a Catholic university, I can assure you that it happens all the time."

"Even a Holocaust Jew?"

Stiles shrugged.

"No, that isn't what bothers me," Selby said.

"What then?" Stiles asked.

Selby held up an index finger in a classic give-me-a-second gesture. "I'm remembering from my childhood. Priests wearing long cassocks attending parties at our house. Both distinctive. One was a huge man with a thick beard and a squeaky voice. The other was thin, wispy even. Slicked back hair and a voice so soft everyone always leaned in to hear what he was saying. And –."

Another hesitation.

"And what?" Ingrid aid impatiently.

"I can almost swear they were both from Georgetown."

Stiles said, "How old were you?"

"I must have been seven, eight, nine."

"Now why would you remember the name of a university at that age?"

"Keep in mind that Elliott was a professor. So I was used to hearing the names of universities. And, because I took an interest in geography, I liked to find out where these schools were that friends of my father taught at. In fact I remember asking one of the priests where his school was located and was confounded by his soft voice and his accent. When the priests had departed I recall having to ask my father to tell me where Georgetown was."

Stiles scoffed. "Yes, but your father had friends at every name university from Atlanta to Halifax."

Selby nodded. "I know, but the coincidence is worth looking into."

Ingrid said, "I don't suppose you remember the priests' names."

"No. Only their school's name stuck with me."

After the three of them had placed their food orders and Alastair had chosen a wine, he said, "Like Miss Sundstrum, I've known Rosa Edelstein for many years. And, while she's no charmer, I can't see her as an art-stealing Nazi either."

"Why not?" Selby asked.

"For the very same reason I can't picture Leonardo Da Vinci painting pornography or the Pope buggering nuns. Completely out of character." Turning to Ingrid, "Pardon my imagination."

The wine arrived and Alastair made a fuss of examining the cork and swirling the taste sample, holding it to the light, inhaling deeply, before downing it and nodding. After the waiter had poured and departed, Stiles toasted Selby and Ingrid. "Good luck to you both in finding the murderer and your paintings." Then, after glasses clinked and the wine sipped, he added, "But I do think you're pissing up the wrong rope, Selby."

"I may be. But think about this. Anymore, at least half the serial killers we read about in the newspapers – after they're caught – turn out to be described by their neighbors, living in the respectable, crime-free neighborhoods they live in, as kind, quiet chaps who walk their dogs, tip their hats to old ladies, buy Girl Scout cookies, never jaywalk, keep their yards mowed, and sit in the front pew at church every Sunday."

39

Monday
August 3, 1992
Fairfax, Virginia

As Selby crossed the Potomac into Virginia and turned west toward Dolly Madison Boulevard and Route 123, he pointed out CIA headquarters to Ingrid.

"Why did you follow your father into the CIA?" she asked.

Selby had not given that issue any thought in years and now found himself wondering why. "You'd have to fathom the workings of the American upper class to understand the answer to that," he said, hoping intimations of ambiguity and complexity might deflect her from pressing him. They didn't.

"So explain these workings to me."

Oh, Christ! Selby thought. To someone from as socialist a country as Sweden this is going to sound weird, I'm sure. "To begin with, there was the simple horror of having to look for a job. Having to ask some stranger for a job, actually. Luckily, I had a way to avoid that particular terror. You see, Ivy League men are expected to call their daddies and then Daddy calls his friends. And, sooner than later, Daddy's son has a job offer. Usually several."

"What's wrong with that?" Ingrid said.

"What's wrong is this. The sons, when they're in college, treat this as an entitlement. Born to privilege, too many of us become dependent on what we here in America call the good-old-boy system. All of us dread, and some of us are incapable of, finding useful careers on our own. We despise meritocracy, despise democracy. We are addicted to being members of a ruling class that sustains itself by taking care of its children, at least male children, often well into middle age."

Ingrid looked puzzled. "I thought Americans prided themselves on this business of raising themselves up by their own bootstraps."

Selby laughed. "Well, yes. Among my peers at Princeton every single one of them would claim to be a self-made man. Yet none of us are. We're all daddies' boys. As for the CIA, it's full of the upper class. Serving in it constitutes a form of public service, *noblesse oblige*. And it's self-serving. We help protect all the Western aristocracies from Bolshevism and socialist egalitarianism."

"Such as we have in Sweden," Ingrid said. "The latter, I mean."

"Indeed! The Swedish menace."

"Now you're mocking yourself," she said. "I think you really despise the system you just described."

"Oh, I mock the system, all right. But I might have perished without it. Using that system is the only survival skill I learned in college. And I think each generation of elders demands it be kept that way."

"Another part of *noblesse oblige*?" Ingrid said.

"Right. The duty of the rich is to look after the children of the rich, but only the children of the rich. That's why my maternal grandfather loathed Franklin Roosevelt so much. FDR not only permitted himself two seconds worth of thought toward the non-rich, but the content of those thoughts was to help such people. To men like my grandfather such behavior was worse than heresy. To them FDR became the Anti-Christ."

"Is this part of the 'Lodges speak only to Cabots and Cabots speak only to God' attitude I learned about when I visited Boston?" Ingrid said.

"Precisely."

"So do you seriously regret having followed your father's career steps?"

"Only because they were my father's. My working for the CIA was okay. Sometimes even satisfying. I always took pleasure in thwarting Yevgeny Votichenko, even when the stakes were small, which they usually were."

"What would you have done, had your father not worked for the CIA?"

"I studied philosophy and mathematics at Princeton, but I had little desire to try to make use of what I learned. Sorry, but I had no interest in art history."

"Why did your father give up art history for espionage?"

"Maybe he caught the bug from Anna Stahlinger," Selby said.

They had just visited the main library and the Art History Department at Georgetown University, where the kind administrative secretary had unearthed what she could regarding members of the department, both faculty and students, in 1953. In the library Selby and Ingrid managed to find a musty copy of Rosa Edelstein's dissertation, entitled *From Bauhaus to Doghouse: Molzahn, Muche, and Schlimmer.*

Ingrid explained to Selby, "All three men -- Johannes Molzahn, Georg Muche, and Oskar Schlimmer -- had paintings in the Degenerate Art Exhibition. They knew each other, having all worked at Walter Gropius' Bauhaus in the early 1930's. Nearly all their Degenerate Art Exhibition works are still missing. By the way, Oskar Schlimmer was from Stuttgart."

More interesting to Selby were the names of Rosa's dissertation co-advisors – Theodosius Rozkosz and Jean-Marcel Troquier. "I'm almost certain these were two of the men who came to dinner parties at our home on the Hudson."

The Art History Department secretary had told them, "Professor Rozkosz died in 1970, well before I began working here. I did find this photo of him that you may borrow if you like. In clearing files a couple years ago I came across several copies. It was taken back in 1968 and didn't mean as much then as it does now."

When Selby and Ingrid looked at the photo of Father Roskosz and another priest, the second man was highly recognizable. Selby turned the photo over and, in a neatly printed hand, read: *July, 1968. Market Square, Old City, Krakow. Father Theodosius Gregor Roskosz with Karol Jozef Cardinal Wojtyla.*

"The Pope," Ingrid said, reading over Selby's arm.

"Wojtyla had just gained his cardinal's hat the previous year," Selby said. "I remember, because the Russians were not pleased when that happened and their grumblings echoed all the way to Berlin. Catholicism in Poland was like an enduring skin rash to them and they were worried that the rash was about to spread. Back then Wojtya was considered a trouble-maker."

The secretary told them stomach cancer had claimed Jean-Marcel Troquier in 1977, shortly after he retired, and that he had returned to his home town in France a month before he died. "Our records show that the only member of the department from 1953 who is still alive is Dominic Orme. I can give him a call and see if he will speak with you. He lives across the river, in Fairfax."

She called and he said he would be pleased to receive Ingrid and Selby at his home, said that, of course, he remembered Rosa Edelstein and had last seen her at an exhibition in Philadelphia three years earlier.

Professor Orme's wife met them at the door and introduced herself as Germaine, telling them she and her husband had celebrated their fortieth wedding anniversary the previous week.

"Nineteen fifty-two," Selby said.

"Yes. Dom had just finished his first year as a member of the Georgetown faculty," she said as she led them into the parlor, where Professor Orme sat in a wheelchair.

"Sorry I can't rise to the occasion," he said as he shook hands. "My knees are wearing out on me. I'm not confined to this contraption, but I use it to get around here in the house. Saves wear and tear. Even so, Germaine's had to find herself a new jitterbug partner. Sit down, sit down."

Selby and Ingrid sat on a worn out sofa. The professor possessed only a few remaining tufts of gray hair, all unruly, a hawk nose lined with broken veins, and chin stubble from not having shaved for a day or three. Yet, Selby noted how clear and bright his eyes were, taking everything in.

"So you're the son of the late, great Elliott Parker. Sorry to learn he passed away. He was truly a fine art historian. Too bad he gave it up for that other, unsavory business, though I must allow that it's definitely more adventurous than art history. Don't you think so, Professor Sundstrum?"

"I find my work to be full of adventure, Doctor Orme. The fact that I'm here right now, for example," Ingrid said.

"Yes, all the missing stuff from the war. I understand. Me? My specialty is Greek and Roman art and architecture. Exciting, but usually in a much different way. Nobody has ever stolen the entire Coliseum or Parthenon."

Ingrid said quietly, "Not for lack of trying. What are all those goodies in the British Museum?"

"*Touché*, Miss Sundstrum."

Mrs. Orme brought coffee and cookies, while her husband rummaged through a boxful of old photos. "My husband should have been a professional photographer instead of an art history professor. You should see the boxes of albums in our basement and attic."

"Here they are. I knew they'd be here. My wife is the best damned photo-file cataloger in the world." He handed a pair of photos to Ingrid.

"How well did you know Rosa Edelstein in 1953?" Selby asked, as Ingrid showed him the photos.

"I was on her thesis committee. Theo and Jean-Marcel were her advisors, but I followed closely what she was researching."

Ingrid asked, "How did you land on her committee?"

"Rosa herself asked me. I warned her that I didn't know squat about the three Germans she planned to write about, but she said that didn't distinguish me from anybody else in the department. So I said I'd do it. Hers was a great story, after all. One of those pull-your-heartstring tales."

"What exactly do you know of her background before she arrived at Georgetown?" Selby said.

"Mostly what she told me. Told all of us. Hiding out in the Bavarian countryside through much of the war. Finally betrayed by neighbors and arrested. Survived the death camp. Nearly starved to death in Munich after the war. Then the Americans found out she knew a bit about art and hired her to help them track down some of the stuff the Nazis had stolen."

"Did she ever mention which Americans helped her?" Selby said.

Professor Orme gave Selby a strange look, then laughed and said, "Why, your father, of course. But then you knew that already. His helping Rosa Edelstein is part of what makes him such a legend."

"Was he instrumental in bringing Rosa to Georgetown?" Selby said.

"*Instrumental* understates the case. *Single-handed* is more like it."

"Why Georgetown?"

Another puzzled look. Then, "I must remind myself, you were but a lad back then. Before and during the war your father worked extensively with Theo Roskosz and Jean-Marcel Troquier, keeping track as best they could of what the Nazis were stealing and where they were taking the goods. So later Georgetown became a natural place to consider. And the two priests were more than glad to help your father out getting her enrolled and heading up her committee."

"Was there ever any explanation of why Rosa wanted to leave Germany?" Selby said.

"Naturally. Think about it. The war was over but there were plenty of Germans left standing. And here was this Jewess who was helping the Yanks undo what Germany had done. Keep in mind that surviving Germans still hated Jews just as much as the dead ones had. Plus, there was something or other about fearing the Russians because of this or that one of her cousins had done to piss the Russians off."

"The Amber Room," Ingrid said quietly.

"That's it! Now I remember. Her cousin was the SS officer who stole the Russians' beloved Amber Room. Dismantled it and shipped it back to the Fatherland. I gather that Elliott was concerned the Russians might try to kidnap Rosa and put her feet to the fire to see if she knew anything about where her cousin had stashed the amber."

"Your knees may be going fuzzy but your mind is still clear, Professor Orme. You've been a great help."

"Thank you, but I'm still not clear about the reason for your interest in Rosa and all this coming-to-Georgetown business," the old man said.

Selby felt sorry he could not be more candid with the man. "We're reassured to know my father was behind Professor Edelstein's arrival in the U.S. We were afraid someone else might have brought her here, using her as a diversion to distract from the movement of stolen art works," Selby said, embarrassed at telling such a cheeky lie.

Dominic Orme appeared dubious. "Who would attempt a maneuver like that?"

"We're not sure, which is why we are making inquiries," Ingrid said, compounding the lie. "The Catholic Church, Odessa --."

"Maybe even the CIA? Or what was it they called themselves back then?" Orme interrupted.

"The OSS," Selby said.

"Sure. Why not the OSS? They hustled von Braun and his rocket-builders here, didn't they?" Orme said.

"Yes," Selby said.

"My God! Do you realize what the implications are for your father in that line of thinking?"

"I'm afraid I do," Selby said.

"Well, let me assure you that Elliott Parker's only intent was to look out for Rosa Edelstein's best interests. Nothing more."

"Thank you, Professor Orme. I appreciate your conviction on that point," Selby said. If only you knew, Selby thought. If only I dared tell you.

On the drive back to Union Station Selby asked Ingrid, "Tell me what thoughts you are having about your own father's role in all of this."

"Keep in mind that my father only knew this woman as Rosa Edelstein," she said. Then, "Damn it! I still can't bring myself to believe Rosa is really Anna Stahlinger. Oh, I know, I know. You've made me begin to doubt. But maybe, too, there really was a death-camp survivor named Rosa Edelstein and she is someone your father took pity on and helped."

Selby said, "I already have Alec Marsden looking into that, as well as checking enrollment records at Philipps-Universität, if they still exist, to see if either an Anna Stahlinger or Rosa Edelstein was ever enrolled there."

"What if they both were?"

"I won't bore you with how often German institutions have engaged in fraud and forgery at the request of American governmental agencies. I also have Alec looking into Dachau records, but I'm certain the name Rosa Edelstein will turn up."

Ingrid said, "All I know is my own father also befriended Rosa Edelstein, but I am as sure as I am sure of anything that he would not have been a friend of Anna Stahlinger."

"Tell me more about him," Selby said as they sat in traffic nearing the Potomac.

"From as far back as I can remember Papa tried to turn me into an artist. I would sit on his lap and watch him draw simple lines on paper to demonstrate perspective. He would hold a pallet and let me mix colors and dab them on pieces of blank canvas with a short-handled brush I could maneuver. For outings we sometimes crossed the Skaggerak to the Danish artists' colony at Skagen, where we would walk the streets and beach and watch artists at work, painting seascapes or tourists' portraits. I had no talent and that fact showed up early on. Yet his interest in my art education never waned. He taught me not only about paintings but about painters. I know Yeats asks how we can distinguish the dancer from the dance, but I learned from my father how to sort artists from their art. Henri de Toulouse-Lautrec was my favorite example. Papa's too, I think. A cripple whose works were full of the life and color of the cabaret. Picasso was another. The opposite. A vile man whose brush touched canvas with such delicacy one might think the stroke had been made by a passing hummingbird."

Ingrid then sat quietly, seemingly lost in memories.

Reluctantly, Selby broke her reverie. "Are you serious then that you still are not convinced Rosa is Anna?"

"No. She may be. But Rosa would know better than to have tried to use my father to further her schemes. Her broker of stolen goods has to be somebody else. I suspect she trusted no one enough and sold them off herself, assuming she sold them. For all we know she simply moved them to another hiding spot."

"Why would she do that?" Selby said.

"We know the Russians visited the farmhouse. She, or someone, killed Karl Vollmer. Maybe Herr Vollmer told her to move the paintings. Perhaps he became frightened at the thought of having them found on his property."

"I think the only thing to do now is to confront her with what we know," Selby said, as they arrived at the car-rental agency near Union Station.

Thursday
August 6, 1992
Stuyvesant, New York

From Washington they had taken trains back to New York City, then on to Stuyvesant, where Selby retrieved one of his cars, a Chrysler convertible. From his parents' estate they drove the next day to Needham, Massachusetts, home to Levitz-Goldman University.

The Art History Department secretary there turned out not to be as accommodating as her counterpart at Georgetown. Faculty addresses were not given out. Period. Rules were rules. As they departed the building a voice called to them. They turned and a young woman, panting from running, approached them.

"Hi! I'm Shiela Gordon. I work part-time in the office you just came from and I overheard your conversation with Miss Officious. I know where Professor Edelstein lives and would gladly give you directions, except --."

"Except --" Selby repeated.

"She's not home this time of year."

"Do you know where we might find her?" Ingrid said.

"Sort of. Just before she retired about five years ago she bought a lakeside house in the Adirondacks. She said she intended to spend part of her summers and all of her autumns there," the young woman said.

"Do you know the name of the town? The name of the lake?" Selby said.

"I'm pretty sure she said the house was on Upper Saranac Lake."

And now, back in Stuyvesant, Selby sat in his father's chair in the small dimly lit study where his father had written so many of his brilliant academic papers and stared at the bill of sale for the long-time family retreat at Lake Saranac. The buyer's name read: Rosa Edelstein. It was dated six years earlier.

Selby remembered turning down his father's offer to deed the house over to Selby, Elliott explaining that he himself was no longer healthy enough to make the four-hour drive. Selby also remembered a few weeks later when Elliott informed him he had sold the lake house to 'a woman I know'.

Elliott must have savored the irony of selling the place to Rosa/Anna, knowing as he did by then – Katherine was dead and he had found Martin Wynerson's letters to her – that his wife and Martin had spent many a day and night at that house during his overseas absence.

"Still have doubts?" Selby asked Ingrid after showing her the sale forms.

"Yes."

"I'm going to see her. Don't feel obliged to come with me."

"Don't be ridiculous. I'm coming, too."

40

Friday
August 7, 1992
Lake Saranac, New York

His trans-Atlantic phone call to Alec Marsden cemented Selby's conviction that Anna Stahlinger was now Rosa Edelstein. The news from Alec even managed to weaken Ingrid's disbelief. Selby was now eager to listen to Rosa Edelstein's explanation when he confronted her with what was turning out to be one of the few missteps she had made along her lengthy trail of murder, theft, and treachery. Or, as Selby mulled over the amateur mistake on the drive from Stuyvesant, perhaps Elliott had committed the blunder. After all, back then the make-up of the OSS, unlike British intelligence and counter-intelligence groups, consisted almost entirely of volunteers brimming with enthusiasm but short on training in the subtleties of deception. Selby mused that both Anna and Elliott could have learned much from studying the British Double-Cross Committee's masterful ruse that came to be know as The Man Who Never Was. Successful scams require attention to fine details.

"Such lovely country," Ingrid repeated again, as Selby drove through the village of Lake Placid. "The 1980 Winter Olympics were held here, weren't they?"

"As well as the 1932 winter games," Selby said.

"Anna Stahlinger skied at Garmisch in 1936, yes?"

"Correct. She's a bit old to want to take up skiing again. Maybe just proximity to the slopes brings back good memories for her. Another half hour and we'll be there."

"In Sweden many people in their eighties cross-country ski. As for good memories, isn't Garmisch where Anna got her nasty scar?" Ingrid said.

"I thought it was from getting beaten by guards at Dachau," Selby teased.

"Okay. Rosa is Anna. But --."

"But what?"

"Nothing."

As they approached the chalet Selby stopped the car and pointed to it.

"You used to own that big place?" Ingrid said.

"My mother inherited it." Pointing again, this time to a late-model, red Mercedes 190 in the chalet's driveway, Selby said, "Being a Dachau survivor obviously hasn't prevented Rosa from appreciating excellent German automotive engineering."

"Maybe it doesn't belong to her," Ingrid said.

"Let's go find out."

Selby's repeated doorbell ringing failed to yield a result. When Ingrid gave him a questioning look he said, "No. I'm not going to pick the lock like I did in Todendorf."

"Good. I'd be embarrassed, if she found out," Ingrid said.

Just then a tall, elderly woman, wearing granny glasses, blue jeans, a red flannel shirt, and a Boston Red Sox cap pulled low on her forehead, peered cautiously from a side of the house. Beneath the cap hung long gray hair the color of tarnished silver. She held pruning shears in one gloved hand, a fistful of shrub branches in the other.

"Yes? What can I –." Then sudden recognition. "Ingrid! Ingrid Sundstrum! What a marvelous surprise!" She dropped the shears and clippings and raised both arms in a welcoming gesture.

"Rosa, you're looking well. How are you?" Ingrid said as she strode to embrace the elder woman.

Hugs and kisses exchanged, the old woman squinted at Selby and said to Ingrid, "Introduce me to your handsome friend."

Ingrid beckoned Selby. "Rosa Edelstein, this is Selby Parker, son of your old and dear friend, Elliott Parker."

Rosa Edelstein stepped forward and shook Selby's hand. Then she stepped back, cocked her head at angle, and finally nodded. "Indeed. Your resemblance to your father is clear." Turning briefly to Ingrid, Rosa nodded. "Did you know Elliott?"

Ingrid shook her head. "I've only seen photographs."

Rosa said to Ingrid, "Tell me what brings you here. And why didn't you let me know you were coming to the States? I gladly would have made plans; dropped everything to accommodate you. You know I would have."

Ingrid gave a sheepish shrug and explained what she and Selby had rehearsed. "Selby invited me to look at his late father's art history papers from before World War II to see if they might be worth donating to a university library. His friend Alastair Stiles recommended me to Selby."

Rosa smiled enigmatically. To Ingrid, "Congratulations!" To Selby, "I was saddened by the death of your father. I considered him a great man. And I apologize for not making it to his funeral. I didn't learn he had died until it was too late for me to go."

Selby said, "The service was small and limited to family members, but thank you for your good intentions," Selby forced himself to say, while thinking: Not so much as a sympathy card.

Rosa said to Selby, "Alastair himself turned you down?"

"Too busy. Too close to me. He thought he might not be capable of an impartial, professional opinion."

"Sorry I didn't know. I would have gladly volunteered," Rosa said. "I don't mean to take anything away from you, Ingrid. In fact, now that I think of it, I may not have been capable of an unbiased assessment either."

Selby thought, I'm sure you'd love to rummage through Dad's papers to see if you can discover any mention about your past life and identity.

"So you came all the way from Sweden. How good of you. Did you know anything about Professor Parker before his son contacted you?" Rosa said.

"Oh, yes. I have been doing considerable work at Galerie Nierendorf in Berlin recently. While he was still at Harvard in the 1930's Professor Parker was well-known to the Nierendorf brothers. A friend and advisor even to Karl Nierendorf, I believe."

Rosa removed her baseball cap and mopped her forehead. "Come with me. Such a thoughtless hostess I am. I was just doing some gardening in the flower beds around my deck. Let me make some iced tea and lemonade. We can sit in the shade and talk more. I bet Mister Parker can even find his own way. I'm sure he told you this grand chalet used to belong to his father."

Ingrid said, "Yes, he told me about it. How his mother's father built it in the 1920's, when he was a prominent banker in Albany."

The chalet had been built on a slope that descended to the lake. Facing the lake at the rear of the house were two decks, an upper and a lower. Rosa Edelstein led Ingrid and Selby up the broad wooden stairway to the upper deck, behind which was the kitchen. Both Ingrid and Selby followed Rosa through the open sliding-glass door into the immense kitchen where Selby remembered watching his mother and her cook, Mrs. Kramer, prepare some of the finest summer food fare Selby could ever recall.

Selby carried a pitcher of iced tea back to the deck and they sat down at a circular table with an umbrella shade. Noting Rosa had carried out a large handbag and placed it at the foot of her chair, Selby positioned himself on Rosa's right, next to her bag, needing no reminders of how cold and brutal this woman had been so often in the past.

"Has much changed around the lake since you were a boy, Mister Parker?" Rosa asked.

Looking out onto the lake, where colorful canoes and small sailboats skimmed gracefully across the chill blue water, Selby said, "Only the generations have changed. I imagine most ownership has stayed within the families who first built here."

Rosa nodded. "I am definitely treated as an outsider. You are right. Most of the occupants around here represent very old money."

"If you want to see old money, lots of old money," Ingrid said, "you should see where Selby lives."

Rosa said to Selby, "Have you kept the home at Stuyvesant?" Selby nodded.

To Ingrid Rosa said, "I've seen it."

Enough pleasantries, Selby decided. "The main reason we're here, Professor Edelstein, is because we are looking for someone and are hoping you can help us find her."

Rosa gave Selby a wary look. "Who might I know that you would be looking for? I'm hardly a social butterfly."

"But you travel some. You've gone to Sweden often to lecture," Selby reminded her.

"Who is it you are looking for?"

Selby paused to sip his tea, then said, "Her name is Anna Stahlinger."

Watching the woman carefully, Selby thought: Oh, she's good. Ice in her veins. Not a hint of self-betrayal.

"Anna Stahlinger?" Rosa repeated slowly.

"Yes."

"I'm afraid I know no one by that name. What led you to suppose I might know this person? Who is she anyway?"

"Coincidentally, she attended the Institute of Art History in Marburg at the very same time you were enrolled there. She had an uncle, Gunther Zeitz, who taught in the math department at Tübingen University, where – again coincidentally – you list your father as having taught. Mathematics also, right?"

Rosa stared at him blankly.

"However, the math professor at Tubingen is listed as Herr Professor Doktor Artur Edelmann, not Edelstein. And the address you gave for him happens to be the address where Gunther Zeitz lived."

"Somebody has been manipulating records at Philipps-Universität," Rosa said.

"I agree completely," Selby said. "And who do you suppose did the manipulating?"

"I have no idea. Obviously somebody trying to discredit me," Rosa said, an edge to her voice.

"Now who would want to discredit you? And why?"

"I don't know who. But clearly someone wants to tie me in some way to this Anna person you say you are looking for. Who is she? What has she done?"

"Anna Stahlinger is a murderer and a thief," Selby said. "She has killed several people; stolen many important paintings."

"I still do not understand why you think I know this woman."

"You would be hard-pressed not to know her, given that the two of you have been so intimately acquainted for the past forty-seven years," Selby said, softly and evenly.

Rosa turned to Ingrid. "Is he mad? Do you believe any of what he is saying?"

Ingrid leaned forward. "I didn't believe him for a very long time, but now I am beginning to."

"What is there to believe?" Rosa said.

"That you are Anna Stahlinger," Ingrid said, leaning even closer to Rosa.

"Preposterous! This is insane. You come to my house and accuse me of being someone I'm not. Worse, accuse me of being a murderer. Get out! Now! Leave me or I will call the police."

Selby slid his chair closer. "We found Karl Vollmer and the crypt full of empty frames. We traced ownership of the Vollmer farm to you and Heinz Sachler. We're prepared to dig up the coffin at Esslingen and run tests on the corpse, assuming there is one. After talking to Franz Strumpf I'm assuming we'll unearth his Aunt Frieda. And we now know you used Lief Sundstrum as your middleman in selling off the paintings."

Ingrid visibly flinched at that bluff and Rosa said to her, "You can't believe that. Lies! All lies! Get out, I say. Get out!"

Selby remained seated. "You are calling my father a liar?"

"Yes! Yes! None of this is true. If he says so, he's a liar."

"Is David Fox a liar, too?" Selby asked.

"Fox? Who is David Fox?"

"You can't have forgotten David Fox. You know who he is. His testimony alone will be enough to hang you." How many more bluffs is this going to take, Selby wondered nervously. "You made a mistake not killing David, too. And I'm surprised that, once you arrived safely in America, you didn't find a way for my father to suffer a fatal accident. What were another couple of lives along the road to protecting yourself and your stolen art collection? Instead, you messed up. Clumsy amateurism has come back to unmask you. The screw-up with the records at Marburg was totally unprofessional. Sloppy. Oh so sloppy. While inventing yourself at Marburg, you should have eradicated all of the real Anna's records. You should never have trusted your memory about Professor Artur Edelmann's name; never have used your uncle's address."

Selby continued, using the information given him by Alec Marsden during the previous day's phone call. "You couldn't get into the graduate art history program at Georgetown without having the equivalent of an American undergraduate degree. And the real Rosa Edelstein from Dachau never went to a university. She worked in her father's bookstore in Munich. In fact, the reason she was sent to Dachau, rather than straight to Auschwitz, was because the Gestapo suspected her of using the bookstore as a message drop-off point for underground anti-Nazi dissidents scattered throughout Munich and Bavaria. The Gestapo believed both that she could be broken and that, even away from the bookstore, she remained a contact and would serve as honey to draw the important radicals they were seeking."

"There was another Rosa Edelstein in Dachau with me. A plant. A Nazi pretending to be a Jewish conduit for communications between enemies of the Reich. She was not convincing and none of us accepted her bookstore tale. Apparently those who rescued us did."

Selby said, "Your facial scar betrays you, Anna. It's become infamous. Everyone who compares the scar on Rosa Edelstein's left cheek with the scar on Anna Stahlinger swears they are identical."

Rosa scoffed. "A scar's a scar."

"No, no," Selby insisted. "Yours has a great deal of character. You ohould have tried to maok it or at least modify it. Why didn't you? Pride? Earned in sports combat as a member of *Die Draufgänger* at Garmisch? You failed to win a medal, but you came away with something, a trophy of sorts. Proof you were a fierce competitor."

From Rosa an adamant "No!" She touched the scar. "This is my reward for refusing to betray my comrades to the SS. It is proof I am a survivor."

"You are a survivor for sure."

Rosa gave Selby a fierce look. "Tell me why you have tracked me down and cast these hideous accusations at me? Your father would be so ashamed of you. Why? What I have done to you?"

"It's what you did to my father. Used him; corrupted him. Poisoned his soul as much as you poisoned your cousin's body."

"I did neither of those things."

Selby ignored her. "And it's what you did to Martin Wynerson. Then afterwards your snake-bite charm paralyzed Elliott's conscience to the point he could not face the truth of who and what you were. A monster. Martin's sister pleaded with my father for more than forty years to tell her the truth about her brother's death and he refused even to acknowledge her pleas. So now I have come to do what he couldn't bring himself to do: expose you."

"You discredit your father unfairly. None of your accusations are true," Rosa said. "None of them!" she screamed.

"When the state police exhume the corpse in Anna Stahlinger's grave in Esslingen whom will they find?" Selby said.

"I repeat: I have no knowledge of this woman. Out of respect for your father I will not phone the police if both of you leave immediately. Ingrid, I don't know how you succumbed to the hallucinations of this madman, but I pity you. Your father, too, was a decent, honorable man. He, too, would be ashamed of you," Rosa said.

Ingrid straightened herself. "Did you kill my father, too? Use him then kill him? Tell me, Anna Stahlinger."

"Stop it. Do not dishonor your father," Rosa said.

"Did you?"

"I need a cigarette," Rosa said and reached for her purse.

Selby grabbed her wrist and squeezed hard. "You don't smoke. You never have. You're an Olympic athlete. Remember?" With his free hand he unzipped her purse and removed a short-barrel .38. "No more killing," he said quietly. "No more."

"Let go of me," she said. "I carry that to protect myself."

"I'm sure," Selby said. "Protect yourself from people who might expose you as Anna Stahlinger."

"I am Rosa Edelstein."

"But you were Anna Stahlinger."

"No!"

Selby spoke softly. "Let go, Anna. Let go the awful burden of wearing a heavy mask. The play has gone on too long. All the pretending, all the clever deceptions. So long, so tiring, I'm sure. But the curtain's come down, Anna. Time to shed the mask, shed the costume."

Suddenly Rosa lunged for the gun in Selby's hand. When he held it away from her she went for his throat with both hands. Ingrid screamed, but Selby quickly broke her grip and sent her reeling backward with a stiff-arm shove. Falling over her chair, Anna crashed to the deck, landing on her back. Stunned, she lay quietly for a moment, then rolled over, buried her face in her hands and began to sob. Ingrid rose from her chair then knelt beside Anna, but Selby waved her off.

"Let her be for a moment," he said. "She's not hurt." He emptied the .38, putting the gun in one pocket, the shells in another.

Anna continued to cry and Selby gestured for Ingrid to sit down and say nothing. Selby sipped tea and waited for the woman's crying to subside. Ingrid fidgeted, then began looking around to see if any neighbors might have witnessed the scene. Then she pulled Anna's chair upright.

Before long Anna's sobbing and heavy breathing slowed. When Anna finally raised herself to one knee Selby knelt and helped her into her chair. He gestured for Ingrid to refill Anna's glass with tea, which she did, sliding it across the table toward her.

Anna drank, then said, in a weak, hoarse voice, "I'm glad… in a way, I guess. Glad it's finally over. You're right. It's been a hellish burden."

"I'm sure. But spare us self-pity. You've left too many bodies floating in your wake to deserve even a tablespoon of sympathy."

"What will happen to me now?"

"I have no idea," Selby said. "We'll turn you over to federal authorities and let them decide which gallows to hang you from."

Anna's eyes widened and her teeth clenched.

"Before we go, I want answers," Ingrid said harshly. "I want to know about my family. Want to know if they helped you in your rotten schemes."

Anna began to laugh. Then said, "Of course they did. All of them. Your grandparents were supposed to be the conduit for the paintings Cousin Rainer stashed in the farm basement. They provided his fake Red Cross papers. Then when they died – and when Rainer was gone – I met with your uncle, Anders." She threw her head back and laughed. "What a twit! I knew he would crumble at the first pressure he felt. Actually, he held out for longer than I imagined. But the Allies kept up the pressure on him. So eventually he had to go."

"You killed Anders?"

"I couldn't just walk away from him. He knew the plan but was going to be too ineffectual to carry it out. I could see that. He had no patience, no backbone to wait the Allies out. Yes, I killed him. What else was I to do?"

"My God!" Ingrid said.

"Your father turned out to be far better suited to my needs. Brilliant, in fact. He deserves an award for being the world's best art fencer."

"No!"

"Oh, yes. He was far better than I expected. Together we earned fortunes. Of course, once the paintings, sculptures, manuscripts, and music scores had all been sold off, our business concluded, I didn't dare trust him after that." Looking at Selby, she said, "Would you?"

"So you killed my father?" Ingrid screamed.

Anna shrugged. "It was nothing personal. I liked your father. Liked him very much. But I had to protect myself. Don't you see?"

"And my father?" Selby said. "Did you try to kill him?"

Anna looked astonished. "Elliott? Are you crazy? How could I even contemplate doing such a horrible thing to a man who helped me more than anyone else in my life? Even more than my parents. Besides, he was in love with me. One doesn't kill someone who is in love with you."

"That didn't stop you from killing your cousin Rainer," Selby pointed out. 'You say Elliott helped you. What all did he do to help you?"

"Anything I asked."

"Did he help you kill your cousin? Help you kill Martin Wynerson?"

"I didn't need help killing either of them, although Elliott had reasons, good and bad, for wishing Martin dead."

So there it was. "What reasons?"

"He knew all about Martin's affair with your mother."

"Who told him?"

"David Fox."

Selby closed his eyes briefly and nodded.

"Elliott was also afraid Martin would discover he had borrowed some of Martin's thinking. Published it as his own."

"My father told you this?"

"I read your father's works. I discovered it for myself."

"And cheerfully pointed his thefts out to him, I'm sure," Selby said.

"It helped keep him under my thumb, as they saying goes."

"I'm surprised he didn't try to kill you."

Anna appeared shocked at such a notion. "He loved me too much to try that."

"Did he help you kill Frieda Strumpf?"

Anna grinned. "No. David Fox helped me kill Frieda. He was glad to be of help killing that tiresome woman."

"Is she the one buried at Esslingen?" Selby asked.

A hearty laugh. "There are two bodies in that grave. Yes, one is Frieda Strumpf."

"And the other?" Selby said.

"Rosa Edelstein."

"Why didn't you kill David Fox? You seem to have been eager to clear up all your loose ends."

"Because Fox anticipated my wanting to kill him. Clever bastard. Instead of trying to kill me first, he decided to blackmail me with threats of exposing me. He said he had hidden evidence of my killing Cousin Rainer and Martin Wynerson, our joint killing of Frieda and Rosa. He said if he went down, I would go down with him." She paused, seeming to be lost in thought. Then she said, "I'm still paying David Fox, you know." Another pause, before spitting out a loud and bitter, "Still!"

"Why did you kill Karl Vollmer?"

"Self-preservation. Just like all the others. Karl would have been a loose end, as you put it."

Ingrid said, "What happened to all the paintings?"

Anna shrugged. "Here, there, and everywhere."

"The Klee?"

"Back where it belongs. Switzerland. And, no. No gaunt-faced, prissy Swiss banker has it. A textile industrialist from Wintertur paid me handsomely for the privilege of hanging it in his wine cellar."

"The Raphael?" Ingrid said.

"Even better justice for *Portrait of a Young Man*. A nobleman from Urbino, no less – Raphael's birthplace – bought it. His wine cellar, too, no doubt has a secret door leading to a private gallery."

Anna looked at Selby and smiled. "On the matter of wine cellars, one of your fancy neighbors on the Hudson, Mister Parker, paid several million dollars for a set of Wagner scores I stole from the *Führer* himself. Originally I sold the scores to the Sundstrums, but then I took them back from Anders and resold them. The man is prominent in New York City music circles. Oh, you should have seen him swoon when I handed them over to him. And now he keeps them in his wine cellar in his mansion downriver from your home. In so many wine cellars, you realize, no matter how excellent and numerous the bottles of wine, they remain mere secondary assets compared with what else lies inside the vaults."

"I'm sure. Now tell us about the Marc?" Selby said.

"No going home for the *Der Turm der blauen Pferde*, alas. No wine cellar for it. Marc's works have proven very much beloved by the Japanese. They admire his mix of vivid color with simple lines." Looking at Ingrid, Anna said, "We held an auction for the Marc in your father's warehouse. Six Japanese businessmen flew in to participate. Every one of them filthy rich. Your father's commission alone would have allowed him to buy half of downtown Malmö. Though you've never mentioned it, the portion of your inheritance that came directly from your father's assets, dear Ingrid, was substantial, I'm sure."

Ingrid looked away.

"Anything else you'd like to tell us?" Selby asked.

"No. I'm suddenly feeling very, very tired. Let us go and do what has to be done." And with that Anna's catharsis came to an end.

"We'll drive you into town and ask the local authorities to hold you. I'll phone the proper federal authorities and request they come to fetch you. Is there anything you need to do here before we leave?" Selby said.

"No. I can't think of anything," Anna said languidly. She waved toward the house. "No need to lock up. The neighbors won't steal anything." The three of them descended the stairs to the back yard and, as they turned toward the front of the house, Anna stopped. "Wait. There is one thing I should see to." She pointed toward the boat dock. "I'd better secure the two boats better. Afternoon winds are predicted and, unless the boats are tied up, bow and stern, they take a beating. Once they broke loose and drifted down the lake."

Selby said, "I'll do it." Then he thought better of that notion, imagining Anna trying to run off. "We'll both do it."

"No, no. I can manage. I promise I'll not try to sail away. You'd catch me in no time, I'm sure."

Selby nodded and watched her walk slowly downhill toward the dock.

"I don't trust her," Ingrid said.

"She'll be all right," Selby assured Ingrid.

The two of them watched as Anna got down on all fours on the dock and retied the stern line of the canoe to a dock cleat. Then she crawled forward and shortened the bow line leading to a small sailboat. Seeming to be satisfied, she stood, walked to the end of the dock and appeared to Selby as if she were peering down into the water.

"What's she doing now?" Ingrid asked.

Selby continued to watch, saying nothing. Suddenly Anna pitched forward into the lake.

"She's fallen!" Ingrid shouted and started forward, only to be restrained by Selby.

"Go back into the house and dial 911," Selby said calmly. "I'll see to her."

"Are you sure?"

"Go."

Ingrid hesitated, but Selby gave her a sharp look until she turned and headed toward the stairs.

Selby then turned, faced the lake, and saw splashing beyond the end of the pier. He took his time removing his sport coat, folding it neatly before placing it on the ground at his feet. Then he began a slow, deliberate walk toward the lake.

Epilogue

Friday
August 14, 1992
Santa Barbara, California

"Did she jump or fall?"

"I don't know."

Selby once again sat in Madeleine Wynerson's small living room with its 1940's décor. The day was warm, Madeleine had opened several windows, and, from outside, came the sounds of children playing, dogs barking. Glancing at his watch, Selby realized he had been talking for nearly an hour, relating the details of his pursuit of the woman who had murdered Martin Wynerson. He had just finished telling of Anna Stahlinger's dogged denials, the matter of the facial-scar comparison, wresting the pistol from her purse, Anna's emotional breakdown and confession. And finally, her toppling into the lake.

"I'm not sure I would have tried to save her," Madeleine said. "On the other hand, I think drowning quickly was too good for her. She deserved worse."

"Perhaps she did," Selby allowed.

Selby had told Madeleine of his failed effort to rescue Anna, that despite his jumping in after her, pulling her from the cold water and administering CPR, she was dead by the time the emergency medical technicians arrived minutes later.

"Whatever Anna Stahlinger's fate, it wouldn't bring back Martin. The important matter is that I now know who killed my brother and why. That she suffered less than she deserved pales compared with my achieving closure." She gave Selby a hard look and added, "Finally."

"I apologize for my father."

Madeleine nodded. "I owe you a great deal, Mister Parker. I'm assuming you will send me a bill for all your efforts."

Selby took a cookie from the tray in front of him, bit it in half, then, holding out the remainder and wiggling it, said, "Paid in full."

"But --."

"My reward in this pursuit was finding out a great deal about my father that I had not known before."

"I'm sorry not all of it was uplifting."

"So am I, but *c'est la vie*. There are multiple dimensions to the old saw that it's a wise child who knows his own father. Now I'm wiser."

"What now for you?" Madeleine said.

"I must now pay my debts to the people who helped me. I don't bake cookies, so they'll all have to settle for a slab of meat, a bottle of wine, and a slice of cheesecake, served in the restaurant of their choice. First, to New York to thank Alastair Stiles. Then on to Berlin to thank Alec Marsden. And finally to Malmö, Sweden, where Ingrid Sundstrum and I still have a great deal to talk about."

"Good for you. I thank you again, though the feeling you've brought me is, quite frankly, inexpressible."

As Selby rose to leave, he said, "I almost forgot. Because Rosa Edelstein was such a prominent academic at Levitz-Goldman, her drowning got quite a lengthy write-up in the *Boston Globe*." Selby fished a clipping from his pocket. "I brought you a copy."

"Thank you."

"And just in case he doesn't subscribe, I also mailed a copy to David Fox, even though I'm sure he'd begin to wonder why Rosa's blackmail checks stopped coming. Beyond that, I have a feeling his neighbors in Gloucester will soon be reading his obituary. When I spot it, I'll send you a copy of his as well."

"Thank you again, Mister Parker."

Selby walked to his car, climbed in, and turned the key. When he looked back toward the house Madeleine stood motionless, leaning against the door frame. As he drove away he looked in his rearview mirror and saw her dab at her eyes, then make a tiny, listless goodbye wave. A moment later he took another look back and in Madeleine's place he swore he could see the ghost of his father standing arm in arm with Anna in the open doorway, each an aged, forlorn *Grauergeist*.

Photo: Lon Porter, Jr.

Jeff Ridenour is a WWII buff, mystery fan, and self-described art history dilettante. Having spent many years living in, and being educated in, California (Stanford), Arizona (ASU), and the state of Washington (UW), he has recently returned to his native Indiana.

www.ingramcontent.com/pod-product-compliance
Lightning Source LLC
Chambersburg PA
CBHW051926020726
47501CB00001B/1